C000107903

ONE THOUSAND & ONE
ARABIAN
NIGHTS
ALADDIN, ALI BABA, SINBAD AND THE TALES OF SCHEHERAZADE

This is a FLAME TREE Book

Publisher & Creative Director: Nick Wells
Editorial Director: Catherine Taylor
Editorial Board: Josie Mitchell, Gillian Whitaker, Taylor Bentley

FLAME TREE PUBLISHING
6 Melbray Mews, Fulham,
London SW6 3NS, United Kingdom
www.flametreepublishing.com

First published 2020

20 22 24 23 21
1 3 5 7 9 10 8 6 4 2

ISBN: 978-1-83964-238-8

The cover image is created by Flame Tree Studio
based on artwork by Slava Gerj and Gabor Ruszkai.

A copy of the CIP data for this book is available from the British Library.

Printed and bound in China

ONE THOUSAND & ONE
ARABIAN NIGHTS
ALADDIN, ALI BABA, SINBAD AND THE TALES OF SCHEHERAZADE

Contents

Foreword

Story's Empire: Around the World with the
One Thousand and One Arabian Nights

THE ONE THOUSAND AND ONE NIGHTS is a famous globetrotter. We all have a notion of what this familiar yet enigmatic stranger from abroad is. It has made itself an intimate part of our life but kept us at an arm's length from its origin, history and identity. From the first instance of Arabic textual reference to a body of tales known as *Hazar Afsaneh*, or 'the thousand tales', in the ninth century AD until today, through further Arabic references in the tenth and eleventh centuries and French-led European discovery of a fifteenth-century Arabic manuscript containing 282 nights of stories, the *Nights* has eluded becoming pinned down as a definitive text ascribable to a known author. It seems always to thrive in translation. The earliest kernel of the *Nights* was purportedly of Indian and Persian origin translated from Persian, and the latest version(s) began to take shape in Antoine Galland's (1646–1715) French translation (1704–17) of the fifteenth-century Arabic text. Galland, perhaps very much like the first Arabic translation, spawned not only more translations but also imitations and, more importantly, a shape-shifting Arabic textual tradition made up of culturally, thematically and generically diverse pre-modern manuscripts and modern printed versions. The written Arabic *Nights* has grown prodigiously over the centuries but it cannot begin to capture the *Nights* stories circulating in an overlapping oral tradition, or in *Nights'* multi-lingual, multi-media diffusion worldwide: in literary writings, anthologies of stories, children's literature, adult literature, the visual and performing arts, music and popular entertainment, to name but a few. The *Nights* is today an international icon that belongs to everyone and no one. It lives in a story's empire that transcends boundaries of text and language; its contours are visible only in the complexly intertwined transnational networks of intercultural circulation of storytelling.

The role of English translators in the making of the global fortunes of the *Nights* is undeniable. From the first anonymous eighteenth-century Grubb Street translation of Galland's French, to Husain Haddawy's 1990 translation of his fifteenth-century manuscript and Malcolm Lyon's 2008 translation of the nineteenth-century Egyptian Bulaq text, English translators, adaptors and artists have creatively fashioned and refashioned the *Nights* for global consumption. The English *Nights* is everywhere in the fabric of our day-to-day, in our cultural and literary life both at home and abroad, on our TV screens, in cinemas, theatres, concert halls and in our books, as children's stories, folk tales, and adult fiction. Richard F. Burton (1821–90), perhaps the most famous – or infamous – English translator of the *Nights*, derives much of his fame from his repackaging and rewording of existing translations of the *Nights* by supplementing the Bulaq text with additional tales but, more importantly, by exaggerating the exotic and erotic features of the *Nights* stories. The affectation of his English and his notorious obsession with sexuality are perhaps what made his translation so influential. The sale of Burton at the Kelly and Walsh bookshop (founded 1870) in Shanghai prompted Chinese and Japanese translations of the *Nights* at the turn of the twentieth century. The Argentine writer Jorge Luis Borges (1899–1986) even claimed that Burton's translation was a major influence on his writing.

In the world of literary fiction, the *Nights* story-within-story narrative technique and the combination of the fantastic and real, both key features of Borges' fiction, are pervasive in magical realism and postmodernism. Scheherazade, the female protagonist of the frametale, is more famous than any historical woman. The most popular stories are, however, 'Sinbad the Sailor', 'Aladdin' and 'Ali Baba and the Forty Thieves', which do not appear in Galland's fifteenth-century manuscript. Galland incorporated 'Sinbad' into his French translation from a later collection he read, and 'Aladdin' and 'Ali Baba' derive from stories he heard from a Syrian storyteller, Hanna Dyab, from Aleppo. Of these stories, 'Sinbad' and 'Aladdin' are, just like the *Nights*, stories of globetrotting, but with a twist. The tales themselves have a life of their own, taking shape and shape-shifting from one translation to another, one medium to another and one culture to another, but they are also about travel. Sinbad is a Baghdadi merchant who sails across the Indian Ocean to trade in India, China, Malaysia and Indonesia, and Aladdin is a Chinese boy who flies to North Africa in order to retrieve his wife and palace from an evil sorcerer. These stories speak for the expansive horizon of the *Nights* and its boundless universe, where wondrous creatures of imaginable and unimaginable species – humans, animals, birds, angels, demons and genies – fly around in a fantastic world on carpets, thrones or simply air, to make love and war but, above all, to marvel at the very adventure that is humanity itself.

Wen-chin Ouyang

Publisher's Note

THE TALES OF the *One Thousand and One Nights* have enchanted audiences for generations, capturing the imaginations of readers and listeners alike with fantastical stories of adventure, magic and romance. Gathered in this book is a carefully selected collection of some of the most significant and beloved narratives, as relayed by Richard F. Burton, Andrew and Nora Lang, Kate Douglas Wiggin, Nora A. Smith and E. Dixon.

Owing to the mixture of sources used in compiling this collection, there may therefore be some inconsistency in translation and spelling, which arise from the text's origins in oral storytelling, leaving it open to interpretation. These narratives, rooted in Arabic, Greek, Persian, Jewish, Indian and Turkish folklore, having been collected over centuries by scholars across Asia and Africa, have then been translated by eighteenth and nineteenth century academics with differing attitudes to the transliteration of Arabic, encouraging further variation. However, some standardization has been attempted where appropriate.

While the order of the stories hews roughly to the chronology of Burton's ten-volume *The Book of the Thousand Nights and a Night* (1885), classic tales such as that of Aladdin and the lamp and the voyages of Sinbad have also been included. Although these were not a part of the original Arabic saga, they featured in Antoine Galland's *Les mille et une nuits* (1704–17), and have been closely associated ever since. As the first European translation of these tales, Galland's work not only had an enormous influence on later translations of these stories, but on literature as a whole, as well as Europe's view of the Islamic world.

We also ask the reader to keep in mind that while these stories are timeless, much of the factual information, opinions, language and style of writing belong to the era in which they were first published.

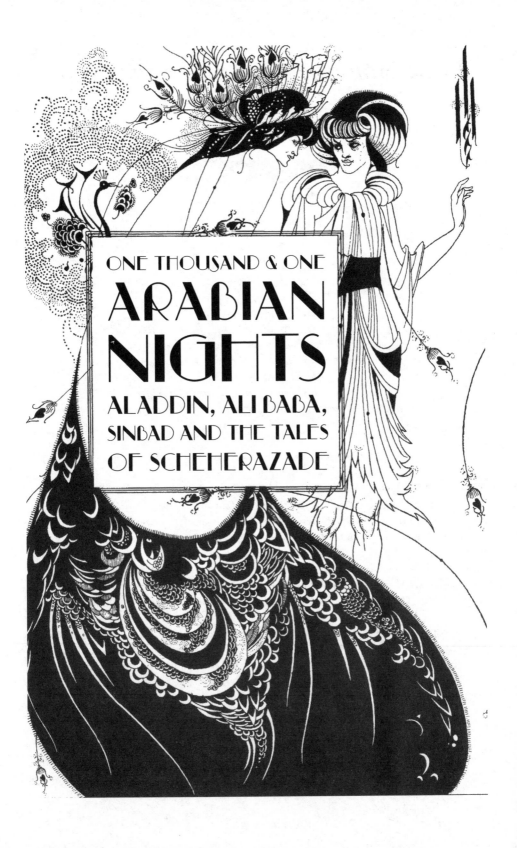

ONE THOUSAND & ONE

ARABIAN NIGHTS

ALADDIN, ALI BABA, SINBAD AND THE TALES OF SCHEHERAZADE

The Story of King Shahryar and His Brother

Richard F. Burton

In the Name of Allah, the Compassionating, the Compassionate!

Praise be to Allah
The Beneficent King
The Creator of the Universe
Lord of the Three Worlds
Who set up the firmament without pillars in its stead
And who stretched out the Earth even as a bed
And grace, and prayer-blessing be upon our Lord Mohammed
Lord of Apostolic Men
And upon his family and companion-train
Prayer and blessings enduring and grace which unto the
day of doom shall remain
Amen!
O Thou of the Three Worlds Sovereign!

AND AFTERWARDS. Verily the works and words of those gone before us have become instances and examples to men of our modern day, that folk may view what admonishing chances befel other folk and may therefrom take warning; and that they may peruse the annals of antique peoples and all that hath betided them, and be thereby ruled and restrained: Praise, therefore, be to Him who hath made the histories of the Past an admonition unto the Present! Now of such instances are the tales called "A Thousand Nights and a Night," together with their far-famed legends and wonders. Therein it is related (but Allah is All-knowing of His hidden things and All-ruling and All-honoured and All-giving and All-gracious and All-merciful!) that, in tide of yore and in time long gone before, there was a King of the Kings of the Banu Sásán in the Islands of India and China, a Lord of armies and guards and servants and dependents. He left only two sons, one in the prime of manhood and the other yet a youth, while both were Knights and Braves, albeit the elder was a doughtier horseman than the younger. So he succeeded to the empire; when he ruled the land and lorded it over his lieges with justice so exemplary that he was beloved by all the peoples of his capital and of his kingdom. His name was King Shahryár, and he made his younger brother, Shah Zamán hight, King of Samarcand in Barbarian-land. These two ceased not to abide in their several realms and the law was ever carried out in their dominions; and each ruled his own kingdom, with equity and fair-dealing to his subjects, in extreme solace and enjoyment; and this condition continually endured for a score of years. But at the end of the twentieth twelvemonth the elder King yearned for a sight of his younger brother and felt that he must look upon him once more. So he took counsel with his Wazir about visiting him, but the Minister, finding the project unadvisable, recommended that a letter be written and a present be sent under his charge to the younger brother with an invitation to visit the elder. Having accepted this advice the King forthwith bade prepare handsome gifts, such as horses with saddles of gem-encrusted gold; Mamelukes, or white slaves; beautiful handmaids, high-breasted virgins, and splendid stuffs and costly. He then wrote a letter to Shah Zaman expressing his warm love and great wish to see him, ending with these words, "We therefore hope of the favour and affection of the beloved brother that he will condescend to bestir himself and turn his face us-wards. Furthermore we have sent our Wazir to make all ordinance for the march, and our one and only desire is to see thee ere we die; but if thou delay or disappoint us we shall not survive the blow. Wherewith peace be upon thee!" Then King Shahryar, having sealed the missive and given it to the Wazir with the offerings aforementioned, commanded him to shorten his skirts and strain his strength and make all expedition in going and returning. "Harkening and obedience!" quoth the Minister, who fell to making ready without stay and packed up his loads and prepared all his requisites without delay. This occupied him three days, and on the dawn of the fourth he took leave of his King and marched right away, over desert and hill-way, stony waste and pleasant lea without halting by night or by day. But whenever he entered a realm whose ruler was subject to his Suzerain, where he was greeted with magnificent gifts of gold and silver and all manner of presents fair and rare, he would tarry there three days, the term of the guest-rite; and, when he left on the fourth, he would be honourably escorted for a whole day's march.

As soon as the Wazir drew near Shah Zaman's court in Samarcand he despatched to report his arrival one of his high officials, who presented himself before the King; and, kissing ground between his hands, delivered his message. Hereupon the King commanded sundry of his Grandees and Lords of his realm to fare forth and meet his brother's Wazir at the distance of a full day's journey; which they did, greeting him respectfully and wishing him all prosperity and forming an escort and a procession. When he entered the city he proceeded straightway to the palace, where he presented himself in the royal presence; and, after kissing ground and praying for the King's health and happiness and for victory over all his enemies, he informed him that his brother was yearning to see him, and prayed for the pleasure of a visit. He then delivered the letter which Shah Zaman took from his hand and read: it contained sundry hints and allusions which required thought; but, when the King had fully comprehended its import, he said, "I hear and I obey the commands of the beloved brother!" adding to the Wazir, "But we will not march till after the third day's hospitality." He appointed for the Minister fitting quarters of the palace; and, pitching tents for the troops, rationed them with whatever they might require of meat and drink and other necessaries. On the fourth day he made ready for wayfare and got together sumptuous presents befitting his elder brother's majesty, and stablished his chief Wazir viceroy of the land during his absence. Then he caused his tents and camels and mules to be brought forth and encamped, with their bales and loads, attendants and guards, within sight of the city, in readiness to set out next morning for his brother's capital. But when the night was half spent he bethought him that he had forgotten in his palace somewhat which he should have brought with him, so he returned privily and entered his apartments, where he found the Queen, his wife, asleep on his own carpet-bed, embracing with both arms a black cook of loathsome aspect and foul with kitchen grease and grime. When he saw this the world waxed black before his sight and he said, "If such case happen while I am yet within sight of the city what will be the doings of this damned whore during my long absence at my brother's court?" So he drew his scymitar and, cutting the two in four pieces with a single blow, left them on the carpet and returned presently to his camp without letting anyone know of what had happened. Then he gave orders for immediate departure and set out at once and began his travel; but he could not help thinking over his wife's treason and he kept ever saying to himself, "How could she do this deed by me? How could she work her own death?," till excessive grief seized him, his colour changed to yellow, his body waxed weak and he was threatened with a dangerous malady, such an one as bringeth men to die. So the Wazir shortened his stages and tarried long at the watering-stations and did his best to solace the King.

Now when Shah Zaman drew near the capital of his brother he despatched vaunt-couriers and messengers of glad tidings to announce his arrival, and Shahryar came forth to meet him with his Wazirs and Emirs and Lords and Grandees of his realm; and saluted him and joyed with exceeding joy and caused the city to be decorated in his honour. When, however, the brothers met, the elder could not but see the change of complexion in the younger and questioned him of his case whereto he replied, "'Tis caused by the travails of wayfare and my case needs care, for I have suffered from the change of water and air! but Allah be praised for reuniting me with a brother so dear and so rare!" On this wise he dissembled and kept his secret, adding, "O King of the time and Caliph of the tide, only toil and moil have tinged my face yellow with bile and hath made my eyes sink deep in my head." Then the two entered the capital in all honour; and the elder brother lodged the younger in a palace overhanging the pleasure garden; and, after a time, seeing his condition still unchanged, he attributed it to his separation from his country and kingdom. So he let him wend his own ways and asked no questions of him till one day when he again said, "O my brother, I see that art grown weaker of body and yellower of colour." "O my brother," replied Shah Zaman "I have an internal wound:" still he would not tell him what he had witnessed in his wife. Thereupon Shahryar summoned doctors and surgeons and bade them treat his brother according to the rules of art, which they did for a whole month; but their sherbets and potions naught availed, for he would dwell upon the deed of his wife, and despondency, instead of diminishing, prevailed, and leechcraft treatment utterly failed.

One day his elder brother said to him, "I am going forth to hunt and course and to take my pleasure and pastime; maybe this would lighten thy heart." Shah Zaman, however, refused, saying, "O my brother, my soul yearneth for naught of this sort and I entreat thy favour to suffer me tarry quietly in this place, being wholly taken up with my malady." So King Shah Zaman passed his night in the palace and, next morning, when his brother had fared forth, he removed from his room and sat him down at one of the lattice-windows overlooking the pleasure grounds; and there he abode thinking with saddest thought over his wife's betrayal and burning sighs issued from his tortured breast. And as he continued in this case lo! a postern of the palace, which was carefully kept private, swung open and out of it came twenty slave girls surrounding his brother's wife who was wondrous fair, a model of beauty and comeliness and symmetry and perfect loveliness and who paced with the grace of a gazelle which panteth for the cooling stream. Thereupon Shah Zaman drew back from the window, but he kept the bevy in sight espying them from a place whence he could not be espied. They walked under the very lattice and advanced a little way into the garden till they came to a jetting fountain amiddlemost a great basin of water; then they stripped off their clothes and behold, ten of them were women, concubines of the King, and the other ten were white slaves. Then they all paired off, each with each: but the Queen, who was left alone, presently cried out in a loud voice, "Here to me, O my lord Saeed!" and then sprang with a drop-leap from one of the trees a big slobbering blackamoor with rolling eyes which showed the whites, a truly hideous sight. He walked boldly up to her and threw his arms round her neck while she embraced him as warmly; then he bussed her and winding his legs round hers, as a button-loop clasps a button, he threw her and enjoyed her. On like wise did the other slaves with the girls till all had satisfied their passions, and they ceased not from kissing and clipping, coupling and carousing till day began to wane; when the Mamelukes rose from the damsels' bosoms and the blackamoor slave dismounted from the Queen's breast; the men resumed their disguises and all, except the negro who swarmed up the tree, entered the palace and closed the postern-door as before. Now, when Shah Zaman saw this conduct of his sister-in-law he said in himself, "By Allah, my calamity is lighter than this! My brother is a greater King among the kings than I am, yet this infamy goeth on in his very palace, and his wife is in love with that filthiest of filthy slaves. But this only showeth that they all do it and that there is no woman but who cuckoldeth her husband, then the curse of Allah upon one and all and upon the fools who lean against them for support or who place the reins of conduct in their hands. So he put away his melancholy and despondency, regret and repine, and allayed his sorrow by constantly repeating those words, adding "'Tis my conviction that no man in this world is safe from their malice!" When supper-time came they brought him the trays and he ate with voracious appetite, for he had long refrained from meat, feeling unable to touch any dish however dainty. Then he returned grateful thanks to Almighty Allah, praising Him and blessing Him, and he spent a most restful night, it having been long since he had savoured the sweet food of sleep.

Next day he broke his fast heartily and began to recover health and strength, and presently regained excellent condition. His brother came back from the chase ten days after, when he rode out to meet him and they saluted each other; and when King Shahryar looked at King Shah Zaman he saw how the hue of health had returned to him, how his face had waxed ruddy and how he ate with an appetite after his late scanty diet. He wondered much and said, "O my brother, I was so anxious that thou wouldst join me in hunting and chasing, and wouldst take thy pleasure and pastime in my dominion!" He thanked him and excused himself; then the two took horse and rode into the city and, when they were seated at their ease in the palace, the food-trays were set before them and they ate their sufficiency. After the meats were removed and they had washed their hands, King Shahryar turned to his brother and said, "My mind is overcome with wonderment at thy condition. I was desirous to carry thee with me to the chase but I saw thee changed in hue, pale and wan to view, and in sore trouble of mind too. But now Alhamdolillah – glory be to God! – I see thy natural colour hath returned to thy face and that thou art again in the best of case. It was my belief that thy sickness came of severance from thy family and friends, and absence from capital and country, so I refrained from troubling thee with further questions. But now I beseech thee to expound to me the cause of thy complaint and thy change of colour, and to explain the reason of thy recovery and the return to the ruddy hue of health which I am wont to view. So speak out and hide naught! When Shah Zaman heard this he bowed ground-wards awhile his head, then raised it and said, "I will tell thee what caused my complaint and my loss of colour; but excuse my acquainting thee with the cause of its return to me and the reason of my complete recovery: indeed I pray thee not to press me for a reply." Said Shahryar, who was much surprised by these words, "Let me hear first what produced thy pallor and thy poor condition." "Know, then, O my brother," rejoined Shah Zaman, "that when thou sentest thy Wazir with the invitation to place myself between thy hands, I made ready and marched out of my city; but presently I minded me having left behind me in the palace a string of jewels intended as a gift to thee. I returned for it alone and found my wife on my carpet-bed and in the arms of a hideous black cook. So I slew the twain and came to thee, yet my thoughts brooded over this business and I lost my bloom and became weak. But excuse me if I still refuse to tell thee what was the reason of my complexion returning." Shahryar shook his head, marvelling with extreme marvel, and with the fire of wrath flaming up from his heart, he cried, "Indeed, the malice of woman is mighty!" Then he took refuge from them with Allah and said, "In very sooth, O my brother, thou hast escaped many an evil by putting thy wife to death, and right excusable were thy wrath and grief for such mishap which never yet befel crowned King like thee. By Allah, had the case been mine, I would not have been satisfied without slaying a thousand women and that way madness lies! But now praise be to Allah who hath tempered to thee thy tribulation, and needs must thou acquaint me with that which so suddenly restored to thee complexion and health, and explain to me what causeth this concealment." "O King of the Age, again I pray thee excuse my so doing!" "Nay, but thou must." "I fear, O my brother, lest the recital cause thee more anger and sorrow than afflicted me." "That were but a better reason," quoth Shahryar, "for telling me the whole history, and I conjure thee by Allah not to keep back aught from me." Thereupon Shah Zaman told him all he had seen, from commencement to conclusion, ending with these words, "When I beheld thy calamity and the treason of thy wife, O my brother, and I reflected that thou art in years my senior and in sovereignty my superior, mine own sorrow was belittled by the comparison, and my mind recovered tone and temper: so throwing off melancholy and despondency, I was able to eat and drink and sleep, and thus I speedily regained health and strength. Such is the truth and the whole truth."

When King Shahryar heard this he waxed wroth with exceeding wrath, and rage was like to strangle him; but presently he recovered himself and said, "O my brother, I would not give thee the lie in this matter, but I cannot credit it till I see it with mine own eyes." "An thou wouldst look upon thy calamity," quoth Shah Zaman, "rise at once and make ready again for hunting and coursing, and then hide thyself with me, so shalt thou witness it and thine eyes shall verify it." "True," quoth the King; whereupon he let make proclamation of his intent to travel, and the troops and tents fared forth without the city, camping within sight, and Shahryar sallied out with them and took seat amidmost his host, bidding the slaves admit no man to him. When night came on he summoned his Wazir and said to him, "Sit thou in my stead and let none wot of my absence till the term of three days." Then the brothers disguised themselves and returned by night with all secrecy to the palace, where they passed the dark hours: and at dawn they seated themselves at the lattice overlooking the pleasure grounds, when presently the Queen and her handmaids came out as before, and passing under the windows made for the fountain. Here they stripped, ten of them being men to ten women, and the King's wife cried out, "Where art thou, O Saeed?" The hideous blackamoor dropped from the tree straightway; and, rushing into her arms without stay or delay, cried out, "I am Sa'ad al-Din Saood!" The lady laughed heartily, and all fell to satisfying their lusts, and remained so occupied for a couple of hours, when the white slaves rose up from the handmaidens' breasts and the blackamoor dismounted from the Queen's bosom: then they went into the basin and, after performing the Ghusl, or complete ablution, donned their dresses and retired as they had done before.

When King Shahryar saw this infamy of his wife and concubines he became as one distraught and he cried out, "Only in utter solitude can man be safe from the doings of this vile world! By Allah, life is naught but one great wrong." Presently he added, "Do not thwart me, O my brother, in what I propose;" and the other answered, "I will not." So he said, "Let us up as we are and depart forthright hence, for we have no concern with Kingship, and let us over-wander Allah's earth, worshipping the Almighty till we find some one to whom the like calamity hath happened; and if we find none then will death be more welcome to us than life." So the two brothers issued from a second private postern of the palace; and they never stinted wayfaring by day and by night, until they reached a tree a-middle of a meadow hard by a spring of sweet water on the shore of the salt sea. Both drank of it and sat down to take their rest; and when an hour of the day had gone by, lo! they heard a mighty roar and uproar in the middle of the main as though the heavens were falling upon the earth; and the sea brake with waves before them, and from it towered a black pillar, which grew and grew till it rose sky-wards and began making for that meadow. Seeing it, they waxed fearful exceedingly and climbed to the top of the tree, which was a lofty; whence they gazed to see what might be the matter. And behold, it was a Jinni, huge of height and burly of breast and bulk, broad of brow and black of blee, bearing on his head a coffer of crystal. He strode to land, wading through the deep, and coming to the tree whereupon were the two Kings, seated himself beneath it. He then set down the coffer on its bottom and out of it drew a casket, with seven padlocks of steel, which he unlocked with seven keys of steel he took from beside his thigh, and out of it a young lady to come was seen, white-skinned and of winsomest mien, of stature fine and thin, and bright as though a moon of the fourteenth night she had been, or the sun raining lively sheen. Even so the poet Utayyah hath excellently said:

> She rose like the morn as she shone through the night
> And she gilded the grove with her gracious sight:
> From her radiance the sun taketh increase when
> She unveileth and shameth the moonshine bright.

Bow down all beings between her hands
As she showeth charms with her veil undight.
And she floodeth cities with torrent tears
When she flasheth her look of leven-light.

The Jinni seated her under the tree by his side and looking at her said, "O choicest love of this heart of mine! O dame of noblest line, whom I snatched away on thy bride night that none might prevent me taking thy maidenhead or tumble thee before I did, and whom none save myself hath loved or hath enjoyed: O my sweetheart! I would lief sleep a little while." He then laid his head upon the lady's thighs; and, stretching out his legs which extended down to the sea, slept and snored and snarked like the roll of thunder. Presently she raised her head towards the tree-top and saw the two Kings perched near the summit; then she softly lifted off her lap the Jinni's pate which she was tired of supporting and placed it upon the ground; then standing upright under the tree signed to the Kings, "Come ye down, ye two, and fear naught from this Ifrít." They were in a terrible fright when they found that she had seen them and answered her in the same manner, "Allah upon thee and by thy modesty, O lady, excuse us from coming down!" But she rejoined by saying, "Allah upon you both that ye come down forthright, and if ye come not, I will rouse upon you my husband, this Ifrit, and he shall do you to die by the illest of deaths;" and she continued making signals to them. So, being afraid, they came down to her and she rose before them and said, "Stroke me a strong stroke, without stay or delay, otherwise will I arouse and set upon you this Ifrit who shall slay you straightway." They said to her, "O our lady, we conjure thee by Allah, let us off this work, for we are fugitives from such and in extreme dread and terror of this thy husband. How then can we do it in such a way as thou desirest?" "Leave this talk: it needs must be so;" quoth she, and she swore them by Him who raised the skies on high, without prop or pillar, that, if they worked not her will, she would cause them to be slain and cast into the sea. Whereupon out of fear King Shahryar said to King Shah Zaman, "O my brother, do thou what she biddeth thee do;" but he replied, "I will not do it till thou do it before I do." And they began disputing about futtering her. Then quoth she to the twain, "How is it I see you disputing and demurring; if ye do not come forward like men and do the deed of kind ye two, I will arouse upon you the Ifrit." At this, by reason of their sore dread of the Jinni, both did by her what she bade them do; and, when they had dismounted from her, she said, "Well done!" She then took from her pocket a purse and drew out a knotted string, whereon were strung five hundred and seventy seal rings, and asked, "Know ye what be these?" They answered her saying, "We know not!" Then quoth she; "These be the signets of five hundred and seventy men who have all futtered me upon the horns of this foul, this foolish, this filthy Ifrit; so give me also your two seal rings, ye pair of brothers. When they had drawn their two rings from their hands and given them to her, she said to them, "Of a truth this Ifrit bore me off on my bride-night, and put me into a casket and set the casket in a coffer and to the coffer he affixed seven strong padlocks of steel and deposited me on the deep bottom of the sea that raves, dashing and clashing with waves; and guarded me so that I might remain chaste and honest, quotha! that none save himself might have connexion with me. But I have lain under as many of my kind as I please, and this wretched Jinni wotteth not that

Destiny may not be averted nor hindered by aught, and that whatso woman willeth the same she fulfilleth however man nilleth. Even so saith one of them:

> *Rely not on women;*
> *Trust not to their hearts,*
> *Whose joys and whose sorrows*
> *Are hung to their parts!*
> *Lying love they will swear thee*
> *Whence guile ne'er departs:*
> *Take Yusuf for sample*
> *'Ware sleights and 'ware smarts!*
> *Iblis ousted Adam*
> *(See ye not?) thro' their arts.*

And another saith:

> *"Stint thy blame, man! 'Twill drive to a passion without bound; My fault is not*
> *so heavy as fault in it hast found.*
> *If true lover I become, then to me there cometh not*
> *Save what happened unto many in the by-gone stound.*
> *For wonderful is he and right worthy of our praise*
> *Who from wiles of female wits kept him safe and kept him sound."*

Hearing these words they marvelled with exceeding marvel, and she went from them to the Ifrit and, taking up his head on her thigh as before, said to them softly, "Now wend your ways and bear yourselves beyond the bounds of his malice." So they fared forth saying either to other, "Allah! Allah!" and, "There be no Majesty and there be no Might save in Allah, the Glorious, the Great; and with Him we seek refuge from women's malice and sleight, for of a truth it hath no mate in might. Consider, O my brother, the ways of this marvellous lady with an Ifrit who is so much more powerful than we are. Now since there hath happened to him a greater mishap than that which befel us and which should bear us abundant consolation, so return we to our countries and capitals, and let us decide never to intermarry with womankind and presently we will show them what will be our action." Thereupon they rode back to the tents of King Shahryar, which they reached on the morning of the third day; and, having mustered the Wazirs and Emirs, the Chamberlains and high officials, he gave a robe of honour to his Viceroy and issued orders for an immediate return to the city. There he sat him upon his throne and sending for the Chief Minister, the father of the two damsels who (Inshallah!) will presently be mentioned, he said, "I command thee to take my wife and smite her to death; for she hath broken her plight and her faith." So he carried her to the place of execution and did her die. Then King Shahryar took brand in hand and repairing to the Serraglio slew all the concubines and their Mamelukes. He also sware himself by a binding oath that whatever wife he married he would abate her maidenhead at night and slay her next morning to make sure of his honour; "For," said he, "there never was nor is there one chaste woman upon the face of earth." Then Shah Zaman prayed for permission to fare homewards; and he went forth equipped and escorted and travelled till he reached his own country. Meanwhile Shahryar commanded his Wazir to bring him the bride of the night that he might go in to her; so he produced a most beautiful girl, the daughter of one of the Emirs and the King went in unto her at eventide and when morning dawned he bade his Minister strike off her head; and the Wazir did accordingly for fear of the Sultan. On this wise he continued for the space of three years; marrying a maiden every night and killing her the next morning, till folk raised an outcry against him and cursed him, praying Allah utterly to destroy him and his rule; and women made an uproar and mothers wept and parents fled with their daughters till there remained not in the city a young person fit for carnal copulation. Presently the King ordered his Chief Wazir, the same who was charged with the executions, to bring him a virgin as was his wont; and the Minister went forth and searched and found none; so he returned home in sorrow and anxiety fearing for his life from the King. Now he had two daughters, Shahrázád and Dunyázád hight, of whom the elder had perused the books, annals and legends of preceding Kings, and the stories, examples and instances of by-gone men and things; indeed it was said that she had collected a thousand books of histories relating to antique races and departed rulers. She had perused the works of the poets and knew them by heart; she had studied philosophy and the sciences, arts and accomplishments; and she was pleasant and polite, wise and witty, well read and well bred. Now on that day she said to her father, "Why do I see thee thus changed and laden with cark and care? Concerning this matter quoth one of the poets:

Tell whoso hath sorrow
Grief never shall last:
E'en as joy hath no morrow
So woe shall go past."

When the Wazir heard from his daughter these words he related to her, from first to last, all that had happened between him and the King. Thereupon said she, "By Allah, O my father, how long shall this slaughter of women endure? Shall I tell thee what is in my mind in order to save both sides from destruction?" "Say on, O my daughter," quoth he, and quoth she, "I wish thou wouldst give me in marriage to this King Shahryar; either I shall live or I shall be a ransom for the virgin daughters of Moslems and the cause of their deliverance from his hands and thine." "Allah upon thee!" cried he in wrath exceeding that lacked no feeding, "O scanty of wit, expose not thy life to such peril! How durst thou address me in words so wide from wisdom and un-far from foolishness? Know that one who lacketh experience in worldly matters readily falleth into misfortune; and whoso considereth not the end keepeth not the world to friend, and the vulgar say: I was lying at mine ease: nought but my officiousness brought me unease." "Needs must thou," she broke in, "make me a doer of this good deed, and let him kill me an he will: I shall only die a ransom for others." "O my daughter," asked he, "and how shall that profit thee when thou shalt have thrown away thy life?" and she answered, "O my father it must be, come of it what will!" The Wazir was again moved to fury and blamed and reproached her, ending with, "In very deed I fear lest the same befal thee which befel the Bull and the Ass with the Husbandman." "And what," asked she, "befel them, O my father?" Whereupon the Wazir began the

Tale of the Bull and the Ass

KNOW, O MY DAUGHTER, that there was once a merchant who owned much money and many men, and who was rich in cattle and camels; he had also a wife and family and he dwelt in the country, being experienced in husbandry and devoted to agriculture. Now Allah Most High had endowed him with understanding the tongues of beasts and birds of every kind, but under pain of death if he divulged the gift to any. So he kept it secret for very fear. He had in his cowhouse a Bull and an Ass each tethered in his own stall one hard by the other. As the merchant was sitting near hand one day with his servants and his children were playing about him, he heard the Bull say to the Ass, "Hail and health to thee O Father of Waking! For that thou enjoyest rest and good ministering; all under thee is clean-swept and fresh-sprinkled; men wait upon thee and feed thee, and thy provaunt is sifted barley and thy drink pure spring-water, while I (unhappy creature!) am led forth in the middle of the night, when they set on my neck the plough and a something called Yoke; and I tire at cleaving the earth from dawn of day till set of sun. I am forced to do more than I can and to bear all manner of ill-treatment from night to night; after which they take me back with my sides torn, my neck flayed, my legs aching and mine eyelids sored with tears. Then they shut me up in the byre and throw me beans and crushed-straw, mixed with dirt and chaff; and I lie in dung and filth and foul stinks through the livelong night. But thou art ever in a place swept and sprinkled and cleansed, and thou art always lying at ease, save when it happens (and seldom enough!) that the master hath some business, when he mounts thee and rides thee to town and returns with thee forthright. So it happens that I am toiling and distrest while thou takest thine ease and thy rest; thou sleepest while I am sleepless; I hunger still while thou eatest thy fill, and I win contempt while thou winnest good will." When the Bull ceased speaking, the Ass turned towards him and said, "O Broad-o'-Brow, O thou lost one! he lied not who dubbed thee Bull-head, for thou, O father of a Bull, hast neither forethought nor contrivance; thou art the simplest of simpletons, and thou knowest naught of good advisers. Hast thou not heard the saying of the wise:

> For others these hardships and labours I bear
> And theirs is the pleasure and mine is the care;
> As the bleacher who blacketh his brow in the sun
> To whiten the raiment which other men wear."

But thou, O fool, art full of zeal and thou toilest and molest before the master; and thou tearest and wearest and slayest thyself for the comfort of another. Hast thou never heard the saw that saith, None to guide and from the way go wide? Thou wendest forth at the call to dawn-prayer and thou returnest not till sundown; and through the livelong day thou endurest all manner hardships; to wit, beating and belabouring and bad language. Now hearken to me, Sir Bull! when they tie thee to thy stinking manger, thou pawest the ground with thy forehand and lashest out with thy hind hoofs and pushest with thy horns and bellowest aloud, so they deem thee contented. And when they throw thee thy fodder thou fallest on it with greed and hastenest to line thy fair fat paunch. But if thou accept my advice it will be better for thee and thou wilt lead an easier life even than mine. When thou goest a-field and they lay the thing called Yoke on thy neck, lie down and rise not again though haply they swinge thee; and, if thou rise, lie down a second time; and when they bring thee home and offer thee thy beans, fall backwards and only sniff at thy meat and withdraw thee and taste it not, and be satisfied with thy crushed straw and chaff; and on this wise feign thou art sick, and cease not doing thus for a day or two days or even three days, so shalt thou have rest from toil and moil." When the Bull heard these words he knew the Ass to be his friend and thanked him, saying, "Right is thy rede;" and prayed that all blessings might requite him, and cried, "O Father Wakener! thou hast made up for my failings." (Now the merchant, O my daughter, understood all that passed between them.) Next day the driver took the Bull, and settling the plough on his neck, made him work as wont; but the Bull began to shirk his ploughing, according to the advice of the Ass, and the ploughman drubbed him till he broke the yoke and made off; but the man caught him up and leathered him till he despaired of his life. Not the less, however, would he do nothing but stand still and drop down till the evening. Then the herd led him home and stabled him in his stall: but he drew back from his manger and neither stamped nor ramped nor butted nor bellowed as he was wont to do; whereat the man wondered. He brought him the beans and husks, but he sniffed at them and left them and lay down as far from them as he could and passed the whole night fasting. The peasant came next morning; and, seeing the manger full of beans, the crushed-straw untasted and the ox lying on his back in sorriest plight, with legs outstretched and swollen belly, he was concerned for him, and said to himself, "By Allah, he hath assuredly sickened and this is the cause why he would not plough yesterday." Then he went to the merchant and reported, "O my master, the Bull is ailing; he refused his fodder last night; nay more, he hath not tasted a scrap of it this morning."

Now the merchant-farmer understood what all this meant, because he had overheard the talk between the Bull and the Ass, so quoth he, "Take that rascal donkey, and set the yoke on his neck, and bind him to the plough and make him do Bull's work." Thereupon the ploughman took the Ass, and worked him through the livelong day at the Bull's task; and, when he failed for weakness, he made him eat stick till his ribs were sore and his sides were sunken and his neck was flayed by the yoke; and when he came home in the evening he could hardly drag his limbs along, either forehand or hind-legs. But as for the Bull, he had passed the day lying at full length and had eaten his fodder with an excellent appetite, and he ceased not calling down blessings on the Ass for his good advice, unknowing what had come to him on his account. So when night set in and the Ass returned to the byre the Bull rose up before him in honour, and said, "May good tidings gladden thy heart, O Father Wakener! through thee I have rested all this day and I have eaten my meat in peace and quiet." But the Ass returned no reply, for wrath and heart-burning and fatigue and the beating he had gotten; and he repented with the most grievous of repentance; and quoth he to himself: "This cometh of my folly in giving good counsel; as the saw saith, I was in joy and gladness, nought save my officiousness brought me this sadness. But I will bear in mind my innate worth and the nobility of my nature; for what saith the poet?

Shall the beautiful hue of the Basil fail
Tho' the beetle's foot o'er the Basil crawl?

> *And though spider and fly be its denizens*
> *Shall disgrace attach to the royal hall?*
> *The cowrie, I ken, shall have currency*
> *But the pearl's clear drop, shall its value fall?*

And now I must take thought and put a trick upon him and return him to his place, else I die." Then he went aweary to his manger, while the Bull thanked him and blessed him. And even so, O my daughter, said the Wazir, thou wilt die for lack of wits; therefore sit thee still and say naught and expose not thy life to such stress; for, by Allah, I offer thee the best advice, which cometh of my affection and kindly solicitude for thee. "O my father," she answered, "needs must I go up to this King and be married to him." Quoth he, "Do not this deed;" and quoth she, "Of a truth I will:" whereat he rejoined, "If thou be not silent and bide still, I will do with thee even what the merchant did with his wife." "And what did he?" asked she. Know then, answered the, that after the return of the Ass the merchant came out on the terrace-roof with his wife and family, for it was a moonlit night and the moon at its full. Now the terrace overlooked the cowhouse and presently, as he sat there with his children playing about him, the trader heard the Ass say to the Bull, "Tell me, O father Broad o' Brow, what thou purposest to do to-morrow?" The Bull answered, "What but continue to follow thy counsel, O Aliboron? Indeed it was as good as good could be and it hath given me rest and repose; nor will I now depart from it one tittle: so, when they bring me my meat, I will refuse it and blow out my belly and counterfeit crank." The Ass shook his head and said, "Beware of so doing, O Father of a Bull!" The Bull asked, "Why," and the Ass answered, "Know that I am about to give thee the best of counsel, for verily I heard our owner say to the herd, If the Bull rise not from his place to do his work this morning and if he retire from his fodder this day, make him over to the butcher that he may slaughter him and give his flesh to the poor, and fashion a bit of leather from his hide. Now I fear for thee on account of this. So take my advice ere a calamity befal thee; and when they bring thee thy fodder eat it and rise up and bellow and paw the ground, or our master will assuredly slay thee: and peace be with thee!" Thereupon the Bull arose and lowed aloud and thanked the Ass, and said, "To-morrow I will readily go forth with them;" and he at once ate up all his meat and even licked the manger. (All this took place and the owner was listening to their talk.) Next morning the trader and his wife went to the Bull's crib and sat down, and the driver came and led forth the Bull who, seeing his owner, whisked his tail and brake wind, and frisked about so lustily that the merchant laughed a loud laugh and kept laughing till he fell on his back. His wife asked him, "Whereat laughest thou with such loud laughter as this?"; and he answered her, "I laughed at a secret something which I have heard and seen but cannot say lest I die my death." She returned, "Perforce thou must discover it to me, and disclose the cause of thy laughing even if thou come by thy death!" But he rejoined, "I cannot reveal what beasts and birds say in their lingo for fear I die. Then quoth she, "By Allah, thou liest! this is a mere pretext: thou laughest at none save me, and now thou wouldest hide somewhat from me. But by the Lord of the Heavens! an thou disclose not the cause I will no longer cohabit with thee: I will leave thee at once." And she sat down and cried. Whereupon quoth the merchant, "Woe betide thee! what means thy weeping? Fear Allah and leave these words and query me no more questions." "Needs must thou tell me the cause of that laugh," said she, and he replied, "Thou wottest that when I prayed Allah to vouchsafe me understanding of the tongues of beasts and birds, I made a vow never to disclose the secret to any Under pain of dying on the spot." "No matter," cried she, "tell me what secret passed between the Bull and the Ass and die this very hour an thou be so minded;" and she ceased not to importune him till he was worn out and clean distraught. So at last he said, "Summon thy father and thy mother and our kith and kin and sundry of our neighbours," which she did; and he sent for the Kazi and his assessors, intending to make his will and reveal to her his secret and die the death; for he loved her with love exceeding because she was his cousin, the daughter of his father's brother, and the mother of his children, and he had lived with her a life of an hundred and twenty years. Then, having assembled all the family and the folk of his neighbourhood, he said to them, "By me there hangeth a strange story, and 'tis such that if I discover the secret to any, I am a dead man." Therefore quoth every one of those present to the woman, "Allah upon thee, leave this sinful obstinacy and recognise the right of this matter, lest haply thy husband and the father of thy children die." But she rejoined, "I will not turn from it till he tell me, even though he come by his death." So they ceased to urge her; and the trader rose from amongst them and repaired to an outhouse to perform the Wuzu-ablution, and he purposed thereafter to return and to tell them his secret and to die.

Now, daughter Shahrazad, that merchant had in his out-houses some fifty hens under one cock, and whilst making ready to farewell his folk he heard one of his many farm-dogs thus address in his own tongue the Cock, who was flapping his wings and crowing lustily and jumping from one hen's back to another and treading all in turn, saying "O Chanticleer! how mean is thy wit and how shameless is thy conduct! Be he disappointed who brought thee up? Art thou not ashamed of thy doings on such a day as this?" "And what," asked the Rooster, "hath occurred this day?," when the Dog answered, "Dost thou not know that our master is this day making ready for his death? His wife is resolved that he shall disclose the secret taught to him by Allah, and the moment he so doeth he shall surely die. We dogs are all a-mourning; but thou clappest thy wings and clarionest thy loudest and treadest hen after hen. Is this an hour for pastime and pleasuring? Art thou not ashamed of thyself?" "Then by Allah," quoth the Cock, "is our master a lack-wit and a man scanty of sense: if he cannot manage matters with a single wife, his life is not worth prolonging. Now I have some fifty Dame Partlets; and I please this and provoke that and starve one and stuff another; and through my good governance they are all well under my control. This our master pretendeth to wit and wisdom, and he hath but one wife, and yet knoweth not how to manage her." Asked the Dog, "What then, O Cock, should the master do to win clear of his strait?" "He should arise forthright," answered the Cock, "and take some twigs from yon mulberry-tree and give her a regular back-basting and rib-roasting till she cry: I repent, O my lord! I will never ask thee a question as long as I live! Then let him beat her once more and soundly, and when he shall have done this he shall sleep free from care and enjoy life. But this master of ours owns neither sense nor judgment." "Now, daughter Shahrazad," continued the Wazir, "I will do to thee as did that husband to that wife." Said Shahrazad, "And what did he do?" He replied, "When the merchant heard the wise words spoken by his Cock to his Dog, he arose in haste and sought his wife's chamber, after cutting for her some mulberry-twigs and hiding them there; and then he called to her, "Come into the closet that I may tell thee the secret while no one seeth me and then die." She entered with him and he locked the door and came down upon her with so sound a beating of back and shoulders, ribs, arms and legs, saying the while, "Wilt thou ever be asking questions about what concerneth thee not?" that she was well nigh senseless. Presently she cried out, "I am of the repentant! By Allah, I will ask thee no more questions, and indeed I repent sincerely and wholesomely." Then she kissed his hand and feet and he led her out of the room submissive as a wife should be. Her parents and all the company rejoiced and sadness and mourning were changed into joy and gladness. Thus the merchant learnt family discipline from his Cock and he and his wife lived together the happiest of lives until death. And thou also, O my daughter! continued the Wazir, "Unless thou turn from this matter I will do by thee what that trader did to his wife." But she answered him with much decision, "I will never desist, O my father, nor shall this tale change my purpose. Leave such talk and tattle. I will not listen to thy words and, if thou deny me, I will marry myself to him despite the nose of thee. And first I will go up to the King myself and alone and I will say to him: I prayed my father to wive me with thee, but he refused, being resolved to disappoint his lord, grudging the like of me to the like of thee." Her father asked, "Must this needs be?" and she answered, "Even so."

Hereupon the Wazir being weary of lamenting and contending, persuading and dissuading her, all to no purpose, went up to King Shahryar and, after blessing him and kissing the ground before him, told him all about his dispute with his daughter from first to last and how he designed to bring her to him that night. The King wondered with exceeding wonder; for he had made an especial exception of the Wazir's daughter, and said to him, "O most faithful of Counsellors, how is this? Thou wottest that I have sworn by the Raiser of the Heavens that after I have gone into her this night I shall say to thee on the morrow's morning: Take her and slay her! and, if thou slay her not, I will slay thee in her stead without fail." "Allah guide thee to glory and lengthen thy life, O King of the age," answered the Wazir, "it is she that hath so determined: all this have I told her and more; but she will not hearken to me and she persisteth in passing this coming night with the King's Majesty." So Shahryar rejoiced greatly and said, "'Tis well; go get her ready and this night bring her to me." The Wazir returned to his daughter and reported to her the command saying, "Allah make not thy father desolate by thy loss!" But Shahrazad rejoiced with exceeding joy and gat ready all she required and said to her younger sister, Dunyazad, "Note well what directions I entrust to thee! When I have gone into the King I will send for thee and when thou comest to me and seest that he hath had his carnal will of me, do thou say to me: O my sister, an thou be not sleepy, relate to me some new story, delectable and delightsome, the better to speed our waking hours;" and I will tell thee a tale which shall be our deliverance, if so Allah please, and which shall turn the King from his blood-thirsty custom." Dunyazad answered "With love and gladness." So when it was night their father the Wazir carried Shahrazad to the King who was gladdened at the sight and asked, "Hast thou brought me my need?" and he answered, "I have." But when the King took her to his bed and fell to toying with her and wished to go in to her she wept; which made him ask, "What aileth thee?" She replied, "O King of the age, I have a younger sister and lief would I take leave of her this night before I see the dawn." So he sent at once for Dunyazad and she came and kissed the ground between his hands, when he permitted her to take her seat near the foot of the couch. Then the King arose and did away with his bride's maidenhead and the three fell asleep. But when it was midnight Shahrazad awoke and signalled to her sister Dunyazad who sat up and said, "Allah upon thee, O my sister, recite to us some new story, delightsome and delectable, wherewith to while away the waking hours of our latter night." "With joy and goodly gree," answered Shahrazad, "if this pious and auspicious King permit me." "Tell on," quoth the King who chanced to be sleepless and restless and therefore was pleased with the prospect of hearing her story. So Shahrazad rejoiced; and thus, on the first night of the Thousand Nights and a Night, she began with the

Tale of the Trader and the Jinni

Richard F. Burton

IT IS RELATED, O auspicious King, that there was a merchant of the merchants who had much wealth, and business in various cities. Now on a day he mounted horse and went forth to recover monies in certain towns, and the heat sore oppressed him; so he sat beneath a tree and, putting his hand into his saddle-bags, took thence some broken bread and dry dates and began to break his fast. When he had ended eating the dates he threw away the stones with force and lo! an Ifrit appeared, huge of stature and brandishing a drawn sword, wherewith he approached the merchant and said, "Stand up that I may slay thee, even as thou slewest my son!" Asked the merchant, "How have I slain thy son?" and he answered, "When thou atest dates and threwest away the stones they struck my son full in the breast as he was walking by, so that he died forthwith." Quoth the merchant, "Verily from Allah we proceeded and unto Allah are we returning. There is no Majesty, and there is no Might save in Allah, the Glorious, the Great! If I slew thy son, I slew him by chance medley. I pray thee now pardon me." Rejoined the Jinni, "There is no help but I must slay thee." Then he seized him and dragged him along and, casting him to the earth, raised the sword to strike him; whereupon the merchant wept, and said, "I commit my case to Allah," and began repeating these couplets:

> Containeth Time a twain of days, this of blessing that of bane
> And holdeth Life a twain of halves, this of pleasure that of pain.
> See'st not when blows the hurricane, sweeping stark and striking strong
> None save the forest giant feels the suffering of the strain?
> How many trees earth nourisheth of the dry and of the green
> Yet none but those which bear the fruits for cast of stone complain.
> See'st not how corpses rise and float on the surface of the tide
> While pearls o' price lie hidden in the deepest of the main!
> In Heaven are unnumberèd the many of the stars
> Yet ne'er a star but Sun and Moon by eclipse is overta'en.
> Well judgest thou the days that saw thy faring sound and well
> And countedst not the pangs and pain whereof Fate is ever fain.
> The nights have kept thee safe and the safety brought thee pride
> But bliss and blessings of the night are 'genderers of bane!

When the merchant ceased repeating his verses the Jinni said to him, "Cut thy words short, by Allah! needs must I slay thee." But the merchant spake him thus, "Know, O thou Ifrit, that I have debts due to me and much wealth and children and a wife and many pledges in hand; so permit me to go home and discharge to every claimant his claim; and I will come back to thee at the head of the new year. Allah be my testimony and surety that I will return to thee; and then thou mayest do with me as thou wilt and Allah is witness to what I say." The Jinni took sure promise of him and let him go; so he returned to his own city and transacted his business and rendered to all men their dues and after informing his wife and children of what had betided him, he appointed a guardian and dwelt with them for a full year. Then he arose, and made the Wuzu-ablution to purify himself before death and took his shroud under his arm and bade farewell to his people, his neighbours and all his kith and kin, and went forth despite his own nose. They then began weeping and wailing and beating their breasts over him; but he travelled until he arrived at the same garden, and the day of his arrival was the head of the New Year. As he sat weeping over what had befallen him, behold, a Shaykh, a very ancient man, drew near leading a chained gazelle; and he saluted that merchant and wishing him long life said, "What is the cause of thy sitting in this place and thou alone and this be a resort of evil spirits?" The merchant related to him what had come to pass with the Ifrit, and the old man, the owner of the gazelle, wondered and said, "By Allah, O brother, thy faith is none other than exceeding faith and thy story right strange; were it graven with gravers on the eye-corners, it were a warner to whoso would be warned." Then seating himself near the merchant he said, "By Allah, O my brother, I will not leave thee until I see what may come to pass with thee and this Ifrit." And presently as he sat and the two were at talk the merchant began to feel fear and terror and exceeding grief and sorrow beyond relief and ever-growing care and extreme despair. And the owner of the gazelle was hard by his side; when behold, a second Shaykh approached them, and with him were two dogs both of greyhound breed and both black. The second old man after saluting them with the salam, also asked them of their tidings and said "What causeth you to sit in this place, a dwelling of the Jánn?"

So they told him the tale from beginning to end, and their stay there had not lasted long before there came up a third Shaykh, and with him a she-mule of bright bay coat; and he saluted them and asked them why they were seated in that place. So they told him the story from first to last: and of no avail, O my master, is a twice-told tale! There he sat down with them, and lo! a dust-cloud advanced and a mighty sand-devil appeared amidmost of the waste. Presently the cloud opened and behold, within it was that Jinni hending in hand a drawn sword, while his eyes were shooting fire-sparks of rage. He came up to them and, haling away the merchant from among them, cried to him, "Arise that I may slay thee, as thou slewest my son, the life-stuff of my liver." The merchant wailed and wept, and the three old men began sighing and crying and weeping and wailing with their companion. Presently the first old man (the owner of the gazelle) came out from among them and kissed the hand of the Ifrit and said, "O Jinni, thou Crown of the Kings of the Jann! were I to tell thee the story of me and this gazelle and thou shouldst consider it wondrous wouldst thou give me a third part of this merchant's blood?" Then quoth the Jinni "Even so, O Shaykh! if thou tell me this tale, and I hold it a marvellous, then will I give thee a third of his blood." Thereupon the old man began to tell

The First Shaykh's Story

KNOW O JINNI! that this gazelle is the daughter of my paternal uncle, my own flesh and blood, and I married her when she was a young maid, and I lived with her well-nigh thirty years, yet was I not blessed with issue by her. So I took me a concubine, who brought to me the boon of a male child fair as the full moon, with eyes of lovely shine and eyebrows which formed one line, and limbs of perfect design. Little by little he grew in stature and waxed tall; and when he was a lad fifteen years old, it became needful I should journey to certain cities and I travelled with great store of goods. But the daughter of my uncle (this gazelle) had learned gramarye and egromancy and clerkly craft from her childhood; so she bewitched that son of mine to a calf, and my handmaid (his mother) to a heifer, and made them over to the herdsman's care. Now when I returned after a long time from my journey and asked for my son and his mother, she answered me, saying "Thy slave-girl is dead, and thy son hath fled and I know not whither he is sped." So I remained for a whole year with grieving heart, and streaming eyes until the time came for the Great Festival of Allah. Then sent I to my herdsman bidding him choose for me a fat heifer; and he brought me one which was the damsel, my handmaid, whom this gazelle had ensorcelled. I tucked up my sleeves and skirt and, taking a knife, proceeded to cut her throat, but she lowed aloud and wept bitter tears. Thereat I marvelled and pity seized me and I held my hand, saying to the herd, "Bring me other than this." Then cried my cousin, "Slay her, for I have not a fatter nor a fairer!" Once more I went forward to sacrifice her, but she again lowed aloud, upon which in ruth I refrained and commanded the herdsmen to slay her and flay her. He killed her and skinned her but found in her neither fat nor flesh, only hide and bone; and I repented when penitence availed me naught. I gave her to the herdsman and said to him, "Fetch me a fat calf;" so he brought my son ensorcelled.

When the calf saw me, he broke his tether and ran to me, and fawned upon me and wailed and shed tears; so that I took pity on him and said to the herdsman, "Bring me a heifer and let this calf go!" Thereupon my cousin (this gazelle) called aloud at me, saying, "Needs must thou kill this calf; this is a holy day and a blessed, whereon naught is slain save what be perfect-pure; and we have not amongst our calves any fatter or fairer than this!" Quoth I, "Look thou upon the condition of the heifer which I slaughtered at thy bidding and how we turn from her in disappointment and she profited us on no wise; and I repent with an exceeding repentance of having killed her: so this time I will not obey thy bidding for the sacrifice of this calf." Quoth she, "By Allah the Most Great, the Compassionating, the Compassionate! there is no help for it; thou must kill him on this holy day, and if thou kill him not to me thou art no man and I to thee am no wife." Now when I heard those hard words, not knowing her object I went up to the calf, knife in hand – And Shahrazad perceived the dawn of day and ceased to say her permitted say. Then quoth her sister to her, "How fair is thy tale, and how grateful, and how sweet and how tasteful!" And Shahrazad answered her, "What is this to that I could tell thee on the coming night, were I to live and the King would spare me?" Then said the King in himself, "By Allah, I will not slay her, until I shall have heard the rest of her tale." So they slept the rest of that night in mutual embrace till day fully brake. Then the King went forth to his audience-hall and the Wazir went up with his daughter's shroud under his arm. The King issued his orders, and promoted this and deposed that, until the end of the day; and he told the Wazir no whit of what had happened. But the Minister wondered thereat with exceeding wonder; and when the Court broke up King Shahryar entered his palace.

Now when it was the Second Night, said Dunyazad to her sister Shahrazad, "O my sister, finish for us that story of the Merchant and the Jinni;" and she answered, "With joy and goodly gree, if the King permit me." Then quoth the King, "Tell thy tale;" and

Shahrazad began in these words: It hath reached me, O auspicious King and Heaven-directed Ruler! that when the merchant purposed the sacrifice of the calf but saw it weeping, his heart relented and he said to the herdsman, "Keep the calf among my cattle." All this the old Shaykh told the Jinni who marvelled much at these strange words. Then the owner of the gazelle continued: O Lord of the Kings of the Jann, this much took place and my uncle's daughter, this gazelle, looked on and saw it, and said, "Butcher me this calf, for surely it is a fat one;" but I bade the herdsman take it away and he took it and turned his face homewards. On the next day as I was sitting in my own house, lo! the herdsman came and, standing before me said, "O my master, I will tell thee a thing which shall gladden thy soul, and shall gain me the gift of good tidings." I answered, "Even so." Then said he, "O merchant, I have a daughter, and she learned magic in her childhood from an old woman who lived with us. Yesterday when thou gavest me the calf, I went into the house to her, and she looked upon it and veiled her face; then she wept and laughed alternately and at last she said: O my father, hath mine honour become so cheap to thee that thou bringest in to me strange men? I asked her: Where be these strange men and why wast thou laughing, and crying?; and she answered, Of a truth this calf which is with thee is the son of our master, the merchant; but he is ensorcelled by his stepdame who bewitched both him and his mother: such is the cause of my laughing; now the reason of his weeping is his mother, for that his father slew her unawares. Then I marvelled at this with exceeding marvel and hardly made sure that day had dawned before I came to tell thee."

When I heard, O Jinni, my herdsman's words, I went out with him, and I was drunken without wine, from the excess of joy and gladness which came upon me, until I reached his house. There his daughter welcomed me and kissed my hand, and forthwith the calf came and fawned upon me as before. Quoth I to the herdsman's daughter, "Is this true that thou sayest of this calf?" Quoth she, "Yea, O my master, he is thy son, the very core of thy heart." I rejoiced and said to her, "O maiden, if thou wilt release him thine shall be whatever cattle and property of mine are under thy father's hand." She smiled and answered, "O my master, I have no greed for the goods nor will I take them save on two conditions; the first that thou marry me to thy son and the second that I may bewitch her who bewitched him and imprison her, otherwise I cannot be safe from her malice and malpractices." Now when I heard, O Jinni, these, the words of the herdsman's daughter, I replied, "Beside what thou askest all the cattle and the household stuff in thy father's charge are thine and, as for the daughter of my uncle, her blood is lawful to thee." When I had spoken, she took a cup and filled it with water: then she recited a spell over it and sprinkled it upon the calf, saying, "If Almighty Allah created thee a calf, remain so shaped, and change not; but if thou be enchanted, return to thy whilom form, by command of Allah Most Highest!" and lo! he trembled and became a man. Then I fell on his neck and said, "Allah upon thee, tell me all that the daughter of my uncle did by thee and by thy mother." And when he told me what had come to pass between them I said, "O my son, Allah favoured thee with one to restore thee, and thy right hath returned to thee." Then, O Jinni, I married the herdsman's daughter to him, and she transformed my wife into this gazelle, saying: Her shape is a comely and by no means loathsome. After this she abode with us night and day, day and night, till the Almighty took her to Himself. When she deceased, my son fared forth to the cities of Hind, even to the city of this man who hath done to thee what hath been done; and I also took this gazelle (my cousin) and wandered with her from town to town seeking tidings of my son, till Destiny drove me to this place where I saw the merchant sitting in tears. Such is my tale! Quoth the Jinni, "This story is indeed strange, and therefore I grant thee the third part of his blood." Thereupon the second old man, who owned the two greyhounds, came up and said, "O Jinni, if I recount to thee what befel me from my brothers, these two hounds, and thou see that it is a tale even more wondrous and marvellous than what thou hast heard, wilt thou grant to me also the third of this man's blood?" Replied the Jinni, "Thou hast my word for it, if thine adventures be more marvellous and wondrous." Thereupon he thus began

The Second Shaykh's Story

KNOW, O LORD of the Kings of the Jann! that these two dogs are my brothers and I am the third. Now when our father died and left us a capital of three thousand gold pieces, I opened a shop with my share, and bought and sold therein, and in like guise did my two brothers, each setting up a shop. But I had been in business no long while before the elder sold his stock for a thousand dinars, and after buying outfit and merchandise, went his ways to foreign parts. He was absent one whole year with the caravan; but one day as I sat in my shop, behold, a beggar stood before me asking alms, and I said to him, "Allah open thee another door!" Whereupon he answered, weeping the while, "Am I so changed that thou knowest me not?" Then I looked at him narrowly, and lo! it was my brother, so I rose to him and welcomed him; then I seated him in my shop and put questions concerning his case. "Ask me not," answered he; "my wealth is awaste and my state hath waxed un-stated!" So I took him to the Hammám-bath and clad him in a suit of my own and gave him lodging in my house. Moreover, after looking over the accounts of my stock-in-trade and the profits of my business, I found that industry had gained me one thousand dinars, while my principal, the head of my wealth, amounted to two thousand. So I shared the whole with him, saying, "Assume that thou hast made no journey abroad but hast remained at home; and be not cast down by thine ill-luck." He took the share in great glee and opened for himself a shop; and matters went on quietly for a few nights and days. But presently my second brother (yon other dog), also setting his heart upon travel, sold off what goods and stock-in-trade he had, and albeit we tried to stay him he would not be stayed: he laid in an outfit for the journey, and fared forth with certain wayfarers. After an absence of a whole year he came back to me, even as my elder brother had come back; and when I said to him, "O my brother, did I not dissuade thee from travel?" he shed tears and cried, "O my brother, this be destiny's decree: here I am a mere beggar, penniless and without a shirt to my back." So I led him to the bath, O Jinni, and clothing him in new clothes of my own wear, I went with him to my shop and served him with meat and drink. Furthermore I said to him, "O my brother, I am wont to cast up my shop-accounts at the head of every year, and whatso I shall find of surplusage is between me and thee." So I proceeded, O Ifrit, to strike a balance and, finding two thousand dinars of profit, I returned praises to the Creator (be He extolled and exalted!) and made over one half to my brother, keeping the other to myself. Thereupon he busied himself with opening a shop and on this wise we abode many days. After a time my brothers began pressing me to travel with them; but I refused, saying, "What gained ye by your voyage that I should gain thereby?" As I would not give ear to them we went back each to his own shop where we bought and sold as before. They kept urging me to travel for a whole twelvemonth, but I refused to do so till full six years were past and gone when I consented with these words, "O my brothers, here am I, your companion of travel: now let me see what monies you have by you." I found, however, that they had not a doit, having squandered their substance in high diet and drinking and carnal delights. Yet I spoke not a word of reproach; so far from it I looked over my shop accounts once more, and sold what goods and stock-in trade were mine; and, finding myself the owner of six thousand ducats, I gladly proceeded to divide that sum into halves, saying to my brothers, "These three thousand gold pieces are for me and for you to trade withal," adding, "Let us bury the other moiety underground that it may be of service in case any harm befal us, in which case each shall take a thousand wherewith to open shops." Both replied, "Right is thy recking;" and I gave to each one his thousand gold pieces, keeping the same sum for myself, to wit, a thousand dinars. We then got ready suitable goods and hired a ship and, having embarked our merchandise, proceeded on our voyage, day following day, a full month, after which we arrived at a city, where we sold our venture; and for every piece of gold we gained ten. And as we turned again to our voyage we found on the shore of the sea a maiden clad in worn and ragged gear, and she kissed my hand and said, "O master, is there kindness in thee and charity? I can make thee a fitting return for them." I answered, "Even so; truly in me are benevolence and good works, even though thou render me no return." Then she said, "Take me to wife, O my master, and carry me to thy city, for I have given myself to thee; so do me a kindness and I am of those who be meet for good works and charity: I will make thee a fitting return for these and be thou not shamed by my condition." When I heard her words, my heart yearned towards her, in such sort as willed it Allah (be He extolled and exalted!); and took her and clothed her and made ready for her a fair resting-place in the vessel, and honourably entreated her.

So we voyaged on, and my heart became attached to her with exceeding attachment, and I was separated from her neither night nor day, and I paid more regard to her than to my brothers. Then they were estranged from me, and waxed jealous of my wealth and the quantity of merchandise I had, and their eyes were opened covetously upon all my property. So they took counsel to murder me and seize my wealth, saying, "Let us slay our brother and all his monies will be ours;" and Satan made this deed seem fair in their sight; so when they found me in privacy (and I sleeping by my wife's side) they took us both up and cast us into the sea. My wife awoke startled from her sleep and, forthright becoming an Ifritah, she bore me up and carried me to an island and disappeared for a short time; but she returned in the morning and said "Here am I, thy faithful slave, who hath made thee due recompense; for I bore thee up in the waters and saved thee from death by command of the Almighty. Know that I am a Jinniyah, and as I saw thee my heart loved thee by will of the Lord, for I am a believer in Allah and in His Apostle (whom Heaven bless and preserve!). Thereupon I came to thee conditioned as thou sawest me and thou didst marry me, and see now I have saved thee from sinking. But I am angered against thy brothers and assuredly I must slay them." When I heard her story I was surprised and, thanking her for all she had done, I said, "But as to slaying my brothers this must not be." Then I told her the tale of what had come to pass with them from the beginning of our lives to the end, and on hearing it quoth she, "This night will I fly as a bird over them and will sink their ship and slay them." Quoth I, "Allah upon thee, do not thus, for the proverb saith, O thou who doest good to him that doth evil, leave the evil doer to his evil deeds. Moreover they are still my brothers." But she rejoined, "By Allah, there is no help for it but I slay them." I humbled myself before her for their pardon, whereupon she bore me up and flew away with me till at last she set me down on the terrace-roof of my own house. I opened the doors and took up what I had hidden in the ground; and after I had saluted the folk I opened my shop and bought me merchandise. Now when night came on I went home, and there I saw these two hounds tied up; and, when they sighted me, they arose and whined and fawned upon me; but ere I knew what happened my wife said, "These two dogs be thy brothers!" I answered, "And who hath done this thing by them?" and she rejoined, "I sent a message to my sister and she entreated them on this wise, nor shall these two be released from their present shape till ten years shall have passed." And now I have arrived at this place on my way to my wife's sister that she may deliver them from this condition, after their having endured it for half a score of years. As I was wending onwards I saw this young man, who acquainted me with what had befallen him, and I determined not to fare hence until I should see what might occur between thee and him. Such is my tale! Then said the Jinni, "Surely this is a strange story and therefor I give thee the third portion of his blood and his crime." Thereupon quoth the third Shaykh, the master of the mare-mule, to the Jinni, "I can tell thee a tale more wondrous than these two, so thou grant me the remainder of his blood and of his offence," and the Jinni answered, "So be it!" Then the old man began

The Third Shaykh's Story

KNOW, O SULTAN and head of the Jann, that this mule was my wife. Now it so happened that I went forth and was absent one whole year; and when I returned from my journey I came to her by night, and saw a black slave lying with her on the carpet-bed, and they were talking, and dallying, and laughing, and kissing and playing the close-buttock game. When she saw me, she rose and came hurriedly at me with a gugglet of water; and, muttering spells over it, she besprinkled me and said, "Come forth from this thy shape into the shape of a dog;" and I became on the instant a dog. She drove me out of the house, and I ran through the doorway nor ceased running until I came to a butcher's stall, where I stopped and began to eat what bones were there. When the stall-owner saw me, he took me and led me into his house, but as soon as his daughter had sight of me she veiled her face from me, crying out, "Dost thou bring men to me and dost thou come in with them to me?" Her father asked, "Where is the man?"; and she answered, "This dog is a man whom his wife hath ensorcelled and I am able to release him." When her father heard her words, he said, "Allah upon thee, O my daughter, release him." So she took a gugglet of water and, after uttering words over it, sprinkled upon me a few drops, saying, "Come forth from that form into thy former form." And I returned to my natural shape. Then I kissed her hand and said, "I wish thou wouldest transform my wife even as she transformed me." Thereupon she gave me some water, saying, "As soon as thou see her asleep, sprinkle this liquid upon her and speak what words thou heardest me utter, so shall she become whatsoever thou desirest." I went to my wife and found her fast asleep; and, while sprinkling the water upon her, I said, "Come forth from that form into the form of a mare-mule." So she became on the instant a she-mule, and she it is whom thou seest with thine eyes, O Sultan and head of the Kings of the Jann! Then the Jinni turned towards her and said, "Is this sooth?" And she nodded her head and replied by signs, "Indeed, 'tis the truth: for such is my tale and this is what hath befallen me." Now when the old man had ceased speaking the Jinni shook with pleasure and gave him the third of the merchant's blood. – And Shahrazad perceived the dawn of day and ceased saying her permitted say. Then quoth Dunyazad, "O, my sister, how pleasant is thy tale, and how tasteful; how sweet and how grateful!" She replied, "And what is this compared with that I could tell thee, the night to come, if I live and the King spare me?" Then thought the King, "By Allah, I will not slay her until I hear the rest of her tale, for truly it is wondrous." So they rested that night in mutual embrace until the dawn. After this the King went forth to his Hall of Estate, and the Wazir and the troops came in and the court was crowded, and the King gave orders and judged and appointed and deposed, bidding and forbidding during the rest of the day. Then the Divan broke up, and King Shahryar entered his palace.

Now when it was the Third Night, and the King had had his will of the Wazir's daughter, Dunyazad, her sister, said to her, "Finish for us that tale of thine;" and she replied, "With joy and goodly gree! It hath reached me, O auspicious King, that when the third old man told a tale to the Jinni more wondrous than the two preceding, the Jinni marvelled with exceeding marvel; and, shaking with delight, cried, "Lo! I have given thee the remainder of the merchant's punishment and for thy sake have I released him." Thereupon the merchant embraced the old men and thanked them, and these Shaykhs wished him joy on being saved and fared forth each one for his own city. Yet this tale is not more wondrous than the fisherman's story." Asked the King, "What is the fisherman's story?" And she answered by relating the tale of

The Story of the Fisherman

Andrew and Nora Lang

SIRE, THERE WAS once upon a time a fisherman so old and so poor that he could scarcely manage to support his wife and three children. He went every day to fish very early, and each day he made a rule not to throw his nets more than four times. He started out one morning by moonlight and came to the sea-shore. He undressed and threw his nets, and as he was drawing them towards the bank he felt a great weight. He though he had caught a large fish, and he felt very pleased. But a moment afterwards, seeing that instead of a fish he only had in his nets the carcase of an ass, he was much disappointed.

Vexed with having such a bad haul, when he had mended his nets, which the carcase of the ass had broken in several places, he threw them a second time. In drawing them in he again felt a great weight, so that he thought they were full of fish. But he only found a large basket full of rubbish. He was much annoyed.

"O Fortune," he cried, "do not trifle thus with me, a poor fisherman, who can hardly support his family!"

So saying, he threw away the rubbish, and after having washed his nets clean of the dirt, he threw them for the third time. But he only drew in stones, shells, and mud. He was almost in despair.

Then he threw his nets for the fourth time. When he thought he had a fish he drew them in with a great deal of trouble. There was no fish however, but he found a yellow pot, which by its weight seemed full of something, and he noticed that it was fastened and sealed with lead, with the impression of a seal. He was delighted. "I will sell it to the founder," he said; "with the money I shall get for it I shall buy a measure of wheat."

He examined the jar on all sides; he shook it to see if it would rattle. But he heard nothing, and so, judging from the impression of the seal and the lid, he thought there must be something precious inside. To find out, he took his knife, and with a little trouble he opened it. He turned it upside down, but nothing came out, which surprised him very much. He set it in front of him, and whilst he was looking at it attentively, such a thick smoke came out that he had to step back a pace or two. This smoke rose up to the clouds, and stretching over the sea and the shore, formed a thick mist, which caused the fisherman much astonishment. When all the smoke was out of the jar it gathered itself together, and became a thick mass in which appeared a genius, twice as large as the largest giant. When he saw such a terrible-looking monster, the fisherman would like to have run away, but he trembled so with fright that he could not move a step.

"Great king of the genii," cried the monster, "I will never again disobey you!"

At these words the fisherman took courage.

"What is this you are saying, great genius? Tell me your history and how you came to be shut up in that vase."

At this, the genius looked at the fisherman haughtily. "Speak to me more civilly," he said, "before I kill you."

"Alas! why should you kill me?" cried the fisherman. "I have just freed you; have you already forgotten that?"

"No," answered the genius; "but that will not prevent me from killing you; and I am only going to grant you one favour, and that is to choose the manner of your death."

"But what have I done to you?" asked the fisherman.

"I cannot treat you in any other way," said the genius, "and if you would know why, listen to my story.

"I rebelled against the king of the genii. To punish me, he shut me up in this vase of copper, and he put on the leaden cover his seal, which is enchantment enough to prevent my coming out. Then he had the vase thrown into the sea. During the first period of my captivity I vowed that if anyone should free me before a hundred years were passed, I would make him rich even after his death. But that century passed, and no one freed me. In the second century I vowed that I would give all the treasures in the world to my deliverer; but he never came.

"In the third, I promised to make him a king, to be always near him, and to grant him three wishes every day; but that century passed away as the other two had done, and I remained in the same plight. At last I grew angry at being captive for so long, and I vowed that if anyone would release me I would kill him at once, and would only allow him to choose in what manner he should die. So you see, as you have freed me to-day, choose in what way you will die."

The fisherman was very unhappy. "What an unlucky man I am to have freed you! I implore you to spare my life."

"I have told you," said the genius, "that it is impossible. Choose quickly; you are wasting time."

The fisherman began to devise a plot.

"Since I must die," he said, "before I choose the manner of my death, I conjure you on your honour to tell me if you really were in that vase?"

"Yes, I was," answered the genius.

"I really cannot believe it," said the fisherman. "That vase could not contain one of your feet even, and how could your whole body go in? I cannot believe it unless I see you do the thing."

Then the genius began to change himself into smoke, which, as before, spread over the sea and the shore, and which, then collecting itself together, began to go back into the vase slowly and evenly till there was nothing left outside. Then a voice came from the vase which said to the fisherman, "Well, unbelieving fisherman, here I am in the vase; do you believe me now?"

The fisherman instead of answering took the lid of lead and shut it down quickly on the vase.

"Now, O genius," he cried, "ask pardon of me, and choose by what death you will die! But no, it will be better if I throw you into the sea whence I drew you out, and I will build a house on the shore to warn fishermen who come to cast their nets here, against fishing up such a wicked genius as you are, who vows to kill the man who frees you."

At these words the genius did all he could to get out, but he could not, because of the enchantment of the lid.

Then he tried to get out by cunning.

"If you will take off the cover," he said, "I will repay you."

"No," answered the fisherman, "if I trust myself to you I am afraid you will treat me as a certain Greek king treated the physician Douban. Listen, and I will tell you."

The Story of the Greek King and the Physician Douban

Andrew and Nora Lang

IN THE COUNTRY of Zouman, in Persia, there lived a Greek king. This king was a leper, and all his doctors had been unable to cure him, when a very clever physician came to his court.

He was very learned in all languages, and knew a great deal about herbs and medicines.

As soon as he was told of the king's illness he put on his best robe and presented himself before the king. "Sire," said he, "I know that no physician has been able to cure your majesty, but if you will follow my instructions, I will promise to cure you without any medicines or outward application."

The king listened to this proposal.

"If you are clever enough to do this," he said, "I promise to make you and your descendants rich for ever."

The physician went to his house and made a polo club, the handle of which he hollowed out, and put in it the drug he wished to use. Then he made a ball, and with these things he went the next day to the king.

He told him that he wished him to play at polo. Accordingly the king mounted his horse and went into the place where he played. There the physician approached him with the bat he had made, saying, "Take this, sire, and strike the ball till you feel your hand and whole body in a glow. When the remedy that is in the handle of the club is warmed by your hand it will penetrate throughout your body. The you must return to your palace, bathe, and go to sleep, and when you awake to-morrow morning you will be cured."

The king took the club and urged his horse after the ball which he had thrown. He struck it, and then it was hit back by the courtiers who were playing with him. When he felt very hot he stopped playing, and went back to the palace, went into the bath, and did all that the physician had said. The next day when he arose he found, to his great joy and astonishment, that he was completely cured. When he entered his audience-chamber all his courtiers, who were eager to see if the wonderful cure had been effected, were overwhelmed with joy.

The physician Douban entered the hall and bowed low to the ground. The king, seeing him, called him, made him sit by his side, and showed him every mark of honour.

That evening he gave him a long and rich robe of state, and presented him with two thousand sequins. The following day he continued to load him with favours.

Now the king had a grand-vizir who was avaricious, and envious, and a very bad man. He grew extremely jealous of the physician, and determined to bring about his ruin.

In order to do this he asked to speak in private with the king, saying that he had a most important communication to make.

"What is it?" asked the king.

"Sire," answered the grand-vizir, "it is most dangerous for a monarch to confide in a man whose faithfulness is not proved, You do not know that this physician is not a traitor come here to assassinate you."

"I am sure," said the king, "that this man is the most faithful and virtuous of men. If he wished to take my life, why did he cure me? Cease to speak against him. I see what it is, you are jealous of him; but do not think that I can be turned against him. I remember well what a vizir said to King Sindbad, his master, to prevent him from putting the prince, his son, to death."

What the Greek king said excited the vizir's curiosity, and he said to him, "Sire, I beg your majesty to have the condescension to tell me what the vizir said to King Sindbad."

"This vizir," he replied, "told King Sindbad that one ought not believe everything that a mother-in-law says, and told him this story."

The Story of the Husband and the Parrot

Andrew and Nora Lang

A GOOD MAN had a beautiful wife, whom he loved passionately, and never left if possible. One day, when he was obliged by important business to go away from her, he went to a place where all kinds of birds are sold and bought a parrot. This parrot not only spoke well, but it had the gift of telling all that had been done before it. He brought it home in a cage, and asked his wife to put it in her room, and take great care of it while he was away. Then he departed. On his return he asked the parrot what had happened during his absence, and the parrot told him some things which made him scold his wife.

She thought that one of her slaves must have been telling tales of her, but they told her it was the parrot, and she resolved to revenge herself on him.

When her husband next went away for one day, she told on slave to turn under the bird's cage a hand-mill; another to throw water down from above the cage, and a third to take a mirror and turn it in front of its eyes, from left to right by the light of a candle. The slaves did this for part of the night, and did it very well.

The next day when the husband came back he asked the parrot what he had seen. The bird replied, "My good master, the lightning, thunder and rain disturbed me so much all night long, that I cannot tell you what I have suffered."

The husband, who knew that it had neither rained nor thundered in the night, was convinced that the parrot was not speaking the truth, so he took him out of the cage and threw him so roughly on the ground that he killed him. Nevertheless he was sorry afterwards, for he found that the parrot had spoken the truth.

"When the Greek king," said the fisherman to the genius, "had finished the story of the parrot, he added to the vizir, "And so, vizir, I shall not listen to you, and I shall take care of the physician, in case I repent as the husband did when he had killed the parrot." But the vizir was determined. "Sire," he replied, "the death of the parrot was nothing. But when it is a question of the life of a king it is better to sacrifice the innocent than save the guilty. It is no uncertain thing, however. The physician, Douban, wishes to assassinate you. My zeal prompts me to disclose this to your Majesty. If I am wrong, I deserve to be punished as a vizir was once punished." "What had the vizir done," said the Greek king, "to merit the punishment?" "I will tell your Majesty, if you will do me the honour to listen," answered the vizir.

The Story of the Vizir Who Was Punished

Andrew and Nora Lang

THERE WAS ONCE upon a time a king who had a son who was very fond of hunting. He often allowed him to indulge in this pastime, but he had ordered his grand-vizir always to go with him, and never to lose sight of him. One day the huntsman roused a stag, and the prince, thinking that the vizir was behind, gave chase, and rode so hard that he found himself alone. He stopped, and having lost sight of it, he turned to rejoin the vizir, who had not been careful enough to follow him. But he lost his way. Whilst he was trying to find it, he saw on the side of the road a beautiful lady who was crying bitterly. He drew his horse's rein, and asked her who she was and what she was doing in this place, and if she needed help. "I am the daughter of an Indian king," she answered, "and whilst riding in the country I fell asleep and tumbled off. My horse has run away, and I do not know what has become of him."

The young prince had pity on her, and offered to take her behind him, which he did. As they passed by a ruined building the lady dismounted and went in. The prince also dismounted and followed her. To his great surprise, he heard her saying to some one inside, "Rejoice my children; I am bringing you a nice fat youth." And other voices replied, "Where is he, mamma, that we may eat him at once, as we are very hungry?"

The prince at once saw the danger he was in. He now knew that the lady who said she was the daughter of an Indian king was an ogress, who lived in desolate places, and who by a thousand wiles surprised and devoured passers-by. He was terrified, and threw himself on his horse. The pretended princess appeared at this moment, and seeing that she had lost her prey, she said to him, "Do not be afraid. What do you want?"

"I am lost," he answered, "and I am looking for the road."

"Keep straight on," said the ogress, "and you will find it."

The prince could hardly believe his ears, and rode off as hard as he could. He found his way, and arrived safe and sound at his father's house, where he told him of the danger he had run because of the grand-vizir's carelessness. The king was very angry, and had him strangled immediately.

"Sire," went on the vizir to the Greek king, "to return to the physician, Douban. If you do not take care, you will repent of having trusted him. Who knows what this remedy, with which he has cured you, may not in time have a bad effect on you?"

The Greek king was naturally very weak, and did not perceive the wicked intention of his vizir, nor was he firm enough to keep to his first resolution.

"Well, vizir," he said, "you are right. Perhaps he did come to take my life. He might do it by the mere smell of one of his drugs. I must see what can be done."

"The best means, sire, to put your life in security, is to send for him at once, and to cut off his head directly he comes," said the vizir.

"I really think," replied the king, "that will be the best way."

He then ordered one of his ministers to fetch the physician, who came at once.

"I have had you sent for," said the king, "in order to free myself from you by taking your life."

The physician was beyond measure astonished when he heard he was to die.

"What crimes have I committed, your majesty?"

"I have learnt," replied the king, "that you are a spy, and intend to kill me. But I will be first, and kill you. Strike," he added to an executioner who was by, "and rid me of this assassin."

At this cruel order the physician threw himself on his knees. "Spare my life," he cried, "and yours will be spared."

The fisherman stopped here to say to the genius: "You see what passed between the Greek king and the physician has just passed between us two. The Greek king," he went on, "had no mercy on him, and the executioner bound his eyes."

All those present begged for his life, but in vain.

The physician on his knees, and bound, said to the king: "At least let me put my affairs in order, and leave my books to persons who will make good use of them. There is one which I should like to present to your majesty. It is very precious, and ought to be kept carefully in your treasury. It contains many curious things the chief being that when you cut off my head, if your majesty will turn to the sixth leaf, and read the third line of the left-hand page, my head will answer all the questions you like to ask it."

The king, eager to see such a wonderful thing, put off his execution to the next day, and sent him under a strong guard to his house. There the physician put his affairs in order, and the next day there was a great crowd assembled in the hall to see his death, and the doings after it. The physician went up to the foot of the throne with a large book in his hand. He carried a basin, on which he spread the covering of the book, and presenting it to the king, said: "Sire, take this book, and when my head is cut off, let it be placed in the basin on the covering of this book; as soon as it is there, the blood will cease to flow. Then open the book, and my head will answer your questions. But, sire, I implore your mercy, for I am innocent."

"Your prayers are useless, and if it were only to hear your head speak when you are dead, you should die."

So saying, he took the book from the physician's hands, and ordered the executioner to do his duty.

The head was so cleverly cut off that it fell into the basin, and directly the blood ceased to flow. Then, to the great astonishment of the king, the eyes opened, and the head said, "Your majesty, open the book." The king did so, and finding that the first leaf stuck against the second, he put his finger in his mouth, to turn it more easily. He did the same thing till he reached the sixth page, and not seeing any writing on it, "Physician," he said, "there is no writing."

"Turn over a few more pages," answered the head. The king went on turning, still putting his finger in his mouth, till the poison in which each page was dipped took effect. His sight failed him, and he fell at the foot of his throne.

When the physician's head saw that the poison had taken effect, and that the king had only a few more minutes to live, "Tyrant," it cried, "see how cruelty and injustice are punished."

Scarcely had it uttered these words than the king died, and the head lost also the little life that had remained in it.

That is the end of the story of the Greek king, and now let us return to the fisherman and the genius.

"If the Greek king," said the fisherman, "had spared the physician, he would not have thus died. The same thing applies to you. Now I am going to throw you into the sea."

"My friend," said the genius, "do not do such a cruel thing. Do not treat me as Imma treated Ateca."

"What did Imma do to Ateca?" asked the fisherman.

"Do you think I can tell you while I am shut up in here?" replied the genius. "Let me out, and I will make you rich."

The hope of being no longer poor made the fisherman give way.

"If you will give me your promise to do this, I will open the lid. I do not think you will dare to break your word."

The genius promised, and the fisherman lifted the lid. He came out at once in smoke, and then, having resumed his proper form, the first thing he did was to kick the vase into the sea. This frightened the fisherman, but the genius laughed and said, "Do not be afraid; I only did it to frighten you, and to show you that I intend to keep my word; take your nets and follow me."

He began to walk in front of the fisherman, who followed him with some misgivings. They passed in front of the town, and went up a mountain and then down into a great plain, where there was a large lake lying between four hills.

When they reached the lake the genius said to the fisherman, "Throw your nets and catch fish."

The fisherman did as he was told, hoping for a good catch, as he saw plenty of fish. What was his astonishment at seeing that there were four quite different kinds, some white, some red, some blue, and some yellow. He caught four, one of each colour. As he had never seen any like them he admired them very much, and he was very pleased to think how much money he would get for them.

"Take these fish and carry them to the Sultan, who will give you more money for them than you have ever had in your life. You can come every day to fish in this lake, but be careful not to throw your nets more than once every day, otherwise some harm will happen to you. If you follow my advice carefully you will find it good."

Saying these words, he struck his foot against the ground, which opened, and when he had disappeared, it closed immediately.

The fisherman resolved to obey the genius exactly, so he did not cast his nets a second time, but walked into the town to sell his fish at the palace.

When the Sultan saw the fish he was much astonished. He looked at them one after the other, and when he had admired them long enough, "Take these fish," he said to his first vizir, "and given them to the clever cook the Emperor of the Greeks sent me. I think they must be as good as they are beautiful."

The vizir took them himself to the cook, saying, "Here are four fish that have been brought to the Sultan. He wants you to cook them."

Then he went back to the Sultan, who told him to give the fisherman four hundred gold pieces. The fisherman, who had never before possessed such a large sum of money at once, could hardly believe his good fortune. He at once relieved the needs of his family, and made good use of it.

But now we must return to the kitchen, which we shall find in great confusion. The cook, when she had cleaned the fish, put them in a pan with some oil to fry them. When she thought them cooked enough on one side she turned them on the other. But scarcely had she done so when the walls of the kitchen opened, and there came out a young and beautiful damsel. She was dressed in an Egyptian dress of flowered satin, and she wore earrings, and a necklace of white pearls, and bracelets of gold set with rubies, and she held a wand of myrtle in her hand.

She went up to the pan, to the great astonishment of the cook, who stood motionless at the sight of her. She struck one of the fish with her rod, "Fish, fish," said she, "are you doing your duty?" The fish answered nothing, and then she repeated her question, whereupon they all raised their heads together and answered very distinctly, "Yes, yes. If you reckon, we reckon. If you pay your debts, we pay ours. If you fly, we conquer, and we are content."

When they had spoken the girl upset the pan, and entered the opening in the wall, which at once closed, and appeared the same as before.

When the cook had recovered from her fright she lifted up the fish which had fallen into the ashes, but she found them as black as cinders, and not fit to serve up to the Sultan. She began to cry.

"Alas! what shall I say to the Sultan? He will be so angry with me, and I know he will not believe me!"

Whilst she was crying the grand-vizir came in and asked if the fish were ready. She told him all that had happened, and he was much surprised. He sent at once for the fisherman, and when he came said to him, "Fisherman, bring me four more fish like you have brought already, for an accident has happened to them so that they cannot be served up to the Sultan."

The fisherman did not say what the genius had told him, but he excused himself from bringing them that day on account of the length of the way, and he promised to bring them next day.

In the night he went to the lake, cast his nets, and on drawing them in found four fish, which were like the others, each of a different colour.

He went back at once and carried them to the grand-vizir as he had promised.

He then took them to the kitchen and shut himself up with the cook, who began to cook them as she had done the four others on the previous day. When she was about to turn them on the other side, the wall opened, the damsel appeared, addressed the same words to the fish, received the same answer, and then overturned the pan and disappeared.

The grand-vizir was filled with astonishment. "I shall tell the Sultan all that has happened," said he. And he did so.

The Sultan was very much astounded, and wished to see this marvel for himself. So he sent for the fisherman, and asked him to procure four more fish. The fisherman asked for three days, which were granted, and he then cast his nets in the lake, and again caught four different coloured fish. The sultan was delighted to see he had got them, and gave him again four hundred gold pieces.

As soon as the Sultan had the fish he had them carried to his room with all that was needed to cook them.

Then he shut himself up with the grand-vizir, who began to prepare them and cook them. When they were done on one side he turned them over on the other. Then the wall of the room opened, but instead of the maiden a black slave came out. He was enormously tall, and carried a large green stick with which he touched the fish, saying in a terrible voice, "Fish, fish, are you doing your duty?" To these words the fish lifting up their heads replied, "Yes, yes. If you reckon, we reckon. If you pay your debts, we pay ours. If you fly, we conquer, and are content."

The black slave overturned the pan in the middle of the room, and the fish were turned to cinders. Then he stepped proudly back into the wall, which closed round him.

"After having seen this," said the Sultan, "I cannot rest. These fish signify some mystery I must clear up."

He sent for the fisherman. "Fisherman," he said, "the fish you have brought us have caused me some anxiety. Where did you get them from?"

"Sire," he answered, "I got them from a lake which lies in the middle of four hills beyond yonder mountains."

"Do you know this lake?" asked the Sultan of the grand-vizir.

"No; though I have hunted many times round that mountain, I have never heard of it," said the vizir.

As the fisherman said it was only three hours' journey away, the sultan ordered his whole court to mount and ride thither, and the fisherman led them.

They climbed the mountain, and then, on the other side, saw the lake as the fisherman had described. The water was so clear that they could see the four kinds of fish swimming about in it. They looked at them for some time, and then the Sultan ordered them to make a camp by the edge of the water.

When night came the Sultan called his vizir, and said to him, "I have resolved to clear up this mystery. I am going out alone, and do you stay here in my tent, and when my ministers come to-morrow, say I am not well, and cannot see them. Do this each day till I return."

The grand-vizir tried to persuade the Sultan not to go, but in vain. The Sultan took off his state robe and put on his sword, and when he saw all was quiet in the camp he set forth alone.

He climbed one of the hills, and then crossed the great plain, till, just as the sun rose, he beheld far in front of him a large building. When he came near to it he saw it was a splendid palace of beautiful black polished marble, covered with steel as smooth as a mirror.

He went to the gate, which stood half open, and went in, as nobody came when he knocked. He passed through a magnificent courtyard and still saw no one, though he called aloud several times.

He entered large halls where the carpets were of silk, the lounges and sofas covered with tapestry from Mecca, and the hangings of the most beautiful Indian stuffs of gold and silver. Then he found himself in a splendid room, with a fountain supported by golden lions. The water out of the lions' mouths turned into diamonds and pearls, and the leaping water almost touched a most beautifully-painted dome. The palace was surrounded on three sides by magnificent gardens, little lakes, and woods. Birds sang in the trees, which were netted over to keep them always there.

Still the Sultan saw no one, till he heard a plaintive cry, and a voice which said, "Oh that I could die, for I am too unhappy to wish to live any longer!"

The Sultan looked round to discover who it was who thus bemoaned his fate, and at last saw a handsome young man, richly clothed, who was sitting on a throne raised slightly from the ground. His face was very sad.

The sultan approached him and bowed to him. The young man bent his head very low, but did not rise.

"Sire," he said to the Sultan, "I cannot rise and do you the reverence that I am sure should be paid to your rank."

"Sir," answered the Sultan, "I am sure you have a good reason for not doing so, and having heard your cry of distress, I am come to offer you my help. Whose is this palace, and why is it thus empty?"

Instead of answering the young man lifted up his robe, and showed the Sultan that, from the waist downwards, he was a block of black marble.

The Sultan was horrified, and begged the young man to tell him his story.

"Willingly I will tell you my sad history," said the young man.

The History of the Young King of the Black Isles

Kate Douglas Wiggin and Nora A. Smith

"YOU MUST KNOW, my lord," said the wretched prisoner, "that my father, named Mahmoud, was monarch of this country. This is the kingdom of the Black Isles, which takes its name from the four small neighbouring mountains; for those mountains were formerly isles, and the capital where the king, my father, resided was situated on the spot now occupied by the lake you have seen. The sequel of my history will inform you of the reason for those changes.

"The king, my father, died when he was seventy years of age; I had no sooner succeeded him than I married, and the lady I chose to share the royal dignity with me was my cousin. I had so much reason to be satisfied with her affection, and, on my part, loved her with so much tenderness, that nothing could surpass the harmony of our union. This lasted five years, at the end of which time I perceived the queen ceased to delight in my attentions.

"One day, after dinner, while she was at the bath, I found myself inclined to repose, and lay down upon a sofa. Two of her ladies, who were then in my chamber, came and sat down, one at my head and the other at my feet, with fans in their hands to moderate the heat, and to prevent the flies from disturbing me. They thought I was asleep, and spoke in whispers; but as I only closed my eyes, I heard all their conversation.

"One of them said to the other, 'Is not the queen wrong, not to love so amiable a prince?' 'Certainly,' replied her companion; 'I do not understand the reason, neither can I conceive why she goes out every night, and leaves him alone! Is it possible that he does not perceive it?' 'Alas!' said the first, 'how should he? She mixes every evening in his liquor the juice of a certain herb, which makes him sleep so sound all night that she has time to go where she pleases, and as day begins to appear she comes and wakes him by the smell of something she puts under his nostrils.'

"You may guess, my lord, how much I was surprised at this conversation, and with what sentiments it inspired me; yet whatever emotion it excited I had sufficient self-command to dissemble, and feigned to awake without having heard a word.

"The queen returned from the bath, we supped together, and she presented me with a cup full of such liquid as I was accustomed to drink; but instead of putting it to my mouth, I went to a window that was open, threw out the water so quickly that she did not perceive it, and returned.

"Soon after, believing that I was asleep, she arose with so little precaution, that she whispered loud enough for me to hear her distinctly, 'Sleep on, and may you never wake again!' and so saying, she dressed herself, and went out of the chamber.

"As soon as the queen, my wife, was gone, I arose in haste, took my cimeter, and followed her so quickly that I soon heard the sound of her feet before me, and then walked softly after her. She passed through several gates, which opened upon her pronouncing some magical words, and the last she opened was that of the garden, which she entered. I stopped at this gate, that she might not perceive me as she passed along a parterre; then looking after her as far as the darkness of the night permitted, I saw her enter a little wood, whose walks were guarded by thick palisadoes. I went thither by another way, and concealing myself, I saw her walking there with a man.

"I did not fail to lend the most attentive ear to their discourse, and heard her address herself thus to her gallant: 'I do not deserve,' she said, 'to be reproached by you for want of diligence. You well know the reason; but if all the proofs of affection I have already given you be not sufficient to convince you of my sincerity, I am ready to give you others more decisive: you need but command me, you know my power; I will, if you desire it, before sunrise convert this great city, and this superb palace, into frightful ruins, inhabited only by wolves, owls, and ravens. If you would have me transport all the stones of those walls so solidly built, beyond Mount Caucasus, the bounds of the habitable world, speak but the word, and all shall be changed.'

"As the queen finished this speech she and her companion came to the end of the walk, turned to enter another, and passed before me. I had already drawn my cimeter, and the man being next me, I struck him on the neck, and brought him to the ground. I concluded I had killed him, and therefore retired speedily without making myself known to the queen, whom I chose to spare, because she was my kinswoman.

"The wound I had given her companion was mortal; but by her enchantments she preserved him in an existence in which he could not be said to be either dead or alive. As I crossed the garden to return to the palace, I heard the queen loudly lamenting, and judging by her cries how much she was grieved, I was pleased that I had spared her life.

"As soon as I had reached my apartment, I went to bed, and being satisfied with having punished the villain who had injured me, fell asleep.

"Next morning I arose, went to my closet, and dressed myself. I afterward held my council. At my return, the queen, clad in mourning, her hair dishevelled, and part of it torn off, presented herself before me, and said: 'I come to beg your majesty not to be surprised to see me in this condition. My heavy affliction is occasioned by intelligence of three distressing events which I have just received.' 'Alas! what are they, madam?' said I. 'The death of the queen, my dear mother,' she replied, 'that of the king, my father, killed in battle, and of one of my brothers, who has fallen down a precipice.'

"I was not displeased that she used these pretexts to conceal the true cause of her grief. 'Madam,' said I, 'so far from blaming, I assure you I heartily commiserate your sorrow. I should feel surprise if you were insensible to such heavy calamities: weep on; your tears are so many proofs of your tenderness; but I hope that time and reflection will moderate your grief.'

"She retired into her apartment, where, giving herself wholly up to sorrow, she spent a whole year in mourning and lamentation. At the end of that period, she begged permission to erect a burying-place for herself, within the bounds of the palace, where she would continue, she told me, to the end of her days: I consented, and she built a stately edifice, and called it the Palace of Tears. When it was finished, she caused the object of her care to be conveyed thither; she had hitherto prevented his dying, by potions which she had administered to him; and she continued to convey them to him herself every day after he came to the Palace of Tears.

"Yet, with all her enchantments, she could not cure the wretch; he was not only unable to walk or support himself, but had also lost the use of his speech, and exhibited no sign of life except in his looks.

"Every day the queen made him two long visits. I was well apprised of this, but pretended ignorance. One day my curiosity induced me to go to the Palace of Tears, to observe how my consort employed herself, and from a place where she could not see me, I heard her thus address the wounded ruffian: 'I am afflicted to the highest degree to behold you in this condition,' she cried, 'I am as sensible as yourself of the tormenting pain you endure; but, dear soul, I am continually speaking to you, and you do not answer me: how long will you remain silent? Speak only one word: alas! the sweetest moments of my life are these I spend here in partaking of your grief.'

"At these words, which were several times interrupted by her sighs, I lost all patience: and discovering myself, came up to her, and said, 'Madam, you have wept enough, it is time to give over this sorrow, which dishonours us both; you have too much forgotten what you owe to me and to yourself.' 'Sire,' said she, 'if you have any kindness or compassion for me left, I beseech you to put no restraint upon me; allow me to indulge my grief, which it is impossible for time to assuage.'

"When I perceived that my remonstrance, instead of restoring her to a sense of duty, served only to increase her anguish, I ceased speaking and retired. She continued every day to visit her charge, and for two whole years abandoned herself to grief and despair.

"I went a second time to the Palace of Tears, while she was there. I concealed myself again, and heard her thus cry out: 'It is now three years since you spoke one word to me; you answer not the proofs I give you of my devotion by my sighs and lamentations. Is it from insensibility, or contempt? O tomb! tell me by what miracle thou becamest the depository of the rarest treasure the world ever contained.'

"I must confess, my lord, I was enraged at these expressions; for, in truth, this adored mortal was by no means what you would imagine him to have been. He was a black Indian, one of the original natives of this country. I was so enraged at the language addressed to him, that I discovered myself, and apostrophising the tomb in my turn, I cried, 'O tomb! why dost thou not swallow up that monster so revolting to human nature, or rather why dost thou not swallow up this pair of monsters?'

"I had scarcely uttered these words, when the queen, who sat by the black, rose up like a fury: 'Miscreant!' said she, 'thou art the cause of my grief; do not think I am ignorant of this, I have dissembled too long. It was thy barbarous hand that brought the object of my fondness into this lamentable condition; and thou hast the cruelty to come and insult me.' 'Yes,' said I, in a rage, 'it was I who chastised that monster, according to his desert; I ought to have treated thee in the same manner; I now repent that I did not; thou hast too long abused my goodness.' As I spoke these words, I drew out my cimeter, and lifted up my hand to punish her; but regarding me steadfastly, she said with a jeering smile, 'Moderate thine anger.' At the same time she pronounced words I did not understand; and afterward added, 'By virtue of my enchantments, I command thee to become half marble and half man.' Immediately, my lord, I became what you see, a dead man among the living, and a living man among the dead. After this cruel sorceress, unworthy of the name of queen, had metamorphosed me thus, and brought me into this hall, by another enchantment she destroyed my capital, which was very flourishing and populous; she annihilated the houses, the public places and markets, and reduced the site of the whole to the lake and desert plain you have seen; the fishes of four colours in the waters are the four kinds of inhabitants, of different religions, which the city contained. The white are the Mussulmans; the red, the Persians, who worship fire; the blue, the Christians; and the yellow, the Jews. The four little hills were the four islands that gave name to this kingdom. I learned all this from the enchantress, who, to add to my affliction, related to me these effects of her rage. But this is not all; her revenge not being satisfied with the destruction of my dominions, and the metamorphosis of my person, she comes every day, and gives me over my naked shoulders a hundred lashes with a whip until I am covered with blood. When she has finished this part of my punishment, she throws over me a coarse stuff of goat's hair, and over that this robe of brocade, not to honour, but to mock me."

When he came to this part of his narrative, the young king could not restrain his tears; and the sultan was himself so affected by the relation, that he could not find utterance for any words of consolation. Shortly after, the young king, lifting up his eyes to heaven, exclaimed, "Mighty creator of all things, I submit myself to Thy judgments, and to the decrees of Thy providence: I endure my calamities with patience, since it is Thy will that things should be as they are; but I hope that Thy infinite goodness will ultimately reward me."

The sultan, greatly moved by the recital of this affecting story, and anxious to avenge the sufferings of the unfortunate prince, said to him: "Inform me whither this perfidious sorceress retires, and where may be found the vile wretch, who is entombed before his death." "My lord," replied the prince, "the Indian, as I have already told you, is lodged in the Palace of Tears, in a superb tomb constructed in the form of a dome: this palace joins the castle on the side in which the gate is placed. As to the queen, I cannot tell you precisely whither she retires, but every day at sunrise she goes to visit her charge, after having executed her bloody vengeance upon me; and you see I am not in a condition to defend myself. She carries to him the potion with which she has hitherto prevented his dying, and always complains of his never having spoken to her since he was wounded."

"Prince," said the sultan, "your condition can never be sufficiently deplored: no one can be more sensibly affected by your misfortune than I am. Never did anything so extraordinary befall any man! One thing only is wanting; the revenge to which you are entitled, and I will omit nothing in my power to effect it."

In his subsequent conversation with the young prince the sultan told him who he was, and for what purpose he had entered the castle; and afterward informed him of a mode of revenge which he had devised. They agreed upon the measures they were to take for accomplishing their design, but deferred the execution of it till the following day. In the meantime, the night being far spent, the sultan took some rest; but the young prince passed the night as usual, without sleep, never having slept since he was enchanted.

Next morning the sultan arose with the dawn, and prepared to execute his design, by proceeding to the Palace of Tears. He found it lighted up with an infinite number of flambeaux of white wax, and perfumed by a delicious scent issuing from several censers of fine gold of admirable workmanship. As soon as he perceived the bed where the Indian lay, he drew his cimeter and deprived him of his wretched life, dragged his corpse into the court of the castle, and threw it into a well. After this he went and lay down in the black's bed, placed his cimeter under the covering, and waited to complete his design.

The queen arrived shortly after. She first went into the chamber of her husband, the king of the Black Islands, stripped him, and with unexampled barbarity gave him a hundred stripes. The unfortunate prince filled the palace with his lamentations, and conjured her in the most affecting tone to take pity on him; but the cruel wretch ceased not till she had given the usual number of blows. "You had no compassion," said she, "and you are to expect none from me."

After the enchantress had given her husband a hundred blows with the whip, she put on again his covering of goat's hair, and his brocade gown over all; she went afterward to the Palace of Tears, and as she entered renewed her tears and lamentations; then approaching the bed, where she thought the Indian lay: "Alas!" said she, addressing herself to the sultan, conceiving him to be the black, "My sun, my life, will you always be silent? Are you resolved to let me die without affording me the comfort of hearing your voice?"

The sultan, as if he had awaked out of a deep sleep, and counterfeiting the pronunciation of the blacks, answered the queen with a grave tone: "There is no strength or power but in God alone, who is almighty." At these words the enchantress, who did not expect them, uttered a loud exclamation of joy. "My dear lord," cried she, "do I not deceive myself; is it certain that I hear you, and that you speak to me?" "Unhappy woman," said the sultan, "art thou worthy that I should answer thee?" "Alas!" replied the queen, "why do you reproach me thus?" "The cries," returned the sultan, "the groans and tears of thy husband, whom thou treatest every day with so much indignity and barbarity, prevent my sleeping night or day. Hadst thou disenchanted him, I should long since have been cured, and have recovered the use of my speech. This is the cause of my silence, of which you complain." "Well," said the enchantress, "to pacify you, I am ready to execute your commands; would you have me restore him?" "Yes," replied the sultan; "make haste to set him at liberty, that I be no longer disturbed by his lamentations." The enchantress went immediately out of the Palace of Tears; she took a cup of water, and pronounced some words over it, which caused it to boil, as if it had been on the fire. She afterward proceeded to the young king, and threw the water upon him, saying: "If the Creator of all things did form thee as thou art at present, or if He be angry with thee, do not change; but if thou art in that condition merely by virtue of my enchantments, resume thy natural shape, and become what thou wast before." She had scarcely spoken these words when the prince, finding himself restored to his former condition, rose up and returned thanks to God. The enchantress then said to him, "Get thee from this castle, and never return on pain of death." The young king, yielding to necessity, went away without replying a word, and retired to a remote place, where he patiently awaited the event of the design which the sultan had so happily begun. Meanwhile the enchantress returned to the Palace of Tears, and supposing that she still spoke to the black, said, "Dear love, I have done what you required; nothing now prevents your rising and giving me the satisfaction of which I have so long been deprived."

The sultan, still counterfeiting the pronunciation of the black, said: "What you have now done is by no means sufficient for my cure; you have only removed a part of the evil; you must cut it up by the root." "My lovely black," resumed the queen, "what do you mean by the root?" "Wretched woman," replied the sultan, "understand you not that I allude to the town and its inhabitants, and the four islands, destroyed by thy enchantments? The fish every night at midnight raise their heads out of the lake, and cry for vengeance against thee and me. This is the true cause of the delay of my cure. Go speedily, restore things to their former state, and at thy return I will give thee my hand, and thou shalt help me to arise."

The enchantress, inspired with hope from these words, cried out in a transport of joy, "My heart, my soul, you shall soon be restored to your health, for I will immediately do as you command me." Accordingly she went that instant, and when she came to the brink of the lake she took a little water in her hand, and sprinkling it, she pronounced some words over the fish and the lake, and the city was immediately restored. The fish became men, women, and children; Mohammedans, Christians, Persians, or Jews; freemen or slaves, as they were before: every one having recovered his natural form. The houses and shops were immediately filled with their inhabitants, who found all things as they were before the enchantment. The sultan's numerous retinue, who found themselves encamped in the largest square, were astonished to see themselves in an instant in the middle of a large, handsome, well-peopled city.

To return to the enchantress: As soon as she had effected this wonderful change, she returned with all expedition to the Palace of Tears, that she might receive her reward. "My dear lord," cried she, as she entered, "I have done all that you required of me, then pray rise and give me your hand." "Come near," said the sultan, still counterfeiting the pronunciation of the black. She did so. "You are not near enough," he continued; "approach nearer." She obeyed. He then rose up, and seizing her by the arm so suddenly that she had not time to discover him, he with a blow of his cimeter cut her in two, so that one half fell one way and the other another. This done, he left the body on the spot, and going out of the Palace of Tears, went to seek the young king of the Black Isles, who waited for him with great impatience. When he found him, "Prince," said he, embracing him, "rejoice; you have now nothing to fear; your cruel enemy is dead."

The young prince returned thanks to the sultan in a manner that sufficiently evinced his gratitude, and in return wished him long life and happiness. "You may henceforward," said the sultan, "dwell peaceably in your capital, unless you will accompany me to mine, which is near: you shall there be welcome, and have as much honour shown you as if you were in your own kingdom." "Potent monarch, to whom I am so much indebted," replied the king, "you think, then, that you are near your capital." "Yes," said the sultan, "I know it is not above four or five hours' journey." "It will take you a whole year to return," said the prince. "I do indeed believe that you came hither from your capital in the time you mention, because mine was enchanted; but since the enchantment is taken off, things are changed: however, this shall not prevent my following you, were it to the utmost corners of the earth. You are my deliverer, and that I may give you proofs of my acknowledgment of this during my whole life, I am willing to accompany you, and to leave my kingdom without regret."

The sultan was extremely surprised to understand that he was so far from his dominions, and could not imagine how it could be, but the young king of the Black Islands convinced him beyond a possibility of doubt. Then the sultan replied: "It is no matter; the trouble of returning to my own country is sufficiently recompensed by the satisfaction of having obliged you, and by acquiring you for a son; for since you will do me the honour to accompany me, as I have no child, I look upon you as such, and from this moment appoint you my heir and successor."

The young prince then employed himself in making preparations for his journey, which were finished in three weeks, to the great regret of his court and subjects, who agreed to receive at his hands one of his nearest kindred for their monarch.

At length the sultan and the young prince began their journey, with a hundred camels laden with inestimable riches from the treasury, followed by fifty handsome gentlemen on horseback, perfectly well mounted and dressed. They had a pleasant journey; and when the sultan, who had sent couriers to give advice of his delay, and of the adventure which had occasioned it, approached his capital, the principal officers came to receive him, and to assure him that his long absence had occasioned no alteration in his empire. The inhabitants also came out in great crowds, received him with acclamations, and made public rejoicings for several days.

The day after his arrival the sultan acquainted his courtiers with his adoption of the king of the Four Black Islands, who was willing to leave a great kingdom to accompany and live with him; and in reward for their loyalty, he made each of them presents according to their rank.

As for the fisherman, as he was the first cause of the deliverance of the young prince, the sultan gave him a plentiful fortune, which made him and his family happy the rest of his days.

The Porter and the Three Ladies of Baghdad

Richard F. Burton

ONCE UPON A TIME there was a Porter in Baghdad, who was a bachelor and who would remain unmarried. It came to pass on a certain day, as he stood about the street leaning idly upon his crate, behold, there stood before him an honourable woman in a mantilla of Mosul silk, broidered with gold and bordered with brocade; her walking-shoes were also purfled with gold and her hair floated in long plaits. She raised her face-veil and, showing two black eyes fringed with jetty lashes, whose glances were soft and languishing and whose perfect beauty was ever blandishing, she accosted the Porter and said in the suavest tones and choicest language, "Take up thy crate and follow me." The Porter was so dazzled he could hardly believe that he heard her aright, but he shouldered his basket in hot haste saying in himself, "O day of good luck! O day of Allah's grace!" and walked after her till she stopped at the door of a house. There she rapped, and presently came out to her an old man, a Nazarene, to whom she gave a gold piece, receiving from him in return what she required of strained wine clear as olive oil; and she set it safely in the hamper, saying, "Lift and follow." Quoth the Porter, "This, by Allah, is indeed an auspicious day, a day propitious for the granting of all a man wisheth." He again hoisted up the crate and followed her; till she stopped at a fruiterer's shop and bought from him Shámi apples and Osmáni quinces and Omani peaches, and cucumbers of Nile growth, and Egyptian limes and Sultáni oranges and citrons; besides Aleppine jasmine, scented myrtle berries, Damascene nenuphars, flower of privet and camomile, blood-red anemones, violets, and pomegranate-bloom, eglantine and narcissus, and set the whole in the Porter's crate, saying, "Up with it." So he lifted and followed her till she stopped at a butcher's booth and said, "Cut me off ten pounds of mutton." She paid him his price and he wrapped it in a banana-leaf, whereupon she laid it in the crate and said "Hoist, O Porter." He hoisted accordingly, and followed her as she walked on till she stopped at a grocer's, where she bought dry fruits and pistachio-kernels, Tihámah raisins, shelled almonds and all wanted for dessert, and said to the Porter, "Lift and follow me." So he up with his hamper and after her till she stayed at the confectioner's, and she bought an earthen platter, and piled it with all kinds of sweetmeats in his shop, open-worked tarts and fritters scented with musk and "soap-cakes," and lemon-loaves and melon-preserves, and "Zaynab's combs," and "ladies' fingers," and "Kazi's tit-bits" and goodies of every description; and placed the platter in the Porter's crate. Thereupon quoth he (being a merry man), "Thou shouldest have told me, and I would have brought with me a pony or a she-camel to carry all this market-stuff." She smiled and gave him a little cuff on the nape saying, "Step out and exceed not in words for (Allah willing!) thy wage will not be wanting." Then she stopped at a perfumer's and took from him ten sorts of waters, rose scented with musk, orange-flower, water-lily, willow flower, violet and five others; and she also bought two loaves of sugar, a bottle for perfume-spraying, a lump of male incense, aloe-wood, ambergris and musk, with candles of Alexandria wax; and she put the whole into the basket, saying, "Up with thy crate and after me." He did so and followed until she stood before the greengrocer's, of whom she bought pickled safflower and olives, in brine and in oil; with tarragon and cream-cheese and hard Syrian cheese; and she stowed them away in the crate saying to the Porter, "Take up thy basket and follow me." He did so and went after her till she came to a fair mansion fronted by a spacious court, a tall, fine place to which columns gave strength and grace: and the gate thereof had two leaves of ebony inlaid with plates of red gold. The lady stopped at the door and, turning her face-veil sideways, knocked softly with her knuckles whilst the Porter stood behind her, thinking of naught save her beauty and loveliness. Presently the door swung back and both leaves were opened, whereupon he looked to see who had opened it; and behold, it was a lady of tall figure, some five feet high; a model of beauty and loveliness, brilliance and symmetry and perfect grace. Her forehead was flower-white; her cheeks like the anemone ruddy bright; her eyes were those of the wild heifer or the gazelle, with eyebrows like the crescent-moon which ends Sha'abán and begins Ramazán; her mouth was the ring of Sulayman, her lips coral-red, and her teeth like a line of strung pearls or of camomile petals. Her throat recalled the antelope's, and her breasts, like two pomegranates of even size, stood at bay as it were; her body rose and fell in waves below her dress like the rolls of a piece of brocade, and her navel would hold an ounce of benzoin ointment. In fine she was like her of whom the poet said: –

> On Sun and Moon of palace cast thy sight
> Enjoy her flower-like face, her fragrant light:
> Thine eyes shall never see in hair so black
> Beauty encase a brow so purely white:
> The ruddy rosy cheek proclaims her claim
> Though fail her name whose beauties we indite:
> As sways her gait I smile at hips so big
> And weep to see the waist they bear so slight.

When the Porter looked upon her his wits were waylaid, and his senses were stormed so that his crate went nigh to fall from his head, and he said to himself, "Never have I in my life seen a day more blessed than this day!" Then quoth the lady-portress to the lady-cateress, "Come in from the gate and relieve this poor man of his load." So the provisioner went in followed by the portress and the Porter and went on till they reached a spacious ground-floor hall, built with admirable skill and beautified with all manner colours and carvings; with upper balconies and groined arches and galleries and cupboards and recesses whose curtains hung before them. In the midst stood a great basin full of water surrounding a fine fountain, and at the upper end on the raised dais was a couch of juniper-wood set with gems and pearls, with a canopy like mosquito-curtains of red satin-silk looped up with pearls as big as filberts and bigger. Thereupon sat a lady bright of blee, with brow beaming brilliancy, the dream of philosophy, whose eyes were fraught with Babel's gramarye and her eyebrows were arched as for archery; her breath breathed ambergris and perfumery and her lips were sugar to taste and carnelian to see. Her stature was straight as the letter ‖ and her face shamed the noon-sun's radiancy; and she was even as a galaxy, or a dome with golden marquetry or a bride displayed in choicest finery or a noble maid of Araby. Right well of her sang the bard when he said: –

> *Her smiles twin rows of pearls display*
> *Chamomile-buds or rimey spray*
> *Her tresses stray as night let down*
> *And shames her light the dawn o' day.*

The third lady rising from the couch stepped forward with graceful swaying gait till she reached the middle of the saloon, when she said to her sisters, "Why stand ye here? take it down from this poor man's head!" Then the cateress went and stood before him, and the portress behind him while the third helped them, and they lifted the load from the Porter's head; and, emptying it of all that was therein, set everything in its place. Lastly they gave him two gold pieces, saying, "Wend thy ways, O Porter." But he went not, for he stood looking at the ladies and admiring what uncommon beauty was theirs, and their pleasant manners and kindly dispositions (never had he seen goodlier); and he gazed wistfully at that good store of wines and sweet-scented flowers and fruits and other matters. Also he marvelled with exceeding marvel, especially to see no man in the place and delayed his going; whereupon quoth the eldest lady, "What aileth thee that goest not; haply thy wage be too little?" And, turning to her sister the cateress, she said, "Give him another dinar!" But the Porter answered, "By Allah, my lady, it is not for the wage; my hire is never more than two dirhams; but in very sooth my heart and my soul are taken up with you and your condition. I wonder to see you single with ne'er a man about you and not a soul to bear you company; and well you wot that the minaret toppleth o'er unless it stand upon four, and you want this same fourth; and women's pleasure without man is short of measure, even as the poet said:

> *Seest not we want for joy four things all told*
> *The harp and lute, the flute and flageolet;*
> *And be they companied with scents four-fold*
> *Rose, myrtle, anemone and violet;*
> *Nor please all eight an four thou wouldst withhold*
> *Good wine and youth and gold and pretty pet.*

You be three and want a fourth who shall be a person of good sense and prudence; smart witted, and one apt to keep careful counsel." His words pleased and amused them much; and they laughed at him and said, "And who is to assure us of that? We are maidens and we fear to entrust our secret where it may not be kept, for we have read in a certain chronicle the lines of one Ibn al-Sumam:

> *Hold fast thy secret and to none unfold*
> *Lost is a secret when that secret's told:*
> *An fail thy breast thy secret to conceal*
> *How canst thou hope another's breast shall hold?*

And Abu Nowás said well on the same subject:

Who trusteth secret to another's hand
Upon his brow deserveth burn of brand!"

When the Porter heard their words he rejoined, "By your lives! I am a man of sense and a discreet, who hath read books and perused chronicles; I reveal the fair and conceal the foul and I act as the poet adviseth:

None but the good a secret keep
And good men keep it unrevealed:
It is to me a well-shut house
With keyless locks and door ensealed."

When the maidens heard his verse and its poetical application addressed to them they said, "Thou knowest that we have laid out all our monies on this place. Now say, hast thou aught to offer us in return for entertainment? For surely we will not suffer thee to sit in our company and be our cup-companion, and gaze upon our faces so fair and so rare without paying a round sum. Wottest thou not the saying:

Sans hope of gain
Love's not worth a grain?"

Whereto the lady-portress added, "If thou bring anything thou art a something; if no thing, be off with thee, thou art a nothing;" but the procuratrix interposed, saying, "Nay, O my sisters, leave teasing him, for by Allah he hath not failed us this day, and had he been other he never had kept patience with me, so whatever be his shot and scot I will take it upon myself." The Porter, overjoyed, kissed the ground before her and thanked her saying, "By Allah, these monies are the first fruits this day hath given me." Hearing this they said, "Sit thee down and welcome to thee," and the eldest lady added, "By Allah, we may not suffer thee to join us save on one condition, and this it is, that no questions be asked as to what concerneth thee not, and frowardness shall be soundly flogged." Answered the Porter, "I agree to this, O my lady, on my head and my eyes be it! Lookye, I am dumb, I have no tongue." Then arose the provisioneress and tightening her girdle set the table by the fountain and put the flowers and sweet herbs in their jars, and strained the wine and ranged the flasks in row and made ready every requisite. Then sat she down, she and her sisters, placing amidst them the Porter who kept deeming himself in a dream; and she took up the wine flagon, and poured out the first cup and drank it off, and likewise a second and a third. After this she filled a fourth cup which she handed to one of her sisters; and, lastly, she crowned a goblet and passed it to the Porter, saying:

Drink the dear draught, drink free and fain
What healeth every grief and pain.

He took the cup in his hand and, louting low, returned his best thanks and improvised:

Drain not the bowl save with a trusty friend
A man of worth whose good old blood all know:

> *For wine, like wind, sucks sweetness from the sweet*
> *And stinks when over stench it haply blow:*

Adding:

> *Drain not the bowl, save from dear hand like thine*
> *The cup recalls thy gifts; thou, gifts of wine.*

After repeating this couplet he kissed their hands and drank and was drunk and sat swaying from side to side and pursued:

> *All drinks wherein is blood the Law unclean*
> *Doth hold save one, the bloodshed of the vine:*
> *Fill! fill! take all my wealth bequeathed or won*
> *Thou fawn! a willing ransom for those eyne.*

Then the cateress crowned a cup and gave it to the portress, who took it from her hand and thanked her and drank. Thereupon she poured again and passed to the eldest lady who sat on the couch, and filled yet another and handed it to the Porter. He kissed the ground before them; and, after drinking and thanking them, he again began to recite:

> *Here! Here! by Allah, here!*
> *Cups of the sweet, the dear!*
> *Fill me a brimming bowl*
> *The Fount o' Life I speer*

Then the Porter stood up before the mistress of the house and said, "O lady, I am thy slave, thy Mameluke, thy white thrall, thy very bondsman;" and he began reciting:

> *A slave of slaves there standeth at thy door*
> *Lauding thy generous boons and gifts galore:*
> *Beauty! may he come in awhile to 'joy*
> *Thy charms? for Love and I part nevermore!*

She said to him, "Drink; and health and happiness attend thy drink." So he took the cup and kissed her hand and recited these lines in sing-song:

> *I gave her brave old wine that like her cheeks*
> *Blushed red or flame from furnace flaring up:*
> *She bussed the brim and said with many a smile*
> *How durst thou deal folk's cheek for folk to sup?*
> *"Drink!" (said I) "these are tears of mine whose tinct*
> *Is heart-blood sighs have boilèd in the cup."*

She answered him in the following couplet:

"An tears of blood for me, friend, thou hast shed
Suffer me sup them, by thy head and eyes!"

Then the lady took the cup, and drank it off to her sisters' health, and they ceased not drinking (the Porter being in the midst of them), and dancing and laughing and reciting verses and singing ballads and ritornellos. All this time the Porter was carrying on with them, kissing, toying, biting, handling, groping, fingering; whilst one thrust a dainty morsel in his mouth, and another slapped him; and this cuffed his cheeks, and that threw sweet flowers at him; and he was in the very paradise of pleasure, as though he were sitting in the seventh sphere among the Houris of Heaven. They ceased not doing after this fashion until the wine played tricks in their heads and worsted their wits; and, when the drink got the better of them, the portress stood up and doffed her clothes till she was mother-naked. However, she let down her hair about her body by way of shift, and throwing herself into the basin disported herself and dived like a duck and swam up and down, and took water in her mouth, and spurted it all over the Porter, and washed her limbs, and between her breasts, and inside her thighs and all around her navel. Then she came up out of the cistern and throwing herself on the Porter's lap said, "O my lord, O my love, what callest thou this article?" pointing to her slit, her solution of continuity. "I call that thy cleft," quoth the Porter, and she rejoined, "Wah! wah! art thou not ashamed to use such a word?" and she caught him by the collar and soundly cuffed him. Said he again, "Thy womb, thy vulva;" and she struck him a second slap crying, "O fie, O fie, this is another ugly word; is there no shame in thee?" Quoth he, "Thy coynte;" and she cried, "O thou! art wholly destitute of modesty?" and thumped him and bashed him. Then cried the Porter, "Thy clitoris," whereat the eldest lady came down upon him with a yet sorer beating, and said, "No;" and he said, "'Tis so," and the Porter went on calling the same commodity by sundry other names, but whatever he said they beat him more and more till his neck ached and swelled with the blows he had gotten; and on this wise they made him a butt and a laughing-stock. At last he turned upon them asking, "And what do you women call this article?" Whereto the damsel made answer, "The basil of the bridges." Cried the Porter, "Thank Allah for my safety: aid me and be thou propitious, O basil of the bridges!" They passed round the cup and tossed off the bowl again, when the second lady stood up; and, stripping off all her clothes, cast herself into the cistern and did as the first had done; then she came out of the water and throwing her naked form on the Porter's lap pointed to her machine and said, "O light of mine eyes, do tell me what is the name of this concern?" He replied as before, "Thy slit;" and she rejoined, "Hath such term no shame for thee?" and cuffed him and buffeted him till the saloon rang with the blows. Then quoth she, "O fie! O fie! how canst thou say this without blushing?" He suggested, "The basil of the bridges;" but she would not have it and she said, "No! no!" and struck him and slapped him on the back of the neck. Then he began calling out all the names he knew, "Thy slit, thy womb, thy coynte, thy clitoris;" and the girls kept on saying, "No! no!" So he said, "I stick to the basil of the bridges;" and all the three laughed till they fell on their backs and laid slaps on his neck and said, "No! no! that's not its proper name." Thereupon he cried, "O my sisters, what is its name?" and they replied, "What sayest thou to the husked sesame-seed?" Then the cateress donned her clothes and they fell again to carousing, but the Porter kept moaning, "Oh! and Oh!" for his neck and shoulders, and the cup passed merrily round and round again for a full hour. After that time the eldest and handsomest lady stood up and stripped off her garments, whereupon the Porter took his neck in hand, and rubbed and shampoo'd it, saying, "My neck and shoulders are on the way of Allah!" Then she threw herself into the basin, and swam and dived, sported and washed; and the Porter looked at her naked figure as though she had been a slice of the moon and at her face with the sheen of Luna when at full, or like the dawn when it brighteneth, and he noted her noble stature and shape, and those glorious forms that quivered as she went; for she was naked as the Lord made her. Then he cried "Alack! Alack!" and began to address her, versifying in these couplets:

> *"If I liken thy shape to the bough when green*
> *My likeness errs and I sore mistake it;*
> *For the bough is fairest when clad the most*
> *And thou art fairest when mother-naked."*

When the lady heard his verses she came up out of the basin and, seating herself upon his lap and knees, pointed to her genitory and said, "O my lordling, what be the name of this?" Quoth he, "The basil of the bridges;" but she said, "Bah, bah!" Quoth he, "The husked sesame;" quoth she, "Pooh, pooh!" Then said he, "Thy womb;" and she cried, "Fie, Fie! art thou not ashamed of thyself?" and cuffed him on the nape of the neck. And whatever name he gave declaring "'Tis so," she beat him and cried "No! no!" till at last he said, "O my sisters, and what is its name?" She replied, "It is entitled the Khan of Abu Mansur;" whereupon the Porter replied, "Ha! ha! O Allah be praised for safe deliverance! O Khan of Abu Mansur!" Then she came forth and dressed and the cup went round a full hour. At last the Porter rose up, and stripping off all his clothes, jumped into the tank and swam about and washed under his bearded chin and armpits, even as they had done. Then he came out and threw himself into the first lady's lap and rested his arms upon the lap of the portress, and reposed his legs in the lap of the cateress and pointed to his prickle and said, "O my mistresses, what is the name of this article?" All laughed at his words till they fell on their backs, and one said, "Thy pintle!" But he replied, "No!" and gave each one of them a bite by way of forfeit. Then said they, "Thy pizzle!" but he cried "No," and gave each of them a hug – And Shahrazad perceived the dawn of day and ceased saying her permitted say.

Now when it was the Tenth Night, quoth her sister Dunyazad, "Finish for us thy story;" and she answered, "With joy and goodly gree." It hath reached me, O auspicious King, that the damsels stinted not saying to the Porter "Thy prickle, thy pintle, thy pizzle," and he ceased not kissing and biting and hugging until his heart was satisfied, and they laughed on till they could no more. At last one said, "O our brother, what, then, is it called?" Quoth he, "Know ye not?" Quoth they, "No!" "Its veritable name," said he, "is mule Burst-all, which browseth on the basil of the bridges, and muncheth the husked sesame, and nighteth in the Khan of Abu Mansur." Then laughed they till they fell on their backs, and returned to their carousal, and ceased not to be after this fashion till night began to fall. Thereupon said they to the Porter, "Bismillah, O our master, up and on with those sorry old shoes of thine and turn thy face and show us the breadth of thy shoulders!" Said he, "By Allah, to part with my soul would be easier for me than departing from you: come let us join night to day, and to-morrow morning we will each wend our own way." "My life on you," said the procuratrix, "suffer him to tarry with us, that we may laugh at him: we may live out our lives and never meet with his like, for surely he is a right merry rogue and a witty." So they said, "Thou must not remain with us this night save on condition that thou submit to our commands, and that whatso thou seest, thou ask no questions thereanent, nor enquire of its cause." "All right," rejoined he, and they said, "Go read the writing over the door." So he rose and went to the entrance and there found written in letters of gold wash; "WHOSO SPEAKETH OF WHAT CONCERNETH HIM NOT, SHALL HEAR WHAT PLEASETH HIM NOT!" The Porter said, "Be ye witnesses against me that I will not speak on whatso concerneth me not." Then the cateress arose, and set food before them and they ate; after which they changed their drinking-place for another, and she lighted the lamps and candles and burned ambergris and aloes-wood, and set on fresh fruit and the wine service, when they fell to carousing and talking of their lovers. And they ceased not to eat and drink and chat, nibbling dry fruits and laughing and playing tricks for the space of a full hour when lo! a knock was heard at the gate. The knocking in no wise disturbed the seance, but one of them rose and went to see what it was and presently returned, saying, "Truly our pleasure for this night is to be perfect." "How is that?" asked they; and she answered, "At the gate be three Persian Kalandars with their beards and heads and eyebrows shaven; and all three blind of the left eye – which is surely a strange chance. They are foreigners from Roum-land with the mark of travel plain upon them; they have just entered Baghdad, this being their first visit to our city; and the cause of their knocking at our door is simply because they cannot find a lodging. Indeed one of them said to me: Haply the owner of this mansion will let us have the key of his stable or some old outhouse wherein we may pass this night; for evening had surprised them and, being strangers in the land, they knew none who would give them shelter. And, O my sisters, each of them is a figure o' fun after his own fashion; and if we let them in we shall have matter to make sport of." She gave not over persuading them till they said to her, "Let them in, and make thou the usual condition with them that they speak not of what concerneth them not, lest they hear what pleaseth them not." So she rejoiced and going to the door presently returned with the three monoculars whose beards and mustachios were clean shaven. They salam'd and stood afar off by way of respect; but the three ladies rose up to them and welcomed them and wished them joy of their safe arrival and made them sit down. The Kalandars looked at the room and saw that it was a pleasant place, clean swept and garnished with flowers; and the lamps were burning and the smoke of perfumes was spiring in air; and beside the dessert and fruits and wine, there were three fair girls who might be maidens; so they exclaimed with one voice, "By Allah, 'tis good!" Then they turned to the Porter and saw that he was a merry-faced wight, albeit he was by no means sober and was sore after his slappings. So they thought that he was one of themselves and said, "A mendicant like us! whether Arab or foreigner." But when the Porter heard these words, he rose up, and fixing his eyes fiercely upon them, said, "Sit ye here without exceeding in talk! Have you not read what is writ over the door? surely it befitteth not fellows who come to us like paupers to wag your tongues at us." "We crave thy pardon, O Fakír," rejoined they, "and our heads are between thy hands." The ladies laughed consumedly at the squabble; and, making peace between the Kalandars and the Porter, seated the new guests before meat and they ate. Then they sat together, and the portress served them with drink; and, as the cup went round merrily, quoth the Porter to the askers, "And you, O brothers mine, have ye no story or rare adventure to amuse us withal?" Now the warmth of wine having mounted to their heads they called for musical instruments; and the portress brought them a tambourine of Mosul, and a lute of Irák, and a Persian harp; and each mendicant took one and tuned it; this the tambourine and those the lute and the harp, and struck up a merry tune while the ladies sang so lustily that there was a great noise. And whilst they were carrying on, behold, some one knocked at the gate, and the portress went to see what was the matter there. Now the cause of that knocking, O King (quoth Shahrazad) was this, the Caliph, Hárún al-Rashíd, had gone forth from the palace, as was his wont now and then, to solace himself in the city that night, and to see and hear what new thing was stirring; he was in merchant's gear, and he was attended by Ja'afar, his Wazir, and by Masrúr his Sworder of Vengeance. As they walked about the city, their way led them towards the house of the three ladies; where they heard the loud noise of musical instruments and singing and merriment; so quoth the Caliph to Ja'afar, "I long to enter this house and hear those songs and see who sing them." Quoth Ja'afar, "O Prince of the Faithful; these folk are surely drunken with wine, and I fear some mischief betide us if we get amongst them." "There is no help but that I go in there," replied the Caliph, "and I desire thee to contrive some pretext for our appearing among them." Ja'afar replied, "I hear and I obey;" and knocked at the door, whereupon the portress came out and opened. Then Ja'afar came forward and kissing the ground before her said, "O my lady, we be merchants from Tiberias-town: we arrived at Baghdad ten days ago; and, alighting at the merchants' caravanserai, we sold all our merchandise. Now a certain trader invited us to an entertainment this night; so we went to his house and he set food before us and we ate: then we sat at wine and wassail with him for an hour or so when he gave us leave to depart; and we went out from him in the shadow of the night and, being strangers, we could not find our way back to our Khan. So haply of your kindness and courtesy you will suffer us to tarry with you this night, and Heaven will reward you!" The portress looked upon them and seeing them dressed like merchants and men of grave looks and solid, she returned to her sisters and repeated to them Ja'afar's story; and they took compassion upon the strangers and said to her, "Let them enter." She opened the door to them, when said they to her, "Have we thy leave to come in?" "Come in," quoth she; and the Caliph entered followed by Ja'afar and Masrur; and when the girls saw them they stood up to them in respect and made them sit down and looked to their wants, saying, "Welcome, and well come and good cheer to the guests, but with one condition!" "What is that?" asked they, and one of the ladies answered, "Speak not of what concerneth you not, lest ye hear what pleaseth you not." "Even so," said they; and sat down to their wine and drank deep. Presently the Caliph looked on the three Kalandars and, seeing them each and every blind of the left eye, wondered at the sight; then he gazed upon the girls and he was startled and he marvelled with exceeding marvel at their beauty and loveliness. They continued to carouse and to converse and said to the Caliph, "Drink!" but he replied, "I am vowed to Pilgrimage;" and drew back from the wine. Thereupon the portress rose and spreading before him a table-cloth worked with gold, set thereon a porcelain bowl into which she poured willow flower water with a lump of snow and a spoonful of sugar-candy. The Caliph thanked her and said in himself, "By Allah, I will recompense her to-morrow for the kind deed she hath done." The others again addressed themselves to conversing and carousing; and, when the wine gat the better of them, the eldest lady who ruled the house rose and making obeisance to them took the cateress by the hand, and said, "Rise, O my sister and let us do what is our devoir." Both answered "Even so!" Then the portress stood up and proceeded to remove the table-service and the remnants of the banquet; and renewed the pastiles and cleared the middle of the saloon. Then she made the Kalandars sit upon a sofa at the side of the estrade, and seated the Caliph and Ja'afar and Masrur on the other side of the saloon; after which she called the Porter, and said, "How scant is thy courtesy! now thou art no stranger; nay, thou art one of the household." So he stood up and, tightening his waist-cloth, asked, "What would ye I do?" and she answered, "Stand in thy place." Then the procuratrix rose and set in the midst of the saloon a low chair and, opening a closet, cried to the Porter, "Come help me," So he went to help her and saw two black bitches with chains round their necks; and she said to him, "Take hold of them;" and he took them and led them into the middle of the saloon. Then the lady of the house arose and tucked up her sleeves above her wrists and, seizing a scourge, said to the Porter, "Bring forward one of the bitches." He brought, her forward, dragging her by the chain, while the bitch wept, and shook her head at the lady who, however, came down upon her with blows on the sconce; and the bitch howled and the lady ceased not beating her till her forearm failed her. Then, casting the scourge from her hand, she pressed the bitch to her bosom and, wiping away her tears with her hands, kissed her head. Then said she to the Porter, "Take her away and bring the second;" and, when he brought her, she did with her as she had done with the first. Now the heart of the Caliph was touched at these cruel doings; his chest straitened and he lost all patience in his desire to know why the two bitches were so beaten. He threw a wink at Ja'afar wishing him to ask, but the Minister turning towards him said by signs, "Be silent!" Then quoth the portress to the mistress of the house, "O my lady, arise and go to thy place that I in turn may do my devoir." She answered, "Even so"; and, taking her seat upon the couch of juniper-wood, pargetted with, gold and silver, said to the portress and cateress, "Now do ye what ye have to do." Thereupon the portress sat upon a low seat by the couch side; but the procuratrix, entering a closet, brought out of it a bag of satin with green fringes and two tassels of gold. She stood up before the lady of the house and shaking the bag drew out from it a lute which she tuned by tightening its pegs; and when it was in perfect order, she began to sing these quatrains:

Ye are the wish, the aim of me
And when, O love, thy sight I see
The heavenly mansion openeth;
But Hell I see when lost thy sight.
From thee comes madness; nor the less
Comes highest joy, comes ecstasy:
Nor in my love for thee I fear
Or shame and blame, or hate and spite.
When Love was throned within my heart
I rent the veil of modesty;
And stints not Love to rend that veil
Garring disgrace on grace to alight;
The robe of sickness then I donned
But rent to rags was secrecy:

Wherefore my love and longing heart
Proclaim your high supremest might;
The tear-drop railing adown my cheek
Telleth my tale of ignomy:
And all the hid was seen by all
And all my riddle ree'd aright.
Heal then my malady, for thou
Art malady and remedy!
But she whose cure is in thy hand
Shall ne'er be free of bane and blight;
Burn me those eyne that radiance rain
Slay me the swords of phantasy;
How many hath the sword of Love
Laid low, their high degree despite?
Yet will I never cease to pine
Nor to oblivion will I flee.
Love is my health, my faith, my joy
Public and private, wrong or right.
O happy eyes that sight thy charms
That gaze upon thee at their gree!
Yea, of my purest wish and will
The slave of Love I'll aye be hight.

When the damsel heard this elegy in quatrains she cried out "Alas! Alas!" and rent her raiment, and fell to the ground fainting; and the Caliph saw scars of the palm-rod on her back and welts of the whip; and marvelled with exceeding wonder. Then the portress arose and sprinkled water on her and brought her a fresh and very fine dress and put it on her. But when the company beheld these doings their minds were troubled, for they had no inkling of the case nor knew the story thereof; so the Caliph said to Ja'afar, "Didst thou not see the scars upon the damsel's body? I cannot keep silence or be at rest till I learn the truth of her condition and the story of this other maiden and the secret of the two black bitches." But Ja'afar answered, "O our lord, they made it a condition with us that we speak not of what concerneth us not, lest we come to hear what pleaseth us not." Then said the portress, "By Allah, O my sister, come to me and complete this service for me." Replied the procuratrix, "With joy and goodly gree;" so she took the lute; and leaned it against her breasts and swept the strings with her finger-tips, and began singing:

Give back mine eyes their sleep long ravishèd
And say me whither be my reason fled:
I learnt that lending to thy love a place
Sleep to mine eyelids mortal foe was made.
They said, "We held thee righteous, who waylaid
Thy soul?" "Go ask his glorious eyes," I said.
I pardon all my blood he pleased to spill
Owning his troubles drove him blood to shed.
On my mind's mirror sun-like sheen he cast
Whose keen reflection fire in vitals bred

> *Waters of Life let Allah waste at will*
> *Suffice my wage those lips of dewy red:*
> *An thou address my love thou'lt find a cause*
> *For plaint and tears or ruth or lustihed.*
> *In water pure his form shall greet your eyne*
> *When fails the bowl nor need ye drink of wine.*

Then she quoted from the same ode:

> *I drank, but the draught of his glance, not wine;*
> *And his swaying gait swayed to sleep these eyne:*
> *'Twas not grape-juice gript me but grasp of Past*
> *'Twas not bowl o'erbowled me but gifts divine:*
> *His coiling curl-lets my soul ennetted*
> *And his cruel will all my wits outwitted.*

After a pause she resumed:

> *If we 'plain of absence what shall we say?*
> *Or if pain afflict us where wend our way?*
> *An I hire a truchman to tell my tale*
> *The lovers' plaint is not told for pay:*
> *If I put on patience, a lover's life*
> *After loss of love will not last a day:*
> *Naught is left me now but regret, repine*
> *And tears flooding cheeks for ever and aye:*
> *O thou who the babes of these eyes hast fled*
> *Thou art homed in heart that shall never stray;*
> *Would heaven I wot hast thou kept our pact*
> *Long as stream shall flow, to have firmest fay?*
> *Or hast forgotten the weeping slave*
> *Whom groans afflict and whom griefs waylay?*
> *Ah, when severance ends and we side by side*
> *Couch, I'll blame thy rigours and chide thy pride!*

Now when the portress heard her second ode she shrieked aloud and said, "By Allah! 'tis right good!"; and laying hands on her garments tore them, as she did the first time, and fell to the ground fainting. Thereupon the procuratrix rose and brought her a second change of clothes after she had sprinkled water on her. She recovered and sat upright and said to her sister the cateress, "Onwards, and help me in my duty, for there remains but this one song." So the provisioneress again brought out the lute and began to sing these verses:

> *How long shall last, how long this rigour rife of woe*
> *May not suffice thee all these tears thou seest flow?*
> *Our parting thus with purpose fell thou dost prolong*
> *Is't not enough to glad the heart of envious foe?*

Were but this lying world once true to lover-heart
He had not watched the weary night in tears of woe:
Oh pity me whom overwhelmed thy cruel will
My lord, my king, 'tis time some ruth to me thou show:
To whom reveal my wrongs, O thou who murdered me?
Sad, who of broken troth the pangs must undergo!
Increase wild love for thee and phrenzy hour by hour
And days of exile minute by so long, so slow;
O Moslems, claim vendetta for this slave of Love
Whose sleep Love ever wastes, whose patience Love lays low:
Doth law of Love allow thee, O my wish! to lie
Lapt in another's arms and unto me cry "Go!"?
Yet in thy presence, say, what joys shall I enjoy
When he I love but works my love to overthrow?

When the portress heard the third song she cried aloud; and, laying hands on her garments, rent them down to the very skirt and fell to the ground fainting a third time, again showing the scars of the scourge. Then said the three Kalandars, "Would Heaven we had never entered this house, but had rather nighted on the mounds and heaps outside the city! for verily our visit hath been troubled by sights which cut to the heart." The Caliph turned to them and asked, "Why so?" and they made answer, "Our minds are sore troubled by this matter." Quoth the Caliph, "Are ye not of the household?" and quoth they, "No; nor indeed did we ever set eyes on the place till within this hour." Hereat the Caliph marvelled and rejoined, "This man who sitteth by you, would he not know the secret of the matter?" and so saying he winked and made signs at the Porter. So they questioned the man but he replied, "By the All-might of Allah, in love all are alike! I am the growth of Baghdad, yet never in my born days did I darken these doors till to-day and my companying with them was a curious matter." "By Allah," they rejoined, "we took thee for one of them and now we see thou art one like ourselves." Then said the Caliph, "We be seven men, and they only three women without even a fourth to help them; so let us question them of their case; and, if they answer us not, fain we will be answered by force." All of them agreed to this except Ja'afar who said, "This is not my recking; let them be; for we are their guests and, as ye know, they made a compact and condition with us which we accepted and promised to keep: wherefore it is better that we be silent concerning this matter; and, as but little of the night remaineth, let each and every of us gang his own gait." Then he winked at the Caliph and whispered to him, "There is but one hour of darkness left and I can bring them before thee to-morrow, when thou canst freely question them all concerning their story." But the Caliph raised his head haughtily and cried out at him in wrath, saying, "I have no patience left for my longing to hear of them: let the Kalandars question them forthright." Quoth Ja'afar, "This is not my rede." Then words ran high and talk answered talk; and they disputed as to who should first put the question, but at last all fixed upon the Porter. And as the jangle increased the house-mistress could not but notice it and asked them, "O ye folk! on what matter are ye talking so loudly?" Then the Porter stood up respectfully before her and said, "O my lady, this company earnestly desire that thou acquaint them with the story of the two bitches and what maketh thee punish them so cruelly; and then thou fallest to weeping over them and kissing them; and lastly they want to hear the tale of thy sister and why she hath been bastinado'd with palm-sticks like a man. These are the questions they charge me to put, and peace be with thee." Thereupon quoth she who was the lady of the house to the guests, "Is this true that he saith on your part?" and all replied, "Yes!" save Ja'afar who kept silence. When she heard these words she cried, "By Allah, ye have wronged us, O our guests, with grievous wronging; for when you came before us we made compact and condition with you, that whoso should speak of what concerneth him not should hear what pleaseth him not. Sufficeth ye not that we took you into our house and fed you with our best food? But the fault is not so much yours as hers who let you in." Then she tucked up her sleeves from her wrists and struck the floor thrice with her hand crying, "Come ye quickly;" and lo! a closet door opened and out of it came seven negro slaves with drawn swords in hand to whom she said, "Pinion me those praters' elbows and bind them each to each." They did her bidding and asked her, "O veiled and virtuous! is it thy high command that we strike off their heads?"; but she answered, "Leave them awhile that I question them of their condition, before their necks feel the sword." "By Allah, O my lady!" cried the Porter, "slay me not for other's sin; all these men offended and deserve the penalty of crime save myself. Now by Allah, our night had been charming had we escaped the mortification of those monocular Kalandars whose entrance into a populous city would convert it into a howling wilderness." Then he repeated these verses:

> How fair is ruth the strong man deigns not smother!
> And fairest fair when shown to weakest brother:
> By Love's own holy tie between us twain,
> Let one not suffer for the sin of other.

When the Porter ended his verse the lady laughed – And Shahrazad perceived the dawn of day and ceased to say her permitted say.

Now when it was the Eleventh Night,

She said, it hath reached me, O auspicious King, that the lady, after laughing at the Porter despite her wrath, came up to the party and spake thus, "Tell me who ye be, for ye have but an hour of life; and were ye not men of rank and, perhaps, notables of your tribes, you had not been so froward and I had hastened your doom." Then said the Caliph, "Woe to thee, O Ja'afar, tell her who we are lest we be slain by mistake; and speak her fair before some horror befal us." "'Tis part of thy deserts," replied he; whereupon the Caliph cried out at him saying, "There is a time for witty words and there is a time for serious work." Then the lady accosted the three Kalandars and asked them, "Are ye brothers?"; when they answered, "No, by Allah, we be naught but Fakirs and foreigners." Then quoth she to one among them, "Wast thou born blind of one eye?"; and quoth he, "No, by Allah, 'twas a marvellous matter and a wondrous mischance which caused my eye to be torn out, and mine is a tale which, if it were written upon the eye-corners with needle-gravers, were a warner to whoso would be warned." She questioned the second and third Kalandar; but all replied like the first, "By Allah, O our mistress, each one of us cometh from a different country, and we are all three the sons of Kings, sovereign Princes ruling over suzerains and capital cities." Thereupon she turned towards them and said, "Let each and every of you tell me his tale in due order and explain the cause of his coming to our place; and if his story please us let him stroke his head and wend his way." The first to come forward was the Hammál, the Porter, who said, "O my lady, I am a man and a porter. This dame, the cateress, hired me to carry a load and took me first to the shop of a vintner; then to the booth of a butcher; thence to the stall of a fruiterer; thence to a grocer who also sold dry fruits; thence to a confectioner and a perfumer-cum-druggist and from him to this place where there happened to me with you what happened. Such is my story and peace be on us all!" At this the lady laughed and said, "Rub thy head and wend thy ways!"; but he cried, "By Allah, I will not stump it till I hear the stories of my companions." Then came forward one of the Monoculars and began to tell her

The First Kalandar's Tale

KNOW, O MY LADY, that the cause of my beard being shorn and my eye being out-torn was as follows. My father was a King and he had a brother who was a King over another city; and it came to pass that I and my cousin, the son of my paternal uncle, were· both born on one and the same day. And years and days rolled on; and, as we grew up, I used to visit my uncle every now and then and to spend a certain number of months with him. Now my cousin and I were sworn friends; for he ever entreated me with exceeding kindness; he killed for me the fattest sheep and strained the best of his wines, and we enjoyed long conversing and carousing. One day when the wine had gotten the better of us, the son of my uncle said to me, "O my cousin, I have a great service to ask of thee; and I desire that thou stay me not in whatso I desire to do!" And I replied, "With joy and goodly will." Then he made me swear the most binding oaths and left me; but after a little while he returned leading a lady veiled and richly apparelled with ornaments worth a large sum of money. Presently he turned to me (the woman being still behind him) and said, "Take this lady with thee and go before me to such a burial ground" (describing it, so that I knew the place), "and enter with her into such a sepulchre and there await my coming." The oaths I swore to him made me keep silence and suffered me not to oppose him; so I led the woman to the cemetery and both I and she took our seats in the sepulchre; and hardly had we sat down when in came my uncle's son, with a bowl of water, a bag of mortar and an adze somewhat like a hoe. He went straight to the tomb in the midst of the sepulchre and, breaking it open with the adze set the stones on one side; then he fell to digging into the earth of the tomb till he came upon a large iron plate, the size of a wicket-door; and on raising it there appeared below it a staircase vaulted and winding. Then he turned to the lady and said to her, "Come now and take thy final choice!" She at once went down by the staircase and disappeared; then quoth he to me, "O son of my uncle, by way of completing thy kindness, when I shall have descended into this place, restore the trap-door to where it was, and heap back the earth upon it as it lay before; and then of thy great goodness mix this unslaked lime which is in the bag with this water which is in the bowl and, after building up the stones, plaster the outside so that none looking upon it shall say: This is a new opening in an old tomb. For a whole year have I worked at this place whereof none knoweth but Allah, and this is the need I have of thee;" presently adding, "May Allah never bereave thy friends of thee nor make them desolate by thine absence, O son of my uncle, O my dear cousin!" And he went down the stairs and disappeared for ever. When he was lost to sight I replaced the iron plate and did all his bidding till the tomb became as it was before; and I worked almost unconsciously for my head was heated with wine. Returning to the palace of my uncle, I was told that he had gone forth a-sporting and hunting; so I slept that night without seeing him; and, when the morning dawned, I remembered the scenes of the past evening and what happened between me and my cousin; I repented of having obeyed him when penitence was of no avail, I still thought, however, that it was a dream. So I fell to asking for the son of my uncle; but there was none to answer me concerning him; and I went out to the grave-yard and the sepulchres, and sought for the tomb under which he was, but could not find it; and I ceased not wandering about from sepulchre to sepulchre, and tomb to tomb, all without success, till night set in. So I returned to the city, yet I could neither eat nor drink; my thoughts being engrossed with my cousin, for that I knew not what was become of him; and I grieved with exceeding grief and passed another sorrowful night, watching until the morning. Then went I a second time to the cemetery, pondering over what the son of mine uncle had done; and, sorely repenting my hearkening to him, went round among all the tombs, but could not find the tomb I sought. I mourned over the past, and remained in my mourning seven days, seeking the place and ever missing the path. Then my torture of scruples grew upon me till I well nigh went mad, and I found no way to dispel my grief save travel and return to my father. So I set out and journeyed homeward; but as I was entering my father's capital a crowd of rioters sprang upon me and pinioned me. I wondered thereat with all wonderment, seeing that I was the son of the Sultan, and these men were my father's subjects and amongst them were some of my own slaves. A great fear fell upon me, and I said to my soul, "Would heaven I knew what hath happened to my father!" I questioned those that bound me of the cause of their so doing, but they returned me no answer. However, after a while one of them said to me (and he had been a hired servant of our house), "Fortune hath been false to thy father; his troops betrayed him and the Wazir who slew him now reigneth in his stead and we lay in wait to seize thee by the bidding of him." I was well-nigh distraught and felt ready to faint on hearing of my father's death; when they carried me off and placed me in presence of the usurper. Now between me and him there was an olden grudge, the cause of which was this. I was fond of shooting with the stone-bow, and it befel one day, as I was standing on the terrace-roof of the palace, that a bird lighted on the top of the Wazir's house when he happened to be there. I shot at the bird and missed the mark; but I hit the Wazir's eye and knocked it out as fate and fortune decreed. Even so saith the poet:

We tread the path where Fate hath led
The path Fate writ we fain must tread:
And man in one land doomed to die
Death no where else shall do him dead.

And on like wise saith another:

Let Fortune have her wanton way
Take heart and all her words obey:
Nor joy nor mourn at anything
For all things pass and no things stay.

Now when I knocked out the Wazir's eye he could not say a single word, for that my father was King of the city; but he hated me ever after and dire was the grudge thus caused between us twain. So when I was set before him hand-bound and pinioned, he straightway gave orders for me to be beheaded. I asked, "For what crime wilt thou put me to death?"; whereupon he answered, "What crime is greater than this?" pointing the while to the place where his eye had been. Quoth I, "This I did by accident not of malice prepense;" and quoth he, "If thou didst it by accident, I will do the like by thee with intention." Then cried he, "Bring him forward," and they brought me up to him, when he thrust his finger into my left eye and gouged it out; whereupon I became one-eyed as ye see me. Then he bade bind me hand and foot, and put me into a chest and said to the sworder, "Take charge of this fellow, and go off with him to the waste lands about the city; then draw thy scymitar and slay him, and leave him to feed the beasts and birds." So the headsman fared forth with me and when he was in the midst of the desert, he took me out of the chest (and I with both hands pinioned and both feet fettered) and was about to bandage my eyes before striking off my head. But I wept with exceeding weeping until I made him weep with me and, looking at him I began to recite these couplets:

> I deemed you coat-o'-mail that should withstand
> The foeman's shafts; and you proved foeman's brand;
> I hoped your aidance in mine every chance
> Though fail my left to aid my dexter hand:
> Aloof you stand and hear the railer's gibe
> While rain their shafts on me the giber-band:
> But an ye will not guard me from my foes
> Stand clear, and succour neither these nor those!

And I also quoted:

> I deemed my brethren mail of strongest steel
> And so they were – from foes to fend my dart!
> I deemed their arrows surest of their aim;
> And so they were – when aiming at my heart!

When the headsman heard my lines (he had been sworder to my sire and he owed me a debt of gratitude) he cried, "O my lord, what can I do, being but a slave under orders?" presently adding, "Fly for thy life and nevermore return to this land, or they will slay thee and slay me with thee, even as the poet said:

> Take thy life and fly whenas evils threat;
> Let the ruined house tell its owner's fate:
> New land for the old thou shalt seek and find
> But to find new life thou must not await.
> Strange that men should sit in the stead of shame,
> When Allah's world is so wide and great!
> And trust not other, in matters grave
> Life itself must act for a life beset:

Ne'er would prowl the lion with maned neck,
Did he reckon on aid or of others reck."

Hardly believing in my escape, I kissed his hand and thought the loss of my eye a light matter in consideration of my escaping from being slain. I arrived at my uncle's capital; and, going in to him, told him of what had befallen my father and myself; whereat he wept with sore weeping and said, "Verily thou addest grief to my grief, and woe to my woe; for thy cousin hath been missing these many days; I wot not what hath happened to him, and none can give me news of him." And he wept till he fainted. I sorrowed and condoled with him; and he would have applied certain medicaments to my eye, but he saw that it was become as a walnut with the shell empty. Then said he, "O my son, better to lose eye and keep life!" After that I could no longer remain silent about my cousin, who was his only son and one dearly loved, so I told him all that had happened. He rejoiced with extreme joyance to hear news of his son and said, "Come now and show me the tomb;" but I replied, "By Allah, O my uncle, I know not its place, though I sought it carefully full many times, yet could not find the site." However, I and my uncle went to the grave-yard and looked right and left, till at last I recognised the tomb and we both rejoiced with exceeding joy. We entered the sepulchre and loosened the earth about the grave; then, upraising the trap-door, descended some fifty steps till we came to the foot of the staircase when lo! we were stopped by a blinding smoke. Thereupon said my uncle that saying whose sayer shall never come to shame, "There is no Majesty and there is no Might, save in Allah, the Glorious, the Great!" and we advanced till we suddenly came upon a saloon, whose floor was strewed with flour and grain and provisions and all manner necessaries; and in the midst of it stood a canopy sheltering a couch. Thereupon my uncle went up to the couch and inspecting it found his son and the lady who had gone down with him into the tomb, lying in each other's embrace; but the twain had become black as charred wood; it was as if they had been cast into a pit of fire. When my uncle saw this spectacle, he spat in his son's face and said, "Thou hast thy deserts, O thou hog! this is thy judgment in the transitory world, and yet remaineth the judgment in the world to come, a durer and a more enduring." – And Shahrazad perceived the dawn of day and ceased saying her permitted say.

Now when it was the Twelfth Night,

She continued, It hath reached me, O auspicious King, that the Kalandar thus went on with his story before the lady and the Caliph and Ja'afar: My uncle struck his son with his slipper as he lay there a black heap of coal. I marvelled at his hardness of heart, and grieving for my cousin and the lady, said, "By Allah, O my uncle, calm thy wrath: dost thou not see that all my thoughts are occupied with this misfortune, and how sorrowful I am for what hath befallen thy son, and how horrible it is that naught of him remaineth but a black heap of charcoal? And is not that enough, but thou must smite him with thy slipper?" Answered he, "O son of my brother, this youth from his boyhood was madly in love with his own sister; and often and often I forbade him from her, saying to myself: They are but little ones. However, when they grew up sin befel between them; and, although I could hardly believe it, I confined him and chided him and threatened him with the severest threats; and the eunuchs and servants said to him: Beware of so foul a thing which none before thee ever did, and which none after thee will ever do; and have a care lest thou be dishonoured and disgraced among the Kings of the day, even to the end of time. And I added: Such a report as this will be spread abroad by caravans, and take heed not to give them cause to talk or I will assuredly curse thee and do thee to death. After that I lodged them apart and shut her up; but the accursed girl loved him with passionate love, for Satan had got the mastery of her as well as of him and made their foul sin seem fair in their sight. Now when my son saw that I separated them, he secretly built this souterrain and furnished it and transported to it victuals, even as thou seest; and, when I had gone out a-sporting, came here with his sister and hid from me. Then His righteous judgment fell upon the twain and consumed them with fire from Heaven; and verily the last judgment will deal them durer pains and more enduring!" Then he wept and I wept with him; and he looked at me and said, "Thou art my son in his stead." And I bethought me awhile of the world and of its chances, how the Wazir had slain my father and had taken his place and had put out my eye; and how my cousin had come to his death by the strangest chance: and I wept again and my uncle wept with me. Then we mounted the steps and let down the iron plate and heaped up the earth over it; and, after restoring the tomb to its former condition, we returned to the palace. But hardly had we sat down ere we heard the tom-toming of the kettle-drum and tantara of trumpets and clash of cymbals; and the rattling of war-men's lances; and the clamours of assailants and the clanking of bits and the neighing of steeds; while the world was canopied with dense dust and sand-clouds raised by the horses' hoofs. We were amazed at sight and sound, knowing not what could be the matter; so we asked and were told us that the Wazir who had usurped my father's kingdom had marched his men; and that after levying his soldiery and taking a host of wild Arabs into service, he had come down upon us with armies like the sands of the sea; their number none could tell and against them none could prevail. They attacked the city unawares; and the citizens, being powerless to oppose them, surrendered the place: my uncle was slain and I made for the suburbs saying to myself, "If thou fall into this villain's hands he will assuredly kill thee." On this wise all my troubles were renewed; and I pondered all that had betided my father and my uncle and I knew not what to do; for if the city people or my father's troops had recognised me they would have done their best to win favour by destroying me; and I could think of no way to escape save by shaving off my beard and my eyebrows. So I shore them off and, changing my fine clothes for a Kalandar's rags, I fared forth from my uncle's capital and made for this city; hoping that peradventure some one would assist me to the presence of the Prince of the Faithful, and the Caliph who is the Viceregent of Allah upon earth. Thus have I come hither that I might tell him my tale and lay my case before him. I arrived here this very night, and was standing in doubt whither I should go, when suddenly I saw this second Kalandar; so I salam'd to him, saying: I am a stranger! and he answered: I too am a stranger! And as we were conversing behold, up came our companion, this third Kalandar, and saluted us saying: I am a stranger! And we answered: We too be strangers! Then we three walked on and together till darkness overtook us and Destiny drave us to your house. Such, then, is the cause of the shaving of my beard and mustachios and eyebrows; and the manner of my losing my right eye. They marvelled much at this tale and the Caliph said to Ja'afar, "By Allah, I have not seen nor have I heard the like of what hath happened to this

Kalandar!" Quoth the lady of the house, "Rub thy head and wend thy ways;" but he replied, "I will not go, till I hear the history of the two others." Thereupon the second Kalandar came forward; and, kissing the ground, began to tell

The Second Kalandar's Tale

KNOW, O MY LADY, that I was not born one-eyed and mine is a strange story; an it were graven with needle-graver on the eye-corners, it were a warner to whoso would be warned. I am a King, son of a King, and was brought up like a Prince. I learned intoning the Koran according the seven schools; and I read all manner books, and held disputations on their contents with the doctors and men of science; moreover I studied star-lore and the fair sayings of poets and I exercised myself in all branches of learning until I surpassed the people of my time; my skill in calligraphy exceeded that of all the scribes; and my fame was bruited abroad over all climes and cities, and all the kings learned to know my name. Amongst others the King of Hind heard of me and sent to my father to invite me to his court, with offerings and presents and rarities such as befit royalties. So my father fitted out six ships for me and my people; and we put to sea and sailed for the space of a full month till we made the land. Then we brought out the horses that were with us in the ships; and, after loading the camels with our presents for the Prince, we set forth inland. But we had marched only a little way, when behold, a dust-cloud up-flew, and grew until it walled the horizon from view. After an hour or so the veil lifted and discovered beneath it fifty horsemen, ravening lions to the sight, in steel armour dight. We observed them straightly and lo! they were cutters-off of the highway, wild as wild Arabs. When they saw that we were only four and had with us but the ten camels carrying the presents, they dashed down upon us with lances at rest. We signed to them, with our fingers, as it were saying, "We be messengers of the great King of Hind, so harm us not!" but they answered on like wise, "We are not in his dominions to obey nor are we subject to his sway." Then they set upon us and slew some of my slaves and put the lave to flight; and I also fled after I had gotten a wound, a grievous hurt, whilst the Arabs were taken up with the money and the presents which were with us. I went forth unknowing whither I went, having become mean as I was mighty; and I fared on until I came to the crest of a mountain where I took shelter for the night in a cave. When day arose I set out again, nor ceased after this fashion till I arrived at a fair city and a well-filled. Now it was the season when Winter was turning away with his rime and to greet the world with his flowers came Prime, and the young blooms were springing and the streams flowed ringing, and the birds were sweetly singing, as saith the poet concerning a certain city when describing it:

> *A place secure from every thought of fear*
> *Safety and peace for ever lord it here:*
> *Its beauties seem to beautify its sons*
> *And as in Heaven its happy folk appear.*

I was glad of my arrival for I was wearied with the way, and yellow of face for weakness and want; but my plight was pitiable and I knew not whither to betake me.

So I accosted a Tailor sitting in his little shop and saluted him; he returned my salam, and bade me kindly welcome and wished me well and entreated me gently and asked me of the cause of my strangerhood. I told him all my past from first to last; and he was concerned on my account and said, "O youth, disclose not thy secret to any: the King of this city is the greatest enemy thy father hath, and there is blood-wit between them and thou hast cause to fear for thy life." Then he set meat and drink before me; and I ate and drank and he with me; and we conversed freely till nightfall, when he cleared me a place in a corner of his shop and brought me a carpet and a coverlet. I tarried with him three days; at the end of which time he said to me, "Knowest thou no calling whereby to win thy living, O my son?" "I am learned in the law," I replied, "and a doctor of doctrine; an adept in art and science, a mathematician and a notable penman." He rejoined, "Thy calling is of no account in our city, where not a soul understandeth science or even writing or aught save money-making." Then said I, "By Allah, I know nothing but what I have mentioned;" and he answered, "Gird thy middle and take thee a hatchet and a cord, and go and hew wood in the wold for thy daily bread, till Allah send thee relief; and tell none who thou art lest they slay thee." Then he bought me an axe and a rope and gave me in charge to certain woodcutters; and with these guardians I went forth into the forest, where I cut fuel-wood the whole of my day and came back in the evening bearing my bundle on my head. I sold it for half a dinar, with part of which I bought provision and laid by the rest. In such work I spent a whole year and when this was ended I went out one day, as was my wont, into the wilderness; and, wandering away from my companions, I chanced on a thickly grown lowland in which there was an abundance of wood. So I entered and I found the gnarled stump of a great tree and loosened the ground about it and shovelled away the earth. Presently my hatchet rang upon a copper ring; so I cleared away the soil and behold, the ring was attached to a wooden trap-door. This I raised and there appeared beneath it a staircase. I descended the steps to the bottom and came to a door, which I opened and found myself in a noble hall strong of structure and beautifully built, where was a damsel like a pearl of great price, whose favour banished from my heart all grief and cark and care; and whose soft speech healed the soul in despair and captivated the wise and ware. Her figure measured five feet in height; her breasts were firm and upright; her cheek a very garden of delight; her colour lively bright; her face gleamed like dawn through curly tresses which gloomed like night, and above the snows of her bosom glittered teeth of a pearly white. As the poet said of one like her:

> Slim-waisted loveling, jetty hair-encrowned
> A wand of willow on a sandy mound:

And as saith another:

> Four things that meet not, save they here unite
> To shed my heart-blood and to rape my sprite:
> Brilliantest forehead; tresses jetty bright;
> Cheeks rosy red and stature beauty-dight.

When I looked upon her I prostrated myself before Him who had created her, for the beauty and loveliness He had shaped in her, and she looked at me and said, "Art thou man or Jinni?" "I am a man," answered I, and she, "Now who brought thee to this place where I have abided five-and-twenty years without even yet seeing man in it." Quoth I (and indeed I found her words wonder-sweet, and my heart was melted to the core by them), "O my lady, my good fortune led me hither for the dispelling of my cark and care." Then I related to her all my mishap from first to last, and my case appeared to her exceeding grievous; so she wept and said, "I will tell thee my story in my turn. I am the daughter of the King Ifitamus, lord of the Islands of Abnús, who married me to my cousin, the son of my paternal uncle; but on my wedding night an Ifrit named Jirjís bin Rajmús, first cousin that is, mother's sister's son, of Iblís, the Foul Fiend, snatched me up and, flying away with me like a bird, set me down in this place, whither he conveyed all I needed of fine stuffs, raiment and jewels and furniture, and meat and drink and other else. Once in every ten days he comes here and lies a single night with me, and then wends his way, for he took me without the consent of his family; and he hath agreed with me that if ever I need him by night or by day, I have only to pass my hand over yonder two lines engraved upon the alcove, and he will appear to me before my fingers cease touching. Four days have now passed since he was here; and, as there remain six days before he come again, say me, wilt thou abide with me five days, and go hence the day before his coming?" I replied "Yes, and yes again! O rare, if all this be not a dream!" Hereat she was glad and, springing to her feet, seized my hand and carried me through an arched doorway to a Hammam-bath, a fair hall and richly decorate. I doffed my clothes, and she doffed hers; then we bathed and she washed me; and when this was done we left the bath, and she seated me by her side upon a high divan, and brought me sherbet scented with musk. When we felt cool after the bath, she set food before me and we ate and fell to talking; but presently she said to me, "Lay thee down and take thy rest, for surely thou must be weary." So I thanked her, my lady, and lay down and slept soundly, forgetting all that had happened to me. When I awoke I found her rubbing and shampooing my feet; so I again thanked her and blessed her and we sat for a while talking. Said she, "By Allah, I was sad at heart, for that I have dwelt alone underground for these five-and-twenty years; and praise be to Allah, who hath sent me some one with whom I can converse!" Then she asked, "O youth, what sayest thou to wine?" and I answered, "Do as thou wilt." Whereupon she went to a cupboard and took out a sealed flask of right old wine and set off the table with flowers and scented herbs and began to sing these lines:

> Had we known of thy coming we fain had dispread
> The cores of our hearts or the balls of our eyes;
> Our cheeks as a carpet to greet thee had thrown
> And our eyelids had strown for thy feet to betread.

Now when she finished her verse I thanked her, for indeed love of her had gotten hold of my heart and my grief and anguish were gone. We sat at converse and carousal till nightfall, and with her I spent the night – such night never spent I in all my life! On the morrow delight followed delight till midday, by which time I had drunken wine so freely that I had lost my wits, and stood up, staggering to the right and to the left, and said "Come, O my charmer, and I will carry thee up from this underground vault and deliver thee from the spell of thy Jinni." She laughed and replied "Content thee and hold thy peace: of every ten days one is for the Ifrit and the other nine are thine." Quoth I (and in good sooth drink had got the better of me), "This very instant will I

break down the alcove whereon is graven the talisman and summon the Ifrit that I
may slay him, for it is a practise of mine to slay Ifrits!" When she heard my words her
colour waxed wan and she said, "By Allah, do not!" and she began repeating:

> This is a thing wherein destruction lies
> I rede thee shun it an thy wits be wise.

And these also:

> O thou who seekest severance, draw the rein
> Of thy swift steed nor seek o'ermuch t' advance;
> Ah stay! for treachery is the rule of life,
> And sweets of meeting end in severance.

I heard her verse but paid no heed to her words, nay, I raised my foot and
administered to the alcove a mighty kick – And Shahrazad perceived the dawn of day
and ceased to say her permitted say.

Now when it was the Thirteenth Night,

She said, it hath reached me, O auspicious King, that the second Kalandar thus
continued his tale to the lady: But when, O my mistress, I kicked that alcove with a
mighty kick, behold, the air starkened and darkened and thundered and lightened;
the earth trembled and quaked and the world became invisible. At once the fumes of
wine left my head: I cried to her, "What is the matter?" and she replied, "The Ifrit is
upon us! did I not warn thee of this? By Allah, thou hast brought ruin upon me; but
fly for thy life and go up by the way thou camest down!" So I fled up the staircase; but,
in the excess of my fear, I forgot sandals and hatchet. And when I had mounted two
steps I turned to look for them, and lo! I saw the earth cleave asunder, and there arose
from it an Ifrit, a monster of hideousness, who said to the damsel, "What trouble and
pother be this wherewith thou disturbest me? What mishap hath betided thee?" "No
mishap hath befallen me" she answered, "save that my breast was straitened and my
heart heavy with sadness: so I drank a little wine to broaden it and to hearten myself;
then I rose to obey a call of Nature, but the wine had gotten into my head and I fell
against the alcove." "Thou liest, like the whore thou art!" shrieked the Ifrit; and he
looked around the hall right and left till he caught sight of my axe and sandals and
said to her, "What be these but the belongings of some mortal who hath been in
thy society?" She answered, "I never set eyes upon them till this moment: they must
have been brought by thee hither cleaving to thy garments." Quoth the Ifrit, "These
words are absurd; thou harlot! thou strumpet!" Then he stripped her stark naked
and, stretching her upon the floor, bound her hands and feet to four stakes, like one
crucified; and set about torturing and trying to make her confess. I could not bear
to stand listening to her cries and groans; so I climbed the stair on the quake with
fear; and when I reached the top I replaced the trap-door and covered it with earth.
Then repented I of what I had done with penitence exceeding; and thought of the
lady and her beauty and loveliness, and the tortures she was suffering at the hands
of the accursed Ifrit, after her quiet life of five-and-twenty years; and how all that
had happened to her was for cause of me. I bethought me of my father and his kingly
estate and how I had become a woodcutter; and how, after my time had been awhile

serene, the world had again waxed turbid and troubled to me. So I wept bitterly and repeated this couplet:

> *What time Fate's tyranny shall most oppress thee*
> *Perpend! one day shall joy thee, one distress thee!*

Then I walked till I reached the home of my friend, the Tailor, whom I found most anxiously expecting me; indeed he was, as the saying goes, on coals of fire for my account. And when he saw me he said, "All night long my heart hath been heavy, fearing for thee from wild beasts or other mischances. Now praise be to Allah for thy safety!" I thanked him for his friendly solicitude and, retiring to my corner, sat pondering and musing on what had befallen me; and I blamed and chided myself for my meddlesome folly and my frowardness in kicking the alcove. I was calling myself to account when behold, my friend, the Tailor, came to me and said, "O youth, in the shop there is an old man, a Persian, who seeketh thee: he hath thy hatchet and thy sandals which he had taken to the woodcutters, saying, I was going out at what time the Mu'azzin began the call to dawn-prayer, when I chanced upon these things and know not whose they are; so direct me to their owner. The woodcutters recognised thy hatchet and directed him to thee: he is sitting in my shop, so fare forth to him and thank him and take thine axe and sandals." When I heard these words I turned yellow with fear and felt stunned as by a blow; and, before I could recover myself, lo! the floor of my private room clove asunder, and out of it rose the Persian who was the Ifrit. He had tortured the lady with exceeding tortures, natheless she would not confess to him aught; so he took the hatchet and sandals and said to her, "As surely as I am Jirjis of the seed of Iblis, I will bring thee back the owner of this and these!" Then he went to the woodcutters with the pretence aforesaid and, being directed to me, after waiting a while in the shop till the fact was confirmed, he suddenly snatched me up as a hawk snatcheth a mouse and flew high in air; but presently descended and plunged with me under the earth (I being aswoon the while), and lastly set me down in the subterranean palace wherein I had passed that blissful night. And there I saw the lady stripped to the skin, her limbs bound to four stakes and blood welling from her sides. At the sight my eyes ran over with tears; but the Ifrit covered her person and said, "O wanton, is not this man thy lover?" She looked upon me and replied, "I wot him not nor have I ever seen him before this hour!" Quoth the Ifrit, "What! this torture and yet no confessing;" and quoth she, "I never saw this man in my born days, and it is not lawful in Allah's sight to tell lies on him." "If thou know him not," said the Ifrit to her, "take this sword and strike off his head." She hent the sword in hand and came close up to me; and I signalled to her with my eyebrows, my tears the while flowing adown my cheeks. She understood me and made answer, also by signs, "How couldest thou bring all this evil upon me?" and I rejoined after the same fashion, "This is the time for mercy and forgiveness." And the mute tongue of my case spake aloud saying:

> *Mine eyes were dragomans for my tongue betied*
> *And told full clear the love I fain would hide:*
> *When last we met and tears in torrents railed*
> *For tongue struck dumb my glances testified:*
> *She signed with eye-glance while her lips were mute*

I signed with fingers and she kenned th' implied:
Our eyebrows did all duty 'twixt us twain;
And we being speechless Love spake loud and plain.

Then, O my mistress, the lady threw away the sword and said, "How shall I strike the neck of one I wot not, and who hath done me no evil? Such deed were not lawful in my law!" and she held her hand. Said the Ifrit, "'Tis grievous to thee to slay thy lover; and, because he hath lain with thee, thou endurest these torments and obstinately refusest to confess. After this it is clear to me that only like loveth and pitieth like." Then he turned to me and asked me, "O man, haply thou also dost not know this woman;" whereto I answered, "And pray who may she be? assuredly I never saw her till this instant." "Then take the sword," said he "and strike off her head and I will believe that, thou wottest her not and will leave thee free to go, and will not deal hardly with thee." I replied, "That will I do;" and, taking the sword went forward sharply and raised my hand to smite. But she signed to me with her eyebrows, "Have I failed thee in aught of love; and is it thus that thou requitest me?" I understood what her looks implied and answered her with an eye-glance, "I will sacrifice my soul for thee." And the tongue of the case wrote in our hearts these lines:

How many a lover with his eyebrows speaketh
To his beloved, as his passion pleadeth:
With flashing eyne his passion he inspireth
And well she seeth what his pleading needeth.
How sweet the look when each on other gazeth;
And with what swiftness and how sure it speedeth:
And this with eyebrows all his passion writeth;
And that with eyeballs all his passion readeth.

Then my eyes filled with tears to overflowing and I cast the sword from my hand saying, "O mighty Ifrit and hero, if a woman lacking wits and faith deem it unlawful to strike off my head, how can it be lawful for me, a man, to smite her neck whom I never saw in my whole life. I cannot do such misdeed though thou cause me drink the cup of death and perdition." Then said the Ifrit, "Ye twain show the good understanding between you; but I will let you see how such doings end." He took the sword, and struck off the lady's hands first, with four strokes, and then her feet; whilst I looked on and made sure of death and she farewelled me with her dying eyes. So the Ifrit cried at her, "Thou whorest and makest me a wittol with thine eyes;" and struck her so that her head went flying. Then turned he to me and said, "O mortal, we have it in our law that, when the wife committeth advowtry it is lawful for us to slay her. As for this damsel I snatched her away on her bride-night when she was a girl of twelve and she knew no one but myself. I used to come to her once in every ten days and lie with her the night, under the semblance of a man, a Persian; and when I was well assured that she had cuckolded me, I slew her. But as for thee I am not well satisfied that thou hast wronged me in her; nevertheless I must not let thee go unharmed; so ask a boon of me and I will grant it." Then I rejoiced, O my lady, with exceeding joy and said, "What boon shall I crave of thee?" He replied, "Ask me this boon; into what shape I shall bewitch thee; wilt thou be a dog, or an ass or an ape?" I rejoined (and indeed I had hoped that mercy might be shown me), "By Allah, spare me, that Allah spare thee for sparing a Moslem and a man who never wronged thee." And I humbled myself before him with exceeding humility, and remained standing in his presence, saying, "I am sore oppressed by circumstance." He replied "Talk me no long talk, it is in my power to slay thee; but I give thee instead thy choice." Quoth I, "O thou Ifrit, it would besit thee to pardon me even as the Envied pardoned the Envier." Quoth he, "And how was that?" and I began to tell him

Tale of the Envier and the Envied

THEY RELATE, O Ifrit, that in a certain city were two men who dwelt in adjoining houses, having a common party-wall; and one of them envied the other and looked on him with an evil eye, and did his utmost endeavour to injure him; and, albeit at all times he was jealous of his neighbour, his malice at last grew on him till he could hardly eat or enjoy the sweet pleasures of sleep. But the Envied did nothing save prosper; and the more the other strove to injure him, the more he got and gained and throve. At last the malice of his neighbour and the man's constant endeavour to work him a harm came to his knowledge; so he said, "By Allah! God's earth is wide enough for its people;" and, leaving the neighbourhood, he repaired to another city where he bought himself a piece of land in which was a dried up draw-well, old and in ruinous condition. Here he built him an oratory and, furnishing it with a few necessaries, took up his abode therein, and devoted himself to prayer and worshipping Allah Almighty; and Fakirs and holy mendicants flocked to him from all quarters; and his fame went abroad through the city and that country side. Presently the news reached his envious neighbour, of what good fortune had befallen him and how the city notables had become his disciples; so he travelled to the place and presented himself at the holy man's hermitage, and was met by the Envied with welcome and greeting and all honour. Then quoth the Envier, "I have a word to say to thee; and this is the cause of my faring hither, and I wish to give thee a piece of good news; so come with me to thy cell." Thereupon the Envied arose and took the Envier by the hand, and they went in to the inmost part of the hermitage; but the Envier said, "Bid thy Fakirs retire to their cells, for I will not tell thee what I have to say, save in secret where none may hear us." Accordingly the Envied said to his Fakirs, "Retire to your private cells;" and, when all had done as he bade them, he set out with his visitor and walked a little way until the twain reached the ruinous old well. And as they stood upon the brink the Envier gave the Envied a push which tumbled him headlong into it, unseen of any; whereupon he fared forth, and went his ways, thinking to have had slain him. Now this well happened to be haunted by the Jann who, seeing the case, bore him up and let him down little by little, till he reached the bottom, when they seated him upon a large stone. Then one of them asked his fellows, "Wot ye who be this man?" and they answered, "Nay." "This man," continued the speaker, "is the Envied hight who, flying from the Envier, came to dwell in our city, and here founded this holy house, and he hath edified us by his litanies and his lections of the Koran; but the Envier set out and journeyed till he rejoined him, and cunningly contrived to deceive him and cast him into the well where we now are. But the fame of this good man hath this very night come to the Sultan of our city who designeth to visit him on the morrow on account of his daughter." "What aileth his daughter?" asked one, and another answered "She is possessed of a spirit; for Maymun, son of Damdam, is madly in love with her; but, if this pious man knew the remedy, her cure would be as easy as could be." Hereupon one of them inquired, "And what is the medicine?" and he replied, "The black tom-cat which is with him in the oratory hath, on the end of his tail, a white spot, the size of a dirham; let him pluck seven white hairs from the spot, then let him fumigate her therewith and the Marid will flee from her and not return; so she shall be sane for the rest of her life. All this took place, O Ifrit, within earshot of the Envied who listened readily. When dawn broke and morn arose in sheen and shone, the Fakirs went to seek the Shaykh and found him climbing up the wall of the well; whereby he was magnified in their eyes. Then, knowing that naught save the black tom-cat could supply him with the remedy required, he plucked the seven tail-hairs from the white spot and laid them by him; and hardly had the sun risen ere the Sultan entered the hermitage, with the great lords of his estate, bidding the rest of his retinue to remain standing outside. The Envied gave him a hearty welcome, and seating him by his side asked him, "Shall I tell thee the cause of thy coming?" The King answered "Yes." He continued, "Thou hast come upon pretext of a visitation; but it is in thy heart to question me of thy daughter." Replied the King, "'Tis even so, O thou holy Shaykh;" and the Envied continued, "Send and fetch her, and I trust to heal her forthright (an such it be the will of Allah!). The King in great joy sent for his daughter, and they brought her pinioned and fettered. The Envied made her sit down behind a curtain and taking out the hairs fumigated her therewith; whereupon that which was in her head cried out and departed from her. The girl was at once restored to her right mind and veiling her face, said, "What hath happened and who brought me hither?" The Sultan rejoiced with a joy which nothing could exceed, and kissed his daughter's eyes, and the holy man's hand; then, turning to his great lords, he asked, "How say ye! What fee deserveth he who hath made my daughter whole?" and all answered "He deserveth her to wife;" and the King said, "Ye speak sooth!" So he married him to her and the Envied thus became son-in-law to the King. And after a little the Wazir died and the King said, "Whom can I make Minister in his stead?" "Thy son-in-law," replied the courtiers. So the Envied became a Wazir; and after a while the Sultan also died and the lieges said, "Whom shall we make King?" and all cried, "The Wazir." So the Wazir was forthright made Sultan, and he became King regnant, a true ruler of men. One day as he had mounted his horse; and, in the eminence of his kinglihood, was riding amidst his Emirs and Wazirs and the Grandees of his realm his eye fell upon his old neighbour, the Envier, who stood afoot on his path; so he turned to one of his Ministers, and said, "Bring hither that man and cause him no affright." The Wazir brought him and the King said, "Give him a thousand miskáls of gold from the treasury, and load him ten camels with goods for trade, and send him under escort to his own town." Then he bade his enemy farewell and sent him away and forbore to punish him for the many and great evils he had done. See, O Ifrit, the mercy of the Envied to the Envier, who had hated him from the beginning and had borne him such bitter malice and never met him without causing him trouble; and had driven him from house and home, and then had journeyed for the sole purpose of taking his life by throwing him into the well. Yet he did not requite his injurious dealing, but forgave him and was bountiful to him. Then I wept before him, O my lady, with sore weeping, never was there sorer, and I recited:

Pardon my fault, for 'tis the wise man's wont
All faults to pardon and revenge forgo:
In sooth all manner faults in me contain
Then deign of goodness mercy-grace to show:
Whoso imploreth pardon from on High
Should hold his hand from sinners here below.

Said the Ifrit, "Lengthen not thy words! As to my slaying thee fear it not, and as to my pardoning thee hope it not; but from my bewitching thee there is no escape." Then he tore me from the ground which closed under my feet and flew with me into the firmament till I saw the earth as a large white cloud or a saucer in the midst of the waters. Presently he set me down on a mountain, and taking a little dust, over which he muttered some magical words, sprinkled me therewith, saying, "Quit that shape and take thou the shape of an ape!" And on the instant I became an ape, a tail-less baboon, the son of a century. Now when he had left me and I saw myself in this ugly and hateful shape, I wept for myself, but resigned my soul to the tyranny of Time and Circumstance, well weeting that Fortune is fair and constant to no man. I descended the mountain and found at the foot a desert plain, long and broad, over which I travelled for the space of a month till my course brought me to the brink of the briny sea. After standing there awhile, I was ware of a ship in the offing which ran before a fair wind making for the shore: I hid myself behind a rock on the beach and waited till the ship drew near, when I leaped on board. I found her full of merchants and passengers and one of them cried, "O Captain, this ill-omened brute will bring us ill-luck!" and another said, "Turn this ill-omened beast out from among us;" the Captain said, "Let us kill it!" another said, "Slay it with the sword;" a third, "Drown it;" and a fourth, "Shoot it with an arrow." But I sprang up and laid hold of the Rais's skirt, and shed tears which poured down my chops. The Captain took pity on me, and said, "O merchants! this ape hath appealed to me for protection and I will protect him; henceforth he is under my charge: so let none do him aught hurt or harm, otherwise there will be bad blood between us." Then he entreated me kindly and whatsoever he said I understood and ministered to his every want and served him as a servant, albeit my tongue would not obey my wishes; so that he came to love me. The vessel sailed on, the wind being fair, for the space of fifty days; at the end of which we cast anchor under the walls of a great city wherein was a world of people, especially learned men, none could tell their number save Allah. No sooner had we arrived than we were visited by certain Mameluke-officials from the King of that city; who, after boarding us, greeted the merchants and giving them joy of safe arrival said, "Our King welcometh you, and sendeth you this roll of paper, whereupon each and every of you must write a line. For ye shall know that the King's Minister, a calligrapher of renown, is dead, and the King hath sworn a solemn oath that he will make none Wazir in his stead who cannot write as well as he could." He then gave us the scroll which measured ten cubits long by a breadth of one, and each of the merchants who knew how to write wrote a line thereon, even to the last of them; after which I stood up (still in the shape of an ape) and snatched the roll out of their hands. They feared lest I should tear it or throw it overboard; so they tried to stay me and scare me, but I signed to them that I could write, whereat all marvelled, saying, "We never yet saw an ape write." And the Captain cried, "Let him write; and if he scribble and scrabble we will kick him out and kill him; but if he write fair and scholarly I will adopt him as my son; for surely I never yet saw a more intelligent and well-mannered monkey than he. Would Heaven my real son were his match in morals and manners." I took the reed, and stretching out my paw, dipped it in ink and wrote, in the hand used for letters, these two couplets:

> *Time hath recorded gifts she gave the great;*
> *But none recorded thine which be far higher;*
> *Allah ne'er orphan men by loss of thee*
> *Who be of Goodness mother, Bounty's sire.*

And I wrote in Rayháni or larger letters elegantly curved:

> *Thou hast a reed of rede to every land,*
> *Whose driving causeth all the world to thrive;*
> *Nil is the Nile of Misraim by thy boons*
> *Who makest misery smile with fingers five.*

Then I wrote in the Suls character:

> *There be no writer who from Death shall fleet,*
> *But what his hand hath writ men shall repeat:*
> *Write, therefore, naught save what shall serve thee when*
> *Thou see't on Judgment-Day an so thou see't!*

Then I wrote in the character Naskh:

> *When to sore parting Fate our love shall doom,*
> *To distant life by Destiny decreed,*
> *We cause the inkhorn's lips to 'plain our pains,*
> *And tongue our utterance with the talking reed.*

And I wrote in the Túmár character:

> *Kingdom with none endures; if thou deny*
> *This truth, where be the Kings of earlier earth?*
> *Set trees of goodliness while rule endures,*
> *And when thou art fallen they shall tell thy worth.*

And I wrote in the character Muhakkak:

> *When oped the inkhorn of thy wealth and fame*
> *Take ink of generous heart and gracious hand;*
> *Write brave and noble deeds while write thou can*
> *And win thee praise from point of pen and brand.*

Then I gave the scroll to the officials and, after we all had written our line, they carried it before the King. When he saw the paper no writing pleased him save my writing; and he said to the assembled courtiers, "Go seek the writer of these lines and dress him in a splendid robe of honour; then mount him on a she-mule, let a band of music precede him and bring him to the presence." At these words they smiled and the King was wroth with them and cried "O accursed! I give you an order and you laugh at me?" "O King," replied they, "if we laugh 'tis not at thee and not without a cause." "And what is it?" asked he; and they answered, "O King, thou orderest us to bring to thy presence the man who wrote these lines; now the truth is that he who wrote them is not of the sons of Adam, but an ape, a tail-less baboon, belonging to the ship-Captain." Quoth he, "Is this true that you say?" Quoth they "Yea! by the rights of thy munificence!" The King marvelled at their words and shook with mirth and said, "I am minded to buy this ape of the Captain." Then he sent messengers to the ship with the mule, the dress, the guard and the state-drums, saying, "Not the less do you clothe him in the robe of honour and mount him on the mule and let him be surrounded by the guards and preceded by the band of music." They came to the ship and took me from the Captain and robed me in the robe of honour and, mounting me on the she-mule, carried me in state-procession through the streets; whilst the people were amazed and amused. And folk said to one another "Halloo! is our Sultan about to make an ape his Minister?"; and came all agog crowding to gaze at me, and the town was astir and turned topsy-turvy on my account. When they brought me up to the King and set me in his presence, I kissed the ground before him three times, and once before the High Chamberlain and great officers, and he bade me be seated, and I sat respectfully on shins and knees, and all who were present marvelled at my fine manners, and the King most of all. Thereupon he ordered the lieges to retire; and, when none remained save the King's majesty, the Eunuch on duty and a little white slave, he bade them set before me the table of food, containing all manner of birds, whatever hoppeth and flieth and treadeth in nest, such as quail and sand-grouse. Then he signed to me to eat with him; so I rose and kissed ground before him, then sat me down and ate with him. And when the table was removed I washed my hands in seven waters and took the reed-case and reed; and wrote instead of speaking these couplets:

> Wail for the little partridges on porringer and plate;
> Cry for the ruin of the fries and stews well marinate:
> Keen as I keen for loved, lost daughters of the Katá-grouse,
> And omelette round the fair enbrownèd fowls agglomerate:
> O fire in heart of me for fish, those deux poissons I saw,
> Bedded on new made scones and cakes in piles to laniate.
> For thee, O vermicelli! aches my very maw! I hold
> Without thee every taste and joy are clean annihilate.
> Those eggs have rolled their yellow eyes in torturing pains of fire
> Ere served with hash and fritters hot, that delicatest cate,
> Praisèd be Allah for His baked and roast and ah! how good
> This pulse, these pot-herbs steeped in oil with eysill combinate!
> When hunger sated was, I elbow-propt fell back upon
> Meat-pudding wherein gleamed the bangles that my wits amate.
> Then woke I sleeping appetite to eat as though in sport
> Sweets from brocaded trays and kickshaws most elaborate.

Be patient, soul of me! Time is a haughty, jealous wight;
To-day he seems dark-lowering and to-morrow fair to sight.

Then I rose and seated myself at a respectful distance while the King read what I had written, and marvelled, exclaiming, "O the miracle, that an ape should be gifted with this graceful style and this power of penmanship! By Allah, 'tis a wonder of wonders!"

Presently they set before the King choice wines in flagons of glass and he drank: then he passed on the cup to me; and I kissed the ground and drank and wrote on it:

With fire they boilèd me to loose my tongue,
And pain and patience gave for fellowship:
Hence comes it hands of men upbear me high
And honey-dew from lips of maid I sip!

And these also:

Morn saith to Night, "withdraw and let me shine;"
So drain we draughts that dull all pain and pine:
I doubt, so fine the glass, the wine so clear,
If 'tis the wine in glass or glass in wine.

The King read my verse and said with a sigh, "Were these gifts in a man, he would excel all the folk of his time and age!" Then he called for the chess-board, and said, "Say, wilt thou play with me?"; and I signed with my head, "Yes." Then I came forward and ordered the pieces and played with him two games, both of which I won. He was speechless with surprise; so I took the pen-case and, drawing forth a reed, wrote on the board these two couplets:

Two hosts fare fighting thro' the livelong day
Nor is their battling ever finishèd,
Until, when darkness girdeth them about,
The twain go sleeping in a single bed.

The King read these lines with wonder and delight and said to his Eunuch, "O Mukbil, go to thy mistress, Sitt al-Husn, and say her, Come, speak the King who biddeth thee hither to take thy solace in seeing this right wondrous ape!" So the Eunuch went out and presently returned with the lady who, when she saw me veiled her face and said, "O my father! hast thou lost all sense of honour? How cometh it thou art pleased to send for me and show me to strange men?" "O Sitt al-Husn," said he, "no man is here save this little foot-page and the Eunuch who reared thee and I, thy father. From whom, then, dost thou veil thy face?" She answered, "This whom thou deemest an ape is a young man, a clever and polite, a wise and learned and the son of a King; but he is ensorcelled and the Ifrit Jirjaris, who is of the seed of Iblis, cast a spell upon him, after putting to death his own wife the daughter of King Ifitamus lord of the Islands of Abnus." The King marvelled at his daughter's words and, turning to me, said, "Is this true that she saith of thee?"; and I signed by a nod of my head the answer "Yea, verily;" and wept sore. Then he asked his daughter "Whence knewest thou that he is ensorcelled?"; and she answered "O my dear papa, there was with me in my childhood an old woman, a wily one and a wise and a witch to boot, and she taught me the theory of magic and its practice; and I took notes in writing and therein waxed perfect, and have committed to memory an hundred and seventy chapters of egromantic formulas, by the least of which I could transport the stones of thy city behind the Mountain Kaf and the Circumambient Main, or make its site an abyss of the sea and its people fishes swimming in the midst of it." "O my daughter," said her father, "I conjure thee, by my life, disenchant this young man, that I may make him my Wazir and marry thee to him, for indeed he is an ingenious youth and a deeply learned." "With joy and goodly gree," she replied and, hending in hand an iron knife whereon was inscribed the name of Allah in Hebrew characters, she described a wide circle – And Shahrazad perceived the dawn of day and ceased saying her permitted say.

Now when it was the Fourteenth Night,

She said, it hath reached me, O auspicious King, that the Kalandar continued his tale thus: O my lady, the King's daughter hent in hand a knife whereon were inscribed Hebrew characters and described a wide circle in the midst of the palace-hall, and therein wrote in Cufic letters mysterious names and talismans; and she uttered words and muttered charms, some of which we understood and others we understood not. Presently the world waxed dark before our sight till we thought that the sky was falling upon our heads, and lo! the Ifrit presented himself in his own shape and aspect. His hands were like many-pronged pitchforks, his legs like the masts of great ships, and his eyes like cressets of gleaming fire. We were in terrible fear of him but the King's daughter cried at him, "No welcome to thee and no greeting, O dog!" whereupon he changed to the form of a lion and said, "O traitress, how is it thou hast broken the oath we sware that neither should contraire other!" "O accursed one," answered she, "how could there be a compact between me and the like of thee?" Then said he, "Take what thou has brought on thyself;" and the lion opened his jaws and rushed upon her; but she was too quick for him; and, plucking a hair from her head, waved it in the air muttering over it the while; and the hair straightway became a trenchant sword-blade, wherewith she smote the lion and cut him in twain. Then the two halves flew away in air and the head changed to a scorpion and the Princess became a huge serpent and set upon the accursed scorpion, and the two fought, coiling and uncoiling, a stiff fight for an hour at least. Then the scorpion changed to a vulture and the serpent became an eagle which set upon the vulture, and hunted him for an hour's time, till he became a black tom-cat, which miauled and grinned and spat. Thereupon the eagle changed into a piebald wolf and these two battled in the palace for a long time, when the cat, seeing himself overcome, changed into a worm and crept into a huge red pomegranate, which lay beside the jetting fountain in the midst of the palace hall. Whereupon the pomegranate swelled to the size of a water-melon in air; and, falling upon the marble pavement of the palace, broke to pieces, and all the grains fell out and were scattered about till they covered the whole floor. Then the wolf shook himself and became a snow-white cock, which fell to picking up the grains purposing not to leave one; but by doom of destiny one seed rolled to the fountain-edge and there lay hid. The cock fell to crowing and clapping his wings and signing to us with his beak as if to ask, "Are any grains left?" But we understood not what he meant, and he cried to us with so loud a cry that we thought the palace would fall upon us. Then he ran over all the floor till he saw the grain which had rolled to the fountain edge, and rushed eagerly to pick it up when behold, it sprang into the midst of the water and became a fish and dived to the bottom of the basin. Thereupon the cock changed to a big fish, and plunged in after the other, and the two disappeared for a while and lo! we heard loud shrieks and cries of pain which made us tremble. After this the Ifrit rose out of the water, and he was as a burning flame; casting fire and smoke from his mouth and eyes and nostrils. And immediately the Princess likewise came forth from the basin and she was one live coal of flaming lowe; and these two, she and he, battled for the space of an hour, until their fires entirely compassed them about and their thick smoke filled the palace. As for us we panted for breath, being well-nigh suffocated, and we longed to plunge into the water fearing lest we be burnt up and utterly destroyed; and the King said, "There is no Majesty and there is no Might save in Allah the Glorious, the Great! Verily we are Allah's and unto Him are we returning! Would Heaven I had not urged my daughter to attempt the disenchantment of this ape-fellow, whereby I have imposed upon her the terrible task of fighting yon accursed Ifrit against whom all the Ifrits in the world could not prevail. And would Heaven we had never seen this ape, Allah never assain nor bless the day of his coming! We thought to do a good deed by him before the face of Allah, and to release him from enchantment, and now we have brought this trouble and travail upon our heart." But I, O my lady, was tongue-tied and powerless to say a word to him. Suddenly, ere we were ware of aught, the Ifrit yelled out from under the flames and, coming up to us as we stood on the estrade, blew fire in our faces. The damsel overtook him and breathed blasts of fire at his face and the sparks from her and from him rained down upon us, and her sparks did us no harm, but one of his sparks alighted upon my eye and destroyed it making me a monocular ape; and another fell on the King's face scorching the lower half, burning off his beard and mustachios and causing his under teeth to fall out; while a third alighted on the Castrato's breast, killing him on the spot. So we despaired of life and made sure of death when lo! a voice repeated the saying, "Allah is most Highest! Allah is most Highest! Aidance and victory to all who the Truth believe; and disappointment and disgrace to all who the religion of Mohammed, the Moon of Faith, unbelieve," The speaker was the Princess who had burnt the Ifrit, and he was become a heap of ashes. Then she came up to us and said, "Reach me a cup of water." They brought it to her and she spoke over it words we understood not, and sprinkling me with it cried, "By virtue of the Truth, and by the Most Great name of Allah, I charge thee return to thy former shape." And behold, I shook and became a man as before, save that I had utterly lost an eye. Then she cried out, "The fire! The fire! O my dear papa an arrow from the accursed hath wounded me to the death, for I am not used to fight with the Jann; had he been a man I had slain him in the beginning. I had no trouble till the time when the pomegranate burst and the grains scattered, but I overlooked the seed wherein was the very life of the Jinni. Had I picked it up he had died on the spot, but as Fate and Fortune decreed, I saw it not; so he came upon me all unawares and there befel between him and me a sore struggle under the earth and high in air and in the water; and, as often as I opened on him a gate, he opened on me another gate and a stronger, till at last he opened on me the gate of fire, and few are saved upon whom the door of fire openeth. But Destiny willed that my cunning prevail over his cunning; and I burned him to death after I vainly exhorted him to embrace the religion of Al-Islam. As for me I am a dead woman; Allah supply my place to you!" Then she called upon Heaven for help and ceased not to implore relief from the fire; when lo! a black spark shot up from her robed feet to her thighs; then it flew to her bosom and thence to her face. When it reached her face she wept and said, "I testify that there is no god but the God and that Mahommed is the Apostle of God!" And we looked at her and saw naught but a heap of ashes by the side of the heap that had been the Ifrit. We mourned for her and I wished I had been in her place, so had I not seen her lovely face who had worked me such weal become ashes; but there is no gainsaying the will of Allah. When the King saw his daughter's terrible death, he plucked out what was left of his beard and beat his face and rent his raiment; and I did as he did and we both wept over her. Then came in the Chamberlains and Grandees and were amazed to find two heaps of ashes and the Sultan in a fainting fit; so they stood round him till he revived and told them what had befallen his daughter from the Ifrit; whereat their grief was right grievous and the women and the slave-girls shrieked and keened, and they continued their lamentations for the space of seven days. Moreover the King bade build over his daughter's ashes a vast vaulted tomb, and burn therein wax tapers and sepulchral lamps: but as for the Ifrit's ashes they scattered them on the winds, speeding them to the curse of Allah. Then the Sultan fell sick of a sickness that well nigh brought him to his death for a month's space; and, when health returned to him and his beard grew again and he had been converted by the mercy of Allah to Al-Islam, he sent for me and said, "O youth, Fate had decreed for us the happiest of lives, safe from all the chances and changes of Time, till thou camest to us, when troubles fell upon us. Would to Heaven we had never seen thee and the foul face of thee! For we took pity on thee and thereby we have lost our all. I have on thy account first lost my daughter who to me was well worth an hundred men; secondly I have suffered that which befel me by reason of the fire and the loss of my teeth, and my Eunuch also was slain. I blame thee not, for it was out of thy power to prevent this: the doom of Allah was on thee as well as on us and thanks be to the Almighty for that my daughter delivered thee, albeit thereby she lost her own life! Go forth now, O my son, from this my city, and suffice thee what hath befallen us through thee, even although 'twas decreed for us. Go forth in peace; and if I ever see thee again I will surely slay thee." And he cried out at me. So I went forth from his presence, O my lady, weeping bitterly and hardly believing in my escape and knowing not whither I should wend. And I recalled all that had befallen me, my meeting the tailor, my love for the damsel in the palace beneath the earth, and my narrow escape from the Ifrit, even after he had determined to do me die; and how I had entered the city as an ape and was now leaving it a man once more. Then I gave thanks to Allah and said, "My eye and not my life!" and before leaving the place I entered the bath and shaved my poll and beard and mustachios and eyebrows; and cast ashes on my head and donned the coarse black woollen robe of a Kalandar. Then I fared forth, O my lady, and every day I pondered all the calamities which had betided me, and I wept and repeated these couplets:

> "I am distraught, yet verily His ruth abides with me,
> Tho' round me gather hosts of ills, whence come I cannot see:

Patient I'll be till Patience self with me impatient wax;
Patient for ever till the Lord fulfil my destiny:
Patient I'll bide without complaint, a wronged and vanquisht man;
Patient as sunparcht wight that spans the desert's sandy sea:
Patient I'll be till Aloe's self unwittingly allow
I'm patient under bitterer things than bitterest aloë:
No bitterer things than aloes or than patience for mankind;
Yet bitterer than the twain to me were Patience' treachery:
My sere and seamed and seared brow would dragoman my sore
If soul could search my sprite and there unsecret secrecy:
Were hills to bear the load I bear they'd crumble 'neath the weight;
'Twould still the roaring wind, 'twould quench the flame-tongue's flagrancy,
And whoso saith the world is sweet certès a day he'll see
With more than aloes' bitterness and aloes' pungency."

Then I journeyed through many regions and saw many a city intending for Baghdad, that I might seek audience, in the House of Peace, with the Commander of the Faithful and tell him all that had befallen me. I arrived here this very night and found my brother in Allah, this first Kalandar, standing about as one perplexed; so I saluted him with "Peace be upon thee," and entered into discourse with him. Presently up came our brother, this third Kalandar, and said to us, "Peace be with you! I am a stranger;" whereto we replied, "And we too be strangers, who have come hither this blessed night." So we all three walked on together, none of us knowing the other's history, till Destiny drave us to this door and we came in to you. Such then is my story and my reason for shaving my beard and mustachios, and this is what caused the loss of my eye. Said the house-mistress "Thy tale is indeed a rare; so rub thy head and wend thy ways;" but he replied, "I will not budge till I hear my companions' stories." Then came forward the third Kalandar, and said, "O illustrious lady! my history is not like that of these my comrades, but more wondrous and far more marvellous. In their case Fate and Fortune came down on them unawares; but I drew down destiny upon my own head and brought sorrow on mine own soul, and shaved my own beard and lost my own eye. Hear then"

The Third Kalandar's Tale

KNOW, O MY LADY, that I also am a King and the Son of a King and my name is Ajíb son of Khazíb. When my father died I succeeded him; and I ruled and did justice and dealt fairly by all my lieges. I delighted in sea trips, for my capital stood on the shore, before which the ocean stretched far and wide; and nearhand were many great islands with sconces and garrisons in the midst of the main. My fleet numbered fifty merchantmen, and as many yachts for pleasance, and an hundred and fifty sail ready fitted for holy war with the Unbelievers. It fortuned that I had a mind to enjoy myself on the islands aforesaid, so I took ship with my people in ten keel; and, carrying with me a month's victual, I set out on a twenty days voyage. But one night a head wind struck us, and the sea rose against us with huge waves; the billows sorely buffetted us and a dense darkness settled round us. We gave ourselves up for lost and I said, "Whoso endangereth his days, e'en an he 'scape deserveth no praise." Then we prayed to Allah and besought Him; but the storm-blasts ceased not to blow against us nor the surges to strike us till morning broke, when the gale fell, the seas sank to mirrory stillness and the sun shone upon us kindly clear. Presently we made an island where we landed and cooked somewhat of food, and ate heartily and took our rest for a couple of days. Then we set out again and sailed other twenty days, the seas broadening and the land shrinking. Presently the current ran counter to us, and we found ourselves in strange waters, where the Captain had lost his reckoning, and was wholly bewildered in this sea; so said we to the look-out man, "Get thee to the mast-head and keep thine eyes open." He swarmed up the mast and looked out and cried aloud, "O Rais, I espy to starboard something dark, very like a fish floating on the face of the sea, and to larboard there is a loom in the midst of the main, now black and now bright." When the Captain heard the look-out's words he dashed his turband on the deck and plucked out his beard and beat his face saying, "Good news indeed! we be all dead men; not one of us can be saved." And he fell to weeping and all of us wept for his weeping and also for our lives; and I said, "O Captain, tell us what it is the look-out saw." "O my Prince," answered he, "know that we lost our course on the night of the storm, which was followed on the morrow by a two-days' calm during which we made no way; and we have gone astray eleven days reckoning from that night, with ne'er a wind to bring us back to our true course. To-morrow by the end of the day we shall come to a mountain of black stone, hight the Magnet Mountain; for thither the currents carry us willy-nilly. As soon as we are under its lea, the ship's sides will open and every nail in plank will fly out and cleave fast to the mountain; for that Almighty Allah hath gifted the loadstone with a mysterious virtue and a love for iron, by reason whereof all which is iron travelleth towards it; and on this mountain is much iron, how much none knoweth save the Most High, from the many vessels which have been lost there since the days of yore. The bright spot upon its summit is a dome of yellow laton from Andalusia, vaulted upon ten columns; and on its crown is a horseman who rideth a horse of brass and holdeth in hand a lance of laton; and there hangeth on his bosom a tablet of lead graven with names and talismans." And he presently added, "And, O King, none destroyeth folk save the rider on that steed, nor will the egromancy be dispelled till he fall from his horse." Then, O my lady, the Captain wept with exceeding weeping and we all made sure of death-doom and each and every one of us farewelled his friend and charged him with his last will and testament in case he might be saved. We slept not that night and in the morning we found ourselves much nearer the Loadstone Mountain, whither the waters drave us with a violent send. When the ships were close under its lea they opened and the nails flew out and all the iron in them sought the Magnet Mountain and clove to it like a network; so that by the end of the day we were all struggling in the waves round about the mountain. Some of us were saved, but more were drowned and even those who had escaped knew not one another, so stupefied were they by the beating of the billows and the raving of the winds. As for me, O my lady, Allah (be His name exalted!) preserved my life that I might suffer whatso He willed to me of hardship, misfortune and calamity; for I scrambled upon a plank from one of the ships, and the wind and waters threw it at the feet of the Mountain. There I found a practicable path leading by steps carven out of the rock to the summit, and I called on the name of Allah Almighty – And Shahrazad perceived the dawn of day and ceased to say her permitted say.

Now when it was the Fifteenth Night,

She continued, It hath reached me, O auspicious King, that the third Kalandar said to the lady (the rest of the party sitting fast bound and the slaves standing with swords drawn over their heads): And after calling on the name of Almighty Allah and passionately beseeching Him, I breasted the ascent, clinging to the steps and notches hewn in the stone, and mounted little by little. And the Lord stilled the wind and aided me in the ascent, so that I succeeded in reaching the summit. There I found no resting-place save the dome, which I entered, joying with exceeding joy at my escape; and made the Wuzu-ablution and prayed a two-bow prayer a thanksgiving to God for my preservation. Then I fell asleep under the dome, and heard in my dream a mysterious Voice saying, "O son of Khazib! when thou wakest from thy sleep dig under thy feet and thou shalt find a bow of brass and three leaden arrows, inscribed with talismans and characts. Take the bow and shoot the arrows at the horseman on the dome-top and free mankind from this sore calamity. When thou hast shot him he shall fall into the sea, and the horse will also drop at thy feet: then bury it in the place of the bow. This done, the main will swell and rise till it is level with the mountain-head, and there will appear on it a skiff carrying a man of laton (other than he thou shalt have shot) holding in his hand a pair of paddles. He will come to thee and do thou embark with him but beware of saying Bismillah or of otherwise naming Allah Almighty. He will row thee for a space of ten days, till he bring thee to certain Islands called the Islands of Safety, and thence thou shalt easily reach a port and find those who will convey thee to thy native land; and all this shall be fulfilled to thee so thou call not on the name of Allah." Then I started up from my sleep in joy and gladness and, hastening to do the bidding of the mysterious Voice, found the bow and arrows and shot at the horseman and tumbled him into the main, whilst the horse dropped at my feet; so I took it and buried it. Presently the sea surged up and rose till it reached the top of the mountain; nor had I long to wait ere I saw a skiff in the offing coming towards me. I gave thanks to Allah; and, when the skiff came up to me, I saw therein a man of brass with a tablet of lead on his breast inscribed with talismans and characts; and I embarked without uttering a word. The boatman rowed on with me through the first day and the second and the third, in all ten whole days, till I caught sight of the Islands of Safety; whereat I joyed with exceeding joy and for stress of gladness exclaimed, "Allah! Allah! In the name of Allah! There is no god but the God and Allah is Almighty." Thereupon the skiff forthwith upset and cast me upon the sea; then it righted and sank deep into the depths. Now I am a fair swimmer, so I swam the whole day till nightfall, when my forearms and shoulders were numbed with fatigue and I felt like to die; so I testified to my Faith, expecting naught but death. The sea was still surging under the violence of the winds, and presently there came a billow like a hillock; and, bearing me up high in air, threw me with a long cast on dry land, that His will might be fulfilled. I crawled up the beach and doffing my raiment wrung it out to dry and spread it in the sunshine: then I lay me down and slept the whole night. As soon as it was day, I donned my clothes and rose to look whither I should walk. Presently I came to a thicket of low trees; and, making a cast round it, found that the spot whereon I stood was an islet, a mere holm, girt on all sides by the ocean; whereupon I said to myself, "Whatso freeth me from one great calamity casteth me into a greater!" But while I was pondering my case and longing for death behold, I saw afar off a ship making for the island; so I clomb a tree and hid myself among the branches. Presently the ship anchored and landed ten slaves, blackamoors, bearing iron hoes and baskets, who walked on till they reached the middle of the island. Here they dug deep into the ground, until they uncovered a plate of metal which they lifted, thereby opening a trap-door. After this they returned to the ship and thence brought bread and flour, honey and fruits, clarified butter, leather bottles containing liquors and many household stuffs; also furniture, table-service and mirrors; rugs, carpets and in fact all needed to furnish a dwelling; and they kept going to and fro, and descending by the trap-door, till they had transported into the dwelling all that was in the ship. After this the slaves again went on board and brought back with them garments as rich as may be, and in the midst of them came an old old man, of whom very little was left, for Time had dealt hardly and harshly with him, and all that remained of him was a bone wrapped in a rag of blue stuff, through which the winds whistled west and east. As saith the poet of him:

> *Time gars me tremble Ah, how sore the baulk!*
> *While Time in pride of strength doth ever stalk:*
> *Time was I walked nor ever felt I tired,*
> *Now am I tired albe I never walk!*

And the Shaykh held by the hand a youth cast in beauty's mould, all elegance and perfect grace; so fair that his comeliness deserved to be proverbial; for he was as a green bough or the tender young of the roe, ravishing every heart with his loveliness and subduing every soul with his coquetry and amorous ways. It was of him the poet spake when he said:

> *Beauty they brought with him to make compare;*
> *But Beauty hung her head in shame and care:*
> *Quoth they, "O Beauty, hast thou seen his like?"*
> *And Beauty cried, "His like? not anywhere!"*

They stinted not their going, O my lady, till all went down by the trap-door and did not reappear for an hour, or rather more; at the end of which time the slaves and the old man came up without the youth and, replacing the iron plate and carefully closing the door-slab, as it was before, they returned to the ship and made sail and were lost to my sight. When they turned away to depart, I came down from the tree and, going to the place I had seen them fill up, scraped off and removed the earth; and in patience possessed my soul till I had cleared the whole of it away. Then appeared the trap-door which was of wood, in shape and size like a millstone; and when I lifted it up it disclosed a winding staircase of stone. At this I marvelled and, descending the steps till I reached the last, found a fair hall, spread with various kinds of carpets and silk stuffs, wherein was a youth sitting upon a raised couch and leaning back on a round cushion with a fan in his hand and nosegays and posies of sweet scented herbs and flowers before him; but he was alone and not a soul near him in the great vault. When he saw me he turned pale; but I saluted him courteously and said, "Set thy mind at ease and calm thy fears; no harm shall come near thee; I am a man like thyself and the son of a King to boot; whom the decrees of Destiny have sent to bear thee company and cheer thee in thy loneliness. But now tell me, what is thy story and what causeth thee to dwell thus in solitude under the ground?" When he was assured that I was of his kind and no Jinni, he rejoiced and his fine colour returned; and, making me draw near to him he said, "O my brother, my story is a strange story and 'tis this. My father is a merchant-jeweller possessed of great wealth, who hath white and black slaves travelling and trading on his account in ships and on camels, and trafficking with the most distant cities; but he was not blessed with a child, not even one. Now on a certain night he dreamed a dream that he should be favoured with a son, who would be short lived; so the morning dawned on my father bringing him woe and weeping. On the following night my mother conceived and my father noted down the date of her becoming pregnant. Her time being fulfilled she bare me; whereat my father rejoiced and made banquets and called together the neighbours and fed the Fakirs and the poor, for that he had been blessed with issue near the end of his days. Then he assembled the astrologers and astronomers who knew the places of the planets, and the wizards and wise ones of the time, and men learned in horoscopes and nativities; and they drew out my birth scheme and said to my father: Thy son shall live to fifteen years, but in his fifteenth there is a sinister aspect; an he safely tide it over he shall attain a great age. And the cause that threateneth him with death is this. In the Sea of Peril standeth the Mountain Magnet hight; on whose summit is a horseman of yellow laton seated on a horse also of brass and bearing on his breast a tablet of lead. Fifty days after this rider shall fall from his steed thy son will die and his slayer will be he who shoots down the horseman, a Prince named Ajib son of King Khazib. My father grieved with exceeding grief to hear these words; but reared me in tenderest fashion and educated me excellently well till my fifteenth year was told. Ten days ago news came to him that the horseman had fallen into the sea and he who shot him down was named Ajib son of King Khazib. My father thereupon wept bitter tears at the need of parting with me and became like one possessed of a Jinni. However, being in mortal fear for me, he built me this place under the earth; and, stocking it with all required for the few days still remaining, he brought me hither in a ship and left me here. Ten are already past and, when the forty shall have gone by without danger to me, he will come and take me away; for he hath done all this only in fear of Prince Ajib. Such, then, is my story and the cause of my loneliness." When I heard his history I marvelled and said in my mind, "I am the Prince Ajib who hath done all this; but as Allah is with me I will surely not slay him!" So said I to him, O my lord, far from thee be this hurt and harm and then, please Allah, thou shalt not suffer cark nor care nor aught disquietude, for I will tarry with thee and serve thee as a servant, and then wend my ways; and, after having borne thee company during the forty days, I will go with thee to thy home where thou shalt give me an escort of some of thy Mamelukes with whom I may journey back to my own city; and the Almighty shall requite thee for me. He was glad to hear these words, when I rose and lighted a large wax-candle and trimmed the lamps and the three lanterns; and I set on meat and drink and sweetmeats. We ate and drank and sat talking over various matters till the greater part of the night was gone; when he lay down to rest and I covered him up and went to sleep myself. Next morning I arose and warmed a little water, then lifted him gently so as to awake him and brought him the warm water wherewith he washed his face and said to me, "Heaven requite thee for me with every blessing, O youth! By Allah, if I get quit of this danger and am saved from him whose name is Ajib bin Khazib, I will make my father reward thee and send thee home healthy and wealthy; and, if I die, then my blessing be upon thee." I answered, "May the day never dawn on which evil shall betide thee; and may Allah make my last day before thy last day!" Then I set before him somewhat of food and we ate; and I got ready perfumes for fumigating the hall, wherewith he was pleased. Moreover I made him a Mankalah-cloth; and we played and ate sweetmeats and we played again and took our pleasure till nightfall, when I rose and lighted the lamps, and set before him somewhat to eat, and sat telling him stories till the hours of darkness were far spent. Then he lay down to rest and I covered him up and rested also. And thus I continued to do, O my lady for days and nights, and affection for him took root in my heart and my sorrow was eased, and I said to myself, The astrologers lied when they predicted that he should be slain by Ajib bin Khazib: by Allah, I will not slay him. I ceased not ministering to him and conversing and carousing with him and telling him all manner tales for thirty-nine days. On the fortieth night the youth rejoiced and said, "O my brother, Alhamdolillah! – praise be to Allah – who hath preserved me from death and this is by thy blessing and the blessing of thy coming to me; and I pray God that He restore thee to thy native land. But now, O my brother, I would thou warm me some water for the Ghusl-ablution and do thou kindly bathe me and change my clothes." I replied, "With love and gladness;" and I heated water in plenty and carrying it in to him washed his body all over, the washing of health, with meal of lupins and rubbed him well and changed his clothes and spread him a high bed whereon he lay down to rest, being drowsy after bathing. Then said he, "O my brother, cut me up a water-melon, and sweeten it with a little sugar-candy." So I went to the store-room and bringing out a fine water-melon I found there, set it on a platter and laid it before him saying, "O my master hast thou not a knife?" "Here it is," answered he, "over my head upon the high shelf." So I got up in haste and taking the knife drew it from its sheath; but my foot slipped in stepping down and I fell heavily upon the youth holding in my hand the knife which hastened to fulfil what had been written on the Day that decided the destinies of man, and buried itself, as if planted, in the youth's heart. He died on the instant. When I saw that he was slain and knew that I had slain him, maugre myself, I cried out with an exceeding loud and bitter cry and beat my face and rent my raiment and said, "Verily we be Allah's and unto Him we be returning, O Moslems! O folk fain of Allah! there remained for this youth but one day of the forty dangerous days which the astrologers and the learned had foretold for him; and the predestined death of this beautiful one was to be at my hand. Would Heaven I had not tried to cut the water-melon. What dire misfortune is this I must bear lief or loath? What a disaster! What an affliction! O Allah mine, I implore thy pardon and declare to Thee my innocence of his death. But what God willeth let that come to pass." – And Shahrazad perceived the dawn of day and ceased to say her permitted say.

Now when it was the Sixteenth Night,

She said, it hath reached me, O auspicious King, that Ajib thus continued his tale to the lady: When I was certified that I had slain him, I arose and ascending the stairs replaced the trap-door and covered it with earth as before. Then I looked out seawards and saw the ship cleaving the waters and making for the island, wherefore I was afeard and said, "The moment they come and see the youth done to death, they will know 'twas I who slew him and will slay me without respite." So I climbed up into a high tree and concealed myself among its leaves; and hardly had I done so when the ship anchored and the slaves landed with the ancient man, the youth's father, and made direct for the place and when they removed the earth they were surprised to see it soft. Then they raised the trap-door and went down and found the youth lying at full length, clothed in fair new garments with a face beaming after the bath, and the knife deep in his heart. At the sight they shrieked and wept and beat their faces, loudly cursing the murderer; whilst a swoon came over the Shaykh so that the slaves deemed him dead, unable to survive his son. At last they wrapped the slain youth in his clothes and carried him up and laid him on the ground covering him with a shroud of silk. Whilst they were making for the ship the old man revived; and, gazing on his son who was stretched out, fell on the ground and strewed dust over his head and smote his face and plucked out his beard; and his weeping redoubled as he thought of his murdered son and he swooned away once more. After awhile a slave went and fetched a strip of silk whereupon they lay the old man and sat down at his head. All this took place and I was on the tree above them watching everything that came to pass; and my heart became hoary before my head waxed grey, for the hard lot which was mine, and for the distress and anguish I had undergone, and I fell to reciting:

> *"How many a joy by Allah's will hath fled*
> *With flight escaping sight of wisest head!*
> *How many a sadness shall begin the day,*
> *Yet grow right gladsome ere the day is sped!*
> *How many a weal trips on the heels of ill,*
> *Causing the mourner's heart with joy to thrill!"*

But the old man, O my lady, ceased not from his swoon till near sunset, when he came to himself and, looking upon his dead son, he recalled what had happened, and how what he had dreaded had come to pass; and he beat his face and head and recited these couplets:

> *"Racked is my heart by parting fro' my friends*
> *And two rills ever fro' my eyelids flow:*
> *With them went forth my hopes, Ah, well away!*
> *What shift remaineth me to say or do?*
> *Would I had never looked upon their sight,*
> *What shift, fair sirs, when paths e'er straiter grow?*
> *What charm shall calm my pangs when this wise burn*
> *Longings of love which in my vitals glow?*
> *Would I had trod with them the road of Death!*
> *Ne'er had befel us twain this parting-blow:*
> *Allah: I pray the Ruthful show me ruth*
> *And mix our lives nor part them evermo'e!*
> *How blest were we as 'neath one roof we dwelt*
> *Conjoined in joys nor recking aught of woe;*
> *Till Fortune shot us with the severance shaft;*
> *Ah who shall patient bear such parting throe?*
> *And dart of Death struck down amid the tribe*
> *The age's pearl that Morn saw brightest show:*

I cried the while his case took speech and said:
Would Heaven, my son, Death mote his doom foreslow!
Which be the readiest road wi' thee to meet
My Son! for whom I would my soul bestow?
If sun I call him no! the sun doth set;
If moon I call him, wane the moons; Ah no!
O sad mischance o' thee, O doom of days,
Thy place none other love shall ever know:
Thy sire distracted sees thee, but despairs
By wit or wisdom Fate to overthrow:
Some evil eye this day hath cast its spell
And foul befal him as it foul befel!"

Then he sobbed a single sob and his soul fled his flesh. The slaves shrieked aloud "Alas, our lord!" and showered dust on their heads and redoubled their weeping and wailing. Presently they carried their dead master to the ship side by side with his dead son and, having transported all the stuff from the dwelling to the vessel, set sail and disappeared from mine eyes. I descended from the tree and, raising the trap-door, went down into the underground dwelling where everything reminded me of the youth; and I looked upon the poor remains of him and began repeating these verses:

Their tracks I see, and pine with pain and pang
And on deserted hearths I weep and yearn:
And Him I pray who doomèd them depart
Some day vouchsafe the boon of safe return.

Then, O my lady, I went up again by the trap-door, and every day I used to wander round about the island and every night I returned to the underground hall. Thus I lived for a month, till at last, looking at the western side of the island, I observed that every day the tide ebbed, leaving shallow water for which the flow did not compensate; and by the end of the month the sea showed dry land in that direction. At this I rejoiced making certain of my safety; so I arose and fording what little was left of the water got me to the main land, where I fell in with great heaps of loose sand in which even a camel's hoof would sink up to the knee. However I emboldened my soul and wading through the sand behold, a fire shone from afar burning with a blazing light. So I made for it hoping haply to find succour and broke out into these verses:

"Belike my Fortune may her bridle turn
And Time bring weal although he's jealous hight;
Forward my hopes, and further all my needs,
And passèd ills with present weals requite."

And when I drew near the fire aforesaid lo! it was a palace with gates of copper burnished red which, when the rising sun shone thereon, gleamed and glistened from afar showing what had seemed to me a fire. I rejoiced in the sight, and sat down over against the gate, but I was hardly settled in my seat before there met me ten young men clothed in sumptuous gear and all were blind of the left eye which appeared as plucked out. They were accompanied by a Shaykh, an old, old man, and much I marvelled at their appearance, and their all being blind of the same eye. When they saw me, they saluted me with the Salam and asked me of my case and my history; whereupon I related to them all what had befallen me, and what full measure of misfortune was mine. Marvelling at my tale they took me to the mansion, where I saw ranged round the hall ten couches each with its blue bedding and coverlet of blue stuff and amiddlemost stood a smaller couch furnished like them with blue and nothing else. As we entered each of the youths took his seat on his own couch and the old man seated himself upon the smaller one in the middle saying to me, "O youth, sit thee down on the floor and ask not of our case nor of the loss of our eyes." Presently he rose up and set before each young man some meat in a charger and drink in a large mazer, treating me in like manner; and after that they sat questioning me concerning my adventures and what had betided me: and I kept telling them my tale till the night was far spent. Then said the young men, "O our Shaykh, wilt not thou set before us our ordinary? The time is come." He replied, "With love and gladness," and rose and entering a closet disappeared, but presently returned bearing on his head ten trays each covered with a strip of blue stuff. He set a tray before each, youth and, lighting ten wax candles, he stuck one upon each tray, and drew off the covers and lo! under them was naught but ashes and powdered charcoal and kettle soot. Then all the young men tucked up their sleeves to the elbows and fell a-weeping and wailing and they blackened their faces and smeared their clothes and buffetted their brows and beat their breasts, continually exclaiming, "We were sitting at our ease but our frowardness brought us unease!" They ceased not to do thus till dawn drew nigh, when the old man rose and heated water for them; and they washed their faces, and donned other and clean clothes. Now when I saw this, O my lady, for very wonderment my senses left me and my wits went wild and heart and head were full of thought, till I forgot what had betided me and I could not keep silence feeling I fain must speak out and question them of these strangenesses; so I said to them, "How come ye to do this after we have been so open-hearted and frolicksome? Thanks be to Allah ye be all sound and sane, yet actions such as these befit none but mad men or those possessed of an evil spirit. I conjure you by all that is dearest to you, why stint ye to tell me your history, and the cause of your losing your eyes and your blackening your faces with ashes and soot?" Hereupon they turned to me and said, "O young man, hearken not to thy youthtide's suggestions and question us no questions." Then they slept and I with them and when they awoke the old man brought us somewhat of food; and, after we had eaten and the plates and goblets had been removed, they sat conversing till nightfall when the old man rose and lit the wax candles and lamps and set meat and drink before us. After we had eaten and drunken we sat conversing and carousing in companionage till the noon of night, when they said to the old man, "Bring us our ordinary, for the hour of sleep is at hand!" So he rose and brought them the trays of soot and ashes; and they did as they had done on the preceding night, nor more, nor less. I abode with them after this fashion for the space of a month during which time they used to blacken their faces with ashes every night, and to wash and change their raiment when the morn was young; and I but marvelled the more and my scruples and curiosity increased to such a point that I had to forego even food and drink. At last, I lost command of myself, for my heart was aflame with fire unquenchable and lowe unconcealable and I said, "O young men, will ye not relieve my trouble and acquaint me with the reason of thus blackening your faces and the meaning of your words: We were sitting at our ease but our frowardness brought us unease?" Quoth they "'Twere better to keep these things secret." Still I was bewildered by their doings to the point of abstaining from eating and drinking and, at last wholly losing patience, quoth I to them, "There is no help for it: ye must acquaint me with what is the reason of these doings." They replied, "We kept our secret only for thy good: to gratify thee will bring down evil upon thee and thou wilt become a monocular even as we are." I repeated, "There is no help for it and, if ye will not, let me leave you and return to mine own people and be at rest from seeing these things, for the proverb saith:

Better ye 'bide and I take my leave:
For what eye sees not heart shall never grieve.

Thereupon they said to me, "Remember, O youth, that should ill befal thee we will not again harbour thee nor suffer thee to abide amongst us;" and bringing a ram they slaughtered it and skinned it. Lastly they gave me a knife saying, "Take this skin and stretch thyself upon it and we will sew it around thee; presently there shall come to thee a certain bird, hight Rukh, that will catch thee up in his pounces and tower high in air and then set thee down on a mountain. When thou feelest he is no longer flying, rip open the pelt with this blade and come out of it; the bird will be scared and will fly away and leave thee free. After this fare for half a day, and the march will place thee at a palace wondrous fair to behold, towering high in air and builded of Khalanj, lign-aloes and sandal-wood, plated with red gold, and studded with all manner emeralds and costly gems fit for seal-rings. Enter it and thou shalt win to thy wish for we have all entered that palace; and such is the cause of our losing our eyes and of our blackening our faces. Were we now to tell thee our stories it would take too long a time; for each and every of us lost his left eye by an adventure of his own." I rejoiced at their words and they did with me as they said; and the bird Rukh bore me off and set me down on the mountain. Then I came out of the skin and walked on till I reached the palace. The door stood open as I entered and found myself in a spacious and goodly hall, wide exceedingly, even as a horse-course; and around it were an hundred chambers with doors of sandal and aloes woods plated with red gold and furnished with silver rings by way of knockers. At the head or upper end of the hall I saw forty damsels, sumptuously dressed and ornamented and one and all bright as moons; none could ever tire of gazing upon them and all so lovely that the most ascetic devotee on seeing them would become their slave and obey their will. When they saw me the whole bevy came up to me and said "Welcome and well come and good cheer to thee, O our lord! This whole month have we been expecting thee. Praised be Allah who hath sent us one who is worthy of us, even as we are worthy of him!" Then they made me sit down upon a high divan and said to me, "This day thou art our lord and master, and we are thy servants and thy handmaids, so order us as thou wilt." And I marvelled at their case. Presently one of them arose and set meat before me and I ate and they ate with me; whilst others warmed water and washed my hands and feet and changed my clothes, and others made ready sherbets and gave us to drink; and all gathered around me being full of joy and gladness at my coming. Then they sat down and conversed with me till nightfall, when five of them arose and laid the trays and spread them with flowers and fragrant herbs and fruits, fresh and dried, and confections in profusion. At last they brought out a fine wine-service with rich old wine; and we sat down to drink and some sang songs and others played the lute and psaltery and recorders and other instruments, and the bowl went merrily round. Hereupon such gladness possessed me that I forgot the sorrows of the world one and all and said, "This is indeed life; O sad that 'tis fleeting!" I enjoyed their company till the time came for rest; and our heads were all warm with wine, when they said, "O our lord, choose from amongst us her who shall be thy bed-fellow this night and not lie with thee again till forty days be past." So I chose a girl fair of face and perfect in shape, with eyes Kohl-edged by nature's hand; hair long and jet black with slightly parted teeth and joining brows: 'twas as if she were some limber graceful branchlet or the slender stalk of sweet basil to amaze and to bewilder man's fancy; even as the poet said of such an one:

> To even her with greeny bough were vain
> Fool he who finds her beauties in the roe:
> When hath the roe those lively lovely limbs
> Or honey dews those lips alone bestow?
> Those eyne, soul-piercing eyne, which slay with love,
> Which bind the victim by their shafts laid low?
> My heart to second childhood they beguiled
> No wonder: love-sick man again is child!

And I repeated to her the maker's words who said:

> None other charms but thine shall greet mine eyes,
> Nor other image can my heart surprize:
> Thy love, my lady, captives all my thoughts
> And on that love I'll die and I'll arise.

So I lay with her that night; none fairer I ever knew; and, when it was morning, the damsels carried me to the Hammam-bath and bathed me and robed me in fairest apparel. Then they served up food, and we ate and drank and the cup went round till nightfall when I chose from among them one fair of form and face, soft-sided and a model of grace, such an one as the poet described when he said:

> On her fair bosom caskets twain I scanned,
> Sealed fast with musk-seals lovers to withstand;
> With arrowy glances stand on guard her eyes,
> Whose shafts would shoot who dares put forth a hand.

With her I spent a most goodly night; and, to be brief, O my mistress, I remained with them in all solace and delight of life, eating and drinking, conversing and carousing and every night lying with one or other of them. But at the head of the new year they came to me in tears and bade me farewell, weeping and crying out and clinging about me; whereat I wondered and said, "What may be the matter? verily you break my heart!" They exclaimed, "Would Heaven we had never known thee; for, though we have companied with many, yet never saw we a pleasanter than thou or a more courteous." And they wept again. "But tell me more clearly," asked I, "what causeth this weeping which maketh my gall-bladder like to burst;" and they answered, "O our lord and master, it is severance which maketh us weep; and thou, and thou only, art the cause of our tears. If thou hearken to us we need never be parted and if thou hearken not we part for ever; but our hearts tell us that thou wilt not listen to our words and this is the cause of our tears and cries." "Tell me how the case standeth?" "Know, O our lord, that we are the daughters of Kings who have met here and have lived together for years; and once in every year we are perforce absent for forty days and afterwards we return and abide here for the rest of the twelvemonth eating and drinking and taking our pleasure and enjoying delights: we are about to depart according to our custom; and we fear lest after we be gone thou contraire our charge and disobey our injunctions. Here now we commit to thee the keys of the palace which containeth forty chambers and thou mayest open of these thirty and nine, but beware (and we conjure thee by Allah and by the lives of us!) lest thou open the fortieth door, for therein is that which shall separate us for ever." Quoth I, "Assuredly I will not open it, if it contain the cause of severance from you." Then one among them came up to me and falling on my neck wept and recited these verses:

> "If Time unite us after absent-while,
> The world harsh frowning on our lot shall smile;
> And if thy semblance deign adorn mine eyes,
> I'll pardon Time past wrongs and by-gone guile."

And I recited the following:

> "When drew she near to bid adieu with heart unstrung,
> While care and longing on that day her bosom wrung;
> Wet pearls she wept and mine like red carnelians rolled
> And, joined in sad rivière, around her neck they hung."

When I saw her weeping I said, "By Allah I will never open that fortieth door, never and no wise!" and I bade her farewell. Thereupon all departed flying away like birds; signalling with their hands farewells as they went and leaving me alone in the palace. When evening drew near I opened the door of the first chamber and entering it found myself in a place like one of the pleasaunces of Paradise. It was a garden with trees of freshest green and ripe fruits of yellow sheen; and its birds were singing clear and keen and rills ran wimpling through the fair terrene. The sight and sounds brought solace to my sprite; and I walked among the trees, and I smelt the breath of the flowers on the breeze; and heard the birdies sing their melodies hymning the One, the Almighty in sweetest litanies; and I looked upon the apple whose hue is parcel red and parcel yellow; as said the poet:

> Apple whose hue combines in union mellow
> My fair's red cheek, her hapless lover's yellow.

Then I looked upon the quince, and inhaled its fragrance which putteth to shame musk and ambergris, even as the poet hath said:

Quince every taste conjoins; in her are found
Gifts which for queen of fruits the Quince have crowned;
Her taste is wine, her scent the waft of musk;
Pure gold her hue, her shape the Moon's fair round.

Then I looked upon the pear whose taste surpasseth sherbet and sugar; and the apricot whose beauty striketh the eye with admiration, as if she were a polished ruby. Then I went out of the place and locked the door as it was before. When it was the morrow I opened the second door; and entering found myself in a spacious plain set with tall date-palms and watered by a running stream whose banks were shrubbed with bushes of rose and jasmine, while privet and eglantine, oxe-eye, violet and lily, narcissus, origane and the winter gilliflower carpeted the borders; and the breath of the breeze swept over these sweet-smelling growths diffusing their delicious odours right and left, perfuming the world and filling my soul with delight. After taking my pleasure there awhile I went from it and, having closed the door as it was before, opened the third door wherein I saw a high open hall pargetted with particoloured marbles and *pietra dura* of price and other precious stones, and hung with cages of sandal-wood and eagle-wood; full of birds which made sweet music, such as the "Thousand-voiced," and the cushat, the merle, the turtle-dove and the Nubian ring-dove. My heart was filled with pleasure thereby; my grief was dispelled and I slept in that aviary till dawn. Then I unlocked the door of the fourth chamber and therein found a grand saloon with forty smaller chambers giving upon it. All their doors stood open: so I entered and found them full of pearls and jacinths and beryls and emeralds and corals and carbuncles, and all manner precious gems and jewels, such as tongue of man may not describe. My thought was stunned at the sight and I said to myself, "These be things methinks united which could not be found save in the treasuries of a King of Kings, nor could the monarchs of the world have collected the like of these!" And my heart dilated and my sorrows ceased, "For," quoth I, "now verily am I the monarch of the age, since by Allah's grace this enormous wealth is mine; and I have forty damsels under my hand nor is there any to claim them save myself." Then I gave not over opening place after place until nine and thirty days were passed and in that time I had entered every chamber except that one whose door the Princesses had charged me not to open. But my thoughts, O my mistress, ever ran on that forbidden fortieth and Satan urged me to open it for my own undoing; nor had I patience to forbear, albeit there wanted of the trysting time but a single day. So I stood before the chamber aforesaid and, after a moment's hesitation, opened the door which was plated with red gold, and entered. I was met by a perfume whose like I had never before smelt; and so sharp and subtle was the odour that it made my senses drunken as with strong wine, and I fell to the ground in a fainting fit which lasted a full hour. When I came to myself I strengthened my heart and, entering, found myself in a chamber whose floor was bespread with saffron and blazing with light from branched candelabra of gold and lamps fed with costly oils, which diffused the scent of musk and ambergris. I saw there also two great censers each big as a mazer-bowl, flaming with lign-aloes, nadd-perfume, ambergris and honied scents; and the place was full of their fragrance. Presently, O my lady, I espied a noble steed, black as the murks of night when murkiest, standing, ready saddled and bridled (and his saddle was of red gold) before two mangers, one of clear crystal wherein was husked sesame, and the other also of crystal containing water of the rose scented with musk. When I saw this I marvelled and said to myself, "Doubtless in this animal must be some wondrous mystery;" and Satan cozened me, so I led him without the palace and mounted him; but he would not stir from his place. So I hammered his sides with my heels, but he moved not, and then I took the rein-whip and struck him withal. When he felt the blow, he neighed a neigh with a sound like deafening thunder and, opening a pair of wings flew up with me in the firmament of heaven far beyond the eyesight of man. After a full hour of flight he descended and alighted on a terrace roof and shaking me off his back lashed me on the face with his tail and gouged out my left eye causing it roll along my cheek. Then he flew away. I went down from the terrace and found myself again amongst the ten one-eyed youths sitting upon their ten couches with blue covers; and they cried out when they saw me, "No welcome to thee, nor aught of good cheer! We all lived of lives the happiest and we ate and drank of the best; upon brocades and cloths of gold we took our rest, and we slept with our heads on beauty's breast, but we could not await one day to gain the delights of a year!" Quoth I, "Behold I have become one like unto you and now I would have you bring me a tray full of blackness, wherewith to blacken my face, and receive me into your society." "No, by Allah," quoth they, "thou shalt not sojourn with us and now get thee hence!" So they drove me away. Finding them reject me thus I foresaw that matters would go hard with me, and I remembered the many miseries which Destiny had written upon my forehead; and I fared forth from among them heavy-hearted and tearful-eyed, repeating to myself these words, "I was sitting at mine ease but my frowardness brought me to unease." Then I shaved beard and mustachios and eyebrows, renouncing the world, and wandered in Kalandar-garb about Allah's earth; and the Almighty decreed safety for me till I arrived at Baghdad, which was on the evening of this very night. Here I met these two other Kalandars standing bewildered; so I saluted them saying, "I am a stranger!" and they answered, "And we likewise be strangers!" By the freak of Fortune we were like to like, three Kalandars and three monoculars all blind of the left eye. Such, O my lady, is the cause of the shearing of my beard and the manner of my losing an eye. Said the lady to him, "Rub thy head and wend thy ways;" but he answered, "By Allah, I will not go until I hear the stories of these others." Then the lady, turning towards the Caliph and Ja'afar and Masrur, said to them, "Do ye also give an account of yourselves, you men!" Whereupon Ja'afar stood forth and told her what he had told the portress as they were entering the house; and when she heard his story of their being merchants and Mosul-men who had outrun the watch, she said, "I grant you your lives each for each sake, and now away with you all." So they all went out and when they were in the street, quoth the Caliph to the Kalandars, "O company, whither go ye now, seeing that the morning hath not yet dawned?" Quoth they, "By Allah, O our lord, we know not where to go." "Come and pass the rest of the night with us," said the Caliph and, turning to Ja'afar, "Take them home with thee and to-morrow bring them to my presence that we may chronicle their adventures." Ja'afar did as the Caliph bade him and the Commander of the Faithful returned to his palace; but sleep gave no sign of visiting him that night and he lay awake pondering the mishaps of the three Kalandar-princes and impatient to know the history of the ladies and the two black bitches. No sooner had morning dawned than he went forth and sat upon the throne of his sovereignty; and, turning to Ja'afar, after all his Grandees and Officers of state were gathered together, he said,

"Bring me the three ladies and the two bitches and the three Kalandars." So Ja'afar fared forth and brought them all before him (and the ladies were veiled); then the Minister turned to them and said in the Caliph's name, "We pardon you your maltreatment of us and your want of courtesy, in consideration of the kindness which forewent it, and for that ye knew us not: now however I would have you to know that ye stand in presence of the fifth of the sons of Abbas, Harun al-Rashid, brother of Caliph Músá al-Hádi, son of Al-Mansúr; son of Mohammed the brother of Al-Saffáh bin Mohammed who was first of the royal house. Speak ye therefore before him the truth and the whole truth!" When the ladies heard Ja'afar's words touching the Commander of the Faithful, the eldest came forward and said, "O Prince of True Believers, my story is one which, were it graven with needle-gravers upon the eye-corners were a warner for whoso would be warned and an example for whoso can take profit from example." – And Shahrazad perceived the dawn of day and ceased to say her permitted say.

Now when it was the Seventeenth Night,

She said, it hath reached me, O auspicious King, that she stood forth before the Commander of the Faithful and began to tell

The Eldest Lady's Tale

VERILY A STRANGE tale is mine and 'tis this: Yon two black bitches are my eldest sisters by one mother and father; and these two others, she who beareth upon her the signs of stripes and the third our procuratrix are my sisters by another mother. When my father died, each took her share of the heritage and, after a while my mother also deceased, leaving me and my sisters-german three thousand dinars; so each daughter received her portion of a thousand dinars and I the same, albe the youngest. In due course of time my sisters married with the usual festivities and lived with their husbands, who bought merchandise with their wives' monies and set out on their travels together. Thus they threw me off. My brothers-in-law were absent with their wives five years, during which period they spent all the money they had and, becoming bankrupt, deserted my sisters in foreign parts amid stranger folk. After five years my eldest sister returned to me in beggar's gear with her clothes in rags and tatters and a dirty old mantilla; and truly she was in the foulest and sorriest plight. At first sight I did not know my own sister; but presently I recognised her and said "What state is this?" "O our sister," she replied, "Words cannot undo the done; and the reed of Destiny hath run through what Allah decreed." Then I sent her to the bath and dressed her in a suit of mine own, and boiled for her a bouillon and brought her some good wine and said to her, "O my sister, thou art the eldest, who still standest to us in the stead of father and mother; and, as for the inheritance which came to me as to you twain, Allah hath blessed it and prospered it to me with increase; and my circumstances are easy, for I have made much money by spinning and cleaning silk; and I and you will share my wealth alike." I entreated her with all kindliness and she abode with me a whole year, during which our thoughts and fancies were always full of our other sister. Shortly after she too came home in yet fouler and sorrier plight than that of my eldest sister; and I dealt by her still more honorably than I had done by the first, and each of them had a share of my substance. After a time they said to me, "O our sister, we desire to marry again, for indeed we have not patience to drag on our days without husbands and to lead the lives of widows bewitched;" and I replied, "O eyes of me! ye have hitherto seen scanty weal in wedlock, for now-a-days good men and true are become rareties and curiosities; nor do I deem your projects advisable, as ye have already made trial of matrimony and have failed." But they would not accept my advice and married without my consent: nevertheless I gave them outfit and dowries out of my money; and they fared forth with their mates. In a mighty little time their husbands played them false and, taking whatever they could lay hands upon, levanted and left them in the lurch. Thereupon they came to me ashamed and in abject case and made their excuses to me, saying, "Pardon our fault and be not wroth with us; for although thou art younger in years yet art thou older in wit; henceforth we will never make mention of marriage; so take us back as thy handmaidens that we may eat our mouthful." Quoth I, "Welcome to you, O my sisters, there is naught dearer to me than you." And I took them in and redoubled my kindness to them. We ceased not to live after this loving fashion for a full year, when I resolved to sell my wares abroad and first to fit me a conveyance for Bassorah; so I equipped a large ship, and loaded her with merchandise and valuable goods for traffic, and with provant and all needful for a voyage, and said to my sisters, "Will ye abide at home whilst I travel, or would ye prefer to accompany me on the voyage?" "We will travel with thee," answered they, "for we cannot bear to be parted from thee." So I divided my monies into two parts, one to accompany me and the other to be left in charge of a trusty person, for, as I said to myself, "Haply some accident may happen to the ship and yet we remain alive; in which case we shall find on our return what may stand us in good stead." I took my two sisters and we went a-voyaging some days and nights; but the master was careless enough to miss his course, and the ship went astray with us and entered a sea other than the sea we sought. For a time we knew naught of this; and the wind blew fair for us ten days, after which the look-out man went aloft to see about him and cried, "Good news!" Then he came down rejoicing and said, "I have seen what seemeth to be a city as 'twere a pigeon." Hereat we rejoiced and, ere an hour of the day had passed, the buildings showed plain in the offing and we asked the Captain, "What is the name of yonder city?" and he answered, "By Allah I wot not, for I never saw it before and never sailed these seas in my life: but, since our troubles have ended in safety, remains for you only to land there with your merchandise and, if you find selling profitable, sell and make your market of what is there; and if not, we will rest here two days and provision ourselves and fare away." So we entered the port and the Captain went up town and was absent awhile, after which he returned to us and said, "Arise; go up into the city and marvel at the works of Allah with His creatures and pray to be preserved from His righteous wrath!" So we landed and going up into the city, saw at the gate men hending staves in hand; but when we drew near them, behold, they had been translated by the anger of Allah and had become stones. Then we entered the city and found all who therein woned into black stones enstoned: not an inhabited house appeared to the espier, nor was there a blower of fire. We were awe struck at the sight and threaded the market streets where we found the goods and gold and silver left lying in their places; and we were glad and said, "Doubtless there is some mystery in all this." Then we dispersed about the thoroughfares and each busied himself with collecting the wealth and money and rich stuffs, taking scanty heed of friend or comrade. As for myself I went up to the

castle which was strongly fortified; and, entering the King's palace by its gate of red
gold, found all the vaiselle of gold and silver, and the King himself seated in the midst
of his Chamberlains and Nabobs and Emirs and Wazirs; all clad in raiment which
confounded man's art. I drew nearer and saw him sitting on a throne incrusted and
inlaid with pearls and gems; and his robes were of gold-cloth adorned with jewels of
every kind, each one flashing like a star. Around him stood fifty Mamelukes, white
slaves, clothed in silks of divers sorts holding their drawn swords in their hands; but
when I drew near to them lo! all were black stones. My understanding was confounded
at the sight, but I walked on and entered the great hall of the Harím, whose walls I
found hung with tapestries of gold-striped silk and spread with silken carpets
embroidered with golden flowers. Here I saw the Queen lying at full length arrayed
in robes purfled with fresh young pearls; on her head was a diadem set with many
sorts of gems each fit for a ring and around her neck hung collars and necklaces. All
her raiment and her ornaments were in natural state but she had been turned into a
black stone by Allah's wrath. Presently I espied an open door for which I made straight
and found leading to it a flight of seven steps. So I walked up and came upon a place
pargetted with marble and spread and hung with gold-worked carpets and tapestry,
amiddlemost of which stood a throne of juniper-wood inlaid with pearls and precious
stones and set with bosses of emeralds. In the further wall was an alcove whose
curtains, bestrung with pearls, were let down and I saw a light issuing therefrom; so
I drew near and perceived that the light came from a precious stone as big as an
ostrich-egg, set at the upper end of the alcove upon a little chryselephantine couch
of ivory and gold; and this jewel, blazing like the sun, cast its rays wide and side. The
couch also was spread with all manner of silken stuffs amazing the gazer with their
richness and beauty. I marvelled much at all this, especially when seeing in that place
candles ready lighted; and I said in my mind, "Needs must some one have lighted
these candles." Then I went forth and came to the kitchen and thence to the buttery
and the King's treasure-chambers; and continued to explore the palace and to pace
from place to place; I forgot myself in my awe and marvel at these matters and I was
drowned in thought till the night came on. Then I would have gone forth, but knowing
not the gate I lost my way, so I returned to the alcove whither the lighted candles
directed me and sat down upon the couch; and wrapping myself in a coverlet, after I
had repeated somewhat from the Koran, I would have slept but could not, for
restlessness possessed me. When night was at its noon I heard a voice chanting the
Koran in sweetest accents; but the tone thereof was weak; so I rose, glad to hear the
silence broken, and followed the sound until I reached a closet whose door stood ajar.
Then peeping through a chink I considered the place and lo! it was an oratory wherein
was a prayer-niche with two wax candles burning and lamps hanging from the ceiling.
In it too was spread a prayer-carpet whereupon sat a youth fair to see; and before him
on its stand was a copy of the Koran, from which he was reading. I marvelled to see
him alone alive amongst the people of the city and entering saluted him; whereupon
he raised his eyes and returned my salam. Quoth I, "Now by the Truth of what thou
readest in Allah's Holy Book, I conjure thee to answer my question." He looked upon
me with a smile and said, "O handmaid of Allah, first tell me the cause of thy coming
hither, and I in turn will tell what hath befallen both me and the people of this city,
and what was the reason of my escaping their doom." So I told him my story whereat
he wondered; and I questioned him of the people of the city, when he replied, "Have

patience with me for awhile, O my sister!" and, reverently closing the Holy Book, he laid it up in a satin bag. Then he seated me by his side; and I looked at him and behold, he was as the moon at its full, fair of face and rare of form, soft-sided and slight, of well-proportioned height, and cheek smoothly bright and diffusing light; in brief a sweet, a sugar-stick, even as saith the poet of the like of him in these couplets:

> That night th' astrologer a scheme of planets drew,
> And lo! a graceful shape of youth appeared in view:
> Saturn had stained his locks with Saturninest jet,
> And spots of nut-brown musk on rosy side-face blew:
> Mars tinctured either cheek with tint of martial red;
> Sagittal shots from eyelids Sagittarius threw:
> Dowered him Mercury with bright mercurial wit;
> Bore off the Bear what all man's evil glances grew:
> Amazed stood Astrophil to sight the marvel-birth
> When louted low the Moon at full to buss the Earth.

And of a truth Allah the Most High had robed him in the raiment of perfect grace and had purfled and fringed it with a cheek all beauty and loveliness, even as the poet saith of such an one:

> By his eyelids shedding perfume and his fine slim waist I swear,
> By the shooting of his shafts barbed with sorcery passing rare;
> By the softness of his sides, and glances' lingering light;
> And brow of dazzling day-tide ray and night within his hair;
> By his eyebrows which deny to who look upon them rest,
> Now bidding now forbidding, ever dealing joy and care;
> By the rose that decks his cheek, and the myrtle of its moss;
> By jacinths bedded in his lips and pearl his smile lays bare;
> By his graceful bending neck and the curving of his breast;
> Whose polished surface beareth those granados, lovely pair;
> By his heavy hips that quiver as he passeth in his pride;
> Or he resteth with that waist which is slim beyond compare;
> By the satin of his skin, by that fine unsullied sprite;
> By the beauty that containeth all things bright and debonnair;
> By that ever-open hand; by the candour of his tongue;
> By noble blood and high degree whereof he's hope and heir;
> Musk from him borrows muskiness she loveth to exhale;
> And all the airs of ambergris through him perfume the air;
> The sun, methinks, the broad bright sun, before my love would pale;
> And sans his splendour would appear a paring of his nail.

I glanced at him with one glance of eyes which caused me a thousand sighs; and my heart was at once taken captive-wise; so I asked him, "O my lord and my love, tell me that whereof I questioned thee;" and he answered, "Hearing is obeying! Know, O handmaid of Allah, that this city was the capital of my father who is the King thou sawest on the throne transfigured by Allah's wrath to a black stone, and the Queen thou foundest in the alcove is my mother. They and all the people of the city were Magians who fire adored in lieu of the Omnipotent Lord and were wont to swear by lowe and heat and shade and light, and the spheres revolving day and night. My father had ne'er a son till he was blest with me near the last of his days; and he reared me till I grew up and prosperity anticipated me in all things. Now it so fortuned there was with us an old woman well stricken in years, a Moslemah who, inwardly believing in Allah and His Apostle, conformed outwardly with the religion of my people; and my father placed thorough confidence in her for that he knew her to be trustworthy and virtuous; and he treated her with ever-increasing kindness believing her to be of his own belief. So when I was well-nigh grown up my father committed me to her charge saying: Take him and educate him and teach him the rules of our faith; let him have the best instructions and cease not thy fostering care of him. So she took me and taught me the tenets of Al-Islam with the divine ordinances of the Wuzu-ablution and the five daily prayers and she made me learn the Koran by rote, often repeating: Serve none save Allah Almighty! When I had mastered this much of knowledge she said to me: O my son, keep this matter concealed from thy sire and reveal naught to him lest he slay thee. So I hid it from him and I abode on this wise for a term of days when the old woman died, and the people of the city redoubled in their impiety and arrogance and the error of their ways. One day, while they were as wont, behold, they heard a loud and terrible sound and a crier crying out with a voice like roaring thunder so every ear could hear, far and near: O folk of this city leave ye your fire-worshipping and adore Allah the All-compassionate King! At this, fear and terror fell upon the citizens and they crowded to my father (he being King of the city) and asked him: What is this awesome voice we have heard, for it hath confounded us with the excess of its terror?; and he answered: Let not a voice fright you nor shake your steadfast sprite nor turn you back from the faith which is right. Their hearts inclined to his words and they ceased not to worship the fire and they persisted in rebellion for a full year from the time they heard the first voice; and on the anniversary came a second cry and a third at the head of the third year, each year once. Still they persisted in their malpractices till one day at break of dawn, judgment and the wrath of Heaven descended upon them with all suddenness, and by the visitation of Allah all were metamorphosed into black stones, they and their beasts and their cattle; and none was saved save myself who at the time was engaged in my devotions. From that day to this I am in the case thou seest, constant in prayer and fasting and reading and reciting the Koran; but I am indeed grown weary by reason of my loneliness, having none to bear me company." Then said I to him (for in very sooth he had won my heart and was the lord of my life and soul), "O youth, wilt thou fare with me to Baghdad city and visit the Olema and men learned in the law and doctors of divinity and get thee increase of wisdom and understanding and theology? And know that she who standeth in thy presence will be thy handmaid, albeit she be head of her family and mistress over men and eunuchs and servants and slaves. Indeed my life was no life before it fell in with thy youth. I have here a ship laden with merchandise; and in very truth Destiny drove me to this city that I might come to the knowledge of these matters, for it was fated that we should meet. And I ceased not to persuade him and speak him fair and use every art till he consented." – And Shahrazad perceived the dawn of day and ceased to say her permitted say.

Now when it was the Eighteenth Night,

She continued, It hath reached me, O auspicious King, that the lady ceased not persuading with soft speech the youth to depart with her till he consented and said "Yes." She slept that night lying at his feet and hardly knowing where she was for excess of joy. As soon as the next morning dawned (she pursued, addressing the Caliph), I arose and we entered the treasuries and took thence whatever was light in weight and great in worth; then we went down side by side from the castle to the city, where we were met by the Captain and my sisters and slaves who had been seeking for me. When they saw me they rejoiced and asked what had stayed me, and I told them all I had seen and related to them the story of the young Prince and the transformation wherewith the citizens had been justly visited. Hereat all marvelled, but when my two sisters (these two bitches, O Commander of the Faithful!) saw me by the side of my young lover they jaloused me on his account and were wroth and plotted mischief against me. We awaited a fair wind and went on board rejoicing and ready to fly for joy by reason of the goods we had gotten, but my own greatest joyance was in the youth; and we waited awhile till the wind blew fair for us and then we set sail and fared forth. Now as we sat talking, my sisters asked me, "And what wilt thou do with this handsome young man?"; and I answered, "I purpose to make him my husband!" Then I turned to him and said, "O my lord, I have that to propose to thee wherein thou must not cross me; and this it is that, when we reach Baghdad, my native city, I offer thee my life as thy handmaiden in holy matrimony, and thou shalt be to me baron and I will be femme to thee." He answered, "I hear and I obey!; thou art my lady and my mistress and whatso thou doest I will not gainsay." Then I turned to my sisters and said, "This is my gain; I content me with this youth and those who have gotten aught of my property let them keep it as their gain with my good will." "Thou sayest and doest well," answered the twain, but they imagined mischief against me. We ceased not spooning before a fair wind till we had exchanged the sea of peril for the seas of safety and, in a few days, we made Bassorah-city, whose buildings loomed clear before us as evening fell. But after we had retired to rest and were sound asleep, my two sisters arose and took me up, bed and all, and threw me into the sea: they did the same with the young Prince who, as he could not swim, sank and was drowned and Allah enrolled him in the noble army of Martyrs. As for me would Heaven I had been drowned with him, but Allah deemed that I should be of the saved; so when I awoke and found myself in the sea and saw the ship making off like a flash of lightning, He threw in my way a piece of timber which I bestrided, and the waves tossed me to and fro till they cast me upon an island coast, a high land and an uninhabited. I landed and walked about the island the rest of the night and, when morning dawned, I saw a rough track barely fit for child of Adam to tread, leading to what proved a shallow ford connecting island and mainland. As soon as the sun had risen I spread my garments to dry in its rays; and ate of the fruits of the island and drank of its waters; then I set out along the foot-track and ceased not walking till I reached the mainland. Now when there remained between me and the city but a two hours' journey behold, a great serpent, the bigness of a date-palm, came fleeing towards me in all haste, gliding along now to the right then to the left till she was close upon me, whilst her tongue lolled ground-wards a span long and swept the dust as she went. She was pursued by a Dragon who was not longer than two lances, and of slender build about the bulk of a spear and, although her terror lent her speed, and she kept wriggling from side to side, he overtook her and seized her by the tail, whereat her tears streamed down and her tongue was thrust out in her agony. I took pity on her and, picking up a stone and calling upon Allah for aid, threw it at the Dragon's head with such force that he died then and there; and the serpent opening a pair of wings flew into the lift and disappeared from before my eyes. I sat down marvelling over that adventure, but I was weary and, drowsiness overcoming me, I slept where I was for a while. When I awoke I found a jet-black damsel sitting at my feet shampooing them; and by her side stood two black bitches (my sisters, O Commander of the Faithful!). I was ashamed before her and, sitting up, asked her, "O my sister, who and what art thou?"; and she answered, "How soon hast thou forgotten me! I am she for whom thou wroughtest a good deed and sowedest the seed of gratitude and slewest her foe; for I am the serpent whom by Allah's aidance thou didst just now deliver from the Dragon. I am a Jinniyah and he was a Jinn who hated me, and none saved my life from him save thou. As soon as thou freedest me from him I flew on the wind to the ship whence thy sisters threw thee, and removed all that was therein to thy house. Then I ordered my attendant Marids to sink the ship and I transformed thy two sisters into these black bitches; for I know all that hath passed between them and thee; but as for the youth, of a truth he is drowned. So saying she flew up with me and the bitches, and presently set us down on the terrace-roof of my house, wherein I found ready stored the whole of what property was in my ship, nor was aught of it missing. Now (continued the serpent that was), I swear by all engraven on the seal-ring of Solomon (with whom be peace!) unless thou deal to each of these bitches three hundred stripes every day I will come and imprison thee for ever under the earth." I answered, "Hearkening and obedience!"; and away she flew. But before going she again charged me saying, "I again swear by Him who made the two seas flow (and this be my second oath) if thou gainsay me I will come and transform thee like thy sisters." Since then I have never failed, O Commander of the Faithful, to beat them with that number of blows till their blood flows with my tears, I pitying them the while, and well they wot that their being scourged is no fault of mine and they accept my excuses. And this is my tale and my history! The Caliph marvelled at her adventures and then signed to Ja'afar who said to the second lady, the Portress, "And thou, how camest thou by the welts and wheals upon thy body?" So she began the

Tale of the Portress

KNOW, O COMMANDER of the Faithful, that I had a father who, after fulfilling his time, deceased and left me great store of wealth. I remained single for a short time and presently married one of the richest of his day. I abode with him a year when he also died, and my share of his property amounted to eighty thousand dinars in gold according to the holy law of inheritance. Thus I became passing rich and my reputation spread far and wide, for I had made me ten changes of raiment, each worth a thousand dinars. One day as I was sitting at home, behold, there came in to me an old woman with lantern jaws and cheeks sucked in, and eyes rucked up, and eyebrows scant and scald, and head bare and bald; and teeth broken by time and mauled, and back bending and neck-nape nodding, and face blotched, and rheum running, and hair like a snake black-and-white-speckled, in complexion a very fright, even as saith the poet of the like of her:

> *Ill-omened hag! unshriven be her sins*
> *Nor mercy visit her on dying bed:*
> *Thousand head-strongest he-mules would her guiles,*
> *Despite their bolting, lead with spider thread.*

And as saith another:

> *A hag to whom th' unlawful lawfullest*
> *And witchcraft wisdom in her sight are grown:*
> *A mischief-making brat, a demon-maid,*
> *A whorish woman and a pimping crone.*

When the old woman entered she salamed to me and kissing the ground before me, said, "I have at home an orphan daughter and this night are her wedding and her displaying. We be poor folks and strangers in this city knowing none inhabitant and we are broken-hearted. So do thou earn for thyself a recompense and a reward in Heaven by being present at her displaying and, when the ladies of this city shall hear that thou art to make act of presence, they also will present themselves; so shalt thou comfort her affliction, for she is sore bruised in spirit and she hath none to look to save Allah the Most High." Then she wept and kissed my feet reciting these couplets:

> *Thy presence bringeth us a grace*
> *We own before thy winsome face:*
> *And wert thou absent ne'er an one*
> *Could stand in stead or take thy place.*

So pity gat hold on me and compassion and I said, "Hearing is consenting and, please Allah, I will do somewhat more for her; nor shall she be shown to her bridegroom save in my raiment and ornaments and jewelry." At this the old woman rejoiced and bowed her head to my feet and kissed them, saying, "Allah requite thee weal, and comfort thy heart even as thou has comforted mine! But, O my lady, do not trouble thyself to do me this service at this hour; be thou ready by supper-time, when I will come and fetch thee." So saying she kissed my hand and went her ways. I set about stringing my pearls and donning my brocades and making my toilette, little recking what Fortune had in womb for me, when suddenly the old woman stood before me, simpering and smiling till she showed every tooth stump, and quoth she, "O my mistress, the city madams have arrived and when I apprized them that thou promisedst to be present, they were glad and they are now awaiting thee and looking eagerly for thy coming and for the honour of meeting thee." So I threw on my mantilla and, making the old crone walk before me and my handmaidens behind me, I fared till we came to a street well watered and swept neat, where the winnowing breeze blew cool and sweet. Here we were stopped by a gate arched over with a dome of marble stone firmly seated on solidest foundation, and leading to a Palace whose walls from earth rose tall and proud, and whose pinnacle was crowned by the clouds, and over the doorway were writ these couplets:

I am the wone where Mirth shall ever smile;
The home of Joyance through my lasting while:
And 'mid my court a fountain jets and flows,
Nor tears nor troubles shall that fount defile:
The marge with royal Nu'uman's bloom is dight,
Myrtle, Narcissus-flower and Chamomile.

Arrived at the gate, before which hung a black curtain, the old woman knocked and it was opened to us; when we entered and found a vestibule spread with carpets and hung around with lamps all alight and wax candles in candelabra adorned with pendants of precious gems and noble ores. We passed on through this passage till we entered a saloon, whose like for grandeur and beauty is not to be found in this world. It was hung and carpeted with silken stuffs, and was illuminated with branches, sconces and tapers ranged in double row, an avenue abutting on the upper or noble end of the saloon, where stood a couch of juniper-wood encrusted with pearls and gems and surmounted by a baldaquin with mosquito-curtains of satin looped up with margarites. And hardly had we taken note of this when there came forth from the baldaquin a young lady and I looked, O Commander of the Faithful, upon a face and form more perfect than the moon when fullest, with a favour brighter than the dawn gleaming with saffron-hued light, even as the poet sang when he said:

Thou pacest the palace a marvel-sight,
A bride for a Kisrá's or Kaisar's night!
Wantons the rose on thy roseate cheek,
O cheek as the blood of the dragon bright!
Slim-waisted, languorous, sleepy-eyed,
With charms which promise all love-delight:
And the tire which attires thy tiara'd brow
Is a night of woe on a morn's glad light.

The fair young girl came down from the estrade and said to me, "Welcome and well come and good cheer to my sister, the dearly-beloved, the illustrious, and a thousand greetings!" Then she recited these couplets:

An but the house could know who cometh 'twould rejoice,
And kiss the very dust whereon thy foot was placed;
And with the tongue of circumstance the walls would say,
"Welcome and hail to one with generous gifts engraced!"

Then sat she down and said to me, "O my sister, I have a brother who hath had sight of thee at sundry wedding-feasts and festive seasons: he is a youth handsomer than I, and he hath fallen desperately in love with thee, for that bounteous Destiny hath garnered in thee all beauty and perfection; and he hath given silver to this old woman that she might visit thee; and she hath contrived on this wise to foregather us twain. He hath heard that thou art one of the nobles of thy tribe nor is he aught less in his; and, being desirous to ally his lot with thy lot, he hath practised this device to bring me in company with thee; for he is fain to marry thee after the ordinance of Allah and his Apostle; and in what is lawful and right there is no shame." When I heard these words and saw myself fairly entrapped in the house, I said, "Hearing is consenting." She was delighted at this and clapped her hands; whereupon a door opened and out of it came a young man blooming in the prime of life, exquisitely dressed, a model of beauty and loveliness and symmetry and perfect grace, with gentle winning manners and eyebrows like a bended bow and shaft on cord, and eyes which bewitched all hearts with sorcery lawful in the sight of the Lord; even as saith some rhymer describing the like of him:

> His face as the face of the young moon shines
> And Fortune stamps him with pearls for signs.

And Allah favour him who said:

> Blest be his beauty; blest the Lord's decree
> Who cast and shaped a thing so bright of blee:
> All gifts of beauty he conjoins in one;
> Lost in his love is all humanity;
> For Beauty's self inscribed on his brow
> "I testify there be no Good but he!"

When I looked at him my heart inclined to him and I loved him; and he sat by my side and talked with me a while, when the young lady again clapped her hands and behold, a side-door opened and out of it came the Kazi with his four assessors as witnesses; and they saluted us and, sitting down, drew up and wrote out the marriage-contract between me and the youth and retired. Then he turned to me and said, "Be our night blessed," presently adding, "O my lady, I have a condition to lay on thee." Quoth I, "O my lord, what is that?" Whereupon he arose and fetching a copy of the Holy Book presented it to me saying, "Swear hereon thou wilt never look at any other than myself nor incline thy body or thy heart to him." I swore readily enough to this and he joyed with exceeding joy and embraced me round the neck while love for him possessed my whole heart. Then they set the table before us and we ate and drank till we were satisfied; but I was dying for the coming of the night. And when night did come he led me to the bride-chamber and slept with me on the bed and continued to kiss and embrace me till the morning – such a night I had never seen in my dreams. I lived with him a life of happiness and delight for a full month, at the end of which I asked his leave to go on foot to the bazar and buy me certain especial stuffs and he gave me permission. So I donned my mantilla and, taking with me the old woman and a slave-girl, I went to the khan of the silk-mercers, where I seated myself in the shop-front of a young merchant whom the old woman recommended, saying to me, "This youth's father died when he was a boy and left him great store of wealth: he hath by him a mighty fine stock of goods and thou wilt find what thou seekest with him, for none in the bazar hath better stuffs than he." Then she said to him, "Show this lady the most costly stuffs thou hast by thee;" and he replied, "Hearkening and obedience!" Then she whispered me, "Say a civil word to him!"; but I replied, "I am pledged to address no man save my lord." And as she began to sound his praise I said sharply to her, "We want nought of thy sweet speeches; our wish is to buy of him whatsoever we need, and return home." So he brought me all I sought and I offered him his money, but he refused to take it saying, "Let it be a gift offered to my guest this day!" Then quoth I to the old woman, "If he will not take the money, give him back his stuff." "By Allah," cried he, "not a thing will I take from thee: I sell it not for gold or for silver, but I give it all as a gift for a single kiss; a kiss more precious to me than everything the shop containeth." Asked the old woman, "What will the kiss profit thee?"; and, turning to me, whispered, "O my daughter, thou hearest what this young fellow saith? What harm will it do thee if he get a kiss from thee and thou gettest what thou seekest at that price?" Replied I, "I take refuge with Allah from such action! Knowest thou not that I am bound by an oath?" But she answered, "Now whist! just let him kiss thee and neither speak to him nor lean over him, so shalt thou keep thine oath and thy silver, and no harm whatever shall befal thee." And she ceased not to persuade me and importune me and make light of the matter till evil entered into my mind and I put my head in the poke and, declaring I would ne'er consent, consented. So I veiled my eyes and held up the edge of my mantilla between me and the people passing and he put his mouth to my cheek under the veil. But while kissing me he bit me so hard a bite that it tore the flesh from my cheek, and blood flowed fast and faintness came over me. The old woman caught me in her arms and, when I came to myself, I found the shop shut up and her sorrowing over me and saying "Thank Allah for averting which might have been worse!" Then she said to me, "Come, take heart and let us go home before the matter become public and thou be dishonoured. And when thou art safe inside the house feign sickness and lie down and cover thyself up; and I will bring thee powders and plasters to cure this bite withal, and thy wound will be healed at the latest in three days." So after a while I arose and I was in extreme distress and terror came full upon me; but I went on little by little till I reached the house when I pleaded illness and lay me down. When it was night my husband came in to me and said, "What hath befallen thee, O my darling, in this excursion of thine?"; and I replied, "I am not well: my head acheth badly." Then he lighted a candle and drew near me and looked hard at me and asked, "What is that wound I see on thy cheek and in the tenderest part too?" And I answered, "When I went out to-day with thy leave to buy stuffs, a camel laden with firewood jostled me and one of the pieces tore my veil and wounded my cheek as thou seest; for indeed the ways of this city are strait." "To-morrow," cried he, "I will go complain to the Governor, so shall he gibbet every fuel-seller in Baghdad." "Allah upon thee," said I, "burden not thy soul with such sin against any man. The fact is I was riding on an ass and it stumbled, throwing me to the ground; and my cheek lighted upon a stick or a bit of glass and got this wound." "Then," said he, "to-morrow I will go up to Ja'afar the Barmaki and tell him the story, so shall he kill every donkey-boy in Baghdad." "Wouldst thou destroy all these men because of my wound," said I, "when this which befel me was by decree of Allah and His destiny?" But he answered, "There is no help for it;" and, springing to his feet, plied me with words and pressed me till I was perplexed and frightened; and I stuttered and stammered and my speech waxed thick and I said, "This is a mere accident by decree of Allah." Then, O Commander of the Faithful, he guessed my case and said, "Thou hast been false to thine oath." He at once cried out with a loud cry, whereupon a door opened and in came seven black slaves whom he commanded to drag me from my bed and throw me down in the middle of the room. Furthermore, he ordered one of them to pinion my elbows and squat upon my head; and a second to sit upon my knees and secure my feet; and drawing his sword he gave it to a third and said, "Strike her, O Sa'ad, and cut her in twain and let each one take half and cast it into the Tigris that the fish may eat her; for such is the retribution due to those who violate their vows and are unfaithful to their love." And he redoubled in wrath and recited these couplets:

> An there be one who shares with me her love,
> I'd strangle Love tho' life by Love were slain;
> Saying, O Soul, Death were the nobler choice,
> For ill is Love when shared 'twixt partners twain.

Then he repeated to the slave, "Smite her, O Sa'ad!" And when the slave who was sitting upon me made sure of the command he bent down to me and said, "O my mistress, repeat the profession of Faith and bethink thee if there be any thing thou wouldst have done; for verily this is the last hour of thy life." "O good slave," said I, "wait but a little while and get off my head that I may charge thee with my last injunctions." Then I raised my head and saw the state I was in, how I had fallen from high degree into lowest disgrace; and into death after life (and such life!) and how I had brought my punishment on myself by my own sin; whereupon the tears streamed from mine eyes and I wept with exceeding weeping. But he looked on me with eyes of wrath, and began repeating:

> Tell her who turneth from our love to work it injury sore,
> And taketh her a fine new love the old love tossing o'er:
> We cry enough o' thee ere thou enough of us shalt cry!
> What past between us doth suffice and haply something more.

When I heard this, O Commander of the Faithful, I wept and looked at him and began repeating these couplets:

> To severance you doom my love and all unmoved remain;
> My tear-sore lids you sleepless make and sleep while I complain:
> You make firm friendship reign between mine eyes and insomny;
> Yet can my heart forget you not, nor tears can I restrain:
> You made me swear with many an oath my troth to hold for aye;
> But when you reigned my bosom's lord you wrought me traitor-bane:
> I loved you like a silly child who wots not what is Love;
> Then spare the learner, let her not be by the master slain!
> By Allah's name I pray you write, when I am dead and gone,
> Upon my tomb, This died of Love whose senses Love had ta'en:
> Then haply one shall pass that way who fire of Love hath felt,
> And treading on a lover's heart with ruth and woe shall melt.

When I ended my verses tears came again; but the poetry and the weeping only added fury to his fury, and he recited:

> 'Twas not satiety bade me leave the dearling of my soul,

But that she sinned a mortal sin which clipt me in its clip:
She sought to let another share the love between us twain,
But my True Faith of Unity refuseth partnership.

When he ceased reciting I wept again and prayed his pardon and humbled myself before him and spoke him softly, saying to myself, "I will work on him with words; so haply he will refrain from slaying me, even though he take all I have." So I complained of my sufferings and began to repeat these couplets:

Now, by thy life and wert thou just my life thou hadst not ta'en,
But who can break the severance-law which parteth lovers twain!
Thou loadest me with heavy weight of longing love, when I
Can hardly bear my chemisette for weakness and for pain:
I marvel not to see my life and soul in ruin lain
I marvel much to see my frame such severance-pangs sustain.

When I ended my verse I wept again; and he looked at me and reviled me in abusive language, repeating these couplets:

Thou wast all taken up with love of other man, not me;
'Twas thine to show me severance-face, 'twas only mine to see:
I'll leave thee for that first thou wast of me to take thy leave
And patient bear that parting blow thou borest so patiently:
E'en as thou soughtest other love, so other love I'll seek,
And make the crime of murdering love thine own atrocity.

When he had ended his verses he again cried out to the slave, "Cut her in half and free us from her, for we have no profit of her." So the slave drew near me, O Commander of the Faithful, and I ceased bandying verses and made sure of death and, despairing of life, committed my affairs to Almighty Allah, when behold, the old woman rushed in and threw herself at my husband's feet and kissed them and wept and said, "O my son, by the rights of my fosterage and by my long service to thee, I conjure thee pardon this young lady, for indeed she hath done nothing deserving such doom. Thou art a very young man and I fear lest her death be laid at thy door; for it is said: Whoso slayeth shall be slain. As for this wanton (since thou deemest her such) drive her out from thy doors, from thy love and from thy heart." And she ceased not to weep and importune him till he relented and said, "I pardon her, but needs must I set on her my mark which shall show upon her all her life." Then he bade the slaves drag me along the ground and lay me out at full length, after stripping me of all my clothes; and when the slaves had so sat upon me that I could not move, he fetched in a rod of quince-tree and came down with it upon my body, and continued beating me on the back and sides till I lost consciousness from excess of pain, and I despaired of life. Then he commanded the slaves to take me away as soon as it was dark, together with the old woman to show them the way and throw me upon the floor of the house wherein I dwelt before my marriage. They did their lord's bidding and cast me down in my old home and went their ways. I did not revive from my swoon till dawn appeared, when I applied myself to the dressing of my wounds with ointments and other medicaments; and I medicined myself, but my sides and ribs still showed signs of the rod as thou hast seen. I lay in weakly case and confined to my bed for four months before I was able to rise and health returned to me. At the end of that time I went to the house where all this had happened and found it a ruin; the street had been pulled down endlong and rubbish-heaps rose where the building erst was; nor could I learn how this had come about. Then I betook myself to this my sister on my father's side and found with her these two black bitches. I saluted her and told her what had betided me and the whole of my story and she said, "O my sister, who is safe from the despite of Time and secure? Thanks be to Allah who hath brought thee off safely;" and she began to say:

> Such is the World, so bear a patient heart
> When riches leave thee and when friends depart!

Then she told me her own story, and what had happened to her with her two sisters and how matters had ended; so we abode together and the subject of marriage was never on our tongues for all these years. After a while we were joined by our other sister, the procuratrix, who goeth out every morning and buyeth all we require for the day and night; and we continued in such condition till this last night. In the morning our sister went out, as usual, to make her market and then befel us what befel from bringing the Porter into the house and admitting these three Kalandar-men.

We entreated them kindly and honourably and a quarter of the night had not passed ere three grave and respectable merchants from Mosul joined us and told us their adventures. We sat talking with them but on one condition which they violated, whereupon we treated them as sorted with their breach of promise, and made them repeat the account they had given of themselves. They did our bidding and we forgave their offence; so they departed from us and this morning we were unexpectedly summoned to thy presence. And such is our story! The Caliph wondered at her words and bade the tale be recorded and chronicled and laid up in his muniment-chambers. – And Shahrazad perceived the dawn of day and ceased saying her permitted say.

Now when it was the Nineteenth Night,

She continued, It hath reached me, O auspicious King, that the Caliph commanded this story and those of the sister and the Kalandars to be recorded in the archives and be set in the royal muniment-chambers. Then he asked the eldest lady, the mistress of the house, "Knowest thou the whereabouts of the Ifritah who spelled thy sisters?"; and she answered, "O Commander of the Faithful, she gave me a ringlet of her hair saying: Whenas thou wouldest see me, burn a couple of these hairs and I will be with thee forthright, even though I were beyond Caucasus-mountain." Quoth the Caliph, "Bring me hither the hair." So she brought it and he threw the whole lock upon the fire. As soon as the odour of the burning hair dispread itself, the palace shook and trembled, and all present heard a rumbling and rolling of thunder and a noise as of wings and lo! the Jinniyah who had been a serpent stood in the Caliph's presence. Now she was a Moslemah, so she saluted him and said, "Peace be with thee O Vicar of Allah;" whereto he replied, "And with thee also be peace and the mercy of Allah and His blessing." Then she continued, "Know that this damsel sowed for me the seed of kindness, wherefor I cannot enough requite her, in that she delivered me from death and destroyed mine enemy. Now I had seen how her sisters dealt with her and felt myself bound to avenge her on them. At first I was minded to slay them, but I feared it would be grievous to her, so I transformed them to bitches; but if thou desire their release, O Commander of the Faithful, I will release them to pleasure thee and her for I am of the Moslems." Quoth the Caliph, "Release them and after we will look into the affair of the beaten lady and consider her case carefully; and if the truth of her story be evidenced I will exact retaliation from him who wronged her." Said the Ifritah, "O Commander of the Faithful, I will forthwith release them and will discover to thee the man who did that deed by this lady and wronged her and took her property, and he is the nearest of all men to thee!" So saying she took a cup of water and muttered a spell over it and uttered words there was no understanding; then she sprinkled some of the water over the faces of the two bitches, saying, "Return to your former human shape!" whereupon they were restored to their natural forms and fell to praising their Creator. Then said the Ifritah, "O Commander of the Faithful, of a truth he who scourged this lady with rods is thy son Al-Amin brother of Al-Maamun; for he had heard of her beauty and loveliness and he played a lover's stratagem with her and married her according to the law and committed the crime (such as it is) of scourging her. Yet indeed he is not to be blamed for beating her, for he laid a condition on her and swore her by a solemn oath not to do a certain thing; however, she was false to her vow and he was minded to put her to death, but he feared Almighty Allah and contented himself with scourging her, as thou hast seen, and with sending her back to her own place. Such is the story of the second lady and the Lord knoweth all." When the Caliph heard these words of the Ifritah, and knew who had beaten the damsel, he marvelled with mighty marvel and said, "Praise be to Allah, the Most High, the Almighty, who hath shown His exceeding mercy towards me, enabling me to deliver these two damsels from sorcery and torture, and vouchsafing to let me know the secret of this lady's history! And now by Allah, we will do a deed which shall be recorded of us after we are no more." Then he summoned his son Al-Amin and questioned him of the story of the second lady, the portress; and he told it in the face of truth; whereupon the Caliph bade call into presence the Kazis and their witnesses and the three Kalandars and the first lady with her sisters german who had been ensorcelled; and he married the three to the three Kalandars whom he knew to be princes and sons of Kings and he appointed them chamberlains about his person, assigning to them stipends and allowances and all that they required, and lodging them in his palace at Baghdad. He returned the beaten lady to his son, Al-Amin, renewing the marriage-contract between them and gave her great wealth and bade rebuild the house fairer than it was before. As for himself he took to wife the procuratrix and lay with her that night: and next day he set apart for her an apartment in his Serraglio, with handmaidens for her service and a fixed daily allowance. And the people marvelled at their Caliph's generosity and natural beneficence and princely wisdom; nor did he forget to send all these histories to be recorded in his annals. When Shahrazad ceased speaking Dunyazad exclaimed, "O my own sister, by Allah in very sooth this is a right pleasant tale and a delectable; never was heard the like of it, but prithee tell me now another story to while away what yet remaineth of the waking hours of this our night." She replied, "With love and gladness if the King give me leave;" and he said, "Tell thy tale and tell it quickly." So she began, in these words,

Tale of the Three Apples

Richard F. Burton

THEY RELATE, O King of the age and lord of the time and of these days, that the Caliph Harun al-Rashid summoned his Wazir Ja'afar one night and said to him, "I desire to go down into the city and question the common folk concerning the conduct of those charged with its governance; and those of whom they complain we will depose from office and those whom they commend we will promote." Quoth Ja'afar, "Hearkening and obedience!" So the Caliph went down with Ja'afar and Eunuch Masrur to the town and walked about the streets and markets and, as they were threading a narrow alley, they came upon a very old man with a fishing-net and crate to carry small fish on his head, and in his hand a staff; and, as he walked at a leisurely pace, he repeated these lines:

> *They say me: Thou shinest a light to mankind*
> *With thy lore as the night which the Moon doth uplight!*
> *I answer, "A truce to your jests and your gibes;*
> *Without luck what is learning? – a poor-devil wight!*
> *If they take me to pawn with my lore in my pouch,*
> *With my volumes to read and my ink-case to write,*
> *For one day's provision they never could pledge me;*
> *As likely on Doomsday to draw bill at sight:"*
> *How poorly, indeed, doth it fare wi' the poor,*
> *With his pauper existence and beggarly plight:*
> *In summer he faileth provision to find;*
> *In winter the fire-pot's his only delight:*
> *The street-dogs with bite and with bark to him rise,*
> *And each losel receives him with bark and with bite:*
> *If he lift up his voice and complain of his wrong,*
> *None pities or heeds him, however he's right;*
> *And when sorrows and evils like these he must brave*
> *His happiest homestead were down in the grave.*

When the Caliph heard his verses he said to Ja'afar, "See this poor man and note his verses, for surely they point to his necessities." Then he accosted him and asked, "O Shaykh, what be thine occupation?" and the poor man answered, "O my lord, I am a fisherman with a family to keep and I have been out between midday and this time; and not a thing hath Allah made my portion wherewithal to feed my family. I cannot even pawn myself to buy them a supper and I hate and disgust my life and I hanker after death." Quoth the Caliph, "Say me, wilt thou return with us to Tigris' bank and cast thy net on my luck, and whatsoever turneth up I will buy of thee for an hundred gold pieces?" The man rejoiced when he heard these words and said, "On my head be it! I will go back with you;" and, returning with them river-wards, made a cast and waited a while; then he hauled in the rope and dragged the net ashore and there appeared in it a chest padlocked and heavy. The Caliph examined it and lifted it finding it weighty; so he gave the fisherman two hundred dinars and sent him about his business; whilst Masrur, aided by the Caliph, carried the chest to the palace and set it down and lighted the candles. Ja'afar and Masrur then broke it open and found therein a basket of palm-leaves corded with red worsted. This they cut open and saw within it a piece of carpet which they lifted out, and under it was a woman's mantilla folded in four, which they pulled out; and at the bottom of the chest they came upon a young lady, fair as a silver ingot, slain and cut into nineteen pieces. When the Caliph looked upon her he cried, "Alas!" and tears ran down his cheeks and turning to Ja'afar he said, "O dog of Wazirs, shall folk be murdered in our reign and be cast into the river to be a burden and a responsibility for us on the Day of Doom? By Allah, we must avenge this woman on her murderer and he shall be made die the worst of deaths!" And presently he added, "Now, as surely as we are descended from the Sons of Abbas, if thou bring us not him who slew her, that we do her justice on him, I will hang thee at the gate of my palace, thee and forty of thy kith and kin by thy side." And the Caliph was wroth with exceeding rage. Quoth Ja'afar, "Grant me three days delay;" and quoth the Caliph, "We grant thee this." So Ja'afar went out from before him and returned to his own house, full of sorrow and saying to himself, "How shall I find him who murdered this damsel, that I may bring him before the Caliph? If I bring other than the murderer, it will be laid to my charge by the Lord: in very sooth I wot not what to do." He kept his house three days and on the fourth day the Caliph sent one of the Chamberlains for him and, as he came into the presence, asked him, "Where is the murderer of the damsel?" to which answered Ja'afar, "O Commander of the Faithful, am I inspector of murdered folk that I should ken who killed her?" The Caliph was furious at his answer and bade hang him before the palace-gate and commanded that a crier cry through the streets of Baghdad, "Whoso would see the hanging of Ja'afar, the Barmaki, Wazir of the Caliph, with forty of the Barmecides, his cousins and kinsmen, before the palace-gate, let him come and let him look!" The people flocked out from all the quarters of the city to witness the execution of Ja'afar and his kinsmen, not knowing the cause. Then they set up the gallows and made Ja'afar and the others stand underneath in readiness for execution, but whilst every eye was looking for the Caliph's signal, and the crowd wept for Ja'afar and his cousins of the Barmecides, lo and behold! a young man fair of face and neat of dress and of favour like the moon raining light, with eyes black and bright, and brow flower-white, and cheeks red as rose and young down where the beard grows, and a mole like a grain of ambergris, pushed his way through the people till he stood immediately before the Wazir and said to him, "Safety to thee from this strait, O Prince of the Emirs and Asylum of the poor! I am the man who slew the woman ye found in the chest, so hang me for her and do her justice on me!" When Ja'afar heard the youth's confession he rejoiced at his own deliverance, but grieved and sorrowed for the fair youth, and whilst they were yet talking behold, another man well stricken in years pressed forwards through the people and thrust his way amid the populace till he came to Ja'afar and the youth, whom he saluted saying, "Ho thou the Wazir and Prince sans-peer! believe not the words of this youth. Of a surety none murdered the damsel but I; take her wreak on me this moment; for, an thou do not thus, I will require it of thee before Almighty Allah." Then quoth the young man, "O Wazir, this is an old man in his dotage who wotteth not whatso he saith ever, and I am he who murdered her, so do thou avenge her on me!" Quoth the old man, "O my son, thou art young and desirest the joys of the world and I am old and weary and surfeited with the world: I will offer my life as a ransom for thee and for the Wazir and his cousins. No one murdered the damsel but I, so Allah upon thee, make haste to hang me, for no life is left in me now that hers is gone."

The Wazir marvelled much at all this strangeness and, taking the young man and the old man, carried them before the Caliph, where, after kissing the ground seven times between his hands, he said, "O Commander of the Faithful, I bring thee the murderer of the damsel!" "Where is he?"; asked the Caliph and Ja'afar answered, "This young man saith, I am the murderer, and this old man giving him the lie saith, I am the murderer, and behold, here are the twain standing before thee." The Caliph looked at the old man and the young man and asked, "Which of you killed the girl?" The young man replied, "No one slew her save I;" and the old man answered, "Indeed none killed her but myself." Then said the Caliph to Ja'afar, "Take the twain and hang them both;" but Ja'afar rejoined, "Since one of them was the murderer, to hang the other were mere injustice." "By Him who raised the firmament and dispread the earth like a carpet," cried the youth, "I am he who slew the damsel;" and he went on to describe the manner of her murder and the basket, the mantilla and the bit of carpet, in fact all that the Caliph had found upon her. So the Caliph was certified that the young man was the murderer; whereat he wondered and asked him, "What was the cause of thy wrongfully doing this damsel to die and what made thee confess the murder without the bastinado, and what brought thee here to yield up thy life, and what made thee say Do her wreak upon me?" The youth answered, "Know, O Commander of the Faithful, that this woman was my wife and the mother of my children; also my first cousin and the daughter of my paternal uncle, this old man who is my father's own brother. When I married her she was a maid and Allah blessed me with three male children by her; she loved me and served me and I saw no evil in her, for I also loved her with fondest love. Now on the first day of this month she fell ill with grievous sickness and I fetched in physicians to her; but recovery came to her little by little and, when I wished her to go to the Hammam-bath, she said: There is a something I long for before I go to the bath and I long for it with an exceeding longing. To hear is to comply, said I. And what is it? Quoth she, I have a queasy craving for an apple, to smell it and bite a bit of it. I replied: Hadst thou a thousand longings I would try to satisfy them! So I went on the instant into the city and sought for apples but could find none; yet, had they cost a gold piece each, would I have bought them. I was vexed at this and went home and said: O daughter of my uncle, by Allah I can find none! She was distressed, being yet very weakly, and her weakness increased greatly on her that night and I felt anxious and alarmed on her account. As soon as morning dawned I went out again and made the round of the gardens, one by one, but found no apples anywhere. At last there met me an old gardener, of whom I asked about them and he answered: O my son, this fruit is a rarity with us and is not now to be found save in the garden of the Commander of the Faithful at Bassorah, where the gardener keepeth it for the Caliph's eating. I returned to my house troubled by my ill-success; and my love for my wife and my affection moved me to undertake the journey. So I gat me ready and set out and travelled fifteen days and nights, going and coming, and brought her three apples which I bought from the gardener for three dinars. But when I went in to my wife and set them before her, she took no pleasure in them and let them lie by her side; for her weakness and fever had increased on her and her malady lasted without abating ten days, after which time she began to recover health. So I left my house and betaking me to my shop sat there buying and selling; and about midday behold, a great ugly black slave, long as a lance and broad as a bench, passed by my shop holding in hand one of the three apples wherewith he was playing. Quoth I: O my good slave, tell me whence thou tookest that apple, that I may get the like of it? He laughed and answered: I got it from my mistress, for I had been absent and on my return I found her lying ill with three apples by her side, and she said to me: My horned wittol of a husband made a journey for them to Bassorah and bought them for three dinars. So I ate and drank with her and took this one from her. When I heard such words from the slave, O Commander of the Faithful, the world grew black before my face, and I arose and locked up my shop and went home beside myself for excess of rage. I looked for the apples and finding only two of the three asked my wife: O my cousin, where is the third apple?; and raising her head languidly she answered: I wot not, O son of my uncle, where 'tis gone! This convinced me that the slave had spoken the truth, so I took a knife and coming behind her got upon her breast without a word said and cut her throat. Then I hewed off her head and her limbs in pieces and, wrapping her in her mantilla and a rag of carpet, hurriedly sewed up the whole which I set in a chest and, locking it tight, loaded it on my he-mule and threw it into the Tigris with my own hands. So Allah upon thee, O Commander of the Faithful, make haste to hang me, as I fear lest she appeal for vengeance on Resurrection Day. For, when I had thrown her into the river and none knew aught of it, as I went back home I found my eldest son crying and yet he knew naught of what I had done with his mother. I asked him: What hath made thee weep, my boy?; and he answered: I took one of the three apples which were by my mammy and went down into the lane to play with my brethren when behold, a big long black slave snatched it from my hand and said, Whence hadst thou this? Quoth I, My father travelled far for it, and brought it from Bassorah for my mother who was ill and two other apples for which he paid three ducats. He took no heed of my words and I asked for the apple a second and a third time, but he cuffed me and kicked me and went off with it. I was afraid lest my mother should swinge me on account of the apple, so for fear of her I went with my brother outside the city and stayed there till evening closed in upon us; and indeed I am in fear of her; and now by Allah, O my father, say nothing to her of this or it may add to her ailment!

When I heard what my child said I knew that the slave was he who had foully slandered my wife, the daughter of my uncle, and was certified that I had slain her wrongfully. So I wept with exceeding weeping and presently this old man, my paternal uncle and her father, came in; and I told him what had happened and he sat down by my side and wept and we ceased not weeping till midnight. We have kept up mourning for her these last five days and we lamented her in the deepest sorrow for that she was unjustly done to die. This came from the gratuitous lying of the slave, the blackamoor, and this was the manner of my killing her; so I conjure thee, by the honour of thine ancestors, make haste to kill me and do her justice upon me, as there is no living for me after her!" The Caliph marvelled at his words and said, "By Allah the young man is excusable: I will hang none but the accursed slave and I will do a deed which shall comfort the ill-at-ease and suffering, and which shall please the

All-glorious King." – And Shahrazad perceived the dawn of day and ceased saying her permitted say.

Now when it was the Twentieth Night,

She said, it hath reached me, O auspicious King, that the Caliph swore he would hang none but the slave, for the youth was excusable. Then he turned to Ja'afar and said to him, "Bring before me this accursed slave who was the sole cause of this calamity; and, if thou bring him not before me within three days, thou shalt be slain in his stead." So Ja'afar fared forth weeping and saying, "Two deaths have already beset me, nor shall the crock come off safe from every shock. In this matter craft and cunning are of no avail; but He who preserved my life the first time can preserve it a second time. By Allah, I will not leave my house during the three days of life which remain to me and let the Truth (whose perfection be praised!) do e'en as He will." So he kept his house three days, and on the fourth day he summoned the Kazis and legal witnesses and made his last will and testament, and took leave of his children weeping. Presently in came a messenger from the Caliph and said to him, "The Commander of the Faithful is in the most violent rage that can be, and he sendeth to seek thee and he sweareth that the day shall certainly not pass without thy being hanged unless the slave be forthcoming." When Ja'afar heard this he wept, and his children and slaves and all who were in the house wept with him. After he had bidden adieu to everybody except his youngest daughter, he proceeded to farewell her; for he loved this wee one, who was a beautiful child, more than all his other children; and he pressed her to his breast and kissed her and wept bitterly at parting from her; when he felt something round inside the bosom of her dress and asked her, "O my little maid, what is in thy bosom pocket?"; "O my father," she replied, "it is an apple with the name of our Lord the Caliph written upon it. Rayhán our slave brought it to me four days ago and would not let me have it till I gave him two dinars for it." When Ja'afar heard speak of the slave and the apple, he was glad and put his hand into his child's pocket and drew out the apple and knew it and rejoiced saying, "O ready Dispeller of trouble!" Then he bade them bring the slave and said to him, "Fie upon thee, Rayhan! whence haddest thou this apple?" "By Allah, O my master," he replied, "though a lie may get a man once off, yet may truth get him off, and well off, again and again. I did not steal this apple from thy palace nor from the gardens of the Commander of the Faithful. The fact is that five days ago, as I was walking along one of the alleys of this city, I saw some little ones at play and this apple in hand of one of them. So I snatched it from him and beat him and he cried and said, O youth this apple is my mother's and she is ill. She told my father how she longed for an apple, so he travelled to Bassorah and bought her three apples for three gold pieces, and I took one of them to play withal. He wept again, but I paid no heed to what he said and carried it off and brought it here, and my little lady bought it of me for two dinars of gold. And this is the whole story." When Ja'afar heard his words he marvelled that the murder of the damsel and all this misery should have been caused by his slave; he grieved for the relation of the slave to himself, while rejoicing over his own deliverance, and he repeated these lines:

If ill betide thee through thy slave,
Make him forthright thy sacrifice:
A many serviles thou shalt find,
But life comes once and never twice.

Then he took the slave's hand and, leading him to the Caliph, related the story from first to last and the Caliph marvelled with extreme astonishment, and laughed till he fell on his back and ordered that the story be recorded and be made public amongst the people. But Ja'afar said, "Marvel not, O Commander of the Faithful, at this adventure, for it is not more wondrous than the History of the Wazir Nur al-Din Ali of Egypt and his brother Shams al-Dín Mohammed." Quoth the Caliph, "Out with it; but what can be stranger than this story?" And Ja'afar answered, "O Commander of the Faithful, I will not tell it thee, save on condition that thou pardon my slave;" and the Caliph rejoined, "If it be indeed more wondrous than that of the three apples, I grant thee his blood, and if not I will surely slay thy slave." So Ja'afar began in these words the

Tale of Nur Al-Din Ali and His Son Badr Al-Din Hasan

Richard F. Burton

KNOW, O COMMANDER of the Faithful, that in times of yore the land of Egypt was ruled by a Sultan endowed with justice and generosity, one who loved the pious poor and companied with the Olema and learned men; and he had a Wazir, a wise and an experienced, well versed in affairs and in the art of government. This Minister, who was a very old man, had two sons, as they were two moons; never man saw the like of them for beauty and grace, the elder called Shams al-Din Mohammed and the younger Nur al-Din Ali; but the younger excelled the elder in seemliness and pleasing semblance, so that folk heard his fame in far countries and men flocked to Egypt for the purpose of seeing him. In course of time their father, the Wazir, died and was deeply regretted and mourned by the Sultan, who sent for his two sons and, investing them with dresses of honour, said to them, "Let not your hearts be troubled, for ye shall stand in your father's stead and be joint Ministers of Egypt." At this they rejoiced and kissed the ground before him and performed the ceremonial mourning for their father during a full month; after which time they entered upon the Wazirate, and the power passed into their hands as it had been in the hands of their father, each doing duty for a week at a time. They lived under the same roof and their word was one; and whenever the Sultan desired to travel they took it by turns to be in attendance on him. It fortuned one night that the Sultan purposed setting out on a journey next morning, and the elder, whose turn it was to accompany him, was sitting conversing with his brother and said to him, "O my brother, it is my wish that we both marry, I and thou, two sisters; and go in to our wives on one and the same night." "Do, O my brother, as thou desirest," the younger replied, "for right is thy recking and surely I will comply with thee in whatso thou sayest." So they agreed upon this and quoth Shams al-Din, "If Allah decree that we marry two damsels and go in to them on the same night, and they shall conceive on their bride-nights and bear children to us on the same day, and by Allah's will thy wife bear thee a son and my wife bear me a daughter, let us wed them either to other, for they will be cousins." Quoth Nur al-Din, "O my brother, Shams al-Din, what dower wilt thou require from my son for thy daughter?" Quoth Shams al-Din, "I will take three thousand dinars and three pleasure gardens and three farms; and it would not be seemly that the youth make contract for less than this." When Nur al-Din heard such demand he said, "What manner of dower is this thou wouldest impose upon my son? Wottest thou not that we are brothers and both by Allah's grace Wazirs and equal in office? It behoveth thee to offer thy daughter to my son without marriage settlement; or, if one need be, it should represent a mere nominal value by way of show to the world: for thou knowest that the masculine is worthier than the feminine, and my son is a male and our memory will be preserved by him, not by thy daughter." "But what," said Shams al-Din, "is she to have?"; and Nur al-Din continued, "Through her we shall not be remembered among the Emirs of the earth; but I see thou wouldest do with me according to the saying: An thou wouldst bluff off a buyer, ask him high price and higher; or as did a man who, they say, went to a friend and asked something of him being in necessity and was answered: Bismillah, in the name of Allah, I will do all what thou requirest but come to-morrow!" Whereupon the other replied in this verse:

> When he who is asked a favour saith "To-morrow,"
> The wise man wots 'tis vain to beg or borrow.

Quoth Shams al-Din, "Basta! I see thee fail in respect to me by making thy son of more account than my daughter; and 'tis plain that thine understanding is of the meanest and that thou lackest manners. Thou remindest me of thy partnership in the Wazirate, when I admitted thee to share with me only in pity for thee, and not wishing to mortify thee; and that thou mightest help me as a manner of assistant. But since thou talkest on this wise, by Allah, I will never marry my daughter to thy son; no, not for her weight in gold!" When Nur al-Din heard his brother's words he waxed wroth and said, "And I too, I will never, never marry my son to thy daughter; no, not to keep from my lips the cup of death." Shams al-Din replied, "I would not accept him as a husband for her, and he is not worth a paring of her nail. Were I not about to travel I would make an example of thee; however when I return thou shalt see, and I will show thee, how I can assert my dignity and vindicate my honour. But Allah doeth whatso He willeth." When Nur al-Din heard this speech from his brother, he was filled with fury and lost his wits for rage; but he hid what he felt and held his peace; and each of the brothers passed the night in a place far apart, wild with wrath against the other. As soon as morning dawned the Sultan fared forth in state and crossed over from Cairo to Jízah and made for the Pyramids, accompanied by the Wazir Shams al-Din, whose turn of duty it was, whilst his brother Nur al-Din, who passed the night in sore rage, rose with the light and prayed the dawn-prayer. Then he betook himself to his treasury and, taking a small pair of saddle-bags, filled them with gold; and he called to mind his brother's threats and the contempt wherewith he had treated him, and he repeated these couplets:

> Travel! and thou shalt find new friends for old ones left behind;
> Toil! for the sweets of human life by toil and moil are found:
> The stay-at-home no honour wins nor aught attains but want;
> So leave thy place of birth and wander all the world around!
> I've seen, and very oft I've seen, how standing water stinks,
> And only flowing sweetens it and trotting makes it sound:
> And were the moon for ever full and ne'er to wax or wane,
> Man would not strain his watchful eyes to see its gladsome round:
> Except the lion leave his lair he ne'er would fell his game;
> Except the arrow leave the bow ne'er had it reached its bound:
> Gold-dust is dust the while it lies untravelled in the mine,
> And aloes-wood mere fuel is upon its native ground:
> And gold shall win his highest worth when from his goal ungoal'd;
> And aloes sent to foreign parts grows costlier than gold.

When he ended his verse he bade one of his pages saddle him his Nubian mare-mule with her padded selle. Now she was a dapple-grey, with ears like reed-pens and legs like columns and a back high and strong as a dome built on pillars; her saddle was of gold-cloth and her stirrups of Indian steel, and her housing of Ispahan velvet; she had trappings which would serve the Chosroës, and she was like a bride adorned for her wedding night. Moreover he bade lay on her back a piece of silk for a seat, and a prayer-carpet under which were his saddle-bags. When this was done he said to his pages and slaves, "I purpose going forth a-pleasuring outside the city on the road to Kalyúb-town, and I shall lie three nights abroad; so let none of you follow me, for there is something straiteneth my breast." Then he mounted the mule in haste; and, taking with him some provaunt for the way, set out from Cairo and faced the open and uncultivated country lying around it. About noontide he entered Bilbays-city, where he dismounted and stayed awhile to rest himself and his mule and ate some of his victual. He bought at Bilbays all he wanted for himself and forage for his mule and then fared on the way of the waste. Towards nightfall he entered a town called Sa'adiyah where he alighted and took out somewhat of his viaticum and ate; then he spread his strip of silk on the sand and set the saddle-bags under his head and slept in the open air; for he was still overcome with anger. When morning dawned he mounted and rode onward till he reached the Holy City, Jerusalem, and thence he made Aleppo, where he dismounted at one of the caravanserais and abode three days to rest himself and the mule and to smell the air. Then, being determined to travel afar and Allah having written safety in his fate, he set out again, wending without wotting whither he was going; and, having fallen in with certain couriers, he stinted not travelling till he had reached Bassorah-city albeit he knew not what the place was. It was dark night when he alighted at the Khan, so he spread out his prayer-carpet and took down the saddle-bags from the back of the mule and gave her with her furniture in charge of the door-keeper that he might walk her about. The man took her and did as he was bid. Now it so happened that the Wazir of Bassorah, a man shot in years, was sitting at the lattice-window of his palace opposite the Khan and he saw the porter walking the mule up and down. He was struck by her trappings of price and thought her a nice beast fit for the riding of Wazirs or even of royalties; and the more he looked the more was he perplexed till at last he said to one of his pages, "Bring hither yon door-keeper." The page went and returned to the Wazir with the porter who kissed the ground between his hands, and the Minister asked him, "Who is the owner of yonder mule and what manner of man is he?"; and he answered, "O my lord, the owner of this mule is a comely young man of pleasant manners, withal grave and dignified, and doubtless one of the sons of the merchants." When the Wazir heard the door-keeper's words he arose forthright; and, mounting his horse, rode to the Khan and went in to Nur al-Din who, seeing the Minister making towards him, rose to his feet and advanced to meet him and saluted him. The Wazir welcomed him to Bassorah and dismounting, embraced him and made him sit down by his side and said, "O my son, whence comest thou and what dost thou seek?" "O my lord," Nur al-Din replied, "I have come from Cairo-city of which my father was whilome Wazir; but he hath been removed to the grace of Allah;" and he informed him of all that had befallen him from beginning to end, adding, "I am resolved never to return home before I have seen all the cities and countries of the world." When the Wazir heard this, he said to him, "O my son, hearken not to the voice of passion lest it cast thee into the pit; for indeed many regions be waste places and I fear for thee the turns of Time." Then he let load the saddle-bags and the silk and prayer-carpets on the mule and carried Nur al-Din to his own house, where he lodged him in a pleasant place and entreated him honourably and made much of him, for he inclined to love him with exceeding love. After a while he said to him, "O my son, here am I left a man in years and have no male children, but Allah hath blessed me with a daughter who eveneth thee in beauty; and I have rejected all her many suitors, men of rank and substance. But affection for thee hath entered into my heart; say me, then, wilt thou be to her a husband? If thou accept this, I will go up with thee to the Sultan of Bassorah and will tell him that thou art my nephew, the son of my brother, and bring thee to be appointed Wazir in my place that I may keep the house for, by Allah, O my son, I am stricken in years and aweary." When Nur al-Din heard the Wazir's words, he bowed his head in modesty and said, "To hear is to obey!" At this the Wazir rejoiced and bade his servants prepare a feast and decorate the great assembly-hall, wherein they were wont to celebrate the marriages of Emirs and Grandees. Then he assembled his friends and the notables of the reign and the merchants of Bassorah and when all stood before him he said to them, "I had a brother who was Wazir in the land of Egypt, and Allah Almighty blessed him with two sons, whilst to me, as well ye wot, He hath given a daughter. My brother charged me to marry my daughter to one of his sons, whereto I assented; and, when my daughter was of age to marry, he sent me one of his sons, the young man now present, to whom I purpose marrying her, drawing up the contract and celebrating the night of unveiling with due ceremony: for he is nearer and dearer to me than a stranger and, after the wedding, if he please he shall abide with me, or if he desire to travel I will forward him and his wife to his father's home." Hereat one and all replied, "Right is thy recking;" and they looked at the bridegroom and were pleased with him. So the Wazir sent for the Kazi and legal witnesses and they wrote out the marriage contract, after which the slaves perfumed the guests with incense, and served them with sherbet of sugar and sprinkled rose-water on them and all went their ways. Then the Wazir bade his servants take Nur al-Din to the Hammam-baths and sent him a suit of the best of his own especial raiment, and napkins and towelry and bowls and perfume-burners and all else that was required. And after the bath, when he came out and donned the dress, he was even as the full moon on the fourteenth night; and he mounted his mule and stayed not till he reached the Wazir's palace. There he dismounted and went in to the Minister and kissed his hands, and the Wazir bade him welcome. – And Shahrazad perceived the dawn of day and ceased to say her permitted say.

Now when it was the Twenty-First Night,

She said, it hath reached me, O auspicious King, that the Wazir stood up to him and welcoming him said, "Arise and go in to thy wife this night, and on the morrow I will carry thee to the Sultan, and pray Allah bless thee with all manner of weal." So Nur al-Din left him and went in to his wife the Wazir's daughter. Thus far concerning him, but as regards his elder brother, Shams al-Din, he was absent with the Sultan a long time and when he returned from his journey he found not his brother; and he asked of his servants and slaves who answered, "On the day of thy departure with the Sultan, thy brother mounted his mule fully caparisoned as for state procession saying: I am going towards Kalyub-town and I shall be absent one day or at most two days; for my breast is straitened, and let none of you follow me." Then he fared forth and from that time to this we have heard no tidings of him. Shams al-Din was greatly troubled at the sudden disappearance of his brother and grieved with exceeding grief at the loss and said to himself, "This is only because I chided and upbraided him the night before my departure with the Sultan; haply his feelings were hurt and he fared forth a-travelling; but I must send after him." Then he went in to the Sultan and acquainted him with what had happened and wrote letters and dispatches, which he sent by running footmen to his deputies in every province. But during the twenty days of his brother's absence Nur al-Din had travelled far and had reached Bassorah; so after diligent search the messengers failed to come at any news of him and returned. Thereupon Shams al-Din despaired of finding his brother and said, "Indeed I went beyond all bounds in what I said to him with reference to the marriage of our children. Would that I had not done so! This all cometh of my lack of wit and want of caution." Soon after this he sought in marriage the daughter of a Cairene merchant and drew up the marriage contract and went in to her. And it so chanced that, on the very same night when Shams al-Din went in to his wife, Nur al-Din also went in to his wife the daughter of the Wazir of Bassorah; this being in accordance with the will of Almighty Allah, that He might deal the decrees of Destiny to His creatures. Furthermore, it was as the two brothers had said; for their two wives became pregnant by them on the same night and both were brought to bed on the same day; the wife of Shams al-Din, Wazir of Egypt, of a daughter, never in Cairo was seen a fairer; and the wife of Nur al-Din of a son, none more beautiful was ever seen in his time, as one of the poets said concerning the like of him:

> That jetty hair, that glossy brow,
> My slender waisted youth, of thine,
> Can darkness round creation throw,
> Or make it brightly shine.
> The dusky mole that faintly shows
> Upon his cheek, ah! blame it not;
> The tulip-flower never blows
> Undarkened by its spot.

And as another also said:

> His scent was musk and his cheek was rose;
> His teeth are pearls and his lips drop wine;
> His form is a brand and his hips a hill;
> His hair is night and his face moonshine.

They named the boy Badr al-Din Hasan and his grandfather, the Wazir of Bassorah, rejoiced in him and, on the seventh day after his birth, made entertainments and spread banquets which would befit the birth of Kings' sons and heirs. Then he took Nur al-Din and went up with him to the Sultan, and his son-in-law, when he came before the presence of the King, kissed the ground between his hands and repeated these verses, for he was ready of speech, firm of sprite and good in heart as he was goodly in form:

> The world's best joys long be thy lot, my lord!
> And last while darkness and the dawn o'erlap:

> *O thou who makest, when we greet thy gifts,*
> *The world to dance and Time his palms to clap.*

Then the Sultan rose up to honour them and, thanking Nur al-Din for his fine compliment, asked the Wazir, "Who may be this young man?"; and the Minister answered, "This is my brother's son," and related his tale from first to last. Quoth the Sultan, "And how comes he to be thy nephew and we have never heard speak of him?" Quoth the Minister, "O our lord the Sultan, I had a brother who was Wazir in the land of Egypt and he died, leaving two sons, whereof the elder hath taken his father's place and the younger, whom thou seest, came to me. I had sworn I would not marry my daughter to any but to him; so when he came I married him to her. Now he is young and I am old; my hearing is dulled and my judgment is easily fooled; wherefore I would solicit our lord the Sultan to set him in my stead, for he is my brother's son and my daughter's husband; and he is fit for the Wazirate, being a man of good counsel and ready contrivance." The Sultan looked at Nur al-Din and liked him, so he stablished him in office as the Wazir had requested and formally appointed him, presenting him with a splendid dress of honour and a she-mule from his private stud; and assigning to him solde, stipends and supplies. Nur al-Din kissed the Sultan's hand and went home, he and his father-in-law, joying with exceeding joy and saying, "All this followeth on the heels of the boy Hasan's birth!" Next day he presented himself before the King and, kissing the ground, began repeating:

> *Grow thy weal and thy welfare day by day:*
> *And thy luck prevail o'er the envier's spite;*
> *And ne'er cease thy days to be white as day,*
> *And thy foeman's day to be black as night!*

The Sultan bade him be seated on the Wazir's seat, so he sat down and applied himself to the business of his office and went into the cases of the lieges and their suits, as is the wont of Ministers; while the Sultan watched him and wondered at his wit and good sense, judgment and insight. Wherefor he loved him and took him into intimacy. When the Divan was dismissed Nur al-Din returned to his house and related what had passed to his father-in-law who rejoiced. And thenceforward Nur al-Din ceased not so to administer the Wazirate that the Sultan would not be parted from him night or day; and increased his stipends and supplies till his means were ample and he became the owner of ships that made trading voyages at his command, as well as of Mamelukes and blackamoor slaves; and he laid out many estates and set up Persian wheels and planted gardens. When his son Hasan was four years of age, the old Wazir deceased, and he made for his father-in-law a sumptuous funeral ceremony ere he was laid in the dust. Then he occupied himself with the education of this son and, when the boy waxed strong and came to the age of seven, he brought him a Fakih, a doctor of law and religion, to teach him in his own house and charged him to give him a good education and instruct him in politeness and good manners. So the tutor made the boy read and retain all varieties of useful knowledge, after he had spent some years in learning the Koran by heart; and he ceased not to grow in beauty and stature and symmetry, even as saith the poet:

In his face-sky shines the fullest moon;
In his cheeks' anemone glows the sun:
He so conquered Beauty that he hath won
All charms of humanity one by one.

The professor brought him up in his father's palace teaching him reading, writing and cyphering, theology and belles lettres. His grandfather the old Wazir had bequeathed to him the whole of his property when he was but four years of age. Now during all the time of his earliest youth he had never left the house, till on a certain day his father, the Wazir Nur al-Din, clad him in his best clothes and, mounting him on a she-mule of the finest, went up with him to the Sultan. The King gazed at Badr al-Din Hasan and marvelled at his comeliness and loved him. As for the city-folk, when he first passed before them with his father, they marvelled at his exceeding beauty and sat down on the road expecting his return, that they might look their fill on his beauty and loveliness and symmetry and perfect grace; even as the poet said in these verses:

As the sage watched the stars, the semblance clear
Of a fair youth on's scroll he saw appear.
Those jetty looks Canopus o'er him threw,
And tinged his temple curls a musky hue;
Mars dyed his ruddy cheek; and from his eyes
The Archer-star his glittering arrow flies;
His wit from Hermes came; and Soha's care,
(The half-seen star that dimly haunts the Bear)
Kept off all evil eyes that threaten and ensnare,
The sage stood mazed to see such fortunes meet,
And Luna kissed the earth beneath his feet.

And they blessed him aloud as he passed and called upon Almighty Allah to bless him. The Sultan entreated the lad with especial favour and said to his father, "O Wazir, thou must needs bring him daily to my presence;" whereupon he replied, "I hear and I obey." Then the Wazir returned home with his son and ceased not to carry him to court till he reached the age of twenty. At that time the Minister sickened and, sending for Badr al-Din Hasan, said to him, "Know, O my son, that the world of the Present is but a house of mortality, while that of the Future is a house of eternity. I wish, before I die, to bequeath thee certain charges and do thou take heed of what I say and incline thy heart to my words." Then he gave him his last instructions as to the properest way of dealing with his neighbours and the due management of his affairs; after which he called to mind his brother and his home and his native land and wept over his separation from those he had first loved. Then he wiped away his tears and, turning to his son, said to him, "Before I proceed, O my son, to my last charges and injunctions, know that I have a brother, and thou hast an uncle, Shams al-Din hight, the Wazir of Cairo, with whom I parted, leaving him against his will. Now take thee a sheet of paper and write upon it whatso I say to thee. Badr al-Din took a fair leaf and set about doing his father's bidding and he wrote thereon a full account of what had happened to his sire first and last; the dates of his arrival at Bassorah and of his foregathering with the Wazir; of his marriage, of his going in to the Minister's daughter and of the birth of his son; brief, his life of forty years from the day of his dispute with his brother, adding the words, "And this is written at my dictation and may Almighty Allah be with him when I am gone!" Then he folded the paper and sealed it and said, "O Hasan, O my son, keep this paper with all care; for it will enable thee to stablish thine origin and rank and lineage and, if anything contrary befal thee, set out for Cairo and ask for thine uncle and show him this paper and say to him that I died a stranger far from mine own people and full of yearning to see him and them." So Badr al-Din Hasan took the document and folded it; and, wrapping it up in a piece of waxed cloth, sewed it like a talisman between the inner and outer cloth of his skull-cap and wound his light turband round it. And he fell to weeping over his father and at parting with him, and he but a boy. Then Nur al-Din lapsed into a swoon, the forerunner of death; but presently recovering himself he said, "O Hasan, O my son, I will now bequeath to thee five last behests. The FIRST BEHEST is, Be over-intimate with none, nor frequent any, nor be familiar with any; so shalt thou be safe from his mischief; for security lieth in seclusion of thought and a certain retirement from the society of thy fellows; and I have heard it said by a poet:

> *In this world there is none thou mayst count upon*
> *To befriend thy case in the nick of need:*
> *So live for thyself nursing hope of none*
> *Such counsel I give thee: enow, take heed!*

The SECOND BEHEST is, O my son: Deal harshly with none lest fortune with thee deal hardly; for the fortune of this world is one day with thee and another day against thee and all worldly goods are but a loan to be repaid. And I have heard a poet say:

> *Take thought nor haste to win the thing thou wilt;*
> *Have ruth on man for ruth thou may'st require:*
> *No hand is there but Allah's hand is higher;*
> *No tyrant but shall rue worse tyrant's ire!*

The THIRD BEHEST is, Learn to be silent in society and let thine own faults distract thine attention from the faults of other men: for it is said: In silence dwelleth safety, and thereon I have heard the lines that tell us:

> *Reserve's a jewel, Silence safety is;*
> *Whenas thou speakest many a word withhold:*
> *For an of Silence thou repent thee once,*
> *Of speech thou shalt repent times manifold.*

The FOURTH BEHEST, O my son, is Beware of wine-bibbing, for wine is the head of all frowardness and a fine solvent of human wits. So shun, and again I say, shun mixing strong liquor; for I have heard a poet say:

> *From wine I turn and whoso wine-cups swill;*
> *Becoming one of those who deem it ill:*
> *Wine driveth man to miss salvation-way,*
> *And opes the gateway wide to sins that kill.*

The FIFTH BEHEST, O my son, is Keep thy wealth and it will keep thee; guard thy money and it will guard thee; and waste not thy substance lest haply thou come to want and must fare a-begging from the meanest of mankind. Save thy dirhams and deem them the sovereignest salve for the wounds of the world. And here again I have heard that one of the poets said:

When fails my wealth no friend will deign befriend:
When wealth abounds all friends their friendship tender:
How many friends lent aid my wealth to spend;
But friends to lack of wealth no friendship render.

On this wise Nur al-Din ceased not to counsel his son Badr al-Din Hasan till his hour came and, sighing one sobbing sigh, his life went forth. Then the voice of mourning and keening rose high in his house and the Sultan and all the grandees grieved for him and buried him; but his son ceased not lamenting his loss for two months, during which he never mounted horse, nor attended the Divan nor presented himself before the Sultan. At last the King, being wroth with him, stablished in his stead one of his Chamberlains and made him Wazir, giving orders to seize and set seals on all Nur al-Din's houses and goods and domains. So the new Wazir went forth with a mighty posse of Chamberlains and people of the Divan, and watchmen and a host of idlers to do this and to seize Badr al-Din Hasan and carry him before the King, who would deal with him as he deemed fit. Now there was among the crowd of followers a Mameluke of the deceased Wazir who, when he had heard this order, urged his horse and rode at full speed to the house of Badr al-Din Hasan; for he could not endure to see the ruin of his old master's son. He found him sitting at the gate with head hung down and sorrowing, as was his wont, for the loss of his father; so he dismounted and kissing his hand said to him, "O my lord and son of my lord, haste ere ruin come and lay waste!" When Hasan heard this he trembled and asked, "What may be the matter?"; and the man answered, "The Sultan is angered with thee and hath issued a warrant against thee, and evil cometh hard upon my track; so flee with thy life!" At these words Hasan's heart flamed with the fire of bale, and his rose-red cheek turned pale, and he said to the Mameluke, "O my brother, is there time for me to go in and get me some worldly gear which may stand me in stead during my strangerhood?" But the slave replied, "O my lord, up at once and save thyself and leave this house, while it is yet time." And he quoted these lines:

Escape with thy life, if oppression betide thee,
And let the house tell of its builder's fate!
Country for country thou'lt find, if thou seek it;
Life for life never, early or late.
It is strange men should dwell in the house of abjection,
When the plain of God's earth is so wide and so great!

At these words of the Mameluke, Badr al-Din covered his head with the skirt of his garment and went forth on foot till he stood outside of the city, where he heard folk saying, "The Sultan hath sent his new Wazir to the house of the old Wazir, now no more, to seal his property and seize his son Badr al-Din Hasan and take him before the presence, that he may put him to death;" and all cried, "Alas for his beauty and his loveliness!" When he heard this he fled forth at hazard, knowing not whither he was going, and gave not over hurrying onwards till Destiny drove him to his father's tomb. So he entered the cemetery and, threading his way through the graves, at last he reached the sepulchre where he sat down and let fall from his head the skirt of his long robe which was made of brocade with a gold-embroidered hem whereon were worked these couplets:

> *O thou whose forehead, like the radiant East,*
> *Tells of the stars of Heaven and bounteous dews:*
> *Endure thine honour to the latest day,*
> *And Time thy growth of glory ne'er refuse!*

While he was sitting by his father's tomb behold, there came to him a Jew as he were a Shroff, a money-changer, with a pair of saddle-bags containing much gold, who accosted him and kissed his hand, saying, "Whither bound, O my lord: 'tis late in the day and thou art clad but lightly and I read signs of trouble in thy face?" "I was sleeping within this very hour," answered Hasan, "when my father appeared to me and chid me for not having visited his tomb; so I awoke trembling and came hither forthright lest the day should go by without my visiting him, which would have been grievous to me." "O my lord," rejoined the Jew "thy father had many merchantmen at sea and, as some of them are now due, it is my wish to buy of thee the cargo of the first ship that cometh into port with this thousand dinars of gold." "I consent," quoth Hasan, whereupon the Jew took out a bag full of gold and counted out a thousand sequins which he gave to Hasan, the son of the Wazir, saying, "Write me a letter of sale and seal it." So Hasan took a pen and paper and wrote these words in duplicate, "The writer, Hasan Badr al-Din, son of Wazir Nur al-Din, hath sold to Isaac the Jew all the cargo of the first of his father's ships which cometh into port, for a thousand dinars, and he hath received the price in advance." And after he had taken one copy the Jew put it into his pouch and went away; but Hasan fell a-weeping as he thought of the dignity and prosperity which had erst been his and he began reciting:

> *This house, my lady, since you left is now a home no more*
> *For me, nor neighbours, since you left, prove kind and neighbourly:*
> *The friend, whilere I took to heart, alas! no more to me*
> *Is friend; and even Luna's self displayeth lunacy:*
> *You left and by your going left the world a waste, a wold,*
> *And lies a gloomy murk upon the face of hill and lea:*
> *O may the raven-bird whose cry our hapless parting croaked*
> *Find ne'er a nesty home and eke shed all his plumery!*
> *At length my patience fails me; and this absence wastes my flesh;*
> *How many a veil by severance rent our eyes are doomèd see:*
> *Ah! shall I ever sight again our fair past nights of yore;*
> *And shall a single house become a home for me once more?*

Then he wept with exceeding weeping and night came upon him; so he leant his head against his father's grave and sleep overcame him: Glory to Him who sleepeth not! He ceased not slumbering till the moon rose, when his head slipped from off the tomb and he lay on his back, with limbs outstretched, his face shining bright in the moonlight. Now the cemetery was haunted day and night by Jinns who were of the True Believers, and presently came out a Jinniyah who, seeing Hasan asleep, marvelled at his beauty and loveliness and cried, "Glory to God! this youth can be none other than one of the Wuldán of Paradise." Then she flew firmament-wards to circle it, as was her custom, and met an Ifrit on the wing who saluted her and she said to him, "Whence comest thou?" "From Cairo," he replied. "Wilt thou come with me and look upon the beauty of a youth who sleepeth in yonder burial place?" she asked, and he answered, "I will." So they flew till they lighted at the tomb and she showed him the youth and said, "Now diddest thou ever in thy born days see aught like this?" The Ifrit looked upon him and exclaimed, "Praise be to Him that hath no equal! But, O my sister, shall I tell thee what I have seen this day?" Asked she, "What is that?" and he answered, "I have seen the counterpart of this youth in the land of Egypt. She is the daughter of the Wazir Shams al-Din and she is a model of beauty and loveliness, of fairest favour and formous form, and dight with symmetry and perfect grace. When she had reached the age of nineteen, the Sultan of Egypt heard of her and, sending for the Wazir her father, said to him: Hear me, O Wazir: it hath reached mine ear that thou hast a daughter and I wish to demand her of thee in marriage. The Wazir replied: O our lord the Sultan, deign accept my excuses and take compassion on my sorrows, for thou knowest that my brother, who was partner with me in the Wazirate, disappeared from amongst us many years ago and we wot not where he is. Now the cause of his departure was that one night, as we were sitting together and talking of wives and children to come, we had words on the matter and he went off in high dudgeon. But I swore that I would marry my daughter to none save to the son of my brother on the day her mother gave her birth, which was nigh upon nineteen years ago. I have lately heard that my brother died at Bassorah, where he had married the daughter of the Wazir and that she bare him a son; and I will not marry my daughter but to him in honour of my brother's memory I recorded the date of my marriage and the conception of my wife and the birth of my daughter; and from her horoscope I find that her name is conjoined with that of her cousin; and there are damsels in foison for our lord the Sultan. The King, hearing his Minister's answer and refusal, waxed wroth with exceeding wrath and cried: When the like of me asketh a girl in marriage of the like of thee, he conferreth an honour, and thou rejectest me and puttest me off with cold excuses! Now, by the life of my head I will marry her to the meanest of my men in spite of the nose of thee! There was in the palace a horse-groom which was a Gobbo with a bunch to his breast and a hunch to his back; and the Sultan sent for him and married him to the daughter of the Wazir, lief or loath, and hath ordered a pompous marriage procession for him and that he go in to his bride this very night. I have now just flown hither from Cairo, where I left the Hunchback at the door of the Hammam-bath amidst the Sultan's white slaves who were waving lighted flambeaux about him. As for the Minister's daughter she sitteth among her nurses and tirewomen, weeping and wailing; for they have forbidden her father to come near her. Never have I seen, O my sister, more hideous being than this Hunchback whilst the young lady is the likest of all folk to this young man, albeit even fairer than he." – And Shahrazad perceived the dawn of day and ceased saying her permitted say.

Now when it was the Twenty-Second Night,

She said, it hath reached me, O auspicious King, that when the Jinni narrated to the Jinniyah how the King had caused the wedding contract to be drawn up between the hunchbacked groom and the lovely young lady who was heart-broken for sorrow; and how she was the fairest of created things and even more beautiful than this youth, the Jinniyah cried at him "Thou liest! this youth is handsomer than any one of his day." The Ifrit gave her the lie again, adding, "By Allah, O my sister, the damsel I speak of is fairer than this; yet none but he deserveth her, for they resemble each other like brother and sister or at least cousins. And, well-away! how she is wasted upon that Hunchback!" Then said she, "O my brother, let us get under him and lift him up and carry him to Cairo, that we may compare him with the damsel of whom thou speakest and so determine whether of the twain is the fairer." "To hear is to obey!" replied he, "thou speakest to the point; nor is there a righter recking than this of thine, and I myself will carry him." So he raised him from the ground and flew with him like a bird soaring in upper air, the Ifritah keeping close by his side at equal speed, till he alighted with him in the city of Cairo and set him down on a stone bench and woke him up. He roused himself and finding that he was no longer at his father's tomb in Bassorah-city he looked right and left and saw that he was in a strange place; and he would have cried out; but the Ifrit gave him a cuff which persuaded him to keep silence. Then he brought him rich raiment and clothed him therein and, giving him a lighted flambeau, said, "Know that I have brought thee hither, meaning to do thee a good turn for the love of Allah: so take this torch and mingle with the people at the Hammam-door and walk on with them without stopping till thou reach the house of the wedding-festival; then go boldly forward and enter the great saloon; and fear none, but take thy stand at the right hand of the Hunchback bridegroom; and, as often as any of the nurses and tirewomen and singing-girls come up to thee, put thy hand into thy pocket which thou wilt find filled with gold. Take it out and throw to them and spare not; for as often as thou thrustest fingers in pouch thou shalt find it full of coin. Give largesse by handsful and fear nothing, but set thy trust upon Him who created thee, for this is not by thine own strength but by that of Allah Almighty, that His decrees may take effect upon his creatures." When Badr al-Din Hasan heard these words from the Ifrit he said to himself, "Would Heaven I knew what all this means and what is the cause of such kindness!" However, he mingled with the people and, lighting his flambeau, moved on with the bridal procession till he came to the bath where he found the Hunchback already on horseback. Then he pushed his way in among the crowd, a veritable beauty of a man in the finest apparel, wearing tarbush and turband and a long-sleeved robe purfled with gold; and, as often as the singing women stopped for the people to give them largesse, he thrust his hand into his pocket and, finding it full of gold, took out a handful and threw it on the tambourine till he had filled it with gold pieces for the music-girls and the tirewomen. The singers were amazed by his bounty and the people marvelled at his beauty and loveliness and the splendour of his dress. He ceased not to do thus till he reached the mansion of the Wazir (who was his uncle), where the Chamberlains drove back the people and forbade them to go forward; but the singing-girls and the tirewomen said, "By Allah we will not enter unless this young man enter with us, for he hath given us length o' life with his largesse and we will not display the bride unless he be present." Therewith they carried him into the bridal hall and made him sit down defying the evil glances of the hunchbacked bridegroom. The wives of the Emirs and Wazirs and Chamberlains and Courtiers all stood in double line, each holding a massy cierge ready lighted; all wore thin face-veils and the two rows right and left extended from the bride's throne to the head of the hall adjoining the chamber whence she was to come forth. When the ladies saw Badr al-Din Hasan and noted his beauty and loveliness and his face that shone like the new moon, their hearts inclined to him and the singing-girls said to all that were present, "Know that this beauty crossed our hands with naught but red gold; so be not chary to do him womanly service and comply with all he says, no matter what he ask." So all the women crowded round Hasan with their torches and gazed on his loveliness and envied him his beauty; and one and all would gladly have lain on his bosom an hour or rather a year. Their hearts were so troubled that they let fall their veils from before their faces and said, "Happy she who belongeth to this youth or to whom he belongeth!"; and they called down curses on the crooked groom and on him who was the cause of his marriage to the girl-beauty; and as often as they blessed Badr al-Din Hasan they damned the Hunchback, saying, "Verily this youth and none else deserveth our Bride: ah, well-away for such a lovely one with this hideous Quasimodo; Allah's curse light on his head and on the Sultan who commanded the marriage!" Then the singing-girls beat their tabrets and lulliloo'd with joy, announcing the appearing of the bride; and the Wazir's daughter came in surrounded by her tirewomen who had made her goodly to look upon; for they had perfumed her and incensed her and adorned her hair; and they had robed her in raiment and ornaments befitting the mighty Chosroes Kings. The most notable part of her dress was a loose robe worn over her other garments: it was diapered in red gold with figures of wild beasts, and birds whose eyes and beaks were of gems, and claws of red rubies and green beryl; and her neck was graced with a necklace of Yamani work, worth thousands of gold pieces, whose bezels were great round jewels of sorts, the like of which was never owned by Kaysar or by Tobba King. And the bride was as the full moon when at fullest on fourteenth night; and as she paced into the hall she was like one of the Houris of Heaven – praise be to Him who created her in such splendour of beauty! The ladies encompassed her as the white contains the black of the eye, they clustering like stars whilst she shone amongst them like the moon when it eats up the clouds. Now Badr al-Din Hasan of Bassorah was sitting in full gaze of the folk, when the bride came forward with her graceful swaying and swimming gait, and her hunchbacked bridegroom stood up to meet and receive her: she, however, turned away from the wight and walked forward till she stood before her cousin Hasan, the son of her uncle. Whereat the people laughed. But when the wedding-guests saw her thus attracted towards Badr Al-Din they made a mighty clamour and the singing-women shouted their loudest; whereupon he put his hand into his pocket and, pulling out a handful of gold, cast it into their tambourines and the girls rejoiced and said, "Could we win our wish this bride were thine!" At this he smiled and the folk came round him, flambeaux in hand like the eyeball round the pupil, while the Gobbo bridegroom was left sitting alone much like a tail-less baboon; for every time they lighted a candle for him it went out willy-nilly, so he was left in darkness and silence and looking at naught but himself. When Badr al-Din Hasan saw the bridegroom sitting lonesome in the dark, and all the wedding-guests with their flambeaux and wax candles crowding about himself, he was bewildered and marvelled much; but when he looked at his cousin, the daughter of his uncle, he rejoiced and felt an inward delight: he longed to greet her and gazed intently on her face which was radiant with light and brilliancy. Then the tirewomen took off her veil and displayed her in the first bridal dress which was of scarlet satin; and Hasan had a view of her which dazzled his sight and dazed his wits, as she moved to and fro, swaying with graceful gait; and she turned the heads of all the guests, women as well as men, for she was even as saith the surpassing poet:

> A sun on wand in knoll of sand she showed,
> Clad in her cramoisy-hued chemisette:
> Of her lips honey-dew she gave me drink,
> And with her rosy cheeks quencht fire she set.

Then they changed that dress and displayed her in a robe of azure; and she reappeared like the full moon when it riseth over the horizon, with her coal-black hair and cheeks delicately fair; and teeth shown in sweet smiling and breasts firm rising and crowning sides of the softest and waist of the roundest. And in this second suit she was as a certain master of high conceits saith of the like of her:

> She came apparelled in an azure vest,
> Ultramarine, as skies are deckt and dight:
> I view'd th' unparallel'd sight, which show'd my eyes
> A moon of Summer on a Winter-night.

Then they changed that suit for another and, veiling her face in the luxuriance of her hair, loosed her lovelocks, so dark, so long that their darkness and length outvied the darkest nights, and she shot through all hearts with the magical shaft of her eye-babes. They displayed her in the third dress and she was as said of her the sayer:

> Veiling her cheeks with hair a-morn she comes,
> And I her mischiefs with the cloud compare:
> Saying, "Thou veilest morn with night!" "Ah no!"
> Quoth she, "I shroud full moon with darkling air!"

Then they displayed her in the fourth bridal dress and she came forward shining like the rising sun and swaying to and fro with lovesome grace and supple ease like a gazelle-fawn. And she clave all hearts with the arrows of her eyelashes, even as saith one who described a charmer like her: ·

> The sun of beauty she to sight appears
> And, lovely-coy, she mocks all loveliness;
> And when he fronts her favour and her smile
> A-morn, the Sun of day in clouds must dress.

Then she came forth in the fifth dress, a very light of loveliness like a wand of waving willow or a gazelle of the thirsty wold. Those locks which stung like scorpions along her cheeks were bent, and her neck was bowed in blandishment, and her hips quivered as she went. As saith one of the poets describing her in verse:

She comes like fullest moon on happy night;
Taper of waist, with shape of magic might:
She hath an eye whose glances quell mankind,
And Ruby on her cheeks reflects his light:
Enveils her hips the blackness of her hair;
Beware of curls that bite with viper-bite!
Her sides are silken-soft, the while the heart
Mere rock behind that surface lurks from sight:
From the fringed curtains of her eyne she shoots
Shafts which at farthest range on mark alight:
When round her neck or waist I throw my arms
Her breasts repel me with their hardened height.
Ah, how her beauty all excels! ah how
That shape transcends the graceful waving bough!

Then they adorned her with the sixth toilette, a dress which was green. And now she shamed in her slender straightness the nut-brown spear; her radiant face dimmed the brightest beams of full moon and she outdid the bending branches in gentle movement and flexile grace. Her loveliness exalted the beauties of earth's four quarters and she broke men's hearts by the significance of her semblance; for she was even as saith one of the poets in these lines:

A damsel 'twas the tirer's art had decked with snares and sleight:
And robed in rays as though the sun from her had borrowed light:
She came before us wondrous clad in chemisette of green,
As veilèd by its leafy screen pomegranate hides from sight:
And when he said "How callest thou the manner of thy dress?"
She answered us in pleasant way with double meaning dight;
"We call this garment crève-cœur; and rightly is it hight,
For many a heart wi' this we broke and conquered many a sprite!"

Then they displayed her in the seventh dress, coloured between safflower and saffron, even as one of the poets saith:

In vest of saffron pale and safflower red
Musk'd, sandal'd, ambergris'd, she came to front:
"Rise!" cried her youth, "go forth and show thyself!"
"Sit!" said her hips, "we cannot bear the brunt!"
And when I craved a bout, her Beauty said
"Do, do!" and said her pretty shame, "Don't, don't!"

Thus they displayed the bride in all her seven toilettes before Hasan al-Basri, wholly neglecting the Gobbo who sat moping alone; and, when she opened her eyes she said, "O Allah make this man my goodman and deliver me from the evil of this hunchbacked groom." As soon as they had made an end of this part of the ceremony they dismissed the wedding guests who went forth, women children and all, and none remained save Hasan and the Hunchback, whilst the tirewomen led the bride into an inner room to change her garb and gear and get her ready for the bridegroom. Thereupon Quasimodo came up to Badr al-Din Hasan and said, "O my lord, thou hast cheered us this night with thy good company and overwhelmed us with thy kindness and courtesy; but now why not get thee up and go?" "Bismillah;" he answered, "In Allah's name so be it!"; and rising, he went forth by the door, where the Ifrit met him and said, "Stay in thy stead, O Badr al-Din, and when the Hunchback goes out to the closet of ease go in without losing time and seat thyself in the alcove; and when the bride comes say to her: 'Tis I am thy husband, for the King devised this trick only fearing for thee the evil eye, and he whom thou sawest is but a Syce, a groom, one of our stablemen. Then walk boldly up to her and unveil her face; for jealousy hath taken us of this matter." While Hasan was still talking with the Ifrit behold, the groom fared forth from the hall and entering the closet of ease sat down on the stool. Hardly had he done this when the Ifrit came out of the tank, wherein the water was, in semblance of a mouse and squeaked out "Zeek!" Quoth the Hunchback, "What ails thee?"; and the mouse grew and grew till it became a coal-black cat and caterwauled "Meeao! Meeao"! Then it grew still more and more till it became a dog and barked out "Owh! Owh!" When the bridegroom saw this he was frightened and exclaimed "Out with thee, O unlucky one!" But the dog grew and swelled till it became an ass-colt that brayed and snorted in his face "Hauk! Hauk!" Whereupon the Hunchback quaked and cried, "Come to my aid, O people of the house!" But behold, the ass-colt grew and became big as a buffalo and walled the way before him and spake with the voice of the sons of Adam, saying, "Woe to thee, O thou Bunch-back, thou stinkard, O thou filthiest of grooms!" Hearing this the groom was seized with a colic and he sat down on the jakes in his clothes with teeth chattering and knocking together. Quoth the Ifrit, "Is the world so strait to thee thou findest none to marry save my lady-love?" But as he was silent the Ifrit continued, "Answer me or I will do thee dwell in the dust!" "By Allah," replied the Gobbo, "O King of the Buffaloes, this is no fault of mine, for they forced me to wed her; and verily I wot not that she had a lover amongst the buffaloes; but now I repent, first before Allah and then before thee." Said the Ifrit to him, "I swear to thee that if thou fare forth from this place, or thou utter a word before sunrise, I assuredly will wring thy neck. When the sun rises wend thy went and never more return to this house." So saying, the Ifrit took up the Gobbo bridegroom and set him head downwards and feet upwards in the slit of the privy, and said to him, "I will leave thee here but I shall be on the look-out for thee till sunrise; and, if thou stir before then, I will seize thee by the feet and dash out thy brains against the wall: so look out for thy life!" Thus far concerning the Hunchback, but as regards Badr al-Din Hasan of Bassorah he left the Gobbo and the Ifrit jangling and wrangling and, going into the house, sat him down in the very middle of the alcove; and behold, in came the bride attended by an old woman who stood at the door and said, "O Father of Uprightness, arise and take what God giveth thee." Then the old woman went away and the bride, Sitt al-Husn or the Lady of Beauty hight, entered the inner part of the alcove broken-hearted and saying in herself, "By Allah I will never yield my person to him; no, not even were he to take my life!" But as she came to the further end she saw Badr al-Din Hasan and she said, "Dearling! art thou still sitting here? By Allah I was wishing that thou wert my bridegroom or, at least, that thou and the hunchbacked horse-groom were partners in me." He replied, "O beautiful lady, how should the Syce have access to thee, and how should he share in thee with me?" "Then," quoth she, "who is my husband, thou or he?" "Sitt al-Husn," rejoined Hasan, "we have not done this for mere fun, but only as a device to ward off the evil eye from thee; for when the tirewomen and singers and wedding guests saw thy beauty being displayed to me, they feared fascination and thy father hired the horse-groom for ten dinars and a porringer of meat to take the evil eye off us; and now he hath received his hire and gone his gait." When the Lady of Beauty heard these words she smiled and rejoiced and laughed a pleasant laugh. Then she whispered him, "By the Lord thou hast quenched a fire which tortured me and now, by Allah, O my little dark-haired darling, take me to thee and press me to thy bosom!" Then she began singing:

> By Allah, set thy foot upon my soul;
> Since long, long years for this alone I long:
> And whisper tale of love in ear of me;
> To me 'tis sweeter than the sweetest song!
> No other youth upon my heart shall lie;
> So do it often, dear, and do it long.

Then she stripped off her outer gear and she threw open her chemise from the neck downwards and showed her parts genital and all the rondure of her hips. When Badr al-Din saw the glorious sight his desires were roused, and he arose and doffed his clothes, and wrapping up in his bag-trousers the purse of gold which he had taken from the Jew and which contained the thousand dinars, he laid it under the edge of the bedding. Then he took off his turband and set it upon the settle atop of his other clothes, remaining in his skull-cap and fine shirt of blue silk laced with gold. Whereupon the Lady of Beauty drew him to her and he did likewise. Then he took her to his embrace and set her legs round his waist and point-blanked that cannon placed where it battereth down the bulwark of maidenhead and layeth it waste. And he found her a pearl unpierced and unthridden and a filly by all men save himself unridden; and he abated her virginity and had joyance of her youth in his virility and presently he withdrew sword from sheath; and then returned to the fray right eath; and when the battle and the siege had finished, some fifteen assaults he had furnished and she conceived by him that very night. Then he laid his hand under her head and she did the same and they embraced and fell asleep in each other's arms, as a certain poet said of such lovers in these couplets:

> Visit thy lover, spurn what envy told;
> No envious churl shall smile on love ensoul'd
> Merciful Allah made no fairer sight
> Than coupled lovers single couch doth hold;
> Breast pressing breast and robed in joys their own,
> With pillowed forearms cast in finest mould:
> And when heart speaks to heart with tongue of love,
> Folk who would part them hammer steel ice-cold:
> If a fair friend thou find who cleaves to thee,
> Live for that friend, that friend in heart enfold.

O ye who blame for love us lover kind
Say, can ye minister to diseasèd mind?

This much concerning Badr al-Din Hasan and Sitt al-Husn his cousin; but as regards the Ifrit, as soon as he saw the twain asleep, he said to the Ifritah, "Arise; slip thee under the youth and let us carry him back to his place ere dawn overtake us; for the day is nearhand." Thereupon she came forward and, getting under him as he lay asleep, took him up clad only in his fine blue shirt, leaving the rest of his garments; and ceased not flying (and the Ifrit vying with her in flight) till the dawn advised them that it had come upon them mid-way, and the Muezzin began his call from the Minaret, "Haste ye to salvation! Haste ye to salvation!" Then Allah suffered His angelic host to shoot down the Ifrit with a shooting star, so he was consumed, but the Ifritah escaped and she descended with Badr al-Din at the place where the Ifrit was burnt, and did not carry him back to Bassorah, fearing lest he come to harm. Now by the order of Him who predestineth all things, they alighted at Damascus of Syria, and the Ifritah set down her burden at one of the city-gates and flew away. When day arose and the doors were opened, the folk who came forth saw a handsome youth, with no other raiment but his blue shirt of gold-embroidered silk and skull-cap, lying upon the ground drowned in sleep after the hard labour of the night which had not suffered him to take his rest. So the folk looking at him said, "O her luck with whom this one spent the night! but would he had waited to don his garments." Quoth another, "A sorry lot are the sons of great families! Haply he but now came forth of the tavern on some occasion of his own and his wine flew to his head, whereby he hath missed the place he was making for and strayed till he came to the gate of the city; and finding it shut lay him down and went to by-by!" As the people were bandying guesses about him suddenly the morning breeze blew upon Badr al-Din and raising his shirt to his middle showed a stomach and navel with something below it, and legs and thighs clear as crystal and smooth as cream. Cried the people, "By Allah he is a pretty fellow!"; and at the cry Badr al-Din awoke and found himself lying at a city-gate with a crowd gathered around him. At this he greatly marvelled and asked, "Where am I, O good folk; and what causeth you thus to gather round me, and what have I had to do with you?"; and they answered, "We found thee lying here asleep during the call to dawn-prayer and this is all we know of the matter, but where diddest thou lie last night?" "By Allah, O good people," replied he, "I lay last night in Cairo." Said somebody, "Thou hast surely been eating Hashísh;" and another, "He is a fool;" and a third, "He is a *citrouille;*" and a fourth asked him, "Art thou out of thy mind? thou sleepest in Cairo and thou wakest in the morning at the gate of Damascus-city!" Cried he, "By Allah, my good people, one and all, I lie not to you: indeed I lay yesternight in the land of Egypt and yesternoon I was at Bassorah." Quoth one, "Well! well!"; and quoth another, "Ho! ho!"; and a third, "So! so!"; and a fourth cried, "This youth is mad, is possessed of the Jinni!" So they clapped hands at him and said to one another, "Alas, the pity of it for his youth: by Allah a madman! and madness is no respecter of persons." Then said they to him, "Collect thy wits and return to thy reason! How couldest thou be in Bassorah yesterday and in Cairo yesternight and withal awake in Damascus this morning?" But he persisted, "Indeed I was a bridegroom in Cairo last night." "Belike thou hast been dreaming," rejoined they, "and sawest all this in thy sleep." So Hasan took thought for a while and said to them, "By Allah, this is no dream; nor vision-like doth it seem! I certainly was in Cairo where they displayed the bride before me, in presence of a third person, the Hunchback groom who was sitting hard by. By Allah, O my brother, this be no dream, and if it were a dream, where is the bag of gold I bore with me and where are my turband and my robe, and my trousers?" Then he rose and entered the city, threading its highways and by-ways and bazar-streets; and the people pressed upon him and jeered at him, crying out "Madman! madman!" till he, beside himself with rage, took refuge in a cook's shop. Now that Cook had been a trifle too clever, that is, a rogue and thief; but Allah had made him repent and turn from his evil ways and open a cook-shop; and all the people of Damascus stood in fear of his boldness and his mischief. So when the crowd saw the youth enter his shop, they dispersed being afraid of him, and went their ways. The Cook looked at Badr al-Din and, noting his beauty and loveliness, fell in love with him forthright and said, "Whence comest thou, O youth? Tell me at once thy tale, for thou art become dearer to me than my soul." So Hasan recounted to him all that had befallen him from beginning to end (but in repetition there is no fruition) and the Cook said, "O my lord Badr al-Din, doubtless thou knowest that this case is wondrous and this story marvellous; therefore, O my son, hide what hath betided thee, till Allah dispel what ills be thine; and tarry with me here the meanwhile, for I have no child and I will adopt thee." Badr al-Din replied, "Be it as thou wilt, O my uncle!" Whereupon the Cook went to the bazar and bought him a fine suit of clothes and made him don it; then fared with him to the Kazi, and formally declared that he was his son. So Badr al-Din Hasan became known in Damascus-city as the Cook's son and he sat with him in the shop to take the silver, and on this wise he sojourned there for a time. Thus far concerning him; but as regards his cousin, the Lady of Beauty, when morning dawned she awoke and missed Badr al-Din Hasan from her side; but she thought that he had gone to the privy and she sat expecting him for an hour or so; when behold, entered her father Shams al-Din Mohammed, Wazir of Egypt. Now he was disconsolate by reason of what had befallen him through the Sultan, who had entreated him harshly and had married his daughter by force to the lowest of his menials and he too a lump of a groom hunchbacked withal, and he said to himself, "I will slay this daughter of mine if of her own free will she have yielded her person to this accursed carle." So he came to the door of the bride's private chamber, and said, "Ho! Sitt al-Husn." She answered him, "Here am I! here am I! O my lord," and came out unsteady of gait after the pains and pleasures of the night; and she kissed his hand, her face showing redoubled brightness and beauty for having lain in the arms of that gazelle, her cousin. When her father, the Wazir, saw her in such case, he asked her, "O thou accursed, art thou rejoicing because of this horse-groom?", and Sitt al-Husn smiled sweetly and answered, "By Allah, don't ridicule me: enough of what passed yesterday when folk laughed at me, and evened me with that groom-fellow who is not worthy to bring my husband's shoes or slippers; nay who is not worth the paring of my husband's nails! By the Lord, never in my life have I nighted a night so sweet as yesternight!, so don't mock by reminding me of the Gobbo." When her parent heard her words he was filled with fury, and his eyes glared and stared, so that little of them showed save the whites and he cried, "Fie upon thee! What words are these? 'Twas the hunchbacked horse-groom who passed the night with thee!" "Allah upon thee," replied the Lady of Beauty, "do not worry me about the Gobbo, Allah damn his father; and leave jesting with me; for this groom was only hired for ten dinars and a porringer of meat and he took his wage and went his way. As for me I entered the bridal-chamber, where I found my true bridegroom sitting, after the singer-women had displayed me to him; the same who had crossed their hands with red gold, till every pauper that was present waxed wealthy; and I passed the night on the breast of my bonny man, a most lively darling, with his black eyes and joined eyebrows." When her parent heard these words the light before his face became night, and he cried out at her saying, "O thou whore! What is this thou tellest me? Where be thy wits?" "O my father," she rejoined, "thou breakest my heart; enough for thee that thou hast been so hard upon me! Indeed my husband who took my virginity is but just now gone to the draught house and I feel that I have conceived by him." The Wazir rose in much marvel and entered the privy where he found the hunchbacked horse-groom with his head in the hole and his heels in the air. At this sight he was confounded and said, "This is none other than he, the rascal Hunchback!" So he called to him, "Ho, Hunchback!" The Gobbo grunted out, *Taghúm! Taghúm!* thinking it was the Ifrit spoke to him; so the Wazir shouted at him and said, "Speak out, or I'll strike off thy pate with this sword." Then quoth the Hunchback, "By Allah, O Shaykh of the Ifrits, ever since thou settest me in this place, I have not lifted my head; so Allah upon thee, take pity and entreat me kindly!" When the Wazir heard this he asked, "What is this thou sayest? I'm the bride's father and no Ifrit." "Enough for thee that thou hast well nigh done me die," answered Quasimodo; "now go thy ways before he come upon thee who hath served me thus. Could ye not marry me to any save the lady-love of buffaloes and the beloved of Ifrits? Allah curse her and curse him who married me to her and was the cause of this my case." – And Shahrazad perceived the dawn of day, and ceased to say her permitted say.

Now when it was the Twenty-third Night,

She said, it hath reached me, O auspicious King, that the hunchbacked groom spake to the bride's father saying, "Allah curse him who was the cause of this my case!" Then said the Wazir to him, "Up and out of this place!" "Am I mad," cried the groom, "that I should go with thee without leave of the Ifrit whose last words to me were: When the sun rises, arise and go thy gait. So hath the sun risen or no?; for I dare not budge from this place till then." Asked the Wazir, "Who brought thee hither?"; and he answered "I came here yesternight for a call of nature and to do what none can do for me, when lo! a mouse came out of the water, and squeaked at me and swelled and waxed gross till it was big as a buffalo, and spoke to me words that entered my ears. Then he left me here and went away, Allah curse the bride and him who married me to her!" The Wazir walked up to him and lifted his head out of the cess-pool hole; and he fared forth running for dear life and hardly crediting that the sun had risen; and repaired to the Sultan to whom he told all that had befallen him with the Ifrit. But the Wazir returned to the bride's private chamber, sore troubled in spirit about her, and said to her, "O my daughter, explain this strange matter to me!" Quoth she, "'Tis simply this. The bridegroom to whom they displayed me yester-eve lay with me all night, and took my virginity and I am with child by him. He is my husband and if thou believe me not, there are his turband, twisted as it was, lying on the settle and his dagger and his trousers beneath the bed with a something, I wot not what, wrapped up in them." When her father heard this he entered the private chamber and found the turband which had been left there by Badr al-Din Hasan, his brother's son, and he took it in hand and turned it over, saying, "This is the turband worn by Wazirs, save that it is of Mosul stuff." So he opened it and, finding what seemed to be an amulet sewn up in the Fez, he unsewed the lining and took it out; then he lifted up the trousers wherein was the purse of the thousand gold pieces and, opening that also, found in it a written paper. This he read and it was the sale-receipt of the Jew in the name of Badr al-Din Hasan, son of Nur al-Din Ali, the Egyptian; and the thousand dinars were also there. No sooner had Shams al-Din read this than he cried out with a loud cry and fell to the ground fainting; and as soon as he revived and understood the gist of the matter he marvelled and said, "There is no god, but the God, whose All-might is over all things! Knowest thou, O my daughter, who it was that became the husband of thy virginity?" "No," answered she, and he said, "Verily he is the son of my brother, thy cousin, and this thousand dinars is thy dowry. Praise be to Allah! and would I wot how this matter came about!" Then opened he the amulet which was sewn up and found therein a paper in the handwriting of his deceased brother, Nur al-Din the Egyptian, father of Badr al-Din Hasan; and, when he saw the handwriting, he kissed it again and again; and he wept and wailed over his dead brother and improvised these lines:

> *I see their traces and with pain I melt,*
> *And on their whilome homes I weep and yearn:*
> *And Him I pray who dealt this parting-blow*
> *Some day he deign vouchsafe a safe return.*

When he ceased versifying, he read the scroll and found in it recorded the dates of his brother's marriage with the daughter of the Wazir of Bassorah, and of his going in to her, and her conception, and the birth of Badr al-Din Hasan and all his brother's history and doings up to his dying day. So he marvelled much and shook with joy and, comparing the dates with his own marriage and going in unto his wife and the birth of his daughter, Sitt al-Husn, he found that they perfectly agreed. So he took the document and, repairing with it to the Sultan, acquainted him with what had passed, from first to last; whereat the King marvelled and commanded the case to be at once recorded. The Wazir abode that day expecting to see his brother's son but he came not; and he waited a second day, a third day and so on to the seventh day, without any tidings of him. So he said, "By Allah, I will do a deed such as none hath ever done before me!"; and he took reed-pen and ink and drew upon a sheet of paper the plan of the whole house, showing whereabouts was the private chamber with the curtain in such a place and the furniture in such another and so on with all that was in the room. Then he folded up the sketch and, causing all the furniture to be collected, he took Badr al-Din's garments and the turband and Fez and robe and purse, and carried the whole to his house and locked them up, against the coming of his nephew, Badr al-Din Hasan, the son of his lost brother, with an iron padlock on which he set his seal. As for the Wazir's daughter, when her tale of months was fulfilled, she bare a son like the full moon, the image of his father in beauty and loveliness and fair proportions and perfect grace. They cut his navel-string and Kohl'd his eyelids to strengthen his eyes, and gave him over to the nurses and nursery governesses, naming him Ajíb, the Wonderful. His day was as a month and his month was as a year; and, when seven years had passed over him, his grandfather sent him to school, enjoining the master to teach him Koran-reading, and to educate him well. He remained at the school four years, till he began to bully his schoolfellows and abuse them and bash them and thrash them and say, "Who among you is like me? I am the son of the Wazir of Egypt!"

At last the boys came in a body to complain to the Monitor of what hard usage they were wont to have from Ajib, and he said to them, "I will tell you somewhat you may do to him so that he shall leave off coming to the school, and it is this. When he enters to-morrow, sit ye down about him and say some one of you to some other: By Allah none shall play with us at this game except he tell us the names of his mamma and his papa; for he who knows not the names of his mother and his father is a bastard, a son of adultery, and he shall not play with us." When morning dawned the boys came to school, Ajib being one of them, and all flocked round him saying, "We will play a game wherein none shall join save he can tell the name of his mamma and his papa." And they all cried, "By Allah, good!" Then quoth one of them, "My name is Májid and my mammy's name is Alawiyah and my daddy's Izz al-Din." Another spoke in like guise and yet a third, till Ajib's turn came, and he said, "My name is Ajib, and my mother's is Sitt al-Husn, and my father's Shams al-Din, the Wazir of Cairo." "By Allah," cried they, "the Wazir is not thy true father." Ajib answered, "The Wazir is my father in very deed." Then the boys all laughed and clapped their hands at him, saying "He does not know who is his papa: get out from among us, for none shall play with us except he know his father's name." Thereupon they dispersed from around him and laughed him to scorn; so his breast was straitened and he well nigh choked with tears and hurt feelings. Then said the Monitor to him, "We know that the Wazir is thy grandfather, the father of thy mother, Sitt al-Husn, and not thy father. As for thy father, neither dost thou know him nor yet do we; for the Sultan married thy mother to the hunchbacked horse-groom; but the Jinni came and slept with her and thou hast no known father. Leave, then, comparing thyself too advantageously with the little ones of the school, till thou know that thou hast a lawful father; for until then thou wilt pass for a child of adultery amongst them. Seest thou not that even a huckster's son knoweth his own sire? Thy grandfather is the Wazir of Egypt; but as for thy father we wot him not and we say indeed that thou hast none. So return to thy sound senses!" When Ajib heard these insulting words from the Monitor and the school boys and understood the reproach they put upon him, he went out at once and ran to his mother, Sitt al-Husn, to complain; but he was crying so bitterly that his tears prevented his speech for a while. When she heard his sobs and saw his tears her heart burned as though with fire for him, and she said, "O my son, why dost thou weep? Allah keep the tears from thine eyes! Tell me what hath betided thee?" So he told her all that he heard from the boys and from the Monitor and ended with asking, "And who, O my mother, is my father?" She answered, "Thy father is the Wazir of Egypt;" but he said, "Do not lie to me. The Wazir is thy father, not mine! who then is my father? Except thou tell me the very truth I will kill myself with this hanger." When his mother heard him speak of his father she wept, remembering her cousin and her bridal night with him and all that occurred there and then, and she repeated these couplets:

> *Love in my heart they lit and went their ways,*
> *And all I love to furthest lands withdrew;*
> *And when they left me sufferance also left,*
> *And when we parted Patience bade adieu:*
> *They fled and flying with my joys they fled,*
> *In very constancy my spirit flew:*
> *They made my eyelids flow with severance tears*

And to the parting-pang these drops are due:
And when I long to see reunion-day,
My groans prolonging sore for ruth I sue:
Then in my heart of hearts their shapes I trace,
And love and longing care and cark renew:
O ye, whose names cling round me like a cloak,
Whose love yet closer than a shirt I drew,
Belovèd ones! how long this hard despite?
How long this severance and this coy shy flight?

Then she wailed and shrieked aloud and her son did the like; and behold, in came the Wazir whose heart burnt within him at the sight of their lamentations and he said, "What makes you weep?" So the Lady of Beauty acquainted him with what happened between her son and the school boys; and he also wept, calling to mind his brother and what had past between them and what had betided his daughter and how he had failed to find out what mystery there was in the matter. Then he rose at once and, repairing to the audience-hall, went straight to the King and told his tale and craved his permission to travel eastward to the city of Bassorah and ask after his brother's son. Furthermore he besought the Sultan to write for him letters patent, authorising him to seize upon Badr al-Din, his nephew and son-in-law, wheresoever he might find him. And he wept before the King, who had pity on him and wrote royal autographs to his deputies in all climes and countries and cities; whereat the Wazir rejoiced and prayed for blessings on him. Then, taking leave of his Sovereign, he returned to his house, where he equipped himself and his daughter and his adopted child Ajib, with all things meet for a long march; and set out and travelled the first day and the second and the third and so forth till he arrived at Damascus-city. He found it a fair place abounding in trees and streams, even as the poet said of it:

When I nighted and dayed in Damascus-town,
Time sware such another he ne'er should view:
And careless we slept under wing of night,
Till dappled Morn 'gan her smiles renew:
And dew-drops on branch in their beauty hung,
Like pearls to be dropt when the Zephyr blew:
And the Lake was the page where birds read and note,
And the clouds set points to what breezes wrote.

The Wazir encamped on the open space called Al-Hasá; and, after pitching tents, said to his servants, "A halt here for two days!" So they went into the city upon their several occasions, this to sell and that to buy; this to go to the Hammam and that to visit the Cathedral-mosque of the Banu Umayyah, the Ommiades, whose like is not in this world. Ajib also went, with his attendant eunuch, for solace and diversion to the city and the servant followed with a quarter-staff of almond-wood so heavy that if he struck a camel therewith the beast would never rise again. When the people of Damascus saw Ajib's beauty and brilliancy and perfect grace and symmetry (for he was a marvel of comeliness and winning loveliness, softer than the cool breeze of the North, sweeter than limpid waters to man in drowth, and pleasanter than the health for which sick man sueth), a mighty many followed him, whilst others ran on before and sat down on the road until he should come up, that they might gaze on him, till, as Destiny had decreed, the Eunuch stopped opposite the shop of Ajib's father, Badr al-Din Hasan. Now his beard had grown long and thick and his wits had ripened during the twelve years which had passed over him, and the Cook and ex-rogue having died, the so-called Hasan of Bassorah had succeeded to his goods and shop, for that he had been formally adopted before the Kazi and witnesses. When his son and the Eunuch stepped before him he gazed on Ajib and, seeing how very beautiful he was, his heart fluttered and throbbed, and blood drew to blood and natural affection spake out and his bowels yearned over him. He had just dressed a conserve of pomegranate grains with sugar, and Heaven-implanted love wrought within him; so he called to his son Ajib and said, "O my lord, O thou who hast gotten the mastery of my heart and my very vitals and to whom my bowels yearn; say me, wilt thou enter my house and solace my soul by eating of my meat?" Then his eyes streamed with tears which he could not stay, for he bethought him of what he had been and what he had become. When Ajib heard his father's words his heart also yearned himwards and he looked at the Eunuch and said to him, "Of a truth, O my good guard, my heart yearns to this cook; he is as one that hath a son far away from him: so let us enter and gladden his heart by tasting of his hospitality. Perchance for our so doing Allah may reunite me with my father." When the Eunuch heard these words he cried, "A fine thing this, by Allah! Shall the sons of Wazirs be seen eating in a common cook-shop? Indeed I keep off the folk from thee with this quarter-staff lest they even look upon thee; and I dare not suffer thee to enter this shop at all." When Hasan of Bassorah heard his speech he marvelled and turned to the Eunuch with the tears pouring down his cheeks; and Ajib said, "Verily my heart loves him!" But he answered, "Leave this talk, thou shalt not go in." Thereupon the father turned to the Eunuch and said, "O worthy sir, why wilt thou not gladden my soul by entering my shop? O thou who art like a chesnut, dark without but white of heart within! O thou of the like of whom a certain poet said * * *" The Eunuch burst out a-laughing and asked – "Said what? Speak out by Allah and be quick about it." So Hasan the Bassorite began reciting these couplets:

> If not master of manners or aught but discreet
> In the household of Kings no trust could he take:
> And then for the Harem! What Eunuch is he
> Whom angels would serve for his service sake.

The Eunuch marvelled and was pleased at these words, so he took Ajib by the hand and went into the cook's shop: whereupon Hasan the Bassorite ladled into a saucer some conserve of pomegranate-grains wonderfully good, dressed with almonds and sugar, saying, "You have honoured me with your company: eat then and health and happiness to you!" Thereupon Ajib said to his father, "Sit thee down and eat with us; so perchance Allah may unite us with him we long for." Quoth Hasan, "O my son, hast thou then been afflicted in thy tender years with parting from those thou lovest?" Quoth Ajib, "Even so, O nuncle mine; my heart burns for the loss of a beloved one who is none other than my father; and indeed I come forth, I and my grandfather, to circle and search the world for him. Oh, the pity of it, and how I long to meet him!" Then he wept with exceeding weeping, and his father also wept seeing him weep and for his own bereavement, which recalled to him his long separation from dear friends and from his mother; and the Eunuch was moved to pity for him. Then they ate together till they were satisfied; and Ajib and the slave rose and left the shop. Hereat Hasan the Bassorite felt as though his soul had departed his body and had gone with them; for he could not lose sight of the boy during the twinkling of an eye, albeit he knew not that Ajib was his son. So he locked up his shop and hastened after them; and he walked so fast that he came up with them before they had gone out of the western gate. The Eunuch turned and asked him, "What ails thee?"; and Badr al-Din answered, "When ye went from me, meseemed my soul had gone with you; and, as I had business without the city-gate, I purposed to bear you company till my matter was ordered and so return." The Eunuch was angered and said to Ajib, "This is just what I feared! we ate that unlucky mouthful (which we are bound to respect), and here is the fellow following us from place to place; for the vulgar are ever the vulgar." Ajib, turning and seeing the Cook just behind him, was wroth and his face reddened with rage and he said to the servant, "Let him walk the highway of the Moslems; but, when we turn off it to our tents, and find that he still follows us, we will send him about his business with a flea in his ear." Then he bowed his head and walked on, the Eunuch walking behind him. But Hasan of Bassorah followed them to the plain Al-Hasa; and, as they drew near to the tents, they turned round and saw him close on their heels; so Ajib was very angry, fearing that the Eunuch might tell his grandfather what had happened. His indignation was the hotter for apprehension lest any say that after he had entered a cook-shop the cook had followed him. So he turned and looked at Hasan of Bassorah and found his eyes fixed on his own, for the father had become a body without a soul; and it seemed to Ajib that his eye was a treacherous eye or that he was some lewd fellow. So his rage redoubled and, stooping down, he took up a stone weighing half a pound and threw it at his father. It struck him on the forehead, cutting it open from eye-brow to eye-brow and causing the blood to stream down: and Hasan fell to the ground in a swoon whilst Ajib and the Eunuch made for the tents. When the father came to himself he wiped away the blood and tore off a strip from his turband and bound up his head, blaming himself the while, and saying, "I wronged the lad by shutting up my shop and following, so that he thought I was some evil-minded fellow." Then he returned to his place where he busied himself with the sale of his sweetmeats; and he yearned after his mother at Bassorah, and wept over her and broke out repeating:

> Unjust it were to bid the World be just
> And blame her not: She ne'er was made for justice:
> Take what she gives thee, leave all grief aside,
> For now to fair and then to foul her lust is.

So Hasan of Bassorah set himself steadily to sell his sweetmeats; but the Wazir, his uncle, halted in Damascus three days and then marched upon Emesa, and passing through that town he made enquiry there and at every place where he rested. Thence he fared on by way of Hamah and Aleppo and thence through Diyár Bakr and Máridin and Mosul, still enquiring, till he arrived at Bassorah-city. Here, as soon as he had secured a lodging, he presented himself before the Sultan, who entreated him with high honour and the respect due to his rank, and asked the cause of his coming. The Wazir acquainted him with his history and told him that the Minister Nur al-Din was his brother; whereupon the Sultan exclaimed, "Allah have mercy upon him!" and added, "My good Sáhib!; he was my Wazir for fifteen years and I loved him exceedingly. Then he died leaving a son who abode only a single month after his father's death; since which time he has disappeared and we could gain no tidings of him. But his mother, who is the daughter of my former Minister, is still among us." When the Wazir Shams al-Din heard that his nephew's mother was alive and well, he rejoiced and said, "O King I much desire to meet her." The King on the instant gave him leave to visit her; so he betook himself to the mansion of his brother, Nur al-Din, and cast sorrowful glances on all things in and around it and kissed the threshold. Then he bethought him of his brother, Nur al-Din Ali, and how he had died in a strange land far from kith and kin and friends; and he wept and repeated these lines:

> I wander 'mid these walls, my Layla's walls,
> And kissing this and other wall I roam:
> 'Tis not the walls or roof my heart so loves,
> But those who in this house had made their home.

Then he passed through the gate into a courtyard and found a vaulted doorway builded of hardest syenite inlaid with sundry kinds of multi-coloured marble. Into this he walked and wandered about the house and, throwing many a glance around, saw the name of his brother, Nur al-Din, written in gold wash upon the walls. So he went up to the inscription and kissed it and wept and thought of how he had been separated from his brother and had now lost him for ever, and he recited these couplets:

> I ask of you from every rising sun,
> And eke I ask when flasheth leven-light:
> Restless I pass my nights in passion-pain,
> Yet ne'er I 'plain me of my painful plight:
> My love! if longer last this parting throe
> Little by little shall it waste my sprite.
> An thou wouldst bless these eyne with sight of thee
> One day on earth, I crave none other sight:
> Think not another could possess my mind
> Nor length nor breadth for other love I find.

Then he walked on till he came to the apartment of his brother's widow, the mother of Badr al-Din Hasan, the Egyptian. Now from the time of her son's disappearance she had never ceased weeping and wailing through the light hours and the dark; and, when the years grew longsome with her, she built for him a tomb of marble in the midst of the saloon and there used to weep for him day and night, never sleeping save thereby. When the Wazir drew near her apartment, he heard her voice and stood behind the door while she addressed the sepulchre in verse and said:

> Answer, by Allah! Sepulchre, are all his beauties gone?
> Hath change the power to blight his charms, that Beauty's paragon?
> Thou art not earth, O Sepulchre! nor art thou sky to me;
> How comes it, then, in thee I see conjoint the branch and moon?

While she was bemoaning herself after this fashion, behold, the Wazir went in to her and saluted her and informed her that he was her husband's brother; and, telling her all that had passed between them, laid open before her the whole story, how her son Badr al-Din Hasan had spent a whole night with his daughter full ten years ago but had disappeared in the morning. And he ended with saying, "My daughter conceived by thy son and bare a male child who is now with me, and he is thy son and thy son's son by my daughter." When she heard the tidings that her boy, Badr al-Din, was still alive and saw her brother-in-law, she rose up to him and threw herself at his feet and kissed them, reciting these lines:

> Allah be good to him that gives glad tidings of thy steps;
> In very sooth for better news mine ears would never sue:
> Were he content with worn-out robe, upon his back I'd throw
> A heart to pieces rent and torn when heard the word Adieu.

Then the Wazir sent for Ajib and his grandmother stood up and fell on his neck and wept; but Shams al-Din said to her, "This is no time for weeping; this is the time to get thee ready for travelling with us to the land of Egypt; haply Allah will reunite me and thee with thy son and my nephew." Replied she, "Hearkening and obedience;" and, rising at once, collected her baggage and treasures and her jewels, and equipped herself and her slave-girls for the march, whilst the Wazir went to take his leave of the Sultan of Bassorah, who sent by him presents and rarities for the Soldan of Egypt. Then he set out at once upon his homeward march and journeyed till he came to Damascus-city where he alighted in the usual place and pitched tents, and said to his suite, "We will halt a se'nnight here to buy presents and rare things for the Soldan." Now Ajib bethought him of the past so he said to the Eunuch, "O Láik, I want a little diversion; come, let us go down to the great bazar of Damascus, and see what hath become of the cook whose sweetmeats we ate and whose head we broke, for indeed he was kind to us and we entreated him scurvily." The Eunuch answered, "Hearing is obeying!" So they went forth from the tents; and the tie of blood drew Ajib towards his father, and forthwith they passed through the gateway, Báb al-Farádís hight, and entered the city and ceased not walking through the streets till they reached the cook-shop, where they found Hasan of Bassorah standing at the door. It was near the time of mid-afternoon prayer and it so fortuned that he had just dressed a confection of pomegranate-grains. When the twain drew near to him and Ajib saw him, his heart yearned towards him, and noticing the scar of the blow, which time had darkened on his brow, he said to him, "Peace be on thee, O man!; know that my heart is with thee." But when Badr al-Din looked upon his son his vitals yearned and his heart fluttered, and he hung his head earthwards and sought to make his tongue give utterance to his words, but he could not. Then he raised his head humbly and suppliant-wise towards his boy and repeated these couplets:

> I longed for my beloved but when I saw his face,
> Abashed I held my tongue and stood with downcast eye;
> And hung my head in dread and would have hid my love,
> But do whatso I would hidden it would not lie:

Volumes of plaints I had prepared, reproach and blame,
But when we met, no single word remembered I.

And then said he to them, "Heal my broken heart and eat of my sweetmeats; for, by Allah, I cannot look at thee but my heart flutters. Indeed I should not have followed thee the other day, but that I was beside myself." "By Allah," answered Ajib, "thou dost indeed love us! We ate in thy house a mouthful when we were here before and thou madest us repent of it, for that thou followedst us and wouldst have disgraced us; so now we will not eat aught with thee save on condition that thou make oath not to go out after us nor dog us. Otherwise we will not visit thee again during our present stay; for we shall halt a week here, whilst my grandfather buys certain presents for the King." Quoth Hasan of Bassorah, "I promise you this." So Ajib and the Eunuch entered the shop, and his father set before them a saucer-full of conserve of pomegranate-grains. Said Ajib, "Sit thee down and eat with us, so haply shall Allah dispel our sorrows." Hasan the Bassorite was joyful and sat down and ate with them; but his eyes kept gazing fixedly on Ajib's face, for his very heart and vitals clove to him; and at last the boy said to him, "Did I not tell thee thou art a most noyous dotard?; so do stint thy staring in my face!" But when Hasan of Bassorah heard his son's words he repeated these lines:

Thou hast some art the hearts of men to clip;
Close-veiled, far-hidden mystery dark and deep:
O thou whose beauties shame the lustrous moon,
Wherewith the saffron Morn fears rivalship!
Thy beauty is a shrine shall ne'er decay;
Whose signs shall grow until they all outstrip;
Must I be thirst-burnt by that Eden-brow
And die of pine to taste that Kausar-lip?

Hasan kept putting morsels into Ajib's mouth at one time and at another time did the same by the Eunuch and they ate till they were satisfied and could no more. Then all rose up and the cook poured water on their hands; and, loosing a silken waist-shawl, dried them and sprinkled them with rose-water from a casting-bottle he had by him. Then he went out and presently returned with a gugglet of sherbet flavoured with rose-water, scented with musk and cooled with snow; and he set this before them saying, "Complete your kindness to me!" So Ajib took the gugglet and drank and passed it to the Eunuch; and it went round till their stomachs were full and they were surfeited with a meal larger than their wont. Then they went away and made haste in walking till they reached the tents, and Ajib went in to his grandmother, who kissed him and, thinking of her son, Badr al-Din Hasan, groaned aloud and wept and recited these lines:

I still had hoped to see thee and enjoy thy sight,
For in thine absence life had lost its kindly light:
I swear my vitals wot none other love but thine
By Allah, who can read the secrets of the sprite!

Then she asked Ajib, "O my son! where hast thou been?"; and he answered, "In Damascus-city;" Whereupon she rose and set before him a bit of scone and a saucer of conserve of pomegranate-grains (which was too little sweetened), and she said to the Eunuch, "Sit down with thy master!" Said the servant to himself, "By Allah, we have no mind to eat: I cannot bear the smell of bread;" but he sat down and so did Ajib, though his stomach was full of what he had eaten already and drunken. Nevertheless he took a bit of the bread and dipped it in the pomegranate-conserve and made shift to eat it, but he found it too little sweetened, for he was cloyed and surfeited, so he said, "Faugh; what be this wild-beast stuff?" "O my son," cried his grandmother, "dost thou find fault with my cookery? I cooked this myself and none can cook it as nicely as I can save thy father, Badr al-Din Hasan." "By Allah, O my lady," Ajib answered, "this dish is nasty stuff; for we saw but now in the city of Bassorah a cook who so dresseth pomegranate-grains that the very smell openeth a way to the heart and the taste would make a full man long to eat; and, as for this mess compared with his, 'tis not worth either much or little." When his grandmother heard his words she waxed wroth with exceeding wrath and looked at the servant – And Shahrazad perceived the dawn of day and ceased to say her permitted say.

Now when it was the Twenty-Fourth Night,

She said, it hath reached me, O auspicious King, that when Ajib's grandmother heard his words, she waxed wroth and looked at the servant and said, "Woe to thee! dost thou spoil my son, and dost take him into common cookshops?" The Eunuch was frightened and denied, saying, "We did not go into the shop; we only passed by it." "By Allah," cried Ajib, "but we *did* go in and we ate till it came out of our nostrils, and the dish was better than thy dish!" Then his grandmother rose and went and told her brother-in-law, who was incensed against the Eunuch, and sending for him asked him, "Why didst thou take my son into a cook-shop?"; and the Eunuch being frightened answered, "We did not go in." But Ajib said, "We *did* go inside and ate conserve of pomegranate-grains till we were full; and the cook gave us to drink of iced and sugared sherbet." At this the Wazir's indignation redoubled and he questioned the Castrato but, as he still denied, the Wazir said to him, "If thou speak sooth, sit down and eat before us." So he came forward and tried to eat, but could not and threw away the mouthful crying "O my lord! I am surfeited since yesterday." By this the Wazir was certified that he had eaten at the cook's and bade the slaves throw him which they did. Then they came down on him with a rib-basting which burned him till he cried for mercy and help from Allah, saying, "O my master, beat me no more and I will tell thee the truth;" whereupon the Wazir stopped the bastinado and said, "Now speak thou sooth." Quoth the Eunuch, "Know then that we did enter the shop of a cook while he was dressing conserve of pomegranate-grains and he set some of it before us: by Allah! I never ate in my life its like, nor tasted aught nastier than this stuff which is now before us." Badr al-Din Hasan's mother was angry at this and said, "Needs must thou go back to the cook and bring me a saucer of conserved pomegranate-grains from that which is in his shop and show it to thy master, that he may say which be the better and the nicer, mine or his." Said the unsexed "I will." So on the instant she gave him a saucer and a half dinar and he returned to the shop and said to the cook, "O Shaykh of all Cooks, we have laid a wager concerning thy cookery in my lord's house, for they have conserve of pomegranate-grains there also; so give me this half-dinar's worth and look to it; for I have eaten a full meal of stick on account of thy cookery, and so do not let me eat aught more thereof." Hasan of Bassorah laughed and answered, "By Allah, none can dress this dish as it should be dressed save myself and my mother, and she at this time is in a far country." Then he ladled out a saucer-full; and, finishing it off with musk and rose-water, put it in a cloth which he sealed and gave it to the Eunuch, who hastened back with it. No sooner had Badr al-Din Hasan's mother tasted it and perceived its fine flavour and the excellence of the cookery, than she knew who had dressed it, and she screamed and fell down fainting. The Wazir, sorely startled, sprinkled rose-water upon her and after a time she recovered and said, "If my son be yet of this world, none dressed this conserve of pomegranate-grains but he; and this Cook is my very son Badr al-Din Hasan; there is no doubt of it nor can there be any mistake, for only I and he knew how to prepare it and I taught him." When the Wazir heard her words he joyed with exceeding joy and said, "Oh the longing of me for a sight of my brother's son! I wonder if the days will ever unite us with him! Yet it is to Almighty Allah alone that we look for bringing about this meeting." Then he rose without stay or delay and, going to his suite said to them, "Be off, some fifty of you with sticks and staves to the Cook's shop and demolish it; then pinion his arms behind him with his own turband, saying: It was thou madest that foul mess of pomegranate-grains! and drag him here perforce but without doing him a harm." And they replied, "It is well." Then the Wazir rode off without losing an instant to the Palace and, foregathering with the Viceroy of Damascus, showed him the Sultan's orders. After careful perusal he kissed the letter, and placing it upon his head said to his visitor, "Who is this offender of thine?" Quoth the Wazir, "A man which is a cook." So the Viceroy at once sent his apparitors to the shop; which they found demolished and everything in it broken to pieces; for whilst the Wazir was riding to the palace his men had done his bidding. Then they awaited his return from the audience, and Hasan of Bassorah who was their prisoner kept saying, "I wonder what they have found in the conserve of pomegranate-grains to bring things to this pass!" When the Wazir returned to them, after his visit to the Viceroy who had given him formal permission to take up his debtor and depart with him, on entering the tents he called for the Cook. They brought him forward pinioned with his turband; and, when Badr al-Din Hasan saw his uncle, he wept with exceeding weeping and said, "O my lord, what is my offence against thee?" "Art thou the man who dressed that conserve of pomegranate-grains?"; asked the Wazir, and he answered "Yes! didst thou find in it aught to call for the cutting off of my head?" Quoth the Wazir, "That were the least of thy deserts!" Quoth the cook, "O my lord, wilt thou not tell me my crime and what aileth the conserve of pomegranate-grains?" "Presently," replied the Wazir and called aloud to his men, saying "Bring hither the camels." So they struck the tents and by the Wazir's orders the servants took Badr al-Din Hasan, and set him in a chest which they padlocked and put on a camel. Then they departed and stinted not journeying till nightfall, when they halted and ate some victual, and took Badr al-Din Hasan out of his chest and gave him a meal and locked him up again. They set out once more and travelled till they reached Kimrah, where they took him out of the box and brought him before the Wazir who asked him, "Art thou he who dressed that conserve of pomegranate-grains?" He answered "Yes, O my lord!"; and the Wazir said "Fetter him!" So they fettered him and returned him to the chest and fared on again till they reached Cairo and lighted at the quarter called Al-Raydaniyah. Then the Wazir gave order to take Badr al-Din Hasan out of the chest and sent for a carpenter and said to him, "Make me a cross of wood for this fellow!" Cried Badr al-Din Hasan, "And what wilt thou do with it?"; and the Wazir replied, "I mean to crucify thee thereon, and nail thee thereto and parade thee all about the city." "And why wilt thou use me after this fashion?" "Because of thy villanous cookery of conserved pomegranate-grains; how durst thou dress it and sell it lacking pepper?" "And for that it lacked pepper wilt thou do all this to me? Is it not enough that thou hast broken my shop and smashed my gear and boxed me up in a chest and fed me only once a day?" "Too little pepper! too little pepper! this is a crime which can be expiated only upon the cross!" Then Badr al-Din Hasan marvelled and fell a-mourning for his life; whereupon the Wazir asked him, "Of what thinkest thou?"; and he answered him, "Of maggoty heads like thine; for an thou had one ounce of sense thou hadst not treated me thus." Quoth the Wazir, "It is our duty to punish thee lest thou do the like again." Quoth Badr al-Din Hasan, "Of a truth my offence were over-punished by the least of what thou hast already done to me; and Allah damn all conserve of pomegranate-grains and curse the hour when I cooked it and would I had died ere this!" But the Wazir rejoined, "There is no help for it: I must crucify a man who sells conserve of pomegranate-grains lacking pepper." All this time the carpenter was shaping the wood and Badr al-Din looked on; and thus they did till night, when his uncle took him and clapped him into the chest, saying, "The thing shall be done to-morrow!" Then he waited till he knew Badr al-Din Hasan to be asleep, when he mounted; and, taking the chest up before him, entered the city and rode on to his own house, where he alighted and said to his daughter, Sitt al-Husn, "Praised be Allah who hath reunited thee with thy husband, the son of thine uncle! Up now, and order the house as it was on thy bridal night." So the servants arose and lit the candles; and the Wazir took out his plan of the nuptial chamber, and directed them what to do till they had set everything in its stead, so that whoever saw it would have no doubt but it was the very night of the marriage. Then he bade them put down Badr al-Din Hasan's turband on the settle, as he had deposited it with his own hand, and in like manner his bag-trousers and the purse which were under the mattress; and told his daughter to undress herself and go to bed in the private chamber as on her wedding-night, adding, "When the son of thine uncle comes in to thee, say to him: Thou hast loitered while going to the privy; and call him to lie by thy side and keep him in converse till day-break, when we will explain the whole matter to him." Then he bade take Badr al-Din Hasan out of the chest, after loosing the fetters from his feet and stripping off all that was on him save the fine shirt of blue silk in which he had slept on his wedding-night; so that he was well nigh naked and trouserless. All this was done whilst he was sleeping on utterly unconscious. Then, by doom of Destiny, Badr al-Din Hasan turned over and awoke; and, finding himself in a lighted vestibule, said to himself, "Surely I am in the mazes of some dream." So he rose and went on a little to an inner door and looked in and lo! he was in the very chamber wherein the bride had been displayed to him; and there he saw the bridal alcove and the settle and his turband and all his clothes. When he saw this he was confounded and kept advancing with one foot, and retiring with the other, saying, "Am I sleeping or waking?" And he began rubbing his forehead and saying (for indeed he was thoroughly astounded), "By Allah, verily this is the chamber of the bride who was displayed before me! Where am I then? I was surely but now in a box!" Whilst he was talking with himself, Sitt al-Husn suddenly lifted the corner of the chamber-curtain and said, "O my lord, wilt thou not come in? Indeed thou hast loitered long in the water-closet." When he heard her words and saw her face he burst out laughing and said, "Of a truth this is a very nightmare among dreams!" Then he went in sighing, and pondered what had come to pass with him and was perplexed about his case, and his affair became yet more obscure to him when he saw his turband and bag-trousers and when, feeling the pocket, he found the purse containing the thousand gold pieces. So he stood still and muttered, "Allah is all knowing! Assuredly I am dreaming a wild waking dream!" Then said the Lady of Beauty to him, "What ails thee to look puzzled and perplexed?"; adding, "Thou wast a very different man during the first of the night!" He laughed and asked her, "How long have I been away from thee?"; and she answered him, "Allah preserve thee and His Holy Name be about thee! Thou didst but go out an hour ago for an occasion and return. Are thy wits clean gone?" When Badr al-Din Hasan heard this, he laughed, and said, "Thou hast spoken truth; but, when I went out from thee, I forgot myself awhile in the draught-house and dreamed that I was a cook at Damascus and abode there ten years; and there came to me a boy who was of the sons of the great, and with him an Eunuch." Here he passed his hand over his forehead and, feeling the scar, cried, "By Allah, O my lady, it must have been true, for he struck my forehead with a stone and cut it open from eye-brow to eye-brow; and here is the mark: so it must have been on wake." Then he added, "But perhaps I dreamt it when we fell asleep, I and thou, in each other's arms, for meseems it was as though I travelled to Damascus without tarbush and trousers and set up as a cook there." Then he was perplexed and considered for awhile, and said, "By Allah, I also fancied that I dressed a conserve of pomegranate-grains and put too little pepper in it. By Allah, I must have slept in the numero-cent and have seen the whole of this in a dream; but how long was that dream!" "Allah upon thee," said Sitt al-Husn, "and what more sawest thou?" So he related all to her; and presently said, "By Allah, had I not woke up they would have nailed me to a cross of wood!" "Wherefore?" asked she; and he answered, "For putting too little pepper in the conserve of pomegranate-grains, and meseemed they demolished my shop and dashed to pieces my pots and pans, destroyed all my stuff and put me in a box; then they sent for the carpenter to fashion a cross for me and would have crucified me thereon. Now Alhamdolillah! thanks be to Allah, for that all this happened to me in sleep, and not on wake." Sitt al-Husn laughed and clasped him to her bosom and he her to his: then he thought again and said, "By Allah, it could not be save while I was awake: truly I know not what to think of it." Then he lay him down and all the night he was bewildered about his case, now saying, "I was dreaming!" and then saying, "I was awake!", till morning, when his uncle Shams al-Din, the Wazir, came to him and saluted him. When Badr al-Din Hasan saw him he said, "By Allah, art thou not he who bade bind my hands behind me and smash my shop and nail me to a cross on a matter of conserved pomegranate-grains because the dish lacked a sufficiency of pepper?" Whereupon the Wazir said to him, "Know, O my son, that truth hath shown it soothfast and the concealed hath been revealed! Thou art the son of my brother, and I did all this with thee to certify myself that thou wast indeed he who went in unto my daughter that night. I could not be sure of this, till I saw that thou knewest the chamber and thy turband and thy trousers and thy gold and the papers in thy writing and in that of thy father, my brother; for I had never seen thee afore that and knew thee not; and as to thy mother I have prevailed upon her to come with me from Bassorah." So saying, he threw himself on his nephew's breast and wept for joy; and Badr al-Din Hasan, hearing these words from his uncle, marvelled with exceeding marvel and fell on his neck and also shed tears for excess of delight. Then said the Wazir to him, "O my son, the sole cause of all this is what passed between me and thy sire;" and he told him the manner of his father wayfaring to Bassorah and all that had occurred to part them. Lastly the Wazir sent for Ajib; and when his father saw him he cried, "And this is he who struck me with the stone!" Quoth the Wazir "This is thy son!" And Badr al-Din Hasan threw himself upon his boy and began repeating:

Long have I wept o'er severance' ban and bane,
Long from mine eyelids tear-rills rail and rain:
And vowèd I if Time re-union bring
My tongue from name of "Severance" I'll restrain:
Joy hath o'ercome me to this stress that I
From joy's revulsion to shed tears am fain:
Ye are so trained to tears, O eyne of me!
You weep with pleasure as you weep with pain.

When he had ended his verse his mother came in and threw herself upon him and began reciting:

When we met we complained,
Our hearts were sore wrung:
But plaint is not pleasant
Fro' messenger's tongue.

Then she wept and related to him what had befallen her since his departure, and he told her what he had suffered, and they thanked Allah Almighty for their reunion. Two days after his arrival the Wazir Shams al-Din went in to the Sultan and, kissing the ground between his hands, greeted him with the greeting due to Kings. The Sultan rejoiced at his return and his face brightened and, placing him hard by his side, asked him to relate all he had seen in his wayfaring and whatso had betided him in his going and coming. So the Wazir told him all that had passed from first to last and the Sultan said, "Thanks be to Allah for thy victory and the winning of thy wish and thy safe return to thy children and thy people! And now I needs must see the son of thy brother, Hasan of Bassorah, so bring him to the audience-hall to-morrow." Shams al-Din replied, "Thy slave shall stand in thy presence to-morrow, Inshallah, if it be God's will." Then he saluted him and, returning to his own house, informed his nephew of the Sultan's desire to see him, whereto replied Hasan, whilome the Bassorite, "The slave is obedient to the orders of his lord." And the result was that next day he accompanied his uncle, Shams al-Din, to the Divan; and, after saluting the Sultan and doing him reverence in most ceremonious obeisance and with most courtly obsequiousness, he began improvising these verses:

The first in rank to kiss the ground shall deign
Before you, and all ends and aims attain:
You are Honour's fount; and all that hope of you,
Shall gain more honour than Hope hoped to gain.

The Sultan smiled and signed to him to sit down. So he took a seat close to his uncle, Shams al-Din, and the King asked him his name. Quoth Badr al-Din Hasan, "The meanest of thy slaves is known as Hasan the Bassorite, who is instant in prayer for thee day and night." The Sultan was pleased at his words and, being minded to test his learning and prove his good breeding, asked him, "Dost thou remember any verses in praise of the mole on the cheek?" He answered, "I do," and began reciting:

When I think of my love and our parting-smart,
My groans go forth and my tears upstart:

He's a mole that reminds me in colour and charms
O' the black o' the eye and the grain of the heart.

The King admired and praised the two couplets and said to him, "Quote something else; Allah bless thy sire and may thy tongue never tire!" So he began:

That cheek-mole's spot they evened with a grain
Of musk, nor did they here the simile strain:
Nay, marvel at the face comprising all
Beauty, nor falling short by single grain.

The King shook with pleasure and said to him, "Say more: Allah bless thy days!" So he began:

O you whose mole on cheek enthroned recalls
A dot of musk upon a stone of ruby,
Grant me your favours! Be not stone at heart!
Core of my heart whose only sustenance you be!

Quoth the King, "Fair comparison, O Hasan! thou hast spoken excellently well and hast proved thyself accomplished in every accomplishment! Now explain to me how many meanings be there in the Arabic language for the word Khál or mole." He replied, "Allah keep the King! Seven and fifty and some by tradition say fifty." Said the Sultan, "Thou sayest sooth," presently adding, "Hast thou knowledge as to the points of excellence in beauty?" "Yes," answered Badr al-Din Hasan, "Beauty consisteth in brightness of face, clearness of complexion, shapeliness of nose, gentleness of eyes, sweetness of mouth, cleverness of speech, slenderness of shape and seemliness of all attributes." But the acme of beauty is in the hair and, indeed, al-Shiháb the Hijazi hath brought together all these items in his doggrel verse of the metre Rajaz and it is this:

Say thou to skin "Be soft," to face "Be fair,"
And gaze, nor shall they blame howso thou stare:
Fine nose in Beauty's list is high esteemed;
Nor less an eye full, bright and debonnair
Eke did they well to laud the lovely lips
(Which e'en the sleep of me will never spare);
A winning tongue, a stature tall and straight;
A seemly union of gifts rarest rare:
But Beauty's acme in the hair one views it;
So hear my strain and with some few excuse it!

The Sultan was captivated by his converse and, regarding him as a friend, asked, "What meaning is there in the saw "Shurayh is foxier than the fox"?" And he answered, "Know, O King (whom Almighty Allah keep!) that the legist Shurayh was wont, during the days of the plague, to make a visitation to Al-Najaf; and, whenever he stood up to pray, there came a fox which would plant himself facing him and which, by mimicking his movements, distracted him from his devotions. Now when this became longsome to him, one day he doffed his shirt and set it upon a cane and shook out the sleeves; then placing his turband on the top and girding its middle with a shawl, he stuck it up in the place where he used to pray. Presently up trotted the fox according to his custom and stood over against the figure, whereupon Shurayh came behind him, and took him." Hence the sayer saith, "Shurayh is foxier than the fox." When the Sultan heard Badr al-Din Hasan's explanation he said to his uncle, Shams al-Din, "Truly this the son of thy brother is perfect in courtly breeding and I do not think that his like can be found in Cairo." At this Hasan arose and kissed the ground before him and sat down again as a Mameluke should sit before his master. When the Sultan had thus assured himself of his courtly breeding and bearing and his knowledge of the liberal arts and belles-lettres, he joyed with exceeding joy and invested him with a splendid robe of honour and promoted him to an office whereby he might better his condition. Then Badr al-Din Hasan arose and, kissing the ground before the King, wished him continuance of glory and asked leave to retire with his uncle, the Wazir Shams al-Din. The Sultan gave him leave and he issued forth and the two returned home, where food was set before them and they ate what Allah had given them. After finishing his meal Hasan repaired to the sitting-chamber of his wife, the Lady of Beauty, and told her what had past between him and the Sultan; whereupon quoth she, "He cannot fail to make thee a cup-companion and give thee largesse in excess and load thee with favours and bounties; so shalt thou, by Allah's blessing, dispread, like the greater light, the rays of thy perfection wherever thou be, on shore or on sea." Said he to her, "I purpose to recite a Kasídah, an ode, in his praise, that he may redouble in affection for me." "Thou art right in thine intent," she answered, "so gather thy wits together and weigh thy words, and I shall surely see my husband favoured with his highest favour." Thereupon Hasan shut himself up and composed these couplets on a solid base and abounding in inner grace and copied them out in a handwriting of the nicest taste. They are as follows:

Mine is a Chief who reached most haught estate,
Treading the pathways of the good and great:
His justice makes all regions safe and sure,
And against froward foes bars every gate:
Bold lion, hero, saint, e'en if you call
Seraph or Sovran he with all may rate!
The poorest suppliant rich from him returns,
All words to praise him were inadequate.
He to the day of peace is saffron Morn,
And murky Night in furious warfare's bate.
Bow 'neath his gifts our necks, and by his deeds
As King of freeborn souls he 'joys his state:
Allah increase for us his term of years,
And from his lot avert all risks and fears!

When he had finished transcribing the lines, he despatched them, in charge of one of his uncle's slaves, to the Sultan, who perused them and his fancy was pleased; so he read them to those present and all praised them with the highest praise. Thereupon he sent for the writer to his sitting chamber and said to him, "Thou art from this day forth my boon-companion and I appoint to thee a monthly solde of a thousand dirhams, over and above that I bestowed on thee aforetime." So Hasan rose and, kissing the ground before the King several times, prayed for the continuance of his greatness and glory and length of life and strength. Thus Badr al-Din Hasan the Bassorite waxed high in honour and his fame flew forth to many regions and he abode in all comfort and solace and delight of life with his uncle and his own folk till Death overtook him. When the Caliph Harun al-Rashid heard this story from the mouth of his Wazir, Ja'afar the Barmecide, he marvelled much and said, "It behoves that these stories be written in letters of liquid gold." Then he set the slave at liberty and assigned to the youth who had slain his wife such a monthly stipend as sufficed to make his life easy; he also gave him a concubine from amongst his own slave-girls and the young man became one of his cup-companions. "Yet this story" (continued Shahrazad) "is in no wise stranger than the tale of the Tailor and the Hunchback and the Jew and the Reeve and the Nazarene, and what betided them." Quoth the King, "And what may that be?" So Shahrazad began, in these words,

Nur Al-Din Ali and the Damsel Anis Al-Jalis

Richard F. Burton

QUOTH SHAHRAZAD: It hath reached me, O auspicious King of intelligence penetrating, that there was, amongst the Kings of Bassorah, a King who loved the poor and needy and cherished his lieges, and gave of his wealth to all who believed in Mohammed (whom Allah bless and assain!), and he was even as one of the poets described him,

> *"A King who when hosts of the foe invade,*
> *Receives them with lance-lunge and sabre-sway;*
> *Writes his name on bosoms in thin red lines,*
> *And scatters the horsemen in wild dismay."*

His name was King Mohammed bin Sulayman al-Zayni, and he had two Wazirs, one called Al-Mu'ín, son of Sáwí and the other Al-Fazl son of Khákán. Now Al-Fazl was the most generous of the people of his age, upright of life, so that all hearts united in loving him and the wise flocked to him for counsel; whilst the subjects used to pray for his long life, because he was a compendium of the best qualities, encouraging the good and lief, and preventing evil and mischief. But the Wazir Mu'ín bin Sáwí on the contrary hated folk and loved not the good and was a mere compound of ill; even as was said of him,

> *"Hold to nobles, sons of nobles! 'tis ever Nature's test*
> *That nobles born of nobles shall excel in noble deed:*
> *And shun the mean of soul, meanly bred, for 'tis the law,*
> *Mean deeds come of men who are mean of blood and breed."*

And as much as the people loved and fondly loved Al-Fazl bin Khákán, so they hated and thoroughly hated the mean and miserly Mu'ín bin Sáwí. It befel one day by the decree of the Decreer, that King Mohammed bin Sulayman al-Zayni, being seated on his throne with his officers of state about him, summoned his Wazir Al-Fazl and said to him, "I wish to have a slave-girl of passing beauty, perfect in loveliness, exquisite in symmetry and endowed with all praiseworthy gifts." Said the courtiers, "Such a girl is not to be bought for less than ten thousand gold pieces:" whereupon the Sultan called out to his treasurer and said, "Carry ten thousand dinars to the house of Al-Fazl bin Khákán." The treasurer did the King's bidding; and the Minister went away, after receiving the royal charge to repair to the slave-bazar every day, and entrust to brokers the matter aforesaid. Moreover the King issued orders that girls worth above a thousand gold pieces should not be bought or sold without being first displayed to the Wazir. Accordingly no broker purchased a slave-girl ere she had been paraded before the minister; but none pleased him, till one day a dealer came to the house and found him taking horse and intending for the palace. So he caught hold of his stirrup saying,

> "O thou, who givest to royal state sweet savour,
> Thou'rt a Wazir shalt never fail of favour!
> Dead Bounty thou hast raised to life for men;
> Ne'er fail of Allah's grace such high endeavour!"

Then quoth he, "O my lord, that surpassing object for whom the gracious mandate was issued is at last found; " and quoth the Wazir, "Here with her to me!" So he went away and returned after a little, bringing a damsel in richest raiment robed, a maid spear-straight of stature and five feet tall; budding of bosom with eyes large and black as by Kohl traced, and dewy lips sweeter than syrup or the sherbet one sips, a virginette smooth cheeked and shapely faced, whose slender waist with massive hips was engraced; a form more pleasing than branchlet waving upon the top-most trees, and a voice softer and gentler than the morning breeze, even as saith one of those who have described her,

> "Strange is the charm which dights her brows like Luna's disk that shine;
> O sweeter taste than sweetest Robb or raisins of the vine.
> A throne th'Empyrean keeps for her in high and glorious state,
> For wit and wisdom, wandlike form and graceful bending line:
> She in the Heaven of her face the seven-fold stars displays,
> That guard her cheeks as satellites against the spy's design:
> If man should cast a furtive glance or steal far look at her,
> His heart is burnt by devil-bolts shot by those piercing eyne."

When the Wazir saw her she made him marvel with excess of admiration, so he turned, perfectly pleased, to the broker and asked, "What is the price of this girl?"; whereto he answered, "Her market-value stands at ten thousand dinars, but her owner swears that this sum will not cover the cost of the chickens she hath eaten, the wine she hath drunken and the dresses of honour bestowed upon her instructor: for she hath learned calligraphy and syntax and etymology; the commentaries of the Koran; the principles of law and religion; the canons of medicine, and the calendar and the art of playing on musical instruments." Said the Wazir, "Bring me her master." So the broker brought him at once and, behold, he was a Persian of whom there was left only what the days had left; for he was as a vulture bald and scald and a wall trembling to its fall. Time had buffetted him with sore smart, yet was he not willing this world to depart; even as said the poet,

> "Time hath shattered all my frame, Oh! how time hath shattered me.
> Time with lordly might can tame Manly strength and vigour free.
> Time was in my youth, that none Sped their way more fleet and fast:
> Time is and my strength is gone, Youth is sped, and speed is past."

The Wazir asked him, "Art thou content to sell this slave-girl to the Sultan for ten thousand dinars?"; and the Persian answered, "By Allah, if I offer her to the King for naught, it were but my devoir." So the Minister bade bring the monies and saw them weighed out to the Persian, who stood up before him and said, "By the leave of our lord the Wazir, I have somewhat to say;" and the Wazir replied, "Out with all thou hast!" "It is my opinion," continued the slave-dealer, "that thou shouldst not carry the maid to the King this day; for she is newly off a journey; the change of air hath affected her and the toils of trouble have fretted her. But keep her quiet in thy palace some ten days, that she may recover her looks and become again as she was. Then send her to the Hammam and clothe her in the richest of clothes and go up with her to the Sultan: this will be more to thy profit." The Wazir pondered the Persian's words and approved of their wisdom; so he carried her to his palace, where he appointed her private rooms, and allowed her every day whatever she wanted of meat and drink and so forth. And on this wise she abode a while. Now the Wazir Al-Fazl had a son like the full moon when sheeniest dight, with face radiant in light, cheeks ruddy bright, and a mole like a dot of ambergris on a downy site; as said of him the poet and said full right,

"A moon which blights you if you dare behold;
A branch which folds you in its waving fold:
Locks of the Zanj and golden glint of hair;
Sweet gait and form a spear to have and hold:
Ah! hard of heart with softest slenderest waist,
That evil tothis weal why not remould?
Were thy form's softness placed in thy heart,
Ne'er would thy lover find thee harsh and cold:
Oh thou accuser! be my love's excuser,
Nor chide if love-pangs deal me woes untold!
I bear no blame: 'tis all my hear and eyne;
So leave thy blaming, let me yearn and pine."

Now the handsome youth knew not the affair of the damsel; and his father had enjoined her closely, saying, "Know, O my daughter, that I have bought thee as a bedfellow for our King, Mohammed bin Sulayman al-Zayni; and I have a son who is a Satan for girls and leaves no maid in the neighbourhood without taking her maidenhead; so be on thy guard against him and beware of letting him see thy face or hear they voice." "Hearkening and obedience," said the girl; and he left her and fared forth. Some days after this it happened by decree of Destiny, that the damsel repaired to the baths in the house, where some of the slave women bathed her; after which she arrayed herself in sumptuous raiment; and her beauty and loveliness were thereby redoubled. Then she went in to the Wazir's wife and kissed her hand; and the dame said to her, "Naiman! May it benefit thee, O Anis al-Jalis! Are not our baths handsome?" "O my mistress," she replied, "I lacked naught there save thy gracious presence." Thereupon the lady said to her slave-women, "Come with us to the Hammam, for it is some days since we went there:" they answered, "To hear is to obey!" and rose and all accompanied her. Now she had set two little slave-girls to keep the door of the private chamber wherein was Anis al-Jalis and had said to them, "Suffer none go in to the damsel." Presently, as the beautiful maiden sat resting in her rooms, suddenly came in the Wazir's son whose name was Nur al-Din Ali, and asked after his mother and her women, to which the two little slave-girls replied, "They are in the Hammam." But the damsel, Anis al-Jalis, had heard from within Nur al-Din Ali's voice and had said to herself, "O would Heaven I saw what like is this youth against whom the Wazir warned me, saying that he hath not left a virgin in the neighbourhood without taking her virginity: by Allah, I do long to have sight of him!" So she sprang to her feet with the freshness of the bath on her and, stepping to the door, looked at Nur al-Din Ali and saw a youth like the moon in its full and the sight bequeathed her a thousand sighs. The young man also glanced at her and the look make him heir to a thousand thoughts of care; and each fell into Love's ready snare. Then he stepped up to the two little slave-girls and cried aloud at them; whereupon both fled before him and stood afar off to see what he would do. And behold, he walked to the door of the damsel's chamber and, opening it, went in and asked her "Art thou she my father bought for me?" and she answered "Yes." Thereupon the youth, who was warm with wine, came up to her and embraced her; then he took her legs and passed them round his waist and she wound her arms about his neck, and met him with kisses and murmurs of pleasure and amorous toyings. Next he sucked her tongue and she sucked his, and lastly, he loosed the strings of her petticoat-trousers and abated her maidenhead. When the two little slave-girls saw their young master get in unto the damsel, Anis al-Jalis, they cried out and shrieked; so as soon as the youth had had his wicked will of her, he rose and fled forth fearing the consequences of his ill-doing. When the Wazir's wife heard the slave-girls' cries, she sprang up and came out of the baths with the perspiration pouring from her face, saying, "What is this unseemly clamour in the house?" Then she came up to the two little slave- girls and asked them saying, "Fie upon you! what is the matter?"; and both answered, "Verily our lord Nur al-Din came in and beat us, so we fled; then he went up to Anis al-Jalis and threw his arms round her and we know not what he did after that; but when we cried out to thee he ran away." Upon this the lady went to Anis al-Jalis and said to her, "What tidings?" "O my lady," she answered, "as I was sitting here lo! a handsome young man came in and said to me: Art thou she my father bought for me?; and I answered Yes; for, by Allah, O mistress mine, I believed that his words were true; and he instantly came in and embraced me." "Did he nought else with thee but this?" quoth the lady, and quoth she, "Indeed he did! But he did it only three times." "He did not leave thee without dishonouring thee!" cried the Wazir's wife and fell to weeping and buffetting her face, she and the girl and all the handmaidens, fearing lest Nur al-Din's father should kill him. Whilst they were thus, in came the Wazir and asked what was the matter, and his wife said to him, "Swear that whatso I tell thee thou wilt attend to it." "I will," answered he. So she related to him what his son had done, whereat he was much concerned and rent his raiment and smote his face till his nose bled, and plucked out his beard by the handful. "Do not kill thyself," said his wife, "I will give thee ten thousand dinars, her price, of my own money." But he raised his head and cried, "Out upon thee! I have no need of her purchase-money: my fear is lest life as well as money go." "O my lord, and how is that?" "Wottest thou not that yonder standeth our enemy Al Mu'ín bin Sáwí who, as soon as he shall hear of this matter, will go up to the Sultan" – And Shahrazad perceived the dawn of day and ceased saying her permitted say.

When it was the Thirty-fifth Night, she continued, It hath reached me, O auspicious King, that the Wazir said to his wife, "Wottest thou not that yonder standeth our enemy

Al-Mu'ín bin Sáwí who, as soon as he hears of this matter will go up to the Sultan and say to him, 'Thy Wazir who, thou wilt have it loveth thee, took from thee ten thousand ducats and bought therewith a slave-girl whose like none ever beheld; but when he saw her, she pleased him and he said to his son, 'Take her: thou art worthier of her than the Sultan.' So he took her and did away with her virginity and she is now in his house.' The King will say, 'Thou liest!' to which he will reply, 'With thy leave I will fall upon him unawares and bring her to thee.' The King will give him warranty for this and he will come down upon the house and will take the girl and present her to the Sultan, who will question her and she will not be able to deny the past. Then mine enemy will say, 'O my lord, thou wottest that I give thee the best of counsel; but I have not found favour in thine eyes.' Thereupon the Sultan will make an example of me, and I shall be a gazing-stock to all the people and my life will be lost." Quoth his wife, "Let none know of this thing which hath happened privily, and commit thy case to Allah and trust in Him to save thee from such strait; for He who knoweth the future shall provide for the future." With this she brought the Wazir a cup of wine and his heart was quieted, and he ceased to feel wrath and fear. Thus far concerning him; but as regards his son Nur al-Din Ali, fearing the consequence of his misdeed he abode his day long in the flower garden and came back only at night to his mother's apartment where he slept; and, rising before dawn, returned to the gardens. He ceased not to do thus for two whole months without showing his face to his parent, till at last his mother said to his father, "O my lord, shall we lose our boy as well as the girl? If matters continue long in this way he will flee from us." "And what to do?" asked he; and she answered, "Do thou watch this night; and, when he cometh, seize on him and frighten him: I will rescue him from thee and do thou make peace with him and give him the damsel to wife, for she loveth him as he loveth her. And I will pay thee her price." So the Minister say up that night and, when his son came, he seized him and throwing him down knelt on his breast and showed as thou he would cut his throat; but his mother ran to the youth's succour and asked her husband, "What wouldest thou do with him?" He answered her, "I will split his weasand." Said the son to the father, "Is my death, then, so light a matter to thee?"; and his father's eyes welled with tears, for natural affection moved him, and he rejoined, "O my son, how light was to thee the loss of my good and my life!" Quoth Nur al-Din, "Hear, O my father, what the poet hath said,

'Forgive me! thee-ward sinned I, but the wise
Ne'er to the sinner shall deny his grace:
Thy foe may pardon sue when lieth he
In lowest, and thou holdest highest place!'"

Thereupon the Wazir rose from off his son's breast saying, "I forgive thee!"; for his heart yearned to him; and the youth kissed the hand of his sire who said, "O my son, were I sure that thou wouldest deal justly by Anis al-Jalis, I would give her to thee." "O my father, what justice am I to do to her?" "I enjoin thee, O my son, not to take another wife or concubine to share with her, nor sell her." "O my father! I swear to thee that verily I will not do her injustice in either way." Having sworn to that effect Nur al-Din went in to the damsel and abode with her a whole year, whilst Allah Almighty caused the King to forget the matter of the maiden; and Al-Mu'ín, though the affair came to his ears, dared not divulge it by reason of the high favour in which his rival stood with the Sultan. At the end of the year Al-Fazl went one day to the public baths; and, as he came out whilst he was still sweating, the air struck him and he caught a cold which turned to a fever; then he took to his bed. His malady gained ground and restlessness was longsome upon him and weakness bound him like a chain; so he called out, "Hither with my son;" and when Nur al-Din Ali came he said to him, "O my son, know that man's lot and means are distributed and decreed; and the end of days by all must be dree'd; and that every soul drain the cup of death is nature's need." The he repeated these lines,

> *"I die my death, but He alone is great who dieth not!*
> *And well I wot, soon shall I die, for death was made my lot:*
> *A King there's not that dies and holds his kingdom in his hand,*
> *For Sovranty the Kingdom is of Him who dieth not."*

Then he continued, "O my son, I have no charge to leave thee save that thou fear Allah and look to the issues of thine acts and bear in mind my injunctions anent Anis al-Jalis." "O my father!" said Nur al-Din, "who is like unto thee? Indeed thou art famed for well doing and preachers offer prayers for thee in their pulpits!" Quoth Al-Fazl, "O my son, I hope that Allah Almighty may grant me acceptance!" Then he pronounced the Two Testimonies, or Professions of the Faith, and was recorded among the blessed. The palace was filled with crying and lamentation and the news of his death reached the King, and the city-people wept, even those at their prayers and women at household cares and the school-children shed tears for Bin- Khákán. Then his son Nur al-Din Ali arose and made ready his funeral, and the Emirs and Wazirs and high Officers of State and city-notables were present, amongst them the Wazir al-Mu'ín bin Sáwí. And as the bier went forth from the house some one in the crowd of mourners began to chant these lines,

> *"On the fifth day I quitted al my friends for evermore,*
> *And they laid me out and washed me on a slab without my door:*
> *They stripped me of the clothes I was ever wont to wear,*
> *And they clothed me in the clothes which till then I never wore.*
> *On four men's necks they bore me and carried me from home*
> *To chapel; and some prayed for him on neck they bore:*
> *They prayed for me a prayer that no prostration knows;*
> *They prayed for me who praised me and were my friends of yore;*
> *And they laid me in a house with a ceiling vaulted o'er,*
> *And Time shall be no more ere it ope to me its door."*

When they had shovelled in the dust over him and the crowd had dispersed, Nur al-Din returned home and he lamented with sobs and tears; and the tongue of the case repeated these couplets,

> *"On the fifth day at even-tide they went away from me:*
> *farewelled them as faring they made farewell my lot:*
> *But my spirit as they went, with them went and so I cried,*

'Ah return ye!' but replied she, 'Alas! return is not
To a framework lere and lorn that lacketh blood and life,
A frame whereof remaineth naught but bones that rattle and rot:
Mine eyes are blind and cannot see quencht by the flowing tear!
Mine ears are dull and lost to sense: they have no power to hear!'"

He abode a long time sorrowing for his father till, one day, as he was sitting at home, there came a knocking at the door; so he rose in haste and opening let in a man, one of his father's intimates and who had been the Wazir's boon-companion. The visitor kissed Nur al-Din's hand and said to him, "O my lord, he who hath left the like of thee is not dead; and this way went also the Chief of the Ancients and the Moderns. O my lord Ali, be comforted and leave sorrowing." Thereupon Nur al-Din rose and going to the guest-saloon transported thither all he needed. Then he assembled his companions and took his handmaid again; and, collecting round him ten of the sons of the merchants, began to eat meat and drink wine, giving entertainment after entertainment and lavishing his presents and his favours. One day his Steward came to him and said, "O my lord Nur al-Din, hast thou not heard the saying, Whoso spendeth and reckoneth not, to poverty wendeth and recketh not?" And he repeated what the poet wrote,

"I look to my money and keep it with care,
For right well I wot 'tis my buckler and brand:
Did I lavish my dirhams on hostilest foes,
I should truck my good luck by mine ill luck trepanned:
So I'll eat it and drink it and joy in my wealth;
And no spending my pennies on others I'll stand:
I will keep my purse close 'gainst whoever he be;
And a niggard in grain a true friend ne'er I fand:
Far better deny him than come to say: Lend,
And five-fold the loan shall return to thy hand!
And he turns face aside and he sidles away,
While I stand like a dog disappointed, unmanned,
Oh, the sorry lot his who hath yellow-boys none,
Though his genius and virtues shine bright as the sun!

O my master," continued the Steward, "this lavish outlay and these magnificent gifts waste away wealth." When Nur al-Din Ali heard these words he looked at his servant and cried, "Of all thou hast spoken I will not heed one single word, for I have heard the saying of the poet who saith,

'An my palm be full of wealth and my wealth I ne'er bestow,
A palsy take my hand and my foot ne'er rise again!
Show my niggard who by niggardise e'er rose to high degree,
Or the generous gifts generally hath slain.'"

And he pursued, "Know, O Steward, it is my desire that so long as thou hast money enough for my breakfast, thou trouble me not with taking thought about my supper."

Thereupon the Steward asked, "Must it be so?"; and he answered, "It must." So the honest man went his way and Nur al-Din Ali devoted himself to extravagance; and, if any of his cup-companions chanced to say, "This is a pretty thing;" he would reply, "'Tis a gift to thee!"; or if another said, "O my lord, such a house is handsome;" he would answer, "Take it: it is thine!" After this reckless fashion he continued to live for a whole year, giving his friends a banquet in the morning and a banquet in the evening and a banquet at midnight, till one day, as the company was sitting together, the damsel Anis al-Jalis repeated these lines,

> "Thou deemedst well of Time when days went well,
> And feardest not what ills might deal thee Fate:
> Thy nights so fair and restful cozened thee,
> For peaceful nights bring woes of heavy weight."

When she had ended her verse behold, somebody knocked at the door. So Nur al-Din rose to open it and one of his boon- companions followed him without being perceived. At the door he found his Steward and asked him, "What is the matter?"; and he answered, "O my lord, what I dreaded for thee hath come to pass!" "How so?" "Know that there remains not a dirham's worth, less or more in my hands. Here are my Daftars and account books showing both income and outlay and the registers of thine original property." When Nur al-Din heard these words he bowed his head and said, "There is no Majesty and there is no Might save in Allah!" When the man who had followed him privily to spy on him heard the Steward's words, he returned to his friends and warned them saying, "Look ye well to what ye do: Nur al-Din is penniless;" and, as the young host came back to his guests, vexation showed itself in his face. Thereupon one of the intimates rose; and, looking at the entertainer, said to him, "O my lord, may be thou wilt give me leave to retire?" "And why so early retirement this day?"; asked he and the other answered him, "My wife is in childbirth and I may not be absent from her: indeed I must return and see how she does." So he gave him leave, whereupon another rose and said, "O my lord Nur al-Din, I wish now to go to my brother's for he circumciseth his son to- day." In short each and every asked permission to retire on some pretence or other, till all the ten were gone leaving Nur al-Din alone. Then he called his slave-girl and said to her, "O Anis al-Jalis, hast thou seen what case is mine?" And he related to her what the Steward had told him. Then quoth she, "O my lord, for many nights I had it in my mind to speak with thee of this matter, but I heard thee repeating,

> 'When the World heaps favours on thee, pass on
> Thy favours to friends ere her hand she stay:
> Largesse never let her when fain she comes,
> Nor niggardise kept her from turning away!'

When I heard these verses I held my peace and cared not to exchange a word with thee." "O Anis al-Jalis," said Nur al-Din, "thou knowest that I have not wasted my wealth save on my friends, especially these ten who have now left me a pauper, and I think they will not abandon and desert me without relief." "By Allah," replied she, "they will not profit thee with aught of aid." Said he, "I will rise at once and go to them and knock at their doors; it may be I shall get from them somewhat wherewith I may trade and leave pastime and pleasuring." So he rose without stay or delay, and repaired to a street wherein all his ten friends lived. He went up to the nearest door and knocked; whereupon a handmaid came out and asked him, "Who art thou?"; and he answered, "Tell thy master that Nur al-Din Ali standeth at the door and saith to him, 'Thy slave kisseth thy hand and awaiteth thy bounty.'" The girl went in and told her master, who cried at her, "Go back and say, 'My master is not at home.'" So she returned to Nur al-Din, and said to him, "O my lord, my master is out." Thereupon he turned away and said to himself, "If this one be a whoreson knave and deny himself, another may not prove himself such knave and whoreson." Then he went up to the next door and sent in a like message to the house-master, who denied himself as the first had done, whereupon he began repeating,

> "He is gone who when to his gate thou go'st,
> Fed thy famisht maw with his boiled and roast."

When he had ended his verse he said, "By Allah, there is no help but that I make trial of them all: perchance there be one amongst them who will stand me in the stead of all the rest." So he went the round of the ten, but not one of them would open his door to him or show himself or even break a bit of bread before him; whereupon he recited,

> "Like a tree is he who in wealth doth wone,
> And while fruits he the folk to his fruit shall run:
> But when bared the tree of what fruit it bare,
> They leave it to suffer from dust and sun.
> Perdition to all of this age! I find
> Ten rogues for every righteous one."

Then he returned to his slave-girl and his grief had grown more grievous and she said to him, "O my lord, did I not tell thee, none would profit thee with aught of aid?" And he replied, "By Allah, not one of them would show me his face or know me!" "O my lord," quoth she, "sell some of the moveables and household stuff, such as pots and pans, little by little; and expend the proceeds until Allah Almighty shall provide." So he sold all of that was in the house till nothing remained when he turned to Anis al-Jalis and asked her "What shall we do now?"; and she answered, "O my lord, it is my advice that thou rise forthwith and take me down to the bazar and sell me. Thou knowest that they father bought me for ten thousand dinars: haply Allah may open thee a way to get the same price, and if it be His will to bring us once more together, we shall meet again." "O Anis al-Jalis," cried he, "by Allah it is no light matter for me to be parted from thee for a single hour!" "By Allah, O my lord," she replied, "nor is it easy to me either, but Need hath its own law, as the poet said,

> 'Need drives a man into devious roads,
> And pathways doubtful of trend and scope:
> No man to a rope will entrust his weight,
> Save for cause that calleth for case of rope.'"

Thereupon he rose to his feet and took her, whilst the tears rolled down his cheek like rain; and he recited with the tongue of the case these lines,

"Stay! grant one parting look before we part,
Nerving my heart this severance to sustain:
But, an this parting deal thee pain and bane,
Leave me to die of love and spare thee pain!"

Then he went down with her to the bazar and delivered her to the broker and said to him, "O Hajj Hasan, I pray thee note the value of her thou hast to cry for sale." "O my lord Nur al- Din," quoth the broker, "the fundamentals are remembered;" adding, "Is not this the Anis al-Jalis whom thy father bought of me for ten thousand dinars?" "Yes," said Nur al-Din. Thereupon the broker went round to the merchants, but found that all had not yet assembled. So he waited till the rest had arrived and the market was crowded with slave-girls of all nations, Turks, Franks and Circassians; Abyssinians, Nubians and Takruris; Tartars, Georgians and others; when he came forward and standing cried aloud, "O merchants! O men of money! every round thing is not a walnut and every long thing a banana is not; all reds are not meat nor all whites fat, nor is every brown thing a date! O merchants, I have here this union-pearl that hath no price: at what sum shall I cry her?" "Cry her at four thousand five hundred dinars," quoth one of the traders. The broker opened the door of sale at the sum named and, as he was yet calling, lo! the Wazir Al-Mu'ín bin Sáwí passed through the bazar and, seeing Nur al-Din Ali waiting at one side, said to himself, "Why is Khákán's son standing about here? Hath this gallows-bird aught remaining wherewith to buy slave-girls?" Then he looked round and, seeing the broker calling out in the market with all the merchants around him, said to himself, "I am sure that he is penniless and hath brought hither the damsel Anis al-Jalis for sale;" adding, "O how cooling and grateful is this to my heart!" Then he called the crier, who came up and kissed the ground before him; and he said to him, "I want this slave-girl whom thou art calling for sale." The broker dared not cross him, so he answered, "O my lord, Bismillah! in Allah's name so be it;" and led forward the damsel and showed her to him. She pleased him much whereat he asked, "O Hasan, what is bidden for this girl?" and he answered, "Four thousand five hundred dinars to open the door of sale." Quoth Al-Mu'ín, "Four thousand five hundred is MY bid." When the merchants heard this, they held back and dared not bid another dirham, wotting what they did of the Wazir's tyranny, violence and treachery. So Al-Mu'ín looked at the broker and said to him, "Why stand still? Go and offer four thousand dinars for me and the five hundred shall be for thyself." Thereupon the broker went to Nur al-Din and said, "O my lord, thy slave is going for nothing!" "And how so?" asked he. The broker answered, "We had opened the biddings for her at four thousand five hundred dinars; when that tyrant, Al-Mu'ín bin Sáwí, passed through the bazar and, as he saw the damsel she pleased him, so he cried to me, 'Call me the buyer at four thousand dinars and thou shalt have five hundred for thyself.' I doubt not but that he knoweth that the damsel if thine, and if he would pay thee down her price at once it were well; but I know his injustice and violence; he will give thee a written order upon some of his agents and will send after thee to say to them, 'Pay him nothing.' So as often as though shalt go in quest of the coin they will say, 'We'll pay thee presently!' and they will put thee off day after day, and thou art proud of spirit; till at last, when they are wearied with thine importunity, they will say, 'Show us the cheque.' Then, as soon as they have got hold of it they will tear it up and so thou wilt lose the girl's price." When Nur al-Din heard this he looked at the broker and asked him, "How shall this matter be managed?"; and he answered, "I will give thee a counsel which, if thou follow, it shall bring thee complete satisfaction." "And what is that?" quoth Nur al-Din. Quoth the broker, "Come thou to me anon when I am standing in the middle of the market and, taking the girl from my hand, give her a sound cuffing and say to her, 'Thou baggage, I have kept my vow and brought thee down to the slave-market, because I swore an oath that I would carry thee from home to the bazar, and make brokers cry thee for sale.' If thou do this, perhaps the device will impose upon the Wazir and the people, and they will believe that thou broughtest her not to the bazar, but for the quittance of thine oath." He replied, "Such were the best way." Then the broker left him and, returning into the midst of the market, took the damsel by the hand, and signed to the Wazir and said, "O my lord, here is her owner." With this up came Nur al-Din Ali and, snatching the girl from the broker's hand, cuffed her soundly and said to her, "Shame on thee, O thou baggage! I have brought thee to the bazar for quittance of mine oath; now get thee home and thwart me no more as is thy wont. Woe to thee! do I need thy price, that I should sell thee? The furniture of my house would fetch thy value many times over!" When Al-Mu'ín saw this he said to Nur al-Din, "Out on thee! Hast thou anything left for selling or buying?" And he would have laid violent hands upon him, but the merchants interposed (for they all loved Nur al-Din), and the young man said to them, "Here am I in your hands and ye all know his tyranny." "By Allah," cried the Wazir, "but for you I had slain him!" Then all signed with significant eyes to Nur al-Din as much as to say, "Take thy wreak of him; not one of us will come between thee and him." Thereupon Nur al-Din, who was stout of heart as he was stalwart of limb, went up to the Wazir and, dragging him over the pommel of his saddle, threw him to the ground. Now there was in that place a puddling- pit for brick-clay, into the midst of which he fell, and Nur al-Din kept pummelling and fisti-cuffing him, and one of the blows fell full on his teeth, and his beard was dyed with his blood. Also there were with the minister ten armed slaves who, seeing their master entreated after this fashion, laid hand on sword-hilt and would have bared blades and fallen on Nur al-Din to cut him down; but the merchants and bystanders said to them, "This is a Wazir and that is the son of a Wazir; haply they will make friends some time or other, in which case you will forfeit the favour of both. Or perchance a blow may befal your lord, and you will all die the vilest of deaths; so it were better for you not to interfere." Accordingly they held aloof and, when Nur al-Din had made an end of thrashing the Wazir, he took his handmaid and fared homewards. Al-Mu'ín also went his ways at once, with his raiment dyed of three colours, black with mud, red with blood and ash coloured with brick-clay. When he saw himself in this state, he bound a bit of matting round his neck and, taking in hand two bundles of coarse Halfah-grass, went up to the palace and standing under the Sultan's windows cried aloud, "O King of the age, I am a wronged man! I am foully wronged!" So they brought him before the King who looked at him; and behold, it was the chief Minister; whereupon he said, "O Wazir who did this deed by thee?" Al-Mu'ín wept and sobbed and repeated these lines,

"Shall the World oppress me when thou art in't?
In the lion's presence shall wolves devour?

Shall the dry all drink of thy tanks and I
Under rain-cloud thirst for the cooling shower?"

"O my lord," cried he, "the like will befal every one who loveth and serveth thee well." "Be quick with thee," quoth the Sultan, "and tell me how this came to pass and who did this deed by one whose honour is part of my honour." Quoth the Wazir, "Know, O my lord, that I went out this day to the slave-market to buy me a cookmaid, when I saw there a damsel, never in my life long saw I a fairer; and I designed to buy her for our lord the Sultan; so I asked the broker of her and of her owner, and he answered, "She belongeth to Ali son of Al-Fazl bin Khákán. Some time ago our lord the Sultan gave his father ten thousand dinars wherewith to buy him a handsome slave-girl, and he bought this maiden who pleased him; so he grudged her to our lord the Sultan and gave her to his own son. When the father died, the son sold all he had of houses and gardens and household gear, and squandered the price till he was penniless. Then he brought the girl to the market that he might sell her, and he handed her over to the broker to cry and the merchants bid higher and higher on her, until the price reached four thousand dinars; whereupon quoth I to myself, 'I will buy this damsel for our lord the Sultan, whose money was paid for her.' So I said to Nur al-Din, 'O my son, sell her to me for four thousand dinars.' When he heard my words he looked at me and cried, 'O ill-omened oldster, I will sell her to a Jew or to a Nazarene, but I will not sell her to thee!' 'I do not buy her for myself,' said I, 'I buy her for our lord and benefactor the Sultan.' Hearing my words he was filled with rage; and, dragging me off my horse (and I a very old man), beat me unmercifully with his fists and buffeted me with his palms till he left me as thou seest, and all this hath befallen me only because I thought to buy this damsel for thee!" Then the Wazir threw himself on the ground and lay there weeping and shivering. When the Sultan saw his condition and heard his story, the vein of rage started out between his eyes and he turned to his body-guard who stood before him, forty white slaves, smiters with the sword, and said to them, "Go down forthright to the house built by the son of Khákán and sack it and raze it and bring to me his son Nur al-Din with the damsel; and drag them both on their faces with their arms pinioned behind them." They replied, "To hear is to obey;" and, arming themselves, they set out for the house of Nur al-Din Ali. Now about the Sultan was a Chamerlain, Alam al-Din Sanjar hight, who had aforetime been Mameluke to Al-Fazl; but he had risen in the world and the Sultan had advanced him to be one of his Chamberlains. When he heard the King's command and saw the enemies make them ready to slay his old master's son, it was grievous to him: so he went out from before the Sultan and, mounting his beast, rode to Nur al-Din's house and knocked at the door. Nur al-Din came out and knowing him would have saluted him: but he said, "O my master this is no time for greeting or treating. Listen to what the poet said,

'Fly, fly with thy life if by ill overtaken!
Let thy house speak thy death by its builder forsaken!
For a land else than this land thou may'st reach, my brother,
But thy life tho'lt ne'er find in this world another.'"

"O Alam al-Din what cheer?" asked Nur al-Din, and he answered, "Rise quickly and fly for thy life, thou and the damsel; for Al- Mu'ín hath set a snare for you both; and, if you fall into his hands, he will slay you. The Sultan hath despatched forty sworders against you and I counsel you to flee ere harm can hurt you." Then Sanjar put his hand to his purse and finding there forty gold pieces took them and gave them to Nur al-Din, saying, "O my lord receive these and journey with them. Had I more I would give them to thee, but this is not the time to take exception." Thereupon Nur al-Din went in to the damsel and told her what had happened, at which she wrung her hands. Then they fared forth at once from the city, and Allah spread over them His veil of protection, so that they reached the river-bank where they found a vessel ready for sea. Her skipper was standing amidships and crying, "Whoso hath aught to do, whether in the way of provisioning or taking leave of his people; or whoso hath forgotten any needful thing, let him do it at once and return, for we are about to sail"; and all of them saying, "There is naught left to be done by us, O captain!", he cried to his crew, "Hallo there! cast off the cable and pull up the mooring- pole!" Quoth Nur al-Din, "Whither bound, O captain?" and quoth he, "To the House of Peace, Baghdad," – -And Shahrazad perceived the dawn of day and ceased to say her permitted say.

When it was the Thirty-sixth Night,
She said, it hath reached me, O auspicious King, that when the skipper answered, "To the House of Peace, Baghdad," Nur al-Din Ali and the damsel went on board, and they launched the craft and shook out the sails, and the ship sped forth as though she were a bird on wing; even as said one of them and said right well,

> "Watch some tall ship, she'll joy the sight of thee,
> The breeze outstripping in her haste to flee;
> As when a bird, with widely-spreading wings,
> Leaveth the sky to settle on the sea."

So the vessel sailed on her fastest and the wind to her was fairest. Thus far concerning them; but as regards the Mamelukes, they went to Nur al-Din's mansion and, breaking open the doors, entered and searched the whole place, but could find no trace of him and the damsel; so they demolished the house and, returning to the Sultan, reported their proceedings; whereupon quoth he, "Make search for them both, wherever they may be;" and they answered, "Hearing is obeying." The Wazir Al-Mu'ín had also gone home after the Sultan had bestowed upon him a robe of honour, and had set his heart at rest by saying, "None shall take blood-wreak for thee save I;" and he had blessed the King and prayed for his long life and prosperity. Then the Sultan bade proclaim about the city, "Oyez, O ye lieges one and all! It is the will of our lord the Sultan that whoso happeneth on Nur al-Din Ali son of Al- Fazl bin Khákán, and bringeth him to the Sultan, shall receive a robe of honour and one thousand gold pieces; and he who hideth him or knoweth his abiding place and informeth not, deserveth whatsoever pains and penalties shall befal him." So all began to search for Nur al-Din Ali, but they could find neither trace nor tidings of him. Meanwhile he and his handmaid sailed on with the wind right aft, till they arrived in safety at Baghdad, and the captain said to them, "This is Baghdad and 'tis the city where security is to be had: Winter with his frosts hath turned away and Prime hath come his roses to display; and the flowers are a- glowing and the trees are blowing and the streams are flowing." So Nur al-Din landed, he and his handmaid and, giving the captain five dinars, walked on a little way till the decrees of Destiny brought them among the gardens, and they came to a place swept and sprinkled, with benches along the walls and hanging jars filled with water. Overhead was a trellis of reed-work and canes shading the whole length of the avenue, and at the upper end was a garden gate, but this was locked. "By Allah," quoth Nur al-Din to the damsel, "right pleasant is this place!"; and she replied, "O my lord sit with me a while on this bench and let us take our ease." So they mounted and sat them down on the bench, after which they washed their faces and hands; and the breeze blew cool on them and they fell asleep and glory be to Him who never sleepeth! Not this garden was named the Garden of Gladness and therein stood a belvedere hight the Palace of Pleasure and the Pavilion of Pictures, the whole belonging to the Caliph Harun al-Rashid who was wont, when his breast was straitened with care, to frequent garden and palace and there to sit. The palace had eighty latticed windows and fourscore lamps hanging round a great candelabrum of gold furnished with wax-candles; and, when the Caliph used to enter, he would order the handmaids to throw open the lattices and light up the rooms; and he would bid Ishak bin Ibrahim the cup-companion and the slave-girls to sing till his breast was broadened and his ailments were allayed. Now the keeper of the garden, Shaykh Ibrahim, was a very old man, and he had found from time to time, when he went out on any business, people pleasuring about the garden gate with their bona robas; at which he was angered with exceeding anger. But he took patience till one day when the Caliph came to his garden; and he complained of this to Harun al-Rashid who said, "Whomsoever thou surprisest about the door of the garden, deal with him as thou wilt." Now on this day the Gardener chanced to be abroad on some occasion and returning found these two sleeping at the gate covered with a single mantilla; whereupon said he, "By Allah, good! These twain know not that the Caliph hath given me leave to slay anyone I may catch at the door; but I will give this couple a shrewd whipping, that none may come near the gate in future." So he cut a green palm-frond and went up to them and, raising his arm till the white of his arm-pit appeared, was about to strike them, when he bethought himself and said, "O Ibrahim, wilt thou beat them unknowing their case? Haply they are strangers or of the Sons of the Road, and the decrees of Destiny have thrown them here. I will uncover their faces and look at them." So he lifted up the mantilla from their heads and said, "They are a handsome couple; it were not fitting that I should beat them." Then he covered their faces again and, going to Nur al-Din's feet, began to rub and shampoo them, whereupon the youth opened his eyes and, seeing an old man of grave and reverend aspect rubbing his feet, he was ashamed and drawing them in, sat up. Then he took Shaykh Ibrahim's hand and kissed it. Quoth the old man, "O my son, whence art thou?"; and quoth he, "O my lord, we two are strangers," and the tears started from his eyes. "O my son," said Shaykh Ibrahim, "know that the Prophet (whom Allah bless and preserve!) hath enjoined honour to the stranger;" and added, "Wilt not thou arise, O my son, and pass into the garden and solace thyself by looking at it and gladden thy heart?" "O my lord," said Nur al-Din, "to whom doth this garden belong?;" and the other replied, "O my son, I have inherited it from my folk." Now his object in saying this was to set them at their ease and induce them to enter the garden. So Nur al-Din thanked him and rose, he and the damsel, and followed him into the garden; and lo! it was a garden, and what a garden! The gate was arched like a great hall and over walls and roof ramped vines with grapes of many colours; the red like rubies and the black like ebonies; and beyond it lay a bower of trelliced boughs growing fruits single and composite, and small birds on branches sang with melodious recite, and the thousand-noted nightingale shrilled with her varied shright; the turtle with her cooing filled the site; the blackbird whistled like human wight and the ring-dove moaned like a drinker in grievous plight. The trees grew in perfection all edible growths and fruited all manner fruits which in pairs were bipartite; with the camphor- apricot, the almond-apricot and the apricot "Khorasani" hight; the plum, like the face of beauty, smooth and bright; the cherry that makes teeth shine clear by her sleight, and the fig of three colours, green, purple and white. There also blossomed the violet as it were sulphur on fire by night; the orange with buds like pink coral and marguerite; the rose whose redness gars the loveliest cheeks blush with despight; and myrtle and gilliflower and lavender with the blood-red anemone from Nu'uman hight. The leaves were all gemmed with tears the clouds had dight; the chamomile smiled showing teeth that bite, and Narcissus with his negro eyes fixed on Rose his sight; the citrons shone with fruits embowled and the lemons like balls of gold; earth was carpeted with flowers tinctured infinite; for Spring was come brightening the place with joy and delight; and the streams ran ringing, to the birds' gay singing, while the rustling breeze upspringing attempered the air to temperance exquisite. Shaykh Ibrahim carried them up into the pavilion, and they gazed on its beauty, and on the lamps aforementioned in the latticed windows; and Nur al-Din, remembering his entertainments of time past, cried, "By Allah, this is a pleasant place; it hath quenched in me anguish which burned as a fire of Ghaza-wood." Then they sat down and Shaykh Ibrahim set food before them; and they ate till they were satisfied and washed their hands: after which Nur al-Din went up to one of the latticed windows, and, calling to his handmaid fell to gazing on the trees laden with all manner fruits. Presently he turned to the Gardener and said to him, "O Shaykh Ibrahim hast thou no drink here, for folk are wont to drink after eating?" The Shaykh brought him sweet water, cool and pleasant, but he said, "This is not the kind of drink I wanted." "Perchance thou wishest for wine?" "Indeed I do, O Shaykh!" "I seek refuge from it with Allah: it is thirteen years since I did this thing, for the Prophet (Abhak) cursed its drinker, presser, seller and carrier!" "Hear two words of me." "Say on." "If yon cursed ass which standeth there be cursed, will aught of his curse alight upon thee?" "By no means!" "Then take this dinar and these two dirhams and mount yonder ass and, halting afar from the wine-shop, call the first man thou seest buying liquor and say to him, 'Take these two dirhams for thyself, and with this dinar buy me some wine and set it on the ass.' So shalt thou be neither the presser, nor the buyer, nor the carrier; and no part of the curse will fall upon thee." At this Shaykh Ibrahim laughed and said, "By Allah, O my son, I never saw one wilier of wit than thou art, nor heard aught sweeter than thy speech." So he did as he was bidden by Nur al-Din who thanked him and said, "We two are now dependent on thee, and it is only meet that thou comply with our wishes; so bring us here what we require." "O my son," replied he, "this is my buttery before thee" (and it was the store-room provided for the Commander of the Faithful); "so go in, and take whatso thou wilt, for there is over and above what thou wantest." Nur al-Din then entered the pantry and found therein vessels of gold and silver and crystal set with all kinds of gems, and was amazed and delighted with what he saw. Then he took out what he needed and set it on and poured the wine into flagons and glass ewers, whilst Shaykh Ibrahim brought them fruit and flowers and aromatic herbs. Then the old man withdrew and sat down at a distance from them, whilst they drank and made merry, till the wine got the better of them, so that their cheeks reddened and their eyes wantoned like the gazelle's; and their locks became dishevelled and their brightness became yet more beautiful. Then said Shaykh Ibrahim to himself, "What aileth me to sit apart from them? Why should I not sit with them? When shall I ever find myself in company with the like of these two that favour two moons?" So he stepped forward and sat down on the edge of the dais, and Nur al-Din said to him, "O my lord, my life on thee, come nearer to us!" He came and sat by them, when Nur al-Din filled a cup and looked towards the Shaykh and said to him, "Drink, that thou mayest try the taste of it!" "I take refuge from it with Allah!" replied he; "for thirteen years I have not done a thing of the kind." Nur al-Din feigned to forget he was there and, drinking off the cup, threw himself on the ground as if the drink had overcome him; whereupon Anis al-Jalis glanced at him and said, "O Shaykh Ibrahim see how this husband of mine treateth me;" and he answered, "O my lady, what aileth him?" "This is how he always serveth me," cried she, "he drinketh awhile, then falleth asleep and leaveth me alone with none to bear me company over my cup nor any to whom I may sing when the bowl goeth round." Quoth the Shaykh (and his mien unstiffened for that his soul inclined towards her), "By Allah, this is not well!" Then she crowned a cup and looking towards him said, "By my life thou must take and drink it, and not refuse to heal my sick heart!" So he put forth his hand and took it and drank it off and she filled a second and set it on the chandelier and said, "O master mine, there is still this one left for thee." "By Allah, I cannot drink it;" cried he, "what I have already drunk is enough for me;" but she rejoined, "By Allah, there is no help for it." So he took the cup and drank; and she filled him a third which he took and was about to drink when behold, Nur al-Din rolled round and sat upright, – And Shahrazad perceived the dawn of day and ceased saying her permitted say.

When it was the Thirty-seventh Night,

She said, it hath reached me, O auspicious King, that Nur al-Din sat upright and said, "Ho, Shaykh Ibrahim, what is this? Did I not adjure thee a while ago and thou refusedst, saying, 'What I! 'tis thirteen years ago since I have done such a thing!'" "By Allah," quoth the Shaykh (and indeed he was abashed), "no sin of mine this, she forced me to do it." Nur al-Din laughed and they sat down again to wine and wassail, but the damsel turned to her master and said in a whisper, "O my lord, drink and do not press him, that I may show thee some sport with him." Then she began to fill her master's cup and he hers and so they did time after time, till at last Shaykh Ibrahim looked at them and said, "What fashion of good fellowship is this? Allah curse the glutton who keepeth the cup to himself! Why dost thou not give me to drink, O my brother? What manners are these, O blessed one?" At this the two laughed until they fell on their backs; then they drank and gave him to drink and ceased not their carousal till a third part of the night was past. Then said the damsel, "O Shaykh Ibrahim, with thy leave I will get up and light one of these candles." "Do so," he replied, "but light no more than one." So she sprang to her feet and, beginning with one candle, lighted all the eighty and sat down again. Presently Nur al-Din said, "O Shaykh Ibrahim, in what favour am I with thee? May I not light one of these lamps?" "Light one," replied he, "and bother me no more in thy turn!" So he rose and lighted one lamp after another, till he had lighted the whole eight and the palace seemed to dance with brilliancy. Quoth the Shaykh (and indeed intoxication had overcome him), "Ye two are bolder than I am." Then he rose to his feet and opened all the lattices and sat down again; and they fell to carousing and reciting verses till the place rang with their noisy mirth. Now Allah, the Decreer who decreeth all things and who for every effect appointeth a cause, had so disposed that the Caliph was at that moment sitting in the light of the moon at one of the windows of his palace overlooking the Tigris. He saw the blaze of the lamps and wax candles reflected in the river and, lifting his eyes, perceived that it came from the Garden Palace which was all ablaze with brilliancy. So he cried, "Here to me with Ja'afar the Barmaki!"; and the last word was hardly spoken ere the Wazir was present before the Commander of the Faithful, who cried at him, "O dog of a Minister, hast thou taken from me this city of Baghdad without saying aught to me?" "What words are these words?" asked Ja'afar; and the Caliph answered, "If Baghdad city were not taken from me, the Palace of Pictures would not be illuminated with lamps and candles, nor would its windows be thrown open. Woe to thee! who durst do a deed like this except the Caliphate had been taken from me?" Quoth Ja'afar (and indeed his side-muscles trembled as he spoke), "Who told thee that the Palace of Pictures was illuminated and the windows thrown open?" "Come hither and see," replied the Caliph. Then Ja'afar came close to the Caliph and, looking towards the garden, saw the palace blazing with illumination that rayed through the gloom of the night; and, thinking that this might have been permitted by the keeper for some reason of his own, he wished to make an excuse for him; so quoth he, "O Commander of the Faithful, Shaykh Ibrahim said to me last week, 'O my lord Ja'afar, I much wish to circumcise my sons during the life of the Commander of the Faithful and thy life.' I asked, 'What dost thou want?'; and he answered, 'Get me leave from the Caliph to hold the festival in the Garden Palace.' So said I to him, 'Go circumcise them and I will see the Caliph and tell him.' Thereupon he went away and I forgot to let thee know." "O Ja'afar," said the Caliph, "thou hast committed two offences against me; first in that thou didst no report to me, secondly, thou didst not give him what he sought; for he came and told thee this only as excuse to ask for some small matter of money, to help him with the outlay; and thou gavest him nothing nor toldest me." "O Commander of the Faithful," said Ja'afar, "I forgot." "Now by the rights of my forefathers and the tombs of my forbears," quoth the Caliph, "I will not pass the rest of this night save in company with him; for truly he is a pious man who frequenteth the Elders of the Faith and the Fakirs and other religious mendicants and entertaineth them; doubtless they are not assembled together and it may be that the prayer of one of them will work us weal both in this world and in the next. Besides, my presence may profit and at any rate be pleasing to Shaykh Ibrahim." "O Commander of the Faithful," quoth Ja'afar, "the greater part of the night is passed, and at this time they will be breaking up." Quoth the Caliph, "It matters not: I needs must go to them." So Ja'afar held his peace, being bewildered and knowing not what to do. Then the Caliph rose to his feet and, taking with him Ja'afar and Masrur the eunuch sworder, the three disguised themselves in merchants' gear and leaving the City-palace, kept threading the streets till they reached the garden. The Caliph went up to the gate and finding it wide open, was surprised and said, "See, O Ja'afar, how Shaykh Ibrahim hath left the gate open at this hour contrary to his custom!" They went in and walked on till they came under the pavilion, when the Caliph said, "O Ja'afar, I wish to look in upon them unawares before I show myself, that I may see what they are about and get sight of the elders; for hitherto I have heard no sound from them, nor even a Fakir calling upon the name of Allah." Then he looked about and, seeing a tall walnut-tree, said to Ja'afar, "I will climb this tree, for its branches are near the lattices and so look in upon them." Thereupon he mounted the tree and ceased not climbing from branch to branch, till he reached a bough which was right opposite one of the windows, and here he took seat and looked inside the palace. He saw a damsel and a youth as they were two moons (glory be to Him who created them and fashioned them!), and by them Shaykh Ibrahim seated cup in hand and saying, "O Princess of fair ones, drinking without music is nothing worth; indeed I have heard a poet say,

> 'Round with bit and little, the bowl and cup,
> Take either than moon in his sheen hath crowned:
> Nor drink without music, for oft I've seen,
> The horse drink best to the whistle's sound!'"

When the Caliph saw this, the vein of wrath started up between his eyes and he came down and said to the Wazir, "O Ja'afar, never beheld I yet men of piety in such case; so do thou mount this tree and look upon them, lest the blessings of the blest be lost to thee." Ja'afar, hearing the words of the Commander of the Faithful and being confounded by them, climbed to the tree- top and looking in, saw Nur al-Din and the damsel, and Shaykh Ibrahim holding in his hand a brimming bowl. At this sight he made sure of death and, descending, stood before the Commander of the Faithful, who said to him, "O Ja'afar, praise be to Allah who hath made us of those that observe external ordinances of Holy Law and hath averted from us the sin of disguising ourselves after the manner of hypocrites!" But Ja'afar could not speak a word for excess of confusion; so the Caliph looked at him and said, "I wonder how they came hither, and who admitted them into my pavilion! But aught like the beauty of this youth and this damsel my eyes never yet saw!" "Thou sayest sooth, O our Lord the Sultan!" replied Ja'afar (and he hoped to propitiate the Caliph Harun al-Rashid). Then quoth the Caliph, "O Ja'afar, let us both mount the branch opposite the window, that we may amuse ourselves with looking at them." So the two climbed the tree and, peering in, heard Shaykh Ibrahim say, "O my lady, I have cast away all gravity mine by the drinking of wine, but 'tis not sweet save with the soft sounds of the lute-strings it combine." "By Allah," replied Anis al-Jalis, "O Shaykh Ibrahim, an we had but some instrument of music our joyance were complete." Hearing this he rose to his feet and the Caliph said to Ja'afar, "I wonder what he is about to do!" and Ja'afar answered, "I know not." The Shaykh disappeared and presently reappeared bringing a lute; and the Caliph took not of it and knew it for that of Abu Ishak the Cup-companion. "By Allah," said the Caliph, "if this damsel sing ill I will crucify all of you; but if she sing well I will forgive them and only gibbet thee." "O Allah cause her to sing vilely!" quoth Ja'afar. Asked the Caliph, "Why so?"; and he answered, "If thou crucify us all together, we shall keep one another company." The Caliph laughed at his speech. Presently the damsel took the lute and, after looking at it and tuning it, she played a measure which made all hearts yearn to her; then she sang these lines,

> "O ye that can aid me, a wretched lover,
> Whom longing burns nor can rest restore me!
> Though all you have done I have well deserved,
> I take refuge with you, so exult not o'er me:
> True, I am weak and low and vile,
> But I'll bear your will and whatso you bore me:

My death at your hands what brings it of glory?
I fear but your sin which of life forlore me!"

Quoth the Caliph, "By Allah, good! O Ja'afar, never in my life have I heard a voice so enchanting as this." "Then haply the Caliph's wrath hath passed away," said Ja'afar, and he replied, "Yes, 'tis gone." Thereupon they descended from the tree, and the Caliph said to Ja'afar, "I wish to go in and sit with them and hear the damsel sing before me." "O Commander of the Faithful," replied Ja'afar, "if thou go in to them they will be terribly troubled, and Shaykh Ibrahim will assuredly die of fright." But the Caliph answered, "O Ja'afar, thou must teach me some device wherewith to delude them and whereby I can foregather with them without their knowing me." So they walked towards the Tigris pondering the matter, and presently came upon a fisherman who stood fishing under the pavilion windows. Now some time before this, the Caliph (being in the pavilion) had called to Shaykh Ibrahim and asked him, "What noise is this I hear under the windows?" and he had answered, "It is voices of fisher folk catching fish:" so quoth the Caliph, "Go down and forbid them this place;" and he forbade them accordingly. However that night a fisherman named Karim, happening to pass by and seeing the garden gate open, said to himself, "This is a time of negligence; and I will take advantage of it to do a bit of fishing." So he took his net and cast it, but he had hardly done so when behold, the Caliph come up single-handed and, standing hard by, knew him and called aloud to him, "Ho, Karim!" The fisherman, hearing himself named, turned round, and seeing the Caliph, trembled and his side-muscles quivered, as he cried, "By Allah, O Commander of the Faithful, I did it not in mockery of the mandate; but poverty and a large family drove me to what thou seest!" Quoth the Caliph, "Make a cast in my name." At this the fisherman was glad and going to the bank threw his net, then waiting till it had spread out at full stretch and settled down, hauled it up and found in it various kinds of fish. The Caliph was pleased and said, "O Karim, doff thy habit." So he put off a gaberdine of coarse woollen stuff patched in an hundred places whereon the lice were rampant, and a turband which had never been untwisted for three years but to which he had sown every rag he came upon. The Caliph also pulled off his person two vests of Alexandrian and Ba'lbak silk, a loose inner robe and a long-sleeved outer coat, and said to the fisherman, "Take them and put them on," while he assumed the foul gaberdine and filthy turband and drew a corner of the head-cloth as a mouth-veil before his face. Then said he to the fisherman, "Get thee about thy business!; and the man kissed the Caliph's feet and thanked him and improvised the following couplets,

"Thou hast granted more favours than ever I craved;
Thou hast satisfied needs which my heart enslaved:
I will thank thee and thank whileas life shall last,
And my bones will praise thee in grave engraved!"

Hardly had the fisherman ended his verse, when the lice began to crawl over the Caliph's skin, and he fell to catching them on his neck with his right and left and throwing them from him, while he cried, "O fisherman, woe to thee! what be this abundance of lice on thy gaberdine." "O my lord," replied he, "they may annoy thee just at first, but before a week is past thou wilt not feel them nor think of them." The

Caliph laughed and said to him, "Out on thee! Shall I leave this gaberdine of thine so long on my body?" Quoth the fisherman, "I would say a word to thee but I am ashamed in presence of the Caliph!"; and quoth he, "Say what thou hast to say." "It passed through my thought, O Commander of the Faithful," said the fisherman, "that, since thou wishest to learn fishing so thou mayest have in hand an honest trade whereby to gain thy livelihood, this my gaberdine besitteth thee right well." The Commander of the Faithful laughed at this speech, and the fisherman went his way. Then the Caliph took up the basket of fish and, strewing a little green grass over it, carried it to Ja'afar and stood before him. Ja'afar thinking him to be Karim the fisherman feared for him and said, "O Karim, what brought thee hither? Flee for thy life, for the Caliph is in the garden to-night and, if he see thee, thy neck is gone." At this the Caliph laughed and Ja'afar recognized him and asked, "Can it be thou, our lord the Sultan?"; and he answered, "Yes, O Ja'afar, and thou art my Wazir and I and thou came hither together; yet thou knowest me not; so how should Shaykh Ibrahim know me, and he drunk? Stay here, till I came back to thee." "To hear is to obey," said Ja'afar. Then the Caliph went up to the door of the pavilion and knocked a gentle knock, whereupon said Nur al-Din," O Shaykh Ibrahim, some one taps at the door." "Who goes there?" cried the Shaykh and the Caliph replied, "It is I, O Shaykh Ibrahim!" "Who art thou," quoth he, and quoth the other, "I am Karim the fisherman: I hear thou hast a feast, so I have brought thee some fish, and of a truth 'tis good fish." When Nur al-Din heard the mention of fish, he was glad, he and the damsel, and they both said to the Shaykh, "O our lord, open the door and let him bring us his fish." So Shaykh Ibrahim opened and the Caliph came in (and he in fisherman guise), and began by saluting them. Said Shaykh Ibrahim, "Welcome to the blackguard, the robber, the dicer! Let us see thy fish." So the Caliph showed them his catch and behold, the fishes were still alive and jumping, whereupon the damsel exclaimed, "By Allah! O my lord, these are indeed fine fish: would they were fried!" and Shaykh Ibrahim rejoined, "By Allah, O my lady, thou art right." Then said he to the Caliph, "O fisherman, why didst thou not bring us the fish ready fried? Up now and cook them and bring them back to us." "On my head be thy commands!" said the Caliph, "I will fry thee a dish and bring it." Said they, "Look sharp." Thereupon he went and ran till he came up to Ja'afar when he called to him, "Hallo, Ja'afar!"; and he replied, "Here am I, O Commander of the Faithful, is all well?" "They want the fish fried," said the Caliph, and Ja'afar answered, "O Commander of the Faithful, give it to me and I'll fry it for them." "By the tombs of my forbears," quoth the Caliph, "none shall fry it but I, with mine own hand!" So he went to the gardener's hut, where he searched and found all that he required, even to salt and saffron and wild marjoram and else besides. Then he turned to the brasier and, setting on the frying-pan, fried a right good fry. When it was done, he laid it on a banana-leaf, and gathering from the garden wind-fallen fruits, limes and lemons, carried the fish to the pavilion and set the dish before them. So the youth and the damsel and Shaykh Ibrahim came forward and ate; after which they washed their hands and Nur al-Din said to the Caliph, "By Allah, O fisherman, thou hast done us a right good deed this night." Then he put hand in pouch and, taking out three of the dinars which Sanjar had given him, said, "O fisherman, excuse me. By Allah had I known thee before that which hath lately befallen me, I had done away the bitterness of poverty from thy heart; but take thou this as the best I can do for thee." Then he threw the gold pieces to the Caliph, who took them and kissed them and put them in pouch. Now his sole object in doing all this was to hear the damsel sing; so he said to Nur al-Din, "Thou hast rewarded me most liberally, but I beg of thy boundless bounty that thou let this damsel sing an air, that I may hear her." So Nur al- Din said, "O Anis al-Jalis!" and she answered "Yes!" and he continued, "By my life, sing us something for the sake of this fisherman who wisheth so much to hear thee." Thereupon she took the lute and struck the strings, after she had screwed them tight and tuned them, and sang these improvised verses,

> *"The fawn of a maid bent her lute in hand*
> *And her music made us right mettlesome:*
> *For her song gave hearing to ears stone-deaf,*
> *While Brava! Brava! exclaimed the dumb."*

Then she played again and played so ravishingly, that she charmed their wits and burst out improvising and singing these couplets,

> *"You have honoured us visiting this our land,*
> *And your splendour illumined the glooms that blent:*
> *So 'tis due that for you I perfume my place*
> *With rose-water, musk and the camphor-scent!"*

Hereupon the Caliph was agitated, and emotion so overpowered him that he could not command himself for excess of pleasure, and he exclaimed, "By Allah, good! by Allah, good! by Allah, good!" Asked Nur al-Din, "O fisherman, doth this damsel please thee?" and the Caliph answered, "Ay, by Allah!" Whereupon said Nur al-Din, "She is a gift to thee, a gift of the generous who repenteth him not of his givings and who will never revoke his gift!" Then he sprang to his feet and, taking a loose robe, threw it over the fisherman and bade him receive the damsel and be gone. But she looked at him and said, "O my lord, art thou faring forth without farewell? If it must be so, at least stay till I bid thee good-bye and make known my case." And she began versifying in these verses,

> *"When love and longing and regret are mine,*
> *Must not this body show of ills a sign?*
> *My love! say not, 'Thou soon shalt be consoled';*
> *When state speaks state none shall allay my pine.*
> *If living man could swim upon his tears,*
> *I first should float on waters of these eyne:*
> *O thou, who in my heart infusedst thy love,*
> *As water mingles in the cup with wine,*
> *This was the fear I feared, this parting blow.*
> *O thou whose love my heart-core ne'er shall tyne!*
> *O Bin Khákán! my sought, my hope, my will,*
> *O thou whose love this breast make wholly thine!*
> *Against thy lord the King thou sinn'dst for me,*
> *And winnedst exile in lands peregrine:*
> *Allah ne'er make my lord repent my loss*
> *To cream o' men thou gavest me, one right digne."*

When she had ended her verses, Nur al-Din answered her with these lines,

> *"She bade me farewell on our parting day,*
> *And she wept in the fire of our bane and pains:*
> *'What wilt thou do when fro' thee I'm gone?'*
> *Quoth I, 'say this to whom life remains!'"*

When the Caliph heard her saying in her verse,

> *"To Karim, the cream of men thou gavest me;"*

his inclination for her redoubled and it seemed a hard matter and a grievous to part them; so quoth he to the youth, "O my lord, truly the damsel said in her verses that thou didst transgress against her master and him who owned her; so tell me, against whom didst thou transgress and who is it hath a claim on thee?" "By Allah, O fisherman," replied Nur al-Din, "there befel me and this damsel a wondrous tale and a marvellous matter: an 't were graven with needle-gravers on the eye-corners it would be a warner to whoso would be warned." Cried the Caliph, "Wilt thou not tell me thy story and acquaint me with thy case? Haply it may bring thee relief, for Allah's aid is ever nearhand." "O fisherman," said Nur al-Din, "Wilt thou hear our history in verse or in prose?" "Prose is a wordy thing, but verses," rejoined the Caliph, "are pearls on string." Then Nur al-Din bowed his head, and made these couplets,

> *"O my friend! reft of rest no repose I command,*
> *And my grief is redoubled in this far land:*
> *Erst I had a father, a kinder ne'er was;*
> *But he died and to Death paid the deodand:*
> *When he went from me, every matter went wrong*
> *Till my heart was nigh-broken, my nature unmanned:*
> *He bought me a handmaid, a sweeting who shamed*
> *A wand of the willow by Zephyr befanned:*
> *I lavisht upon her mine heritage,*
> *And spent like a nobleman puissant and grand:*
> *Then to sell her compelled, my sorrow increased;*
> *The parting was sore but I mote not gainstand:*
> *Now as soon as the crier had called her, there bid*
> *A wicked old fellow, a fiery brand:*
> *So I raged with a rage that I could not restrain,*
> *And snatched her from out of his hireling's hand;*
> *When the angry curmudgeon made ready for blows,*
> *And the fire of a fight kindled he and his band,*
> *I smote him in fury with right and with left,*
> *And his hide, till well satisfied, curried and tanned:*
> *Then in fear I fled forth and lay hid in my house,*
> *To escape from the snares which my foeman had spanned:*
> *So the King of the country proclaimed my arrest;*
> *When access to me a good Chamberlain fand:*

And warned me to flee from the city afar,
Disappear, disappoint what my enemies planned:
Then we fled from our home 'neath the wing of the night,
And sought us a refuge by Baghdad strand:
Of my riches I've nothing on thee to bestow,
O Fisher, except the fair gift thou hast scanned:
The loved of my soul, and when I from her part,
Know for sure that I give thee the blood of my heart."

When he had ended his verse, the Caliph said to him, "O my lord Nur al-Din, explain to me thy case more fully," So he told him the whole story from beginning to end, and the Caliph said to him, "Whither dost thou now intend?" "Allah's world is wide," replied he. Quoth the Caliph, "I will write thee a letter to carry to the Sultan Mohammed bin Sulayman al-Zayni, which when he readeth, he will not hurt nor harm thee in aught." – -And Shahrazad perceived the dawn of day and ceased saying her permitted say.

When it was the Thirty-eighth Night, she continued, It hath reached me, O auspicious King, that when the Caliph said to Nur al-Din Ali, "I will write thee a letter to carry to the Sultan Mohammed bin Sulayman al-Zayni, which when he readeth, he will not hurt nor harm thee in aught," Nur al-Din asked "What! is there in the world a fisherman who writeth to Kings? Such a thing can never be!"; and the Caliph answered, "Thou sayest sooth, but I will tell thee the reason. Know that I and he learnt in the same school under one schoolmaster, and that I was his monitor. Since that time Fortune befriended him and he is become a Sultan, while Allah hath abased me and made me a fisherman; yet I never send to him to ask aught but he doeth my desire; nay, though I should ask of him a thousand favours every day, he would comply." When Nur al-Din heard this he said, "Good! write that I may see." So the Caliph took ink-case and reed-pen and wrote as follows, – "In the name of Allah, the Compassionating, the Compassionate! But after. This letter is written by Harun al-Rashid, son of Al-Mahdi, to his highness Mohammed bin Sulayman al-Zayni, whom I have encompassed about with my favour and made my viceroy in certain of my dominions. The bearer of these presents is Nur al-Din Ali, son of Fazl bin Khákán the Wazir. As soon as they come to thy hand divest thyself forthright of the kingly dignity and invest him therewith; so oppose not my commandment and peace be with thee." He gave the letter to Nur al-Din, who took it and kissed it, then put it in his turband and set out at once on his journey. So far concerning him; but as regards the Caliph, Shaykh Ibrahim stared to him (and he still in fisher garb) and said, "O vilest of fishermen, thou hast brought us a couple of fish worth a score of half-dirhams, and hast gotten three dinars for them; and thinkest thou to take the damsel to boot?" When the Caliph heard this, he cried out at him, and signed to Masrur who discovered himself and rushed in upon him. Now Ja'afar had sent one of the gardener-lads to the doorkeeper of the palace to fetch a suit of royal raiment for the Prince of the Faithful; so the man went and, returning with the suit, kissed the ground before the Caliph and gave it him. Then he threw of the clothes he had on and donned kingly apparel. Shaykh Ibrahim was still sitting upon his chair and the Caliph tarried to behold what would come next. But seeing the Fisherman become the Caliph, Shaykh Ibrahim was utterly confounded and he could do nothing but bite his finger- ends and say, "Would I knew whether am I asleep or am I awake!" At last the Caliph looked at him and cried, "O Shaykh Ibrahim, what state is this in which I see thee?" Thereupon he recovered from his drunkenness and, throwing himself upon the ground, repeated these verses,

> *"Pardon the sinful ways I did pursue;*
> *Ruth from his lord to every slave is due:*
> *Confession pays the fine that sin demands;*
> *Where, then, is that which grace and mercy sue?"*

The Caliph forgave him and bade carry the damsel to the city- palace, where he set apart for her an apartment and appointed slaves to serve her, saying to her, "Know that we have sent thy lord to be Sultan in Bassorah and, Almighty Allah willing, we will dispatch him the dress of investiture and thee with it." Meanwhile, Nur al-Din Ali ceased not travelling till he reached Bassorah, where he repaired to the Sultan's palace and he shouted a long shout. The Sultan heard him and sent for him; and when he came into his presence, he kissed the ground between his hands and, producing the letter, presented it to him. Seeing the superscription in the writing of the Commander of the Faithful, the Sultan rose to his feet and kissed it three times; and after reading it said, "I hear and I obey Allah Almighty and the Commander of the Faithful!" Then he summoned the four Kazis and the Emirs and was about to divest himself of the rule royal, when behold, in came Al Mu'ín bin Sáwí. The Sultan gave him the Caliph's letter and he read it, then tore it to pieces and putting it into his mouth, chewed it and spat it out. "Woe to thee," quoth the Sultan (and indeed he was sore angered); "what induced thee to do this deed?" "Now by thy life! O our lord the Sultan," replied Mu'ín, "this man hath never foregathered with the Caliph nor with his Wazir; but he is a gallows-bird, a limb of Satan, a knave who, having come upon a written paper in the Caliph's hand, some idle scroll, hath made it serve his own end. The Caliph would surely not send him to take the Sultanate from thee without the imperial autograph and the diploma of investiture, and he certainly would have despatched with him a Chamberlain or a Minister. But he hath come alone and he never came from the Caliph, no, never! never! never!" "What is to be done?" asked the Sultan, and the Minister answered, "Leave him to me and I will take him and keep him away from thee, and send him in charge of a Chamberlain to Baghdad-city. Then, if what he says be sooth, they will bring us back autograph and investiture; and if not, I will take my due out of this debtor." When the Sultan heard the Minister's words he said, "Hence with thee and him too." Al Mu'ín took trust of him from the King and, carrying him to his own house, cried out to his pages who laid him flat and beat him till he fainted. Then he let put upon his feet heavy shackles and carried him to the jail, where he called the jailor, one Kutayt, who came and kissed the ground before him. Quoth the Wazir, "O Kutayt, I wish thee to take this fellow and throw him into one of the underground cells in the prison and torture him night and day." "To hear is to obey," replied the jailor and, taking Nur al-Din into the prison, locked the door upon him. Then he gave orders to sweep a bench behind the door and, spreading on it a sitting-rug and a leather-cloth, seated Nur al-Din thereon and loosed his shackles and entreated him kindly. The Wazir sent every day enjoining the jailor to beat him, but he abstained from this, and so continued to do for forty days. On the forty-first day there came a present from the Caliph; which when the Sultan saw, it pleased him and he consulted his Ministers on the matter, when one of them said, "Perchance this present was for the new Sultan." Cried Al-Mu'ín, "We should have done well had we put him to death at his first coming;" and the Sultan cried "By Allah, thou hast reminded me of him! Go down to the prison and fetch him, and I will strike off his head." "To hear is to obey," replied Al-Mu'ín: then he stood up and said, "I will make proclamation in the city: Whoso would solace himself with seeing the beheading of Nur al-Din bin al-Fazl bin Khákán, let him repair to the palace! So follower and followed, great and small will flock to the spectacle, and I shall heal my heart and harm my foe." "Do as thou wilt," said the Sultan. The Wazir went off (and he was glad and gay), and ordered the Chief of Police to make the afore-mentioned proclamation. When the people heard the crier, they all sorrowed and wept, even the little ones at school and the traders in their shops; and some strove to get places for seeing the sight, whilst others went to the prison with the object of escorting him thence. Presently, the Wazir came with ten Mamelukes to the jail and Kutayt the jailor asked him, "Whom seekest thou, O our lord the Wazir?"; whereto he answered, "Bring me out that gallows- bird." But the jailor said, "He is in the sorriest of plights for the much beating I have given him." Then he went into the prison and found Nur al-Din repeating these verses,

> "Who shall support me in calamities,
> When fail all cures and greater cares arise?
> Exile hath worm my heart, my vitals torn;
> The World to foes hath turned my firm allies.
> O folk, will not one friend amidst you all
> Wail o'er my woes, and cry to hear my cries?
> Death and it agonies seem light to me,
> Since life has lost all joys and jollities:
> O Lord of Mustafa, that Science-sea,
> Sole Intercessor, Guide all-ware, all-wise!
> I pray thee free me and my fault forego,
> And from me drive mine evil and my woe."

The jailor stripped off his clean clothes and, dressing him in two filthy vests, carried him to the Wazir. Nur al-Din looked at him and saw it was his foe that sought to compass his death; so he wept and said, "Art thou, then, so secure against the World? Hast thou not heard the saying of the poet,

> 'Kisras and Caesars in a bygone day
> Stored wealth; where it is, and ah! where are they?'

O Wazir," he continued, "know that Allah (be He extolled and exalted!) will do whatso He will!" "O Ali," replied he, "thinkest thou to frighten me with such talk? I mean this very day to smite thy neck despite the noses of the Bassorah folk and I care not; let the days do as they please; nor will I turn me to thy counsel but rather to what the poet saith,

> 'Leave thou the days to breed their ban and bate,
> And make thee strong t' upbear the weight of Fate.'

And also how excellently saith another,
'Whoso shall see the death-day of his foe,
One day surviving, wins his bestest wish.'

Then he ordered his attendants to mount Nur al-Din upon the bare back of a mule; and they said to the youth (for truly it was irksome to them), "Let us stone him and cut him down thou our lives go for it." But Nur al-Din said to them, "Do not so: have ye not heard the saying of the poet,

'Needs must I bear the term by Fate decreed,
And when that day be dead needs must I die:
If lions dragged me to their forest-lair,
Safe should I live till draw my death-day nigh.'

Then they proceeded to proclaim before Nur al-Din, "This is the least of the retribution for him who imposeth upon Kings with forgeries." And they ceased not parading him round about Bassorah, till they made him stand beneath the palace-windows and set him upon the leather of blood, and the sworder came up to him and said, "O my lord, I am but a slave commanded in this matter: an thou have any desire, tell it me that I may fulfil it, for now there remaineth of they life only so much as may be till the Sultan shall put his face out of the lattice." Thereupon Nur al-Din looked to the right and to the left, and before him and behind him and began improvising,

"The sword, the sworder and the blood-skin waiting me I sight,
And cry, Alack, mine evil fate! ah, my calamity!
How is't I see no loving friend with eye of sense or soul?
What! no one here? I cry to all: will none reply to me?
The time is past that formed my life, my death term draweth nigh,
Will no man win the grace of God showing me clemency;
And look with pity on my state, and clear my dark despair,
E'en with a draught of water dealt to cool death's agony?"

The people fell to weeping over him; and the headsman rose and brought him a draught of water; but the Wazir sprang up from his place and smote the gugglet with his hand and broke it: then he cried out at the executioner and bade him strike off Nur al-Din's head. So he bound the eyes of the doomed man and folk clamoured at the Wazir and loud wailings were heard and much questioning of man and man. At this moment behold, rose a dense dust-cloud filling sky and wold; and when the Sultan, who was sitting in the palace, descried this, he said to his suite, "Go and see what yon cloud bringeth:" Replied Al Mu'ín, "Not till we have smitten this fellow's neck;" but the Sultan said, "Wait ye till we see what this meaneth." Now the dust-cloud was the dust of J'afar the Barmecide, Wazir to the Caliph, and his host; and the cause of his coming was as follows. The Caliph passed thirty days without calling to mind the matter of Nur al-Din Ali, and none reminded him of it, till one night, as he passed by the chamber of Anis al-Jalis, he heard her weeping and singing with a soft sweet voice these lines of the poet,

"In thought I see thy form when farthest far or nearest near;
And on my tongue there dwells a name which man shall ne'er unhear."

Then her weeping redoubled; when lo! the Caliph opened the door and, entering the chamber, found Anis al-Jalis in tears. When she saw him she fell to the ground and kissing his feet three times repeated these lines,

> *"O fertile root and noble growth of trunk;*
> *Ripe-fruitful branch of never sullied race;*
> *I mind thee of what pact thy bounty made;*
> *Far be 't from thee thou should'st forget my case!"*

Quoth the Caliph, "Who art thou?" and she replied, "I am she whom Ali bin Khákán gave thee in gift, and I wish the fulfilment of thy promise to send me to him with the robe of honour; for I have now been thirty days without tasting the food of sleep." Thereupon the Caliph sent for Ja'afar and said to him, "O Ja'afar, 'tis thirty days since we have had news of Nur al-Din bin Khákán, and I cannot suppose that the Sultan hath slain him; but, by the life of my head and by the sepulchres of my forefathers, if aught of foul play hath befallen him, I will surely make an end of him who was the cause of it, though he be the dearest of all men to myself! So I desire that thou set out for Bassorah within this hour and bring me tidings of my cousin, King Mohammed bin Sulayman al-Zayni, and how he had dealt with Nur al-Din Ali bin Khákán;" adding, "If thou tarry longer on the road than shall suffice for the journey, I will strike off they head. Furthermore, do thou tell the son of my uncle the whole story of Nur al-Din, and how I sent him with my written orders; and if thou find, O my cousin, that the King hath done otherwise than as I commanded, bring him and the Wazir Al-Mu'ín bin Sáwí to us in whatsoever guise thou shalt find them." "Hearing and obedience," replied Ja'afar and, making ready on the instant, he set out for Bassorah where the news of his coming had foregone him and had reached to the ears of King Mohammed. When Ja'afar arrived and saw the crushing and crowding of the lieges, he asked, "What means all this gathering?" so they told him what was doing in the matter of Nur al-Din; whereupon he hastened to go to the Sultan and saluting him, acquainted him with the cause why he came and the Caliph's resolve, in case of any foul play having befallen the youth, to put to death whoso should have brought it about. Then he took into custody the King and the Wazir and laid them in ward and, giving order for the release of Nur al-Din Ali, enthroned him as Sultan in the stead of Mohammed bin Sulayman. After this Ja'afar abode three days in Bassorah, the usual guest-time, and on the morning of the fourth day, Nur al-Din Ali turned to him and said, "I long for the sight of the Commander of the Faithful." Then said Ja'afar to Mohammed bin Sulayman, "Make ready to travel, for we will say the dawn-prayer and mount Baghdad-wards;" and he replied, "To hear is to obey." Then they prayed and they took horse and set out, all of them, carrying with them the Wazir, Al-Mu'ín bin Sáwí, who began to repent him of what he had done. Nur al-Din rode by Ja'afar's side and they stinted not faring on till they arrived at Baghdad, the House of Peace, and going in to the Caliph told him how they had found Nur al-Din nigh upon death. Thereupon the Caliph said to the youth, "Take this sword and smite with it the neck of thine enemy." So he took the sword from his hand and stepped up to Al-Mu'ín who looked at him and said, "I did according to my mother's milk, do thou according to thine." Upon this Nur al-Din cast the sword from his hand and said to the Caliph, "O Commander of the Faithful, he hath beguiled me with his words;" and he repeated this couplet,

"By craft and sleight I snared him when he came;
A few fair words aye trap the noble-game!"

"Leave him then," cried the Caliph and, turning to Masrur said, "Rise thou and smite his neck." So Masrur drew his sword and struck off his head. Then quoth the Caliph to Nur al-Din Ali, "Ask a boon of me." "O my lord," answered he, "I have no need of the Kingship of Bassorah; my sole desire is to be honoured by serving thee and by seeing the countenance." "With love and gladness," said the Caliph. Then he sent for the damsel, Anis al-Jalis, and bestowed plentiful favours upon them both and gave them one of his palaces in Baghdad, and assigned stipends and allowances, and made Nur al-Din Ali bin Fazl bin Khákán, one of his cup-companions; and he abode with the Commander of the Faithful enjoying the pleasantest of lives till death overtook him.

The Little Hunchback

Andrew and Nora Lang

IN THE KINGDOM of Kashgar, which is, as everybody knows, situated on the frontiers of Great Tartary, there lived long ago a tailor and his wife who loved each other very much. One day, when the tailor was hard at work, a little hunchback came and sat at the entrance of the shop, and began to sing and play his tambourine. The tailor was amused with the antics of the fellow, and thought he would take him home to divert his wife. The hunchback having agreed to his proposal, the tailor closed his shop and they set off together.

When they reached the house they found the table ready laid for supper, and in a very few minutes all three were sitting before a beautiful fish which the tailor's wife had cooked with her own hands. But unluckily, the hunchback happened to swallow a large bone, and, in spite of all the tailor and his wife could do to help him, died of suffocation in an instant. Besides being very sorry for the poor man, the tailor and his wife were very much frightened on their own account, for if the police came to hear of it the worthy couple ran the risk of being thrown into prison for wilful murder. In order to prevent this dreadful calamity they both set about inventing some plan which would throw suspicion on some one else, and at last they made up their minds that they could do no better than select a Jewish doctor who lived close by as the author of the crime. So the tailor picked up the hunchback by his head while his wife took his feet and carried him to the doctor's house. Then they knocked at the door, which opened straight on to a steep staircase. A servant soon appeared, feeling her way down the dark staircase and inquired what they wanted.

"Tell your master," said the tailor, "that we have brought a very sick man for him to cure; and," he added, holding out some money, "give him this in advance, so that he may not feel he is wasting his time." The servant remounted the stairs to give the message to the doctor, and the moment she was out of sight the tailor and his wife carried the body swiftly after her, propped it up at the top of the staircase, and ran home as fast as their legs could carry them.

Now the doctor was so delighted at the news of a patient (for he was young, and had not many of them), that he was transported with joy.

"Get a light," he called to the servant, "and follow me as fast as you can!" and rushing out of his room he ran towards the staircase. There he nearly fell over the body of the hunchback, and without knowing what it was gave it such a kick that it rolled right to the bottom, and very nearly dragged the doctor after it. "A light! a light!" he cried again, and when it was brought and he saw what he had done he was almost beside himself with terror.

"Holy Moses!" he exclaimed, "why did I not wait for the light? I have killed the sick man whom they brought me; and if the sacred Ass of Esdras does not come to my aid I am lost! It will not be long before I am led to jail as a murderer."

Agitated though he was, and with reason, the doctor did not forget to shut the house door, lest some passers-by might chance to see what had happened. He then took up the corpse and carried it into his wife's room, nearly driving her crazy with fright.

"It is all over with us!" she wailed, "if we cannot find some means of getting the body out of the house. Once let the sun rise and we can hide it no longer! How were you driven to commit such a terrible crime?"

"Never mind that," returned the doctor, "the thing is to find a way out of it."

For a long while the doctor and his wife continued to turn over in their minds a way of escape, but could not find any that seemed good enough. At last the doctor gave it up altogether and resigned himself to bear the penalty of his misfortune.

But his wife, who had twice his brains, suddenly exclaimed, "I have thought of something! Let us carry the body on the roof of the house and lower it down the chimney of our neighbour the Mussulman." Now this Mussulman was employed by the Sultan, and furnished his table with oil and butter. Part of his house was occupied by a great storeroom, where rats and mice held high revel.

The doctor jumped at his wife's plan, and they took up the hunchback, and passing cords under his armpits they let him down into the purveyor's bed-room so gently that he really seemed to be leaning against the wall. When they felt he was touching the ground they drew up the cords and left him.

Scarcely had they got back to their own house when the purveyor entered his room. He had spent the evening at a wedding feast, and had a lantern in his hand. In the dim light it cast he was astonished to see a man standing in his chimney, but being naturally courageous he seized a stick and made straight for the supposed thief. "Ah!" he cried, "so it is you, and not the rats and mice, who steal my butter. I'll take care that you don't want to come back!"

So saying he struck him several hard blows. The corpse fell on the floor, but the man only redoubled his blows, till at length it occurred to him it was odd that the thief should lie so still and make no resistance. Then, finding he was quite dead, a cold fear took possession of him. "Wretch that I am," said he, "I have murdered a man. Ah, my revenge has gone too far. Without the help of Allah I am undone! Cursed be the goods which have led me to my ruin." And already he felt the rope round his neck.

But when he had got over the first shock he began to think of some way out of the difficulty, and seizing the hunchback in his arms he carried him out into the street, and leaning him against the wall of a shop he stole back to his own house, without once looking behind him.

A few minutes before the sun rose, a rich Christian merchant, who supplied the palace with all sorts of necessaries, left his house, after a night of feasting, to go to the bath. Though he was very drunk, he was yet sober enough to know that the dawn was at hand, and that all good Mussulmen would shortly be going to prayer. So he hastened his steps lest he should meet some one on his way to the mosque, who, seeing his condition, would send him to prison as a drunkard. In his haste he jostled against the hunchback, who fell heavily upon him, and the merchant, thinking he was being attacked by a thief, knocked him down with one blow of his fist. He then called loudly for help, beating the fallen man all the while.

The chief policeman of the quarter came running up, and found a Christian ill-treating a Mussulman. "What are you doing?" he asked indignantly.

"He tried to rob me," replied the merchant, "and very nearly choked me."

"Well, you have had your revenge," said the man, catching hold of his arm. "Come, be off with you!"

As he spoke he held out his hand to the hunchback to help him up, but the hunchback never moved. "Oho!" he went on, looking closer, "so this is the way a Christian has the impudence to treat a Mussulman!" and seizing the merchant in a firm grasp he took him to the inspector of police, who threw him into prison till the judge should be out of bed and ready to attend to his case. All this brought the merchant to his senses, but the more he thought of it the less he could understand how the hunchback could have died merely from the blows he had received.

The merchant was still pondering on this subject when he was summoned before the chief of police and questioned about his crime, which he could not deny. As the hunchback was one of the Sultan's private jesters, the chief of police resolved to defer sentence of death until he had consulted his master. He went to the palace to demand an audience, and told his story to the Sultan, who only answered,

"There is no pardon for a Christian who kills a Mussulman. Do your duty."

So the chief of police ordered a gallows to be erected, and sent criers to proclaim in every street in the city that a Christian was to be hanged that day for having killed a Mussulman.

When all was ready the merchant was brought from prison and led to the foot of the gallows. The executioner knotted the cord firmly round the unfortunate man's neck and was just about to swing him into the air, when the Sultan's purveyor dashed through the crowd, and cried, panting, to the hangman,

"Stop, stop, don't be in such a hurry. It was not he who did the murder, it was I."

The chief of police, who was present to see that everything was in order, put several questions to the purveyor, who told him the whole story of the death of the hunchback, and how he had carried the body to the place where it had been found by the Christian merchant.

"You are going," he said to the chief of police, "to kill an innocent man, for it is impossible that he should have murdered a creature who was dead already. It is bad enough for me to have slain a Mussulman without having it on my conscience that a Christian who is guiltless should suffer through my fault."

Now the purveyor's speech had been made in a loud voice, and was heard by all the crowd, and even if he had wished it, the chief of police could not have escaped setting the merchant free.

"Loose the cords from the Christian's neck," he commanded, turning to the executioner, "and hang this man in his place, seeing that by his own confession he is the murderer."

The hangman did as he was bid, and was tying the cord firmly, when he was stopped by the voice of the Jewish doctor beseeching him to pause, for he had something very important to say. When he had fought his way through the crowd and reached the chief of police,

"Worshipful sir," he began, "this Mussulman whom you desire to hang is unworthy of death; I alone am guilty. Last night a man and a woman who were strangers to me knocked at my door, bringing with them a patient for me to cure. The servant opened it, but having no light was hardly able to make out their faces, though she readily agreed to wake me and to hand me the fee for my services. While she was telling me her story they seem to have carried the sick man to the top of the staircase and then left him there. I jumped up in a hurry without waiting for a lantern, and in the darkness I fell against something, which tumbled headlong down the stairs and never stopped till it reached the bottom. When I examined the body I found it was quite dead, and the corpse was that of a hunchback Mussulman. Terrified at what we had done, my wife and I took the body on the roof and let it down the chimney of our neighbour the purveyor, whom you were just about to hang. The purveyor, finding him in his room, naturally thought he was a thief, and struck him such a blow that the man fell down and lay motionless on the floor. Stooping to examine him, and finding him stone dead, the purveyor supposed that the man had died from the blow he had received; but of course this was a mistake, as you will see from my account, and I only am the murderer; and although I am innocent of any wish to commit a crime, I must suffer for it all the same, or else have the blood of two Musselmans on my conscience. Therefore send away this man, I pray you, and let me take his place, as it is I who am guilty."

On hearing the declaration of the Jewish doctor, the chief of police commanded that he should be led to the gallows, and the Sultan's purveyor go free. The cord was placed round the Jew's neck, and his feet had already ceased to touch the ground when the voice of the tailor was heard beseeching the executioner to pause one moment and to listen to what he had to say.

"Oh, my lord," he cried, turning to the chief of police, "how nearly have you caused the death of three innocent people! But if you will only have the patience to listen to my tale, you shall know who is the real culprit. If some one has to suffer, it must be me! Yesterday, at dusk, I was working in my shop with a light heart when the little hunchback, who was more than half drunk, came and sat in the doorway. He sang me several songs, and then I invited him to finish the evening at my house. He accepted my invitation, and we went away together. At supper I helped him to a slice of fish, but in eating it a bone stuck in his throat, and in spite of all we could do he died in a few minutes. We felt deeply sorry for his death, but fearing lest we should be held responsible, we carried the corpse to the house of the Jewish doctor. I knocked, and desired the servant to beg her master to come down as fast as possible and see a sick man whom we had brought for him to cure; and in order to hasten his movements I placed a piece of money in her hand as the doctor's fee. Directly she had disappeared I dragged the body to the top of the stairs, and then hurried away with my wife back to our house. In descending the stairs the doctor accidentally knocked over the corpse, and finding him dead believed that he himself was the murderer. But now you know the truth set him free, and let me die in his stead."

The chief of police and the crowd of spectators were lost in astonishment at the strange events to which the death of the hunchback had given rise.

"Loosen the Jewish doctor," said he to the hangman, "and string up the tailor instead, since he has made confession of his crime. Really, one cannot deny that this is a very singular story, and it deserves to be written in letters of gold."

The executioner speedily untied the knots which confined the doctor, and was passing the cord round the neck of the tailor, when the Sultan of Kashgar, who had missed his jester, happened to make inquiry of his officers as to what had become of him.

"Sire," replied they, "the hunchback having drunk more than was good for him, escaped from the palace and was seen wandering about the town, where this morning he was found dead. A man was arrested for having caused his death, and held in custody till a gallows was erected. At the moment that he was about to suffer punishment, first one man arrived, and then another, each accusing themselves of the murder, and this went on for a long time, and at the present instant the chief of police is engaged in questioning a man who declares that he alone is the true assassin."

The Sultan of Kashgar no sooner heard these words than he ordered an usher to go to the chief of police and to bring all the persons concerned in the hunchback's death, together with the corpse, that he wished to see once again. The usher hastened on his errand, but was only just in time, for the tailor was positively swinging in the air, when his voice fell upon the silence of the crowd, commanding the hangman to cut down the body. The hangman, recognising the usher as one of the king's servants, cut down the tailor, and the usher, seeing the man was safe, sought the chief of police and gave him the Sultan's message. Accordingly, the chief of police at once set out for the palace, taking with him the tailor, the doctor, the purveyor, and the merchant, who bore the dead hunchback on their shoulders.

When the procession reached the palace the chief of police prostrated himself at the feet of the Sultan, and related all that he knew of the matter. The Sultan was so much struck by the circumstances that he ordered his private historian to write down an exact account of what had passed, so that in the years to come the miraculous escape of the four men who had thought themselves murderers might never be forgotten.

The Sultan asked everybody concerned in the hunchback's affair to tell him their stories. Among others was a prating barber, whose tale of one of his brothers follows.

The Story of the Barber's Fifth Brother

Andrew and Nora Lang

AS LONG AS our father lived Alnaschar was very idle. Instead of working for his bread he was not ashamed to ask for it every evening, and to support himself next day on what he had received the night before. When our father died, worn out by age, he only left seven hundred silver drachmas to be divided amongst us, which made one hundred for each son. Alnaschar, who had never possessed so much money in his life, was quite puzzled to know what to do with it. After reflecting upon the matter for some time he decided to lay it out on glasses, bottles, and things of that sort, which he would buy from a wholesale merchant. Having bought his stock he next proceeded to look out for a small shop in a good position, where he sat down at the open door, his wares being piled up in an uncovered basket in front of him, waiting for a customer among the passers-by.

In this attitude he remained seated, his eyes fixed on the basket, but his thoughts far away. Unknown to himself he began to talk out loud, and a tailor, whose shop was next door to his, heard quite plainly what he was saying.

"This basket," said Alnaschar to himself, "has cost me a hundred drachmas – all that I possess in the world. Now in selling the contents piece by piece I shall turn two hundred, and these hundreds I shall again lay out in glass, which will produce four hundred. By this means I shall in course of time make four thousand drachmas, which will easily double themselves. When I have got ten thousand I will give up the glass trade and become a jeweller, and devote all my time to trading in pearls, diamonds, and other precious stones. At last, having all the wealth that heart can desire, I will buy a beautiful country house, with horses and slaves, and then I will lead a merry life and entertain my friends. At my feasts I will send for musicians and dancers from the neighbouring town to amuse my guests. In spite of my riches I shall not, however, give up trade till I have amassed a capital of a hundred thousand drachmas, when, having become a man of much consideration, I shall request the hand of the grand-vizir's daughter, taking care to inform the worthy father that I have heard favourable reports of her beauty and wit, and that I will pay down on our wedding day thousand gold pieces. Should the vizir refuse my proposal, which after all is hardly to be expected, I will seize him by the beard and drag him to my house."

When I shall have married his daughter I will give her ten of the best eunuchs that can be found for her service. Then I shall put on my most gorgeous robes, and mounted on a horse with a saddle of fine gold, and its trappings blazing with diamonds, followed by a train of slaves, I shall present myself at the house of the grand-vizir, the people casting down their eyes and bowing low as I pass along. At the foot of the grand-vizir's staircase I shall dismount, and while my servants stand in a row to right and left I shall ascend the stairs, at the head of which the grand-vizir will be waiting to receive me. He will then embrace me as his son-in-law, and giving me his seat will place himself below me. This being done (as I have every reason to expect), two of my servants will enter, each bearing a purse containing a thousand pieces of gold. One of these I shall present to him saying, "Here are the thousand gold pieces that I offered for your daughter's hand, and here," I shall continue, holding out the second purse, "are another thousand to show you that I am a man who is better than his word." After hearing of such generosity the world will talk of nothing else.

I shall return home with the same pomp as I set out, and my wife will send an officer to compliment me on my visit to her father, and I shall confer on the officer the honour of a rich dress and a handsome gift. Should she send one to me I shall refuse it and dismiss the bearer. I shall never allow my wife to leave her rooms on any pretext whatever without my permission, and my visits to her will be marked by all the ceremony calculated to inspire respect. No establishment will be better ordered than mine, and I shall take care always to be dressed in a manner suitable to my position. In the evening, when we retire to our apartments, I shall sit in the place of honour, where I shall assume a grand demeanour and speak little, gazing straight before me, and when my wife, lovely as the full moon, stands humbly in front of my chair I shall pretend not to see her. Then her women will say to me, "Respected lord and master, your wife and slave is before you waiting to be noticed. She is mortified that you never deign to look her way; she is tired of standing so long. Beg her, we pray you, to be seated." Of course I shall give no signs of even hearing this speech, which will vex them mightily. They will throw themselves at my feet with lamentations, and at length I will raise my head and throw a careless glance at her, then I shall go back to my former attitude. The women will think that I am displeased at my wife's dress and will lead her away to put on a finer one, and I on my side shall replace the one I am wearing with another yet more splendid. They will then return to the charge, but this time it will take much longer before they persuade me even to look at my wife. It is as well to begin on my wedding-day as I mean to go on for the rest of our lives.

The next day she will complain to her mother of the way she has been treated, which will fill my heart with joy. Her mother will come to seek me, and, kissing my hands with respect, will say, "My lord" (for she could not dare to risk my anger by using the familiar title of "son-in-law"), "My lord, do not, I implore you, refuse to look upon my daughter or to approach her. She only lives to please you, and loves you with all her soul." But I shall pay no more heed to my mother-in-law's words than I did to those of the women. Again she will beseech me to listen to her entreaties, throwing herself this time at my feet, but all to no purpose. Then, putting a glass of wine into my wife's hand, she will say to her, "There, present that to him yourself, he cannot have the cruelty to reject anything offered by so beautiful a hand," and my wife will take it and offer it to me tremblingly with tears in her eyes, but I shall look in the other direction. This will cause her to weep still more, and she will hold out the glass crying, "Adorable husband, never shall I cease my prayers till you have done me the favour to drink." Sick of her importunities, these words will goad me to fury. I shall dart an angry look at her and give her a sharp blow on the cheek, at the same time giving her a kick so violent that she will stagger across the room and fall on to the sofa.

"My brother," pursued the barber, "was so much absorbed in his dreams that he actually did give a kick with his foot, which unluckily hit the basket of glass. It fell into the street and was instantly broken into a thousand pieces."

His neighbour the tailor, who had been listening to his visions, broke into a loud fit of laughter as he saw this sight.

"Wretched man!" he cried, "you ought to die of shame at behaving so to a young wife who has done nothing to you. You must be a brute for her tears and prayers not to touch your heart. If I were the grand-vizir I would order you a hundred blows from a bullock whip, and would have you led round the town accompanied by a herald who should proclaim your crimes."

The accident, so fatal to all his profits, had restored my brother to his senses, and seeing that the mischief had been caused by his own insufferable pride, he rent his clothes and tore his hair, and lamented himself so loudly that the passers-by stopped to listen. It was a Friday, so these were more numerous than usual. Some pitied Alnaschar, others only laughed at him, but the vanity which had gone to his head had disappeared with his basket of glass, and he was loudly bewailing his folly when a lady, evidently a person of consideration, rode by on a mule. She stopped and inquired what was the matter, and why the man wept. They told her that he was a poor man who had laid out all his money on this basket of glass, which was now broken. On hearing the cause of these loud wails the lady turned to her attendant and said to him, "Give him whatever you have got with you." The man obeyed, and placed in my brother's hands a purse containing five hundred pieces of gold. Alnaschar almost died of joy on receiving it. He blessed the lady a thousand times, and, shutting up his shop where he had no longer anything to do, he returned home.

He was still absorbed in contemplating his good fortune, when a knock came to his door, and on opening it he found an old woman standing outside.

"My son," she said, "I have a favour to ask of you. It is the hour of prayer and I have not yet washed myself. Let me, I beg you, enter your house, and give me water."

My brother, although the old woman was a stranger to him, did not hesitate to do as she wished. He gave her a vessel of water and then went back to his place and his thoughts, and with his mind busy over his last adventure, he put his gold into a long and narrow purse, which he could easily carry in his belt. During this time the old woman was busy over her prayers, and when she had finished she came and prostrated herself twice before my brother, and then rising called down endless blessings on his head. Observing her shabby clothes, my brother thought that her gratitude was in reality a hint that he should give her some money to buy some new ones, so he held out two pieces of gold. The old woman started back in surprise as if she had received an insult. "Good heavens!" she exclaimed, "what is the meaning of this? Is it possible that you take me, my lord, for one of those miserable creatures who force their way into houses to beg for alms? Take back your money. I am thankful to say I do not need it, for I belong to a beautiful lady who is very rich and gives me everything I want."

My brother was not clever enough to detect that the old woman had merely refused the two pieces of money he had offered her in order to get more, but he inquired if she could procure him the pleasure of seeing this lady.

"Willingly," she replied; "and she will be charmed to marry you, and to make you the master of all her wealth. So pick up your money and follow me."

Delighted at the thought that he had found so easily both a fortune and a beautiful wife, my brother asked no more questions, but concealing his purse, with the money the lady had given him, in the folds of his dress, he set out joyfully with his guide.

They walked for some distance till the old woman stopped at a large house, where she knocked. The door was opened by a young Greek slave, and the old woman led my brother across a well-paved court into a well-furnished hall. Here she left him to inform her mistress of his presence, and as the day was hot he flung himself on a pile of cushions and took off his heavy turban. In a few minutes there entered a lady, and my brother perceived at the first glance that she was even more beautiful and more richly dressed than he had expected. He rose from his seat, but the lady signed to him to sit down again and placed herself beside him. After the usual compliments had passed between them she said, "We are not comfortable here, let us go into another room," and passing into a smaller chamber, apparently communicating with no other, she continued to talk to him for some time. Then rising hastily she left him, saying, "Stay where you are, I will come back in a moment."

He waited as he was told, but instead of the lady there entered a huge black slave with a sword in his hand. Approaching my brother with an angry countenance he exclaimed, "What business have you here?" His voice and manner were so terrific that Alnaschar had not strength to reply, and allowed his gold to be taken from him, and even sabre cuts to be inflicted on him without making any resistance. As soon as he was let go, he sank on the ground powerless to move, though he still had possession of his senses. Thinking he was dead, the black ordered the Greek slave to bring him some salt, and between them they rubbed it into his wounds, thus giving him acute agony, though he had the presence of mind to give no sign of life. They then left him, and their place was taken by the old woman, who dragged him to a trapdoor and threw him down into a vault filled with the bodies of murdered men.

At first the violence of his fall caused him to lose consciousness, but luckily the salt which had been rubbed into his wounds had by its smarting preserved his life, and little by little he regained his strength. At the end of two days he lifted the trapdoor during the night and hid himself in the courtyard till daybreak, when he saw the old woman leave the house in search of more prey. Luckily she did not observe him, and when she was out of sight he stole from this nest of assassins and took refuge in my house.

I dressed his wounds and tended him carefully, and when a month had passed he was as well as ever. His one thought was how to be revenged on that wicked old hag, and for this purpose he had a purse made large enough to contain five hundred gold pieces, but filled it instead with bits of glass. This he tied round him with his sash, and, disguising himself as an old woman, he took a sabre, which he hid under his dress.

One morning as he was hobbling through the streets he met his old enemy prowling to see if she could find anyone to decoy. He went up to her and, imitating the voice of a woman, he said, "Do you happen to have a pair of scales you could lend me? I have just come from Persia and have brought with me five hundred gold pieces, and I am anxious to see if they are the proper weight."

"Good woman," replied the old hag, "you could not have asked anyone better. My son is a money-changer, and if you will follow me he will weigh them for you himself. Only we must be quick or he will have gone to his shop." So saying she led the way to the same house as before, and the door was opened by the same Greek slave.

Again my brother was left in the hall, and the pretended son appeared under the form of the black slave. "Miserable crone," he said to my brother, "get up and come with me," and turned to lead the way to the place of murder. Alnaschar rose too, and drawing the sabre from under his dress dealt the black such a blow on his neck that his head was severed from his body. My brother picked up the head with one hand, and seizing the body with the other dragged it to the vault, when he threw it in and sent the head after it. The Greek slave, supposing that all had passed as usual, shortly arrived with the basin of salt, but when she beheld Alnaschar with the sabre in his hand she let the basin fall and turned to fly. My brother, however, was too quick for her, and in another instant her head was rolling from her shoulders. The noise brought the old woman running to see what was the matter, and he seized her before she had time to escape. "Wretch!" he cried, "do you know me?"

"Who are you, my lord?" she replied trembling all over. "I have never seen you before."

"I am he whose house you entered to offer your hypocritical prayers. Don't you remember now?"

She flung herself on her knees to implore mercy, but he cut her in four pieces.

There remained only the lady, who was quite ignorant of all that was taking place around her. He sought her through the house, and when at last he found her, she nearly fainted with terror at the sight of him. She begged hard for life, which he was generous enough to give her, but he bade her to tell him how she had got into partnership with the abominable creatures he had just put to death.

"I was once," replied she, "the wife of an honest merchant, and that old woman, whose wickedness I did not know, used occasionally to visit me. 'Madam,' she said to me one day, 'we have a grand wedding at our house to-day. If you would do us the honour to be present, I am sure you would enjoy yourself.' I allowed myself to be persuaded, put on my richest dress, and took a purse with a hundred pieces of gold. Once inside the doors I was kept by force by that dreadful black, and it is now three years that I have been here, to my great grief."

"That horrible black must have amassed great wealth," remarked my brother.

"Such wealth," returned she, "that if you succeed in carrying it all away it will make you rich for ever. Come and let us see how much there is."

She led Alnaschar into a chamber filled with coffers packed with gold, which he gazed at with an admiration he was powerless to conceal. "Go," she said, "and bring men to carry them away."

My brother did not wait to be told twice, and hurried out into the streets, where he soon collected ten men. They all came back to the house, but what was his surprise to find the door open, and the room with the chests of gold quite empty. The lady had been cleverer than himself, and had made the best use of her time. However, he tried to console himself by removing all the beautiful furniture, which more than made up for the five hundred gold pieces he had lost.

Unluckily, on leaving the house, he forgot to lock the door, and the neighbours, finding the place empty, informed the police, who next morning arrested Alnaschar as a thief. My brother tried to bribe them to let him off, but far from listening to him they tied his hands, and forced him to walk between them to the presence of the judge. When they had explained to the official the cause of complaint, he asked Alnaschar where he had obtained all the furniture that he had taken to his house the day before.

"Sir," replied Alnaschar, "I am ready to tell you the whole story, but give, I pray you, your word, that I shall run no risk of punishment."

"That I promise," said the judge. So my brother began at the beginning and related all his adventures, and how he had avenged himself on those who had betrayed him. As to the furniture, he entreated the judge at least to allow him to keep part to make up for the five hundred pieces of gold which had been stolen from him.

The judge, however, would say nothing about this, and lost no time in sending men to fetch away all that Alnaschar had taken from the house. When everything had been moved and placed under his roof he ordered my brother to leave the town and never more to enter it on peril of his life, fearing that if he returned he might seek justice from the Caliph. Alnaschar obeyed, and was on his way to a neighbouring city when he fell in with a band of robbers, who stripped him of his clothes and left him naked by the roadside. Hearing of his plight, I hurried after him to console him for his misfortunes, and to dress him in my best robe. I then brought him back disguised, under cover of night, to my house, where I have since given him all the care I bestow on my other brothers.

The Story of the Barber's Sixth Brother

Andrew and Nora Lang

THERE NOW REMAINS for me to relate to you the story of my sixth brother, whose name was Schacabac. Like the rest of us, he inherited a hundred silver drachmas from our father, which he thought was a large fortune, but through ill-luck, he soon lost it all, and was driven to beg. As he had a smooth tongue and good manners, he really did very well in his new profession, and he devoted himself specially to making friends with the servants in big houses, so as to gain access to their masters.

One day he was passing a splendid mansion, with a crowd of servants lounging in the courtyard. He thought that from the appearance of the house it might yield him a rich harvest, so he entered and inquired to whom it belonged.

"My good man, where do you come from?" replied the servant. "Can't you see for yourself that it can belong to nobody but a Barmecide?" for the Barmecides were famed for their liberality and generosity. My brother, hearing this, asked the porters, of whom there were several, if they would give him alms. They did not refuse, but told him politely to go in, and speak to the master himself.

My brother thanked them for their courtesy and entered the building, which was so large that it took him some time to reach the apartments of the Barmecide. At last, in a room richly decorated with paintings, he saw an old man with a long white beard, sitting on a sofa, who received him with such kindness that my brother was emboldened to make his petition.

"My lord," he said, "you behold in me a poor man who only lives by the help of persons as rich and as generous as you."

Before he could proceed further, he was stopped by the astonishment shown by the Barmecide. "Is it possible," he cried, "that while I am in Bagdad, a man like you should be starving? That is a state of things that must at once be put an end to! Never shall it be said that I have abandoned you, and I am sure that you, on your part, will never abandon me."

"My lord," answered my brother, "I swear that I have not broken my fast this whole day."

"What, you are dying of hunger?" exclaimed the Barmecide. "Here, slave; bring water, that we may wash our hands before meat!" No slave appeared, but my brother remarked that the Barmecide did not fail to rub his hands as if the water had been poured over them.

Then he said to my brother, "Why don't you wash your hands too?" and Schacabac, supposing that it was a joke on the part of the Barmecide (though he could see none himself), drew near, and imitated his motion.

When the Barmecide had done rubbing his hands, he raised his voice, and cried, "Set food before us at once, we are very hungry." No food was brought, but the

Barmecide pretended to help himself from a dish, and carry a morsel to his mouth, saying as he did so, "Eat, my friend, eat, I entreat. Help yourself as freely as if you were at home! For a starving man, you seem to have a very small appetite."

"Excuse me, my lord," replied Schacabac, imitating his gestures as before, "I really am not losing time, and I do full justice to the repast."

"How do you like this bread?" asked the Barmecide. "I find it particularly good myself."

"Oh, my lord," answered my brother, who beheld neither meat nor bread, "never have I tasted anything so delicious."

"Eat as much as you want," said the Barmecide. "I bought the woman who makes it for five hundred pieces of gold, so that I might never be without it."

After ordering a variety of dishes (which never came) to be placed on the table, and discussing the merits of each one, the Barmecide declared that having dined so well, they would now proceed to take their wine. To this my brother at first objected, declaring that it was forbidden; but on the Barmecide insisting that it was out of the question that he should drink by himself, he consented to take a little. The Barmecide, however, pretended to fill their glasses so often, that my brother feigned that the wine had gone into his head, and struck the Barmecide such a blow on the head, that he fell to the ground. Indeed, he raised his hand to strike him a second time, when the Barmecide cried out that he was mad, upon which my brother controlled himself, and apologised and protested that it was all the fault of the wine he had drunk. At this the Barmecide, instead of being angry, began to laugh, and embraced him heartily. "I have long been seeking," he exclaimed, "a man of your description, and henceforth my house shall be yours. You have had the good grace to fall in with my humour, and to pretend to eat and to drink when nothing was there. Now you shall be rewarded by a really good supper."

Then he clapped his hands, and all the dishes were brought that they had tasted in imagination before and during the repast, slaves sang and played on various instruments. All the while Schacabac was treated by the Barmecide as a familiar friend, and dressed in a garment out of his own wardrobe.

Twenty years passed by, and my brother was still living with the Barmecide, looking after his house, and managing his affairs. At the end of that time his generous benefactor died without heirs, so all his possessions went to the prince. They even despoiled my brother of those that rightly belonged to him, and he, now as poor as he had ever been in his life, decided to cast in his lot with a caravan of pilgrims who were on their way to Mecca. Unluckily, the caravan was attacked and pillaged by the Bedouins, and the pilgrims were taken prisoners. My brother became the slave of a man who beat him daily, hoping to drive him to offer a ransom, although, as Schacabac pointed out, it was quite useless trouble, as his relations were as poor as himself. At length the Bedouin grew tired of tormenting, and sent him on a camel to the top of a high barren mountain, where he left him to take his chance. A passing caravan, on its way to Bagdad, told me where he was to be found, and I hurried to his rescue, and brought him in a deplorable condition back to the town.

"This," – continued the barber, – "is the tale I related to the Caliph, who, when I had finished, burst into fits of laughter.

"Well were you called `the Silent,'" said he; "no name was ever better deserved. But for reasons of my own, which it is not necessary to mention, I desire you to leave the town, and never to come back."

"I had of course no choice but to obey, and travelled about for several years until I heard of the death of the Caliph, when I hastily returned to Bagdad, only to find that all my brothers were dead. It was at this time that I rendered to the young cripple the important service of which you have heard, and for which, as you know, he showed such profound ingratitude, that he preferred rather to leave Bagdad than to run the risk of seeing me. I sought him long from place to place, but it was only to-day, when I expected it least, that I came across him, as much irritated with me as ever" – So saying the tailor went on to relate the story of the lame man and the barber, which has already been told.

"When the barber," he continued, "had finished his tale, we came to the conclusion that the young man had been right, when he had accused him of being a great chatter-box. However, we wished to keep him with us, and share our feast, and we remained at table till the hour of afternoon prayer. Then the company broke up, and I went back to work in my shop.

"It was during this interval that the little hunchback, half drunk already, presented himself before me, singing and playing on his drum. I took him home, to amuse my wife, and she invited him to supper. While eating some fish, a bone got into his throat, and in spite of all we could do, he died shortly. It was all so sudden that we lost our heads, and in order to divert suspicion from ourselves, we carried the body to the house of a Jewish physician. He placed it in the chamber of the purveyor, and the purveyor propped it up in the street, where it was thought to have been killed by the merchant.

"This, Sire, is the story which I was obliged to tell to satisfy your highness. It is now for you to say if we deserve mercy or punishment; life or death?"

The Sultan of Kashgar listened with an air of pleasure which filled the tailor and his friends with hope. "I must confess," he exclaimed, "that I am much more interested in the stories of the barber and his brothers, and of the lame man, than in that of my own jester. But before I allow you all four to return to your own homes, and have the corpse of the hunchback properly buried, I should like to see this barber who has earned your pardon. And as he is in this town, let an usher go with you at once in search of him."

The usher and the tailor soon returned, bringing with them an old man who must have been at least ninety years of age. "O Silent One," said the Sultan, "I am told that you know many strange stories. Will you tell some of them to me?"

"Never mind my stories for the present," replied the barber, "but will your Highness graciously be pleased to explain why this Jew, this Christian, and this Mussulman, as well as this dead body, are all here?"

"What business is that of yours?" asked the Sultan with a smile; but seeing that the barber had some reasons for his question, he commanded that the tale of the hunchback should be told him.

"It is certainly most surprising," cried he, when he had heard it all, "but I should like to examine the body." He then knelt down, and took the head on his knees, looking at it attentively. Suddenly he burst into such loud laughter that he fell right backwards, and when he had recovered himself enough to speak, he turned to the Sultan. "The man is no more dead than I am," he said; "watch me." As he spoke he drew a small case of medicines from his pocket and rubbed the neck of the hunchback with some ointment made of balsam. Next he opened the dead man's mouth, and by the help of a pair of pincers drew the bone from his throat. At this the hunchback sneezed, stretched himself and opened his eyes.

The Sultan and all those who saw this operation did not know which to admire most, the constitution of the hunchback who had apparently been dead for a whole night and most of one day, or the skill of the barber, whom everyone now began to look upon as a great man. His Highness desired that the history of the hunchback should be written down, and placed in the archives beside that of the barber, so that they might be associated in people's minds to the end of time. And he did not stop there; for in order to wipe out the memory of what they had undergone, he commanded that the tailor, the doctor, the purveyor and the merchant, should each be clothed in his presence with a robe from his own wardrobe before they returned home. As for the barber, he bestowed on him a large pension, and kept him near his own person.

Aladdin and the Wonderful Lamp

Andrew and Nora Lang

THERE ONCE LIVED a poor tailor, who had a son called Aladdin, a careless, idle boy who would do nothing but play all day long in the streets with little idle boys like himself. This so grieved the father that he died; yet, in spite of his mother's tears and prayers, Aladdin did not mend his ways. One day, when he was playing in the streets as usual, a stranger asked him his age, and if he were not the son of Mustapha the tailor.

"I am, sir," replied Aladdin; "but he died a long while ago."

On this the stranger, who was a famous African magician, fell on his neck and kissed him, saying: "I am your uncle, and knew you from your likeness to my brother. Go to your mother and tell her I am coming."

Aladdin ran home, and told his mother of his newly found uncle.

"Indeed, child," she said, "your father had a brother, but I always thought he was dead."

However, she prepared supper, and bade Aladdin seek his uncle, who came laden with wine and fruit. He presently fell down and kissed the place where Mustapha used to sit, bidding Aladdin's mother not to be surprised at not having seen him before, as he had been forty years out of the country. He then turned to Aladdin, and asked him his trade, at which the boy hung his head, while his mother burst into tears. On learning that Aladdin was idle and would learn no trade, he offered to take a shop for him and stock it with merchandise. Next day he bought Aladdin a fine suit of clothes, and took him all over the city, showing him the sights, and brought him home at nightfall to his mother, who was overjoyed to see her son so fine.

Next day the magician led Aladdin into some beautiful gardens a long way outside the city gates. They sat down by a fountain, and the magician pulled a cake from his girdle, which he divided between them. They then journeyed onwards till they almost reached the mountains. Aladdin was so tired that he begged to go back, but the magician beguiled him with pleasant stories, and led him on in spite of himself.

At last they came to two mountains divided by a narrow valley.

"We will go no farther," said the false uncle. "I will show you something wonderful; only do you gather up sticks while I kindle a fire."

When it was lit the magician threw on it a powder he had about him, at the same time saying some magical words. The earth trembled a little and opened in front of them, disclosing a square flat stone with a brass ring in the middle to raise it by. Aladdin tried to run away, but the magician caught him and gave him a blow that knocked him down.

"What have I done, uncle?" he said piteously; whereupon the magician said more kindly: "Fear nothing, but obey me. Beneath this stone lies a treasure which is to be yours, and no one else may touch it, so you must do exactly as I tell you."

At the word treasure, Aladdin forgot his fears, and grasped the ring as he was told, saying the names of his father and grandfather. The stone came up quite easily and some steps appeared.

"Go down," said the magician; "at the foot of those steps you will find an open door leading into three large halls. Tuck up your gown and go through them without touching anything, or you will die instantly. These halls lead into a garden of fine fruit trees. Walk on till you come to a niche in a terrace where stands a lighted lamp. Pour out the oil it contains and bring it to me."

He drew a ring from his finger and gave it to Aladdin, bidding him prosper.

Aladdin found everything as the magician had said, gathered some fruit off the trees, and, having got the lamp, arrived at the mouth of the cave. The magician cried out in a great hurry:

"Make haste and give me the lamp." This Aladdin refused to do until he was out of the cave. The magician flew into a terrible passion, and throwing some more powder on the fire, he said something, and the stone rolled back into its place.

The magician left Persia for ever, which plainly showed that he was no uncle of Aladdin's, but a cunning magician who had read in his magic books of a wonderful lamp, which would make him the most powerful man in the world. Though he alone knew where to find it, he could only receive it from the hand of another. He had picked out the foolish Aladdin for this purpose, intending to get the lamp and kill him afterwards.

For two days Aladdin remained in the dark, crying and lamenting. At last he clasped his hands in prayer, and in so doing rubbed the ring, which the magician had forgotten to take from him. Immediately an enormous and frightful genie rose out of the earth, saying:

"What wouldst thou with me? I am the Slave of the Ring, and will obey thee in all things."

Aladdin fearlessly replied: "Deliver me from this place!" whereupon the earth opened, and he found himself outside. As soon as his eyes could bear the light he went home, but fainted on the threshold. When he came to himself he told his mother what had passed, and showed her the lamp and the fruits he had gathered in the garden, which were in reality precious stones. He then asked for some food.

"Alas! child," she said, "I have nothing in the house, but I have spun a little cotton and will go and sell it."

Aladdin bade her keep her cotton, for he would sell the lamp instead. As it was very dirty she began to rub it, that it might fetch a higher price. Instantly a hideous genie appeared, and asked what she would have. She fainted away, but Aladdin, snatching the lamp, said boldly:

"Fetch me something to eat!"

The genie returned with a silver bowl, twelve silver plates containing rich meats, two silver cups, and two bottles of wine. Aladdin's mother, when she came to herself, said:

"Whence comes this splendid feast?"

"Ask not, but eat," replied Aladdin.

So they sat at breakfast till it was dinner-time, and Aladdin told his mother about the lamp. She begged him to sell it, and have nothing to do with devils.

"No," said Aladdin, "since chance has made us aware of its virtues, we will use it and the ring likewise, which I shall always wear on my finger." When they had eaten all the genie had brought, Aladdin sold one of the silver plates, and so on till none were left. He then had recourse to the genie, who gave him another set of plates, and thus they lived for many years.

One day Aladdin heard an order from the Sultan proclaimed that everyone was to stay at home and close his shutters while the princess, his daughter, went to and from the bath. Aladdin was seized by a desire to see her face, which was very difficult, as she always went veiled. He hid himself behind the door of the bath, and peeped through a chink. The princess lifted her veil as she went in, and looked so beautiful that Aladdin fell in love with her at first sight. He went home so changed that his mother was frightened. He told her he loved the princess so deeply that he could not live without her, and meant to ask her in marriage of her father. His mother, on hearing this, burst out laughing, but Aladdin at last prevailed upon her to go before the Sultan and carry his request. She fetched a napkin and laid in it the magic fruits from the enchanted garden, which sparkled and shone like the most beautiful jewels. She took these with her to please the Sultan, and set out, trusting in the lamp. The grand-vizir and the lords of council had just gone in as she entered the hall and placed herself in front of the Sultan. He, however, took no notice of her. She went every day for a week, and stood in the same place.

When the council broke up on the sixth day the Sultan said to his vizir: "I see a certain woman in the audience-chamber every day carrying something in a napkin. Call her next time, that I may find out what she wants."

Next day, at a sign from the vizir, she went up to the foot of the throne, and remained kneeling till the Sultan said to her: "Rise, good woman, and tell me what you want."

She hesitated, so the Sultan sent away all but the vizir, and bade her speak freely, promising to forgive her beforehand for anything she might say. She then told him of her son's violent love for the princess.

"I prayed him to forget her," she said, "but in vain; he threatened to do some desperate deed if I refused to go and ask your Majesty for the hand of the princess. Now I pray you to forgive not me alone, but my son Aladdin."

The Sultan asked her kindly what she had in the napkin, whereupon she unfolded the jewels and presented them.

He was thunderstruck, and turning to the vizir said: "What sayest thou? Ought I not to bestow the princess on one who values her at such a price?"

The vizir, who wanted her for his own son, begged the Sultan to withhold her for three months, in the course of which he hoped his son would contrive to make him a richer present. The Sultan granted this, and told Aladdin's mother that, though he consented to the marriage, she must not appear before him again for three months.

Aladdin waited patiently for nearly three months, but after two had elapsed his mother, going into the city to buy oil, found everyone rejoicing, and asked what was going on.

"Do you not know," was the answer, "that the son of the grand-vizir is to marry the Sultan's daughter to-night?"

Breathless, she ran and told Aladdin, who was overwhelmed at first, but presently bethought him of the lamp. He rubbed it, and the genie appeared, saying: "What is thy will?"

Aladdin replied: "The Sultan, as thou knowest, has broken his promise to me, and the vizir's son is to have the princess. My command is that to-night you bring hither the bride and bridegroom."

"Master, I obey," said the genie.

Aladdin then went to his chamber, where, sure enough at midnight the genie transported the bed containing the vizir's son and the princess.

"Take this new-married man," he said, "and put him outside in the cold, and return at daybreak."

Whereupon the genie took the vizir's son out of bed, leaving Aladdin with the princess.

"Fear nothing," Aladdin said to her; "you are my wife, promised to me by your unjust father, and no harm shall come to you."

The princess was too frightened to speak, and passed the most miserable night of her life, while Aladdin lay down beside her and slept soundly. At the appointed hour the genie fetched in the shivering bridegroom, laid him in his place, and transported the bed back to the palace.

Presently the Sultan came to wish his daughter good-morning. The unhappy vizir's son jumped up and hid himself, while the princess would not say a word, and was very sorrowful.

The Sultan sent her mother to her, who said: "How comes it, child, that you will not speak to your father? What has happened?"

The princess sighed deeply, and at last told her mother how, during the night, the bed had been carried into some strange house, and what had passed there. Her mother did not believe her in the least, but bade her rise and consider it an idle dream.

The following night exactly the same thing happened, and next morning, on the princess's refusing to speak, the Sultan threatened to cut off her head. She then confessed all, bidding him ask the vizir's son if it were not so. The Sultan told the vizir to ask his son, who owned the truth, adding that, dearly as he loved the princess, he had rather die than go through another such fearful night, and wished to be separated from her. His wish was granted, and there was an end of feasting and rejoicing.

When the three months were over, Aladdin sent his mother to remind the Sultan of his promise. She stood in the same place as before, and the Sultan, who had forgotten Aladdin, at once remembered him, and sent for her. On seeing her poverty the Sultan felt less inclined than ever to keep his word, and asked the vizir's advice, who counselled him to set so high a value on the princess that no man living could come up to it.

The Sultan then turned to Aladdin's mother, saying: "Good woman, a Sultan must remember his promises, and I will remember mine, but your son must first send me forty basins of gold brimful of jewels, carried by forty black slaves, led by as many white ones, splendidly dressed. Tell him that I await his answer." The mother of Aladdin bowed low and went home, thinking all was lost.

She gave Aladdin the message, adding: "He may wait long enough for your answer!"

"Not so long, mother, as you think," her son replied "I would do a great deal more than that for the princess."

He summoned the genie, and in a few moments the eighty slaves arrived, and filled up the small house and garden.

Aladdin made them set out to the palace, two and two, followed by his mother. They were so richly dressed, with such splendid jewels in their girdles, that everyone crowded to see them and the basins of gold they carried on their heads.

They entered the palace, and, after kneeling before the Sultan, stood in a half-circle round the throne with their arms crossed, while Aladdin's mother presented them to the Sultan.

He hesitated no longer, but said: "Good woman, return and tell your son that I wait for him with open arms."

She lost no time in telling Aladdin, bidding him make haste. But Aladdin first called the genie.

"I want a scented bath," he said, "a richly embroidered habit, a horse surpassing the Sultan's, and twenty slaves to attend me. Besides this, six slaves, beautifully dressed, to wait on my mother; and lastly, ten thousand pieces of gold in ten purses."

No sooner said than done. Aladdin mounted his horse and passed through the streets, the slaves strewing gold as they went. Those who had played with him in his childhood knew him not, he had grown so handsome.

When the Sultan saw him he came down from his throne, embraced him, and led him into a hall where a feast was spread, intending to marry him to the princess that very day.

But Aladdin refused, saying, "I must build a palace fit for her," and took his leave.

Once home he said to the genie: "Build me a palace of the finest marble, set with jasper, agate, and other precious stones. In the middle you shall build me a large hall with a dome, its four walls of massy gold and silver, each side having six windows, whose lattices, all except one, which is to be left unfinished, must be set with diamonds and rubies. There must be stables and horses and grooms and slaves; go and see about it!"

The palace was finished by next day, and the genie carried him there and showed him all his orders faithfully carried out, even to the laying of a velvet carpet from Aladdin's palace to the Sultan's. Aladdin's mother then dressed herself carefully, and walked to the palace with her slaves, while he followed her on horseback. The Sultan sent musicians with trumpets and cymbals to meet them, so that the air resounded with music and cheers. She was taken to the princess, who saluted her and treated her with great honour. At night the princess said good-bye to her father, and set out on the carpet for Aladdin's palace, with his mother at her side, and followed by the hundred slaves. She was charmed at the sight of Aladdin, who ran to receive her.

"Princess," he said, "blame your beauty for my boldness if I have displeased you."

She told him that, having seen him, she willingly obeyed her father in this matter. After the wedding had taken place Aladdin led her into the hall, where a feast was spread, and she supped with him, after which they danced till midnight.

Next day Aladdin invited the Sultan to see the palace. On entering the hall with the four-and-twenty windows, with their rubies, diamonds, and emeralds, he cried:

"It is a world's wonder! There is only one thing that surprises me. Was it by accident that one window was left unfinished?"

"No, sir, by design," returned Aladdin. "I wished your Majesty to have the glory of finishing this palace."

The Sultan was pleased, and sent for the best jewelers in the city. He showed them the unfinished window, and bade them fit it up like the others.

"Sir," replied their spokesman, "we cannot find jewels enough."

The Sultan had his own fetched, which they soon used, but to no purpose, for in a month's time the work was not half done. Aladdin, knowing that their task was vain, bade them undo their work and carry the jewels back, and the genie finished the window at his command. The Sultan was surprised to receive his jewels again and visited Aladdin, who showed him the window finished. The Sultan embraced him, the envious vizir meanwhile hinting that it was the work of enchantment.

Aladdin had won the hearts of the people by his gentle bearing. He was made captain of the Sultan's armies, and won several battles for him, but remained modest and courteous as before, and lived thus in peace and content for several years.

But far away in Africa the magician remembered Aladdin, and by his magic arts discovered that Aladdin, instead of perishing miserably in the cave, had escaped, and had married a princess, with whom he was living in great honour and wealth. He knew that the poor tailor's son could only have accomplished this by means of the lamp, and travelled night and day till he reached the capital of China, bent on Aladdin's ruin. As he passed through the town he heard people talking everywhere about a marvellous palace.

"Forgive my ignorance," he asked, "what is this palace you speak of?"

"Have you not heard of Prince Aladdin's palace," was the reply, "the greatest wonder of the world? I will direct you if you have a mind to see it."

The magician thanked him who spoke, and having seen the palace knew that it had been raised by the genie of the lamp, and became half mad with rage. He determined to get hold of the lamp, and again plunge Aladdin into the deepest poverty.

Unluckily, Aladdin had gone a-hunting for eight days, which gave the magician plenty of time. He bought a dozen copper lamps, put them into a basket, and went to the palace, crying: "New lamps for old!" followed by a jeering crowd.

The princess, sitting in the hall of four-and-twenty windows, sent a slave to find out what the noise was about, who came back laughing, so that the princess scolded her.

"Madam," replied the slave, "who can help laughing to see an old fool offering to exchange fine new lamps for old ones?"

Another slave, hearing this, said: "There is an old one on the cornice there which he can have."

Now this was the magic lamp, which Aladdin had left there, as he could not take it out hunting with him. The princess, not knowing its value, laughingly bade the slave take it and make the exchange.

She went and said to the magician: "Give me a new lamp for this."

He snatched it and bade the slave take her choice, amid the jeers of the crowd. Little he cared, but left off crying his lamps, and went out of the city gates to a lonely place, where he remained till nightfall, when he pulled out the lamp and rubbed it. The genie appeared, and at the magician's command carried him, together with the palace and the princess in it, to a lonely place in Africa.

Next morning the Sultan looked out of the window towards Aladdin's palace and rubbed his eyes, for it was gone. He sent for the vizir, and asked what had become of the palace. The vizir looked out too, and was lost in astonishment. He again put it down to enchantment, and this time the Sultan believed him, and sent thirty men on horseback to fetch Aladdin in chains. They met him riding home, bound him, and forced him to go with them on foot. The people, however, who loved him, followed, armed, to see that he came to no harm. He was carried before the Sultan, who ordered the executioner to cut off his head. The executioner made Aladdin kneel down, bandaged his eyes, and raised his scimitar to strike.

At that instant the vizir, who saw that the crowd had forced their way into the courtyard and were scaling the walls to rescue Aladdin, called to the executioner to stay his hand. The people, indeed, looked so threatening that the Sultan gave way and ordered Aladdin to be unbound, and pardoned him in the sight of the crowd.

Aladdin now begged to know what he had done.

"False wretch!" said the Sultan, "come hither," and showed him from the window the place where his palace had stood.

Aladdin was so amazed that he could not say a word.

"Where is my palace and my daughter?" demanded the Sultan. "For the first I am not so deeply concerned, but my daughter I must have, and you must find her or lose your head."

Aladdin begged for forty days in which to find her, promising if he failed to return and suffer death at the Sultan's pleasure. His prayer was granted, and he went forth sadly from the Sultan's presence. For three days he wandered about like a madman, asking everyone what had become of his palace, but they only laughed and pitied him. He came to the banks of a river, and knelt down to say his prayers before throwing himself in. In so doing he rubbed the magic ring he still wore.

The genie he had seen in the cave appeared, and asked his will.

"Save my life, genie," said Aladdin, "and bring my palace back."

"That is not in my power," said the genie; "I am only the slave of the ring; you must ask the slave of the lamp."

"Even so," said Aladdin "but thou canst take me to the palace, and set me down under my dear wife's window." He at once found himself in Africa, under the window of the princess, and fell asleep out of sheer weariness.

He was awakened by the singing of the birds, and his heart was lighter. He saw plainly that all his misfortunes were owing to the loss of the lamp, and vainly wondered who had robbed him of it.

That morning the princess rose earlier than she had done since she had been carried into Africa by the magician, whose company she was forced to endure once a day. She, however, treated him so harshly that he dared not live there altogether. As she was dressing, one of her women looked out and saw Aladdin. The princess ran and opened the window, and at the noise she made Aladdin looked up. She called to him to come to her, and great was the joy of these lovers at seeing each other again.

After he had kissed her Aladdin said: "I beg of you, Princess, in God's name, before we speak of anything else, for your own sake and mine, tell me what has become of an old lamp I left on the cornice in the hall of four-and-twenty windows, when I went a-hunting."

"Alas!" she said "I am the innocent cause of our sorrows," and told him of the exchange of the lamp.

"Now I know," cried Aladdin, "that we have to thank the African magician for this! Where is the lamp?"

"He carries it about with him," said the princess, "I know, for he pulled it out of his breast to show me. He wishes me to break my faith with you and marry him, saying that you were beheaded by my father's command. He is forever speaking ill of you, but I only reply by my tears. If I persist, I doubt not that he will use violence."

Aladdin comforted her, and left her for a while. He changed clothes with the first person he met in the town, and having bought a certain powder returned to the princess, who let him in by a little side door.

"Put on your most beautiful dress," he said to her, "and receive the magician with smiles, leading him to believe that you have forgotten me. Invite him to sup with you, and say you wish to taste the wine of his country. He will go for some, and while he is gone I will tell you what to do."

She listened carefully to Aladdin, and when he left her arrayed herself gaily for the first time since she left China. She put on a girdle and head-dress of diamonds, and seeing in a glass that she looked more beautiful than ever, received the magician, saying to his great amazement: "I have made up my mind that Aladdin is dead, and that all my tears will not bring him back to me, so I am resolved to mourn no more, and have therefore invited you to sup with me; but I am tired of the wines of China, and would fain taste those of Africa."

The magician flew to his cellar, and the princess put the powder Aladdin had given her in her cup. When he returned she asked him to drink her health in the wine of Africa, handing him her cup in exchange for his as a sign she was reconciled to him.

Before drinking the magician made her a speech in praise of her beauty, but the princess cut him short saying:

"Let me drink first, and you shall say what you will afterwards." She set her cup to her lips and kept it there, while the magician drained his to the dregs and fell back lifeless.

The princess then opened the door to Aladdin, and flung her arms round his neck, but Aladdin put her away, bidding her to leave him, as he had more to do. He then went to the dead magician, took the lamp out of his vest, and bade the genie carry the palace and all in it back to China. This was done, and the princess in her chamber only felt two little shocks, and little thought she was at home again.

The Sultan, who was sitting in his closet, mourning for his lost daughter, happened to look up, and rubbed his eyes, for there stood the palace as before! He hastened thither, and Aladdin received him in the hall of the four-and-twenty windows, with the princess at his side. Aladdin told him what had happened, and showed him the dead body of the magician, that he might believe. A ten days' feast was proclaimed, and it seemed as if Aladdin might now live the rest of his life in peace; but it was not to be.

The African magician had a younger brother, who was, if possible, more wicked and more cunning than himself. He travelled to China to avenge his brother's death, and went to visit a pious woman called Fatima, thinking she might be of use to him. He entered her cell and clapped a dagger to her breast, telling her to rise and do his bidding on pain of death. He changed clothes with her, coloured his face like hers, put on her veil and murdered her, that she might tell no tales. Then he went towards the palace of Aladdin, and all the people thinking he was the holy woman, gathered round him, kissing his hands and begging his blessing. When he got to the palace there was such a noise going on round him that the princess bade her slave look out of the window and ask what was the matter. The slave said it was the holy woman, curing people by her touch of their ailments, whereupon the princess, who had long desired to see Fatima, sent for her. On coming to the princess the magician offered up a prayer for her health and prosperity. When he had done the princess made him sit by her, and begged him to stay with her always. The false Fatima, who wished for nothing better, consented, but kept his veil down for fear of discovery. The princess showed him the hall, and asked him what he thought of it.

"It is truly beautiful," said the false Fatima. "In my mind it wants but one thing."

"And what is that?" said the princess.

"If only a roc's egg," replied he, "were hung up from the middle of this dome, it would be the wonder of the world."

After this the princess could think of nothing but a roc's egg, and when Aladdin returned from hunting he found her in a very ill humour. He begged to know what was amiss, and she told him that all her pleasure in the hall was spoilt for the want of a roc's egg hanging from the dome.

"It that is all," replied Aladdin, "you shall soon be happy."

He left her and rubbed the lamp, and when the genie appeared commanded him to bring a roc's egg. The genie gave such a loud and terrible shriek that the hall shook.

"Wretch!" he cried, "is it not enough that I have done everything for you, but you must command me to bring my master and hang him up in the midst of this dome? You and your wife and your palace deserve to be burnt to ashes; but this request does not come from you, but from the brother of the African magician whom you destroyed. He is now in your palace disguised as the holy woman – whom he murdered. He it was who put that wish into your wife's head. Take care of yourself, for he means to kill you." So saying the genie disappeared.

Aladdin went back to the princess, saying his head ached, and requesting that the holy Fatima should be fetched to lay her hands on it. But when the magician came near, Aladdin, seizing his dagger, pierced him to the heart.

"What have you done?" cried the princess. "You have killed the holy woman!"

"Not so," replied Aladdin, "but a wicked magician," and told her of how she had been deceived.

After this Aladdin and his wife lived in peace. He succeeded the Sultan when he died, and reigned for many years, leaving behind him a long line of kings.

The Adventures of Haroun-al-Raschid, Caliph of Bagdad

Andrew and Nora Lang

THE CALIPH HAROUN-AL-RASCHID sat in his palace, wondering if there was anything left in the world that could possibly give him a few hours' amusement, when Giafar the grand-vizir, his old and tried friend, suddenly appeared before him. Bowing low, he waited, as was his duty, till his master spoke, but Haroun-al-Raschid merely turned his head and looked at him, and sank back into his former weary posture.

Now Giafar had something of importance to say to the Caliph, and had no intention of being put off by mere silence, so with another low bow in front of the throne, he began to speak.

"Commander of the Faithful," said he, "I have taken on myself to remind your Highness that you have undertaken secretly to observe for yourself the manner in which justice is done and order is kept throughout the city. This is the day you have set apart to devote to this object, and perhaps in fulfilling this duty you may find some distraction from the melancholy to which, as I see to my sorrow, you are a prey."

"You are right," returned the Caliph, "I had forgotten all about it. Go and change your coat, and I will change mine."

A few moments later they both re-entered the hall, disguised as foreign merchants, and passed through a secret door, out into the open country. Here they turned towards the Euphrates, and crossing the river in a small boat, walked through that part of the town which lay along the further bank, without seeing anything to call for their interference. Much pleased with the peace and good order of the city, the Caliph and his vizir made their way to a bridge, which led straight back to the palace, and had already crossed it, when they were stopped by an old and blind man, who begged for alms.

The Caliph gave him a piece of money, and was passing on, but the blind man seized his hand, and held him fast.

"Charitable person," he said, "whoever you may be grant me yet another prayer. Strike me, I beg of you, one blow. I have deserved it richly, and even a more severe penalty."

The Caliph, much surprised at this request, replied gently: "My good man, that which you ask is impossible. Of what use would my alms be if I treated you so ill?" And as he spoke he tried to loosen the grasp of the blind beggar.

"My lord," answered the man, "pardon my boldness and my persistence. Take back your money, or give me the blow which I crave. I have sworn a solemn oath that I will receive nothing without receiving chastisement, and if you knew all, you would feel that the punishment is not a tenth part of what I deserve."

Moved by these words, and perhaps still more by the fact that he had other business to attend to, the Caliph yielded, and struck him lightly on the shoulder. Then he continued his road, followed by the blessing of the blind man. When they were out of earshot, he said to the vizir, "There must be something very odd to make that man act so – I should like to find out what is the reason. Go back to him; tell him who I am, and order him to come without fail to the palace to-morrow, after the hour of evening prayer."

So the grand-vizir went back to the bridge; gave the blind beggar first a piece of money and then a blow, delivered the Caliph's message, and rejoined his master.

They passed on towards the palace, but walking through a square, they came upon a crowd watching a young and well-dressed man who was urging a horse at full speed round the open space, using at the same time his spurs and whip so unmercifully that the animal was all covered with foam and blood. The Caliph, astonished at this proceeding, inquired of a passer-by what it all meant, but no one could tell him anything, except that every day at the same hour the same thing took place.

Still wondering, he passed on, and for the moment had to content himself with telling the vizir to command the horseman also to appear before him at the same time as the blind man.

The next day, after evening prayer, the Caliph entered the hall, and was followed by the vizir bringing with him the two men of whom we have spoken, and a third, with whom we have nothing to do. They all bowed themselves low before the throne and then the Caliph bade them rise, and ask the blind man his name.

"Baba-Abdalla, your Highness," said he.

"Baba-Abdalla," returned the Caliph, "your way of asking alms yesterday seemed to me so strange, that I almost commanded you then and there to cease from causing such a public scandal. But I have sent for you to inquire what was your motive in making such a curious vow. When I know the reason I shall be able to judge whether you can be permitted to continue to practise it, for I cannot help thinking that it sets a very bad example to others. Tell me therefore the whole truth, and conceal nothing."

These words troubled the heart of Baba-Abdalla, who prostrated himself at the feet of the Caliph. Then rising, he answered: "Commander of the Faithful, I crave your pardon humbly, for my persistence in beseeching your Highness to do an action which appears on the face of it to be without any meaning. No doubt, in the eyes of men, it has none; but I look on it as a slight expiation for a fearful sin of which I have been guilty, and if your Highness will deign to listen to my tale, you will see that no punishment could atone for the crime."

The Story of the Blind Baba-Abdalla

Andrew and Nora Lang

I WAS BORN, Commander of the Faithful, in Bagdad, and was left an orphan while I was yet a very young man, for my parents died within a few days of each other. I had inherited from them a small fortune, which I worked hard night and day to increase, till at last I found myself the owner of eighty camels. These I hired out to travelling merchants, whom I frequently accompanied on their various journeys, and always returned with large profits.

One day I was coming back from Balsora, whither I had taken a supply of goods, intended for India, and halted at noon in a lonely place, which promised rich pasture for my camels. I was resting in the shade under a tree, when a dervish, going on foot towards Balsora, sat down by my side, and I inquired whence he had come and to what place he was going. We soon made friends, and after we had asked each other the usual questions, we produced the food we had with us, and satisfied our hunger.

While we were eating, the dervish happened to mention that in a spot only a little way off from where we were sitting, there was hidden a treasure so great that if my eighty camels were loaded till they could carry no more, the hiding place would seem as full as if it had never been touched.

At this news I became almost beside myself with joy and greed, and I flung my arms round the neck of the dervish, exclaiming: "Good dervish, I see plainly that the riches of this world are nothing to you, therefore of what use is the knowledge of this treasure to you? Alone and on foot, you could carry away a mere handful. But tell me where it is, and I will load my eighty camels with it, and give you one of them as a token of my gratitude."

Certainly my offer does not sound very magnificent, but it was great to me, for at his words a wave of covetousness had swept over my heart, and I almost felt as if the seventy-nine camels that were left were nothing in comparison.

The dervish saw quite well what was passing in my mind, but he did not show what he thought of my proposal.

"My brother," he answered quietly, "you know as well as I do, that you are behaving unjustly. It was open to me to keep my secret, and to reserve the treasure for myself. But the fact that I have told you of its existence shows that I had confidence in you, and that I hoped to earn your gratitude for ever, by making your fortune as well as mine. But before I reveal to you the secret of the treasure, you must swear that, after we have loaded the camels with as much as they can carry, you will give half to me, and let us go our own ways. I think you will see that this is fair, for if you present me with forty camels, I on my side will give you the means of buying a thousand more."

I could not of course deny that what the dervish said was perfectly reasonable, but, in spite of that, the thought that the dervish would be as rich as I was unbearable to me. Still there was no use in discussing the matter, and I had to accept his conditions or bewail to the end of my life the loss of immense wealth. So I collected my camels and we set out together under the guidance of the dervish. After walking some time, we reached what looked like a valley, but with such a narrow entrance that my camels could only pass one by one. The little valley, or open space, was shut up by two mountains, whose sides were formed of straight cliffs, which no human being could climb.

When we were exactly between these mountains the dervish stopped.

"Make your camels lie down in this open space," he said, "so that we can easily load them; then we will go to the treasure."

I did what I was bid, and rejoined the dervish, whom I found trying to kindle a fire out of some dry wood. As soon as it was alight, he threw on it a handful of perfumes, and pronounced a few words that I did not understand, and immediately a thick column of smoke rose high into the air. He separated the smoke into two columns, and then I saw a rock, which stood like a pillar between the two mountains, slowly open, and a splendid palace appear within.

But, Commander of the Faithful, the love of gold had taken such possession of my heart, that I could not even stop to examine the riches, but fell upon the first pile of gold within my reach and began to heap it into a sack that I had brought with me.

The dervish likewise set to work, but I soon noticed that he confined himself to collecting precious stones, and I felt I should be wise to follow his example. At length the camels were loaded with as much as they could carry, and nothing remained but to seal up the treasure, and go our ways.

Before, however, this was done, the dervish went up to a great golden vase, beautifully chased, and took from it a small wooden box, which he hid in the bosom of his dress, merely saying that it contained a special kind of ointment. Then he once more kindled the fire, threw on the perfume, and murmured the unknown spell, and the rock closed, and stood whole as before.

The next thing was to divide the camels, and to charge them with the treasure, after which we each took command of our own and marched out of the valley, till we reached the place in the high road where the routes diverge, and then we parted, the dervish going towards Balsora, and I to Bagdad. We embraced each other tenderly, and I poured out my gratitude for the honour he had done me, in singling me out for this great wealth, and having said a hearty farewell we turned our backs, and hastened after our camels.

I had hardly come up with mine when the demon of envy filled my soul. "What does a dervish want with riches like that?" I said to myself. "He alone has the secret of the treasure, and can always get as much as he wants," and I halted my camels by the roadside, and ran back after him.

I was a quick runner, and it did not take me very long to come up with him. "My brother," I exclaimed, as soon as I could speak, "almost at the moment of our leave-taking, a reflection occurred to me, which is perhaps new to you. You are a dervish by profession, and live a very quiet life, only caring to do good, and careless of the things of this world. You do not realise the burden that you lay upon yourself, when you gather into your hands such great wealth, besides the fact that no one, who is not accustomed to camels from his birth, can ever manage the stubborn beasts. If you are wise, you will not encumber yourself with more than thirty, and you will find those trouble enough."

"You are right," replied the dervish, who understood me quite well, but did not wish to fight the matter. "I confess I had not thought about it. Choose any ten you like, and drive them before you."

I selected ten of the best camels, and we proceeded along the road, to rejoin those I had left behind. I had got what I wanted, but I had found the dervish so easy to deal with, that I rather regretted I had not asked for ten more. I looked back. He had only gone a few paces, and I called after him.

"My brother," I said, "I am unwilling to part from you without pointing out what I think you scarcely grasp, that large experience of camel-driving is necessary to anybody who intends to keep together a troop of thirty. In your own interest, I feel sure you would be much happier if you entrusted ten more of them to me, for with my practice it is all one to me if I take two or a hundred."

As before, the dervish made no difficulties, and I drove off my ten camels in triumph, only leaving him with twenty for his share. I had now sixty, and anyone might have imagined that I should be content.

But, Commander of the Faithful, there is a proverb that says, "the more one has, the more one wants." So it was with me. I could not rest as long as one solitary camel remained to the dervish; and returning to him I redoubled my prayers and embraces, and promises of eternal gratitude, till the last twenty were in my hands.

"Make a good use of them, my brother," said the holy man. "Remember riches sometimes have wings if we keep them for ourselves, and the poor are at our gates expressly that we may help them."

My eyes were so blinded by gold, that I paid no heed to his wise counsel, and only looked about for something else to grasp. Suddenly I remembered the little box of ointment that the dervish had hidden, and which most likely contained a treasure more precious than all the rest. Giving him one last embrace, I observed accidentally, "What are you going to do with that little box of ointment? It seems hardly worth taking with you; you might as well let me have it. And really, a dervish who has given up the world has no need of ointment!"

Oh, if he had only refused my request! But then, supposing he had, I should have got possession of it by force, so great was the madness that had laid hold upon me. However, far from refusing it, the dervish at once held it out, saying gracefully, "Take it, my friend, and if there is anything else I can do to make you happy you must let me know."

Directly the box was in my hands I wrenched off the cover. "As you are so kind," I said, "tell me, I pray you, what are the virtues of this ointment?"

"They are most curious and interesting," replied the dervish. "If you apply a little of it to your left eye you will behold in an instant all the treasures hidden in the bowels of the earth. But beware lest you touch your right eye with it, or your sight will be destroyed for ever."

His words excited my curiosity to the highest pitch. "Make trial on me, I implore you," I cried, holding out the box to the dervish. "You will know how to do it better than I! I am burning with impatience to test its charms."

The dervish took the box I had extended to him, and, bidding me shut my left eye, touched it gently with the ointment. When I opened it again I saw spread out, as it were before me, treasures of every kind and without number. But as all this time I had been obliged to keep my right eye closed, which was very fatiguing, I begged the dervish to apply the ointment to that eye also.

"If you insist upon it I will do it," answered the dervish, "but you must remember what I told you just now – that if it touches your right eye you will become blind on the spot."

Unluckily, in spite of my having proved the truth of the dervish's words in so many instances, I was firmly convinced that he was now keeping concealed from me some hidden and precious virtue of the ointment. So I turned a deaf ear to all he said.

"My brother," I replied smiling, "I see you are joking. It is not natural that the same ointment should have two such exactly opposite effects."

"It is true all the same," answered the dervish, "and it would be well for you if you believed my word."

But I would not believe, and, dazzled by the greed of avarice, I thought that if one eye could show me riches, the other might teach me how to get possession of them. And I continued to press the dervish to anoint my right eye, but this he resolutely declined to do.

"After having conferred such benefits on you," said he, "I am loth indeed to work you such evil. Think what it is to be blind, and do not force me to do what you will repent as long as you live."

It was of no use. "My brother," I said firmly, "pray say no more, but do what I ask. You have most generously responded to my wishes up to this time, do not spoil my recollection of you for a thing of such little consequence. Let what will happen I take it on my own head, and will never reproach you."

"Since you are determined upon it," he answered with a sigh, "there is no use talking," and taking the ointment he laid some on my right eye, which was tight shut. When I tried to open it heavy clouds of darkness floated before me. I was as blind as you see me now!

"Miserable dervish!" I shrieked, "so it is true after all! Into what a bottomless pit has my lust after gold plunged me. Ah, now that my eyes are closed they are really opened. I know that all my sufferings are caused by myself alone! But, good brother, you, who are so kind and charitable, and know the secrets of such vast learning, have you nothing that will give me back my sight?"

"Unhappy man," replied the dervish, "it is not my fault that this has befallen you, but it is a just chastisement. The blindness of your heart has wrought the blindness of your body. Yes, I have secrets; that you have seen in the short time that we have known each other. But I have none that will give you back your sight. You have proved yourself unworthy of the riches that were given you. Now they have passed into my hands, whence they will flow into the hands of others less greedy and ungrateful than you."

The dervish said no more and left me, speechless with shame and confusion, and so wretched that I stood rooted to the spot, while he collected the eighty camels and proceeded on his way to Balsora. It was in vain that I entreated him not to leave me, but at least to take me within reach of the first passing caravan. He was deaf to my prayers and cries, and I should soon have been dead of hunger and misery if some merchants had not come along the track the following day and kindly brought me back to Bagdad.

From a rich man I had in one moment become a beggar; and up to this time I have lived solely on the alms that have been bestowed on me. But, in order to expiate the sin of avarice, which was my undoing, I oblige each passer-by to give me a blow.

This, Commander of the Faithful, is my story.

When the blind man had ended the Caliph addressed him: "Baba-Abdalla, truly your sin is great, but you have suffered enough. Henceforth repent in private, for I will see that enough money is given you day by day for all your wants."

At these words Baba-Abdalla flung himself at the Caliph's feet, and prayed that honour and happiness might be his portion for ever.

The Story of Sidi-Nouman

Andrew and Nora Lang

THE CALIPH, Haroun-al-Raschid, was much pleased with the tale of the blind man and the dervish, and when it was finished he turned to the young man who had ill-treated his horse, and inquired his name also. The young man replied that he was called Sidi-Nouman.

"Sidi-Nouman," observed the Caliph, "I have seen horses broken all my life long, and have even broken them myself, but I have never seen any horse broken in such a barbarous manner as by you yesterday. Every one who looked on was indignant, and blamed you loudly. As for myself, I was so angry that I was very nearly disclosing who I was, and putting a stop to it at once. Still, you have not the air of a cruel man, and I would gladly believe that you did not act in this way without some reason. As I am told that it was not the first time, and indeed that every day you are to be seen flogging and spurring your horse, I wish to come to the bottom of the matter. But tell me the whole truth, and conceal nothing."

Sidi-Nouman changed colour as he heard these words, and his manner grew confused; but he saw plainly that there was no help for it. So he prostrated himself before the throne of the Caliph and tried to obey, but the words stuck in his throat, and he remained silent.

The Caliph, accustomed though he was to instant obedience, guessed something of what was passing in the young man's mind, and sought to put him at his ease. "Sidi-Nouman," he said, "do not think of me as the Caliph, but merely as a friend who would like to hear your story. If there is anything in it that you are afraid may offend me, take courage, for I pardon you beforehand. Speak then openly and without fear, as to one who knows and loves you."

Reassured by the kindness of the Caliph, Sidi-Nouman at length began his tale.

"Commander of the Faithful," said he, "dazzled though I am by the lustre of your Highness' presence, I will do my best to satisfy your wishes. I am by no means perfect, but I am not naturally cruel, neither do I take pleasure in breaking the law. I admit that the treatment of my horse is calculated to give your Highness a bad opinion of me, and to set an evil example to others; yet I have not chastised it without reason, and I have hopes that I shall be judged more worthy of pity than punishment."

Commander of the Faithful, I will not trouble to describe my birth; it is not of sufficient distinction to deserve your Highness' attention. My ancestors were careful people, and I inherited enough money to enable me to live comfortably, though without show.

Having therefore a modest fortune, the only thing wanting to my happiness was a wife who could return my affection, but this blessing I was not destined to get; for on the very day after my marriage, my bride began to try my patience in every way that was most hard to bear.

Now, seeing that the customs of our land oblige us to marry without ever beholding the person with whom we are to pass our lives, a man has of course no right to complain as long as his wife is not absolutely repulsive, or is not positively deformed. And whatever defects her body may have, pleasant ways and good behaviour will go far to remedy them.

The first time I saw my wife unveiled, when she had been brought to my house with the usual ceremonies, I was enchanted to find that I had not been deceived in regard to the account that had been given me of her beauty. I began my married life in high spirits, and the best hopes of happiness.

The following day a grand dinner was served to us but as my wife did not appear, I ordered a servant to call her. Still she did not come, and I waited impatiently for some time. At last she entered the room, and she took our places at the table, and plates of rice were set before us.

I ate mine, as was natural, with a spoon, but great was my surprise to notice that my wife, instead of doing the same, drew from her pocket a little case, from which she selected a long pin, and by the help of this pin conveyed her rice grain by grain to her mouth.

"Amina," I exclaimed in astonishment, "is that the way you eat rice at home? And did you do it because your appetite was so small, or did you wish to count the grains so that you might never eat more than a certain number? If it was from economy, and you are anxious to teach me not to be wasteful, you have no cause for alarm. We shall never ruin ourselves in that way! Our fortune is large enough for all our needs, therefore, dear Amina, do not seek to check yourself, but eat as much as you desire, as I do!"

In reply to my affectionate words, I expected a cheerful answer; yet Amina said nothing at all, but continued to pick her rice as before, only at longer and longer intervals. And, instead of trying the other dishes, all she did was to put every now and then a crumb, of bread into her mouth, that would not have made a meal for a sparrow.

I felt provoked by her obstinacy, but to excuse her to myself as far as I could, I suggested that perhaps she had never been used to eat in the company of men, and that her family might have taught her that she ought to behave prudently and discreetly in the presence of her husband. Likewise that she might either have dined already or intend to do so in her own apartments. So I took no further notice, and when I had finished left the room, secretly much vexed at her strange conduct.

The same thing occurred at supper, and all through the next day, whenever we ate together. It was quite clear that no woman could live upon two or three bread-crumbs and a few grains of rice, and I determined to find out how and when she got food. I pretended not to pay attention to anything she did, in the hope that little by little she would get accustomed to me, and become more friendly; but I soon saw that my expectations were quite vain.

One night I was lying with my eyes closed, and to, all appearance sound asleep, when Amina arose softly, and dressed herself without making the slightest sound. I could not imagine what she was going to do, and as my curiosity was great I made up my mind to follow her. When she was fully dressed, she stole quietly from the room.

The instant she had let the curtain fall behind her, I flung a garment on my shoulders and a pair of slippers on my feet. Looking from a lattice which opened into the court, I saw her in the act of passing through the street door, which she carefully left open.

It was bright moonlight, so I easily managed to keep her in sight, till she entered a cemetery not far from the house. There I hid myself under the shadow of the wall, and crouched down cautiously; and hardly was I concealed, when I saw my wife approaching in company with a ghoul – one of those demons which, as your Highness is aware, wander about the country making their lairs in deserted buildings and springing out upon unwary travellers whose flesh they eat. If no live being goes their way, they then betake themselves to the cemeteries, and feed upon the dead bodies.

I was nearly struck dumb with horror on seeing my wife with this hideous female ghoul. They passed by me without noticing me, began to dig up a corpse which had been buried that day, and then sat down on the edge of the grave, to enjoy their frightful repast, talking quietly and cheerfully all the while, though I was too far off to hear what they said. When they had finished, they threw back the body into the grave, and heaped back the earth upon it. I made no effort to disturb them, and returned quickly to the house, when I took care to leave the door open, as I had previously found it. Then I got back into bed, and pretended to sleep soundly.

A short time after Amina entered as quietly as she had gone out. She undressed and stole into bed, congratulating herself apparently on the cleverness with which she had managed her expedition.

As may be guessed, after such a scene it was long before I could close my eyes, and at the first sound which called the faithful to prayer, I put on my clothes and went to the mosque. But even prayer did not restore peace to my troubled spirit, and I could not face my wife until I had made up my mind what future course I should pursue in regard to her. I therefore spent the morning roaming about from one garden to another, turning over various plans for compelling my wife to give up her horrible ways; I thought of using violence to make her submit, but felt reluctant to be unkind to her. Besides, I had an instinct that gentle means had the best chance of success; so, a little soothed, I turned towards home, which I reached about the hour of dinner.

As soon as I appeared, Amina ordered dinner to be served, and we sat down together. As usual, she persisted in only picking a few grains of rice, and I resolved to speak to her at once of what lay so heavily on my heart.

"Amina," I said, as quietly as possible, "you must have guessed the surprise I felt, when the day after our marriage you declined to eat anything but a few morsels of rice, and altogether behaved in such a manner that most husbands would have been deeply wounded. However I had patience with you, and only tried to tempt your appetite by the choicest dishes I could invent, but all to no purpose. Still, Amina, it seems to me that there be some among them as sweet to the taste as the flesh of a corpse?"

I had no sooner uttered these words than Amina, who instantly understood that I had followed her to the grave-yard, was seized with a passion beyond any that I have ever witnessed. Her face became purple, her eyes looked as if they would start from her head, and she positively foamed with rage.

I watched her with terror, wondering what would happen next, but little thinking what would be the end of her fury. She seized a vessel of water that stood at hand, and plunging her hand in it, murmured some words I failed to catch. Then, sprinkling it on my face, she cried madly:

"Wretch, receive the reward of your prying, and become a dog."

The words were not out of her mouth when, without feeling conscious that any change was passing over me, I suddenly knew that I had ceased to be a man. In the greatness of the shock and surprise – for I had no idea that Amina was a magician – I never dreamed of running away, and stood rooted to the spot, while Amina grasped a stick and began to beat me. Indeed her blows were so heavy, that I only wonder they did not kill me at once. However they succeeded in rousing me from my stupor, and I dashed into the court-yard, followed closely by Amina, who made frantic dives at me, which I was not quick enough to dodge. At last she got tired of pursuing me, or else a new trick entered into her head, which would give me speedy and painful death; she opened the gate leading into the street, intending to crush me as I passed through. Dog though I was, I saw through her design, and stung into presence of mind by the greatness of the danger, I timed my movements so well that I contrived to rush through, and only the tip of my tail received a squeeze as she banged the gate.

I was safe, but my tail hurt me horribly, and I yelped and howled so loud all along the streets, that the other dogs came and attacked me, which made matters no better. In order to avoid them, I took refuge in a cookshop, where tongues and sheep's heads were sold.

At first the owner showed me great kindness, and drove away the other dogs that were still at my heels, while I crept into the darkest corner. But though I was safe for the moment, I was not destined to remain long under his protection, for he was one of those who hold all dogs to be unclean, and that all the washing in the world will hardly purify you from their contact. So after my enemies had gone to seek other prey, he tried to lure me from my corner in order to force me into the street. But I refused to come out of my hole, and spent the night in sleep, which I sorely needed, after the pain inflicted on me by Amina.

I have no wish to weary your Highness by dwelling on the sad thoughts which accompanied my change of shape, but it may interest you to hear that the next morning my host went out early to do his marketing, and returned laden with the sheep's heads, and tongues and trotters that formed his stock in trade for the day. The smell of meat attracted various hungry dogs in the neighbourhood, and they gathered round the door begging for some bits. I stole out of my corner, and stood with them.

In spite of his objection to dogs, as unclean animals, my protector was a kind-hearted man, and knowing I had eaten nothing since yesterday, he threw me bigger and better bits than those which fell to the share of the other dogs. When I had finished, I tried to go back into the shop, but this he would not allow, and stood so firmly at the entrance with a stout stick, that I was forced to give it up, and seek some other home.

A few paces further on was a baker's shop, which seemed to have a gay and merry man for a master. At that moment he was having his breakfast, and though I gave no signs of hunger, he at once threw me a piece of bread. Before gobbling it up, as most dogs are in the habit of doing, I bowed my head and wagged my tail, in token of thanks, and he understood, and smiled pleasantly. I really did not want the bread at all, but felt it would be ungracious to refuse, so I ate it slowly, in order that he might see that I only did it out of politeness. He understood this also, and seemed quite willing to let me stay in his shop, so I sat down, with my face to the door, to show that I only asked his protection. This he gave me, and indeed encouraged me to come into the house itself, giving me a corner where I might sleep, without being in anybody's way.

The kindness heaped on me by this excellent man was far greater than I could ever have expected. He was always affectionate in his manner of treating me, and I shared his breakfast, dinner and supper, while, on my side, I gave him all the gratitude and attachment to which he had a right.

I sat with my eyes fixed on him, and he never left the house without having me at his heels; and if it ever happened that when he was preparing to go out I was asleep, and did not notice, he would call "Rufus, Rufus," for that was the name he gave me.

Some weeks passed in this way, when one day a woman came in to buy bread. In paying for it, she laid down several pieces of money, one of which was bad. The baker perceived this, and declined to take it, demanding another in its place. The woman, for her part, refused to take it back, declaring it was perfectly good, but the baker would have nothing to do with it. "It is really such a bad imitation," he exclaimed at last, "that even my dog would not be taken in. Here Rufus! Rufus!" and hearing his voice, I jumped on to the counter. The baker threw down the money before me, and said, "Find out if there is a bad coin." I looked at each in turn, and then laid my paw on the false one, glancing at the same time at my master, so as to point it out.

The baker, who had of course been only in joke, was exceedingly surprised at my cleverness, and the woman, who was at last convinced that the man spoke the truth, produced another piece of money in its place. When she had gone, my master was so pleased that he told all the neighbours what I had done, and made a great deal more of it than there really was.

The neighbours, very naturally, declined to believe his story, and tried me several times with all the bad money they could collect together, but I never failed to stand the test triumphantly.

Soon, the shop was filled from morning till night, with people who on the pretence of buying bread came to see if I was as clever as I was reported to be. The baker drove a roaring trade, and admitted that I was worth my weight in gold to him.

Of course there were plenty who envied him his large custom, and many was the pitfall set for me, so that he never dared to let me out of his sight. One day a woman, who had not been in the shop before, came to ask for bread, like the rest. As usual, I was lying on the counter, and she threw down six coins before me, one of which was false. I detected it at once, and put my paw on it, looking as I did so at the woman. "Yes," she said, nodding her head. "You are quite right, that is the one." She stood gazing at me attentively for some time, then paid for the bread, and left the shop, making a sign for me to follow her secretly.

Now my thoughts were always running on some means of shaking off the spell laid on me, and noticing the way in which this woman had looked at me, the idea entered my head that perhaps she might have guessed what had happened, and in this I was not deceived. However I let her go on a little way, and merely stood at the door watching her. She turned, and seeing that I was quite still, she again beckoned to me.

The baker all this while was busy with his oven, and had forgotten all about me, so I stole out softly, and ran after the woman.

When we came to her house, which was some distance off, she opened the door and then said to me, "Come in, come in; you will never be sorry that you followed me." When I had entered she fastened the door, and took me into a large room, where a beautiful girl was working at a piece of embroidery. "My daughter," exclaimed my guide, "I have brought you the famous dog belonging to the baker which can tell good money from bad. You know that when I first heard of him, I told you I was sure he must be really a man, changed into a dog by magic. To-day I went to the baker's, to prove for myself the truth of the story, and persuaded the dog to follow me here. Now what do you say?"

"You are right, mother," replied the girl, and rising she dipped her hand into a vessel of water. Then sprinkling it over me she said, "If you were born dog, remain dog; but if you were born man, by virtue of this water resume your proper form." In one moment the spell was broken. The dog's shape vanished as if it had never been, and it was a man who stood before her.

Overcome with gratitude at my deliverance, I flung myself at her feet, and kissed the hem of her garment. "How can I thank you for your goodness towards a stranger, and for what you have done? Henceforth I am your slave. Deal with me as you will!"

Then, in order to explain how I came to be changed into a dog, I told her my whole story, and finished with rendering the mother the thanks due to her for the happiness she had brought me.

"Sidi-Nouman," returned the daughter, "say no more about the obligation you are under to us. The knowledge that we have been of service to you is ample payment. Let us speak of Amina, your wife, with whom I was acquainted before her marriage. I was aware that she was a magician, and she knew too that I had studied the same art, under the same mistress. We met often going to the same baths, but we did not like each other, and never sought to become friends. As to what concerns you, it is not enough to have broken your spell, she must be punished for her wickedness. Remain for a moment with my mother, I beg," she added hastily, "I will return shortly."

Left alone with the mother, I again expressed the gratitude I felt, to her as well as to her daughter.

"My daughter," she answered, "is, as you see, as accomplished a magician as Amina herself, but you would be astonished at the amount of good she does by her knowledge. That is why I have never interfered, otherwise I should have put a stop to it long ago." As she spoke, her daughter entered with a small bottle in her hand.

"Sidi-Nouman," she said, "the books I have just consulted tell me that Amina is not home at present, but she should return at any moment. I have likewise found out by their means, that she pretends before the servants great uneasiness as to your absence. She has circulated a story that, while at dinner with her, you remembered some important business that had to be done at once, and left the house without shutting the door. By this means a dog had strayed in, which she was forced to get rid of by a stick. Go home then without delay, and await Amina's return in your room. When she comes in, go down to meet her, and in her surprise, she will try to run away. Then have this bottle ready, and dash the water it contains over her, saying boldly, "Receive the reward of your crimes." That is all I have to tell you."

Everything happened exactly as the young magician had foretold. I had not been in my house many minutes before Amina returned, and as she approached I stepped in front of her, with the water in my hand. She gave one loud cry, and turned to the door, but she was too late. I had already dashed the water in her face and spoken the magic words. Amina disappeared, and in her place stood the horse you saw me beating yesterday.

This, Commander of the Faithful, is my story, and may I venture to hope that, now you have heard the reason of my conduct, your Highness will not think this wicked woman too harshly treated?

"Sidi-Nouman," replied the Caliph, "your story is indeed a strange one, and there is no excuse to be offered for your wife. But, without condemning your treatment of her,

I wish you to reflect how much she must suffer from being changed into an animal, and I hope you will let that punishment be enough. I do not order you to insist upon the young magician finding the means to restore your wife to her human shape, because I know that when once women such as she begin to work evil they never leave off, and I should only bring down on your head a vengeance far worse than the one you have undergone already."

The Story of Ali Colia, Merchant of Bagdad

Andrew and Nora Lang

IN THE REIGN of Haroun-al-Raschid, there lived in Bagdad a merchant named Ali Cogia, who, having neither wife nor child, contented himself with the modest profits produced by his trade. He had spent some years quite happily in the house his father had left him, when three nights running he dreamed that an old man had appeared to him, and reproached him for having neglected the duty of a good Mussulman, in delaying so long his pilgrimage to Mecca.

Ali Cogia was much troubled by this dream, as he was unwilling to give up his shop, and lose all his customers. He had shut his eyes for some time to the necessity of performing this pilgrimage, and tried to atone to his conscience by an extra number of good works, but the dream seemed to him a direct warning, and he resolved to put the journey off no longer.

The first thing he did was to sell his furniture and the wares he had in his shop, only reserving to himself such goods as he might trade with on the road. The shop itself he sold also, and easily found a tenant for his private house. The only matter he could not settle satisfactorily was the safe custody of a thousand pieces of gold which he wished to leave behind him.

After some thought, Ali Cogia hit upon a plan which seemed a safe one. He took a large vase, and placing the money in the bottom of it, filled up the rest with olives. After corking the vase tightly down, he carried it to one of his friends, a merchant like himself, and said to him:

"My brother, you have probably heard that I am staffing with a caravan in a few days for Mecca. I have come to ask whether you would do me the favour to keep this vase of olives for me till I come back?"

The merchant replied readily, "Look, this is the key of my shop: take it, and put the vase wherever you like. I promise that you shall find it in the same place on your return."

A few days later, Ali Cogia mounted the camel that he had laden with merchandise, joined the caravan, and arrived in due time at Mecca. Like the other pilgrims he visited the sacred Mosque, and after all his religious duties were performed, he set out his goods to the best advantage, hoping to gain some customers among the passers-by.

Very soon two merchants stopped before the pile, and when they had turned it over, one said to the other:

"If this man was wise he would take these things to Cairo, where he would get a much better price than he is likely to do here."

Ali Cogia heard the words, and lost no time in following the advice. He packed up his wares, and instead of returning to Bagdad, joined a caravan that was going to Cairo.

The results of the journey gladdened his heart. He sold off everything almost directly, and bought a stock of Egyptian curiosities, which he intended selling at Damascus; but as the caravan with which he would have to travel would not be starting for another six weeks, he took advantage of the delay to visit the Pyramids, and some of the cities along the banks of the Nile.

Now the attractions of Damascus so fascinated the worthy Ali, that he could hardly tear himself away, but at length he remembered that he had a home in Bagdad, meaning to return by way of Aleppo, and after he had crossed the Euphrates, to follow the course of the Tigris.

But when he reached Mossoul, Ali had made such friends with some Persian merchants, that they persuaded him to accompany them to their native land, and even as far as India, and so it came to pass that seven years had slipped by since he had left Bagdad, and during all that time the friend with whom he had left the vase of olives had never once thought of him or of it. In fact, it was only a month before Ali Cogia's actual return that the affair came into his head at all, owing to his wife's remarking one day, that it was a long time since she had eaten any olives, and would like some.

"That reminds me," said the husband, "that before Ali Cogia went to Mecca seven years ago, he left a vase of olives in my care. But really by this time he must be dead, and there is no reason we should not eat the olives if we like. Give me a light, and I will fetch them and see how they taste."

"My husband," answered the wife, "beware, I pray, of your doing anything so base! Supposing seven years have passed without news of Ali Cogia, he need not be dead for all that, and may come back any day. How shameful it would be to have to confess that you had betrayed your trust and broken the seal of the vase! Pay no attention to my idle words, I really have no desire for olives now. And probably after all this while they are no longer good. I have a presentiment that Ali Cogia will return, and what will he think of you? Give it up, I entreat."

The merchant, however, refused to listen to her advice, sensible though it was. He took a light and a dish and went into his shop.

"If you will be so obstate," said his wife, "I cannot help it; but do not blame me if it turns out ill."

When the merchant opened the vase he found the topmost olives were rotten, and in order to see if the under ones were in better condition he shook some out into the dish. As they fell out a few of the gold pieces fell out too.

The sight of the money roused all the merchant's greed. He looked into the vase, and saw that all the bottom was filled with gold. He then replaced the olives and returned to his wife.

"My wife," he said, as he entered the room, "you were quite right; the olives are rotten, and I have recorked the vase so well that Ali Cogia will never know it has been touched."

"You would have done better to believe me," replied the wife. "I trust that no harm will come of it."

These words made no more impression on the merchant than the others had done; and he spent the whole night in wondering how he could manage to keep the gold if Ali Cogia should come back and claim his vase. Very early next morning he went out and bought fresh new olives; he then threw away the old ones, took out the gold and hid it, and filled up the vase with the olives he had bought. This done he recorked the vase and put it in the same place where it had been left by Ali Cogia.

A month later Ali Cogia re-entered Bagdad, and as his house was still let he went to an inn; and the following day set out to see his friend the merchant, who received him with open arms and many expressions of surprise. After a few moments given to inquiries Ali Cogia begged the merchant to hand him over the vase that he had taken care of for so long.

"Oh certainly," said he, "I am only glad I could be of use to you in the matter. Here is the key of my shop; you will find the vase in the place where you put it."

Ali Cogia fetched his vase and carried it to his room at the inn, where he opened it. He thrust down his hand but could feel no money, but still was persuaded it must be there. So he got some plates and vessels from his travelling kit and emptied out the olives. To no purpose. The gold was not there. The poor man was dumb with horror, then, lifting up his hands, he exclaimed, "Can my old friend really have committed such a crime?"

In great haste he went back to the house of the merchant. "My friend," he cried, "you will be astonished to see me again, but I can find nowhere in this vase a thousand pieces of gold that I placed in the bottom under the olives. Perhaps you may have taken a loan of them for your business purposes; if that is so you are most welcome. I will only ask you to give me a receipt, and you can pay the money at your leisure."

The merchant, who had expected something of the sort, had his reply all ready. "Ali Cogia," he said, "when you brought me the vase of olives did I ever touch it?"

"I gave you the key of my shop and you put it yourself where you liked, and did you not find it in exactly the same spot and in the same state? If you placed any gold in it, it must be there still. I know nothing about that; you only told me there were olives. You can believe me or not, but I have not laid a finger on the vase."

Ali Cogia still tried every means to persuade the merchant to admit the truth. "I love peace," he said, "and shall deeply regret having to resort to harsh measures. Once more, think of your reputation. I shall be in despair if you oblige me to call in the aid of the law."

"Ali Cogia," answered the merchant, "you allow that it was a vase of olives you placed in my charge. You fetched it and removed it yourself, and now you tell me it contained a thousand pieces of gold, and that I must restore them to you! Did you ever say anything about them before? Why, I did not even know that the vase had olives in it! You never showed them to me. I wonder you have not demanded pearls or diamonds. Retire, I pray you, lest a crowd should gather in front of my shop."

By this time not only the casual passers-by, but also the neighbouring merchants, were standing round, listening to the dispute, and trying every now and then to smooth matters between them. But at the merchant's last words Ali Cogia resolved to lay the cause of the quarrel before them, and told them the whole story. They heard him to the end, and inquired of the merchant what he had to say.

The accused man admitted that he had kept Ali Cogia's vase in his shop; but he denied having touched it, and swore that as to what it contained he only knew what Ali Cogia had told him, and called them all to witness the insult that had been put upon him.

"You have brought it on yourself," said Ali Cogia, taking him by the arm, "and as you appeal to the law, the law you shall have! Let us see if you will dare to repeat your story before the Cadi."

Now as a good Mussulman the merchant was forbidden to refuse this choice of a judge, so he accepted the test, and said to Ali Cogia, "Very well; I should like nothing better. We shall soon see which of us is in the right."

So the two men presented themselves before the Cadi, and Ali Cogia again repeated his tale. The Cadi asked what witnesses he had. Ali Cogia replied that he had not taken this precaution, as he had considered the man his friend, and up to that time had always found him honest.

The merchant, on his side, stuck to his story, and offered to swear solemnly that not only had he never stolen the thousand gold pieces, but that he did not even know they were there. The Cadi allowed him to take the oath, and pronounced him innocent.

Ali Cogia, furious at having to suffer such a loss, protested against the verdict, declaring that he would appeal to the Caliph, Haroun-al-Raschid, himself. But the Cadi paid no attention to his threats, and was quite satisfied that he had done what was right.

Judgment being given the merchant returned home triumphant, and Ali Cogia went back to his inn to draw up a petition to the Caliph. The next morning he placed himself on the road along which the Caliph must pass after mid-day prayer, and stretched out his petition to the officer who walked before the Caliph, whose duty it was to collect such things, and on entering the palace to hand them to his master. There Haroun-al-Raschid studied them carefully.

Knowing this custom, Ali Cogia followed the Caliph into the public hall of the palace, and waited the result. After some time the officer appeared, and told him that the Caliph had read his petition, and had appointed an hour the next morning to give him audience. He then inquired the merchant's address, so that he might be summoned to attend also.

That very evening, the Caliph, with his grand-vizir Giafar, and Mesrour, chief of the eunuchs, all three disguised, as was their habit, went out to take a stroll through the town.

Going down one street, the Caliph's attention was attracted by a noise, and looking through a door which opened into a court he perceived ten or twelve children playing in the moonlight. He hid himself in a dark corner, and watched them.

"Let us play at being the Cadi," said the brightest and quickest of them all; "I will be the Cadi. Bring before me Ali Cogia, and the merchant who robbed him of the thousand pieces of gold."

The boy's words recalled to the Caliph the petition he had read that morning, and he waited with interest to see what the children would do.

The proposal was hailed with joy by the other children, who had heard a great deal of talk about the matter, and they quickly settled the part each one was to play. The Cadi took his seat gravely, and an officer introduced first Ali Cogia, the plaintiff, and then the merchant who was the defendant.

Ali Cogia made a low bow, and pleaded his cause point by point; concluding by imploring the Cadi not to inflict on him such a heavy loss.

The Cadi having heard his case, turned to the merchant, and inquired why he had not repaid Ali Cogia the sum in question.

The false merchant repeated the reasons that the real merchant had given to the Cadi of Bagdad, and also offered to swear that he had told the truth.

"Stop a moment!" said the little Cadi, "before we come to oaths, I should like to examine the vase with the olives. Ali Cogia," he added, "have you got the vase with you?" and finding he had not, the Cadi continued, "Go and get it, and bring it to me."

So Ali Cogia disappeared for an instant, and then pretended to lay a vase at the feet of the Cadi, declaring it was his vase, which he had given to the accused for safe custody; and in order to be quite correct, the Cadi asked the merchant if he recognised it as the same vase. By his silence the merchant admitted the fact, and the Cadi then commanded to have the vase opened. Ali Cogia made a movement as if he was taking off the lid, and the little Cadi on his part made a pretence of peering into a vase.

"What beautiful olives!" he said, "I should like to taste one," and pretending to put one in his mouth, he added, "they are really excellent!

"But," he went on, "it seems to me odd that olives seven years old should be as good as that! Send for some dealers in olives, and let us hear what they say!"

Two children were presented to him as olive merchants, and the Cadi addressed them. "Tell me," he said, "how long can olives be kept so as to be pleasant eating?"

"My lord," replied the merchants, "however much care is taken to preserve them, they never last beyond the third year. They lose both taste and colour, and are only fit to be thrown away."

"If that is so," answered the little Cadi, "examine this vase, and tell me how long the olives have been in it."

The olive merchants pretended to examine the olives and taste them; then reported to the Cadi that they were fresh and good.

"You are mistaken," said he, "Ali Cogia declares he put them in that vase seven years ago."

"My lord," returned the olive merchants, "we can assure you that the olives are those of the present year. And if you consult all the merchants in Bagdad you will not find one to give a contrary opinion."

The accused merchant opened his mouth as if to protest, but the Cadi gave him no time. "Be silent," he said, "you are a thief. Take him away and hang him." So the game ended, the children clapping their hands in applause, and leading the criminal away to be hanged.

Haroun-al-Raschid was lost in astonishment at the wisdom of the child, who had given so wise a verdict on the case which he himself was to hear on the morrow. "Is there any other verdict possible?" he asked the grand-vizir, who was as much impressed as himself. "I can imagine no better judgment."

"If the circumstances are really such as we have heard," replied the grand-vizir, "it seems to me your Highness could only follow the example of this boy, in the method of reasoning, and also in your conclusions."

"Then take careful note of this house," said the Caliph, "and bring me the boy to-morrow, so that the affair may be tried by him in my presence. Summon also the Cadi, to learn his duty from the mouth of a child. Bid Ali Cogia bring his vase of olives, and see that two dealers in olives are present." So saying the Caliph returned to the palace.

The next morning early, the grand-vizir went back to the house where they had seen the children playing, and asked for the mistress and her children. Three boys appeared, and the grand-vizir inquired which had represented the Cadi in their game of the previous evening. The eldest and tallest, changing colour, confessed that it was he, and to his mother's great alarm, the grand-vizir said that he had strict orders to bring him into the presence of the Caliph.

"Does he want to take my son from me?" cried the poor woman; but the grand-vizir hastened to calm her, by assuring her that she should have the boy again in an hour, and she would be quite satisfied when she knew the reason of the summons. So she dressed the boy in his best clothes, and the two left the house.

When the grand-vizir presented the child to the Caliph, he was a little awed and confused, and the Caliph proceeded to explain why he had sent for him. "Approach, my son," he said kindly. "I think it was you who judged the case of Ali Cogia and the merchant last night? I overheard you by chance, and was very pleased with the way you conducted it. To-day you will see the real Ali Cogia and the real merchant. Seat yourself at once next to me."

The Caliph being seated on his throne with the boy next him, the parties to the suit were ushered in. One by one they prostrated themselves, and touched the carpet at the foot of the throne with their foreheads. When they rose up, the Caliph said: "Now speak. This child will give you justice, and if more should be wanted I will see to it myself."

Ali Cogia and the merchant pleaded one after the other, but when the merchant offered to swear the same oath that he had taken before the Cadi, he was stopped by the child, who said that before this was done he must first see the vase of olives.

At these words, Ali Cogia presented the vase to the Caliph, and uncovered it. The Caliph took one of the olives, tasted it, and ordered the expert merchants to do the same. They pronounced the olives good, and fresh that year. The boy informed them that Ali Cogia declared it was seven years since he had placed them in the vase; to which they returned the same answer as the children had done.

The accused merchant saw by this time that his condemnation was certain, and tried to allege something in his defence. The boy had too much sense to order him to be hanged, and looked at the Caliph, saying, "Commander of the Faithful, this is not a game now; it is for your Highness to condemn him to death and not for me."

Then the Caliph, convinced that the man was a thief, bade them take him away and hang him, which was done, but not before he had confessed his guilt and the place in which he had hidden Ali Cogia's money. The Caliph ordered the Cadi to learn how to deal out justice from the mouth of a child, and sent the boy home, with a purse containing a hundred pieces of gold as a mark of his favour.

The Enchanted Horse

Andrew and Nora Lang

IT WAS THE Feast of the New Year, the oldest and most splendid of all the feasts in the Kingdom of Persia, and the day had been spent by the king in the city of Schiraz, taking part in the magnificent spectacles prepared by his subjects to do honour to the festival. The sun was setting, and the monarch was about to give his court the signal to retire, when suddenly an Indian appeared before his throne, leading a horse richly harnessed, and looking in every respect exactly like a real one.

"Sire," said he, prostrating himself as he spoke, "although I make my appearance so late before your Highness, I can confidently assure you that none of the wonders you have seen during the day can be compared to this horse, if you will deign to cast your eyes upon him."

"I see nothing in it," replied the king, "except a clever imitation of a real one; and any skilled workman might do as much."

"Sire," returned the Indian, "it is not of his outward form that I would speak, but of the use that I can make of him. I have only to mount him, and to wish myself in some special place, and no matter how distant it may be, in a very few moments I shall find myself there. It is this, Sire, that makes the horse so marvellous, and if your Highness will allow me, you can prove it for yourself."

The King of Persia, who was interested in every thing out of the common, and had never before come across a horse with such qualities, bade the Indian mount the animal, and show what he could do. In an instant the man had vaulted on his back, and inquired where the monarch wished to send him.

"Do you see that mountain?" asked the king, pointing to a huge mass that towered into the sky about three leagues from Schiraz; "go and bring me the leaf of a palm that grows at the foot."

The words were hardly out of the king's mouth when the Indian turned a screw placed in the horse's neck, close to the saddle, and the animal bounded like lightning up into the air, and was soon beyond the sight even of the sharpest eyes. In a quarter of an hour the Indian was seen returning, bearing in his hand the palm, and, guiding his horse to the foot of the throne, he dismounted, and laid the leaf before the king.

Now the monarch had no sooner proved the astonishing speed of which the horse was capable than he longed to possess it himself, and indeed, so sure was he that the Indian would be quite ready to sell it, that he looked upon it as his own already.

"I never guessed from his mere outside how valuable an animal he was," he remarked to the Indian, "and I am grateful to you for having shown me my error," said he. "If you will sell it, name your own price."

"Sire," replied the Indian, "I never doubted that a sovereign so wise and accomplished as your Highness would do justice to my horse, when he once knew its power; and I even went so far as to think it probable that you might wish to possess it. Greatly as I prize it, I will yield it up to your Highness on one condition. The horse was not constructed by me, but it was given me by the inventor, in exchange for my only daughter, who made me take a solemn oath that I would never part with it, except for some object of equal value."

"Name anything you like," cried the monarch, interrupting him. "My kingdom is large, and filled with fair cities. You have only to choose which you would prefer, to become its ruler to the end of your life."

"Sire," answered the Indian, to whom the proposal did not seem nearly so generous as it appeared to the king, "I am most grateful to your Highness for your princely offer, and beseech you not to be offended with me if I say that I can only deliver up my horse in exchange for the hand of the princess your daughter."

A shout of laughter burst from the courtiers as they heard these words, and Prince Firouz Schah, the heir apparent, was filled with anger at the Indian's presumption. The king, however, thought that it would not cost him much to part from the princess in order to gain such a delightful toy, and while he was hesitating as to his answer the prince broke in.

"Sire," he said, "it is not possible that you can doubt for an instant what reply you should give to such an insolent bargain. Consider what you owe to yourself, and to the blood of your ancestors."

"My son," replied the king, "you speak nobly, but you do not realise either the value of the horse, or the fact that if I reject the proposal of the Indian, he will only make the same to some other monarch, and I should be filled with despair at the thought that anyone but myself should own this Seventh Wonder of the World. Of course I do not say that I shall accept his conditions, and perhaps he may be brought to reason, but meanwhile I should like you to examine the horse, and, with the owner's permission, to make trial of its powers."

The Indian, who had overheard the king's speech, thought that he saw in it signs of yielding to his proposal, so he joyfully agreed to the monarch's wishes, and came forward to help the prince to mount the horse, and show him how to guide it: but, before he had finished, the young man turned the screw, and was soon out of sight.

They waited some time, expecting that every moment he might be seen returning in the distance, but at length the Indian grew frightened, and prostrating himself before the throne, he said to the king, "Sire, your Highness must have noticed that the prince, in his impatience, did not allow me to tell him what it was necessary to do in order to return to the place from which he started. I implore you not to punish me for what was not my fault, and not to visit on me any misfortune that may occur."

"But why," cried the king in a burst of fear and anger, "why did you not call him back when you saw him disappearing?"

"Sire," replied the Indian, "the rapidity of his movements took me so by surprise that he was out of hearing before I recovered my speech. But we must hope that he will perceive and turn a second screw, which will have the effect of bringing the horse back to earth."

"But supposing he does!" answered the king, "what is to hinder the horse from descending straight into the sea, or dashing him to pieces on the rocks?"

"Have no fears, your Highness," said the Indian; "the horse has the gift of passing over seas, and of carrying his rider wherever he wishes to go."

"Well, your head shall answer for it," returned the monarch, "and if in three months he is not safe back with me, or at any rate does not send me news of his safety, your life shall pay the penalty." So saying, he ordered his guards to seize the Indian and throw him into prison.

Meanwhile, Prince Firouz Schah had gone gaily up into the air, and for the space of an hour continued to ascend higher and higher, till the very mountains were not distinguishable from the plains. Then he began to think it was time to come down, and took for granted that, in order to do this, it was only needful to turn the screw the reverse way; but, to his surprise and horror, he found that, turn as he might, he did not make the smallest impression. He then remembered that he had never waited to ask how he was to get back to earth again, and understood the danger in which he stood. Luckily, he did not lose his head, and set about examining the horse's neck with great care, till at last, to his intense joy, he discovered a tiny little peg, much smaller than the other, close to the right ear. This he turned, and found him-self dropping to the earth, though more slowly than he had left it.

It was now dark, and as the prince could see nothing, he was obliged, not without some feeling of disquiet, to allow the horse to direct his own course, and midnight was already passed before Prince Firouz Schah again touched the ground, faint and weary from his long ride, and from the fact that he had eaten nothing since early morning.

The first thing he did on dismounting was to try to find out where he was, and, as far as he could discover in the thick darkness, he found himself on the terraced roof of a huge palace, with a balustrade of marble running round. In one corner of the terrace stood a small door, opening on to a staircase which led down into the palace.

Some people might have hesitated before exploring further, but not so the prince. "I am doing no harm," he said, "and whoever the owner may be, he will not touch me when he sees I am unarmed," and in dread of making a false step, he went cautiously down the staircase. On a landing, he noticed an open door, beyond which was a faintly lighted hall.

Before entering, the prince paused and listened, but he heard nothing except the sound of men snoring. By the light of a lantern suspended from the roof, he perceived a row of black guards sleeping, each with a naked sword lying by him, and he understood that the hall must form the ante-room to the chamber of some queen or princess.

Standing quite still, Prince Firouz Schah looked about him, till his eyes grew accustomed to the gloom, and he noticed a bright light shining through a curtain in one corner. He then made his way softly towards it, and, drawing aside its folds, passed into a magnificent chamber full of sleeping women, all lying on low couches, except one, who was on a sofa; and this one, he knew, must be the princess.

Gently stealing up to the side of her bed he looked at her, and saw that she was more beautiful than any woman he had ever beheld. But, fascinated though he was, he was well aware of the danger of his position, as one cry of surprise would awake the guards, and cause his certain death.

So sinking quietly on his knees, he took hold of the sleeve of the princess and drew her arm lightly towards him. The princess opened her eyes, and seeing before her a handsome well-dressed man, she remained speechless with astonishment.

This favourable moment was seized by the prince, who bowing low while he knelt, thus addressed her:

"You behold, madame, a prince in distress, son to the King of Persia, who, owing to an adventure so strange that you will scarcely believe it, finds himself here, a suppliant for your protection. But yesterday, I was in my father's court, engaged in the celebration of our most solemn festival; to-day, I am in an unknown land, in danger of my life."

Now the princess whose mercy Prince Firouz Schah implored was the eldest daughter of the King of Bengal, who was enjoying rest and change in the palace her father had built her, at a little distance from the capital. She listened kindly to what he had to say, and then answered:

"Prince, be not uneasy; hospitality and humanity are practised as widely in Bengal as they are in Persia. The protection you ask will be given you by all. You have my word for it." And as the prince was about to thank her for her goodness, she added quickly, "However great may be my curiosity to learn by what means you have travelled here so speedily, I know that you must be faint for want of food, so I shall give orders to my women to take you to one of my chambers, where you will be provided with supper, and left to repose."

By this time the princess's attendants were all awake, and listening to the conversation. At a sign from their mistress they rose, dressed themselves hastily, and snatching up some of the tapers which lighted the room, conducted the prince to a large and lofty room, where two of the number prepared his bed, and the rest went down to the kitchen, from which they soon returned with all sorts of dishes. Then, showing him cupboards filled with dresses and linen, they quitted the room.

During their absence the Princess of Bengal, who had been greatly struck by the beauty of the prince, tried in vain to go to sleep again. It was of no use: she felt broad awake, and when her women entered the room, she inquired eagerly if the prince had all he wanted, and what they thought of him.

"Madame," they replied, "it is of course impossible for us to tell what impression this young man has made on you. For ourselves, we think you would be fortunate if the king your father should allow you to marry anyone so amiable. Certainly there is no one in the Court of Bengal who can be compared with him."

These flattering observations were by no means displeasing to the princess, but as she did not wish to betray her own feelings she merely said, "You are all a set of chatterboxes; go back to bed, and let me sleep."

When she dressed the following morning, her maids noticed that, contrary to her usual habit, the princess was very particular about her toilette, and insisted on her hair being dressed two or three times over. "For," she said to herself, "if my appearance was not displeasing to the prince when he saw me in the condition I was, how much more will he be struck with me when he beholds me with all my charms."

Then she placed in her hair the largest and most brilliant diamonds she could find, with a necklace, bracelets and girdle, all of precious stones. And over her shoulders her ladies put a robe of the richest stuff in all the Indies, that no one was allowed to wear except members of the royal family. When she was fully dressed according to her wishes, she sent to know if the Prince of Persia was awake and ready to receive her, as she desired to present herself before him.

When the princess's messenger entered his room, Prince Firouz Schah was in the act of leaving it, to inquire if he might be allowed to pay his homage to her mistress: but on hearing the princess's wishes, he at once gave way. "Her will is my law," he said, "I am only here to obey her orders."

In a few moments the princess herself appeared, and after the usual compliments had passed between them, the princess sat down on a sofa, and began to explain to the prince her reasons for not giving him an audience in her own apartments. "Had I done so," she said, "we might have been interrupted at any hour by the chief of the eunuchs, who has the right to enter whenever it pleases him, whereas this is forbidden ground. I am all impatience to learn the wonderful accident which has procured the pleasure of your arrival, and that is why I have come to you here, where no one can intrude upon us. Begin then, I entreat you, without delay."

So the prince began at the beginning, and told all the story of the festival of Nedrouz held yearly in Persia, and of the splendid spectacles celebrated in its honour. But when he came to the enchanted horse, the princess declared that she could never have imagined anything half so surprising. "Well then," continued the prince, "you can easily understand how the King my father, who has a passion for all curious things, was seized with a violent desire to possess this horse, and asked the Indian what sum he would take for it.

"The man's answer was absolutely absurd, as you will agree, when I tell you that it was nothing less than the hand of the princess my sister; but though all the bystanders laughed and mocked, and I was beside myself with rage, I saw to my despair that my father could not make up his mind to treat the insolent proposal as it deserved. I tried to argue with him, but in vain. He only begged me to examine the horse with a view (as I quite understood) of making me more sensible of its value."

"To please my father, I mounted the horse, and, without waiting for any instructions from the Indian, turned the peg as I had seen him do. In an instant I was soaring upwards, much quicker than an arrow could fly, and I felt as if I must be getting so near the sky that I should soon hit my head against it! I could see nothing beneath me, and for some time was so confused that I did not even know in what direction I was travelling. At last, when it was growing dark, I found another screw, and on turning it, the horse began slowly to sink towards the earth. I was forced to trust to chance, and to see what fate had in store, and it was already past midnight when I found myself on the roof of this palace. I crept down the little staircase, and made directly for a light which I perceived through an open door – I peeped cautiously in, and saw, as you will guess, the eunuchs lying asleep on the floor. I knew the risks I ran, but my need was so great that I paid no attention to them, and stole safely past your guards, to the curtain which concealed your doorway.

"The rest, Princess, you know; and it only remains for me to thank you for the kindness you have shown me, and to assure you of my gratitude. By the law of nations, I am already your slave, and I have only my heart, that is my own, to offer you. But what am I saying? My own? Alas, madame, it was yours from the first moment I beheld you!"

The air with which he said these words could have left no doubt on the mind of the princess as to the effect of her charms, and the blush which mounted to her face only increased her beauty.

"Prince," returned she as soon as her confusion permitted her to speak, "you have given me the greatest pleasure, and I have followed you closely in all your adventures, and though you are positively sitting before me, I even trembled at your danger in the upper regions of the air! Let me say what a debt I owe to the chance that has led you to my house; you could have entered none which would have given you a warmer welcome. As to your being a slave, of course that is merely a joke, and my reception must itself have assured you that you are as free here as at your father's court. As to your heart," continued she in tones of encouragement, "I am quite sure that must have been disposed of long ago, to some princess who is well worthy of it, and I could not think of being the cause of your unfaithfulness to her."

Prince Firouz Schah was about to protest that there was no lady with any prior claims, but he was stopped by the entrance of one of the princess's attendants, who announced that dinner was served, and, after all, neither was sorry for the interruption.

Dinner was laid in a magnificent apartment, and the table was covered with delicious fruits; while during the repast richly dressed girls sang softly and sweetly to stringed instruments. After the prince and princess had finished, they passed into a small room hung with blue and gold, looking out into a garden stocked with flowers and arbutus trees, quite different from any that were to be found in Persia.

"Princess," observed the young man, "till now I had always believed that Persia could boast finer palaces and more lovely gardens than any kingdom upon earth. But my eyes have been opened, and I begin to perceive that, wherever there is a great king he will surround himself with buildings worthy of him."

"Prince," replied the Princess of Bengal, "I have no idea what a Persian palace is like, so I am unable to make comparisons. I do not wish to depreciate my own palace, but I can assure you that it is very poor beside that of the King my father, as you will agree when you have been there to greet him, as I hope you will shortly do."

Now the princess hoped that, by bringing about a meeting between the prince and her father, the King would be so struck with the young man's distinguished air and fine manners, that he would offer him his daughter to wife. But the reply of the Prince of Persia to her suggestion was not quite what she wished.

"Madame," he said, "by taking advantage of your proposal to visit the palace of the King of Bengal, I should satisfy not merely my curiosity, but also the sentiments of respect with which I regard him. But, Princess, I am persuaded that you will feel with me, that I cannot possibly present myself before so great a sovereign without the attendants suitable to my rank. He would think me an adventurer."

"If that is all," she answered, "you can get as many attendants here as you please. There are plenty of Persian merchants, and as for money, my treasury is always open to you. Take what you please."

Prince Firouz Schah guessed what prompted so much kindness on the part of the princess, and was much touched by it. Still his passion, which increased every moment, did not make him forget his duty. So he replied without hesitation:

"I do not know, Princess, how to express my gratitude for your obliging offer, which I would accept at once if it were not for the recollection of all the uneasiness the King my father must be suffering on my account. I should be unworthy indeed of all the love he showers upon me, if I did not return to him at the first possible moment. For, while I am enjoying the society of the most amiable of all princesses, he is, I am quite convinced, plunged in the deepest grief, having lost all hope of seeing me again. I am sure you will understand my position, and will feel that to remain away one instant longer than is necessary would not only be ungrateful on my part, but perhaps even a crime, for how do I know if my absence may not break his heart?

"But," continued the prince, "having obeyed the voice of my conscience, I shall count the moments when, with your gracious permission, I may present myself before the King of Bengal, not as a wanderer, but as a prince, to implore the favour of your hand. My father has always informed me that in my marriage I shall be left quite free, but I am persuaded that I have only to describe your generosity, for my wishes to become his own."

The Princess of Bengal was too reasonable not to accept the explanation offered by Prince Firouz Schah, but she was much disturbed at his intention of departing at once, for she feared that, no sooner had he left her, than the impression she had made on him would fade away. So she made one more effort to keep him, and after assuring him that she entirely approved of his anxiety to see his father, begged him to give her a day or two more of his company.

In common politeness the prince could hardly refuse this request, and the princess set about inventing every kind of amusement for him, and succeeded so well that two months slipped by almost unnoticed, in balls, spectacles and in hunting, of which, when unattended by danger, the princess was passionately fond. But at last, one day, he declared seriously that he could neglect his duty no longer, and entreated her to put no further obstacles in his way, promising at the same time to return, as soon as he could, with all the magnificence due both to her and to himself.

"Princess," he added, "it may be that in your heart you class me with those false lovers whose devotion cannot stand the test of absence. If you do, you wrong me; and were it not for fear of offending you, I would beseech you to come with me, for my life can only be happy when passed with you. As for your reception at the Persian Court, it will be as warm as your merits deserve; and as for what concerns the King of Bengal, he must be much more indifferent to your welfare than you have led me to believe if he does not give his consent to our marriage."

The princess could not find words in which to reply to the arguments of the Prince of Persia, but her silence and her downcast eyes spoke for her, and declared that she had no objection to accompanying him on his travels.

The only difficulty that occurred to her was that Prince Firouz Schah did not know how to manage the horse, and she dreaded lest they might find themselves in the same plight as before. But the prince soothed her fears so successfully, that she soon had no other thought than to arrange for their flight so secretly, that no one in the palace should suspect it.

This was done, and early the following morning, when the whole palace was wrapped in sleep, she stole up on to the roof, where the prince was already awaiting her, with his horse's head towards Persia. He mounted first and helped the princess up behind; then, when she was firmly seated, with her hands holding tightly to his belt, he touched the screw, and the horse began to leave the earth quickly behind him.

He travelled with his accustomed speed, and Prince Firouz Schah guided him so well that in two hours and a half from the time of starting, he saw the capital of Persia lying beneath him. He determined to alight neither in the great square from which he had started, nor in the Sultan's palace, but in a country house at a little distance from the town. Here he showed the princess a beautiful suite of rooms, and begged her to rest, while he informed his father of their arrival, and prepared a public reception worthy of her rank. Then he ordered a horse to be saddled, and set out.

All the way through the streets he was welcomed with shouts of joy by the people, who had long lost all hope of seeing him again. On reaching the palace, he found the Sultan surrounded by his ministers, all clad in the deepest mourning, and his father almost went out of his mind with surprise and delight at the mere sound of his son's voice. When he had calmed down a little, he begged the prince to relate his adventures.

The prince at once seized the opening thus given him, and told the whole story of his treatment by the Princess of Bengal, not even concealing the fact that she had fallen in love with him. "And, Sire," ended the prince, "having given my royal word that you would not refuse your consent to our marriage, I persuaded her to return with me on the Indian's horse. I have left her in one of your Highness's country houses, where she is waiting anxiously to be assured that I have not promised in vain."

As he said this the prince was about to throw himself at the feet of the Sultan, but his father prevented him, and embracing him again, said eagerly:

"My son, not only do I gladly consent to your marriage with the Princess of Bengal, but I will hasten to pay my respects to her, and to thank her in my own person for the benefits she has conferred on you. I will then bring her back with me, and make all arrangements for the wedding to be celebrated to-day."

So the Sultan gave orders that the habits of mourning worn by the people should be thrown off and that there should be a concert of drums, trumpets and cymbals. Also that the Indian should be taken from prison, and brought before him.

His commands were obeyed, and the Indian was led into his presence, surrounded by guards. "I have kept you locked up," said the Sultan, "so that in case my son was lost, your life should pay the penalty. He has now returned; so take your horse, and begone for ever."

The Indian hastily quitted the presence of the Sultan, and when he was outside, he inquired of the man who had taken him out of prison where the prince had really been all this time, and what he had been doing. They told him the whole story, and how the Princess of Bengal was even then awaiting in the country palace the consent of the Sultan, which at once put into the Indian's head a plan of revenge for the treatment he had experienced. Going straight to the country house, he informed the doorkeeper who was left in charge that he had been sent by the Sultan and by the Prince of Persia to fetch the princess on the enchanted horse, and to bring her to the palace.

The doorkeeper knew the Indian by sight, and was of course aware that nearly three months before he had been thrown into prison by the Sultan; and seeing him at liberty, the man took for granted that he was speaking the truth, and made no difficulty about leading him before the Princess of Bengal; while on her side, hearing that he had come from the prince, the lady gladly consented to do what he wished.

The Indian, delighted with the success of his scheme, mounted the horse, assisted the princess to mount behind him, and turned the peg at the very moment that the prince was leaving the palace in Schiraz for the country house, followed closely by the Sultan and all the court. Knowing this, the Indian deliberately steered the horse right above the city, in order that his revenge for his unjust imprisonment might be all the quicker and sweeter.

When the Sultan of Persia saw the horse and its riders, he stopped short with astonishment and horror, and broke out into oaths and curses, which the Indian heard quite unmoved, knowing that he was perfectly safe from pursuit. But mortified and furious as the Sultan was, his feelings were nothing to those of Prince Firouz Schah, when he saw the object of his passionate devotion being borne rapidly away. And while he was struck speechless with grief and remorse at not having guarded her better, she vanished swiftly out of his sight. What was he to do? Should he follow his father into the palace, and there give reins to his despair? Both his love and his courage alike forbade it; and he continued his way to the palace.

The sight of the prince showed the doorkeeper of what folly he had been guilty, and flinging himself at his master's feet, implored his pardon. "Rise," said the prince, "I am the cause of this misfortune, and not you. Go and find me the dress of a dervish, but beware of saying it is for me."

At a short distance from the country house, a convent of dervishes was situated, and the superior, or scheih, was the doorkeeper's friend. So by means of a false story made up on the spur of the moment, it was easy enough to get hold of a dervish's dress, which the prince at once put on, instead of his own. Disguised like this and concealing about him a box of pearls and diamonds he had intended as a present to the princess, he left the house at nightfall, uncertain where he should go, but firmly resolved not to return without her.

Meanwhile the Indian had turned the horse in such a direction that, before many hours had passed, it had entered a wood close to the capital of the kingdom of Cashmere. Feeling very hungry, and supposing that the princess also might be in want of food, he brought his steed down to the earth, and left the princess in a shady place, on the banks of a clear stream.

At first, when the princess had found herself alone, the idea had occurred to her of trying to escape and hide herself. But as she had eaten scarcely anything since she had left Bengal, she felt she was too weak to venture far, and was obliged to abandon her design. On the return of the Indian with meats of various kinds, she began to eat voraciously, and soon had regained sufficient courage to reply with spirit to his insolent remarks. Goaded by his threats she sprang to her feet, calling loudly for help, and luckily her cries were heard by a troop of horsemen, who rode up to inquire what was the matter.

Now the leader of these horsemen was the Sultan of Cashmere, returning from the chase, and he instantly turned to the Indian to inquire who he was, and whom he had with him. The Indian rudely answered that it was his wife, and there was no occasion for anyone else to interfere between them.

The princess, who, of course, was ignorant of the rank of her deliverer, denied altogether the Indian's story. "My lord," she cried, "whoever you may be, put no faith in this impostor. He is an abominable magician, who has this day torn me from the Prince of Persia, my destined husband, and has brought me here on this enchanted horse." She would have continued, but her tears choked her, and the Sultan of Cashmere, convinced by her beauty and her distinguished air of the truth of her tale, ordered his followers to cut off the Indian's head, which was done immediately.

But rescued though she was from one peril, it seemed as if she had only fallen into another. The Sultan commanded a horse to be given her, and conducted her to his own palace, where he led her to a beautiful apartment, and selected female slaves to wait on her, and eunuchs to be her guard. Then, without allowing her time to thank him for all he had done, he bade her repose, saying she should tell him her adventures on the following day.

The princess fell asleep, flattering herself that she had only to relate her story for the Sultan to be touched by compassion, and to restore her to the prince without delay. But a few hours were to undeceive her.

When the King of Cashmere had quitted her presence the evening before, he had resolved that the sun should not set again without the princess becoming his wife, and at daybreak proclamation of his intention was made throughout the town, by the sound of drums, trumpets, cymbals, and other instruments calculated to fill the heart with joy. The Princess of Bengal was early awakened by the noise, but she did not for one moment imagine that it had anything to do with her, till the Sultan, arriving as soon as she was dressed to inquire after her health, informed her that the trumpet blasts she heard were part of the solemn marriage ceremonies, for which he begged her to prepare. This unexpected announcement caused the princess such terror that she sank down in a dead faint.

The slaves that were in waiting ran to her aid, and the Sultan himself did his best to bring her back to consciousness, but for a long while it was all to no purpose. At length her senses began slowly to come back to her, and then, rather than break faith with the Prince of Persia by consenting to such a marriage, she determined to feign madness. So she began by saying all sorts of absurdities, and using all kinds of strange gestures, while the Sultan stood watching her with sorrow and surprise. But as this sudden seizure showed no sign of abating, he left her to her women, ordering them to take the greatest care of her. Still, as the day went on, the malady seemed to become worse, and by night it was almost violent.

Days passed in this manner, till at last the Sultan of Cashmere decided to summon all the doctors of his court to consult together over her sad state. Their answer was that madness is of so many different kinds that it was impossible to give an opinion on the case without seeing the princess, so the Sultan gave orders that they were to be introduced into her chamber, one by one, every man according to his rank.

This decision had been foreseen by the princess, who knew quite well that if once she allowed the physicians to feel her pulse, the most ignorant of them would discover that she was in perfectly good health, and that her madness was feigned, so as each man approached, she broke out into such violent paroxysms, that not one dared to lay a finger on her. A few, who pretended to be cleverer than the rest, declared that they could diagnose sick people only from sight, ordered her certain potions, which she made no difficulty about taking, as she was persuaded they were all harmless.

When the Sultan of Cashmere saw that the court doctors could do nothing towards curing the princess, he called in those of the city, who fared no better. Then he had recourse to the most celebrated physicians in the other large towns, but finding that the task was beyond their science, he finally sent messengers into the other neighbouring states, with a memorandum containing full particulars of the princess's madness, offering at the same time to pay the expenses of any physician who would come and see for himself, and a handsome reward to the one who should cure her. In answer to this proclamation many foreign professors flocked into Cashmere, but they naturally were not more successful than the rest had been, as the cure depended neither on them nor their skill, but only on the princess herself.

It was during this time that Prince Firouz Schah, wandering sadly and hopelessly from place to place, arrived in a large city of India, where he heard a great deal of talk about the Princess of Bengal who had gone out of her senses, on the very day that she was to have been married to the Sultan of Cashmere. This was quite enough to induce him to take the road to Cashmere, and to inquire at the first inn at which he lodged in the capital the full particulars of the story. When he knew that he had at last found the princess whom he had so long lost, he set about devising a plan for her rescue.

The first thing he did was to procure a doctor's robe, so that his dress, added to the long beard he had allowed to grow on his travels, might unmistakably proclaim his profession. He then lost no time in going to the palace, where he obtained an audience of the chief usher, and while apologising for his boldness in presuming to think that he could cure the princess, where so many others had failed, declared that he had the secret of certain remedies, which had hitherto never failed of their effect.

The chief usher assured him that he was heartily welcome, and that the Sultan would receive him with pleasure; and in case of success, he would gain a magnificent reward.

When the Prince of Persia, in the disguise of a physician, was brought before him, the Sultan wasted no time in talking, beyond remarking that the mere sight of a doctor threw the princess into transports of rage. He then led the prince up to a room under the roof, which had an opening through which he might observe the princess, without himself being seen.

The prince looked, and beheld the princess reclining on a sofa with tears in her eyes, singing softly to herself a song bewailing her sad destiny, which had deprived her, perhaps for ever, of a being she so tenderly loved. The young man's heart beat fast as he listened, for he needed no further proof that her madness was feigned, and that it was love of him which had caused her to resort to this species of trick. He softly left his hiding-place, and returned to the Sultan, to whom he reported that he was sure from certain signs that the princess's malady was not incurable, but that he must see her and speak with her alone.

The Sultan made no difficulty in consenting to this, and commanded that he should be ushered in to the princess's apartment. The moment she caught sight of his physician's robe, she sprang from her seat in a fury, and heaped insults upon him. The prince took no notice of her behaviour, and approaching quite close, so that his words might be heard by her alone, he said in a low whisper, "Look at me, princess, and you will see that I am no doctor, but the Prince of Persia, who has come to set you free."

At the sound of his voice, the Princess of Bengal suddenly grew calm, and an expression of joy overspread her face, such as only comes when what we wish for most and expect the least suddenly happens to us. For some time she was too enchanted to speak, and Prince Firouz Schah took advantage of her silence to explain to her all that had occurred, his despair at watching her disappear before his very eyes, the oath he had sworn to follow her over the world, and his rapture at finally discovering her in the palace at Cashmere. When he had finished, he begged in his turn that the princess would tell him how she had come there, so that he might the better devise some means of rescuing her from the tyranny of the Sultan.

It needed but a few words from the princess to make him acquainted with the whole situation, and how she had been forced to play the part of a mad woman in order to escape from a marriage with the Sultan, who had not had sufficient politeness even to ask her consent. If necessary, she added, she had resolved to die sooner than permit herself to be forced into such a union, and break faith with a prince whom she loved.

The prince then inquired if she knew what had become of the enchanted horse since the Indian's death, but the princess could only reply that she had heard nothing about it. Still she did not suppose that the horse could have been forgotten by the Sultan, after all she had told him of its value.

To this the prince agreed, and they consulted together over a plan by which she might be able to make her escape and return with him into Persia. And as the first step, she was to dress herself with care, and receive the Sultan with civility when he visited her next morning.

The Sultan was transported with delight on learning the result of the interview, and his opinion of the doctor's skill was raised still higher when, on the following day, the princess behaved towards him in such a way as to persuade him that her complete cure would not be long delayed. However he contented himself with assuring her how happy he was to see her health so much improved, and exhorted her to make every use of so clever a physician, and to repose entire confidence in him. Then he retired, without awaiting any reply from the princess.

The Prince of Persia left the room at the same time, and asked if he might be allowed humbly to inquire by what means the Princess of Bengal had reached Cashmere, which was so far distant from her father's kingdom, and how she came to be there alone. The Sultan thought the question very natural, and told him the same story that the Princess of Bengal had done, adding that he had ordered the enchanted horse to be taken to his treasury as a curiosity, though he was quite ignorant how it could be used.

"Sire," replied the physician, "your Highness's tale has supplied me with the clue I needed to complete the recovery of the princess. During her voyage hither on an enchanted horse, a portion of its enchantment has by some means been communicated to her person, and it can only be dissipated by certain perfumes of which I possess the secret. If your Highness will deign to consent, and to give the court and the people one of the most astonishing spectacles they have ever witnessed, command the horse to be brought into the big square outside the palace, and leave the rest to me. I promise that in a very few moments, in presence of all the assembled multitude, you shall see the princess as healthy both in mind and body as ever she was in her life. And in order to make the spectacle as impressive as possible, I would suggest that she should be richly dressed and covered with the noblest jewels of the crown."

The Sultan readily agreed to all that the prince proposed, and the following morning he desired that the enchanted horse should be taken from the treasury, and brought into the great square of the palace. Soon the rumour began to spread through the town, that something extraordinary was about to happen, and such a crowd began to collect that the guards had to be called out to keep order, and to make a way for the enchanted horse.

When all was ready, the Sultan appeared, and took his place on a platform, surrounded by the chief nobles and officers of his court. When they were seated, the Princess of Bengal was seen leaving the palace, accompanied by the ladies who had been assigned to her by the Sultan. She slowly approached the enchanted horse, and with the help of her ladies, she mounted on its back. Directly she was in the saddle, with her feet in the stirrups and the bridle in her hand, the physician placed around the horse some large braziers full of burning coals, into each of which he threw a perfume composed of all sorts of delicious scents. Then he crossed his hands over his breast, and with lowered eyes walked three times round the horse, muttering the while certain words. Soon there arose from the burning braziers a thick smoke which almost concealed both the horse and princess, and this was the moment for which he had been waiting. Springing lightly up behind the lady, he leaned forward and turned the peg, and as the horse darted up into the air, he cried aloud so that his words were heard by all present, "Sultan of Cashmere, when you wish to marry princesses who have sought your protection, learn first to gain their consent."

It was in this way that the Prince of Persia rescued the Princess of Bengal, and returned with her to Persia, where they descended this time before the palace of the King himself. The marriage was only delayed just long enough to make the ceremony as brilliant as possible, and, as soon as the rejoicings were over, an ambassador was sent to the King of Bengal, to inform him of what had passed, and to ask his approbation of the alliance between the two countries, which he heartily gave.

The Talking Bird, the Singing Tree, and the Golden Water

Kate Douglas Wiggin and Nora A. Smith

THERE WAS AN emperor of Persia named Kosrouschah, who, when he first came to his crown, in order to obtain a knowledge of affairs, took great pleasure in night excursions, attended by a trusty minister. He often walked in disguise through the city, and met with many adventures, one of the most remarkable of which happened to him upon his first ramble, which was not long after his accession to the throne of his father.

After the ceremonies of his father's funeral rites and his own inauguration were over, the new sultan, as well from inclination as from duty, went out one evening attended by his grand vizier, disguised like himself, to observe what was transacting in the city. As he was passing through a street in that part of the town inhabited only by the meaner sort, he heard some people talking very loud; and going close to the house whence the noise proceeded, and looking through a crack in the door, perceived a light, and three sisters sitting on a sofa, conversing together after supper. By what the eldest said he presently understood the subject of their conversation was wishes: "for," said she, "since we are talking about wishes, mine shall be to have the sultan's baker for my husband, for then I shall eat my fill of that bread, which by way of excellence is called the sultan's; let us see if your tastes are as good as mine." "For my part," replied the second sister, "I wish I was wife to the sultan's chief cook, for then I should eat of the most excellent dishes; and as I am persuaded that the sultan's bread is common in the palace, I should not want any of that; therefore you see," addressing herself to her eldest sister, "that I have a better taste than you." The youngest sister, who was very beautiful, and had more charms and wit than the two elder, spoke in her turn: "For my part, sisters," said she, "I shall not limit my desires to such trifles, but take a higher flight; and since we are upon wishing, I wish to be the emperor's queen-consort. I would make him father of a prince, whose hair should be gold on one side of his head, and silver on the other; when he cried, the tears from his eyes should be pearls; and when he smiled, his vermilion lips should look like a rosebud fresh-blown."

The three sisters' wishes, particularly that of the youngest, seemed so singular to the sultan, that he resolved to gratify them in their desires; but without communicating his design to his grand vizier, he charged him only to take notice of the house, and bring the three sisters before him the following day.

The grand vizier, in executing the emperor's orders, would but just give the sisters time to dress themselves to appear before his majesty, without telling them the reason. He brought them to the palace, and presented them to the emperor, who said to them, "Do you remember the wishes you expressed last night, when you were all in so pleasant a mood? Speak the truth; I must know what they were." At these unexpected words of the emperor, the three sisters were much confounded. They cast down their eyes and blushed, and the colour which rose in the cheeks of the youngest quite captivated the emperor's heart. Modesty, and fear lest they might have offended by their conversation, kept them silent. The emperor, perceiving their confusion, said to encourage them, "Fear nothing, I did not send for you to distress you; and since I see that without my intending it, this is the effect of the question I asked, as I know the wish of each, I will relieve you from your fears. You," added he, "who wished to be my wife, shall have your desire this day; and you," continued he, addressing himself to the two elder sisters, "shall also be married to my chief baker and cook."

As soon as the sultan had declared his pleasure, the youngest sister, setting her elders an example, threw herself at the emperor's feet to express her gratitude. "Sir," said she, "my wish, since it is come to your majesty's knowledge, was expressed only in the way of conversation and amusement. I am unworthy of the honour you do me, and supplicate your pardon for my presumption." The other two sisters would have excused themselves also, but the emperor, interrupting them, said, "No, no; it shall be as I have declared; the wishes of all shall be fulfilled." The nuptials were all celebrated that day, as the emperor had resolved, but in a different manner. The youngest sister's were solemnized with all the rejoicings usual at the marriages of the emperors of Persia; and those of the other two sisters according to the quality and distinction of their husbands; the one as the sultan's chief baker, and the other as head cook.

The two elder felt strongly the disproportion of their marriages to that of their younger sister. This consideration made them far from being content, though they were arrived at the utmost height of their late wishes, and much beyond their hopes. They gave themselves up to an excess of jealousy, which not only disturbed their joy, but was the cause of great trouble and affliction to the queen-consort, their younger sister. They had not an opportunity to communicate their thoughts to each other on the preference the emperor had given her, but were altogether employed in preparing themselves for the celebration of their marriages. Some days afterward, when they had an opportunity of seeing each other at the public baths, the eldest said to the other: "Well, what say you to our sister's great fortune? Is not she a fine person to be a queen!" "I must own," said the other sister, "I cannot conceive what charms the emperor could discover to be so bewitched by her. Was it a reason sufficient for him not to cast his eyes on you, because she was somewhat younger? You were as worthy of his throne, and in justice he ought to have preferred you."

"Sister," said the elder, "I should not have regretted if his majesty had but pitched upon you; but that he should choose that little simpleton really grieves me. But I will revenge myself; and you, I think, are as much concerned as I; therefore, I propose that we should contrive measures and act in concert: communicate to me what you think the likeliest way to mortify her, while I, on my side, will inform you what my desire of revenge shall suggest to me." After this wicked agreement, the two sisters saw each other frequently, and consulted how they might disturb and interrupt the happiness of the queen. They proposed a great many ways, but in deliberating about the manner of executing them, found so many difficulties that they durst not attempt them. In the meantime, with a detestable dissimulation, they often went together to make her visits, and every time showed her all the marks of affection they could devise, to persuade her how overjoyed they were to have a sister raised to so high a fortune. The queen, on her part, constantly received them with all the demonstrations of esteem they could expect from so near a relative. Some time after her marriage, the expected birth of an heir gave great joy to the queen and emperor, which was communicated to all the court, and spread throughout the empire. Upon this news the two sisters came to pay their compliments, and proffered their services, desiring her, if not provided with nurses, to accept of them.

The queen said to them most obligingly: "Sisters, I should desire nothing more, if it were in my power to make the choice. I am, however, obliged to you for your goodwill, but must submit to what the emperor shall order on this occasion. Let your husbands employ their friends to make interest, and get some courtier to ask this favour of his majesty, and if he speaks to me about it, be assured that I shall not only express the pleasure he does me but thank him for making choice of you."

The two husbands applied themselves to some courtiers, their patrons, and begged of them to use their interest to procure their wives the honour they aspired to. Those patrons exerted themselves so much in their behalf that the emperor promised them to consider of the matter, and was as good as his word; for in conversation with the queen he told her that he thought her sisters were the most proper persons to be about her, but would not name them before he had asked her consent. The queen, sensible of the deference the emperor so obligingly paid her, said to him, "Sir, I was prepared to do as your majesty might please to command. But since you have been so kind as to think of my sisters, I thank you for the regard you have shown them for my sake, and therefore I shall not dissemble that I had rather have them than strangers." The emperor therefore named the queen's two sisters to be her attendants; and from that time they went frequently to the palace, overjoyed at the opportunity they would have of executing the detestable wickedness they had meditated against the queen.

Shortly afterward a young prince, as bright as the day, was born to the queen; but neither his innocence nor beauty could move the cruel hearts of the merciless sisters. They wrapped him up carelessly in his cloths and put him into a basket, which they abandoned to the stream of a small canal that ran under the queen's apartment, and declared that she had given birth to a puppy. This dreadful intelligence was announced to the emperor, who became so angry at the circumstance, that he was likely to have occasioned the queen's death, if his grand vizier had not represented to him that he could not, without injustice, make her answerable for the misfortune.

In the meantime, the basket in which the little prince was exposed was carried by the stream beyond a wall which bounded the prospect of the queen's apartment, and from thence floated with the current down the gardens. By chance the intendant of the emperor's gardens, one of the principal officers of the kingdom, was walking in the garden by the side of this canal, and, perceiving a basket floating, called to a gardener who was not far off, to bring it to shore that he might see what it contained. The gardener, with a rake which he had in his hand, drew the basket to the side of the canal, took it up, and gave it to him. The intendant of the gardens was extremely surprised to see in the basket a child, which, though he knew it could be but just born, had very fine features. This officer had been married several years, but though he had always been desirous of having children, Heaven had never blessed him with any. This accident interrupted his walk: he made the gardener follow him with the child, and when he came to his own house, which was situated at the entrance to the gardens of the palace, went into his wife's apartment. "Wife," said he, "as we have no children of our own, God has sent us one. I recommend him to you; provide him a nurse, and take as much care of him as if he were our own son; for, from this moment, I acknowledge him as such." The intendant's wife received the child with great joy, and took particular pleasure in the care of him. The intendant himself would not inquire too narrowly whence the infant came. He saw plainly it came not far off from the queen's apartment, but it was not his business to examine too closely into what had passed, nor to create disturbances in a place where peace was so necessary.

The following year another prince was born, on whom the unnatural sisters had no more compassion than on his brother, but exposed him likewise in a basket and set him adrift in the canal, pretending, this time, that the sultana had given birth to a cat. It was happy also for this child that the intendant of the gardens was walking by the canal side, for he had it carried to his wife, and charged her to take as much care of it as of the former, which was as agreeable to her inclination as it was to his own.

The emperor of Persia was more enraged this time against the queen than before, and she had felt the effects of his anger if the grand vizier's remonstrances had not prevailed. The third year the queen gave birth to a princess, which innocent babe underwent the same fate as her brothers, for the two sisters, being determined not to desist from their detestable schemes till they had seen the queen cast off and humbled, claimed that a log of wood had been born and exposed this infant also on the canal. But the princess, as well as her brothers, was preserved from death by the compassion and charity of the intendant of the gardens.

Kosrouschah could no longer contain himself, when he was informed of the new misfortune. He pronounced sentence of death upon the wretched queen and ordered the grand vizier to see it executed.

The grand vizier and the courtiers who were present cast themselves at the emperor's feet, to beg of him to revoke the sentence. "Your majesty, I hope, will give me leave," said the grand vizier, "to represent to you, that the laws which condemn persons to death were made to punish crimes; the three extraordinary misfortunes of the queen are not crimes, for in what can she be said to have contributed toward them? Your majesty may abstain from seeing her, but let her live. The affliction in which she will spend the rest of her life, after the loss of your favour, will be a punishment sufficiently distressing."

The emperor of Persia considered with himself, and, reflecting that it was unjust to condemn the queen to death for what had happened, said: "Let her live then; I will spare her life, but it shall be on this condition: that she shall desire to die more than once every day. Let a wooden shed be built for her at the gate of the principal mosque, with iron bars to the windows, and let her be put into it, in the coarsest habit; and every Mussulman that shall go into the mosque to prayers shall heap scorn upon her. If any one fail, I will have him exposed to the same punishment; and that I may be punctually obeyed, I charge you, vizier, to appoint persons to see this done." The emperor pronounced his sentence in such a tone that the grand vizier durst not further remonstrate; and it was executed, to the great satisfaction of the two envious sisters. A shed was built, and the queen, truly worthy of compassion, was put into it and exposed ignominiously to the contempt of the people, which usage she bore with a patient resignation that excited the compassion of those who were discriminating and judged of things better than the vulgar.

The two princes and the princess were, in the meantime, nursed and brought up by the intendant of the gardens and his wife with the tenderness of a father and mother; and as they advanced in age, they all showed marks of superior dignity, which discovered itself every day by a certain air which could only belong to exalted birth. All this increased the affections of the intendant and his wife, who called the eldest prince Bahman, and the second Perviz, both of them names of the most ancient emperors of Persia, and the princess, Periezade, which name also had been borne by several queens and princesses of the kingdom.

As soon as the two princes were old enough, the intendant provided proper masters to teach them to read and write; and the princess, their sister, who was often with them, showing a great desire to learn, the intendant, pleased with her quickness, employed the same master to teach her also. Her vivacity and piercing wit made her, in a little time, as great a proficient as her brothers. From that time the brothers and sister had the same masters in geography, poetry, history, and even the secret sciences, and made so wonderful a progress that their tutors were amazed, and frankly owned that they could teach them nothing more. At the hours of recreation, the princess learned to sing and play upon all sorts of instruments; and when the princes were learning to ride she would not permit them to have that advantage over her, but went through all the exercises with them, learning to ride also, to bend the bow, and dart the reed or javelin, and oftentimes outdid them in the race and other contests of agility.

The intendant of the gardens was so overjoyed to find his adopted children so accomplished in all the perfections of body and mind, and that they so well requited the expense he had been at in their education, that he resolved to be at a still greater; for, as he had until then been content simply with his lodge at the entrance of the garden, and kept no country-house, he purchased a mansion at a short distance from the city, surrounded by a large tract of arable land, meadows, and woods. As the house was not sufficiently handsome nor convenient, he pulled it down, and spared no expense in building a more magnificent residence. He went every day to hasten, by his presence, the great number of workmen he employed, and as soon as there was an apartment ready to receive him, passed several days together there when his presence was not necessary at court; and by the same exertions, the interior was furnished in the richest manner, in consonance with the magnificence of the edifice. Afterward he made gardens, according to a plan drawn by himself. He took in a large extent of ground, which he walled around, and stocked with fallow deer, that the princes and princess might divert themselves with hunting when they chose.

When this country seat was finished and fit for habitation, the intendant of the gardens went and cast himself at the emperor's feet, and, after representing how long he had served, and the infirmities of age which he found growing upon him, begged that he might be permitted to resign his charge into his majesty's disposal and retire. The emperor gave him leave, with the more pleasure, because he was satisfied with his long services, both in his father's reign and his own, and when he granted it, asked what he should do to recompense him. "Sir," replied the intendant of the gardens, "I have received so many obligations from your majesty and the late emperor, your father, of happy memory, that I desire no more than the honour of dying in your favour." He took his leave of the emperor and retired with the two princes and the princess to the country retreat he had built. His wife had been dead some years, and he himself had not lived above six months with his charges before he was surprised by so sudden a death that he had not time to give them the least account of the manner in which he had discovered them. The Princes Bahman and Perviz, and the Princess Periezade, who knew no other father than the intendant of the emperor's gardens, regretted and bewailed him as such, and paid all the honours in his funeral obsequies which love and filial gratitude required of them. Satisfied with the plentiful fortune he had left them, they lived together in perfect union, free from the ambition of distinguishing themselves at court, or aspiring to places of honour and dignity, which they might easily have obtained.

One day when the two princes were hunting, and the princess had remained at home, a religious old woman came to the gate, and desired leave to go in to say her prayers, it being then the hour. The servants asked the princess's permission, who ordered them to show her into the oratory, which the intendant of the emperor's gardens had taken care to fit up in his house, for want of a mosque in the neighbourhood. She bade them, also, after the good woman had finished her prayers, to show her the house and gardens and then bring her to the hall.

The old woman went into the oratory, said her prayers, and when she came out two of the princess's women invited her to see the residence, which civility she accepted, followed them from one apartment to another, and observed, like a person who understood what belonged to furniture, the nice arrangement of everything. They conducted her also into the garden, the disposition of which she found so well planned, that she admired it, observing that the person who had formed it must have been an excellent master of his art. Afterward she was brought before the princess, who waited for her in the great hall, which in beauty and richness exceeded all that she had admired in the other apartments.

As soon as the princess saw the devout woman, she said to her: "My good mother, come near and sit down by me. I am overjoyed at the happiness of having the opportunity of profiting for some moments by the example and conversation of such a person as you, who have taken the right way by dedicating yourself to the service of God. I wish every one were as wise."

The devout woman, instead of sitting on a sofa, would only sit upon the edge of one. The princess would not permit her to do so, but rising from her seat and taking her by the hand, obliged her to come and sit by her. The good woman, sensible of the civility, said: "Madam, I ought not to have so much respect shown me; but since you command, and are mistress of your own house, I will obey you." When she had seated herself, before they entered into any conversation, one of the princess's women brought a low stand of mother-of-pearl and ebony, with a china dish full of cakes upon it, and many others set round it full of fruits in season, and wet and dry sweetmeats.

The princess took up one of the cakes, and presenting her with it, said: "Eat, good mother, and make choice of what you like best; you had need to eat after coming so far." "Madam," replied the good woman, "I am not used to eat such delicacies, but will not refuse what God has sent me by so liberal a hand as yours."

While the devout woman was eating, the princess ate a little too, to bear her company, and asked her many questions upon the exercise of devotion which she practised and how she lived; all of which she answered with great modesty. Talking of various things, at last the princess asked her what she thought of the house, and how she liked it.

"Madam," answered the devout woman, "I must certainly have very bad taste to disapprove anything in it, since it is beautiful, regular, and magnificently furnished with exactness and judgment, and all its ornaments adjusted in the best manner. Its situation is an agreeable spot, and no garden can be more delightful; but yet, if you will give me leave to speak my mind freely, I will take the liberty to tell you that this house would be incomparable if it had three things which are wanting to complete it." "My good mother," replied the Princess Periezade, "what are those? I entreat you to tell me what they are; I will spare nothing to get them."

"Madam," replied the devout woman, "the first of these three things is the Talking Bird, so singular a creature, that it draws round it all the songsters of the neighbourhood which come to accompany its voice. The second is the Singing Tree, the leaves of which are so many mouths which form an harmonious concert of different voices and never cease. The third is the Golden Water, a single drop of which being poured into a vessel properly prepared, it increases so as to fill it immediately, and rises up in the middle like a fountain, which continually plays, and yet the basin never overflows."

"Ah! my good mother," cried the princess, "how much am I obliged to you for the knowledge of these curiosities! I never before heard there were such rarities in the world; but as I am persuaded that you know, I expect that you should do me the favour to inform me where they are to be found."

"Madam," replied the good woman, "I should be unworthy the hospitality you have shown me if I should refuse to satisfy your curiosity on that point, and am glad to have the honour to tell you that these curiosities are all to be met with in the same spot on the confines of this kingdom, toward India. The road lies before your house, and whoever you send needs but follow it for twenty days, and on the twentieth only let him ask the first person he meets where the Talking Bird, the Singing Tree, and the Golden Water are, and he will be informed." After saying this, she rose from her seat, took her leave, and went her way.

The Princess Periezade's thoughts were so taken up with the Talking Bird, Singing Tree, and Golden Water, that she never perceived the devout woman's departure, till she wanted to ask her some question for her better information; for she thought that what she had been told was not a sufficient reason for exposing herself by undertaking a long journey. However, she would not send after her visitor, but endeavoured to remember all the directions, and when she thought she had recollected every word, took real pleasure in thinking of the satisfaction she should have if she could get these curiosities into her possession; but the difficulties she apprehended and the fear of not succeeding made her very uneasy.

She was absorbed in these thoughts when her brothers returned from hunting, who, when they entered the great hall, instead of finding her lively and gay, as she was wont to be, were amazed to see her so pensive and hanging down her head as if something troubled her.

"Sister," said Prince Bahman, "what is become of all your mirth and gaiety? Are you not well? or has some misfortune befallen you? Tell us, that we may know how to act, and give you some relief. If any one has affronted you, we will resent his insolence."

The princess remained in the same posture some time without answering, but at last lifted up her eyes to look at her brothers, and then held them down again, telling them nothing disturbed her.

"Sister," said Prince Bahman, "you conceal the truth from us; there must be something of consequence. It is impossible we could observe so sudden a change if nothing was the matter with you. You would not have us satisfied with the evasive answer you have given; do not conceal anything, unless you would have us suspect that you renounce the strict union which has hitherto subsisted between us."

The princess, who had not the smallest intention to offend her brothers, would not suffer them to entertain such a thought, but said: "When I told you nothing disturbed me, I meant nothing that was of importance to you, but to me it is of some consequence; and since you press me to tell you by our strict union and friendship, which are so dear to me, I will. You think, and I always believed so too, that this house was so complete that nothing was wanting. But this day I have learned that it lacks three rarities which would render it so perfect that no country seat in the world could be compared with it. These three things are the Talking Bird, the Singing Tree, and the Golden Water." After she had informed them wherein consisted the excellency of these rarities, "A devout woman," added she, "has made this discovery to me, told me the place where they are to be found, and the way thither. Perhaps you may imagine these things of little consequence; that without these additions our house will always be thought sufficiently elegant, and that we can do without them. You may think as you please, but I cannot help telling you that I am persuaded they are absolutely necessary, and I shall not be easy without them. Therefore, whether you value them or not, I desire you to consider what person you may think proper for me to send in search of the curiosities I have mentioned."

"Sister," replied Prince Bahman, "nothing can concern you in which we have not an equal interest. It is enough that you desire these things to oblige us to take the same interest; but if you had not, we feel ourselves inclined of our own accord and for our own individual satisfaction. I am persuaded my brother is of the same opinion, and therefore we ought to undertake this conquest, for the importance and singularity of the undertaking deserve that name. I will take the charge upon myself; only tell me the place and the way to it, and I will defer my journey no longer than till to-morrow."

"Brother," said Prince Perviz, "it is not proper that you, who are the head of our family, should be absent. I desire my sister should join with me to oblige you to abandon your design, and allow me to undertake it. I hope to acquit myself as well as you, and it will be a more regular proceeding." "I am persuaded of your goodwill, brother," replied Prince Bahman, "and that you would succeed as well as myself in this journey; but I have resolved and will undertake it. You shall stay at home with our sister, and I need not recommend her to you."

The next morning Bahman mounted his horse, and Perviz and the princess embraced and wished him a good journey. But in the midst of their adieus, the princess recollected what she had not thought of before. "Brother," said she, "I had quite forgotten the accidents which attend travellers. Who knows whether I shall ever see you again? Alight, I beseech you, and give up this journey. I would rather be deprived of the sight and possession of the Talking Bird, the Singing Tree, and the Golden Water, than run the risk of never seeing you more."

"Sister," replied Bahman, smiling at her sudden fears, "my resolution is fixed. The accidents you speak of befall only those who are unfortunate; but there are more who are not so. However, as events are uncertain, and I may fail in this undertaking, all I can do is to leave you this knife."

Bahman pulling a knife from his vestband, and presenting it to the princess in the sheath, said: "Take this knife, sister, and give yourself the trouble sometimes to pull it out of the sheath; while you see it clean as it is now, it will be a sign that I am alive;

but if you find it stained with blood, then you may believe me dead and indulge me with your prayers."

The princess could obtain nothing more of Bahman. He bade adieu to her and Prince Perviz for the last time and rode away. When he got into the road, he never turned to the right hand nor to the left, but went directly forward toward India. The twentieth day he perceived on the roadside a hideous old man, who sat under a tree near a thatched house, which was his retreat from the weather.

His eyebrows were as white as snow, as was also the hair of his head; his whiskers covered his mouth, and his beard and hair reached down to his feet. The nails of his hands and feet were grown to an extensive length, while a flat, broad umbrella covered his head. He had no clothes, but only a mat thrown round his body. This old man was a dervish for so many years retired from the world to give himself up entirely to the service of God that at last he had become what we have described.

Prince Bahman, who had been all that morning very attentive, to see if he could meet with anybody who could give him information of the place he was in search of, stopped when he came near the dervish, alighted, in conformity to the directions which the devout woman had given the Princess Periezade, and leading his horse by the bridle, advanced toward him and saluting him, said: "God prolong your days, good father, and grant you the accomplishment of your desires."

The dervish returned the prince's salutation, but so unintelligibly that he could not understand one word he said and Prince Bahman, perceiving that this difficulty proceeded from the dervish's whiskers hanging over his mouth, and unwilling to go any further without the instructions he wanted, pulled out a pair of scissors he had about him, and having tied his horse to a branch of the tree, said: "Good dervish, I want to have some talk with you, but your whiskers prevent my understanding what you say; and if you will consent, I will cut off some part of them and of your eyebrows, which disfigure you so much that you look more like a bear than a man."

The dervish did not oppose the offer, and when the prince had cut off as much hair as he thought fit, he perceived that the dervish had a good complexion, and that he was not as old as he seemed. "Good dervish," said he, "if I had a glass I would show you how young you look: you are now a man, but before, nobody could tell what you were."

The kind behaviour of Prince Bahman made the dervish smile and return his compliment. "Sir," said he, "whoever you are, I am obliged by the good office you have performed, and am ready to show my gratitude by doing anything in my power for you. You must have alighted here upon some account or other. Tell me what it is, and I will endeavour to serve you."

"Good dervish," replied Prince Bahman, "I am in search of the Talking Bird, the Singing Tree, and the Golden Water; I know these three rarities are not far from hence, but cannot tell exactly the place where they are to be found; if you know, I conjure you to show me the way, that I may not lose my labour after so long a journey."

The prince, while he spoke, observed that the dervish changed countenance, held down his eyes, looked very serious, and remained silent, which obliged him to say to him again: "Good father, tell me whether you know what I ask you, that I may not lose my time, but inform myself somewhere else."

At last the dervish broke silence. "Sir," said he to Prince Bahman, "I know the way you ask of me; but the regard which I conceived for you the first moment I saw you, and which is grown stronger by the service you have done me, kept me in suspense as to whether I should give you the satisfaction you desire." "What motive can hinder you?" replied the prince; "and what difficulties do you find in so doing?" "I will tell you," replied the dervish; "the danger to which you are going to expose yourself is greater than you may suppose. A number of gentlemen of as much bravery as you can possibly possess have passed this way, and asked me the same question. When I had used all my endeavours to persuade them to desist, they would not believe me; at last I yielded to their importunities; I was compelled to show them the way, and I can assure you they have all perished, for I have not seen one come back. Therefore, if you have any regard for your life, take my advice, go no farther, but return home."

Prince Bahman persisted in his resolution. "I will not suppose," said he to the dervish, "but that your advice is sincere. I am obliged to you for the friendship you express for me; but whatever may be the danger, nothing shall make me change my intention: whoever attacks me, I am well armed, and can say I am as brave as any one." "But they who will attack you are not to be seen," replied the dervish; "how will you defend yourself against invisible persons?" "It is no matter," answered the prince, "all you say shall not persuade me to do anything contrary to my duty. Since you know the way, I conjure you once more to inform me."

When the dervish found he could not prevail upon Prince Bahman, and that he was obstinately bent to pursue his journey, notwithstanding his friendly remonstrance, he put his hand into a bag that lay by him and pulled out a bowl, which he presented to him. "Since I cannot prevail on you to attend to my advice," said he, "take this bowl and when you are on horseback throw it before you, and follow it to the foot of a mountain, where it will stop. As soon as the bowl stops, alight, leave your horse with the bridle over his neck, and he will stand in the same place till you return. As you ascend you will see on your right and left a great number of large black stones, and will hear on all sides a confusion of voices, which will utter a thousand abuses to discourage you, and prevent your reaching the summit of the mountain. Be not afraid; but, above all things, do not turn your head to look behind you, for in that instant you will be changed into such a black stone as those you see, which are all youths who have failed in this enterprise. If you escape the danger of which I give you but a faint idea, and get to the top of the mountain, you will see a cage, and in that cage is the bird you seek; ask him which are the Singing Tree and the Golden Water, and he will tell you. I have nothing more to say; this is what you have to do, and if you are prudent you will take my advice and not expose your life. Consider once more while you have time that the difficulties are almost insuperable."

"I am obliged to you for your advice," replied Prince Bahman, after he had received the bowl, "but cannot follow it. However, I will endeavour to conform myself to that part of it which bids me not to look behind me, and I hope to come and thank you when I have obtained what I am seeking." After these words, to which the dervish made no other answer than that he should be overjoyed to see him again, the prince mounted his horse, took leave of the dervish with a respectful salute, and threw the bowl before him.

The bowl rolled away with as much swiftness as when Prince Bahman first hurled it from his hand, which obliged him to put his horse to the same pace to avoid losing sight of it, and when it had reached the foot of the mountain it stopped. The prince alighted from his horse, laid the bridle on his neck, and having first surveyed the mountain and seen the black stones, began to ascend, but had not gone four steps before he heard the voices mentioned by the dervish, though he could see nobody. Some said: "Where is that fool going? Where is he going? What would he have? Do not let him pass." Others: "Stop him, catch him, kill him:" and others with a voice like thunder: "Thief! assassin! murderer!" while some in a gibing tone cried: "No, no, do not hurt him; let the pretty fellow pass, the cage and bird are kept for him."

Notwithstanding all these troublesome voices, Prince Bahman ascended with resolution for some time, but the voices redoubled with so loud a din, both behind and before, that at last he was seized with dread, his legs trembled under him, he staggered, and finding that his strength failed him, he forgot the dervish's advice, turned about to run down the hill, and was that instant changed into a black stone; a metamorphosis which had happened to many before him who had attempted the ascent. His horse, likewise, underwent the same change.

From the time of Prince Bahman's departure, the Princess Periezade always wore the knife and sheath in her girdle, and pulled it out several times in a day, to know whether her brother was alive. She had the consolation to understand he was in perfect health and to talk of him frequently with Prince Perviz. On the fatal day that Prince Bahman was transformed into a stone, as Prince Perviz and the princess were talking together in the evening, as usual, the prince desired his sister to pull out the knife to know how their brother did. The princess readily complied, and seeing the blood run down the point was seized with so much horror that she threw it down. "Ah! my dear brother," cried she, "I have been the cause of your death, and shall never see you more! Why did I tell you of the Talking Bird, Singing Tree, and Golden Water; or rather, of what importance was it to me to know whether the devout woman thought this house ugly or handsome, or complete or not? I wish to Heaven she had never addressed herself to me!"

Prince Perviz was as much afflicted at the death of Prince Bahman as the princess, but not to waste time in needless regret, as he knew that she still passionately desired possession of the marvellous treasures, he interrupted her, saying: "Sister, our regret for our brother is vain; our lamentations cannot restore him to life; it is the will of God; we must submit and adore the decrees of the Almighty without searching into them. Why should you now doubt of the truth of what the holy woman told you? Do you think she spoke to you of three things that were not in being, and that she invented them to deceive you who had received her with so much goodness and civility? Let us rather believe that our brother's death is owing to some error on his part, or some accident which we cannot conceive. It ought not therefore to prevent us from pursuing our object. I offered to go this journey, and am now more resolved than ever; his example has no effect upon my resolution; to-morrow I will depart."

The princess did all she could to dissuade Prince Perviz, conjuring him not to expose her to the danger of losing two brothers; but he was obstinate, and all the remonstrances she could urge had no effect upon him. Before he went, that she might know what success he had, he left her a string of a hundred pearls, telling her that if they would not run when she should count them upon the string, but remain fixed, that would be a certain sign he had undergone the same fate as his brother; but at the same time told her he hoped it would never happen, but that he should have the delight of seeing her again.

Prince Perviz, on the twentieth day after his departure, met the same dervish in the same place as his brother Bahman had done before him. He went directly up to him, and after he had saluted, asked him if he could tell him where to find the Talking Bird, the Singing Tree, and the Golden Water. The dervish urged the same remonstrances as he had done to Prince Bahman, telling him that a young gentleman, who very much resembled him, was with him a short time before; that, overcome by his importunity, he had shown him the way, given him a guide, and told him how he should act to succeed, but that he had not seen him since, and doubted not but he had shared the same fate as all other adventurers.

"Good dervish," answered Prince Perviz, "I know whom you speak of; he was my elder brother, and I am informed of the certainty of his death, but know not the cause." "I can tell you," replied the dervish; "he was changed into a black stone, as all I speak of have been; and you must expect the same transformation, unless you observe more exactly than he has done the advice I gave him, in case you persist in your resolution, which I once more entreat you to renounce."

"Dervish," said Prince Perviz, "I cannot sufficiently express how much I am obliged for the concern you take in my life, who am a stranger to you, and have done nothing to deserve your kindness; but I thoroughly considered this enterprise before I undertook it; therefore I beg of you to do me the same favour you have done my brother. Perhaps I may have better success in following your directions." "Since I cannot prevail with you," said the dervish, "to give up your obstinate resolution, if my age did not prevent me, and I could stand, I would get up to reach you a bowl I have here, which will show you the way."

Without giving the dervish time to say more, the prince alighted from his horse and went to the dervish, who had taken a bowl out of his bag, in which he had a great many, and gave it him, with the same directions he had given Prince Bahman; and after warning him not to be discouraged by the voices he should hear, however threatening they might be, but to continue his way up the hill till he saw the cage and bird, he let him depart.

Prince Perviz thanked the dervish, and when he had remounted and taken leave, threw the bowl before his horse, and spurring him at the same time, followed it. When the bowl came to the bottom of the hill it stopped, the prince alighted, and stood some time to recollect the dervish's directions. He encouraged himself, and began to walk up with a resolution to reach the summit; but before he had gone above six steps, he heard a voice, which seemed to be near, as of a man behind him, say in an insulting tone: "Stay, rash youth, that I may punish you for your presumption."

Upon this affront the prince, forgetting the dervish's advice, clapped his hand upon his sword, drew it, and turned about to revenge himself; but had scarcely time to see that nobody followed him before he and his horse were changed into black stones.

In the meantime the Princess Periezade, several times a day after her brother's departure, counted her chaplet. She did not omit it at night, but when she went to bed put it about her neck, and in the morning when she awoke counted over the pearls again to see if they would slide.

The day that Prince Perviz was transformed into a stone she was counting over the pearls as she used to do, when all at once they became immovably fixed, a certain token that the prince, her brother, was dead. As she had determined what to do in case it should so happen, she lost no time in outward demonstrations of grief, which she concealed as much as possible, but having disguised herself in man's apparel, she mounted her horse the next morning, armed and equipped, having told her servants she should return in two or three days, and took the same road that her brothers had done.

The princess, who had been used to ride on horseback in hunting, supported the fatigue of so long a journey better than most ladies could have done; and as she made the same stages as her brothers, she also met with the dervish on the twentieth day. When she came near him, she alighted from her horse, leading him by the bridle, went and sat down by the dervish, and after she had saluted him, said: "Good dervish, give me leave to rest myself; and do me the favour to tell me if you have not heard that there are somewhere in this neighbourhood a Talking Bird, a Singing Tree, and Golden Water."

"Princess," answered the dervish, "for so I must call you, since by your voice I know you to be a woman disguised in man's apparel, I know the place well where these things are to be found; but what makes you ask me this question?"

"Good dervish," replied the princess, "I have had such a flattering relation of them given me, that I have a great desire to possess them." "Madam," replied the dervish, "you have been told the truth. These curiosities are more singular than they have been represented, but you have not been made acquainted with the difficulties which must be surmounted in order to obtain them. If you had been fully informed of these, you would not have undertaken so dangerous an enterprise. Take my advice, return, and do not urge me to contribute toward your ruin."

"Good father," said the princess, "I have travelled a great way, and should be sorry to return without executing my design. You talk of difficulties and danger of life, but you do not tell me what those difficulties are, and wherein the danger consists. This is what I desire to know, that I may consider and judge whether I can trust my courage and strength to brave them."

The dervish repeated to the princess what he had said to the Princes Bahman and Perviz, exaggerating the difficulties of climbing up to the top of the mountain, where she was to make herself mistress of the Bird, which would inform her of the Singing Tree and Golden Water. He magnified the din of the terrible threatening voices which she would hear on all sides of her, and the great number of black stones alone sufficient to strike terror. He entreated her to reflect that those stones were so many brave gentlemen, so metamorphosed for having omitted to observe the principal condition of success in the perilous undertaking, which was not to look behind them before they had got possession of the cage.

When the dervish had done, the princess replied: "By what I comprehend from your discourse, the difficulties of succeeding in this affair are, first, the getting up to the cage without being frightened at the terrible din of voices I shall hear; and, secondly, not to look behind me. For this last, I hope I shall be mistress enough of myself to observe it; as to the first, I own that voices, such as you represent them to be, are capable of striking terror into the most undaunted; but as in all enterprises and dangers every one may use stratagem, I desire to know of you if I may use any in one of so great importance." "And what stratagem is it you would employ?" said the dervish. "To stop my ears with cotton," answered the princess, "that the voices, however terrible, may make the less impression upon my imagination, and my mind remain free from that disturbance which might cause me to lose the use of my reason."

"Princess," replied the dervish, "of all the persons who have addressed themselves to me for information, I do not know that ever one made use of the contrivance you propose. All I know is that they all perished. If you persist in your design, you may make the experiment. You will be fortunate if it succeeds, but I would advise you not to expose yourself to the danger."

"My good father," replied the princess, "I am sure my precaution will succeed, and am resolved to try the experiment. Nothing remains for me but to know which way I must go, and I conjure you not to deny me that information." The dervish exhorted her again to consider well what she was going to do; but finding her resolute, he took out a bowl, and presenting it to her, said: "Take this bowl, mount your horse again, and when you have thrown it before you, follow it through all its windings, till it stops at the bottom of the mountain; there alight and ascend the hill. Go, you know the rest."

After the princess had thanked the dervish, and taken her leave of him, she mounted her horse, threw the bowl before her, and followed it till it stopped at the foot of the mountain.

She then alighted, stopped her ears with cotton, and after she had well examined the path leading to the summit began with a moderate pace and walked up with intrepidity. She heard the voices and perceived the great service the cotton was to her. The higher she went, the louder and more numerous the voices seemed, but they were not capable of making any impression upon her. She heard a great many affronting speeches and raillery very disagreeable to a woman, which she only laughed at. "I mind not," said she to herself, "all that can be said, were it worse; I only laugh at them and shall pursue my way." At last, she climbed so high that she could perceive the cage and the Bird which endeavoured, in company with the voices, to frighten her, crying in a thundering tone, notwithstanding the smallness of its size: "Retire, fool, and approach no nearer."

The princess, encouraged by this sight, redoubled her speed, and by effort gained the summit of the mountain, where the ground was level; then running directly to the cage and clapping her hand upon it, cried: "Bird, I have you, and you shall not escape me."

While Periezade was pulling the cotton out of her ears the Bird said to her: "Heroic princess, be not angry with me for joining with those who exerted themselves to preserve my liberty. Though in a cage, I was content with my condition; but since I am destined to be a slave, I would rather be yours than any other person's, since you have obtained me so courageously. From this instant, I swear entire submission to all your commands. I know who you are. You do not; but the time will come when I shall do you essential service, for which I hope you will think yourself obliged to me. As a proof of my sincerity, tell me what you desire and I am ready to obey you."

The princess's joy was the more inexpressible, because the conquest she had made had cost her the lives of two beloved brothers, and given her more trouble and danger than she could have imagined. "Bird," said she, "it was my intention to have told you that I wish for many things which are of importance, but I am overjoyed that you have shown your goodwill and prevented me. I have been told that there is not far off a Golden Water, the property of which is very wonderful; before all things, I ask you to tell me where it is." The Bird showed her the place, which was just by, and she went and filled a little silver flagon which she had brought with her. She returned at once and said: "Bird, this is not enough; I want also the Singing Tree; tell me where it is." "Turn about," said the Bird, "and you will see behind you a wood where you will find the tree." The princess went into the wood, and by the harmonious concert she heard, soon knew the tree among many others, but it was very large and high. She came back again and said: "Bird, I have found the Singing Tree, but I can neither pull it up by the roots nor carry it." The Bird replied: "It is not necessary that you should take it up; it will be sufficient to break off a branch and carry it to plant in your garden; it will take root as soon as it is put into the earth, and in a little time will grow to as fine a tree as that you have seen."

When the princess had obtained possession of the three things for which she had conceived so great a desire, she said again: "Bird, what you have yet done for me is not sufficient. You have been the cause of the death of my two brothers, who must be among the black stones I saw as I ascended the mountain. I wish to take the princes home with me."

The Bird seemed reluctant to satisfy the princess in this point, and indeed made some difficulty to comply. "Bird," said the princess, "remember you told me that you were my slave. You are so; and your life is in my disposal." "That I cannot deny," answered the bird; "but although what you now ask is more difficult than all the rest, yet I will do it for you. Cast your eyes around," added he, "and look if you can see a little pitcher." "I see it already," said the princess. "Take it then," said he, "and as you descend the mountain, sprinkle a little of the water that is in it upon every black stone."

The princess took up the pitcher accordingly, carried with her the cage and Bird, the flagon of Golden Water, and the branch of the Singing Tree, and as she descended the mountain, threw a little of the water on every black stone, which was changed immediately into a man; and as she did not miss one stone, all the horses, both of her brothers and of the other gentlemen, resumed their natural forms also. She instantly recognised Bahman and Perviz, as they did her, and ran to embrace her. She returned their embraces and expressed her amazement. "What do you here, my dear brothers?" said she, and they told her they had been asleep. "Yes," replied she, "and if it had not been for me, perhaps you might have slept till the day of judgment. Do not you remember that you came to fetch the Talking Bird, the Singing Tree, and the Golden Water, and did not you see, as you came along, the place covered with black stones? Look and see if there be any now. The gentlemen and their horses who surround us, and you yourselves, were these black stones. If you desire to know how this wonder was performed," continued she, showing the pitcher, which she set down at the foot of the mountain, "it was done by virtue of the water which was in this pitcher, with which I sprinkled every stone. After I had made the Talking Bird (which you see in this cage) my slave, by his directions I found out the Singing Tree, a branch of which I have now in my hand; and the Golden Water, with which this flagon is filled; but being still unwilling to return without taking you with me, I constrained the Bird, by the power I had over him, to afford me the means. He told me where to find this pitcher, and the use I was to make of it."

The Princes Bahman and Perviz learned by this relation the obligation they had to their sister, as did all the other gentlemen, who expressed to her that, far from envying her happiness in the conquest she had made, and which they all had aspired to, they thought they could not better express their gratitude for restoring them to life again, than by declaring themselves her slaves, and that they were ready to obey her in whatever she should command.

"Gentlemen," replied the princess, "if you had given any attention to my words, you might have observed that I had no other intention in what I have done than to recover my brothers; therefore, if you have received any benefit, you owe me no obligation, and I have no further share in your compliment than your politeness toward me, for which I return you my thanks. In other respects, I regard each of you as quite as free as you were before your misfortunes, and I rejoice with you at the happiness which has accrued to you by my means. Let us, however, stay no longer in a place where we have nothing to detain us, but mount our horses and return to our respective homes."

The princess took her horse, which stood in the place where she had left him. Before she mounted, Prince Bahman desired her to give him the cage to carry. "Brother," replied the princess, "the Bird is my slave and I will carry him myself; if you will take the pains to carry the branch of the Singing Tree, there it is; only hold the cage while I get on horseback." When she had mounted her horse, and Prince Bahman had given her the cage, she turned about and said to Prince Perviz: "I leave the flagon of Golden Water to your care, if it will not be too much trouble for you to carry it," and Prince Perviz accordingly took charge of it with pleasure.

When Bahman, Perviz, and all the gentlemen had mounted their horses, the princess waited for some of them to lead the way. The two princes paid that compliment to the gentlemen, and they again to the princess, who, finding that none of them would accept the honour, but that it was reserved for her, addressed herself to them and said: "Gentlemen, I expect that some of you should lead the way:" to which one who was nearest to her, in the name of the rest, replied: "Madam, were we ignorant of the respect due to your sex, yet after what you have done for us there is no deference we would not willingly pay you, notwithstanding your modesty; we entreat you no longer to deprive us of the happiness of following you."

"Gentlemen," said the princess, "I do not deserve the honour you do me, and accept it only because you desire it." At the same time she led the way, and the two princes and the gentlemen followed.

This illustrious company called upon the dervish as they passed, to thank him for his reception and wholesome advice, which they had all found to be sincere. He was dead, however; whether of old age, or because he was no longer necessary to show the way to obtaining the three rarities, did not appear. They pursued their route, but lessened in their numbers every day. The gentlemen who, as we said before, had come from different countries, after severally repeating their obligations to the princess and her brothers, took leave of them one after another as they approached the road by which they had come.

As soon as the princess reached home, she placed the cage in the garden, and the Bird no sooner began to warble than he was surrounded by nightingales, chaffinches, larks, linnets, goldfinches, and every species of birds of the country. The branch of the Singing Tree was no sooner set in the midst of the parterre, a little distance from the house, than it took root and in a short time became a large tree, the leaves of which gave as harmonious a concert as those of the parent from which it was gathered. A large basin of beautiful marble was placed in the garden, and when it was finished, the princess poured into it all the Golden Water from the flagon, which instantly increased and swelled so much that it soon reached up to the edges of the basin, and afterward formed in the middle a fountain twenty feet high, which fell again into the basin perpetually, without running over.

The report of these wonders was presently spread abroad, and as the gates of the house and those of the gardens were shut to nobody, a great number of people came to admire them.

Some days after, when the Princes Bahman and Perviz had recovered from the fatigue of their journey, they resumed their former way of living; and as their usual diversion was hunting, they mounted their horses and went for the first time since their return, not to their own demesne, but two or three leagues from their house. As they pursued their sport, the emperor of Persia came in pursuit of game upon the same ground. When they perceived, by the number of horsemen in different places, that he would soon be up, they resolved to discontinue their chase, and retire to avoid encountering him; but in the very road they took they chanced to meet him in so narrow a way that they could not retreat without being seen. In their surprise they had only time to alight and prostrate themselves before the emperor, without lifting up their heads to look at him. The emperor, who saw they were as well mounted and dressed as if they had belonged to his court, had a curiosity to see their faces. He stopped and commanded them to rise. The princes rose up and stood before him with an easy and graceful air, accompanied with modest countenances. The emperor took some time to view them before he spoke, and after he had admired their good air and mien, asked them who they were and where they lived.

"Sir," said Prince Bahman, "we are the sons of the late intendant of your majesty's gardens, and live in a house which he built a little before he died, till we should be fit to serve your majesty and ask of you some employ when opportunity offered."

"By what I perceive," replied the emperor, "you love hunting." "Sir," replied Prince Bahman, "it is our common exercise, and what none of your majesty's subjects who intend to bear arms in your armies, ought, according to the ancient custom of the kingdom, to neglect." The emperor, charmed with so prudent an answer, said: "Since it is so, I should be glad to see your expertness in the chase; choose your own game."

The princes mounted their horses again and followed the emperor, but had not gone far before they saw many wild beasts together. Prince Bahman chose a lion and Prince Perviz a bear, and pursued them with so much intrepidity that the emperor was surprised. They came up with their game nearly at the same time, and darted their javelins with so much skill and address that they pierced the one the lion and the other the bear so effectually that the emperor saw them fall one after the other. Immediately afterward Prince Bahman pursued another bear, and Prince Perviz another lion, and killed them in a short time, and would have beaten out for fresh game, but the emperor would not let them, and sent to them to come to him. When they approached he said: "If I had given you leave, you would soon have destroyed all my game; but it is not that which I would preserve, but your persons; for I am so well assured your bravery may one time or other be serviceable to me, that from this moment your lives will be always dear to me."

The emperor, in short, conceived so great a kindness for the two princes, that he invited them immediately to make him a visit, to which Prince Bahman replied: "Your majesty does us an honour we do not deserve, and we beg you will excuse us."

The emperor, who could not comprehend what reason the princes could have to refuse this token of his favour, pressed them to tell him why they excused themselves. "Sir," said Prince Bahman, "we have a sister younger than ourselves, with whom we live in such perfect union, that we undertake nothing before we consult her, nor she anything without asking our advice." "I commend your brotherly affection," answered the emperor. "Consult your sister, meet me to-morrow, and give me an answer."

The princes went home, but neglected to speak of their adventure in meeting the emperor and hunting with him, and also of the honour he had done them, yet did not the next morning fail to meet him at the place appointed. "Well," said the emperor, "have you spoken to your sister, and has she consented to the pleasure I expect of seeing you?" The two princes looked at each other and blushed. "Sir," said Prince Bahman, "we beg your majesty to excuse us, for both my brother and I forgot." "Then remember to-day," replied the emperor, "and be sure to bring me an answer to-morrow."

The princes were guilty of the same fault a second time, and the emperor was so good-natured as to forgive their negligence; but to prevent their forgetfulness the third time, he pulled three little golden balls out of a purse, and put them into Prince Bahman's bosom. "These balls," said he, smiling, "will prevent your forgetting a third time what I wish you to do for my sake; since the noise they will make by falling on the floor when you undress will remind you, if you do not recollect it before." The event happened just as the emperor foresaw; and without these balls the princes had not thought of speaking to their sister of this affair, for as Prince Bahman unloosed his girdle to go to bed the balls dropped on the floor, upon which he ran into Prince Perviz's chamber, when both went into the Princess Periezade's apartment, and after they had asked her pardon for coming at so unseasonable a time, they told her all the circumstances of their meeting the emperor.

The princess was somewhat surprised at this intelligence. "Your meeting with the emperor," said she, "is happy and honourable and may in the end be highly advantageous to you, but it places me in an awkward position. It was on my account, I know, you refused the emperor, and I am infinitely obliged to you for doing so. I know by this that you would rather be guilty of incivility toward the emperor than violate the union we have sworn to each other. You judge right, for if you had once gone you would insensibly have been engaged to devote yourselves to him. But do you think it an easy matter absolutely to refuse the emperor what he seems so earnestly to desire? Monarchs will be obeyed in their desires, and it may be dangerous to oppose them; therefore, if to follow my inclination I should dissuade you from obeying him, it may expose you to his resentment, and may render myself and you miserable. These are my sentiments; but before we conclude upon anything let us consult the Talking Bird and hear what he says; he is penetrating, and has promised his assistance in all difficulties."

The princess sent for the cage, and after she had related the circumstances to the Bird in the presence of her brothers, asked him what they should do in this perplexity. The Bird answered: "The princes, your brothers, must conform to the emperor's pleasure, and in their turn invite him to come and see your house."

"But, Bird," replied the princess, "my brothers and I love one another, and our friendship is yet undisturbed. Will not this step be injurious to that friendship?" "Not at all," replied the Bird; "it will tend rather to cement it." "Then," answered the princess, "the emperor will see me." The Bird told her it was necessary he should, and that everything would go better afterward.

Next morning the princes met the emperor hunting, who asked them if they had remembered to speak to their sister. Prince Bahman approached and answered: "Sir, we are ready to obey you, for we have not only obtained our sister's consent with great ease, but she took it amiss that we should pay her that deference in a matter wherein our duty to your majesty was concerned. If we have offended, we hope you will pardon us." "Do not be uneasy," replied the emperor. "I highly approve of your conduct, and hope you will have the same deference and attachment to my person, if I have ever so little share in your friendship." The princes, confounded at the emperor's goodness, returned no other answer but a low obeisance.

The emperor, contrary to his usual custom, did not hunt long that day. Presuming that the princes possessed wit equal to their courage and bravery, he longed with impatience to converse with them more at liberty. He made them ride on each side of him, an honour which was envied by the grand vizier, who was much mortified to see them preferred before him.

When the emperor entered his capital, the eyes of the people, who stood in crowds in the streets, were fixed upon the two Princes Bahman and Perviz; and they were earnest to know who they might be.

All, however, agreed in wishing that the emperor had been blessed with two such handsome princes, and said that his children would have been about the same age, if the queen had not been so unfortunate as to lose them.

The first thing the emperor did when he arrived at his palace was to conduct the princes into the principal apartments, who praised without affectation the beauty and symmetry of the rooms, and the richness of the furniture and ornaments. Afterward a magnificent repast was served up, and the emperor made them sit with him, which they at first refused; but finding it was his pleasure, they obeyed.

The emperor, who had himself much learning, particularly in history, foresaw that the princes, out of modesty and respect, would not take the liberty of beginning any conversation. Therefore, to give them an opportunity, he furnished them with subjects all dinner-time. But whatever subject he introduced, they shewed so much wit, judgment, and discernment, that he was struck with admiration. "Were these my own children," said he to himself, "and I had improved their talents by suitable education, they could not have been more accomplished or better informed." In short, he took such great pleasure in their conversation, that, after having sat longer than usual, he led them into his closet, where he pursued his conversation with them, and at last said: "I never supposed that there were among my subjects in the country youths so well brought up, so lively, so capable; and I never was better pleased with any conversation than yours; but it is time now we should relax our minds with some diversion; and as nothing is more capable of enlivening the mind than music, you shall hear a vocal and instrumental concert which may not be disagreeable to you."

The emperor had no sooner spoken than the musicians, who had orders to attend, entered, and answered fully the expectations the princes had been led to entertain of their abilities. After the concerts, an excellent farce was acted, and the entertainment was concluded by dancers of both sexes.

The two princes, seeing night approach, prostrated themselves at the emperor's feet; and having first thanked him for the favours and honours he had heaped upon them, asked his permission to retire; which was granted by the emperor, who, in dismissing them, said: "I give you leave to go; but remember, you will be always welcome, and the oftener you come the greater pleasure you will do me."

Before they went out of the emperor's presence, Prince Bahman said: "Sir, may we presume to request that your majesty will do us and our sister the honour to pass by our house, and refresh yourself after your fatigue, the first time you take the diversion of hunting in that neighbourhood? It is not worthy of your presence; but monarchs sometimes have vouchsafed to take shelter in a cottage." "My children," replied the emperor, "your house cannot be otherwise than beautiful and worthy of its owners. I will call and see it with pleasure, which will be the greater for having for my hosts you and your sister, who is already dear to me from the account you give me of the rare qualities with which she is endowed: and this satisfaction I will defer no longer than to-morrow. Early in the morning I will be at the place where I shall never forget that I first saw you. Meet me, and you shall be my guides."

When the Princes Bahman and Perviz had returned home, they gave the princess an account of the distinguished reception the emperor had given them, and told her that they had invited him to do them the honour, as he passed by, to call at their house, and that he had appointed the next day.

"If it be so," replied the princess, "we must think of preparing a repast fit for his majesty; and for that purpose I think it would be proper we should consult the Talking Bird, who will tell us, perhaps, what meats the emperor likes best." The princes approved of her plan, and after they had retired she consulted the Bird alone. "Bird," said she, "the emperor will do us the honour to-morrow to come and see our house, and we are to entertain him; tell us what we shall do to acquit ourselves to his satisfaction."

"Good mistress," replied the Bird, "you have excellent cooks, let them do the best they can; but above all things, let them prepare a dish of cucumbers stuffed full of pearls, which must be set before the emperor in the first course before all the other dishes."

"Cucumbers stuffed full of pearls!" cried Princess Periezade with amazement; "surely, Bird, you do not know what you say; it is an unheard of dish. The emperor may admire it as a piece of magnificence, but he will sit down to eat, and not to admire pearls; besides, all the pearls I possess are not enough for such a dish."

"Mistress," said the Bird, "do what I say, and be not uneasy about what may happen. Nothing but good will follow. As for the pearls, go early to-morrow morning to the foot of the first tree on your right hand in the park, dig under it, and you will find more than you want."

That night the princess ordered a gardener to be ready to attend her, and the next morning early, led him to the tree which the Bird had told her of, and bade him dig at its foot. When the gardener came to a certain depth, he found some resistance to the spade, and presently discovered a gold box about a foot square, which he showed the princess. "This," said she, "is what I brought you for; take care not to injure it with the spade."

When the gardener took up the box, he gave it into the princess's hands, who, as it was only fastened with neat little hasps, soon opened it, and found it full of pearls of a moderate size, but equal and fit for the use that was to be made of them. Very well satisfied with having found this treasure, after she had shut the box again, she put it under her arm and went back to the house, while the gardener threw the earth into the hole at the foot of the tree as it had been before.

The Princes Bahman and Perviz, who, as they were dressing themselves in their own apartments, saw their sister in the garden earlier than usual, as soon as they could get out went to her, and met her as she was returning with a gold box under her arm, which much surprised them. "Sister," said Bahman, "you carried nothing with you when we saw you before with the gardener, and now we see you have a golden box; is this some treasure found by the gardener, and did he come and tell you of it?"

"No, brother," answered the princess, "I took the gardener to the place where this casket was concealed, and showed him where to dig; but you will be more amazed when you see what it contains."

The princess opened the box, and when the princes saw that it was full of pearls, which, though small, were of great value, they asked her how she came to the knowledge of this treasure. "Brothers," said she, "come with me and I will tell you." The princess, as they returned to the house, gave them an account of her having consulted the Bird, as they had agreed she should, and the answer he had given her; the objection she had raised to preparing a dish of cucumbers stuffed full of pearls, and how he had told her where to find this box. The sister and brothers formed many conjectures to penetrate into what the Bird could mean by ordering them to prepare such a dish; but after much conversation, they agreed to follow his advice exactly.

As soon as the princess entered the house, she called for the head cook; and after she had given him directions about the entertainment for the emperor, said to him: "Besides all this, you must dress an extraordinary dish for the emperor's own eating, which nobody else must have anything to do with besides yourself. This dish must be of cucumbers stuffed with these pearls:" and at the same time she opened him the box, and showed him the jewels.

The chief cook, who had never heard of such a dish, started back, and showed his thoughts by his looks; which the princess penetrating, said: "I see you take me to be mad to order such a dish, which one may say with certainty was never made. I know this as well as you; but I am not mad, and give you these orders with the most perfect recollection. You must invent and do the best you can, and bring me back what pearls are left." The cook could make no reply, but took the box and retired; and afterward the princess gave directions to all the domestics to have everything in order, both in the house and gardens, to receive the emperor.

Next day the two princes went to the place appointed, and as soon as the emperor of Persia arrived the chase began and lasted till the heat of the sun obliged him to leave off. While Prince Bahman stayed to conduct the emperor to their house, Prince Perviz rode before to show the way, and when he came in sight of the house, spurred his horse, to inform the princess that the emperor was approaching; but she had been told by some servants whom she had placed to give notice, and the prince found her waiting ready to receive him.

When the emperor had entered the court-yard and alighted at the portico, the princess came and threw herself at his feet, and the two princes informed him she was their sister, and besought him to accept her respects.

The emperor stooped to raise her, and after he had gazed some time on her beauty, struck with her fine person and dignified air, he said: "The brothers are worthy of the sister, and she worthy of them; since, if I may judge of her understanding by her person, I am not amazed that the brothers would do nothing without their sister's consent; but," added he, "I hope to be better acquainted with you, my daughter, after I have seen the house."

"Sir," said the princess, "it is only a plain country residence, fit for such people as we are, who live retired from the great world. It is not to be compared with the magnificent palaces of emperors." "I cannot perfectly agree with you in opinion," said the emperor very obligingly, "for its first appearance makes me suspect you; however,

I will not pass my judgment upon it till I have seen it all; therefore be pleased to conduct me through the apartments."

The princess led the emperor through all the rooms except the hall; and, after he had considered them very attentively, and admired their variety, "My daughter," said he to the princess, "do you call this a country house? The finest and largest cities would soon be deserted if all country houses were like yours. I am no longer surprised that you despise the town. Now let me see the garden, which I doubt not is answerable to the house."

The princess opened a door which led into the garden, and the first object which presented itself to the emperor's view was the golden fountain. Surprised at so rare an object, he asked from whence that wonderful water, which gave so much pleasure to behold, had been procured; where was its source, and by what art it was made to play so high. He said he would presently take a nearer view of it.

The princess then led him to the spot where the harmonious tree was planted; and there the emperor heard a concert, different from all he had ever heard before; and stopping to see where the musicians were, he could discern nobody far or near, but still distinctly heard the music which ravished his senses. "My daughter," said he to the princess, "where are the musicians whom I hear? Are they under ground, or invisible in the air? Such excellent performers will hazard nothing by being seen; on the contrary, they would please the more."

"Sir," answered the princess, smiling, "they are not musicians, but the leaves of the tree your majesty sees before you, which form this concert; and if you will give yourself the trouble to go a little nearer, you will be convinced, and the voices will be the more distinct."

The emperor went nearer and was so charmed with the sweet harmony that he would never have been tired with hearing it, but that his desire to have a nearer view of the fountain of golden water forced him away. "Daughter," said he, "tell me, I pray you, whether this wonderful tree was found in your garden by chance, or was a present made to you, or have you procured it from some foreign country? It must certainly have come from a great distance, otherwise curious as I am after natural rarities I should have heard of it. What name do you call it by?"

"Sir," replied the princess, "this tree has no other name than that of the Singing Tree, and is not a native of this country. It would at present take up too much time to tell your majesty by what adventures it came here; its history is connected with the Golden Water and the Talking Bird, which came to me at the same time, and which your majesty may presently see. But if it be agreeable to your majesty, after you have rested yourself and recovered the fatigue of hunting, which must be the greater because of the sun's intense heat, I will do myself the honour of relating it to you."

"My daughter," replied the emperor, "my fatigue is so well recompensed by the wonderful things you have shown me, that I do not feel it in the least. Let me see the Golden Water, for I am impatient to see and admire afterward the Talking Bird."

When the emperor came to the Golden Water, his eyes were fixed so steadfastly upon the fountain, that he could not take them off. At last, addressing himself to the princess, he said: "As you tell me, daughter, that this water has no spring or communication, I conclude that it is foreign, as well as the Singing Tree."

"Sir," replied the princess, "it is as your majesty conjectures; and to let you know that this water has no communication with any spring, I must inform you that the basin is one entire stone, so that the water cannot come in at the sides or underneath. But what your majesty will think most wonderful is that all this water proceeded but from one small flagon, emptied into this basin, which increased to the quantity you see, by a property peculiar to itself, and formed this fountain." "Well," said the emperor, going from the fountain, "this is enough for one time. I promise myself the pleasure to come and visit it often; but now let us go and see the Talking Bird."

As he went toward the hall, the emperor perceived a prodigious number of singing birds in the trees around, filling the air with their songs and warblings, and asked why there were so many there and none on the other trees in the garden. "The reason, sir," answered the princess, "is because they come from all parts to accompany the song of the Talking Bird, which your majesty may see in a cage in one of the windows of the hall we are approaching; and if you attend, you will perceive that his notes are sweeter than those of any of the other birds, even the nightingale's."

The emperor went into the hall; and as the Bird continued singing, the princess raised her voice, and said, "My slave, here is the emperor, pay your compliments to him." The Bird left off singing that instant, when all the other birds ceased also, and said: "The emperor is welcome; God prosper him and prolong his life!" As the entertainment was served on the sofa near the window where the Bird was placed, the sultan replied, as he was taking his seat: "Bird, I thank you, and am overjoyed to find in you the sultan and king of birds."

As soon as the emperor saw the dish of cucumbers set before him, thinking they were prepared in the best manner, he reached out his hand and took one; but when he cut it, was in extreme surprise to find it stuffed with pearls. "What novelty is this?" said he; "and with what design were these cucumbers stuffed thus with pearls, since pearls are not to be eaten?" He looked at his hosts to ask them the meaning when the Bird interrupting him, said: "Can your majesty be in such great astonishment at cucumbers stuffed with pearls, which you see with your own eyes, and yet so easily believe that the queen, your wife, gave birth to a dog, a cat, and a piece of wood?" "I believed those things," replied the emperor, "because the attendants assured me of the facts." "Those attendants, sir," replied the Bird, "were the queen's two sisters, who, envious of her happiness in being preferred by your majesty before them, to satisfy their envy and revenge, have abused your majesty's credulity. If you interrogate them, they will confess their crime. The two brothers and the sister whom you see before you are your own children, whom they exposed, and who were taken in by the intendant of your gardens, who provided nurses for them, and took care of their education."

This speech presently cleared up the emperor's understanding. "Bird," cried he, "I believe the truth which you discover to me. The inclination which drew me to them told me plainly they must be of my own blood. Come then, my sons, come, my daughter, let me embrace you, and give you the first marks of a father's love and tenderness." The emperor then rose, and after having embraced the two princes and the princess, and mingled his tears with theirs, said: "It is not enough, my children; you must embrace each other, not as the children of the intendant of my gardens, to whom I have been so much obliged for preserving your lives, but as my own children, of the royal blood of the monarchs of Persia, whose glory, I am persuaded you will maintain."

After the two princes and princess had embraced mutually with new satisfaction, the emperor sat down again with them, and finished his meal in haste; and when he had done, said: "My children, you see in me your father; to-morrow I will bring the queen, your mother, therefore prepare to receive her."

The emperor afterward mounted his horse, and returned with expedition to his capitol. The first thing he did, as soon as he had alighted and entered his palace, was to command the grand vizier to seize the queen's two sisters. They were taken from their houses separately, convicted, and condemned to death; which sentence was put in execution within an hour.

In the meantime, the Emperor Kosrouschah, followed by all the lords of his court who were then present, went on foot to the door of the great mosque; and after he had taken the queen out of the strict confinement she had languished under for so many years, embracing her in the miserable condition to which she was then reduced, said to her with tears in his eyes: "I come to entreat your pardon for the injustice I have done you, and to make you the reparation I ought; which I have begun, by punishing the unnatural wretches who put the abominable cheat upon me; and I hope you will look upon it as complete, when I present to you two accomplished princes and a lovely princess, our children. Come and resume your former rank, with all the honours which are your due." All this was done and said before great crowds of people who flocked from all parts at the first news of what was passing, and immediately spread the joyful intelligence through the city.

Next morning early the emperor and queen, whose mournful humiliating dress was changed for magnificent robes, went with all their court to the house built by the intendant of the gardens, where the emperor presented the Princes Bahman and Perviz, and the Princess Periezade to their enraptured mother. "These, much injured wife," said he, "are the two princes your sons, and the princess your daughter; embrace them with the same tenderness I have done, since they are worthy both of me and you." The tears flowed plentifully down their cheeks at these tender embraces, especially the queen's, from the comfort and joy of having two such princes for her sons, and such a princess for her daughter, on whose account she had so long endured the severest afflictions.

The two princes and the princess had prepared a magnificent repast for the emperor and queen and their court. As soon as that was over, the emperor led the queen into the garden, and shewed her the Harmonious Tree and the beautiful effect of the Golden Fountain. She had seen the Bird in his cage, and the emperor had spared no panegyric in his praise during the repast.

When there was nothing to detain the emperor any longer, he took horse, and with the Princes Bahman and Perviz on his right hand, and the queen consort and the princess at his left, preceded and followed by all the officers of his court, according to their rank, returned to his capital. Crowds of people came out to meet them, and with acclamations of joy ushered them into the city, where all eyes were fixed not only upon the queen, and her royal children, but also upon the Bird, which the princess carried before her in his cage, admiring his sweet notes, which had drawn all the other birds about him, and followed him flying from tree to tree in the country, and from one house top to another in the city. The Princes Bahman and Perviz and the Princess Periezade were at length brought to the palace with pomp, and nothing was to be seen or heard all that night but illuminations and rejoicings both in the palace and in the utmost parts of the city, which lasted many days, and were continued throughout the empire of Persia, as intelligence of the joyful event reached the several provinces.

The Story of Gulnare of the Sea

Kate Douglas Wiggin and Nora A. Smith

THERE WAS, in olden time, and in an ancient age and period, in the land of the Persians, a king named Shahzeman, and the place of his residence was Khorassan. He had not been blest, during his whole life, with a male child nor a female; and he reflected upon this, one day, and lamented that the greater portion of his life had passed, and he had no heir to take the kingdom after him as he had inherited it from his fathers and forefathers. So the utmost grief befell him on this account.

Now while he was sitting one day, one of his mamelukes came in to him, and said to him: "O my lord, at the door is a slave-girl with a merchant: none more beautiful than she hath been seen." And he replied: "Bring to me the merchant and the slave-girl." The merchant and the slave-girl therefore came to him; and when he saw her, he found her to resemble the lance in straightness and slenderness. She was wrapped in a garment of silk embroidered with gold, and the merchant uncovered her face, whereupon the place was illuminated by her beauty, and there hung down from her forehead seven locks of hair reaching to her anklets. The King, therefore, wondered at the sight of her, and at her beauty, and her stature and justness of form; and he said to the merchant: "O sheikh, for how much is this damsel to be sold?" The merchant answered: "O my lord, I purchased her for two thousand pieces of gold of the merchant who owned her before me, and I have been for three years travelling with her, and she hath cost, to the period of her arrival at this place, three thousand pieces of gold; and she is a present from me unto thee." Upon this, the king conferred upon him a magnificent robe of honour, and gave orders to present him with ten thousand pieces of gold. So he took them, and kissed the hands of the king, thanking him for his beneficence, and departed. Then the king committed the damsel to the tirewomen, saying to them: "Amend the state of this damsel, and deck her, and furnish for her a private chamber, and take her into it." He also gave orders to his chamberlains that everything which she required should be conveyed to her. The seat of government where he resided was on the shore of the sea, and his city was called the White City. And they conducted the damsel into a private chamber, which chamber had windows overlooking the sea; and the king commanded his chamberlains to close all the doors upon her after taking to her all that she required.

The king then went in to visit the damsel; but she rose not to him, nor took any notice of him. So the king said: "It seemeth that she hath been with people who have not taught her good manners." And looking at the damsel, he saw her to be a person surpassing in loveliness, her face was like the disk of the moon at the full, or the shining sun in the clear sky; and he wondered at her beauty, extolling the perfection of God, the Creator: then the king advanced to the damsel, and seated himself by her side, pressed her to his bosom, and kissed her lips, which he found to be sweeter than honey. After this, he gave orders to bring tables of the richest viands, comprising dishes of every kind; and he ate, and put morsels into her mouth until she was satisfied; but she spoke not a single word. The king talked to her, and inquired of her her name; but she was silent, not uttering a word, nor returning him an answer, ceasing not to hang down her head toward the ground; and what protected her from the anger of the king was her beauty, and her tenderness of manner. So the king said within himself: "Extolled be the perfection of God, the Creator of this damsel! How elegant is she, saving that she doth not speak!" – Then the king asked the female slaves whether she had spoken; and they answered him: "From the time of her arrival to the present moment she hath not spoken one word, and we have not heard her talk." The king therefore caused some of them to come, and sing to her, and make merry with her, thinking that then she might perhaps speak. Accordingly the female slaves played before her with all kinds of musical instruments, and enacted sports and other performances, and they sang so that every one who was present was moved with delight, except the damsel, who looked at them and was silent, neither laughing nor speaking. So the heart of the king was contracted. He however inclined to her entirely, paying no regard to others, but relinquishing all the rest of his favourites.

He remained with her a whole year, which seemed as one day, and still she spoke not; and he said to her one day, when his passion was excessive: "O desire of souls, verily the love that I have for thee is great, and I have relinquished for thy sake all my worldly portion, and been patient with thee a whole year. I beg God that He will, in His grace, soften thy heart toward me, and that thou mayest speak to me. Or, if thou be dumb, inform me by a sign, that I may give up hope of thy speaking. I also beg of God that He will bless thee with a son that may inherit my kingdom after me; for I am solitary, having none to be my heir, and my age hath become great. I conjure thee, then, by Allah, if thou love me, that thou return me a reply." And upon this, the damsel hung her head toward the ground, meditating. Then she raised her head, and smiled in the face of the king, whereat it appeared to the king that lightning filled the private chamber; and she said: "O magnanimous King, God hath answered thy prayer; for I am about to bring thee a child, and the time is almost come. And were it not that I knew this thing, I had not spoken to thee one word." And when the king heard what she said, his face brightened up with happiness, and he kissed her hands by reason of the violence of his joy, and said: "Praise be to God who hath favoured me with things that I desired; the first, thy speaking; and the second, thy information that thou art about to bring me a child." Then the king arose and went forth from her, and seated himself upon the throne of his kingdom in a state of exceeding happiness; and he ordered the vizier to give out to the poor and the needy a hundred thousand pieces of gold as a thank-offering to God. So the vizier did as the king had commanded him. And after that, the king went in to the damsel, and embraced her, saying to her: "O my mistress, wherefore hath been this silence, seeing that thou hast been with me a whole year, awake and asleep, yet hast not spoken to me, except on this day?"

The damsel answered: "Hear, O King of the age, and know that I am a poor person, a stranger, broken-hearted: I have become separated from my mother, and my family, and my brother." And when the king heard her words, he knew her desire, and he replied: "As to thy saying that thou art poor, there is no occasion for such an assertion; for all my kingdom and possessions are at thy service, and as to thy saying, 'I have become separated from my mother and my family and my brother' – inform me in what place they are, and I will send to them, and bring them to thee." So she said to him:

"Know, O King, that my name is Gulnare (*Pomegranate Flower*) of the Sea. My father was one of the Kings of the Sea, and he died, and left to us the kingdom; but while we were enjoying it, another of the kings came upon us, and took the kingdom from our hands. I have also a brother named Saleh, and my mother is of the women of the sea; and I quarrelled with my brother, and swore that I would throw myself into the hands of a man of the inhabitants of the land. Accordingly I came forth from the sea, and sat upon the shore of an island in the moonlight, and there passed by a man who took me and sold me to this man from whom thou tookest me, and he was an excellent, virtuous man, a person of religion and fidelity and kindness. But had not thy heart loved me, and hadst thou not preferred me above all thy wives, I had not remained with thee one hour; for I should have cast myself into the sea from this window, and gone to my mother and my people. I was ashamed, however, to go to them; for they would imagine evil of me, and would not believe me, even though I should swear to them, were I to tell them that a king had purchased me with his money, and chosen me in preference to his other wives and all that his right hand possessed. This is my story, and peace be on thee!" And when he heard her words, he thanked her, and kissed her between the eyes, and said to her: "By Allah, O my mistress, and light of my eyes, I cannot endure separation from thee for one hour; and if thou quit me, I shall die instantly. How then shall the affair be?" She answered: "O my master, the time of the birth is near, and my family must come." "And how," said the king, "do they walk in the sea without being wetted?" She answered: "We walk in the sea as ye walk upon the land, through the influence of the names engraved upon the seal of Solomon, the son of David, upon both of whom be peace! But, O King, when my family and my brethren come, I will inform them that thou boughtest me with thy money, and hast treated me with beneficence, and it will be meet that thou confirm my assertion to them. They will also see thy state with their eyes, and will know that thou art a king, the son of a king." And thereupon the king said: "O my mistress, do what seemeth fit to thee, and what thou wishest; for I will comply with thy desire in all that thou wilt do." And the damsel said: "Know, O King of the age, that we walk in the sea with our eyes open, and see what is in it, and we see the sun, and the moon, and the stars, and the sky as on the face of the earth, and this hurteth us not. Know also, that in the sea are many peoples and various forms of all the kinds that are on the land; and know, moreover, that all that is on the land, in comparison with what is in the sea, is a very small matter." And the king wondered at her words.

Then the damsel took a bit of aloes-wood and, having lighted a fire in a perfuming-vessel, threw into it that bit, and she proceeded to speak words which no one understood; whereupon a great smoke arose, while the king looked on. After this, she said to the king: "O my lord, arise and conceal thyself in a closet, that I may shew thee my brother and my mother and my family without their seeing thee; for I desire to bring them, and thou shalt see in this place, at this time, a wonder, and shalt marvel at the various shapes and strange forms that God hath created." So the king arose immediately, and entered a closet, and looked to see what she would do. And she proceeded to burn perfume and repeat spells until the sea foamed and was agitated, and there came forth from it a young man of comely form, of beautiful countenance, like the moon at the full, with shining forehead, and red cheeks, and hair resembling pearls and jewels; he was, of all the creation, the most like to his sister, and the tongue of the case itself seemed to recite in his praise these verses:

The moon becometh perfect once in each month; but the loveliness of thy face is perfect every day.

Its abode is in the heart of one sign at a time; but thine abode is in all hearts at once.

Afterward, there came forth from the sea a grizzly-haired old woman, and with her five damsels, resembling moons and bearing a likeness to the damsel whose name was Gulnare. Then the king saw the young man and the old woman and the damsels walk upon the surface of the water until they came to Gulnare; and when they drew near to the window, and she beheld them, she rose to them and met them with joy. On their seeing her, they knew her, and they went in to her and embraced her, weeping violently; and they said to her: "O Gulnare, how is it that thou leavest us for four years, and we know not the place in which thou art? By Allah, we had no delight in food nor in drink a single day, weeping night and day on account of the excess of our longing to see thee." Then the damsel began to kiss the hand of her brother, and the hand of her mother, and so also the hands of the daughters of her uncle, and they sat with her awhile, asking her respecting her state, and the things that had happened to her, and her present condition.

So she said to them: "Know ye, that when I quitted you, and came forth from the sea, I sat upon the shore of an island, and a man took me, and sold me to a merchant, and the merchant brought me to this city, and sold me to its king for ten thousand pieces of gold. Then he treated me with attention, and forsook all his favourites for my sake, and was diverted by his regard for me from everything that he possessed and what was in his city." And when her brother heard her words, he said: "Praise be to God who hath reunited us! But it is my desire, O my sister, that thou wouldst arise and go with us to our country and our family." So when the king heard the words of her brother, his reason fled in consequence of his fear lest the damsel should accept the proposal of her kindred, and he could not prevent her, though he was inflamed with love of her; wherefore he became perplexed in violent fear of her separation. But as to the damsel Gulnare, on hearing the words of her brother she said: "By Allah, O my brother, the man who purchased me is the king of this city, and he is a great king, and a man of wisdom, generous, of the utmost liberality. He hath treated me with honour, and he is a person of kindness, and of great wealth, but hath no male child nor a female. He hath shewn me favour too, and acted well to me in every respect; and from the day when I came to him to the present time, I have not heard from him a word to grieve my heart; but he hath not ceased to treat me with courtesy, and I am living with him in the most perfect of enjoyments. Moreover, if I quitted him, he would perish: for he can never endure my separation even for a single hour. I also, if I quitted him, should die of my love for him in consequence of his kindness to me during the period of my residence with him; for if my father were living, my condition with him would not be like my condition with this great, glorious king. God (whose name be exalted!) afflicted me not, but compensated me well; and as the king hath not a male child nor a female, I beg God to bless me with a son that may inherit of this great king these palaces and possessions." And when her brother, and the daughters of her uncle, heard her words, their eyes became cheerful thereat, and they said to her: "O Gulnare, thou art acquainted with our affection for thee, and thou art assured that thou art the dearest of all persons to us, and art certain that we desire for thee comfort, without trouble or toil. Therefore if thou be not in a state of comfort, arise and accompany us to our country and our family; but if thou be comfortable here, in honour and happiness, this is our desire and wish." And Gulnare replied: "By Allah, I am in a state of the utmost enjoyment, in honour and desirable happiness." So when the king heard these words from her, he rejoiced, and he thanked her for them; his love for her penetrated to his heart's core, and he knew that she loved him as he loved her, and that she desired to remain with him to see his child which she was to bring to him.

Then the damsel Gulnare of the Sea gave orders to the female slaves to bring forward viands of all kinds; and Gulnare herself was the person who superintended the preparation of the viands in the kitchen. So the female slaves brought to them the viands, and the sweetmeats, and the fruits; and she ate with her family. But afterward they said to her: "O Gulnare, thy master is a man who is a stranger to us, and we have entered his abode without his permission, and thou praisest to us his excellence, and hast also brought to us his food, and we have eaten, but have not seen him, nor hath he seen us, nor come into our presence, nor eaten with us, that the bond of bread and salt might be established between us." And they all desisted from eating, and were enraged at her, and fire began to issue from their mouths as from cressets. So when the king beheld this, his reason fled, in consequence of the violence of his fear of them. Then Gulnare rose to them, and soothed their hearts; after which she walked along until she entered the closet in which was the king her master; and she said to him: "O my master, didst thou see, and didst thou hear my thanks to thee, and my praise of thee in the presence of my family; and didst thou hear what they said to me, that they desired to take me with them to our family and our country?" The king answered her: "I heard and saw. May God recompense thee! By Allah, I knew not the extent of the love that thou feelest for me until this blessed hour." She replied: "O my master, is the recompense of beneficence aught but beneficence? How then could my heart be happy to quit thee, and to depart from thee? Now I desire of thy goodness that thou come and salute my family, that they may see thee, and that pleasure and mutual friendship may ensue. For know, O King, that my brother and my mother and the daughters of my uncle have conceived a great love for thee in consequence of my praising thee to them, and they have said, 'We will not depart from thee to our country until we have an interview with the king, and salute him.'" And the king said to her: "I hear and obey; for this is what I desire." He then rose from his place, and went to them, and saluted them with the best salutation; and they hastened to rise to him; they met him in the most polite manner, and he sat with them in the pavilion, ate with them at the table, and remained with them for a period of thirty days. Then they desired to return to their country and abode. So they took leave of the king and Queen Gulnare of the Sea, and departed from them, after the king had treated them with the utmost honour.

After this, Gulnare gave birth to a boy, resembling the moon at the full, whereat the king experienced the utmost happiness, because he had not before been blessed with a son nor a daughter during his life. They continued the rejoicings, and the decoration of the city, for a period of seven days, in the utmost happiness and enjoyment; and on the seventh day, the mother of Gulnare, and her brother, and the daughters of her uncle, all came, when they knew that she had given birth to her child. The king met them, rejoicing at their arrival, and said to them: "I said that I would not name my son until ye should come, and that ye should name him according to your knowledge." And they named him Bedr Basim (*Smiling Full Moon*), all of them agreeing as to this name. They then presented the boy to his maternal uncle, Saleh, who took him upon his hands, and, rising with him from among them, walked about the palace to the right and left; after which he went forth with him from the palace, descended with him to the sea, and walked on until he became concealed from the eye of the king. So when the king saw that he had taken his son, and disappeared from him at the bottom of the sea, he despaired of him, and began to weep and wail. But Gulnare, seeing him in this state, said to him, "O King of the age, fear not nor grieve for thy son; for I love my child more than thou, and my child is with my brother; therefore fear not his being drowned. If my brother knew that any injury would betide the little one, he had not done what he hath done; and presently he will bring thee thy son safe, if it be the will of God, whose name be exalted!" And but a short time had elapsed when the sea was agitated, and the uncle of the little one came forth from it, having with him the king's son safe, and he flew from the sea until he came to them, with the little one in his arms, silent, and his face resembling the moon in the night of its fulness. Then the uncle of the little one looked toward the king, and said to him: "Perhaps thou fearedst some injury to thy son when I descended into the sea, having him with me." So he replied: "Yes, O my master, I feared for him, and I did not imagine that he would ever come forth from it safe." And Saleh said to him: "O King of the Land, we applied to his eyes a lotion that we know, and repeated over him the names engraved upon the seal of Solomon, the son of David; for when a child is born among us, we do to him as I have told thee. Fear not therefore, on his account, drowning, nor suffocation, nor all the seas if he descend into them. Like as ye walk upon the land, we walk in the sea."

He then took forth from his pocket a case, written upon, and sealed; and he broke its seal, and scattered its contents, whereupon there fell from it strung jewels, consisting of all kinds of jacinths and other gems, together with three hundred oblong emeralds, and three hundred oblong large jewels, of the size of the eggs of the ostrich, the light of which was more resplendent than the light of the sun and the moon. And he said: "O King of the age, these jewels and jacinths are a present from me unto thee; for we never brought thee a present, because we knew not the place of Gulnare's abode. So when we saw thee to have become united to her, and that we all had become one, we brought thee this present; and after every period of a few days, we will bring thee the like of it. For these jewels and jacinths with us are more plentiful than the gravel upon the land, and we know the excellent among them, and the bad, and the places where they are found, and they are easy of access to us." – And when the king looked at those jewels, his reason was confounded and his mind was bewildered, and he said: "By Allah, one of these jewels is worth my kingdom!" Then the king thanked Saleh of the Sea for his generosity, and looking toward the Queen Gulnare said to her: "I am abashed at thy brother; for he hath shewn favour to me, and presented me with this magnificent present, which the people of the earth would fail to procure." So Gulnare thanked her brother for that which he had done; but her brother said: "O King of the age, to thank thee hath been incumbent on us; for thou hast treated my sister with beneficence, and we have entered thine abode, and eaten of thy provision." Then Saleh said: "If we stood serving thee, O King of the age, a thousand years, regarding nothing else, we could not requite thee, and our doing so would be but a small thing in comparison with thy desert." And Saleh remained with the king, he and his mother and the daughters of his uncle, forty days; after which he arose and kissed the ground before the king, the husband of his sister. So the king said to him: "What dost thou desire, O Saleh?" And he answered: "O King of the age, we desire of thy goodness that thou wouldst give us permission to depart; for we have become desirous of seeing again our family and our country and our relations and our homes. We will not, however, relinquish the service of thee, nor that of my sister nor the son of my sister; and by Allah, O King of the age, to quit you is not pleasant to my heart; but how can we act, when we have been reared in the sea, and the land is not agreeable to us?" So when the king heard his words, he rose upon his feet, and bade farewell to Saleh of the Sea and his mother and the daughters of his uncle, and they wept together on account of the separation. Then they said to the king: "We will never relinquish you, but after every period of a few days we will visit you." And after this, they flew toward the sea, and descended into it, and disappeared.

The king treated Gulnare with beneficence, and honoured her exceedingly, and the little one grew up well; and his maternal uncle, with his grandmother and the daughters of his uncle, after every period of a few days used to come to the residence of the king, and to remain with him a month, and then return to their places. The boy ceased not to increase in beauty and loveliness until his age became fifteen years; and he was incomparable in his perfect beauty, and his stature and his justness of form. He had learned writing and reading, and history and grammar and philology, and archery; and he learned to play with the spear; and he also learned horsemanship, and all that the sons of the kings required. There was not one of the children of the inhabitants of the city, men and women, that talked not of the charms of that young man; for he was of surpassing loveliness and perfection; and the king loved him greatly. Then the king summoned the vizier and the emeers, and the lords of the empire, and the great men of the kingdom, and made them swear by binding oaths that they would make Bedr Basim king over them after his father; so they swore to him by binding oaths, and rejoiced thereat; and the king himself was beneficent to the people, courteous in speech and of auspicious aspect. And on the following day, the king mounted, together with the lords of the empire and all the emeers, and all the soldiers, and they ceased not to proceed until they arrived at the vestibule of the palace; the king's son riding. Thereupon he alighted, and his father embraced him, he and the emeers, and they seated him upon the throne of the kingdom, while his father stood, as also did the emeers, before him. Then Bedr Basim judged the people, displaced the tyrannical and invested the just, and continued to give judgment until near midday, when he rose from the throne of the kingdom, and went in to his mother, Gulnare of the Sea, having upon his head the crown, and resembling the moon. So when his mother saw him, and the king before him, she rose to him and kissed him, and congratulated him on his elevation to the dignity of sultan; and she offered up a prayer in favour of him and his father for length of life, and victory over their enemies. He then sat with his mother and rested; and when the time of afternoon-prayers arrived, he rode with the emeers before him until he came to the horse-course, where he played with arms till the time of nightfall, together with his father and the lords of his empire; after which he returned to the palace, with all the people before him. Every day he used to ride to the horse-course; and when he returned, he sat to judge the people, and administered justice between the emeer and the poor man. He ceased not to do thus for a whole year; and after that, he used to ride to the chase, and go about through the cities and provinces that were under his rule making proclamation of safety and security, and doing as do the kings; and he was incomparable among the people of his age in glory and courage, and in justice to the people.

Now it came to pass that the old king, the father of Bedr Basim, fell sick one day, whereupon his heart throbbed, and he felt that he was about to be removed to the mansion of eternity. Then his malady increased so that he was at the point of death. He therefore summoned his son, and charged him to take care of his subjects and his mother and all the lords of his empire and all the dependants. He also made them swear, and covenanted with them a second time, that they would obey his son; and he confided in their oaths. And after this he remained a few days, and was admitted to the mercy of God, whose name be exalted! His son Bedr Basim, and his wife Gulnare and the emeers and viziers and the lords of the empire, mourned over him; and they made for him a tomb, and buried him in it, and continued the ceremonies of mourning for him a whole month. Saleh, the brother of Gulnare, and her mother, and the daughters of her uncle, also came, and consoled them for the loss of the king; and they said: "O Gulnare, if the king hath died, he hath left this ingenuous youth, and he who hath left such as he is hath not died. This is he who hath not an equal, the crushing lion, and the splendid moon." Then the lords of the empire, and the grandees, went in to the King Bedr Basim, and said to him: "O King, there is no harm in mourning for the king; but mourning becometh not any save women; therefore trouble not thy heart and ours by mourning for thy father; for he hath died and left thee, and he who hath left such as thou art hath not died." They proceeded to address him with soft words, and to console him, and after that they conducted him into the bath; and when he came forth from the bath, he put on a magnificent suit woven of gold, adorned with jewels and jacinths, and he put the royal crown upon his head, seated himself upon the throne of his kingdom, and performed the affairs of the people, deciding equitably between the strong and the weak, and exacting for the poor man his due from the emeer; wherefore the people loved him exceedingly. Thus he continued to do for the space of a whole year; and after every short period, his family of the sea visited him; so his life was pleasant, and his eye was cheerful: and he ceased not to live in this state until he was visited by the terminator of delights and the separator of companions. This is the end of their story. The mercy of God be on them all!

Prince Beder and the Princess Giauhara

E. Dixon

YOUNG PRINCE BEDER was brought up and educated in the palace under the care of the King and Queen of Persia. He gave them great pleasure as he advanced in years by his agreeable manners, and by the justness of whatever he said; King Saleh his uncle, the queen his grandmother, and the princesses his relations, came from time to time to see him. He was easily taught to read and write, and was instructed in all the sciences that became a prince of his rank.

When he arrived at the age of fifteen he was very wise and prudent. The king, who had almost from his cradle discovered in him these virtues so necessary for a monarch, and who moreover began to perceive the infirmities of old age coming upon himself every day, would not wait till death gave him possession of the throne, but purposed to resign it to him. He had no great difficulty to make his council consent to it; and the people heard this with so much the more joy, because they considered Prince Beder worthy to govern them. They saw that he treated all mankind with that goodness which invited them to approach him; that he heard favourably all who had anything to say to him; that he answered everybody with a goodness that was peculiar to him; and that he refused nobody anything that had the least appearance of justice.

The day for the ceremony was appointed. In the midst of the whole assembly, which was larger than usual, the King of Persia, then sitting on his throne, came down from it, took the crown from off his head, put it on that of Prince Beder, and having seated him in his place, kissed his hand, as a token that he resigned his authority to him. After which he took his place among the crowd of viziers and emirs below the throne.

Hereupon the viziers, emirs, and other principal officers, came immediately and threw themselves at the new king's feet, taking each the oath of fidelity according to their rank. Then the grand vizier made a report of various important matters, on which the young king gave judgment with admirable prudence and sagacity that surprised all the council. He next turned out several governors convicted of mal-administration, and put others in their place, with wonderful and just discernment. He at length left the council, accompanied by the late king his father, and went to see his mother, Queen Gulnare. The queen no sooner saw him coming with his crown upon his head, than she ran to him, and embraced him with tenderness, wishing him a long and prosperous reign.

The first year of his reign King Beder acquitted himself of all his royal functions with great care. Above all, he took care to inform himself of the state of his affairs, and all that might in any way contribute towards the happiness of his people. Next year, having left the administration to his council, under the direction of the old king his father, he went out of his capital, under pretext of diverting himself with hunting; but his real intention was to visit all the provinces of his kingdom, that he might reform all abuses there, establish good order and discipline everywhere, and take from all ill-minded princes, his neighbours, any opportunities of attempting any thing against the security and tranquillity of his subjects, by showing himself on his frontiers.

It required no less than a whole year for this young king to carry out his plans. Soon after his return, the old king his father fell so dangerously ill that he knew at once he should never recover. He waited for his last moment with great tranquillity, and his only care was to recommend the ministers and other lords of his son's court to remain faithful to him: and there was not one but willingly renewed his oath as freely as at first. He died, at length, to the great grief of King Beder and Queen Gulnare, who caused his corpse to be borne to a stately mausoleum, worthy of his rank and dignity.

The funeral ended, King Beder found no difficulty in complying with that ancient custom in Persia to mourn for the dead a whole month, and not to be seen by anybody during all that time. He would have mourned the death of his father his whole life, had it been right for a great prince thus to abandon himself to grief. During this interval the queen, mother to Queen Gulnare, and King Saleh, together with the princesses their relations, arrived at the Persian court, and shared their affliction, before they offered any consolation.

When the month was expired, the king could not refuse admittance to the grand vizier and the other lords of his court, who besought him to lay aside his mourning, to show himself to his subjects, and take upon him the administration of affairs as before.

He showed such great reluctance at their request, that the grand vizier was forced to take upon himself to say to him; 'Sir, neither our tears nor yours are capable of restoring life to the good king your father, though we should lament him all our days. He has undergone the common law of all men, which subjects them to pay the indispensable tribute of death. Yet we cannot say absolutely that he is dead, since we see him in your sacred person. He did not himself doubt, when he was dying, but that he should revive in you, and to your majesty it belongs to show that he was not deceived.'

King Beder could no longer oppose such pressing entreaties: he laid aside his mourning; and after he had resumed the royal habit and ornaments, he began to provide for the necessities of his kingdom and subjects with the same care as before his father's death. He acquitted himself with universal approbation: and as he was exact in maintaining the ordinances of his predecessor, the people did not feel they had changed their sovereign.

King Saleh, who had returned to his dominions in the sea with the queen his mother and the princesses, no sooner saw that King Beder had resumed the government, at the end of the month than he came alone to visit him; and King Beder and Queen Gulnare were overjoyed to see him.

One evening when they rose from table, they talked of various matters. King Saleh began with the praises of the king his nephew, and expressed to the queen his sister how glad he was to see him govern so prudently, all of which had acquired him great reputation, not among his neighbours only, but more remote princes. King Beder, who could not bear to hear himself so well spoken of, and not being willing, through good manners, to interrupt the king his uncle, turned on one side to sleep, leaning his head against a cushion that was behind him.

'Sister,' said King Saleh, 'I wonder you have not thought of marrying him ere this: if I mistake not, he is in his twentieth year; and, at that age, no prince like him ought to be suffered to be without a wife. I will think of a wife for him myself, since you will not, and marry him to some princess of our lower world that may be worthy of him.'

'Brother,' replied Queen Gulnare, 'I have never thought of it to this very moment, and I am glad you have spoken of it to me. I like your proposing one of our princesses; and I desire you to name one so beautiful and accomplished that the king my son may be obliged to love her.'

'I know one that will suit,' replied King Saleh, softly; 'but I see many difficulties to be surmounted, not on the lady's part, as I hope, but on that of her father. I need only mention to you the Princess Giauhara, daughter of the king of Samandal.'

'What?' replied Queen Gulnare, 'is not the Princess Giauhara yet married? I remember to have seen her before I left your palace; she was then about eighteen months old, and surprisingly beautiful, and must needs be the wonder of the world. The few years she is older than the king my son ought not to prevent us from doing our utmost to bring it about. Let me but know the difficulties that are to be surmounted, and we will surmount them.'

'Sister,' replied King Saleh, 'the greatest difficulty is, that the King of Samandal is insupportably vain, looking upon all others as his inferiors: it is not likely we shall easily get him to enter into this alliance. For my part, I will go to him in person, and demand of him the princess his daughter; and, in case he refuses her, we will address ourselves elsewhere, where we shall be more favourably heard. For this reason, as you may perceive,' added he, 'it is as well for the king my nephew not to know anything of our design, lest he should fall in love with the Princess Giauhara, till we have got the consent of the King of Samandal, in case, after all, we should not be able to obtain her for him.' They discoursed a little longer upon this point, and, before they parted, agreed that King Saleh should forthwith return to his own dominions, and demand the Princess Giauhara of the King of Samandal her father, for the King of Persia his nephew.

Now King Beder had heard what they said, and he immediately fell in love with the Princess Giauhara without having even seen her, and he lay awake thinking all night. Next day King Saleh took leave of Queen Gulnare and the king his nephew. The young king, who knew the king his uncle would not have departed so soon but to go and promote his happiness without loss of time, changed colour when he heard him mention his departure. He resolved to desire his uncle to bring the princess away with him: but only asked him to stay with him one day more, that they might hunt together. The day for hunting was fixed, and King Beder had many opportunities of being alone with his uncle, but he had not the courage to open his mouth. In the heat of the chase, when King Saleh was separated from him, and not one of his officers and attendants was near, he alighted near a rivulet; and having tied his horse to a tree, which, with several others growing along the banks, afforded a very pleasing shade, he laid himself down on the grass. He remained a good while absorbed in thought, without speaking a word.

King Saleh, in the meantime, missing the king his nephew, began to be much concerned to know what had become of him. He therefore left his company to go in search of him, and at length perceived him at a distance. He had observed the day before, and more plainly that day, that he was not so lively as he used to be; and that if he was asked a question, he either answered not at all, or nothing to the purpose. As soon as King Saleh saw him lying in that disconsolate posture, he immediately guessed he had heard what passed between him and Queen Gulnare. He hereupon alighted at some distance from him, and having tied his horse to a tree, came upon him so softly, that he heard him say to himself:

'Amiable princess of the kingdom of Samandal, I would this moment go and offer you my heart, if I knew where to find you.'

King Saleh would hear no more; he advanced immediately, and showed himself to King Beder. 'From what I see, nephew,' said he, 'you heard what the queen your mother and I said the other day of the Princess Giauhara. It was not our intention you should have known anything, and we thought you were asleep.'

'My dear uncle,' replied King Beder, 'I heard every word, but was ashamed to disclose to you my weakness. I beseech you to pity me, and not wait to procure me the consent of the divine Giauhara till you have gained the consent of the King of Samandal that I may marry his daughter.'

These words of the King of Persia greatly embarrassed King Saleh. He represented to him how difficult it was, and that he could not well do it without carrying him along with him; which might be of dangerous consequence, since his presence was so absolutely necessary in his kingdom. He begged him to wait. But these reasons were not sufficient to satisfy the King of Persia.

'Cruel Uncle,' said he, 'I find you do not love me so much as you pretended, and that you had rather see me die than grant the first request I ever made you.'

'I am ready to convince your majesty,' replied King Saleh, 'that I would do anything to serve you; but as for carrying you along with me, I cannot do that till I have spoken to the queen your mother. What would she say of you and me? If she consents, I am ready to do all you would have me, and I will join my entreaties to yours.'

'If you do really love me,' replied the King of Persia impatiently, 'as you would have me believe you do, you must return to your kingdom immediately, and carry me along with you.'

King Saleh, finding himself obliged to yield to his nephew, drew from his finger a ring, on which were engraven the same mysterious names that were upon Solomon's seal, that had wrought so many wonders by their virtue. 'Here, take this ring,' said he, 'put it upon your finger, and fear neither the waters of the sea, nor their depth.'

The King of Persia took the ring, and when he had put it on his finger, King Saleh said to him, 'Do as I do.' At the same time they both mounted lightly up into the air, and made towards the sea which was not far distant, whereinto they both plunged.

The sea-king was not long in getting to his palace with the King of Persia, whom he immediately carried to the queen's apartment, and presented him to her. The King of Persia kissed the queen his grandmother's hands, and she embraced him with great joy. 'I do not ask you how you are,' said she to him; 'I see you are very well, and I am rejoiced at it; but I desire to know how is my daughter, your mother, Queen Gulnare?'

The King of Persia told her the queen his mother was in perfect health. Then the queen presented him to the princesses; and while he was in conversation with them, she left him, and went with King Saleh, who told her how the King of Persia was fallen in love with the Princess Giauhara, and that he had brought him along with him, without being able to hinder it.

Although King Saleh was, to do him justice, perfectly innocent, yet the queen could hardly forgive his indiscretion in mentioning the Princess Giauhara before him. 'Your imprudence is not to be forgiven,' said she to him: 'can you think that the King of Samandal, whose character is so well known, will have greater consideration for you than the many other kings he has refused his daughter to with such evident contempt? Would you have him send you away with the same confusion?'

'Madam,' replied King Saleh, 'I have already told you it was contrary to my intention that the king, my nephew, should hear what I related of the Princess Giauhara to the queen my sister. The fault is committed; I will therefore do all that I can to remedy it. I hope, madam, you will approve of my resolution to go myself and wait upon the King of Samandal, with a rich present of precious stones, and demand of him the princess, his daughter, for the King of Persia, your grandson. I have some reason to believe he will not refuse me, but will be pleased at an alliance with one of the greatest potentates of the earth.'

'It were to have been wished,' replied the queen, 'that we had not been under a necessity of making this demand, since the success of our attempt is not so certain as we could desire; but since my grandson's peace and content depend upon it, I freely give my consent. But, above all, I charge you, since you well know the temper of the King of Samandal, that you take care to speak to him with due respect, and in a manner that cannot possibly offend him.'

The queen prepared the present herself, composed of diamonds, rubies, emeralds, and strings of pearl; all of which she put into a very neat and very rich box. Next morning, King Saleh took leave of her majesty and the King of Persia, and departed with a chosen and small troop of officers and other attendants. He soon arrived at the kingdom and the palace of the King of Samandal, who rose from his throne as soon as he perceived him; and King Saleh, forgetting his character for some moments, though knowing whom he had to deal with, prostrated himself at his feet, wishing him the accomplishment of all his desires. The King of Samandal immediately stooped to raise him up, and after he had placed him on his left hand, he told him he was welcome, and asked him if there was anything he could do to serve him.

'Sir,' answered King Saleh, 'though I should have no other motive than that of paying my respects to the most potent, most prudent, and most valiant prince in the world, feeble would be my expressions how much I honour your majesty.' Having, spoken these words, he took the box of jewels from one of his servants and having opened it, presented it to the king, imploring him to accept it for his sake.

'Prince,' replied the King of Samandal, 'you would not make me such a present unless you had a request to propose. If there be anything in my power, you may freely command it, and I shall feel the greatest pleasure in granting it. Speak, and tell me frankly wherein I can serve you.'

'I must own,' replied King Saleh, 'I have a boon to ask of your majesty; and I shall take care to ask nothing but what is in your power to grant. The thing depends so absolutely on yourself, that it would be to no purpose to ask it of any other. I ask it then with all possible earnestness, and I beg of you not to refuse it me.'

'If it be so,' replied the King of Samandal, 'you have nothing to do but acquaint me what it is, and you shall see after what manner I can oblige when it is in my power.'

'Sir,' said King Saleh, 'after the confidence your majesty has been pleased to encourage me to put in your goodwill, I will not dissemble any longer. I came to beg of you to honour our house with your alliance by the marriage of your honourable daughter the Princess Giauhara, and to strengthen the good understanding that has so long subsisted between our two crowns.'

At these words the King of Samandal burst out laughing falling back in his throne against a cushion that supported him, and with an imperious and scornful air, said to King Saleh: 'King Saleh, I have always hitherto thought you a prince of great sense; but what you say convinces me how much I was mistaken. Tell me, I beseech you, where was your discretion, when you imagined to yourself so great an absurdity as you have just now proposed to me? Could you conceive a thought only of aspiring in marriage to a princess, the daughter of so great and powerful a king as I am? You ought to have considered better beforehand the great distance between us, and not run the risk of losing in a moment the esteem I always had for your person.'

King Saleh was extremely nettled at this affronting, answer, and had much ado to restrain his resentment; however, he replied, with all possible moderation, 'God reward your majesty as you deserve! I have the honour to inform you, I do not demand the princess your daughter in marriage for myself; had I done so your majesty and the princess ought to have been so far from being offended, that you should have thought it an honour done to both. Your majesty well knows I am one of the kings of the sea as well as yourself; that the kings, my ancestors, yield not in antiquity to any other royal families; and that the kingdom I inherit from them is no less potent and flourishing than it has ever been. If your majesty had not interrupted me, you had soon understood that the favour I ask of you was not for myself, but for the young King of Persia, my nephew, whose power and grandeur, no less than his personal good qualities, cannot be unknown to you. Everybody acknowledges the Princess Giauhara to be the most beautiful person in the world: but it is no less true that the young King of Persia, my nephew, is the best and most accomplished prince on the land. Thus the favour that is asked being likely to redound both to the honour of your majesty and the princess your daughter, you ought not to doubt that your consent to an alliance so equal will be unanimously approved in all the kingdoms of the sea. The princess is worthy of the King of Persia, and the King of Persia is no less worthy of her. No king or prince in the world can dispute her with him.'

The King of Samandal would not have let King Saleh go on so long after this rate, had not the rage he put him in deprived him of all power of speech. It was some time before he could find his tongue, so much was he transported with passion. At length, however, he broke into outrageous language, unworthy of a great king. 'Dog!' cried he, 'dare you talk to me after this manner, and so much as mention my daughter's name in my presence? Can you think the son of your sister Gulnare worthy to come in competition with my daughter? Who are you? Who was your father? Who is your sister? And who your nephew? Was not his father a dog, and a son of a dog, like you? Guards, seize the insolent wretch, and cut off his head.'

The few officers that were about the King of Samandal were immediately going to obey his orders, when King Saleh, who was nimble and vigorous, got from them before they could draw their sabres; and having reached the palace gate, he there found a thousand men of his relations and friends, well armed and equipped, who had just arrived. The queen his mother having considered the small number of attendants he took with him, and, moreover, foreseeing the bad reception he would probably have from the King of Samandal, had sent these troops to protect and defend him in case of danger, ordering them to make haste. Those of his relations who were at the head of this troop had reason to rejoice at their seasonable arrival, when they beheld him and his attendants come running in great disorder and pursued. 'Sir,' cried his friends, the moment he joined them, 'what is the matter? We are ready to revenge you: you need only command us.'

King Saleh related his case to them in as few words as he could, and putting himself at the head of a large troop, he, while some seized on the gates, re-entered the palace as before. The few officers and guards who had pursued him being soon dispersed, he re-entered the King of Samandal's apartment, who, being abandoned by his attendants, was soon seized. King Saleh left sufficient guards to secure his person, and then went from apartment to apartment, in search of the Princess Giauhara. But that princess, on the first alarm, had, together with her women, sprung up to the surface of the sea, and escaped to a desert island.

While this was passing in the palace of the King of Samandal, those of King Saleh's attendants who had fled at the first menaces of that king put the queen mother into terrible consternation upon relating the danger her son was in. King Beder, who was by at that time, was the more concerned, in that he looked upon himself as the principal author of all the mischief: therefore, not caring to abide in the queen's presence any longer, he darted up from the bottom of the sea; and, not knowing how to find his way to the kingdom of Persia, he happened to light on the island where the Princess Giauhara had taken refuge.

The prince, not a little disturbed in mind, went and seated himself under the shade of a large tree. Whilst he was endeavouring to recover himself, he heard somebody talking, but was too far off to understand what was said. He arose and advanced softly towards the place whence the sound came, where, among the branches, he perceived a most beautiful lady. 'Doubtless,' said he, within himself, stopping and considering her with great attention, 'this must be the Princess Giauhara, whom fear has obliged to abandon her father's palace.' This said, he came forward, and approached the princess with profound reverence. 'Madam,' said he, 'a greater happiness could not have befallen me than this opportunity to offer you my most humble services. I beseech you, therefore, madam, to accept them, it being impossible that a lady in this solitude should not want assistance.'

'True, my lord,' replied Giauhara very sorrowfully, 'it is not a little extraordinary for a lady of my rank to be in this situation. I am a princess, daughter of the King of Samandal, and my name is Giauhara. I was in my father's palace, when all of a sudden I heard a dreadful noise: news was immediately brought me that King Saleh, I know not for what reason, had forced his way into the palace, seized the king my father, and murdered all the guards that made any resistance. I had only time to save myself, and escaped hither from his violence.'

At these words of the princess, King Beder began to be concerned that he had quitted his grandmother so hastily, without staying to hear from her an explanation of the news that had been brought her. But he was, on the other hand, overjoyed to find that the king, his uncle, had rendered himself master of the King of Samandal's person, not doubting but that he would consent to give up the princess for his liberty. 'Adorable princess,' continued he, 'your concern is most just, but it is easy to put an end both to that and to your father's captivity. You will agree with me when I tell you that I am Beder, King of Persia, and King Saleh is my uncle; I assure you, madam, he has no design to seize upon the king your father's dominions; his only intent is to obtain his consent that I may have the honour and happiness of being his son-in-law. I had already given my heart to you, and now, far from repenting of what I have done, I beg of you to be assured that I will love you as long as I live. Permit me, then, beauteous princess! to have the honour to go and present you to the king my uncle; and the king your father shall no sooner have consented to our marriage, than King Saleh will leave him sovereign of his dominions as before.'

This declaration of King Beder did not produce the effect he expected. When the princess heard from his own mouth that he had been the occasion of the ill-treatment her father had suffered, of the grief and fright she had endured, and especially the necessity she was reduced to of flying her country, she looked upon him as an enemy with whom she ought to have nothing whatever to do.

King Beder, believing himself arrived at the very pinnacle of happiness, stretched forth his hand, and taking that of the princess' stooped down to kiss it, when she, pushing him back, said, 'Wretch, quit that form of a man, and take that of a white bird, with a red bill and feet.' Upon her pronouncing these words, King Beder was immediately changed into a bird of that sort, to his great surprise and mortification. 'Take him,' said she to one of her women, 'and carry him to the Dry Island.' This island was only one frightful rock, where there was not a drop of water to be had.

The waiting-woman took the bird, and in executing her princess's orders had compassion on King Beder's destiny. 'It would be a great pity,' said she to herself, 'to let a prince, so worthy to live, die of hunger and thirst. The princess, so good and gentle, will, it may be, repent of this cruel order when she comes to herself: it were better that I carried him to a place where he may die a natural death.' She accordingly carried him to a well-frequented island, and left him in a charming plain, planted with all sorts of fruit trees, and watered by several rivulets.

Let us return to King Saleh. After he had sought a good while for the Princess Giauhara, and ordered others to seek for her, to no purpose, he caused the King of Samandal to be shut up in his own palace, under a strong guard; and having given the necessary orders for governing the kingdom in his absence, he returned to give the queen his mother an account of what he had done. The first thing he asked upon his arrival was of the whereabouts of the king his nephew, and he learned with great surprise and vexation that he had disappeared.

'News being brought me,' said the queen, 'of the danger you were in at the palace of the King of Samandal, whilst I was giving orders to send other troops to avenge you, he disappeared. He must have been frightened at hearing of your being in so great danger, and did not think himself in sufficient safety with us.'

This news exceedingly afflicted King Saleh, who now repented of his being so easily wrought upon by King Beder as to carry him away with him without his mother's consent. Whilst he was in this suspense about his nephew, he left his kingdom under the administration of his mother, and went to govern that of the King of Samandal, whom he continued to keep under great vigilance, though with all due respect to his rank.

The same day that King Saleh returned to the kingdom of Samandal, Queen Gulnare, mother to King Beder, arrived at the court of the queen her mother. The princess was not at all surprised to find her son did not return the same day he set out, it being not uncommon for him to go further than he proposed in the heat of the chase; but when she saw that he returned neither the next day, nor the day after, she began to be alarmed. This alarm was increased when the officers, who had accompanied the king, and were obliged to return after they had for a long time sought in vain for both him and his uncle, came and told her majesty they must of necessity have come to some harm, or be together in some place which they could not guess, since they could hear no tidings of them. Their horses, indeed, they had found, but as for their persons, they knew not where to look for them. The queen, hearing this, had resolved to dissemble and conceal her affliction, bidding the officers to search once more with their utmost diligence; but in the mean time, saying nothing to anybody, she plunged into the sea, to satisfy herself as to the suspicion she had that King Saleh must have carried away his nephew along with him.

This great queen would have been more affectionately received by the queen her mother, had she not, upon first sight of her, guessed the occasion of her coming. 'Daughter,' said she, 'I plainly perceive you are not come hither to visit me; you come to inquire after the king your son; and the only news I can tell you will augment both your grief and mine. I no sooner saw him arrive in our territories, than I rejoiced; yet, when I came to understand he had come away without your knowledge, I began to share with you the concern you must needs feel.' Then she related to her with what zeal King Saleh went to demand the Princess Giauhara in marriage for King Beder, and what had happened, till her son disappeared. 'I have sent diligently after him,' added she, 'and the king my son, who is but just gone to govern the kingdom of Samandal, has done all that lay in his power. All our endeavours have hitherto proved unsuccessful, but we must hope nevertheless to see him again, perhaps when we least expect it.'

Queen Gulnare was not satisfied with this hope; she looked upon the king her dear son as lost, and lamented him bitterly, laying all the blame upon the king his uncle. The queen her mother made her consider the necessity of not yielding too much to her grief. 'The king your brother,' said she, 'ought not, it is true, to have talked to you so imprudently about that marriage, nor ever have consented to carry away the king my grandson, without acquainting you first; yet, since it is not certain that the King of Persia is absolutely lost, you ought to neglect nothing to preserve his kingdom for him: lose, then, no more time, but return to your capital; your presence there will be necessary, and it will not be hard for you to preserve the public peace, by causing it to be published that the King of Persia was gone to visit his grandmother.'

Queen Gulnare yielded. She took leave of the queen her mother, and was back in the palace of the capital of Persia before she had been missed. She immediately despatched persons to recall the officers she had sent after the king, and to tell them she knew where his majesty was, and that they should soon see him again. She also governed with the prime minister and council as quietly as if the king had been present.

To return to King Beder, whom the Princess Giauhara's waiting-woman had carried and left in the island before mentioned; that monarch was not a little surprised when he found himself alone, and under the form of a bird. He felt yet more unhappy that he knew not where he was, nor in what part of the world the kingdom of Persia lay. He was forced to remain where he was, and live upon such food as birds of his kind were wont to eat, and to pass the night on a tree.

A few days after, a peasant that was skilled in taking birds with nets chanced to come to the place where he was; when perceiving so fine a bird, the like of which he had never seen before, he began greatly to rejoice. He employed all his art to catch him, and at length succeeded. Overjoyed at so great a prize, which he looked upon as of more worth than all the other birds, because so rare, he shut it up in a cage, and carried it to the city. As soon as he was come into the market, a citizen stops him, and asked him how much he wanted for that bird.

Instead of answering, the peasant asked the citizen what he would do with him in case he should buy him? 'What wouldst thou have me to do with him,' answered the citizen, 'but roast and eat him?'

'If that be the case,' replied the peasant, 'I suppose you would think me very well paid if you gave me the smallest piece of silver for him. I set a much higher value upon him, and you should not have him for a piece of gold. Although I am advanced in years, I never saw such a bird in my life. I intend to make a present of him to the king; he will know the value of him better than you.'

Without staying any longer in the market, the peasant went directly to the palace, and placed himself exactly before the king's apartment. His majesty, being at a window where he could see all that passed in the court, no sooner cast his eyes on this beautiful bird, than he sent an officer to buy it for him. The officer, going to the peasant, asked him how much he wanted for that bird. 'If it be for his majesty,' answered the peasant, 'I humbly beg of him to accept it of me as a present, and I desire you to carry it to him.' The officer took the bird to the king, who found it so great a rarity that he ordered the same officer to take ten pieces of gold, and carry them to the peasant, who departed very well satisfied. The king ordered the bird to be put into a magnificent cage, and gave it seed and water in rich vessels.

His majesty being then ready to go hunting, had not time to consider the bird, therefore had it brought to him as soon as he came back. The officer brought the cage, and the king, that he might better see the bird, took it out himself, and perched it upon his hand. Looking earnestly at it, he asked the officer if he had seen it eat. 'Sir,' replied the officer, 'your majesty may observe the vessel with his food is still full, and he has not touched any of it.' Then the king ordered him meat of various sorts, that he might take what he liked best.

The table being spread, and dinner served up just as the king had given these orders, the bird, flapping his wings, hopped off the king's hand, and flew on to the table, where he began to peck the bread and victuals, sometimes on one plate, and sometimes on another. The king was so surprised, that he immediately sent the officer to desire the queen to come and see this wonder. The officer related it to her majesty, and she came forthwith: but she no sooner saw the bird, than she covered her face with her veil, and would have retired. The king, surprised at her proceeding, asked the reason of it.

'Sir,' answered the queen, 'your majesty will no longer be surprised when you understand that this bird is not, as you take it, a bird, but a man.'

'Madam,' said the king, more astonished than before, 'you are making fun of me; you shall never persuade me that a bird can be a man.'

'Sir,' replied the queen, 'far be it from me to make fun of your majesty; nothing is more certain than what I have had the honour to tell you. I can assure your majesty it is the King of Persia, named Beder, son of the celebrated Gulnare, princess of one of the largest kingdoms of the sea, nephew of Saleh, king of that kingdom, and grandson of Queen Farasche, mother of Gulnare and Saleh; and it was the Princess Giauhara, daughter of the King of Samandal, who thus metamorphosed him into a bird.' That the king might no longer doubt of what she affirmed, she told him the whole story, how and for what reason the Princess Giauhara, had thus revenged herself for the ill-treatment of King Saleh towards the king of Samandal, her father.

The king had less difficulty in believing this assertion of the queen in that he knew her to be a skilful magician, one of the greatest in the world. And as she knew everything which took place, he was always by her means timely informed of the designs of the kings his neighbours against him, and prevented them. His majesty had compassion on the King of Persia, and earnestly besought his queen to break the enchantment, that he might return to his own form.

The queen consented to it with great willingness. 'Sir,' said she to the king, 'be pleased to take the bird into your room, and I will show you a king worthy of the consideration you have for him.' The bird, which had ceased eating, and attended to what the king and queen said, would not give his majesty the trouble to take him, but hopped into the room before him; and the queen came in soon after, with a vessel full of water in her hand. She pronounced over the vessel some words unknown to the king, till the water began to boil, when she took some of it in her hand, and, sprinkling a little upon the bird, said, 'By virtue of these holy and mysterious words I have just pronounced, quit that form of a bird, and reassume that which thou hast received from thy Creator.'

The words were scarcely out of the queen's mouth, when, instead of a bird, the king saw a young prince. King Beder immediately fell on his knees, and thanked God for the favour that had been bestowed upon him. Then he took the king's hand, who helped him up, and kissed it in token of gratitude; but the king embraced him with great joy. He would then have made his acknowledgments to the queen, but she had already retired to her apartment. The king made him sit at the table with him, and, after dinner was over, prayed him to relate how the Princess Giauhara could have had the inhumanity to transform into a bird so amiable a prince as he was; and the King of Persia immediately told him. When he had done, the king, provoked at the proceeding of the princess, could not help blaming her. 'It was commendable,' said he, 'in the Princess of Samandal to feel hurt at the king her father's ill-treatment; but to carry her vengeance so far, and especially against a prince who was not guilty, was what she will never be able to justify herself for. But let us have done with this discourse, and tell me, I beseech you, in what I can further serve you.'

'Sir,' answered King Beder, 'my obligation to your majesty is so great, that I ought to remain with you all my life to testify my gratitude; but since your majesty sets no limits to your generosity, I entreat you to grant me one of your ships to transport me to Persia, where I fear my absence, which has been but too long, may have occasioned some disorder, and that the queen my mother, from whom I concealed my departure, may be dead of grief, under the uncertainty whether I am alive or dead.'

The king granted what he desired with the best grace imaginable, and immediately gave orders for equipping one of his largest ships, and the best sailor in his numerous fleet. The ship was soon furnished with all its crew, provisions, and ammunition; and as soon as the wind became fair, King Beder embarked, after having taken leave of the king, and thanked him for all his favours.

The ship sailed before the wind for ten days; on the eleventh day the wind changed, and becoming very violent, there followed a furious tempest. The ship was not only driven out of its course, but so violently tossed, that all its masts went by the board; and driving along at the pleasure of the wind, it at length struck against a rock and split open.

The greater part of the people were instantly drowned. Some few were saved by swimming, and others by getting on pieces of the wreck. King Beder was among the latter, and, after having been tossed about for some time by the waves and currents, he at length perceived himself near the shore, and not far from a city that seemed large. He exerted his remaining strength to reach the land, and was at length fortunate to come so near as to be able to touch the ground with his feet. He immediately abandoned his piece of wood, which had been of so great service to him; but when he came near the shore he was greatly surprised to see horses, camels, mules, asses, oxen, cows, bulls, and other animals crowding to the shore to oppose his landing. He had the utmost difficulty to conquer their obstinacy and force his way; but at length he succeeded, and sheltered himself among the rocks till he had recovered his breath, and dried his clothes in the sun.

When the prince advanced to enter the city, he met with the same opposition from these animals, who seemed to want to make him understand that it was dangerous to proceed.

King Beder, however, got into the city soon after, and saw many fair and spacious streets, but was surprised to find no man there. This made him think it was not without cause that so many animals had opposed his passage. Going forward, nevertheless, he observed several shops open, which gave him reason to believe the place was not so destitute of inhabitants as he imagined. He approached one of these shops, where several sorts of fruits were exposed to sale, and saluted very courteously an old man that was sitting there.

The old man, who was busy about something, lifted up his head, and seeing a youth who had an appearance of grandeur, started, and asked him whence he came, and what business had brought him there. King Beder satisfied him in a few words; and the old man further asked him if he had met anybody on the road. 'You are the first person I have seen,' answered the king; 'and I cannot comprehend how so fine and large a city comes to be without inhabitants.'

'Come in, sir; stay no longer upon the threshold,' replied the old man, 'or peradventure some misfortune may happen to you. I will satisfy your curiosity at leisure, and give you the reason why it is necessary you should take this precaution.'

King Beder would not be bidden twice: he entered the shop, and sat down by the old man. The latter knew he must want food, therefore immediately presented him with what was necessary to recover his strength; and although King Beder was very anxious to know why he had taken the precaution to make him enter the shop, the old man nevertheless would not tell him anything till he had done eating, for fear the sad things he had to relate might take away his appetite. At last he said to him, 'You have great reason to thank God you got hither without any misfortune.'

'Alas! why?' replied king Beder, very much surprised and alarmed.

'Because,' answered he, 'this city is called the City of Enchantments, and is governed not by a king, but by a queen, who is a notorious and dangerous sorceress. You will be convinced of this,' added he, 'when you know that these horses, mules, and other animals that you have seen are so many men, like you and me, whom she has transformed by her diabolical art. And when young men like you enter the city, she has persons stationed to stop and bring them, either by fair means or force, before her. She receives them in the most obliging manner; she caresses them, regales them, and lodges them magnificently. But she does not suffer them long to enjoy this happiness. There is not one of them whom she has not transformed into some animal or bird at the end of forty days. You told me all these animals opposed your landing and entering, the city. This was the only way they could make you comprehend the danger you were going to expose yourself to, and they did all in their power to save you.'

This account exceedingly afflicted the young King of Persia. 'Alas!' cried he, 'to what extremities has my ill-fortune reduced me! I am hardly freed from one enchantment, which I look back upon with horror, but I find myself exposed to another much more terrible.' This gave him occasion to relate his story to the old man more at length, and to acquaint him with his birth, quality, his falling in love with the Princess of Samandal, and her cruelty in changing him into a bird the very moment he had seen her and declared his love to her.

When the prince came to speak of his good fortune in finding a queen who broke the enchantment, the old man, to encourage him, said, 'Notwithstanding all I told you of the magic queen, that ought not to give you the least disquiet, since I am generally beloved throughout the city, and am not unknown to the queen herself, who has much respect for me; therefore it was singularly fortunate that you addressed yourself to me rather than elsewhere. You are secure in my house, where I advise you to continue, if you think fit; and provided you do not stray from hence, I dare assure you you will have no just cause to complain; so that you are under no sort of constraint whatsoever.'

King Beder thanked the old man for his kind reception, and the protection he was pleased so readily to afford him. He sat down at the entrance of the shop, where he no sooner appeared than his youth and handsome looks drew the eyes of all that passed that way. Many stopped and complimented the old man on his having acquired so fine a slave, as they imagined the king to be; and they were the more surprised, because they could not comprehend how so beautiful a youth could escape the queen's knowledge. 'Believe not,' said the old man, 'that this is a slave; you all know that I am not rich enough. He is my nephew, son of a brother of mine that is dead; and as I had no children of my own, I sent for him to keep me company.'

They congratulated his good fortune in having so fine a young man for his relation; but could not help telling him they feared the queen would take him from him. 'You know her well,' said they, 'and you cannot be ignorant of the danger to which you are exposed, after all the examples you have seen. How grieved would you be if she should serve him as she has done so many others that we know of!'

'I am obliged to you,' replied the old man, 'for your good will towards me, and I heartily thank you for your care; but I shall never entertain the least thought that the queen will do me any injury, after all the kindness she has professed for me. In case she happens to hear of this young man, and speaks to me about him, I doubt not she will cease to think of him, so soon as she comes to know he is my nephew.'

The old man was exceedingly glad to hear the commendations they bestowed on the young King of Persia. He became as fond of him as if he had been his own son. They had lived about a month together, when, King Beder sitting at the shop-door, after his ordinary manner, Queen Labe (so was this magic queen named) happened to come by with great pomp. The young king no sooner perceived the guards coming before her, than he arose, and, going into the shop, asked the old man what all that show meant. 'The queen is coming by,' answered he, 'but stand still and fear nothing.'

The queen's guards, clothed in purple uniform, and well armed and mounted, marched in four files, with their sabres drawn, to the number of a thousand, and every one of their officers, as they passed by the shop, saluted the old man: then followed a like number habited in brocaded silk, and better mounted, whose officers did the old man the like honour. Next came as many young ladies on foot, equally beautiful, richly dressed, and set off with precious stones. They marched gravely, with half pikes in their hands; and in the midst of them appeared Queen Labe, on a horse glittering with diamonds, with a golden saddle, and a harness of inestimable value. All the young ladies saluted the old man as they passed by him; and the queen, struck with the good mien of King Beder, stopped as soon as she came before the shop. 'Abdallah' (so was the old man named), said she to him, 'tell me, I beseech thee, does that beautiful and charming slave belong to thee? and is it long that thou hast been in possession of him?'

Abdallah, before he answered the queen, threw himself on the ground, and rising again, said, 'Madam, it is my nephew, son of a brother I had, who has not long been dead. Having no children, I look upon him as my son, and sent for him to come and comfort me, intending to leave him what I have when I die.'

Queen Labe, who had never yet seen any one to compare with King Beder, thought immediately of getting the old man to abandon him to her. 'Father,' quoth she, 'will you not oblige me so far as to make me a present of this young man? Do not refuse me, I conjure you; and I swear by the fire and the light, I will make him so great and powerful that no individual in the world ever arrived at such good fortune. Although my purpose were to do evil to all mankind, yet he shall be the sole exception. I trust you will grant me what I desire, more on the account of the friendship I know you have for me, than for the esteem you know I always had, and shall ever have for you.'

'Madam,' replied the good Abdallah, 'I am infinitely obliged to your majesty for all your kindness, and the honours you propose to do my nephew. He is not worthy to approach so great a queen, and I humbly beseech your majesty to excuse him.'

'Abdallah,' replied the queen, 'I all along flattered myself you loved me; and I could never have thought you would have given me so evident a token of your slighting my request. But I here swear once more by the fire and light, and even by whatsoever is most sacred in my religion, that I will pass on no farther till I have conquered your obstinacy. I understand very well what raises your apprehensions; but I promise you shall never have any occasion to repent having obliged me in so sensible a manner.'

Old Abdallah was exceedingly grieved, both on his own account and King Beder's, for being in a manner forced to obey the queen. 'Madam,' replied he, 'I would not willingly have your majesty entertain an ill opinion of the respect I have for you, and my zeal always to do whatever I can to oblige you. I put entire confidence in your royal word, and I do not in the least doubt but you will keep it. I only beg of your majesty to delay doing this great honour to my nephew till you shall again pass this way.'

'That shall be to-morrow,' said the queen, who inclined her head, as a token of being pleased, and so went forward towards her palace.

When Queen Labe and all her attendants were out of sight, the good Abdallah said to King Beder, 'Son, (for so he was wont to call him, for fear of some time or other betraying him when he spoke of him in public), 'it has not been in my power, as you may have observed, to refuse the queen what she demanded of me with so great earnestness, for fear I might force her to employ her magic both against you and myself openly or secretly, and treat you, as much from resentment to you as to me, with more signal cruelty than all those she has had in her power before. But I have some reason to believe she will treat you well, as she promised, on account of that particular esteem she professes for me. This you may have seen by the respect shown, and the honours paid me by all her court. She would be a fiendish creature indeed, if she should deceive me; but she shall not deceive me unrevenged, for I know how to be even with her.'

These assurances, which appeared very doubtful, were not sufficient to raise King Beder's spirits. 'After all you have told me of this queen's wickedness,' replied he, 'you cannot wonder if I am somewhat fearful to approach her: I might, it may be, make little of all you could tell me of her, did I not know by experience what it is to be at the mercy of a sorceress. The condition I was in, through the enchantment of the Princess Giauhara, and from whence I was delivered only to enter almost immediately into another, has made me look upon such a fate with horror.'

'Son,' replied old Abdallah, 'do not afflict yourself; for though I must own there is no great faith to be put in the promises and oaths of so perfidious a queen, yet I must withal tell you that her power extends not to me. She knows it well herself; and that is the reason, and no other, that she pays me such great respect. I can quickly hinder her from doing you the least harm, if she should be perfidious enough to attempt it. You may depend upon me; and, provided you follow exactly the advice I shall give you before I hand you over to her, she shall have no more power over you than she has over me.'

The magic queen did not fail to pass by the old man's shop the next day, with the same pomp as the day before, and Abdallah waited for her with great respect. 'Father,' cried she, stopping just before him, 'you may judge of my impatience to have your nephew with me, by my punctual coming to put you in mind of your promise. I know you are a man of your word, and I cannot think you will break it with me.'

Abdallah, who fell on his face as soon as he saw the queen approaching, rose up when she had done speaking; and as he wanted nobody to hear what he had a mind to say to her, he advanced with great respect as far as her horse's head, and then said softly, 'Powerful queen! I am persuaded your majesty will not be offended at my seeming unwillingness to trust my nephew with you yesterday, since you cannot be ignorant of the reasons I had for it; but I implore you to lay aside the secrets of that art which you possess in so wonderful a degree. I regard my nephew as my own son; and your majesty would reduce me to despair if you should deal with him as you have done with others.'

'I promise you I will not,' replied the queen; 'and I once more repeat the oath I made yesterday, that neither you nor your nephew shall have any cause to be offended with me. I see plainly,' added she, 'you are not yet well enough acquainted with me; you never saw me yet but through a veil; but as I find your nephew worthy of my friendship, I will show you I am not in any way unworthy of his.' With that she threw off her veil and showed King Beder, who came near her with Abdallah, incomparable beauty.

But King Beder was little charmed. 'It is not enough,' said he within himself, 'to be beautiful; one's actions ought to correspond.'

Whilst King Beder was making these reflections, with his eyes fixed on Queen Labe, the old man turned towards him, and taking him by the arm, presented him to her majesty. 'Here he is, madam,' said he, 'and I beg of your majesty once more to remember he is my nephew, and to let him come and see me sometimes.' The queen promised he should; and to give a further mark of her gratitude, she caused a bag of a thousand pieces of gold to be given him. He excused himself at first from receiving them, but she insisted absolutely upon it, and he could not refuse her. She had caused a horse to be brought (as richly harnessed as her own) for the King of Persia.

When King Beder was mounted, he would have taken his place behind the queen, but she would not suffer him, and made him ride on her left hand. She looked at Abdallah, and after having made him an inclination with her head, she set forward on her march.

Instead of observing a satisfaction in the people's faces at the sight of their sovereign, King Beder took notice that they looked at her with contempt, and even cursed her. 'The sorceress,' said some, 'has got a new subject to exercise her wickedness upon: will Heaven never deliver the world from her tyranny?' 'Poor stranger!' cried out others, 'thou art much deceived if thou thinkest thine happiness will last long. It is only to render thy fall most terrible that thou art raised so high.' This talk gave King Beder to understand that Abdallah had told him nothing but the truth of Queen Labe: but as it now depended no longer on himself to escape the mischief, he committed himself to divine Providence and the will of Heaven respecting his fate.

The magic queen arrived at her palace; she alighted, and giving her hand to King Beder, entered with him, accompanied by her women and the officers. She herself showed him all her apartments, where there was nothing to be seen but massy gold, precious stones, and furniture of wonderful magnificence. Then she led him out into a balcony, from whence he observed a garden of surprising beauty. King Beder commended all he saw, but so that he might not be discovered to be any other than old Abdallah's nephew. They discoursed of indifferent matters, till the queen was informed that dinner was upon the table.

The queen and King Beder arose, and sat down at the table, which was of massy gold, and the dishes of the same metal. They began to eat, but drank hardly at all till the dessert came, when the queen caused a cup to be filled for her with excellent wine. She took it and drank to King Beder's health; and then, without putting it out of her hand, caused it to be filled again, and presented it to him. King Beder received it with profound respect, and by a very low bow signified to her majesty that he in return drank to her health.

At the same time ten of Queen Labe's women entered with musical instruments, with which they made an agreeable concert. At length both began so to be heated with wine, that King Beder forgot he had to do with a magic queen, and looked upon her only as the most beautiful queen he ever saw.

Next morning the women who had served the king presented him with fine linen and a magnificent robe. The queen likewise, who was more splendidly dressed than the day before, came to receive him, and they went together to her apartments, where they had a good repast brought them, and spent the remainder of the day in walking in the garden, and in various other amusements.

Queen Labe treated King Beder after this manner for forty days, as she had been accustomed to do to all the others. The fortieth night she arose without making any noise and came into his room; but he was awake, and perceiving she had some design upon him, watched all her motions. She opened a chest, from whence she took a little box full of a certain yellow powder; taking some of the powder, she laid a train of it across the chamber, and it immediately flowed in a rivulet of water, to the great astonishment of King Beder. He trembled with fear, but still pretended to sleep, that the sorceress might not discover he was awake.

Queen Labe next took up some of the water in a vessel, and poured it into a basin, where there was flour, with which she made a paste, and kneaded it for a long time: then she mixed with it certain drugs, which she took from different boxes, and made a cake, which she put into a covered baking-pan. As she had taken care first of all to make a good fire, she took some of the coals, and set the pan upon them; and while the cake was baking, she put up the vessels and boxes in their places again; and on her pronouncing certain words, the rivulet, which ran along the end of the room, appeared no more. When the cake was baked, she took it off the coals, and carried it into her room, without the least suspicion that he had seen anything of what she had done.

King Beder, whom the pleasures and amusements of a court had made forget his good host Abdallah, began now to think of him again, and believed he had more than ordinary occasion for his advice, after all he had seen the queen do that night. As soon as he was up, therefore, he expressed a great desire to go and see his uncle, and begged her majesty to permit him. 'What! my dear Beder,' cried the queen, 'are you then already tired, I will not say with living in so superb a palace as mine is, where you must find so many pleasures, but with the company of a queen who is so fond of you as I am?'

'Great queen!' answered King Beder, 'how can I be tired of so many favours and graces as your majesty perpetually heaps upon me? I must own, however, it is partly for this reason, that, my uncle loving me so tenderly, as I well know he does, and I having been absent from him now forty days, without once seeing him, I would not give him reason to think that I consent to remain longer without seeing him.'

'Go,' said the queen, 'you have my consent; but do not be long before you return.' This said, she ordered him a horse richly caparisoned, and he departed.

Old Abdallah was overjoyed to see King Beder; he embraced him tenderly, and King Beder did the same. As soon as they had sat down, 'Well,' said Abdallah to the king, 'how have you been, and how have you passed your time with that infidel sorceress?'

'Hitherto,' answered King Beder, 'I must needs own she has been extraordinarily kind to me, but I observed something last night which gives me just reason to suspect that all her kindness hitherto is but dissimulation.' He related to Abdallah how and after what manner he had seen her make the cake; and then added, 'Hitherto, I must needs confess I had almost forgotten, not only you, but all the advice you gave me concerning the wickedness of this queen; but this last action of hers gives me reason to fear she does not intend to observe any of her promises or solemn oaths to you. I thought of you immediately, and I esteem myself happy in that I have obtained permission to come to you.'

'You are not mistaken,' replied old Abdallah with a smile, which showed he did not himself believe she would have acted otherwise, 'nothing is capable of obliging a treacherous person to amend. But fear nothing. I know the way to make the mischief she intends for you fall upon herself. You are alarmed in time; and you could not have done better than to have recourse to me. It is her ordinary practice to keep her lovers only forty days, and after that time, instead of sending them home, to turn them into animals, to stock her forests and parks; but I thought of measures yesterday to prevent her doing you the same harm. The earth has borne this monster long enough, and it is now high time she should be treated as she deserves.'

So saying, Abdallah put two cakes into King Beder's hands, bidding him keep them to make use of as he should direct. 'You told me,' continued he, 'the sorceress made a cake last night; it was for you to eat, depend upon it; but take great care you do not touch it. Nevertheless, do not refuse to receive it when she offers it you; but instead of tasting it, break off part of one of the two I shall give you, unobserved, and eat that. As soon as she thinks you have swallowed it, she will not fail to attempt transforming you into some animal, but she will not succeed; when she sees that she will immediately turn the thing into a joke, as if what she had done was only to frighten you. But she will conceal a mortal grief in her heart, and think she omitted something in the composition of her cake. As for the other cake, you shall make a present of it to her and press her to eat it; which she will not refuse to do, were it only to convince you she does not mistrust you, though she has given you so much reason to mistrust her. When she has eaten of it, take a little water in the hollow of your hand, and throwing it in her face, say, "Quit that form you now wear, and take that of such and such an animal" as you think fit; which done, come to me with the animal, and I will tell you what you shall do afterwards.'

King Beder thanked Abdallah in the most expressive terms, and took his leave of him and returned to the palace. Upon his arrival, he understood that the queen waited for him with great impatience in the garden. He went to her, and she no sooner perceived him, than she came in great haste to meet him. 'My dear Beder!' said she, 'it seems ages since I have been separated from you. If you had stayed ever so little longer, I was preparing to come and fetch you.'

'Madam,' replied King Beder, 'I can assure your majesty I was no less impatient to rejoin you; but I could not refuse to stay a little longer with an uncle that loves me, and had not seen me for so long a time. He would have kept me still longer, but I tore myself away from him, to come where love calls me. Of all he prepared for me, I have only brought away this cake, which I desire your majesty to accept.' King Beder had wrapped up one of the two cakes in a handkerchief very neatly, took it out, and presented it to the queen, saying, 'I beg your majesty to accept it.'

'I do accept it with all my heart,' replied the queen, 'and will eat it with pleasure for your and your good uncle's sake; but before I taste it, I desire you for my sake to eat a piece of this, which I have made for you during your absence.'

'Fair queen,' answered King Beder, receiving it with great respect, I cannot sufficiently acknowledge the favour you do me.'

King Beder then artfully substituted in the place of the queen's cake the other which old Abdallah had given him, and having broken off a piece, he put it in his mouth, and cried, while he was eating, 'Ah! queen, I never tasted anything so charming in my life.'

Being near a cascade, as the sorceress saw him swallow one bit of the cake, and ready to eat another, she took a little water in the palm of her hand, throwing it in the king's face, said, 'Wretch! quit that form of a man, and take that of a vile horse, blind and lame.'

These words not having the desired effect, the sorceress was strangely surprised to find King Beder still in the same form, and that he only started for fear. Her cheeks reddened; and as she saw that she had missed her aim, 'Dear Beder,' cried she, 'this is nothing; recover yourself. I did not intend you any harm; I only did it to see what you would say.'

'Powerful queen,' replied King Beder, 'persuaded as I am that what your majesty did was only to divert yourself, yet I could not help being surprised. But, madam,' continued he, 'let us drop this, and since I have eaten your cake, would you do me the favour to taste mine?'

Queen Labe, who could not better justify herself than by showing this mark of confidence in the King of Persia, broke off a piece of his cake, and ate it. She had no sooner swallowed it than she appeared much troubled, and remained as it were motionless. King Beder lost no time, but took water out of the same basin, and throwing it in her face, cried, 'Abominable sorceress! quit that form of a woman, and be turned instantly into a mare.'

The same instant Queen Labe was transformed into a very beautiful mare; and her confusion was so great to find herself in that condition, that she shed tears in great abundance, which perhaps no mare before had ever been known to do. She bowed her head to the feet of King Beder, thinking to move him to compassion; but though he could have been so moved, it was absolutely out of his power to repair the mischief he had done. He led her into the stable belonging to the palace, and put her into the hands of a groom, to bridle and saddle; but of all the bridles which the groom tried upon her, not one would fit her. This made him cause two horses to be saddled, one for the groom, and the other for himself; and the groom led the mare after him to old Abdallah's.

Abdallah, seeing at a distance King Beder coming with the mare, doubted not but he had done what he advised him. 'Hateful sorceress!' said he immediately to himself in a transport of joy, 'Heaven has at length punished thee as thou deservest.' King Beder alighted at Abdallah's door, and entered the shop, embracing and thanking him for all the signal services he had done him. He related to him the whole matter, and told him that he could find no bridle fit for the mare. Abdallah, who had one for every horse, bridled the mare himself, and as soon as King Beder had sent back the groom with the two horses, he said to him, 'My lord, you have no reason to stay any longer in this city: mount the mare, and return to your kingdom. I have but one thing more to recommend to you; and that is, if you should ever happen to part with the mare, be sure not to give up the bridle.' King Beder promised to remember it; and having taken leave of the good old man, he departed.

The young King of Persia no sooner got out of the city, than he began to reflect with joy on the deliverance he had had, and that he had the sorceress in his power, who had given him so much cause to tremble. Three days after he arrived at a great city, where, entering the suburbs, he met a venerable old man. 'Sir,' said the old man, stopping him, 'may I presume to ask from what part of the world you come?' The king stopped to tell him, and as they were discoursing together, an old woman came up; who, stopping likewise, wept and sighed bitterly at the sight of the mare.

King Beder and the old man left off discoursing, to look at the old woman, whom the king asked what cause she had to lament so much, 'Alas! sir,' replied she, 'it is because your mare resembles so perfectly one my son had, which I still mourn the loss of on his account. I should think yours were the same, did I not know she was dead. Sell her to me, I beseech you: I will give you more than she is worth, and thank you too.'

'Good woman,' replied King Beder, 'I am heartily sorry I cannot comply with your request: my mare is not to be sold.'

'Alas! sir,' continued the old woman, 'do not refuse me this favour. My son and I will certainly die with grief if you do not grant it.'

'Good mother,' replied the king, 'I would grant it with all my heart, if I was disposed to part with so good a beast; but if I were so disposed, I believe you would hardly give a thousand pieces of gold for her, and I could not sell her for less.'

'Why should I not give so much?' replied the old woman: 'if that be the lowest price, you need only say you will take it, and I will fetch you the money.'

King Beder, seeing the old woman so poorly dressed, could not imagine she could find the money; therefore to try her, he said, 'Go, fetch me the money, and the mare is yours.' The old woman immediately unloosed a purse she had fastened to her girdle, and desiring him to alight, bade him tell over the money, and in case he found it came short of the sum demanded, she said her house was not far off, and she could quickly fetch the rest.

The surprise of King Beder, at the sight of this purse, was not small. 'Good woman,' said he, 'do you not perceive I have been bantering you all this while? I assure you my mare is not to be sold.'

The old man, who had been witness to all that was said, now began to speak. 'Son,' quoth he to King Beder, 'it is necessary you should know one thing, which I find you are ignorant of; and that is, that in this city it is not permitted to any one to tell a lie, on any account whatsoever, on pain of death. You cannot refuse taking this good woman's money, and delivering your mare, when she gives you the sum according to the agreement; and this you had better do without any noise, than expose yourself to what may happen.'

King Beder, sorely afflicted to find himself thus trapped by his rash offer, alighted with great regret. The old woman stood ready to seize the bridle, and immediately unbridled the mare, and taking some water in her hand, from a stream that ran in the middle of the street, she threw it in the mare's face, uttering these words, 'Daughter, quit that strange shape, and re-assume thine own.' The transformation was effected in a moment, and King Beder, who swooned as soon as he saw Queen Labe appear, would have fallen to the ground, if the old man had not caught him.

The old woman, who was mother to Queen Labe, and had instructed her in all her magic secrets, had no sooner embraced her daughter, than to show her fury, she whistled. Immediately rose a genie of gigantic form and stature. This genie took King Beder on one shoulder, and the old woman with the magic queen on the other, and transported them in a few minutes to the palace of Queen Labe in the City of Enchantments.

The magic queen immediately fell upon King Beder, 'Is it thus, ungrateful wretch,' said she, 'that thou and thy unworthy uncle repay me for all the kindnesses I have done for you? I shall soon make you both feel what you deserve.' She said no more, but taking water in her hand, threw it in his face with these words, 'Come out of that shape, and take that of a vile owl.' These words were followed by the effect, and immediately she commanded one of her women to shut up the owl in a cage, and give him neither meat nor drink.

The woman took the cage, and without regarding what the queen ordered, gave him both meat and drink; and being old Abdallah's friend, she sent him word privately how the queen had treated his nephew, and of her design to destroy both him and King Beder, that he might give orders to prevent it and save himself.

Abdallah knew no common measures would do with Queen Labe: he therefore did but whistle after a certain manner, and there immediately arose a vast giant, with four wings, who, presenting himself before him, asked what he wanted. 'Lightning,' said Abdallah to him (for so was the genie called), 'I command you to preserve the life of King Beder, son of Queen Gulnare. Go to the palace of the magic queen, and transport immediately to the capital of Persia the compassionate woman who has the cage in custody, so that she may inform Queen Gulnare of the danger the king her son is in, and the occasion he has for her assistance. Take care not to frighten her when you come before her and tell her from me what she ought to do.'

Lightning immediately disappeared, and got in an instant to the palace of the magic queen. He instructed the woman, lifted her up into the air, and transported her to the capital of Persia, where he placed her on the terrace near the apartment where Queen Gulnare was. She went downstairs to the apartment, and she there found Queen Gulnare and Queen Farasche her mother lamenting their misfortunes. She made them a profound obeisance and they soon understood the great need that King Beder was in of their assistance.

Queen Gulnare was so overjoyed at the news, that rising from her seat, she went and embraced the good woman, telling her how much she was obliged to her for the service she had done.

Then immediately going out, she commanded the trumpets to sound, and the drums to beat, to acquaint the city that the King of Persia would suddenly return safe to his kingdom. She then went again, and found King Saleh her brother, whom Queen Farasche had caused to come speedily thither by a certain fumigation. 'Brother,' said she to him, 'the king your nephew, my dear son, is in the City of Enchantments, under the power of Queen Labe. Both you and I must go to deliver him, for there is no time to be lost.'

King Saleh forthwith assembled a powerful body of his marine troops, who soon rose out of the sea. He also called to his assistance the genies, his allies, who appeared with a much more numerous army than his own. As soon as the two armies were joined, he put himself at the head of them, with Queen Farasche, Queen Gulnare, and the princesses. They then lifted themselves up into the air, and soon poured down on the palace and City of Enchantments, where the magic queen, her mother, and all the adorers of fire, were destroyed in an instant.

Queen Gulnare had ordered the woman who brought her the news of Queen Labe's transforming and imprisoning her son to follow her closely, and bade her go, and in the confusion, seize the cage, and bring it to her. This order was executed as she wished, and Queen Gulnare was no sooner in possession of the cage than she opened it and took out the owl, saying, as she sprinkled a little water upon him, 'My dear son, quit that strange form, and resume thy natural one of a man.'

In a moment Queen Gulnare no more saw the hideous owl, but King Beder her son. She immediately embraced him with an excess of joy. She could not find in her heart to let him go; and Queen Farasche was obliged to force him from her in her turn. After her, he was likewise embraced by the king his uncle and his relations.

Queen Gulnare's first care was to look out for old Abdallah, to whom she had been indebted for the recovery of the King of Persia. When he was brought to her, she said,

'My obligations to you, sir, have been so great, that there is nothing in my power that I would not freely do for you, as a token of my acknowledgment. Do but tell me in what I can serve you.'

'Great queen,' replied Abdallah, 'if the lady whom I sent to your majesty will but consent to the marriage I offer her, and the King of Persia will give me leave to reside at his court, I will spend the remainder of my days in his service.'

Then the queen turned to the lady, who was present, and finding that she was not averse to the match proposed, she caused them to join hands, and the King of Persia and she took care of their welfare.

This marriage occasioned the King of Persia to speak thus to the queen: 'Madam,' said he, 'I am heartily glad of this match which your majesty has just made. There remains one more, which I desire you to think of.'

Queen Gulnare did not at first comprehend what marriage he meant; but after a little considering, she said, 'Of yours, you mean, son? I consent to it with all my heart.' Then turning, and looking on her brother's sea attendants, and the genies who were still present, 'Go,' said she, 'and traverse both sea and land, to find out the most lovely and amiable princess, worthy of the king my son, and come and tell us.'

'Madam,' replied King Beder, 'it is to no purpose for them to take all that pains. You have no doubt heard that I have already given my heart to the Princess of Samandal. I have seen her, and do not repent of the present I then made her. In a word, neither earth nor sea, in my opinion, can furnish a princess like her. It is true that she treated me in a way that would have extinguished any affection less strong than mine. But I hold her excused; she could not treat me with less rigour, after I had had the king her father imprisoned. But it may be the King of Samandal has changed his mind; and his daughter the princess may consent to love me when she sees her father has agreed to it.'

'Son,' replied Queen Gulnare, 'if only the Princess Giauhara can make you happy, it is not my design to oppose you. The king your uncle need only have the King of Samandal brought, and we shall soon see whether he be still of the same untractable temper.'

Strictly as the King of Samandal had been kept during his captivity by King Saleh's orders, yet he always had great respect shown him, and was become very familiar with the officers who guarded him. King Saleh caused a chafing-dish of coals to be brought, into which he threw a certain composition, uttering at the same time some mysterious words. As soon as the smoke began to arise, the palace shook, and immediately the King of Samandal, with King Saleh's officers, appeared. The King of Persia cast himself at the King of Samandal's feet, and kneeling said, 'It is no longer King Saleh that demands of your majesty the honour of your alliance for the King of Persia; it is the King of Persia himself that humbly begs that boon; and I am sure your majesty will not persist in being the cause of the death of a king who can no longer live if he does not share life with the amiable Princess Giauhara.'

The King of Samandal did not long suffer the King of Persia to remain at his feet. He embraced him and obliging him to rise, said, 'I should be very sorry to have contributed in the least to the death of a monarch who is so worthy to live. If it be true that so precious a life cannot be preserved without my daughter, live, sir,' said he, 'she is yours. She has always been obedient to my will, and I cannot think she will now oppose it.' Speaking these words, he ordered one of his officers, whom King Saleh had permitted to be about him, to go and look for the Princess Giauhara, and bring her to him immediately.

The princess had remained where the King of Persia had left her. The officer soon perceived her, and brought her with her women. The King of Samandal embraced her, and said, 'Daughter, I have provided a husband for you; it is the King of Persia you see there, the most accomplished monarch at present in the universe. The preference he has given you over all other Princesses obliges us both to express our gratitude.'

'Sir,' replied the Princess Giauhara, 'your majesty well knows I never have presumed to disobey your will in anything; I shall always be ready to obey you; and I hope the King of Persia will forget my ill-treatment of him, and consider it was duty, not inclination, that forced me to it.'

The wedding was celebrated in the palace of the City of Enchantments, with the greater solemnity in that all the lovers of the magic queen, who resumed their original forms as soon as ever that queen ceased to live, came to return their thanks to the King of Persia, Queen Gulnare, and King Saleh. They were all sons of kings or princes, or persons of high rank.

King Saleh at length conducted the King of Samandal to his dominions, and put him in possession of them. The King of Persia returned to his capital with Queen Gulnare, Queen Farasche, and the princesses; and Queen Farasche and the princesses continued there till King Saleh came to reconduct them to his kingdom under the waves of the sea.

The Story of Ali Baba and the Forty Thieves

Kate Douglas Wiggin and Nora A. Smith

IN A TOWN in Persia, there lived two brothers, one named Cassim, the other Ali Baba. Their father left them scarcely anything; but as he had divided his little property equally between them, it would seem that their fortune ought to have been equal; but chance determined otherwise.

Cassim married a wife, who soon after became heiress to a large sum, and to a warehouse full of rich goods; so that he all at once became one of the richest and most considerable merchants, and lived at his ease. Ali Baba, on the other hand, who had married a woman as poor as himself, lived in a very wretched habitation, and had no other means to maintain his wife and children but his daily labour of cutting wood, and bringing it to town to sell, upon three asses, which were his whole substance.

One day, when Ali Baba was in the forest, and had just cut wood enough to load his asses, he saw at a distance a great cloud of dust, which seemed to be driven toward him: he observed it very attentively, and distinguished soon after a body of horse. Though there had been no rumour of robbers in that country, Ali Baba began to think that they might prove such, and without considering what might become of his asses, was resolved to save himself. He climbed up a large, thick tree, whose branches, at a little distance from the ground, were so close to one another that there was but little space between them. He placed himself in the middle, from whence he could see all that passed without being discovered; and the tree stood at the base of a single rock, so steep and craggy that nobody could climb up it.

The troop, who were all well mounted and armed, came to the foot of this rock, and there dismounted. Ali Baba counted forty of them, and, from their looks and equipage, was assured that they were robbers. Nor was he mistaken in his opinion; for they were a troop of banditti, who, without doing any harm to the neighbourhood, robbed at a distance, and made that place their rendezvous; but what confirmed him in his opinion was, that every man unbridled his horse, tied him to some shrub, and hung about his neck a bag of corn which they brought behind them. Then each of them took his saddle wallet, which seemed to Ali Baba to be full of gold and silver from its weight. One, who was the most personable amongst them, and whom he took to be their captain, came with his wallet on his back under the tree in which Ali Baba was concealed, and making his way through some shrubs, pronounced these words so distinctly: "Open, Sesame," that Ali Baba heard him. As soon as the captain of the robbers had uttered these words, a door opened in the rock; and after he had made all his troop enter before him, he followed them, when the door shut again of itself. The robbers stayed some time within the rock, and Ali Baba, who feared that some one, or all of them together, might come out and catch him, if he should endeavour to make his escape, was obliged to sit patiently in the tree. He was nevertheless tempted to get down, mount one of their horses, and lead another, driving his asses before him with all the haste he could to town; but the uncertainty of the event made him choose the safest course.

At last the door opened again, and the forty robbers came out. As the captain went in last, he came out first, and stood to see them all pass by him, when Ali Baba heard him make the door close by pronouncing these words: *"Shut, Sesame."* Every man went and bridled his horse, fastened his wallet, and mounted again; and when the captain saw them all ready, he put himself at their head, and they returned the way they had come. Ali Baba did not immediately quit his tree; for, said he to himself, they may have forgotten something and may come back again, and then I shall be taken. He followed them with his eyes as far as he could see them; and afterward stayed a considerable time before he descended. Remembering the words the captain of the robbers used to cause the door to open and shut, he had the curiosity to try if his pronouncing them would have the same effect. Accordingly, he went among the shrubs, and perceiving the door concealed behind them, stood before it, and said: *"Open, Sesame!"* The door instantly flew wide open. Ali Baba, who expected a dark dismal cavern, was surprised to see it well lighted and spacious, in the form of a vault, which received the light from an opening at the top of the rock. He saw all sorts of provisions, rich bales of silk stuff, brocade, and valuable carpeting, piled upon one another; gold and silver ingots in great heaps, and money in bags. The sight of all these riches made him suppose that this cave must have been occupied for ages by robbers, who had succeeded one another. Ali Baba did not stand long to consider what he should do, but went immediately into the cave, and as soon as he had entered, the door shut of itself, but this did not disturb him, because he knew the secret to open it again. He never regarded the silver, but made the best use of his time in carrying out as much of the gold coin as he thought his three asses could carry. He collected his asses, which were dispersed, and when he had loaded them with the bags, laid wood over in such a manner that they could not be seen. When he had done he stood before the door, and pronouncing the words: *"Shut, Sesame!"* the door closed after him, for it had shut of itself while he was within, but remained open while he was out. He then made the best of his way to town.

When Ali Baba got home, he drove his asses into a little yard, shut the gates very carefully, threw off the wood that covered the bags, carried them into his house, and ranged them in order before his wife, who sat on a sofa. His wife handled the bags, and finding them full of money, suspected that her husband had been robbing, insomuch that she could not help saying: "Ali Baba, have you been so unhappy as to – " "Be quiet, wife," interrupted Ali Baba, "do not frighten yourself; I am no robber, unless he may be one who steals from robbers. You will no longer entertain an ill opinion of me, when I shall tell you my good fortune." He then emptied the bags, which raised such a great heap of gold as dazzled his wife's eyes; and when he had done, told her the whole adventure from beginning to end; and, above all, recommended her to keep it secret. The wife, cured of her fears, rejoiced with her husband at their good fortune, and would count all the gold piece by piece. "Wife," replied Ali Baba, "you do not know what you undertake, when you pretend to count the money; you will never have done. I will dig a hole, and bury it; there is no time to be lost." "You are in the right, husband," replied she; "but let us know, as nigh as possible, how much we have. I will borrow a small measure in the neighbourhood, and measure it, while you dig the hole." "What you are going to do is to no purpose, wife," said Ali Baba; "if you would take my advice, you had better let it alone; but keep the secret, and do what you please." Away the wife ran to her brother-in-law Cassim, who lived just by, but was not then at home; and addressing herself to his wife, desired her to lend her a measure for a little while. Her sister-in-law asked her, whether she would have a great or a small one. The wife asked for a small one. The sister-in-law agreed to lend one, but as she knew Ali Baba's poverty, she was curious to know what sort of grain his wife wanted to measure, and artfully putting some suet at the bottom of the measure, brought it to her with an excuse, that she was sorry that she had made her stay so long, but that she could not find it sooner. Ali Baba's wife went home, set the measure upon the heap of gold, filled it and emptied it often upon the sofa, till she had done: when she was very well satisfied to find the number of measures amounted to so many as they did, and went to tell her husband, who had almost finished digging the hole. While Ali Baba was burying the gold, his wife, to show her exactness and diligence to her sister-in-law, carried the measure back again, but without taking notice that a piece of gold had stuck to the bottom. "Sister," said she, giving it to her again, "you see that I have not kept your measure long; I am obliged to you for it, and return it with thanks."

As soon as her sister-in-law was gone, Cassim's wife looked at the bottom of the measure, and was inexpressibly surprised to find a piece of gold stuck to it. Envy immediately possessed her breast. "What!" said she, "has Ali Baba gold so plentiful as to measure it? Where has that poor wretch got all this wealth?" Cassim, her husband, was not at home, but at his counting-house, which he left always in the evening. His wife waited for him, and thought the time an age; so great was her impatience to tell him the circumstance, at which she guessed he would be as much surprised as herself.

When Cassim came home, his wife said to him: "Cassim, I know you think yourself rich, but you are much mistaken; Ali Baba is infinitely richer than you; he does not count his money, but measures it." Cassim desired her to explain the riddle, which she did, by telling him the stratagem she had used to make the discovery, and showed him the piece of money, which was so old that they could not tell in what prince's reign it was coined. Cassim, instead of being pleased, conceived a base envy at his brother's prosperity; he could not sleep all that night, and went to him in the morning before sunrise, although after he had married the rich widow, he had never treated him as a brother, but neglected him. "Ali Baba," said he, accosting him, "you are very reserved in your affairs; you pretend to be miserably poor, and yet you measure gold." "How, brother?" replied Ali Baba; "I do not know what you mean: explain yourself." "Do not pretend ignorance," replied Cassim, showing him the piece of gold his wife had given him. "How many of these pieces," added he, "have you? My wife found this at the bottom of the measure you borrowed yesterday."

By this discourse, Ali Baba perceived that Cassim and his wife, through his own wife's folly, knew what they had so much reason to conceal; but what was done could not be recalled; therefore, without shewing the least surprise or trouble, he confessed all, told his brother by what chance he had discovered this retreat of the thieves, in what place it was; and offered him part of his treasure to keep the secret. "I expect as much," replied Cassim haughtily; "but I must know exactly where this treasure is, and how I may visit it myself when I choose; otherwise I will go and inform against you, and then you will not only get no more, but will lose all you have, and I shall have a share for my information."

Ali Baba, more out of his natural good temper, than frightened by the menaces of his unnatural brother, told him all he desired, and even the very words he was to use to gain admission into the cave.

Cassim, who wanted no more of Ali Baba, left him, resolving to be beforehand with him, and hoping to get all the treasure to himself. He rose the next morning long before the sun, and set out for the forest with ten mules bearing great chests, which he designed to fill; and followed the road which Ali Baba had pointed out to him. He was not long before he reached the rock, and found out the place by the tree, and other marks, which his brother had given him. When he reached the entrance of the cavern, he pronounced the words: *"Open, Sesame!"* and the door immediately opened, and when he was in, closed upon him. In examining the cave, he was in great admiration to find much more riches than he had apprehended from Ali Baba's account. He was so covetous, and greedy of wealth, that he could have spent the whole day in feasting his eyes with so much treasure, if the thought that he came to carry some away had not hindered him. He laid as many bags of gold as he could carry at the door of the cavern, but his thoughts were so full of the great riches he should possess, that he could not think of the necessary word to make it open, but instead of *"Sesame,"* said: *"Open, Barley!"* and was much amazed to find that the door remained fast shut. He named several sorts of grain, but still the door would not open. Cassim had never expected such an incident, and was so alarmed at the danger he was in, that the more he endeavoured to remember the word *"Sesame,"* the more his memory was confounded, and he had as much forgotten it as if he had never heard it mentioned. He threw down the bags he had loaded himself with and walked distractedly up and down the cave, without having the least regard to the riches that were round him. About noon the robbers chanced to visit their cave, and at some distance from it saw Cassim's mules straggling about the rock, with great chests on their backs. Alarmed at this novelty, they galloped full speed to the cave. They drove away the mules, which Cassim had neglected to fasten, and they strayed through the forest so far, that they were soon out of sight. The robbers never gave themselves the trouble to pursue them, being more concerned to know to whom they belonged, and while some of them searched about the rock, the captain and the rest went directly to the door, with their naked sabres in their hands, and pronouncing the proper words, it opened.

Cassim, who heard the noise of the horses' feet from the middle of the cave, never doubted of the arrival of the robbers, and his approaching death; but was resolved to make one effort to escape from them. To this end he rushed to the door, and no sooner heard the word *Sesame*, which he had forgotten, and saw the door open, than he ran out and threw the leader down, but could not escape the other robbers, who with their sabres soon deprived him of life. The first care of the robbers after this was to examine the cave. They found all the bags which Cassim had brought to the door, to be ready to load his mules, and carried them again to their places, without missing what Ali Baba had taken away before. Then holding a council, and deliberating upon this occurrence, they guessed that Cassim, when he was in, could not get out again; but could not imagine how he had entered. It came into their heads that he might have got down by the top of the cave; but the aperture by which it received light was so high, and the rocks so inaccessible without, that they gave up this conjecture. That he came in at the door they could not believe, however, unless he had the secret of making it open. In short, none of them could imagine which way he had entered; for they were all persuaded nobody knew their secret, little imagining that Ali Baba had watched them. It was a matter of the greatest importance to them to secure their riches. They agreed therefore to cut Cassim's body into quarters, to hang two on one side and two on the other, within the door of the cave, to terrify any person who should attempt again to enter. They had no sooner taken this resolution than they put it in execution, and when they had nothing more to detain them, left the place of their hoards well closed. They then mounted their horses, went to beat the roads again, and to attack the caravans they might meet.

In the meantime, Cassim's wife was very uneasy when night came, and her husband was not returned. She ran to Ali Baba in alarm, and said: "I believe, brother-in-law, that you know Cassim, your brother, is gone to the forest, and upon what account; it is now night, and he is not returned; I am afraid some misfortune has happened to him." Ali Baba, who had expected that his brother, after what he had said, would go to the forest, had declined going himself that day, for fear of giving him any umbrage; therefore told her, without any reflection upon her husband's unhandsome behaviour, that she need not frighten herself, for that certainly Cassim would not think it proper to come into the town till the night should be pretty far advanced.

Cassim's wife, considering how much it concerned her husband to keep the business secret, was the more easily persuaded to believe her brother-in-law. She went home again, and waited patiently till midnight. She repented of her foolish curiosity, and cursed her desire of penetrating into the affairs of her brother and sister-in-law. She spent all the night in weeping; and as soon as it was day, went to them, telling them, by her tears, the cause of her coming. Ali Baba did not wait for his sister-in-law to desire him to go and see what was become of Cassim, but departed immediately with his three asses, begging of her first to moderate her affliction. He went to the forest, and when he came near the rock, having seen neither his brother nor the mules in his way, was seriously alarmed at finding some blood spilt near the door, which he took for an ill omen; but when he had pronounced the word, and the door had opened, he was struck with horror at the dismal sight of his brother's body. Without adverting to the little fraternal affection his brother had shewn for him, Ali Baba went into the cave to find something to enshroud his remains, and having loaded one of his asses with them, covered them over with wood. The other two asses he loaded with bags of gold, covering them with wood also as before; and then bidding the door shut, came away; but was so cautious as to stop some time at the end of the forest, that he might not go into the town before night. When he came home, he drove the two asses loaded with gold into his little yard, and left the care of unloading them to his wife, while he led the other to his sister-in-law's house.

Ali Baba knocked at the door, which was opened by Morgiana, an intelligent slave, fruitful in inventions to insure success in the most difficult undertakings: and Ali Baba knew her to be such. When he came into the court, he unloaded the ass, and taking Morgiana aside, said to her: "The first thing I ask of you is an inviolable secrecy, both for your mistress's sake and mine. Your master's body is contained in these two bundles, and our business is, to bury him as if he had died a natural death. Go, tell your mistress I want to speak with her; and mind what I have said to you."

Morgiana went to her mistress, and Ali Baba followed her. "Well, brother," said she, with impatience, "what news do you bring me of my husband? I perceive no comfort in your countenance." "Sister," answered Ali Baba, "I cannot satisfy your inquiries unless you hear my story without speaking a word; for it is of as great importance to you as to me to keep what has happened secret." "Alas!" said she, "this preamble lets me know that my husband is not to be found; but at the same time I know the necessity of secrecy, and I must constrain myself: say on, I will hear you."

Ali Baba then detailed the incidents of his journey, till he came to the finding of Cassim's body. "Now," said he, "sister, I have something to relate which will afflict you the more, because it is what you so little expect; but it cannot now be remedied; if my endeavours can comfort you, I offer to put that which God hath sent me to what you have, and marry you: assuring you that my wife will not be jealous, and that we shall live happily together. If this proposal is agreeable to you, we must think of acting so that my brother should appear to have died a natural death. I think you may leave the management of the business to Morgiana, and I will contribute all that lies in my power to your consolation." What could Cassim's widow do better than accept of this proposal? for though her first husband had left behind him a plentiful substance, his brother was now much richer, and by the discovery of this treasure might be still more so. Instead, therefore, of rejecting the offer, she regarded it as the sure means of comfort; and drying up her tears, which had begun to flow abundantly, and suppressing the outcries usual with women who have lost their husbands, showed Ali Baba that she approved of his proposal. Ali Baba left the widow, recommended to Morgiana to act her part well, and then returned home with his ass.

Morgiana went out at the same time to an apothecary, and asked for a sort of lozenges which he prepared, and were very efficacious in the most dangerous disorders. The apothecary inquired who was ill at her master's? She replied with a sigh, her good master Cassim himself: that they knew not what his disorder was, but that he could neither eat nor speak. After these words, Morgiana carried the lozenges home with her, and the next morning went to the same apothecary's again, and with tears in her eyes, asked for an essence which they used to give to sick people only when at the last extremity. "Alas!" said she, taking it from the apothecary, "I am afraid that this remedy will have no better effect than the lozenges; and that I shall lose my good master." On the other hand, as Ali Baba and his wife were often seen to go between Cassim's and their own house all that day, and to seem melancholy, nobody was surprised in the evening to hear the lamentable shrieks and cries of Cassim's wife and Morgiana, who gave out everywhere that her master was dead. The next morning, soon after day appeared, Morgiana, who knew a certain old cobbler that opened his stall early, before other people, went to him, and bidding him good morrow, put a piece of gold into his hand. "Well," said Baba Mustapha, which was his name, and who was a merry old fellow, looking at the gold, "this is good hansel: what must I do for it? I am ready."

"Baba Mustapha," said Morgiana, "you must take with you your sewing tackle, and go with me; but I must tell you, I shall blindfold you when you come to such a place." Baba Mustapha seemed to hesitate a little at these words. "Oh! oh!" replied he, "you would have me do something against my conscience or against my honour?" "God forbid!" said Morgiana, putting another piece of gold into his hand, "that I should ask anything that is contrary to your honour; only come along with me, and fear nothing."

Baba Mustapha went with Morgiana, who, after she had bound his eyes with a handkerchief, conveyed him to her deceased master's house, and never unloosed his eyes till he had entered the room where she had put the corpse together. "Baba Mustapha," said she, "you must make haste and sew these quarters together; and when you have done, I will give you another piece of gold." After Baba Mustapha had finished his task, she blindfolded him again, gave him the third piece of gold as she had promised, and recommending secrecy to him, carried him back to the place where she first bound his eyes, pulled off the bandage, and let him go home, but watched him that he returned toward his stall, till he was quite out of sight, for fear he should have the curiosity to return and track her.

By the time Morgiana had warmed some water to wash the body, Ali Baba came with incense to embalm it, after which it was sewn up in a winding-sheet. Not long after, the joiner, according to Ali Baba's orders, brought the bier, which Morgiana received at the door, and helped Ali Baba to put the body into it; when she went to the mosque to inform the imaum that they were ready. The people of the mosque, whose business it was to wash the dead, offered to perform their duty, but she told them that it was done already. Morgiana had scarcely got home before the imaum and the other ministers of the mosque arrived. Four neighbours carried the corpse on their shoulders to the burying-ground, following the imaum, who recited some prayers. Morgiana, as a slave to the deceased, followed the corpse, weeping, beating her breast, and tearing her hair; and Ali Baba came after with some neighbours, who often relieved the others in carrying the corpse to the burying-ground. Cassim's wife stayed at home mourning, uttering lamentable cries with the women of the neighbourhood, who came according to custom during the funeral, and joining their lamentations with hers, filled the quarter far and near with sorrow. In this manner Cassim's melancholy death was concealed and hushed up between Ali Baba, his wife, Cassim's widow, and Morgiana, with so much contrivance, that nobody in the city had the least knowledge or suspicion of the cause of it.

Three or four days after the funeral, Ali Baba removed his few goods openly to the widow's house; but the money he had taken from the robbers he conveyed thither by night: soon after the marriage with his sister-in-law was published, and as these marriages are common in the Mussulman religion, nobody was surprised. As for Cassim's warehouse, Ali Baba gave it to his own eldest son, promising that if he managed it well, he would soon give him a fortune to marry very advantageously according to his situation.

Let us now leave Ali Baba to enjoy the beginning of his good fortune, and return to the forty robbers. They came again at the appointed time to visit their retreat in the forest; but great was their surprise to find Cassim's body taken away, with some of their bags of gold. "We are certainly discovered," said the captain, "and if we do not speedily apply some remedy, shall gradually lose all the riches which we have, with so much pains and danger, been so many years amassing together. All that we can think of the loss which we have sustained is, that the thief whom we surprised had the secret of opening the door, and we arrived luckily as he was coming out: but his body being removed, and with it some of our money, plainly shows that he had an accomplice; and as it is likely that there were but two who had discovered our secret, and one has been caught, we must look narrowly after the other. What say you, my lads?" All the robbers thought the captain's proposal so advisable, that they unanimously approved of it, and agreed that they must lay all other enterprises aside, to follow this closely, and not give it up till they had succeeded.

"I expected no less," said the captain, "from your fidelity: but, first of all, one of you who is artful, and enterprising, must go into the town disguised as a traveller, to try if he can hear any talk of the strange death of the man whom we have killed, as he deserved; and endeavour to find out who he was, and where he lived. This is a matter of the first importance for us to ascertain, that we may do nothing which we may have reason to repent of, by discovering ourselves in a country where we have lived so long unknown. But to warn him who shall take upon himself this commission, and to prevent our being deceived by his giving us a false report, I ask you all, if you do not think that in case of treachery, or even error of judgment, he should suffer death?" Without waiting for the suffrages of his companions, one of the robbers started up, and said: "I submit to this condition, and think it an honour to expose my life, by taking the commission upon me; but remember, at least, if I do not succeed, that I neither wanted courage nor good will to serve the troop." After this robber had received great commendations from the captain, he disguised himself, and taking his leave of the troop that night, went into the town just at daybreak; and walked up and down, till accidentally he came to Baba Mustapha's stall, which was always open before any of the shops.

Baba Mustapha was seated with an awl in his hand, just going to work. The robber saluted him, bidding him good morrow; and perceiving that he was old, said: "Honest man, you begin to work very early: is it possible that one of your age can see so well? I question, even if it were somewhat lighter, whether you could see to stitch."

"Certainly," replied Baba Mustapha, "you must be a stranger, and do not know me; for old as I am, I have extraordinarily good eyes; and you will not doubt it when I tell you that I sewed a dead body together in a place where I had not so much light as I have now." The robber was overjoyed to think that he had addressed himself, at his first coming into the town, to a man who in all probability could give him the intelligence he wanted. "A dead body!" replied he with affected amazement. "What could you sew up a dead body for? You mean you sewed up his winding-sheet." "No, no," answered Baba Mustapha, "I perceive your meaning; you want to have me speak out, but you shall know no more." The robber wanted no farther assurance to be persuaded that he had discovered what he sought. He pulled out a piece of gold, and putting it into Baba Mustapha's hand, said to him: "I do not want to learn your secret, though I can assure you I would not divulge it, if you trusted me with it; the only thing which I desire of you is, to do me the favour to shew me the house where you stitched up the dead body."

"If I were disposed to do you that favour," replied Baba Mustapha, holding the money in his hand, ready to return it, "I assure you I cannot. I was taken to a certain place, where I was blinded, I was then led to the house, and afterward brought back again in the same manner; you see, therefore, the impossibility of my doing what you desire."

"Well," replied the robber, "you may, however, remember a little of the way that you were led blindfolded. Come, let me blind your eyes at the same place. We will walk together; perhaps you may recognise some part; and as everybody ought to be paid for his trouble, there is another piece of gold for you; gratify me in what I ask you." So saying, he put another piece of gold into his hand.

The two pieces of gold were great temptations to Baba Mustapha. He looked at them a long time in his hand, without saying a word, thinking with himself what he should do; but at last he pulled out his purse, and put them in. "I cannot assure you," said he to the robber, "that I can remember the way exactly; but since you desire, I will try what I can do." At these words Baba Mustapha rose up, to the great joy of the robber, and without shutting his shop, where he had nothing valuable to lose, he led the robber to the place where Morgiana had bound his eyes. "It was here," said Baba Mustapha, "I was blindfolded; and I turned as you see me." The robber, who had his handkerchief ready, tied it over his eyes, walked by him till he stopped, partly leading, and partly guided by him. "I think," said Baba Mustapha, "I went no farther," and he had now stopped directly at Cassim's house, where Ali Baba then lived. The thief, before he pulled off the band, marked the door with a piece of chalk, which he had ready in his hand; and then asked him if he knew whose house that was; to which Baba Mustapha replied, that as he did not live in that neighbourhood he could not tell. The robber, finding he could discover no more from Baba Mustapha, thanked him for the trouble he had taken, and left him to go back to his stall, while he returned to the forest, persuaded that he should be very well received. A little after the robber and Baba Mustapha had parted, Morgiana went out of Ali Baba's house upon some errand, and upon her return, seeing the mark the robber had made, stopped to observe it. "What can be the meaning of this mark?" said she to herself. "Somebody intends my master no good: however, with whatever intention it was done, it is advisable to guard against the worst." Accordingly, she fetched a piece of chalk, and marked two or three doors on each side in the same manner, without saying a word to her master or mistress.

In the meantime the thief rejoined his troop in the forest, and recounted to them his success. All the robbers listened to him with the utmost satisfaction; when the captain, after commending his diligence, addressing himself to them all, said: "Comrades, we have no time to lose: let us set off well armed; but that we may not excite any suspicion, let only one or two go into the town together, and join at our rendezvous, which shall be the great square. In the meantime, our comrade who brought us the good news, and I, will go and find out the house, that we may consult what had best be done."

This plan was approved of by all, and they were soon ready. They filed off in parties of two each, and got into the town without being in the least suspected. The captain, and he who had visited the town in the morning as spy, came in the last. He led the captain into the street where he had marked Ali Baba's residence; and when they came to the first of the houses which Morgiana had marked, he pointed it out. But the captain observed that the next door was chalked in the same manner: and shewing it to his guide, asked him which house it was, that, or the first? The guide was so confounded, that he knew not what answer to make; but still more puzzled, when he saw five or six houses similarly marked. He assured the captain, with an oath, that he had marked but one, and could not tell who had chalked the rest so that he could not distinguish the house which the cobbler had stopped at.

The captain, finding that their design had proved abortive, went directly to the place of rendezvous, and told the first of his troop whom he met that they had lost their labour, and must return to their cave. When the troop was all got together, the captain told them the reason of their returning; and presently the conductor was declared by all worthy of death. He condemned himself, acknowledging that he ought to have taken better precaution, and prepared to receive the stroke from him who was appointed to cut off his head. Another of the gang, who promised himself that he should succeed better, immediately presented himself, and his offer being accepted, he went and corrupted Baba Mustapha, as the other had done; and being shewn the house, marked it in a place more remote from sight, with red chalk.

Not long after, Morgiana, whose eyes nothing could escape, went out, and seeing the red chalk, and arguing with herself as she had done before, marked the other neighbours' houses in the same place and manner. The robber, at his return to his company, valued himself much on the precaution he had taken, which he looked upon as an infallible way of distinguishing Ali Baba's house from the others; and the captain and all of them thought it must succeed. They conveyed themselves into the town with the same precaution as before; but when the robber and his captain came to the street, they found the same difficulty: at which the captain was enraged, and the robber in as great confusion as his predecessor. Thus the captain and his troop were forced to retire a second time, and much more dissatisfied; while the unfortunate robber, who had been the author of the mistake, underwent the same punishment; which he willingly submitted to.

The captain, having lost two brave fellows of his troop, was afraid of diminishing it too much by pursuing this plan to get information of the residence of their plunderer. He found by their example that their heads were not so good as their hands on such occasions; and therefore resolved to take upon himself the important commission. Accordingly, he went and addressed himself to Baba Mustapha, who did him the same service he had done to the other robbers. He did not set any particular mark on the house, but examined and observed it so carefully, by passing often by it, that it was impossible for him to mistake it.

The captain, well satisfied with his attempt, and informed of what he wanted to know, returned to the forest; and when he came into the cave, where the troop waited for him, said: "Now, comrades, nothing can prevent our full revenge, as I am certain of the house, and in my way hither I have thought how to put it into execution, but if any one can form a better expedient, let him communicate it." He then told them his contrivance; and as they approved of it, ordered them to go into the villages about, and buy nineteen mules, with thirty-eight large leather jars, one full of oil, and the others empty. In two or three days' time the robbers had purchased the mules and jars, and as the mouths of the jars were rather too narrow for his purpose, the captain caused them to be widened; and after having put one of his men into each, with the weapons which he thought fit, leaving open the seam which had been undone to leave them room to breathe, he rubbed the jars on the outside with oil from the full vessel. Things being thus prepared, when the nineteen mules were loaded with thirty-seven robbers in jars, and the jar of oil, the captain, as their driver, set out with them, and reached the town by the dusk of the evening, as he had intended. He led them through the streets till he came to Ali Baba's, at whose door he designed to have knocked; but was prevented by his sitting there after supper to take a little fresh air. He stopped his mules, addressed himself to him, and said: "I have brought some oil a great way, to sell at to-morrow's market; and it is now so late that I do not know where to lodge. If I should not be troublesome to you, do me the favour to let me pass the night with you, and I shall be very much obliged by your hospitality."

Though Ali Baba had seen the captain of the robbers in the forest, and had heard him speak, it was hardly possible to know him in the disguise of an oil-merchant. He told him he should be welcome, and immediately opened his gates for the mules to go into the yard. At the same time he called to a slave, and ordered him, when the mules were unloaded, to put them into the stable, and give them fodder; and then went to Morgiana, to bid her get a good supper. He did more. When he saw the captain had unloaded his mules, and that they were put into the stables as he had ordered, and he was looking for a place to pass the night in the air, he brought him into the hall where he received his company, telling him he would not suffer him to be in the court. The captain excused himself on pretence of not being troublesome; but really to have room to execute his design, and it was not till after the most pressing importunity that he yielded. Ali Baba, not content to keep company, till supper was ready, with the man who had a design on his life, continued talking with him till it was ended, and repeating his offer of service. The captain rose up at the same time with his host; and while Ali Baba went to speak to Morgiana he withdrew into the yard, under pretence of looking at his mules. Ali Baba, after charging Morgiana afresh to take care of his guest, said to her: "To-morrow morning I design to go to the bath before day; take care my bathing linens be ready, give them to Abdoollah," which was the slave's name, "and make me some good broth against I return." After this he went to bed.

In the meantime, the captain went from the stable to give his people orders what to do; and beginning at the first jar, and so on to the last, said to each man: "As soon as I throw some stones out of the chamber window where I lie, do not fail to cut the jar open with the knife you have about you for the purpose, and come out, and I will immediately join you." After this he returned into the house, when Morgiana, taking up a light, conducted him to his chamber, where she left him; and he, to avoid any suspicion, put the light out soon after, and laid himself down in his clothes, that he might be the more ready to rise.

Morgiana, remembering Ali Baba's orders, got his bathing linens ready, and ordered Abdoollah to set on the pot for the broth; but while she was preparing it, the lamp went out, and there was no more oil in the house, nor any candles. What to do she did not know, for the broth must be made. Abdoollah seeing her very uneasy, said: "Do not fret and tease yourself, but go into the yard, and take some oil out of one of the jars." Morgiana thanked Abdoollah for his advice, took the oil-pot, and went into the yard; when as she came nigh the first jar, the robber within said softly: "Is it time?" Though the robber spoke low, Morgiana was struck with the voice the more, because the captain, when he unloaded the mules, had taken the lids off this and all the other jars to give air to his men, who were ill enough at their ease, almost wanting room to breathe. As much surprised as Morgiana naturally was at finding a man in a jar, instead of the oil she wanted, many would have made such an outcry as to have given an alarm; whereas Morgiana comprehending immediately the importance of keeping silence, and the necessity of applying a speedy remedy without noise, conceived at once the means, and collecting herself without shewing the least emotion, answered: "Not yet, but presently." She went in this manner to all the jars, giving the same answer, till she came to the jar of oil.

By this means, Morgiana found that her master Ali Baba, who thought that he had entertained an oil merchant, had admitted thirty-eight robbers into his house, regarding this pretended merchant as their captain. She made what haste she could to fill her oil-pot, and returned into her kitchen; where, as soon as she had lighted her lamp, she took a great kettle, went again to the oil-jar, filled the kettle, set it on a large wood-fire, and as soon as it boiled went and poured enough into every jar to stifle and destroy the robber within.

When this action, worthy of the courage of Morgiana, was executed without any noise, she returned into the kitchen with the empty kettle; and having put out the great fire she had made to boil the oil, and leaving just enough to make the broth, put out the lamp also, and remained silent; resolving not to go to rest till she had observed what might follow through a window of the kitchen, which opened into the yard.

She had not waited long before the captain of the robbers got up, opened the window, and finding no light, and hearing no noise, or any one stirring in the house, gave the appointed signal, by throwing little stones, several of which hit the jars, as he doubted not by the sound they gave. He then listened, but not hearing or perceiving anything whereby he could judge that his companions stirred, he began to grow very uneasy, threw stones again a second and also a third time, and could not comprehend the reason that none of them should answer his signal. Much alarmed, he went softly down into the yard, and going to the first jar, whilst asking the robber, whom he thought alive, if he was in readiness, smelt the hot boiled oil, which sent forth a steam out of the jar. Hence he suspected that his plot to murder Ali Baba and plunder his house was discovered. Examining all the jars one after another, he found that all the members of his gang were dead; and by the oil he missed out of the last jar guessed the means and manner of their death. Enraged to despair at having failed in his design, he forced the lock of a door that led from the yard to the garden, and climbing over the walls, made his escape.

When Morgiana heard no noise, and found, after waiting some time, that the captain did not return, she concluded that he had chosen rather to make his escape by the garden than the street door, which was double-locked. Satisfied and pleased to have succeeded so well, in saving her master and family, she went to bed.

Ali Baba rose before day, and, followed by his slave, went to the baths, entirely ignorant of the important event which had happened at home; for Morgiana had not thought it safe to wake him before, for fear of losing her opportunity; and after her successful exploit she thought it needless to disturb him.

When he returned from the baths, the sun was risen; he was very much surprised to see the oil jars and that the merchant was not gone with the mules. He asked Morgiana, who opened the door, and had let all things stand as they were, that he might see them, the reason of it. "My good master," answered she, "God preserve you and all your family; you will be better informed of what you wish to know when you have seen what I have to show you, if you will but give yourself the trouble to follow me."

As soon as Morgiana had shut the door, Ali Baba followed her; when she requested him to look into the first jar and see if there was any oil. Ali Baba did so, and seeing a man, started back in alarm, and cried out. "Do not be afraid," said Morgiana; "the man you see there can neither do you nor anybody else any harm. He is dead." "Ah, Morgiana!" said Ali Baba, "what is it you show me? Explain yourself." "I will," replied Morgiana; "moderate your astonishment, and do not excite the curiosity of your neighbours. Look into all the other jars."

Ali Baba examined all the other jars, and when he came to that which had the oil in, found it prodigiously sunk, and stood for some time motionless, sometimes looking at the jars, and sometimes at Morgiana, without saying a word, so great was his surprise: at last, when he had recovered himself, he said: "And what is become of the merchant?"

"Merchant!" answered she, "he is as much one as I am; I will tell you who he is, and what is become of him: but you had better hear the story in your own chamber; for it is time for your health that you had your broth after your bathing."

While Ali Baba retired to his chamber, Morgiana went into the kitchen to fetch the broth, but before he would drink it, he first entreated her to satisfy his impatience, and tell him what had happened, with all the circumstances; and she obeyed him.

"This," she said, when she had completed her story, "is the account you asked of me; and I am convinced it is the consequence of what I observed some days ago, but did not think fit to acquaint you with; for when I came in one morning early I found our street door marked with white chalk, and the next morning with red; upon which, both times without knowing what was the intention of those chalks, I marked two or three neighbours' doors on each side in the same manner. If you reflect on this, and what has since happened, you will find it to be a plot of the robbers of the forest, of whose gang there are two wanting, and now they are reduced to three: all this shows that they had sworn your destruction, and it is proper you should be upon your guard, while there is one of them alive: for my part, I shall neglect nothing necessary to your preservation, as I am in duty bound."

When Morgiana had left off speaking, Ali Baba was so sensible of the great service she had done him, that he said to her: "I will not die without rewarding you as you deserve; I owe my life to you, and for the first token of my acknowledgment, give you your liberty from this moment, till I can complete your recompense as I intend. I am persuaded with you, that the forty robbers have laid snares for my destruction. God, by your means, has delivered me from them as yet, and I hope will continue to preserve me from their wicked designs, and deliver the world from their persecution. All that we have to do is to bury the bodies of these pests of mankind immediately, and with all the secrecy imaginable, that nobody may suspect what is become of them. But that labour Abdoollah and I will undertake."

Ali Baba's garden was very long, and shaded at the farther end by a great number of large trees. Under these he and the slave dug a trench, long and wide enough to hold all the robbers. Afterward they lifted the bodies out of the jars, took away their weapons, carried them to the end of the garden, laid them in the trench, and levelled the ground again. When this was done, Ali Baba hid the jars and weapons; and as he had no occasion for the mules, he sent them at different times to be sold in the market by his slave.

While Ali Baba took these measures to prevent the public from knowing how he came by his riches in so short a time, the captain of the forty robbers returned to the forest with inconceivable mortification; and in his confusion at his ill success, so contrary to what he had promised himself, entered the cave, not being able, all the way from the town, to come to any resolution how to revenge himself of Ali Baba.

The loneliness of the gloomy cavern became frightful to him. "Where are you, my brave lads," cried he, "old companions of my watchings, inroads, and labour? What can I do without you? Did I collect you only to lose you by so base a fate, and so unworthy of your courage! Had you died with your sabres in your hands, like brave men, my regret had been less! When shall I enlist so gallant a troop again? And if I could, can

I undertake it without exposing so much gold and treasure to him who hath already enriched himself out of it? I cannot, I ought not to think of it, before I have taken away his life. I will undertake that alone, which I could not accomplish with your powerful assistance; and when I have taken measures to secure this treasure from being pillaged, I will provide for it new masters and successors after me, who shall preserve and augment it to all posterity." This resolution being taken, he was not at a loss how to execute his purpose; but full of hopes, slept all that night very quietly.

When he awoke early next morning, he dressed himself, agreeably to the project he had formed, went to the town, and took a lodging in a khan. As he expected what had happened at Ali Baba's might make a great noise, he asked his host what news there was in the city? Upon which the innkeeper told him a great many circumstances, which did not concern him in the least. He judged by this, that the reason why Ali Baba kept his affairs so secret, was for fear people should know where the treasure lay; and because he knew his life would be sought on account of it. This urged him the more to neglect nothing to rid himself of so cautious an enemy.

The captain now assumed the character of a merchant, and conveyed gradually a great many sorts of rich stuffs and fine linen to his lodging from the cavern, but with all the necessary precautions imaginable to conceal the place whence he brought them. In order to dispose of the merchandise, when he had amassed them together, he took a warehouse, which happened to be opposite to Cassim's, which Ali Baba's son had occupied since the death of his uncle.

He took the name of Khaujeh Houssain, and as a newcomer, was, according to custom, extremely civil and complaisant to all the merchants his neighbours. Ali Baba's son was from his vicinity one of the first to converse with Khaujeh Houssain, who strove to cultivate his friendship more particularly when, two or three days after he was settled, he recognised Ali Baba, who came to see his son, and stopped to talk with him as he was accustomed to do. When he was gone, the impostor learnt from his son who he was. He increased his assiduities, caressed him in the most engaging manner, made him some small presents, and often asked him to dine and sup with him.

Ali Baba's son did not choose to lie under such obligation to Khaujeh Houssain, without making the like return; but was so much straitened for want of room in his house, that he could not entertain him so well as he wished; he therefore acquainted his father Ali Baba with his intention, and told him that it did not look well for him to receive such favours from Khaujeh Houssain without inviting him in return.

Ali Baba, with great pleasure, took the treat upon himself. "Son," said he, "to-morrow being Friday, which is a day that the shops of such great merchants as Khaujeh Houssain and yourself are shut, get him to take a walk with you, and as you come back, pass by my door and call in. It will look better to have it happen accidentally, than if you gave him a formal invitation. I will go and order Morgiana to provide a supper."

The next day Ali Baba's son and Khaujeh Houssain met by appointment, took their walk, and as they returned, Ali Baba's son led Khaujeh Houssain through the street where his father lived; and when they came to the house, stopped and knocked at the door. "This, sir," said he, "is my father's house; who, from the account I have given him of your friendship, charged me to procure him the honour of your acquaintance."

Though it was the sole aim of Khaujeh Houssain to introduce himself into Ali Baba's house, that he might kill him without hazarding his own life or making any noise; yet he excused himself, and offered to take his leave. But a slave having opened the door, Ali Baba's son took him obligingly by the hand, and in a manner forced him in.

Ali Baba received Khaujeh Houssain with a smiling countenance, and in the most obliging manner. He thanked him for all the favours he had done his son; adding withal, the obligation was the greater, as he was a young man not much acquainted with the world.

Khaujeh Houssain returned the compliment, by assuring Ali Baba, that though his son might not have acquired the experience of older men, he had good sense equal to the knowledge of many others. After a little more conversation on different subjects, he offered again to take his leave; when Ali Baba, stopping him, said: "Where are you going, sir, in so much haste? I beg you would do me the honour to sup with me, though what I have to give you is not worth your acceptance; but such as it is, I hope you will accept it as heartily as I give it." "Sir," replied Khaujeh Houssain, "I am thoroughly persuaded of your good will; and if I ask the favour of you not to take it ill that I do not accept your obliging invitation, I beg of you to believe that it does not proceed from any slight or intention to affront, but from a reason which you would approve if you knew it.

"And what may that reason be, sir," replied Ali Baba, "if I may be so bold as to ask you?" "It is," answered Khaujeh Houssain, "that I can eat no victuals that have any salt in them; therefore judge how I should feel at your table." "If that is the only reason," said Ali Baba, "it ought not to deprive me of the honour of your company at supper; for, in the first place, there is no salt ever put into my bread, and as to the meat we shall have to-night, I promise you there shall be none in that. Therefore you must do me the favour to stay. I will return immediately."

Ali Baba went into the kitchen, and ordered Morgiana to put no salt to the meat that was to be dressed that night; and to make quickly two or three ragouts besides what he had ordered, but be sure to put no salt in them.

Morgiana, who was always ready to obey her master, could not help seeming somewhat dissatisfied at his strange order. "Who is this difficult man," said she, "who eats no salt with his meat? Your supper will be spoiled, if I keep it back so long." "Do not be angry, Morgiana," replied Ali Baba; "he is an honest man; therefore do as I bid you."

Morgiana obeyed, though with no little reluctance, and had a curiosity to see this man who ate no salt. To this end, when she had finished what she had to do in the kitchen, she helped Abdoollah to carry up the dishes; and looking at Khaujeh Houssain, knew him at first sight, notwithstanding his disguise, to be the captain of the robbers, and examining him very carefully, perceived that he had a dagger under his garment. "I am not in the least amazed," said she to herself, "that this wicked wretch, who is my master's greatest enemy, would eat no salt with him, since he intends to assassinate him; but I will prevent him."

Morgiana, while they were eating, made the necessary preparations for executing one of the boldest acts ever meditated, and had just determined, when Abdoollah came for the dessert of fruit, which she carried up, and as soon as he had taken the meat away, set upon the table; after that, she placed three glasses by Ali Baba, and going out, took Abdoollah with her to sup, and to give Ali Baba the more liberty of conversation with his guest.

Khaujeh Houssain, or rather the captain of the robbers, thought he had now a favourable opportunity of being revenged on Ali Baba. "I will," said he to himself, "make the father and son both drunk: the son, whose life I intend to spare, will not be able to prevent my stabbing his father to the heart; and while the slaves are at supper, or asleep in the kitchen, I can make my escape over the gardens as before."

Instead of going to supper, Morgiana, who had penetrated the intentions of the counterfeit Khaujeh Houssain, would not give him time to put his villainous design into execution, but dressed herself neatly with a suitable head-dress like a dancer, girded her waist with a silver-gilt girdle, to which there hung a poniard with a hilt and guard of the same metal, and put a handsome mask on her face. When she had thus disguised herself, she said to Abdoollah: "Take your tabor, and let us go and divert our master and his son's guest, as we do sometimes when he is alone."

Abdoollah took his tabor and played all the way into the hall before Morgiana, who when she came to the door made a low obeisance, with a deliberate air, in order to draw attention, and by way of asking leave to exhibit her skill. Abdoollah, seeing that his master had a mind to say something, left off playing. "Come in, Morgiana," said Ali Baba, "and let Khaujeh Houssain see what you can do, that he may tell us what he thinks of you. But, sir," said he, turning toward his guest, "do not think that I put myself to any expense to give you this diversion, since these are my slave and my cook and housekeeper; and I hope you will not find the entertainment they give us disagreeable."

Khaujeh Houssain, who did not expect this diversion after supper, began to fear he should not be able to improve the opportunity he thought he had found: but hoped, if he now missed his aim, to secure it another time, by keeping up a friendly correspondence with the father and son; therefore, though he could have wished Ali Baba would have declined the dance, he had the complaisance to express his satisfaction at what he saw pleased his host.

As soon as Abdoollah saw that Ali Baba and Khaujeh Houssain had done talking, he began to play on the tabor, and accompanied it with an air; to which Morgiana, who was an excellent performer, danced in such a manner as would have created admiration in any other company besides that before which she now exhibited, among whom, perhaps, none but the false Khaujeh Houssain was in the least attentive to her, the rest having seen her so frequently.

After she had danced several dances with equal propriety and grace, she drew the poniard, and holding it in her hand, began a dance, in which she outdid herself, by the many different figures, light movements, and the surprising leaps and wonderful exertions with which she accompanied it. Sometimes she presented the poniard to one person's breast, sometimes to another's, and oftentimes seemed to strike her own. At last, as if she was out of breath, she snatched the tabor from Abdoollah with her left hand, and holding the dagger in her right, presented the other side of the tabor, after the manner of those who get a livelihood by dancing, and solicit the liberality of the spectators.

Ali Baba put a piece of gold into the tabor, as did also his son: and Khaujeh Houssain, seeing that she was coming to him, had pulled his purse out of his bosom to make her a present; but while he was putting his hand into it, Morgiana, with a courage and resolution worthy of herself, plunged the poniard into his heart. Ali Baba and his son, shocked at this action, cried out aloud. "Unhappy wretch!" exclaimed Ali Baba, "what have you done to ruin me and my family?" "It was to preserve, not to ruin you," answered Morgiana; "for see here," continued she (opening the pretended Khaujeh Houssain's garment, and showing the dagger), "what an enemy you had entertained! Look well at him, and you will find him to be both the fictitious oil-merchant, and the captain of the gang of forty robbers. Remember, too, that he would eat no salt with you; and what would you have more to persuade you of his wicked design? Before I saw him, I suspected him as soon as you told me you had such a guest. I knew him, and you now find that my suspicion was not groundless."

Ali Baba, who immediately felt the new obligation he had to Morgiana for saving his life a second time, embraced her: "Morgiana," said he, "I gave you your liberty, and then promised you that my gratitude should not stop there, but that I would soon give you higher proofs of its sincerity, which I now do by making you my daughter-in-law." Then addressing himself to his son, he said: "I believe you, son, to be so dutiful a child, that you will not refuse Morgiana for your wife. You see that Khaujeh Houssain sought your friendship with a treacherous design to take away my life; and, if he had succeeded, there is no doubt but he would have sacrificed you also to his revenge. Consider, that by marrying Morgiana you marry the preserver of my family and your own."

The son, far from showing any dislike, readily consented to the marriage; not only because he would not disobey his father, but also because it was agreeable to his inclination.

After this, they thought of burying the captain of the robbers with his comrades, and did it so privately that nobody discovered their bones till many years after, when no one had any concern in the publication of this remarkable history.

A few days afterward, Ali Baba celebrated the nuptials of his son and Morgiana with great solemnity, a sumptuous feast, and the usual dancing and spectacles; and had the satisfaction to see that his friends and neighbours, whom he invited, had no knowledge of the true motives of the marriage; but that those who were not unacquainted with Morgiana's good qualities commended his generosity and goodness of heart.

Ali Baba forbore, after this marriage, from going again to the robbers' cave, as he had done, for fear of being surprised, from the time he had brought away his brother Cassim's mangled remains. He had kept away after the death of the thirty-seven robbers and their captain, supposing the other two, whom he could get no account of, might be alive.

At the year's end, when he found that they had not made any attempt to disturb him, he had the curiosity to make another journey, taking the necessary precautions for his safety. He mounted his horse, and when he came to the cave, and saw no footsteps of men or beasts, looked upon it as a good sign. He alighted, tied his horse to a tree, then approaching the entrance and pronouncing the words, *Open, Sesame!* the door opened. He entered the cavern, and by the condition he found things in, judged that nobody had been there since the false Khaujeh Houssain, when he had fetched the goods for his shop; that the gang of forty robbers was completely destroyed, and no longer doubted that he was the only person in the world who had the secret of opening the cave, so that all the treasure was at his sole disposal. Having brought with him a wallet, he put into it as much gold as his horse would carry, and returned to town.

Afterward Ali Baba carried his son to the cave, and taught him the secret, which they handed down to their posterity, who, using their good fortune with moderation, lived in great honour and splendour.

The History of Codadad and His Brothers

Kate Douglas Wiggin and Nora A. Smith

THERE FORMERLY REIGNED in the city of Harran a most magnificent and potent sultan, who loved his subjects, and was equally beloved by them. He was endued with all virtues, and wanted nothing to complete his happiness but an heir. He continually prayed to Heaven for a child; and one night in his sleep, a prophet appeared to him and said: "Your prayers are heard; you have obtained what you have desired; rise as soon as you awake, go to your prayers, and make two genuflexions; then walk into the garden of your palace, call your gardener, and bid him bring you a pomegranate; eat as many of the seeds as you please, and your wishes shall be accomplished."

The sultan calling to mind his dream when he awoke, returned thanks to Heaven, got up, prayed, made two genuflexions, and then went into his garden, where he took fifty pomegranate seeds, which he counted, and ate. Some time afterward forty-nine of his wives presented him with sons, each one as vigorous as a young palm-tree, but Pirouzè, the fiftieth wife, remained childless. The sultan, therefore, took an aversion to this lady and would have had her put to death had not his vizier prevented him, advising rather that she be sent to Samaria, to her brother, Sultan Samer, with orders that she be well treated.

Not long after Pirouzè had been retired to her brother's country, a most beautiful prince was born to her. The prince of Samaria wrote immediately to the sultan of Harran, to acquaint him with the birth of a son, and to congratulate him on the occasion. The sultan was much rejoiced at this intelligence, and answered Prince Samer as follows: "Cousin, all my other wives have each presented me with a prince. I desire you to educate the child of Pirouzè, to give him the name of Codadad, and to send him to me when I may apply for him."

The prince of Samaria spared nothing that might improve the education of his nephew. He taught him to ride, draw the bow, and all other accomplishments becoming the son of a sovereign; so that Codadad, at eighteen years of age, was looked upon as a prodigy. The young prince, being inspired with a courage worthy his birth, said one day to his mother: "Madam, I begin to grow weary of Samaria; I feel a passion for glory; give me leave to seek it amidst the perils of war. My father the sultan of Harran has many enemies. Why does he not call me to his assistance? Must I spend my life in sloth, when all my brothers have the happiness to be fighting by his side?" "My son," answered Pirouzè, "I am no less impatient to have your name become famous; I could wish you had already signalised yourself against your father's enemies; but we must wait till he requires it." "No, madam," replied Codadad, "I have already waited too long. I burn to see the sultan, and am tempted to offer him my service, as a young stranger: no doubt but he will accept of it, and I will not discover myself till I have performed some glorious actions." Pirouzè approved of his generous resolutions, and Codadad departed from Samaria, as if he had been going to the chase, without acquainting Prince Samer, lest he should thwart his design.

He was mounted on a white charger, who had a bit and shoes of gold, his housing was of blue satin embroidered with pearls; the hilt of his cimeter was of one single diamond, and the scabbard of sandalwood, adorned with emeralds and rubies, and on his shoulder he carried his bow and quiver. In this equipage, which greatly set off his handsome person, he arrived at the city of Harran, and soon found means to offer his service to the sultan; who being charmed with his beauty, and perhaps indeed by natural sympathy, gave him a favourable reception, and asked his name and quality. "Sir," answered Codadad, "I am son to an emir of Grand Cairo; an inclination to travel has made me quit my country, and understanding that you were engaged in war, I am come to your court to offer your majesty my service." The sultan, upon hearing this, shewed him extraordinary kindness, and gave him a command in his army.

The young prince soon gained the esteem of the officers, and was admired by the soldiers. Having no less wit than courage, he so far advanced himself in the sultan's esteem, as to become his favourite. All the ministers and other courtiers daily resorted to Codadad, and were so eager to purchase his friendship, that they neglected the sultan's sons. The princes could not but resent this conduct, and all conceived an implacable hatred against him; but the sultan's affection daily increasing, he was never weary of giving him fresh testimonies of his regard. He always would have him near his person; and to shew his high opinion of his wisdom and prudence, committed to his care the other princes, though he was of the same age as they; so that Codadad was made governor of his brothers.

This only served to heighten their hatred. "Is it come to this," said they, "that the sultan, not satisfied with loving a stranger more than us, will have him to be our governor, and not allow us to act without his leave? This is not to be endured. We must rid ourselves of this foreigner." "Let us go together," said one of them, "and despatch him." "No, no," answered another; "we had better be cautious how we sacrifice ourselves. His death would render us odious to the sultan. Let us destroy him by some stratagem. We will ask his permission to hunt, and, when at a distance from the palace, proceed to some other city and stay there some time. The sultan will wonder at our absence, and perceiving we do not return, perhaps put the stranger to death, or at least will banish him from court, for suffering us to leave the palace."

All the princes applauded this artifice. They went together to Codadad, and desired him to allow them to take the diversion of hunting, promising to return the same day. Pirouzè's son was taken in the snare, and granted the permission his brothers desired. They set out, but never returned. They had been three days absent, when the sultan asked Codadad where the princes were, for it was long since he had seen them. "Sir," answered Codadad, after making a profound reverence, "they have been hunting these three days, but they promised me they would return sooner." The sultan grew uneasy, and his uneasiness increased when he perceived the princes did not return the next day. He could not check his anger: "Indiscreet stranger," said he to Codadad, "why did you let my sons go without bearing them company? Go, seek them immediately, and bring them to me, or your life shall be forfeited."

These words chilled with alarm Pirouzè's unfortunate son. He armed himself, departed from the city, and like a shepherd who had lost his flock, searched the country for his brothers, inquiring at every village whether they had been seen; but hearing no news of them, abandoned himself to the most lively grief. He was inconsolable for having given the princes permission to hunt, or for not having borne them company.

After some days spent in fruitless search, he came to a plain of prodigious extent, in the midst whereof was a palace built of black marble. He drew near, and at one of the windows beheld a most beautiful lady; but set off with no other ornament than her own charms; for her hair was dishevelled, her garments torn, and on her countenance appeared all the marks of affliction. As soon as she saw Codadad, and judged he might hear her, she directed her discourse to him, saying: "Young man, depart from this fatal place, or you will soon fall into the hands of the monster that inhabits it: a black, who feeds only on human blood, resides in this palace; he seizes all persons whom their ill fate conducts to this plain, and shuts them up in his dungeons, whence they are never released, but to be devoured by him."

"Madam," answered Codadad, "tell me who you are, and be not concerned for myself." "I am a lady of quality of Grand Cairo," replied the captive; "I was passing by this castle yesterday, on my way to Bagdad, and met with the black, who killed all my attendants, and brought me hither. I beg of you," she cried, "to make your escape: the black will soon return; he is gone out to pursue some travellers he espied at a distance on the plain. Lose no time, but fly."

She had scarcely done speaking before the black appeared. He was of monstrous bulk, and of a dreadful aspect, mounted on a large Tartar horse, and bore a heavy cimeter, that none but himself could wield. The prince seeing him, was amazed at his gigantic stature, directed his prayers to Heaven to assist him, then drew his own cimeter, and firmly awaited his approach. The monster, despising so inconsiderable an enemy, called to him to submit without fighting. Codadad by his conduct shewed that he was resolved to defend his life; for rushing upon the black, he wounded him on the knee. The monster, feeling himself wounded, uttered such a dreadful yell as made all the plain resound. He grew furious and foamed with rage, and raising himself on his stirrups, made at Codadad with his dreadful cimeter. The blow was so violent, that it would have put an end to the young prince, had not he avoided it by a sudden spring. The cimeter made a horrible hissing in the air: but, before the black could have time to make a second blow, Codadad struck him on his right arm with such force that he cut it off. The dreadful cimeter fell with the hand that held it, and the black, yielding under the violence of the stroke, lost his stirrups, and made the earth shake with the weight of his fall. The prince alighted at the same time, and cut off his enemy's head. Just then the lady, who had been a spectator of the combat, and was still offering up her earnest prayers to Heaven for the young hero, uttered a shriek of joy, and said to Codadad: "Prince and Deliverer, finish the work you have begun; the black has the keys of this castle, take them and deliver me out of prison."

The prince searched the wretch as he lay stretched on the ground, and found several keys. He opened the first door, and entered a court, where he saw the lady coming to meet him; she would have cast herself at his feet, the better to express her gratitude, but he would not permit her. She commended his valour, and extolled him above all the heroes in the world. He returned her compliments; and she appeared still more lovely to him near, than she had done at a distance. I know not whether she felt more joy at being delivered from the desperate danger she had been in, than he for having done so considerable a service to so beautiful a person.

Their conversation was interrupted by dismal cries and groans. "What do I hear?" said Codadad; "whence come these miserable lamentations, which pierce my ears?" "My lord," said the lady, pointing to a little door in the court, "they come from thence. There are I know not how many wretched persons whom fate has thrown into the hands of the black. They are all chained, and the monster drew out one every day to devour."

"It is an addition to my joy," answered the young prince, "to understand that my victory will save the lives of those unfortunate beings. Come with me, madam, to partake in the satisfaction of giving them their liberty." Having so said, they advanced toward the door of the dungeon, where Codadad, pitying them, and impatient to put an end to their sufferings, presently put one of the keys into the lock. The noise made all the unfortunate captives, who concluded it was the black coming, according to custom, to seize one of them to devour, redouble their cries and groans.

In the meantime, the prince had opened the door; he went down a steep staircase into a deep vault, which received some feeble light from a little window, and in which there were above a hundred persons, bound to stakes. "Unfortunate travellers," said he to them, "who only expected the moment of an approaching death, give thanks to Heaven which has this day delivered you by my means. I have slain the black by whom you were to be devoured, and am come to knock off your chains." The prisoners hearing these words, gave a shout of mingled joy and surprise. Codadad and the lady began to unbind them; and as soon as any of them were loose, they helped to take off the fetters from the rest; so that in a short time they were all at liberty.

They then kneeled down, and having returned thanks to Codadad for what he had done for them, went out of the dungeon; but when they were come into the court, how was the prince surprised to see among the prisoners those he was in search of, and almost without hopes to find! "Princes," cried he, "is it you whom I behold? May I flatter myself that it is in my power to restore you to the sultan your father, who is inconsolable for the loss of you? Are you all here alive? Alas! the death of one of you will suffice to damp the joy I feel for having delivered you."

The forty-nine princes all made themselves known to Codadad, who embraced them one after another, and told them how uneasy their father was on account of their absence. They gave their deliverer all the commendations he deserved, as did the other prisoners, who could not find words expressive enough to declare their gratitude. Codadad, with them, searched the whole castle, where was immense wealth: curious silks, gold brocades, Persian carpets, China satins, and an infinite quantity of other goods, which the black had taken from the caravans he had plundered, a considerable part whereof belonged to the prisoners Codadad had then liberated. Every man knew and claimed his property. The prince restored them their own, and divided the rest of the merchandise among them. Then he said to them: "How will you carry away your goods? We are here in a desert place, and there is no likelihood of your getting horses." "My lord," answered one of the prisoners, "the black robbed us of our camels, as well as of our goods, and perhaps they may be in the stables of this castle." "That is not unlikely," replied Codadad; "let us examine." Accordingly they went to the stables, where they not only found the camels, but also the horses belonging to the sultan of Harran's sons. All the merchants, overjoyed that they had recovered their goods and camels, together with their liberty, thought of nothing but prosecuting their journey; but first repeated their thanks to their deliverer.

When they were gone, Codadad, directing his discourse to the lady, said: "What place, madam, do you desire to go to? I intend to bear you company to the spot you shall choose for your retreat, and I question not but that all these princes will do the same." The sultan of Harran's sons protested to the lady, that they would not leave her till she was restored to her friends.

"Princes," said she, "I am of a country too remote from here; and, besides that, it would be abusing your generosity to oblige you to travel so far. I must confess that I have left my native country for ever. I told you that I was a lady of Grand Cairo; but since you have shewn me so much favour, I should be much in the wrong in concealing the truth from you: I am a sultan's daughter. A usurper has possessed himself of my father's throne, after having murdered him, and I have been forced to fly to save my life."

Codadad and his brothers requested the princess to tell them her story, and after thanking them for their repeated protestations of readiness to serve her, she could not refuse to satisfy their curiosity, and began the recital of her adventures in the following manner.

"There was in a certain island," said the princess, "a great city called Deryabar, governed by a magnificent and virtuous sultan, who had no children, which was the only blessing wanting to make him happy. He continually addressed his prayers to Heaven, but Heaven only partially granted his requests, for the queen his wife, after a long expectation, brought forth a daughter.

"I am that unfortunate princess; my father was rather grieved than pleased at my birth; but he submitted to the will of God, and caused me to be educated with all possible care, being resolved, since he had no son, to teach me the art of ruling, that I might supply his place after his death.

"There was, at the court of Deryabar, an orphan youth of good birth whom the sultan, my father, had befriended and educated according to his rank. He was very handsome, and, not wanting ability, found means to please my father, who conceived a great friendship for him. All the courtiers perceived it, and guessed that the young man might in the end be my husband. In this idea, and looking on him already as heir to the crown, they made their court to him, and every one endeavoured to gain his favour. He soon saw into their designs, and forgetting the distance there was between our conditions, flattered himself with the hopes that my father was fond enough of him to prefer him before all the princes in the world. He went farther; for the sultan not offering me to him as soon as he could have wished, he had the boldness to ask me of him. Whatever punishment his insolence deserved, my father was satisfied with telling him he had other thoughts in relation to me. The youth was incensed at this refusal; he resented the contempt, as if he had asked some maid of ordinary extraction, or as if his birth had been equal to mine. Nor did he stop here, but resolved to be revenged on the sultan, and with unparalleled ingratitude conspired against him. In short, he murdered him, and caused himself to be proclaimed sovereign of Deryabar. The grand vizier, however, while the usurper was butchering my father came to carry me away from the palace, and secured me in a friend's house, till a vessel he had provided was ready to sail. I then left the island, attended only by a governess and that generous minister, who chose rather to follow his master's daughter than to submit to a tyrant.

"The grand vizier designed to carry me to the courts of the neighbouring sultans, to implore their assistance, and excite them to revenge my father's death; but Heaven did not concur in a resolution we thought so just. When we had been but a few days at sea, there arose such a furious storm, that our vessel, carried away by the violence of the winds and waves, was dashed in pieces against a rock. My governess, the grand vizier, and all that attended me, were swallowed up by the sea. I lost my senses; and whether I was thrown upon the coast, or whether Heaven wrought a miracle for my deliverance, I found myself on shore when my senses returned.

"In my despair and horror I was on the point of casting myself into the sea again; when I heard behind me a great noise of men and horses. I looked about to see what it might be, and espied several armed horsemen, among whom was one mounted on an Arabian charger. He had on a garment embroidered with silver, a girdle set with precious stones, and a crown of gold on his head. Though his habit had not convinced me that he was chief of the company, I should have judged it by the air of grandeur which appeared in his person. He was a young man extraordinarily well shaped, and perfectly beautiful. Surprised to see a young lady alone in that place, he sent some of his officers to ask who I was. I answered only by weeping. The shore being covered with the wreck of our ship, they concluded that I was certainly some person who had escaped from the vessel. This conjecture excited the curiosity of the officers, who began to ask me a thousand questions, with assurances that their master was a generous prince, and that I should receive protection at his court.

"The sultan, impatient to know who I was, grew weary of waiting the return of his officers, and drew near to me. He gazed on me very earnestly, and observing that I did not cease weeping, without being able to return an answer to their questions, he forbade them troubling me any more; and directing his discourse to me: 'Madam,' said he, 'I conjure you to moderate your excessive affliction. I dare assure you that, if your misfortunes are capable of receiving any relief, you shall find it in my dominions. You shall live with the queen my mother, who will endeavour by her kindness to ease your affliction. I know not yet who you are, but I find I already take an interest in your welfare.'

"I thanked the young sultan for his goodness to me, accepted his obliging offer; and to convince him that I was not unworthy of them, told him my condition. When I had done speaking, the prince assured me that he was deeply concerned at my misfortunes. He then conducted me to his palace, and presented me to the queen his mother, to whom I was obliged again to repeat my misfortunes. The queen seemed very sensible of my trouble, and conceived extreme affection for me. On the other hand, the sultan her son fell desperately in love with me, and soon offered me his hand and his crown. I was so taken up with the thoughts of my calamities, that the prince, though so lovely a person, did not make so great an impression on me as he might have done at another time. However, gratitude prevailing, I did not refuse to make him happy, and our nuptials were concluded with all imaginable splendour.

"While the people were taken up with the celebration of their sovereign's nuptials, a neighbouring prince, his enemy, made a descent by night on the island with a great number of troops and surprised and cut to pieces my husband's subjects. We escaped very narrowly, for he had already entered the palace with some of his followers; but we found means to slip away and to get to the sea-coast, where we threw ourselves into a fishing-boat which we had the good fortune to meet with. Two days we were driven about by the winds, without knowing what would become of us. The third day we espied a vessel making toward us under sail. We rejoiced at first, believing it had been a merchant-ship which might take us aboard; but what was our consternation, when, as it drew near, we saw ten or twelve armed pirates appear on the deck. Having boarded, five or six of them leaped into our boat, seized us, bound the prince, and conveyed us into their ship, where they immediately took off my veil. My youth and features touched them, and they all declared how much they were charmed at the sight of me. Instead of casting lots, each of them claimed the preference, and me as his right. The dispute grew warm, they came to blows, and fought like madmen. The deck was soon covered with dead bodies, and they were all killed but one, who, being left sole possessor of me, said: 'You are mine. I will carry you to Grand Cairo, to deliver you to a friend of mine, to whom I have promised a beautiful slave. But who,' added he, looking upon the sultan, my husband, 'is that man? What relation does he bear to you? Are you allied by blood or love?' 'Sir,' answered I, 'he is my husband.' 'If so,' replied the pirate, 'in pity I must rid myself of him: it would be too great an affliction to him to see you disposed of to another.' Having spoken these words, he took up the unhappy prince, who was bound, and threw him into the sea, notwithstanding all my endeavours to prevent him.

"I shrieked in a dreadful manner at the sight of what he had done, and had certainly cast myself into the sea also, but that the pirate held me. He saw my design, and therefore bound me with cords to the main-mast, then hoisting sail, made toward the land, and got ashore. He unbound me and led me to a little town, where he bought camels, tents, and slaves, and then set out for Grand Cairo, designing, as he still said, to present me to his friend, according to his promise.

"We had been several days upon the road, when, as we were crossing this plain yesterday, we descried the black who inhabited this castle. At a distance we took him for a tower, and when near us, could scarcely believe him to be a man. He drew his huge cimeter, and summoned the pirate to yield himself prisoner, with all his slaves and the lady he was conducting. You know the end of this dreadful adventure and can foresee what would have been my fate had you, generous prince, not come to my deliverance."

As soon as the princess had finished the recital of her adventures, Codadad declared to her that he was deeply concerned at her misfortunes. "But, madam," added he, "it shall be your own fault if you do not live at ease for the future. The sultan of Harran's sons offer you a safe retreat in the court of their father; be pleased to accept of it, and if you do not disdain the affection of your deliverer, permit me to assure you of it, and to espouse you before all these princes; let them be witnesses to our contract." The princess consented, and the marriage was concluded that very day in the castle, where they found all sorts of provisions, with an abundance of delicious wine and other liquors.

They all sat down at table; and after having eaten and drunk plentifully, took with them the rest of the provisions, and set out for the sultan of Harran's court. They travelled several days, encamping in the pleasantest places they could find, and were within one day's journey of Harran, when Codadad, directing his discourse to all his company, said: "Princes, I have too long concealed from you who I am. Behold your brother Codadad! I, as well as you, received my being from the sultan of Harran, the prince of Samaria brought me up, and the Princess Pirouzè is my mother. Madam," added he, addressing himself to the princess of Deryabar, "do you also forgive me for having concealed my birth from you? Perhaps, by discovering it sooner, I might have prevented some disagreeable reflections, which may have been occasioned by a match you may have thought unequal." "No, sir," answered the princess "the opinion I at first conceived of you heightened every moment and you did not stand in need of the extraction you now discover to make me happy."

The princes congratulated Codadad on his birth, and expressed much satisfaction at being made acquainted with it. But in reality, instead of rejoicing, their hatred of so amiable a brother was increased. They met together at night, and forgetting that had it not been for the brave son of Pirouzè they must have been devoured by the black, agreed among themselves to murder him. "We have no other course to choose," said one of them, "for the moment our father shall come to understand that this stranger, of whom he is already so fond, is our brother, he will declare him his heir, and we shall all be obliged to obey and fall down before him." He added much more, which made such an impression on their unnatural minds, that they immediately repaired to Codadad, then asleep, stabbed him repeatedly, and leaving him for dead in the arms of the princess of Deryabar, proceeded on their journey to the city of Harran, where they arrived the next day.

The sultan their father conceived the greater joy at their return, because he had despaired of ever seeing them again: he asked what had been the occasion of their stay. But they took care not to acquaint him with it, making no mention either of the black or of Codadad; and only said, that being curious to see different countries, they had spent some time in the neighbouring cities.

In the meantime Codadad lay in his tent weltering in his blood and little differing from a dead man, with the princess his wife, who seemed to be in not much better condition than himself. She rent the air with her dismal shrieks, tore her hair, and bathing her husband's body with her tears, "Alas! Codadad, my dear Codadad," cried she, "is it you whom I behold just departing this life? Can I believe these are your brothers who have treated you so unmercifully, those brothers whom thy valour had saved? O Heaven! which has condemned me to lead a life of calamities, if you will not permit me to have a consort, why did you permit me to find one? Behold, you have now robbed me of two, just as I began to be attached to them."

By these and other moving expressions the afflicted princess of Deryabar vented her sorrow, fixing her eyes on the unfortunate Codadad, who could not hear her; but he was not dead, and his consort, observing that he still breathed, ran to a large town she espied in the plain, to inquire for a surgeon. She was directed to one, who went immediately with her; but when they came to the tent, they could not find Codadad, which made them conclude he had been dragged away by some wild beast to be devoured. The princess renewed her complaints and lamentations in a most affecting manner. The surgeon was moved, and being unwilling to leave her in so distressed a condition, proposed to her to return to the town, offering her his house and service.

She suffered herself to be prevailed upon. The surgeon conducted her to his house, and without knowing, as yet, who she was, treated her with all imaginable courtesy and respect. He used all his endeavours to comfort her, but it was vain to think of removing her sorrow. "Madam," said he to her one day, "be pleased to recount to me your misfortunes; tell me your country and your condition. Perhaps I may give you some good advice, when I am acquainted with all the circumstances of your calamity."

The surgeon's words were so efficacious, that they wrought on the princess, who recounted to him all her adventures; and when she had done, the surgeon directed his discourse to her: "Madam," said he, "you ought not thus to give way to your sorrow; you ought rather to arm yourself with resolution, and perform what the duty of a wife requires of you. You are bound to avenge your husband. If you please, I will wait on you as your attendant. Let us go to the sultan of Harran's court; he is a good and a just prince. You need only represent to him in lively colours, how Prince Codadad has been treated by his brothers. I am persuaded he will do you justice." "I submit to your reasoning," answered the princess; "it is my duty to endeavour to avenge Codadad; and since you are so generous as to offer to attend me, I am ready to set out." No sooner had she fixed this resolution, than the surgeon ordered two camels to be made ready, on which the princess and he mounted, and repaired to Harran.

They alighted at the first caravanserai they found, and inquired of the host the news at court. "Deryabar," said he, "is in very great perplexity. The sultan had a son, who lived long with him as a stranger, and none can tell what is become of the young prince. One of the sultan's wives, named Pirouzè, is his mother; she has made all possible inquiry, but to no purpose. The sultan has forty-nine other sons, all by different mothers, but not one of them has virtue enough to comfort him for the death of Codadad; I say, his death, because it is impossible he should be still alive, since no intelligence has been heard of him, notwithstanding so much search has been made."

The surgeon, having heard this account from the host, concluded that the best course the princess of Deryabar could take was to wait upon Pirouzè; but that step required much precaution: for it was to be feared that if the sultan of Harran's sons should happen to hear of the arrival of their sister-in-law and her design, they might cause her to be conveyed away before she could discover herself. The surgeon weighed all these circumstances, and therefore, that he might manage matters with discretion, desired the princess to remain in the caravanserai, whilst he repaired to the palace, to observe which might be the safest way to conduct her to Pirouzè.

He went accordingly into the city, and was walking toward the palace, when he beheld a lady mounted on a mule richly accoutred. She was followed by several ladies mounted also on mules, with a great number of guards and black slaves. All the people formed a lane to see her pass along, and saluted her by prostrating themselves on the ground. The surgeon paid her the same respect, and then asked a calendar, who happened to stand by him, whether that lady was one of the sultan's wives. "Yes, brother," answered the calendar, "she is, and the most honoured and beloved by the people, because she is the mother of Prince Codadad, of whom you must have heard."

The surgeon asked no more questions, but followed Pirouzè to a mosque, into which she went to distribute alms, and assist at the public prayers which the sultan had ordered to be offered up for the safe return of Codadad. The surgeon broke through the throng and advanced to Pirouzè's guards. He waited the conclusion of the prayers, and when the princess went out, stepped up to one of her slaves, and whispered him in the ear: "Brother, I have a secret of moment to impart to the Princess Pirouzè: may not I be introduced into her apartment?" "If that secret," answered the slave, "relates to Prince Codadad I dare promise you shall have audience of her; but if it concern not him, it is needless for you to be introduced; for her thoughts are all engrossed by her son." "It is only about that dear son," replied the surgeon, "that I wish to speak to her." "If so," said the slave, "you need but follow us to the palace, and you shall soon have the opportunity."

Accordingly, as soon as Pirouzè was returned to her apartment, the slave acquainted her that a person unknown had some important information to communicate to her, and that it related to Prince Codadad. No sooner had he uttered these words, than Pirouzè expressed her impatience to see the stranger. The slave immediately conducted him into the princess's closet who ordered all her women to withdraw, except two, from whom she concealed nothing. As soon as she saw the surgeon, she asked him eagerly what news he had to tell her of Codadad. "Madam," answered the surgeon, after having prostrated himself on the ground, "I have a long account to give you, and such as will surprise you." He then related all the particulars of what had passed between Codadad and his brothers, which she listened to with eager attention; but when he came to speak of the murder, the tender mother fainted away on her sofa, as if she had herself been stabbed like her son. Her two women soon brought her to herself and the surgeon continued his relation; and when he had concluded, Pirouzè said to him: "Go back to the princess of Deryabar, and assure her from me that the sultan shall soon own her for his daughter-in-law; and as for yourself, your services shall be rewarded as liberally as they deserve."

When the surgeon was gone, Pirouzè remained on the sofa in such a state of affliction as may easily be imagined; and yielding to her tenderness at the recollection of Codadad, "O my son!" said she, "I must never then expect to see you more! Unfortunate Codadad, why did you leave me?" While she uttered these words, she wept bitterly, and her two attendants, moved by her grief, mingled their tears with hers.

Whilst they were all three in this manner vying in affliction, the sultan came into the closet, and seeing them in this condition, asked Pirouzè whether she had received any bad news concerning Codadad. "Alas! sir," said she, "all is over, my son has lost his life, and to add to my sorrow, I cannot pay him the funeral rites; for, in all probability, wild beasts have devoured him." She then told him all she had heard from the surgeon, and did not fail to enlarge on the inhuman manner in which Codadad had been murdered by his brothers.

The sultan did not give Pirouzè time to finish her relation, but transported with anger, and giving way to his passion, "Madam," said he to the princess, "those perfidious wretches who cause you to shed these tears, and are the occasion of mortal grief to their father, shall soon feel the punishment due to their guilt." The sultan, having spoken these words, with indignation in his countenance, went directly to the presence-chamber, where all his courtiers attended, and such of the people as had petitions to present to him. They were alarmed to see him in passion, and thought his anger had been kindled against them. He ascended the throne, and causing his grand vizier to approach, "Hassan," said he, "go immediately, take a thousand of my guards, and seize all the princes, my sons; shut them up in the tower used as a prison for murderers, and let this be done in a moment." All who were present trembled at this extraordinary command; and the grand vizier, without uttering a word, laid his hand on his head, to express his obedience, and hastened from the hall to execute his orders. In the meantime the sultan dismissed those who attended for audience, and declared he would not hear of any business for a month to come. He was still in the hall when the vizier returned. "Are all my sons," demanded he, "in the tower?" "They are, sir," answered the vizier; "I have obeyed your orders." "This is not all," replied the sultan, "I have farther commands for you:" and so saying he went out of the hall of audience, and returned to Pirouzè's apartment, the vizier following him. He asked the princess where Codadad's widow had taken up her lodging. Pirouzè's women told him, for the surgeon had not forgotten that in his relation. The sultan then turning to his minister, "Go," said he, "to this caravanserai, and conduct a young princess who lodges there, with all the respect due to her quality, to my palace."

The vizier was not long in performing what he was ordered. He mounted on horseback with all the emirs and courtiers, and repaired to the caravanserai, where the princess of Deryabar was lodged, whom he acquainted with his orders; and presented her, from the sultan, with a fine white mule, whose saddle and bridle were adorned with gold, rubies, and diamonds. She mounted, and proceeded to the palace. The surgeon attended her, mounted on a beautiful Tartar horse which the vizier had provided for him. All the people were at their windows, or in the streets, to see the cavalcade; and it being given out that the princess, whom they conducted in such state to court, was Codadad's wife, the city resounded with acclamations, the air rung with shouts of joy, which would have been turned into lamentations had that prince's fatal adventure been known, so much was he beloved by all.

The princess of Deryabar found the sultan at the palace gate waiting to receive her: he took her by the hand and led her to Pirouzè's apartment, where a very moving scene took place. Codadad's wife found her affliction redouble at the sight of her husband's father and mother; as, on the other hand, those parents could not look on their son's wife without being much affected. She cast herself at the sultan's feet, and having bathed them with tears, was so overcome with grief that she was not able to speak. Pirouzè was in no better state, and the sultan, moved by these affecting objects, gave way to his own feelings and wept. At length the princess of Deryabar, being somewhat recovered, recounted the adventure of the castle and Codadad's disaster. Then she demanded justice for the treachery of the princes. "Yes, madam," said the sultan, "those ungrateful wretches shall perish; but Codadad's death must be first made public, that the punishment of his brothers may not cause my subjects to rebel; and though we have not my son's body, we will not omit paying him the last duties." This said, he directed his discourse to the vizier, and ordered him to cause to be erected a dome of white marble, in a delightful plain, in the midst of which the city of Harran stands. Then he appointed the princess of Deryabar a suitable apartment in his palace, acknowledging her for his daughter-in-law.

Hassan caused the work to be carried on with such diligence, and employed so many workmen, that the dome was soon finished. Within it was erected a tomb, which was covered with gold brocade. When all was completed, the sultan ordered prayers to be said, and appointed a day for the obsequies of his son.

On that day all the inhabitants of the city went out upon the plain to see the ceremony performed. The gate of the dome was then closed, and all the people returned to the city. Next day there were public prayers in all the mosques, and the same was continued for eight days successively. On the ninth the king resolved to cause the princes his sons to be beheaded. The people, incensed at their cruelty toward Codadad, impatiently expected to see them executed. The scaffolds were erecting, but the execution was respited, because, on a sudden, intelligence was brought that the neighbouring princes who had before made war on the sultan of Harran, were advancing with more numerous forces than on the first invasion, and were then not far from the city. This news gave new cause to lament the loss of Codadad, who had signalised himself in the former war against the same enemies. The sultan, nothing dismayed, formed a considerable army, and being too brave to await the enemies' attack within his walls, marched out to meet them. They, on their side, being informed that the sultan of Harran was marching to engage them, halted in the plain, and formed their army.

As soon as the sultan discovered them, he also drew up his forces, and ranged them in order of battle. The signal was given, and he attacked them with extraordinary vigour; nor was the opposition inferior. Much blood was shed on both sides, and the victory long remained dubious; but at length it seemed to incline to the sultan of Harran's enemies, who, being more numerous, were upon the point of surrounding him, when a great body of cavalry appeared on the plain, and approached the two armies. The sight of this fresh party daunted both sides, neither knowing what to think of them; but their doubts were soon cleared; for they fell upon the flank of the sultan of Harran's enemies with such a furious charge, that they soon broke and routed them. Nor did they stop here; they pursued them, and cut most of them in pieces.

The sultan of Harran, who had attentively observed all that passed, admired the bravery of this strange body of cavalry, whose unexpected arrival had given the victory to his army. But, above all, he was charmed with their chief, whom he had seen fighting with a more than ordinary valour. He longed to know the name of the generous hero. Impatient to see and thank him, he advanced toward him, but perceived he was coming to prevent him. The two princes drew near, and the sultan of Harran, discovering Codadad in the brave warrior who had just defeated his enemies, became motionless with joy and surprise. "Father," said Codadad to him, "you have sufficient cause to be astonished at the sudden appearance of a man whom perhaps you concluded to be dead. I should have been so, had not Heaven preserved me still to serve you against your enemies." "O my son," cried the sultan, "is it possible that you are restored to me? Alas! I despaired of seeing you more." So saying, he stretched out his arms to the young prince, who flew to such a tender embrace.

"I know all, my son," said the sultan again, after having long held him in his arms. "I know what return your brothers have made you for delivering them out of the hands of the black; but you shall be revenged to-morrow. Let us now go to the palace where your mother, who has shed so many tears on your account, expects to rejoice with us on the defeat of our enemies. What a joy will it be to her to be informed that my victory is your work!" "Sir," said Codadad, "give me leave to ask how you could know the adventure of the castle? Have any of my brothers, repenting, owned it to you?" "No," answered the sultan; "the princess of Deryabar has given us an account of everything, for she is in my palace, and came thither to demand justice against your brothers." Codadad was transported with joy, to learn that the princess his wife was at the court. "Let us go, sir," cried he to his father in rapture, "let us go to my mother, who waits for us. I am impatient to dry her tears, as well as those of the princess of Deryabar."

The sultan immediately returned to the city with his army, and re-entered his palace victorious, amidst the acclamations of the people, who followed him in crowds, praying to Heaven to prolong his life, and extolling Codadad to the skies. They found Pirouzè and her daughter-in-law waiting to congratulate the sultan; but words cannot express the transports of joy they felt when they saw the young prince with him: their embraces were mingled with tears of a very different kind from those they had before shed for him. When they had sufficiently yielded to all the emotions that the ties of blood and love inspired, they asked Codadad by what miracle he came to be still alive.

He answered that a peasant mounted on a mule happening accidentally to come into the tent where he lay senseless, and perceiving him alone and stabbed in several places, had made him fast on his mule, and carried him to his house, where he applied to his wounds certain herbs, which recovered him. "When I found myself well," added he, "I returned thanks to the peasant, and gave him all the diamonds I had. I then made for the city of Harran; but being informed by the way that some neighbouring princes had gathered forces, and were on their march against the sultan's subjects, I made myself known to the villagers, and stirred them up to undertake his defence. I armed a great number of young men, and heading them, happened to arrive at the time when the two armies were engaged."

When he had done speaking, the sultan said: "Let us return thanks to God for having preserved Codadad; but it is requisite that the traitors who would have destroyed him should perish." "Sir," answered the generous prince, "though they are wicked and ungrateful, consider they are your own flesh and blood: they are my brothers; I forgive their offence, and beg you to pardon them." This generosity drew tears from the sultan, who caused the people to be assembled, and declared Codadad his heir. He then ordered the princes, who were prisoners, to be brought out loaded with irons. Pirouzè's son struck off their chains, and embraced them all successively with as much sincerity and affection as he had done in the black's castle. The people were charmed with Codadad's generosity, and loaded him with applause. The surgeon was next nobly rewarded in requital of the services he had done the princess of Deryabar and the court of Harran remained thereafter in perfect joy and felicity.

The Story of Sinbad the Voyager

Kate Douglas Wiggin and Nora A. Smith

IN THE REIGN of the Caliph Haroun-al-Raschid, there lived at Bagdad a poor porter called Hindbad. One day, when the weather was excessively hot, he was employed to carry a heavy burden from one end of the town to the other. Having still a great way to go, he came into a street where a refreshing breeze blew on his face, and the pavement was sprinkled with rose water. As he could not desire a better place to rest, he took off his load, and sat upon it, near a large mansion.

He was much pleased that he stopped in this place; for the agreeable smell of wood of aloes, and of pastils, that came from the house, mixing with the scent of the rose-water, completely perfumed the air. Besides, he heard from within a concert of instrumental music, accompanied with the harmonious notes of nightingales. This charming melody, and the smell of savoury dishes, made the porter conclude there was a feast within. His business seldom leading him that way, he knew not to whom the mansion belonged; but to satisfy his curiosity he went to some of the servants, whom he saw standing at the gate in magnificent apparel, and asked the name of the proprietor. "How," replied one of them, "do you live in Bagdad, and know not that this is the house of Sinbad the sailor, that famous voyager, who has sailed round the world?" The porter, who had heard of this Sinbad's riches, lifted up his eyes to Heaven, and said, loud enough to be heard: "Almighty creator of all things, consider the difference between Sinbad and me! I am every day exposed to fatigues and calamities, and can scarcely get barley-bread for myself and my family, whilst happy Sinbad expends immense riches and leads a life of pleasure. What has he done to obtain a lot so agreeable? And what have I done to deserve one so wretched?"

Whilst the porter was thus indulging his melancholy, a servant came out of the house, and taking him by the arm, bade him follow him, for Sinbad, his master, wanted to speak to him.

The servants brought him into a great hall, where a number of people sat round a table, covered with all sorts of savoury dishes. At the upper end sat a venerable gentleman, with a long white beard, and behind him stood a number of officers and domestics, all ready to attend his pleasure. This personage was Sinbad. The porter, whose fear was increased at the sight of so many people, and of a banquet so sumptuous, saluted the company trembling. Sinbad bade him draw near, and seating him at his right hand, served him himself, and gave him a cup of excellent wine.

When the repast was over, Sinbad addressed his conversation to Hindbad, and inquired his name and employment. "My lord," answered he, "my name is Hindbad." "I am very glad to see you," replied Sinbad; "but I wish to hear from your own mouth what it was you lately said in the street." Sinbad had himself heard the porter complain through the window, and this it was that induced him to have him brought in.

At this request, Hindbad hung down his head in confusion, and replied: "My lord, I confess that my fatigue put me out of humour, and occasioned me to utter some indiscreet words, which I beg you to pardon." "Do not think I am so unjust," resumed Sinbad, "as to resent such a complaint, but I must rectify your error concerning myself. You think, no doubt, that I have acquired, without labour and trouble, the ease which I now enjoy. But do not mistake; I did not attain to this happy condition, without enduring for several years more trouble of body and mind than can well be imagined. Yes, gentlemen," he added, speaking to the whole company, "I can assure you my troubles were so extraordinary, that they were calculated to discourage the most covetous from undertaking such voyages as I did, to acquire riches. Perhaps you have never heard a distinct account of my wonderful adventures; and since I have this opportunity, I will give you a faithful account of them, not doubting but it will be acceptable."

The First Voyage

"I INHERITED FROM my father considerable property, the greater part of which I squandered in my youth in dissipation; but I perceived my error, and reflected that riches were perishable, and quickly consumed by such ill managers as myself, I further considered, that by my irregular way of living I wretchedly misspent my time; which is, of all things, the most valuable. Struck with these reflections, I collected the remains of my fortune, and sold all my effects by public auction. I then entered into a contract with some merchants, who traded by sea. I took the advice of such as I thought most capable, and resolving to improve what money I had, I embarked with several merchants on board a ship which we had jointly fitted out.

"We set sail, and steered our course toward the Indies through the Persian Gulf, which is formed by the coasts of Arabia Felix on the right, and by those of Persia on the left. At first I was troubled with sea-sickness, but speedily recovered my health, and was not afterward subject to that complaint.

"In our voyage we touched at several islands, where we sold or exchanged our goods. One day, whilst under sail, we were becalmed near a small island, but little elevated above the level of the water, and resembling a green meadow. The captain ordered his sails to be furled, and permitted such persons as were so inclined to land; of which number I was one.

"But while we were enjoying ourselves in eating and drinking, and recovering ourselves from the fatigue of the sea, the island on a sudden trembled, and shook us terribly.

"The motion was perceived on board the ship, and we were called upon to re-embark speedily, or we should all be lost; for what we took for an island proved to be the back of a sea monster. The nimblest got into the sloop, others betook themselves to swimming; but for myself, I was still upon the back of the creature when he dived into the sea, and I had time only to catch hold of a piece of wood that we had brought out of the ship. Meanwhile, the captain, having received those on board who were in the sloop, and taken up some of those that swam, resolved to improve the favourable gale that had just risen, and hoisting his sails, pursued his voyage, so that it was impossible for me to recover the ship.

"Thus was I exposed to the mercy of the waves all the rest of the day and the following night. By this time I found my strength gone, and despaired of saving my life, when happily a wave threw me against an island. The bank was high and rugged; so that I could scarcely have got up, had it not been for some roots of trees, which chance placed within reach. Having gained the land, I lay down upon the ground half dead, until the sun appeared. Then, though I was very feeble, both from hard labour and want of food, I crept along to find some herbs fit to eat, and had the good luck not only to procure some, but likewise to discover a spring of excellent water, which contributed much to recover me. After this I advanced farther into the island, and at last reached a fine plain, where at a great distance I perceived some horses feeding. I went toward them, and as I approached heard the voice of a man, who immediately appeared, and asked me who I was. I related to him my adventure, after which, taking me by the hand, he led me into a cave, where there were several other people, no less amazed to see me than I was to see them.

"I partook of some provisions which they offered me. I then asked them what they did in such a desert place, to which they answered, that they were grooms belonging to the Maha-raja, sovereign of the island, and that every year, at the same season they brought thither the king's horses for pasturage. They added, that they were to return home on the morrow, and had I been one day later, I must have perished, because the inhabited part of the island was at a great distance, and it would have been impossible for me to have got thither without a guide.

"Next morning they returned to the capital of the island, took me with them, and presented me to the Maha-raja. He asked me who I was, and by what adventure I had come into his dominions. After I had satisfied him, he told me he was much concerned for my misfortune, and at the same time ordered that I should want nothing; which commands his officers were so generous as to see exactly fulfilled.

"Being a merchant, I frequented men of my own profession, and particularly inquired for those who were strangers, that perchance I might hear news from Bagdad, or find an opportunity to return. They put a thousand questions respecting my country; and I, being willing to inform myself as to their laws and customs, asked them concerning everything which I thought worth knowing.

"There belongs to this king an island named Cassel. They assured me that every night a noise of drums was heard there, whence the mariners fancied that it was the residence of Degial. I determined to visit this wonderful place, and in my way thither saw fishes of one hundred and two hundred cubits long, that occasion more fear than hurt, for they are so timorous, that they will fly upon the rattling of two sticks or boards. I saw likewise other fish about a cubit in length, that had heads like owls.

"As I was one day at the port after my return, a ship arrived, and as soon as she cast anchor, they began to unload her, and the merchants on board ordered their goods to be carried into the custom-house. As I cast my eye upon some bales, and looked to the name, I found my own, and perceived the bales to be the same that I had embarked at Bussorah. I also knew the captain; but being persuaded that he believed me to be drowned, I went, and asked him whose bales these were. He replied that they belonged to a merchant of Bagdad, called Sinbad, who came to sea with him; but had unfortunately perished on the voyage, and that he had resolved to trade with the bales, until he met with some of his family, to whom he might return the profit. 'I am that Sinbad,' said I, 'whom you thought to be dead, and those bales are mine.'

"When the captain heard me speak thus, 'Heavens!' he exclaimed, 'whom can we trust in these times? There is no faith left among men. I saw Sinbad perish with my own eyes, as did also the passengers on board, and yet you tell me you are that Sinbad. What impudence is this? You tell a horrible falsehood, in order to possess yourself of what does not belong to you.' 'Have patience,' replied I; 'do me the favour to hear what I have to say.' Then I told him how I had escaped, and by what adventure I met with the grooms of the Maha-raja, who had brought me to his court.

"The captain was at length persuaded that I was no cheat; for there came people from his ship who knew me, and expressed much joy at seeing me alive. At last he recollected me himself, and embracing me, 'Heaven be praised,' said he, 'for your happy escape. I cannot express the joy it affords me; there are your goods, take and do with them as you please.' I thanked him, acknowledged his probity, and offered him part of my goods as a present, which he generously refused.

"I took out what was most valuable in my bales, and presented them to the Maha-raja, who, knowing my misfortune, asked me how I came by such rarities. I acquainted him with the circumstance of their recovery. He was pleased at my good luck, accepted my present, and in return gave me one much more considerable. Upon this, I took leave of him, and went aboard the same ship, after I had exchanged my goods for the commodities of that country. I carried with me wood of aloes, sandal, camphire, nutmegs, cloves, pepper, and ginger. We passed by several islands, and at last arrived at Bussorah, from whence I came to this city, with the value of one hundred thousand sequins. My family and I received one another with sincere affection. I bought slaves and a landed estate, and built a magnificent house. Thus I settled myself, resolving to forget the miseries I had suffered, and to enjoy the pleasures of life."

Sinbad stopped here, and ordered the musicians to proceed with their concert, which the story had interrupted. The company continued enjoying themselves till the evening, when Sinbad sent for a purse of a hundred sequins, and giving it to the porter, said: "Take this, Hindbad, return to your home, and come back to-morrow to hear more of my adventures." The porter went away, astonished at the honour done, and the present made him. The account of this adventure proved very agreeable to his wife and children, who did not fail to return thanks to God for what providence had sent them by the hand of Sinbad.

Hindbad put on his best apparel next day, and returned to the bountiful traveller, who welcomed him heartily. When all the guests had arrived, dinner was served. When it was ended, Sinbad, addressing himself to the company, said, "Gentlemen, be pleased to listen to the adventures of my second voyage; they deserve your attention even more than those of the first." Upon this every one held his peace, and Sinbad proceeded.

The Second Voyage

"I DESIGNED, after my first voyage, to spend the rest of my days at Bagdad, but it was not long ere I grew weary of an indolent life. My inclination to trade revived. I bought goods proper for the commerce I intended, and put to sea a second time with merchants of known probity. We embarked on board a good ship, and after recommending ourselves to God, set sail. We traded from island to island, and exchanged commodities with great profit. One day we landed on an island covered with several sorts of fruit-trees, but we could see neither man nor animal. We went to take a little fresh air in the meadows, along the streams that watered them. Whilst some diverted themselves with gathering flowers, and others fruits, I took my wine and provisions, and sat down near a stream betwixt two high trees which formed a thick shade. I made a good meal, and afterward fell asleep. I cannot tell how long I slept, but when I awoke the ship was gone.

"I got up and looked around me, but could not see one of the merchants who landed with me. I perceived the ship under sail, but at such a distance, that I lost sight of her in a short time.

"In this sad condition, I was ready to die with grief. I cried out in agony, and threw myself upon the ground, where I lay some time in despair. I upbraided myself a hundred times for not being content with the produce of my first voyage, that might have sufficed me all my life. But all this was in vain, and my repentance came too late.

"At last I resigned myself to the will of God. Not knowing what to do, I climbed up to the top of a lofty tree, from whence I looked about on all sides, to see if I could discover anything that could give me hopes. When I gazed toward the sea I could see nothing but sky and water; but looking over the land I beheld something white; and coming down, I took what provision I had left, and went toward it, the distance being so great that I could not distinguish what it was.

"As I approached, I thought it to be a white dome, of a prodigious height and extent; and when I came up to it, I touched it, and found it to be very smooth. I went round to see if it was open on any side, but saw that it was not, and that there was no climbing up to the top, as it was so smooth. It was at least fifty paces round.

"By this time the sun was about to set, and all of a sudden the sky became as dark as if it had been covered with a thick cloud. I was much astonished at this sudden darkness, but much more when I found it occasioned by a bird of a monstrous size, that came flying toward me. I remembered that I had often heard mariners speak of a miraculous bird called the roc, and conceived that the great dome which I so much admired must be its egg. As I perceived the roc coming, I crept close to the egg, so that I had before me one of the bird's legs, which was as big as the trunk of a tree. I tied myself strongly to it with my turban, in hopes that next morning she would carry me with her out of this desert island. After having passed the night in this condition, the bird flew away as soon as it was daylight, and carried me so high, that I could not discern the earth; she afterward descended with so much rapidity that I lost my senses. But when I found myself on the ground, I speedily untied the knot, and had scarcely done so, when the roc, having taken up a serpent of a monstrous length in her bill, flew away.

"The spot where she left me was encompassed on all sides by mountains, that seemed to reach above the clouds, and so steep that there was no possibility of getting out of the valley. This was a new perplexity: so that when I compared this place with the desert island from which the roc had brought me I found that I had gained nothing by the change.

"As I walked through this valley, I perceived it was strewed with diamonds, some of which were of a surprising bigness. I took pleasure in looking upon them; but shortly saw at a distance such objects as greatly diminished my satisfaction, namely, a great number of serpents, so monstrous, that the least of them was capable of swallowing an elephant. They retired in the daytime to their dens, where they hid themselves from the roc, their enemy, and came out only in the night.

"I spent the day in walking about in the valley, resting myself at times in such places as I thought most convenient. When night came on, I went into a cave, where I thought I might repose in safety. I secured the entrance with a great stone to preserve me from the serpents; but not so far as to exclude the light. I supped on part of my provisions, but the serpents, which began hissing round me, put me into such extreme fear, that I could not sleep. When day appeared, the serpents retired, and I came out of the cave trembling. I can justly say, that I walked upon diamonds, without feeling any inclination to touch them. At last I sat down, and notwithstanding my apprehensions, not having closed my eyes during the night, fell asleep, after having eaten a little more of my provision. But I had scarcely shut my eyes, when something that fell by me with a great noise awaked me. This was a large piece of raw meat; and at the same time I saw several others fall down from the rocks in different places.

"I had always regarded as fabulous what I had heard sailors and others relate of the valley of diamonds, and of the stratagems employed by merchants to obtain jewels from thence; but now I found that they had stated nothing but truth. For the fact is, that the merchants come to the neighbourhood of this valley when the eagles have young ones; and, throwing great joints of meat into the valley, the diamonds upon whose points they fall stick to them; the eagles, which are stronger in this country than anywhere else, pounce with great force upon those pieces of meat, and carry them to their nests on the rocks to feed their young; the merchants at this time run to the nests, drive off the eagles by their shouts, and take away the diamonds that stick to the meat.

"Until I perceived the device I had concluded it to be impossible for me to leave this abyss, which I regarded as my grave; but now I changed my opinion, and began to think upon the means of my deliverance. I began to collect the largest diamonds I could find, and put them into the leather bag in which I used to carry my provisions. I afterward took the largest of the pieces of meat, tied it close round me with the cloth of my turban, and then laid myself upon the ground with my face downward, the bag of diamonds being made fast to my girdle.

"I had scarcely placed myself in this posture when the eagles came. Each of them seized a piece of meat, and one of the strongest having taken me up, with the piece of meat to which I was fastened, carried me to his nest on the top of the mountain. The merchants immediately began their shouting to frighten the eagles; and when they had obliged them to quit their prey, one of them came to the nest where I was. He was much alarmed when he saw me; but recovering himself, instead of inquiring how I came thither, began to quarrel with me, and asked, why I stole his goods. 'You will treat me,' replied I, 'with more civility when you know me better. Do not be uneasy, I have diamonds enough for you and myself, more than all the other merchants together. What ever they have, they owe to chance, but I selected for myself in the bottom of the valley those which you see in this bag.' I had scarcely done speaking, when the other merchants came crowding about us, much astonished to see me; but they were much more surprised when I told them my story.

"They conducted me to their encampment, and there having opened my bag, they were surprised at the largeness of my diamonds, and confessed that in all the courts which they had visited they had never seen any of such size and perfection. I prayed the merchant who owned the nest to which I had been carried (for every merchant had his own), to take as many for his share as he pleased. He contented himself with one, and that the least of them; and when I pressed him to take more, 'No,' said he, 'I am very well satisfied with this, which is valuable enough to save me the trouble of making any more voyages, and will raise as great a fortune as I desire.'

"I spent the night with the merchants, to whom I related my story a second time, for the satisfaction of those who had not heard it. I could not moderate my joy when I found myself delivered from the danger I have mentioned. I thought myself in a dream, and could scarcely believe myself out of danger.

"The merchants had thrown their pieces of meat into the valley for several days, and each of them being satisfied with the diamonds that had fallen to his lot, we left the place the next morning and travelled near high mountains, where there were serpents of a prodigious length, which we had the good fortune to escape. We took shipping at the first port we reached, and touched at the isle of Roha, where the trees grow that yield camphire. This tree is so large, and its branches so thick, that one hundred men may easily sit under its shade. The juice of which the camphire is made exudes from a hole bored in the upper part of the tree, is received in a vessel, where it thickens to a consistency, and becomes what we call camphire; after the juice is thus drawn out, the tree withers and dies.

"In this island is also found the rhinoceros, an animal less than the elephant, but larger than the buffalo. It has a horn upon its nose, about a cubit in length; this horn is solid, and cleft through the middle. The rhinoceros fights with the elephant, runs his horn into his belly, and carries him off upon his head; but the blood and the fat of the elephant running into his eyes, and making him blind, he falls to the ground; and then, strange to relate! the roc comes and carries them both away in her claws, for food for her young ones.

"In this island I exchanged some of my diamonds for merchandise. From hence we went to other ports, and at last, having touched at several trading towns of the continent, we landed at Bussorah, from whence I proceeded to Bagdad. There I immediately gave large presents to the poor, and lived honourably upon the vast riches I had gained with so much fatigue."

Thus Sinbad ended his relation, gave Hindbad another hundred sequins, and invited him to come the next day to hear the account of the third voyage.

The Third Voyage

"I SOON LOST the remembrance of the perils I had encountered in my two former voyages," said Sinbad, "and being in the flower of my age, I grew weary of living without business, and went from Bagdad to Bussorah with the richest commodities of the country. There I embarked again with some merchants. We made a long voyage and touched at several ports, where we carried on a considerable trade. One day, being out in the main ocean, we were overtaken by a dreadful tempest, which drove us from our course. The tempest continued several days, and brought us before the port of an island, which the captain was very unwilling to enter, but we were obliged to cast anchor. When we had furled our sails, the captain told us that this, and some other neighbouring islands, were inhabited by hairy savages, who would speedily attack us; and, though they were but dwarfs, yet we must make no resistance, for they were more in number than the locusts; and if we happened to kill one of them they would all fall upon us and destroy us.

"We soon found that what he had told us was but too true; an innumerable multitude of frightful savages, about two feet high, covered all over with red hair, came swimming towards us, and encompassed our ship. They spoke to us as they came near, but we understood not their language and they climbed up the sides of the ship with such agility as surprised us. They took down our sails, cut the cables, and hauling to the shore, made us all get out, and afterward carried the ship into another island, from whence they had come.

"We went forward into the island, where we gathered some fruits and herbs to prolong our lives as long as we could; but we expected nothing but death. As we advanced, we perceived at a distance a vast pile of buildings, and made toward it. We found it to be a palace, elegantly built, and very lofty, with a gate of ebony, which we forced open. We entered the court, where we saw before us a large apartment, with a porch, having on one side a heap of human bones, and on the other a vast number of roasting spits. We trembled at this spectacle, and being fatigued with travelling, fell to the ground, seized with deadly apprehension, and lay a long time motionless.

"The sun set, the gate of the apartment opened with a loud crash, and there came out the horrible figure of a black man, as tall as a lofty palm-tree. He had but one eye, and that in the middle of his forehead, where it looked as red as a burning coal. His fore-teeth were very long and sharp, and stood out of his mouth, which was as deep as that of a horse. His upper lip hung down upon his breast. His ears resembled those of an elephant, and covered his shoulders; and his nails were as long and crooked as the talons of the greatest birds. At the sight of so frightful a giant we became insensible, and lay like dead men.

"At last we came to ourselves, and saw him sitting in the porch looking at us. When he had considered us well, he advanced toward us, and laying his hand upon me, took me up by the nape of my neck, and turned me round as a butcher would do a sheep's head. After having examined me, and perceiving me to be so lean that I had nothing but skin and bone, he let me go. He took up all the rest one by one, and viewed them in the same manner. The captain being the fattest, he held him with one hand, as I would do a sparrow, and thrust a spit through him; he then kindled a great fire, roasted, and ate him in his apartment for his supper. Having finished his repast, he returned to his porch, where he lay and fell asleep, snoring louder than thunder. He slept thus till morning. As to ourselves, it was not possible for us to enjoy any rest, so that we passed the night in the most painful apprehension that can be imagined. When day appeared the giant awoke, got up, went out, and left us in the palace.

"When we thought him at a distance, we broke the melancholy silence we had preserved the whole of the night, and filled the palace with our lamentations and groans.

"We spent the day in traversing the island, supporting ourselves with fruits and herbs as we had done the day before. In the evening we sought for some place of shelter, but found none; so that we were forced, whether we would or not, to go back to the palace.

"The giant failed not to return, and supped once more upon one of our companions, after which he slept and snored till day, and then went out and left us as before. Our situation appeared to us so dreadful that several of my comrades designed to throw themselves into the sea, rather than die so painful a death, upon which one of the company answered that it would be much more reasonable to devise some method to rid ourselves of the monster.

"Having thought of a project for this purpose, I communicated it to my comrades, who approved it. 'Brethren,' said I, 'you know there is much timber floating upon the coast; if you will be advised by me, let us make several rafts capable of bearing us. In the meantime, we will carry out the design I proposed to you for our deliverance from the giant, and if it succeed, we may remain here patiently awaiting the arrival of some ship; but if it happen to miscarry, we will take to our rafts and put to sea.' My advice was approved, and we made rafts capable of carrying three persons on each.

"We returned to the palace toward the evening, and the giant arrived shortly after. We were forced to submit to seeing another of our comrades roasted, but at last we revenged ourselves on the brutish giant in the following manner. After he had finished his supper he lay down on his back and fell asleep. As soon as we heard him snore, according to his custom, nine of the boldest among us, and myself, took each of us a spit, and putting the points of them into the fire till they were burning hot, we thrust them into his eye all at once and blinded him. The pain made him break out into a frightful yell: he started up, and stretched out his hands, in order to sacrifice some of us to his rage: but we ran to such places as he could not reach; and after having sought for us in vain, he groped for the gate and went out, howling in agony.

"We quitted the palace after the giant and came to the shore, where we had left our rafts, and put them immediately to sea. We waited till day, in order to get upon them in case the giant should come toward us with any guide of his own species; but we hoped if he did not appear by sunrise, and gave over his howling, which we still heard, that he would prove to be dead; and if that happened, we resolved to stay in that island, and not to risk our lives upon the rafts. But day had scarcely appeared when we perceived our cruel enemy, accompanied with two others almost of the same size, leading him; and a great number more coming before him at a quick pace.

"We did not hesitate to take to our rafts, and put to sea with all the speed we could. The giants, who perceived this, took up great stones, and running to the shore, entered the water up to the middle, and threw so exactly that they sunk all the rafts but that I was upon; and all my companions, except the two with me, were drowned. We rowed with all our might, and escaped the giants, but when we got out to sea we were exposed to the mercy of the waves and winds, and spent that night and the following day under the most painful uncertainty as to our fate; but next morning we had the good fortune to be thrown upon an island, where we landed with much joy. We found excellent fruit, which afforded us great relief and recruited our strength.

"At night we went to sleep on the sea shore; but were awakened by the noise of a serpent of surprising length and thickness, whose scales made a rustling noise as he wound himself along. It swallowed up one of my comrades, notwithstanding his loud cries, and the efforts he made to extricate himself from it; dashing him several times against the ground, it crushed him, and we could hear it gnaw and tear the poor wretch's bones, though we had fled to a considerable distance.

"As we walked about, when day returned, we saw a tall tree, upon which we designed to pass the following night, for our security; and having satisfied our hunger with fruit, we mounted it before the dusk had fallen. Shortly after, the serpent came hissing to the foot of the tree; raised itself up against the trunk of it, and meeting with my comrade, who sat lower than I, swallowed him at once, and went off.

"I remained upon the tree till it was day, and then came down, more like a dead man than one alive, expecting the same fate as my two companions. This filled me with horror, and I advanced some steps to throw myself into the sea; but I withstood this dictate of despair, and submitted myself to the will of God.

"In the meantime I collected a great quantity of small wood, brambles, and dry thorns, and making them up into faggots, made a wide circle with them round the tree, and also tied some of them to the branches over my head. Having done this, when the evening came I shut myself up within this circle, feeling that I had neglected nothing which could preserve me from the cruel destiny with which I was threatened. The serpent failed not to come at the usual hour, and went round the tree, seeking for an opportunity to devour me, but was prevented by the rampart I had made; so that he lay till day, like a cat watching in vain for a mouse that has fortunately reached a place of safety. When day appeared he retired, but I dared not to leave my fort until the sun arose.

"I felt so much fatigued by the labour to which it had put me, and suffered so much from the serpent's poisonous breath, that death seemed more eligible to me than the horrors of such a state. I came down from the tree, and was going to throw myself into the sea, when God took compassion on me and I perceived a ship at a considerable distance. I called as loud as I could, and taking the linen from my turban, displayed it, that they might observe me. This had the desired effect; the crew perceived me, and the captain sent his boat for me. As soon as I came on board, the merchants and seamen flocked about me, to know how I came into that desert island; and after I had related to them all that had befallen me, the oldest among them said that they had often heard of the giants that dwelt in that island, that they were cannibals; and as to the serpents, they added, that there were abundance of them that hid themselves by day, and came abroad by night. After having testified their joy at my escaping so many dangers, they brought me the best of their provisions; and the captain, seeing that I was in rags, was so generous as to give me one of his own suits. We continued at sea for some time, touched at several islands, and at last landed at that of Salabat, where sandal wood is obtained, which is of great use in medicine. We entered the port, and came to anchor. The merchants began to unload their goods, in order to sell or exchange them. In the meantime, the captain came to me and said: 'Brother, I have here some goods that belonged to a merchant, who sailed some time on board this ship, and he being dead, I design to dispose of them for the benefit of his heirs.' The bales he spoke of lay on the deck, and showing them to me, he said: 'There are the goods; I hope you will take care to sell them, and you shall have factorage.' I thanked him for thus affording me an opportunity of employing myself, because I hated to be idle.

"The clerk of the ship took an account of all the bales, with the names of the merchants to whom they belonged, and when he asked the captain in whose name he should enter those he had given me the charge of, 'Enter them,' said the captain, 'in the name of Sinbad.' I could not hear myself named without some emotion; and looking steadfastly on the captain, I knew him to be the person who, in my second voyage, had left me in the island where I fell asleep.

"I was not surprised that he, believing me to be dead, did not recognise me. 'Captain,' said I, 'was the merchant's name, to whom those bales belonged, Sinbad?' 'Yes,' replied he, 'that was his name; he came from Bagdad, and embarked on board my ship at Bussorah.' 'You believe him, then, to be dead?' said I. 'Certainly,' answered he. 'No, captain,' resumed I; 'look at me, and you may know that I am Sinbad.'

"The captain, having considered me attentively, recognised me. 'God be praised,' said he, embracing me, 'I rejoice that fortune has rectified my fault. There are your goods, which I always took care to preserve.' I took them from him, and made him the acknowledgments to which he was entitled.

"From the isle of Salabat, we went to another, where I furnished myself with cloves, cinnamon, and other spices. As we sailed from this island, we saw a tortoise twenty cubits in length and breadth. We observed also an amphibious animal like a cow, which gave milk; its skin is so hard, that they usually make bucklers of it.

"In short, after a long voyage I arrived at Bussorah, and from thence returned to Bagdad, with so much wealth that I knew not its extent. I gave a great deal to the poor, and bought another considerable estate in addition to what I had already."

Thus Sinbad finished the history of his third voyage; gave another hundred sequins to Hindbad, and invited him to dinner again the next day to hear the story of his fourth series of adventures.

The Fourth Voyage

"**THE PLEASURES** which I enjoyed after my third voyage had not charms sufficient to divert me from another. My passion for trade, and my love of novelty, again prevailed. I therefore settled my affairs, and having provided a stock of goods fit for the traffic I designed to engage in, I set out on my journey. I took the route of Persia, travelled over several provinces, and then arrived at a port, where I embarked. We hoisted our sails, and touched at several ports of the continent, and then put out to sea; when we were overtaken by such a sudden gust of wind, as obliged the captain to lower his yards, and take all other necessary precautions to prevent the danger that threatened us. But all was in vain; our endeavours had no effect, the sails were split in a thousand pieces, and the ship was stranded; several of the merchants and seamen were drowned, and the cargo was lost.

"I had the good fortune, with several of the merchants and mariners, to get upon some planks, and we were carried by the current to an island which lay before us. There we found fruit and spring water, which preserved our lives. We stayed all night near the place where we had been cast ashore and next morning, as soon as the sun was up, advancing into the island, saw some houses, which we approached. As soon as we drew near, we were encompassed by a great number of negroes, who seized us and carried us to their respective habitations.

"I, and five of my comrades, were carried to one place; here they made us sit down, and gave us a certain herb, which they made signs to us to eat. My comrades, not taking notice that the blacks ate none of it themselves, thought only of satisfying their hunger, and ate with greediness. But I, suspecting some trick, would not so much as taste it, which happened well for me; for in a little time after, I perceived my companions had lost their senses, and that when they spoke to me, they knew not what they said.

"The negroes fed us afterward with rice, prepared with oil of cocoa-nuts; and my comrades, who had lost their reason, ate of it greedily. I also partook of it, but very sparingly. They gave us that herb at first on purpose to deprive us of our senses, that we might not be aware of the sad destiny prepared for us; and they supplied us with rice to fatten us; for, being cannibals, their design was to eat us as soon as we grew fat. This accordingly happened, for they devoured my comrades, who were not sensible of their condition; but my senses being entire, you may easily guess that instead of growing fat I grew leaner every day. The fear of death under which I laboured caused me to fall into a languishing distemper, which proved my safety; for the negroes, having eaten my companions, seeing me to be withered, and sick, deferred my death.

"Meanwhile I had much liberty, so that scarcely any notice was taken of what I did, and this gave me an opportunity one day to get at a distance from the houses and to make my escape. An old man, who saw me and suspected my design, called to me as loud as he could to return; but I redoubled my speed, and quickly got out of sight. At that time there was none but the old man about the houses, the rest being abroad, and not to return till night, which was usual with them. Therefore, being sure that they could not arrive in time enough to pursue me, I went on till night, when I stopped to rest a little, and to eat some of the provisions I had secured; but I speedily set forward again, and travelled seven days, avoiding those places which seemed to be inhabited, and lived for the most part upon cocoa-nuts, which served me both for meat and drink. On the eighth day I came near the sea, and saw some white people like myself, gathering pepper, of which there was great plenty in that place. This I took to be a good omen, and went to them without any scruple. They came to meet me as soon as they saw me, and asked me in Arabic who I was, and whence I came. I was overjoyed to hear them speak in my own language, and satisfied their curiosity by giving them an account of my shipwreck, and how I fell into the hands of the negroes. 'Those negroes,' replied they, 'eat men, and by what miracle did you escape their cruelty?' I related to them the circumstances I have just mentioned, at which they were wonderfully surprised.

"I stayed with them till they had gathered their quantity of pepper, and then sailed with them to the island from whence they had come. They presented me to their king, who was a good prince. He had the patience to hear the relation of my adventures; and he afterward gave me clothes, and commanded care to be taken of me.

"The island was very well peopled, plentiful in everything, and the capital a place of great trade. This agreeable retreat was very comfortable to me, after my misfortunes, and the kindness of this generous prince completed my satisfaction. In a word, there was not a person more in favour with him than myself; and consequently every man in court and city sought to oblige me; so that in a very little time I was looked upon rather as a native than a stranger.

"I observed one thing which to me appeared very extraordinary. All the people, the king himself not excepted, rode their horses without bridle or stirrups. This made me one day take the liberty to ask the king how it came to pass. His Majesty answered, that I talked to him of things which nobody knew the use of in his dominions.

"I went immediately to a workman, and gave him a model for making the stock of a saddle. When that was done, I covered it myself with velvet and leather, and embroidered it with gold. I afterward went to a smith, who made me a bit, according to the pattern I showed him, and also some stirrups. When I had all things completed, I presented them to the king, and put them upon one of his horses. His Majesty mounted immediately, and was so pleased with them, that he testified his satisfaction by large presents.

"As I paid my court very constantly to the king, he said to me one day: 'Sinbad, I love thee and I have one thing to demand of thee, which thou must grant.' 'Sir,' answered I, 'there is nothing but I will do, as a mark of my obedience to your Majesty.' 'I have a mind thou shouldst marry,' replied he, 'that so thou mayest stay in my dominions, and think no more of thy own country.' I durst not resist the prince's will, and he gave me one of the ladies of his court, noble, beautiful, and rich. The ceremonies of marriage being over, I went and dwelt with my wife, and for some time we lived together in perfect harmony. I was not, however, satisfied with my banishment, therefore designed to make my escape the first opportunity, and to return to Bagdad.

"At this time the wife of one of my neighbours fell sick, and died. I went to see and comfort him in his affliction, and finding him absorbed in sorrow, I said to him as soon as I saw him: 'God preserve you and grant you a long life.' 'Alas!' replied he, 'how do you think I should obtain the favour you wish me? I have not above an hour to live.' 'Pray,' said I, 'do not entertain such a melancholy thought; I hope I shall enjoy your company many years.' 'I wish you,' he replied, 'a long life; but my days are at an end, for I must be buried this day with my wife. This is a law which our ancestors established in this island, and it is always observed. The living husband is interred with the dead wife, and the living wife with the dead husband. Nothing can save me; every one must submit to this law.'

"While he was giving me an account of this barbarous custom, the very relation of which chilled my blood, his kindred, friends, and neighbours came in a body to assist at the funeral. They dressed the corpse of the woman in her richest apparel, and all her jewels, as if it had been her wedding day; then they placed her in an open coffin, and began their march to the place of burial, the husband walking at the head of the company. They proceeded to a high mountain, and when they had reached the place of their destination, they took up a large stone, which covered the mouth of a deep pit, and let down the corpse with all its apparel and jewels. Then the husband embracing his kindred and friends, suffered himself, without resistance, to be put into another open coffin with a pot of water, and seven small loaves, and was let down in the same manner. The ceremony being over, the aperture was again covered with the stone, and the company returned.

"It is needless for me to tell you that I was a melancholy spectator of this funeral, while the rest were scarcely moved, the custom was to them so familiar. I could not forbear communicating to the king my sentiment respecting the practice: 'Sir,' I said, 'I cannot but feel astonished at the strange usage observed in this country, of burying the living with the dead. I have been a great traveller, and seen many countries, but never heard of so cruel a law.' 'What do you mean, Sinbad?' replied the king: 'it is a common law. I shall be interred with the queen, my wife, if she die first.' 'But, sir,' said I, 'may I presume to ask your Majesty, if strangers be obliged to observe this law?' 'Without doubt,' returned the king; 'they are not exempted, if they be married in this island.'

"I returned home much depressed by this answer; for the fear of my wife's dying first and that I should be interred alive with her, occasioned me very uneasy reflections. But there was no remedy; I must have patience, and submit to the will of God. I trembled, however, at every little indisposition of my wife, and, alas! in a little time my fears were realised, for she fell sick and died.

"The king and all his court expressed their wish to honour the funeral with their presence, and the most considerable people of the city did the same. When all was ready for the ceremony, the corpse was put into a coffin with all her jewels and her most magnificent apparel. The procession began, and as second actor in this doleful tragedy, I went next the corpse, with my eyes full of tears, bewailing my deplorable fate. Before we reached the mountain, I made an attempt to affect the minds of the spectators: I addressed myself to the king first, and then to all those that were round me; bowing before them to the earth, and kissing the border of their garments, I prayed them to have compassion upon me. 'Consider,' said I, 'that I am a stranger, and ought not to be subject to this rigorous law, and that I have another wife and children in my own country.' Although I spoke in the most pathetic manner, no one was moved by my address; on the contrary, they ridiculed my dread of death as cowardly, made haste to let my wife's corpse into the pit, and lowered me down the next moment in an open coffin with a vessel full of water and seven loaves.

"As I approached the bottom, I discovered by the aid of the little light that came from above the nature of this subterranean place; it seemed an endless cavern, and might be about fifty fathoms deep.

"Instead of losing my courage and calling death to my assistance in that miserable condition, however, I felt still an inclination to live, and to do all I could to prolong my days. I went groping about, for the bread and water that was in my coffin, and took some of it. Though the darkness of the cave was so great that I could not distinguish day and night, yet I always found my coffin again, and the cave seemed to be more spacious than it had appeared to be at first. I lived for some days upon my bread and water, which being all spent, I at last prepared for death.

"I was offering up my last devotions when I heard something tread, and breathing or panting as it walked. I advanced toward that side from whence I heard the noise, and on my approach the creature puffed and blew harder, as if running away from me. I followed the noise, and the thing seemed to stop sometimes, but always fled and blew as I approached. I pursued it for a considerable time, till at last I perceived a light, resembling a star; I went on, sometimes lost sight of it, but always found it again, and at last discovered that it came through a hole in the rock, large enough to admit a man.

"Upon this, I stopped some time to rest, being much fatigued with the rapidity of my progress: afterward coming up to the hole, I got through, and found myself upon the seashore. I leave you to guess the excess of my joy: it was such that I could scarcely persuade myself that the whole was not a dream.

"But when I was recovered from my surprise, and convinced of the reality of my escape, I perceived what I had followed to be a creature which came out of the sea, and was accustomed to enter the cavern when the tides were high.

"I examined the mountain, and found it to be situated betwixt the sea and the town, but without any passage to or communication with the latter; the rocks on the sea side being high and perpendicularly steep. I prostrated myself on the shore to thank God for this mercy, and afterward entered the cave again to fetch bread and water, which I ate by daylight with a better appetite than I had done since my interment in the dark cavern.

"I returned thither a second time, and groped among the coffins for all the diamonds, rubies, pearls, gold bracelets, and rich stuffs I could find; these I brought to the shore, and tying them up neatly into bales, I laid them together upon the beach, waiting till some ship might appear.

"After two or three days, I perceived a ship just come out of the harbour, making for the place where I was. I made a sign with the linen of my turban, and called to the crew as loud as I could. They heard me, and sent a boat to bring me on board, when they asked by what misfortune I came thither; I told them that I had suffered shipwreck two days before, and made shift to get ashore with the goods they saw. It was fortunate for me that these people did not consider the place where I was, nor inquire into the probability of what I told them; but without hesitation took me on board. When I came to the ship, the captain was so well pleased to have saved me, and so much taken up with his own affairs, that he also took the story of my pretended shipwreck upon trust, and generously refused some jewels which I offered him.

"We passed by several islands, and among others that called the isle of Bells, about ten days' sail from Serendib, and six from that of Kela, where we landed. This island produces lead mines, Indian canes, and excellent camphire.

"The King of the isle of Kela is very rich and powerful, and the isle of Bells, which is about two days' journey in extent, is also subject to him. The inhabitants are so barbarous that they still eat human flesh. After we had finished our traffic in that island, we put to sea again, and touched at several other ports; at last I arrived happily at Bagdad with infinite riches. Out of gratitude to God for His mercies, I contributed liberally toward the support of several mosques, and the subsistence of the poor, and gave myself up to the society of my kindred and friends, enjoying myself with them in festivities and amusements."

Here Sinbad finished the relation of his fourth voyage. He made a new present of one hundred sequins to Hindbad, whom he requested to return with the rest next day at the same hour to dine with him, and hear the story of his fifth voyage. Hindbad and the other guests took their leave and retired. Next morning when they all met, they sat down at table, and when dinner was over, Sinbad began the relation of his fifth voyage as follows:

The Fifth Voyage

"ALL THE TROUBLES and calamities I had undergone," said he, "could not cure me of my inclination to make new voyages. I therefore bought goods, departed with them for the best seaport; and that I might not be obliged to depend upon a captain, but have a ship at my own command, I remained there till one was built on purpose. When the ship was ready, I went on board with my goods: but not having enough to load her, I agreed to take with me several merchants of different nations with their merchandise.

"We sailed with the first fair wind, and after a long navigation, the first place we touched at was a desert island, where we found an egg of a roc, equal in size to that I formerly mentioned. There was a young roc in it just ready to be hatched, and its bill had begun to appear. The merchants whom I had taken on board, and who landed with me, broke the egg with hatchets, pulled out the young roc, piecemeal, and roasted it. I had earnestly entreated them not to meddle with the egg, but they would not listen to me.

"Scarcely had they finished their repast, when there appeared in the air at a considerable distance from us two great clouds. The captain whom I had hired to navigate my ship, said they were the male and female roc that belonged to the young one and pressed us to re-embark with all speed, to prevent the misfortune which he saw would otherwise befall us. We hastened on board, and set sail with all possible expedition.

"In the meantime, the two rocs approached with a frightful noise, which they redoubled when they saw the egg broken, and their young one gone. They flew back in the direction they had come, and disappeared for some time, while we made all the sail we could to endeavour to prevent that which unhappily befell us.

"They soon returned, and we observed that each of them carried between its talons rocks of a monstrous size. When they came directly over my ship, they hovered, and one of them let fall a stone, but by the dexterity of the steersman it missed us. The other roc, to our misfortune, threw his burden so exactly upon the middle of the ship, as to split it into a thousand pieces. The mariners and passengers were all crushed to death, or sank. I myself was of the number of the latter; but as I came up again, I fortunately caught hold of a piece of the wreck, and swimming sometimes with one hand, and sometimes with the other, I came to an island, and got safely ashore.

"I sat down upon the grass, to recover myself from my fatigue, after which I went into the island to explore it. I found trees everywhere, some of them bearing green, and others ripe fruits, and streams of fresh pure water. I ate of the fruits, which I found excellent; and drank of the water, which was very good.

"When I was a little advanced into the island, I saw an old man, who appeared very weak and infirm. He was sitting on the bank of a stream, and at first I took him to be one who had been shipwrecked like myself. I went toward him and saluted him, but he only slightly bowed his head. I asked him why he sat so still, but instead of answering me, he made a sign for me to take him upon my back, and carry him over the brook, signifying that it was to gather fruit.

"I believed him really to stand in need of my assistance, took him upon my back, and having carried him over, bade him get down, and for that end stooped, that he might get off with ease; but instead of doing so (which I laugh at every time I think of it) the old man, who to me appeared quite decrepit, clasped his legs nimbly about my neck. He sat astride upon my shoulders, and held my throat so tight, that I thought he would have strangled me, the apprehension of which made me swoon and fall down.

"Notwithstanding my fainting, the ill-natured old fellow kept fast about my neck, but opened his legs a little to give me time to recover my breath. When I had done so, he thrust one of his feet against my stomach, and struck me so rudely on the side with the other that he forced me to rise up against my will. Having arisen, he made me walk under the trees, and forced me now and then to stop, to gather and eat fruit. He never left me all day, and when I lay down to rest at night, laid himself down with me, holding always fast about my neck. Every morning he pushed me to make me awake, and afterward obliged me to get up and walk, and pressed me with his feet.

"One day I found in my way several dry calabashes that had fallen from a tree. I took a large one, and after cleaning it, pressed into it some juice of grapes, which abounded in the island; having filled the calabash, I put it by in a convenient place, and going thither again some days after, I tasted it, and found the wine so good, that it soon made me forget my sorrow, gave me new vigour, and so exhilarated my spirits, that I began to sing and dance as I walked along.

"The old man, perceiving the effect which this liquor had upon me, and that I carried him with more ease than before, made me a sign to give him some of it. I handed him the calabash, and the liquor pleasing his palate, he drank it all off. There being a considerable quantity of it, he became intoxicated, and the fumes getting up into his head, he began to sing after his manner, and to dance, thus loosening his legs from about me by degrees. Finding that he did not press me as before, I threw him upon the ground, where he lay without motion; I then took up a great stone, and crushed him.

"I was extremely glad to be thus freed forever from this troublesome fellow. I now walked toward the beach, where I met the crew of a ship that had cast anchor, to take in water. They were surprised to see me, but more so at hearing the particulars of my adventures. 'You fell,' said they, 'into the hands of the Old Man of the Sea, and are the first who ever escaped strangling by his malicious tricks. He never quits those he has once made himself master of till he has destroyed them, and he has made this island notorious by the number of men he has slain.'

"After having informed me of these things, they carried me with them to the ship, and the captain received me with great kindness, when they told him what had befallen me. He put out again to sea, and after some days' sail, we arrived at the harbour of a great city.

"One of the merchants who had taken me into his friendship invited me to go along with him, and carried me to a place appointed for the accommodation of foreign merchants. He gave me a large bag, and having recommended me to some people of the town, who used to gather cocoa-nuts, desired them to take me with them. 'Go,' said he, 'follow them, and act as you see them do, but do not separate from them, otherwise you may endanger your life.' Having thus spoken, he gave me provisions for the journey, and I went with them.

"We came to a thick forest of cocoa-trees, very lofty, with trunks so smooth that it was not possible to climb to the branches that bore the fruit. When we entered the forest we saw a great number of apes of several sizes, who fled as soon as they perceived us, and climbed up to the top of the trees with surprising swiftness.

"The merchants with whom I was, gathered stones and threw them at the apes on the trees. I did the same, and the apes out of revenge threw cocoa-nuts at us so fast, and with such gestures, as sufficiently testified their anger and resentment. We gathered up the cocoa-nuts, and from time to time threw stones to provoke the apes; so that by this stratagem we filled our bags with cocoa-nuts, which it had been impossible otherwise to have done.

"When we had gathered our number, we returned to the city, where the merchant who had sent me to the forest gave me the value of the cocoas I brought: 'Go on,' said he, 'and do the like every day, until you have got money enough to carry you home.' I thanked him for his advice, and gradually collected as many cocoa-nuts as produced me a considerable sum.

"The vessel in which I had come sailed with some merchants who loaded her with cocoa-nuts. I embarked in her all the nuts I had, and when she was ready to sail took leave of the merchant who had been so kind to me.

"We sailed toward the islands, where pepper grows in great plenty. From thence we went to the isle of Comari, where the best species of wood of aloes grows. I exchanged my cocoa in those two islands for pepper and wood of aloes, and went with other merchants a pearl-fishing. I hired divers, who brought me up some that were very large and pure. I embarked in a vessel that happily arrived at Bussorah; from thence

I returned to Bagdad, where I made vast sums from my pepper, wood of aloes, and pearls. I gave the tenth of my gains in alms, as I had done upon my return from my other voyages, and endeavoured to dissipate my fatigues by amusements of different kinds."

When Sinbad had finished his story, he ordered one hundred sequins to be given to Hindbad, who retired with the other guests; but next morning the same company returned to dine; when Sinbad requested their attention, and gave the following account of his sixth voyage:

The Sixth Voyage

"YOU LONG WITHOUT doubt to know," said he, "how, after having been shipwrecked five times, and escaped so many dangers, I could resolve again to tempt fortune, and expose myself to new hardships. I am, myself, astonished at my conduct when I reflect upon it, and must certainly have been actuated by my destiny. But be that as it may, after a year's rest I prepared for a sixth voyage, notwithstanding the entreaties of my kindred, who did all in their power to dissuade me.

"Instead of taking my way by the Persian Gulf, I travelled once more through several provinces of Persia and the Indies, and arrived at a seaport, where I embarked in a ship, the captain of which was bound on a long voyage. It was long indeed, for the captain and pilot lost their course. They, however, at last discovered where they were, but we had no reason to rejoice at the circumstance. Suddenly we saw the captain quit his post, uttering loud lamentations. He threw off his turban, pulled his beard, and beat his head like a madman. We asked him the reason, and he answered, that he was in the most dangerous place in all the ocean. 'A rapid current carries the ship along with it,' said he, 'and we shall all perish in less than a quarter of an hour. Pray to God to deliver us from this peril; we cannot escape, if He do not take pity on us.' At these words he ordered the sails to be lowered; but all the ropes broke, and the ship was carried by the current to the foot of an inaccessible mountain, where she struck and went to pieces, yet in such a manner that we saved our lives, our provisions, and the best of our goods.

"This being over, the captain said to us: 'God has done what pleased Him. Each of us may dig his grave, and bid the world adieu; for we are all in so fatal a place, that none shipwrecked here ever returned to their homes.' His discourse afflicted us sensibly, and we embraced each other, bewailing our deplorable lot.

"The mountain at the foot of which we were wrecked formed part of the coast of a very large island. It was covered with wrecks, with human bones, and with a vast quantity of goods and riches. In all other places, rivers run from their channels into the sea, but here a river of fresh water runs out of the sea into a dark cavern, whose entrance is very high and spacious. What is most remarkable in this place is, that the stones of the mountain are of crystal, rubies, or other precious stones. Here is also a sort of fountain of pitch or bitumen, that runs into the sea, which the fish swallow, and turn into ambergris: and this the waves throw up on the beach in great quantities. Trees also grow here, most of which are wood of aloes, equal in goodness to those of Comari.

"To finish the description of this place, which may well be called a gulf, since nothing ever returns from it, it is not possible for ships to get off when once they approach within a certain distance. If they be driven thither by a wind from the sea, the wind and the current impel them; and if they come into it when a land-wind blows, the height of the mountain stops the wind, and occasions a calm, so that the force of the current carries them ashore: and what completes the misfortune is, that there is no possibility of ascending the mountain, or of escaping by sea.

"We continued upon the shore in a state of despair, and expected death every day. At first we divided our provisions as equally as we could, and thus every one lived a longer or shorter time, according to his temperance, and the use he made of his provisions.

"I survived all my companions, yet when I buried the last, I had so little provision remaining that I thought I could not long endure and I dug a grave, resolving to lie down in it because there was no one left to inter me.

"But it pleased God once more to take compassion on me, and put it in my mind to go to the bank of the river which ran into the great cavern. Considering its probable course with great attention, I said to myself: 'This river, which runs thus under ground, must somewhere have an issue. If I make a raft, and leave myself to the current, it will convey me to some inhabited country, or I shall perish. If I be drowned, I lose nothing, but only change one kind of death for another.'

"I immediately went to work upon large pieces of timber and cables, for I had choice of them, and tied them together so strongly that I soon made a very solid raft. When I had finished, I loaded it with rubies, emeralds, ambergris, rock-crystal, and bales of rich stuffs. Having balanced my cargo exactly, and fastened it well to the raft, I went on board with two oars that I had made, and leaving it to the course of the river, resigned myself to the will of God.

"As soon as I entered the cavern I lost all light, and the stream carried me I knew not whither. Thus I floated some days in perfect darkness, and once found the arch so low, that it very nearly touched my head, which made me cautious afterward to avoid the like danger. All this while I ate nothing but what was just necessary to support nature; yet, notwithstanding my frugality, all my provisions were spent. Then a pleasing stupor seized upon me. I cannot tell how long it continued; but when I revived, I was surprised to find myself in an extensive plain on the brink of a river, where my raft was tied, amidst a great number of negroes. I got up as soon as I saw them, and saluted them. They spoke to me, but I did not understand their language. I was so transported with joy, that I knew not whether I was asleep or awake; but being persuaded that I was not asleep, I recited aloud the following words in Arabic: 'Call upon the Almighty, He will help thee; thou needest not perplex thyself about anything else: shut thy eyes, and while thou art asleep, God will change thy bad fortune into good.'

"One of the blacks, who understood Arabic, hearing me speak thus, came toward me and said: 'Brother, be not surprised to see us; we are inhabitants of this country, and came hither to-day to water our fields. We observed something floating upon the water, and, perceiving your raft, one of us swam into the river and brought it hither, where we fastened it, as you see, until you should awake. Pray tell us your history, for it must be extraordinary; how did you venture yourself into this river, and whence did you come?' I begged of them first to give me something to eat, and then I would satisfy their curiosity. They gave me several sorts of food, and when I had satisfied my hunger, I related all that had befallen me, which they listened to with attentive surprise. As soon as I had finished, they told me, by the person who spoke Arabic and interpreted to them what I said, that it was one of the most wonderful stories they had ever heard, and that I must go along with them, and tell it to their king myself; it being too extraordinary to be related by any other than the person to whom the events had happened.

"They immediately sent for a horse, which was brought in a little time; and having helped me to mount, some of them walked before to shew the way, while the rest took my raft and cargo and followed.

"We marched till we came to the capital of Serendib, for it was in that island I had landed. The blacks presented me to their king; I approached his throne, and saluted him as I used to do the Kings of the Indies; that is to say, I prostrated myself at his feet. The prince ordered me to rise, received me with an obliging air, and made me sit down near him.

"I related to the king all that I have told you, and his majesty was so surprised and pleased, that he commanded my adventures to be written in letters of gold, and laid up in the archives of his kingdom. At last my raft was brought in, and the bales opened in his presence: he admired the quantity of wood of aloes and ambergris; but, above all, the rubies and emeralds, for he had none in his treasury that equalled them.

"Observing that he looked on my jewels with pleasure, I fell prostrate at his feet, and took the liberty to say to him: 'Sir, not only my person is at your majesty's service, but the cargo of the raft, and I would beg of you to dispose of it as your own.' He answered me with a smile: 'Sinbad, I will take care not to covet anything of yours, or to take anything from you that God has given you; far from lessening your wealth, I design to augment it, and will not let you quit my dominions without marks of my liberality.' He then charged one of his officers to take care of me, and ordered people to serve me at his own expense. The officer was very faithful in the execution of his commission, and caused all the goods to be carried to the lodgings provided for me.

"I went every day at a set hour to make my court to the king, and spent the rest of my time in viewing the city, and what was most worthy of notice.

"The capital of Serendib stands at the end of a fine valley, in the middle of the island, encompassed by mountains the highest in the world. Rubies and several sorts of minerals abound, and the rocks are for the most part composed of a metalline stone made use of to cut and polish other precious stones. All kinds of rare plants and trees grow there, especially cedars and cocoa-nut. There is also a pearl-fishing in the mouth of its principal river; and in some of its valleys are found diamonds. I made, by way of devotion, a pilgrimage to the place where Adam was confined after his banishment from Paradise, and had the curiosity to go to the top of the mountain.

"When I returned to the city, I prayed the king to allow me to return to my own country, and he granted me permission in the most honourable manner. He would needs force a rich present upon me; and when I went to take my leave of him, he gave me one much more considerable, and at the same time charged me with a letter for the Commander of the Faithful, our sovereign, saying to me: 'I pray you give this present from me, and this letter, to the Caliph, and assure him of my friendship.' I took the present and letter and promised his majesty punctually to execute the commission with which he was pleased to honour me.

"The letter from the King of Serendib was written on the skin of a certain animal of great value, because of its being so scarce, and of a yellowish colour. The characters of this letter were of azure, and the contents as follows:

"'*The King of the Indies, before whom march one hundred elephants, who lives in a palace that shines with one hundred thousand rubies, and who has in his treasury twenty thousand crowns enriched with diamonds, to Caliph Haroun-al-Raschid:*

"'*Though the present we send you be inconsiderable, receive it, however, as a brother, in consideration of the hearty friendship which we bear for you, and of which we are willing to give you proof. We desire the same part in your friendship, considering that we believe it to be our merit, being of the same dignity with yourself. We conjure you this in quality of a brother. Adieu.'*

"The present consisted, first, of one single ruby made into a cup, about half a foot high, an inch thick, and filled with round pearls of half a drachm each; the skin of a serpent, whose scales were as large as an ordinary piece of gold, and had the virtue to preserve from sickness those who lay upon it; fifty thousand drachms of the best wood of aloes, with thirty grains of camphire as big as pistachios and a female slave of ravishing beauty, whose apparel was all covered over with jewels.

"The ship set sail, and after a very successful navigation we landed at Bussorah, and from thence I went to Bagdad, where the first thing I did was to acquit myself of my commission.

"I took the king of Serendib's letter and went to present myself at the gate of the Commander of the Faithful, followed by the beautiful slave, and such of my own family as carried the gifts. I stated the reason of my coming, and was immediately conducted to the throne of the caliph. I made my reverence, and, after a short speech, gave him the letter and present. When he had read what the king of Serendib wrote to him, he asked me if the prince were really so rich and potent as he represented himself in his letter. I prostrated myself a second time, and rising again, said: 'Commander of the Faithful, I can assure your majesty he doth not exceed the truth. Nothing is more worthy of admiration than the magnificence of his palace. When the prince appears in public he has a throne fixed on the back of an elephant, and marches betwixt two ranks of his ministers, favourites, and other people of his court; before him, upon the same elephant, an officer carries a golden lance in his hand; and behind the throne there is another, who stands upright, with a column of gold, on the top of which is an emerald half a foot long and an inch thick; before him march a guard of one thousand men, clad in cloth of gold and silk, and mounted on elephants richly caparisoned.

"While the king is on his march, the officer who is before him on the same elephant cries from time to time, with a loud voice: 'Behold the great monarch, the potent and redoubtable Sultan of the Indies, whose palace is covered with one hundred thousand rubies, and who possesses twenty thousand crowns of diamonds. Behold the monarch greater than Solomon, and the powerful Maha-raja.' After he has pronounced those words, the officer behind the throne cries in his turn: 'This monarch, so great and so powerful, must die, must die, must die.' And the officer before replies: 'Praise be to him who liveth for ever.'

"Furthermore, the King of Serendib is so just that there are no judges in his dominions. His people have no need of them. They understand and observe justice rigidly of themselves.'

"The caliph was much pleased with my account. 'The wisdom of that king,' said he, 'appears in his letter, and after what you tell me, I must confess, that his wisdom is worthy of his people, and his people deserve so wise a prince.' Having spoken thus, he dismissed me, and sent me home with a rich present."

Sinbad left off, and his company retired, Hindbad having first received one hundred sequins; and next day they returned to hear the relation of his seventh and last voyage.

The Seventh and Last Voyage

"BEING RETURNED from my sixth voyage," said Sinbad, "I absolutely laid aside all thoughts of travelling; for, besides that my age now required rest, I was resolved no more to expose myself to such risks as I had encountered; so that I thought of nothing but to pass the rest of my days in tranquillity. One day, however, as I was treating my friends, one of my servants came and told me that an officer of the caliph's inquired for me. I rose from table, and went to him. 'The caliph,' said he, 'has sent me to tell you that he must speak with you.' I followed the officer to the palace, where, being presented to the caliph, I saluted him by prostrating myself at his feet. 'Sinbad,' said he to me, 'I stand in need of your service; you must carry my answer and present to the King of Serendib. It is but just I should return his civility.'

"This command of the caliph was to me like a clap of thunder. 'Commander of the Faithful,' I replied, 'I am ready to do whatever your majesty shall think fit to command; but I beseech you most humbly to consider what I have undergone. I have also made a vow never to go out of Bagdad.' Hence I took occasion to give him a full and particular account of all my adventures, which he had the patience to hear out.

"As soon as I had finished, 'I confess,' said he, 'that the things you tell me are very extraordinary, yet you must for my sake undertake this voyage which I propose to you. You will only have to go to the isle of Serendib, and deliver the commission which I give you, for you know it would not comport with my dignity to be indebted to the king of that island.' Perceiving that the caliph insisted upon my compliance, I submitted, and told him that I was willing to obey. He was very well pleased, and ordered me one thousand sequins for the expenses of my journey.

"I prepared for my departure in a few days, and as soon as the caliph's letter and present were delivered to me, I went to Bussorah, where I embarked, and had a very happy voyage. Having arrived at the isle of Serendib, I acquainted the king's ministers with my commission, and prayed them to get me speedy audience. They did so, and I was conducted to the palace, where I saluted the king by prostration, according to custom. That prince knew me immediately, and testified very great joy at seeing me, 'Sinbad,' said he, 'you are welcome; I have many times thought of you since you departed; I bless the day on which we see one another once more.' I made my compliments to him, and after having thanked him for his kindness, delivered the caliph's letter and present, which he received with all imaginable satisfaction.

"The caliph's present was a complete suit of cloth of gold, valued at one thousand sequins; fifty robes of rich stuff, a hundred of white cloth, the finest of Cairo, Suez, and Alexandria; a vessel of agate broader than deep, an inch thick, and half a foot wide, the bottom of which represented in bas-relief a man with one knee on the ground, who held a bow and an arrow, ready to discharge at a lion. He sent him also a rich tablet, which, according to tradition, belonged to the great Solomon. The caliph's letter was as follows:

"'Greeting, in the name of the sovereign guide of the right way, from the dependant on God, Haroun-al-Raschid, whom God hath set in the place of vicegerent to his prophet, after his ancestors of happy memory, to the potent and esteemed Raja of Serendib:

'We received your letter with joy, and send you this from our imperial residence, the garden of superior wits. We hope when you look upon it, you will perceive our good intention and be pleased with it. Adieu.'

"The King of Serendib was highly gratified that the caliph answered his friendship. A little time after this audience, I solicited leave to depart, and had much difficulty to obtain it. I procured it, however, at last, and the king, when he dismissed me, made me a very considerable present. I embarked immediately to return to Bagdad, but had not the good fortune to arrive there so speedily as I had hoped. God ordered it otherwise.

"Three or four days after my departure, we were attacked by corsairs, who easily seized upon our ship, because it was no vessel of force. Some of the crew offered resistance, which cost them their lives. But for myself and the rest, who were not so imprudent, the corsairs saved us on purpose to make slaves of us.

"We were all stripped, and instead of our own clothes, they gave us sorry rags, and carried us into a remote island, where they sold us.

"I fell into the hands of a rich merchant, who, as soon as he bought me, carried me to his house, treated me well, and clad me handsomely for a slave. Some days after, not knowing who I was, he asked me if I understood any trade. I answered, that I was no mechanic, but a merchant, and that the corsairs who sold me, had robbed me of all I possessed. 'But tell me,' replied he, 'can you shoot with a bow?' I answered, that the bow was one of my exercises in my youth. He gave me a bow and arrows, and, taking me behind him upon an elephant, carried me to a thick forest some leagues from the town. We penetrated a great way into the wood, and he bade me alight; then, shewing me a great tree, 'Climb up that,' said he, 'and shoot at the elephants as you see them pass by, for there is a prodigious number of them in this forest, and if any of them fall, come and give me notice.' Having spoken this, he left me victuals, and returned to the town, and I continued upon the tree all night.

"I saw no elephant during the night, but next morning, as soon as the sun was up, I perceived a great number. I shot several arrows among them, and at last one of the elephants fell, when the rest retired immediately, and left me at liberty to go and acquaint my patron with my booty. When I had informed him, he gave me a good meal, commended my dexterity, and caressed me highly. We went afterwards together to the forest, where we dug a hole for the elephant; my patron designing to return when it had fallen to pieces and take its teeth to trade with.

"I continued this employment for two months, and killed an elephant every day, getting sometimes upon one tree, and sometimes upon another. One morning, as I looked for the elephants, I perceived with extreme amazement that, instead of passing by me across the forest as usual, they stopped, and came to me with a horrible noise, in such number that the plain was covered, and shook under them. They encompassed the tree in which I was concealed, with their trunks extended, and all fixed their eyes upon me. At this alarming spectacle I continued immovable, and was so much terrified, that my bow and arrows fell out of my hand.

"My fears were not without cause; for after the elephants had stared upon me some time, one of the largest of them put his trunk round the foot of the tree, plucked it up, and threw it on the ground. I fell with the tree; and the elephant, taking me up with his trunk, laid me on his back, where I sat more like one dead than alive, with my quiver on my shoulder. He put himself afterward at the head of the rest, who followed him in troops, carried me a considerable way, then laid me down on the ground, and retired with all his companions. After having lain some time, and seeing the elephants gone, I got up, and found I was upon a long and broad hill, almost covered with the bones and teeth of elephants. I confess to you, that this object furnished me with abundance of reflections. I admired the instinct of those animals; I doubted not but that was their burying-place, and that they carried me thither on purpose to tell me that I should forbear to persecute them, since I did it only for their teeth. I did not stay on the hill, but turned toward the city, and, after having travelled a day and a night, I came to my patron.

"As soon as he saw me, 'Ah, poor Sinbad,' exclaimed he, 'I was in great trouble to know what was become of you. I have been at the forest, where I found a tree newly pulled up, and a bow and arrows on the ground, and I despaired of ever seeing you more. Pray tell me what befell you, and by what good chance you are still alive.' I satisfied his curiosity, and going both of us next morning to the hill, he found to his great joy that what I had told him was true. We loaded the elephant which had carried us with as many teeth as he could bear; and when we were returned, 'Brother,' said my patron, 'for I will treat you no more as my slave, after having made such a discovery as will enrich me, God bless you with all happiness and prosperity. I declare before Him, that I give you your liberty. I concealed from you what I am now going to tell you.

"'The elephants of our forest have every year killed a great many slaves, whom we sent to seek ivory. God has delivered you from their fury, and has bestowed that favour upon you only. It is a sign that He loves you, and has some use for your service in the world. You have procured me incredible wealth. Formerly we could not procure ivory but by exposing the lives of our slaves, and now our whole city is enriched by your means. I could engage all our inhabitants to contribute toward making your fortune, but I will have the glory of doing it myself.'

"To this obliging declaration I replied: 'Patron, God preserve you. Your giving me my liberty is enough to discharge what you owe me, and I desire no other reward for the service I had the good fortune to do to you, and your city, but leave to return to my own country.' 'Very well,' said he, 'the monsoon will in a little time bring ships for ivory. I will then send you home, and give you wherewith to bear your charges.' I thanked him again for my liberty and his good intentions toward me. I stayed with him expecting the monsoon; and during that time, we made so many journeys to the hill that we filled all our warehouses with ivory. The other merchants, who traded in it, did the same, for it could not be long concealed from them.

"The ships arrived at last, and my patron, himself having made choice of the ship wherein I was to embark, loaded half of it with ivory on my account, laid in provisions in abundance for my passage, and besides obliged me to accept a present of some curiosities of the country of great value. After I had returned him a thousand thanks for all his favours, I went aboard. We set sail, and as the adventure which procured me this liberty was very extraordinary, I had it continually in my thoughts.

"We stopped at some islands to take in fresh provisions. Our vessel being come to a port on the main land in the Indies, we touched there, and not being willing to venture by sea to Bussorah, I landed my proportion of the ivory, resolving to proceed on my journey by land. I made vast sums by my ivory, bought several rarities for presents, and when my equipage was ready, set out in company with a large caravan of merchants. I was a long time on the way, and suffered much, but endured all with patience, when I considered that I had nothing to fear from the seas, from pirates, from serpents, or from the other perils to which I had been exposed.

"All these fatigues ended at last, and I arrived safe at Bagdad. I went immediately to wait upon the caliph, and gave him an account of my embassy. That prince said he had been uneasy as I was so long in returning, but that he always hoped God would preserve me. When I told him the adventure of the elephants, he seemed much surprised, and would never have given any credit to it had he not known my veracity. He deemed this story, and the other relations I had given him, to be so curious, that he ordered one of his secretaries to write them in characters of gold, and lay them up in his treasury. I retired well satisfied with the honours I received, and the presents which he gave me; and ever since I have devoted myself wholly to my family, kindred and friends."

Sinbad here finished the relation of his seventh and last voyage, and then, addressing himself to Hindbad, "Well, friend," said he, "did you ever hear of any person that suffered so much as I have done, or of any mortal that has gone through so many vicissitudes? Is it not reasonable that, after all this, I should enjoy a quiet and pleasant life?" As he said this, Hindbad drew near to him, and kissing his hand, said, "I must acknowledge sir, that you have gone through many imminent dangers; my troubles are not comparable to yours; if they afflict me for a time, I comfort myself with the thoughts of the profit I get by them. You not only deserve a quiet life, but are worthy of all the riches you enjoy, because you make of them such a good and generous use. May you therefore continue to live in happiness till the day of your death!" Sinbad then gave him one hundred sequins more, received him into the number of his friends and desired him to quit his porter's employment, and come and dine every day with him, that he might have ample reason to remember Sinbad the voyager and his adventures.

The Three Princes and the Princess Nouronnihar

E. Dixon

THERE WAS ONCE a sultan of India who had three sons. These, with the princess his niece, were the ornaments of his court. The eldest of the princes was called Houssain, the second Ali, the youngest Ahmed, and the princess his niece, Nouronnihar. The Princess Nouronnihar was the daughter of the younger brother of the sultan, to whom the sultan in his lifetime allowed a considerable revenue. But that prince had not been married long before he died, and left the princess very young. The sultan, out of brotherly love and friendship, took upon himself the care of his niece's education, and brought her up in his palace with the three princes, where her singular beauty and personal accomplishments, joined to a sprightly disposition and irreproachable conduct, distinguished her among all the princesses of her time.

The sultan, her uncle, proposed to get her married, when she arrived at a proper age, to some neighbouring prince, and was thinking seriously about it, when he perceived that the three princes his sons had all fallen in love with her. He was very much concerned, owing to the difficulty he foresaw whether the two younger would consent to yield to their elder brother. He spoke to each of them apart; and after having remonstrated on the impossibility of one princess being the wife of three persons, and the troubles they would create if they persisted, he did all he could to persuade them to abide by a declaration of the princess in favour of one of them; or to suffer her to be married to a foreign prince. But as he found them obstinate, he sent for them all together, and said to them, 'Children, since I have not been able to persuade you no longer to aspire to marry the princess your cousin; and as I have no inclination to force her to marry any of you, I have thought of a plan which will please you all, and preserve union among you, if you will but follow my advice. I think it would be best, if every one travelled separately into a different country, so that you might not meet each other: and as you know I delight in every thing that is rare and singular, I promise my niece in marriage to him that shall bring me the most extraordinary curiosity; and for travelling expenses, I will give each of you a sum befitting your rank and the purchase of the curiosity you search.'

As the three princes were always submissive and obedient to the sultan's will, and each flattered himself that fortune would favour him, they all consented. The sultan gave them the money he promised; and that very day they issued orders in preparation for their travels, and took leave of the sultan, that they might be ready to set out early the next morning. They all went out at the same gate of the city, each dressed like a merchant, attended by a trusty officer dressed like a slave, all well mounted and equipped. They went the first day's journey together; and slept at the first inn, where the road divided into three different tracks. At night when they were at supper together, they agreed to travel for a year, and to make that inn their rendezvous; that the first that came should wait for the rest; that as they had all three taken leave together of the sultan, they should all return together. The next morning by break of day, after they had embraced and wished each other good success, they mounted their horses, and each took a different road.

Prince Houssain, the eldest brother, who had heard wonders of the extent, strength, riches, and splendour of the kingdom of Bisnagar, bent his course towards the Indian coast; and, after three months travelling with different caravans, sometimes over deserts and barren mountains, and sometimes through populous and fertile countries, he arrived at Bisnagar, the capital of the kingdom of that name and the residence of its king. He lodged at a khan appointed for foreign merchants; and having learnt that there were four principal quarters where merchants of all sorts kept their shops, in the midst of which stood the castle, or rather the king's palace, as the centre of the city, surrounded by three courts, and each gate two leagues distant from the other, he went to one of these quarters the next day.

Prince Houssain could not see this quarter without admiration. It was large, and divided into several streets, all vaulted and shaded from the sun, and yet very light. The shops were all of the same size and proportion; and all that dealt in the same sort of merchandise, as well as the craftsmen, lived in one street.

The multitude of shops stocked with the finest linens from several parts of India, some painted in the brightest colours, with men, landscapes, trees, and flowers; silks and brocades from Persia, China, and other places; porcelain from Japan and China, foot carpets of all sizes, – all this surprised him so much that he knew not how to believe his own eyes; but when he came to the shops of the goldsmiths and jewellers (for those two trades were exercised by the same merchants), he was dazzled by the lustre of the pearls, diamonds, rubies, emeralds, and other precious stones exposed for sale. But if he was amazed at seeing so many riches in one place, he was much more surprised when he came to judge of the wealth of the whole kingdom by considering that except the Brahmins and ministers of the idols, who profess a life retired from worldly vanity, there was not an Indian, man or woman, through the extent of that kingdom, who did not wear necklaces, bracelets, and ornaments about their legs and feet, made of pearls and other precious stones.

Another thing Prince Houssain particularly admired was the great number of rose-sellers, who crowded the streets; for the Indians are such lovers of that flower, that not one will stir without a nosegay in his hand, or a garland on his head; and the merchants keep them in pots in their shops, so that the air of the whole quarter, however large, is perfectly perfumed.

After Prince Houssain had run through the quarter, street by street, his thoughts fully occupied by the riches he had seen, he was very much tired, and a merchant civilly invited him to sit down in his shop. He accepted the offer; but had not been seated long before he saw a crier pass by with a piece of carpet on his arm, about six feet square, and cry it at thirty purses. The prince called to the crier, and asked to see the carpet, which seemed to him to be valued at an exorbitant price, not only for its size, but the meanness of the stuff. When he had examined it well, he told the crier that he could not comprehend how so small and poor a piece could be priced so high.

The crier, who took him for a merchant, replied, 'Sir, if this price seems so extravagant to you, your amazement will be greater when I tell you I have orders to raise it to forty purses, and not to part with it for less.'

'Certainly,' answered Prince Houssain, 'it must have something very extraordinary about it, which I know nothing of.'

'You have guessed right, sir,' replied the crier, 'and will own as much when you come to know that whoever sits on this piece of carpet may be transported in an instant wherever he desires to go without being stopped by any obstacle.'

At this the Prince of the Indies, considering that the principal motive of his journey was to carry some singular curiosity home to the sultan his father, thought that be could not meet with anything which could give him more satisfaction. 'If the carpet,' said he to the crier, 'has the virtue you assign it, I shall not think forty purses too much but shall make you a present besides.'

'Sir,' replied the crier, 'I have told you the truth; and it will be an easy matter to convince you of it, as soon as you have made the bargain for forty purses, by experiment. But as I suppose you have not so much with you, and that I must go with you to the khan where you lodge, with the leave of the master of the shop we will go into his back shop, and I will spread the carpet; and when we have both sat down, and you have formed the wish to be transported into your room at the khan, if we are not transported thither it shall be no bargain. As to your present, as I am paid for my trouble by the seller, I shall receive it as a favour, and be very much obliged to you for it.'

The prince accepted the conditions, and concluded the bargain; and having obtained the master's leave, they went into his back shop; they both sat down on the carpet, and as soon as the prince wished to be transported into his room at the khan, he found himself and the crier there, and as he wanted no more convincing proof of the virtue of the carpet, he counted to the crier forty purses of gold, and gave him twenty pieces for himself.

In this manner Prince Houssain became the possessor of the carpet, and was overjoyed that on his arrival at Bisnagar he had found so rare a treasure, which he never doubted would gain him the Princess Nouronnihar. In short he looked upon it as an impossible thing for the princes, his younger brothers, to meet with anything to compare with it. It was in his power, by sitting on this carpet, to be at the place of rendezvous that very day; but as he was obliged to wait for his brothers, as they had agreed, and as he was curious to see the King of Bisnagar and his court, and to learn about the laws, customs, and religion of the kingdom, he chose to make a longer abode there.

It was a custom of the King of Bisnagar to give audience to all strange merchants once a week; and Prince Houssain, who remained incognito, saw him often; and as he was handsome, clever, and extremely polite, he easily distinguished himself among the merchants, and was preferred before them all by the sultan, who asked him about the Sultan of the Indies, and the government, strength, and riches of his dominions.

The rest of his time the prince spent in seeing what was most remarkable in and about the city; and among other things he visited a temple, all built of brass. It was ten cubits square, and fifteen high; and the greatest ornament to it was an idol of the height of a man, of massy gold: its eyes were two rubies, set so artificially, that it seemed to look at those who looked at it, on whichever side they turned. Besides this, there was another not less curious, in a village in the midst of a plain of about ten acres, which was a delicious garden full of roses and the choicest flowers, surrounded with a small wall breast high, to keep the cattle out. In the midst of this plain was raised a terrace, a man's height, so nicely paved that the whole pavement seemed to be but one single stone. A temple was erected in the middle of this terrace, with a dome about fifty cubits high, which might be seen for several leagues round. It was thirty cubits long, and twenty broad, built of red marble, highly polished. The inside of the dome was adorned with three rows of fine paintings, in good taste: and there was not a place in the whole temple but was embellished with paintings, bas-reliefs, and figures of idols from top to bottom.

Every night and morning there were ceremonies performed in this temple, which were always succeeded by sports, concerts, dancing, singing, and feasts. The ministers of the temple and the inhabitants of the place had nothing to live on but the offerings of pilgrims, who came in crowds from the most distant parts of the kingdom to perform their vows.

Prince Houssain was also spectator of a solemn feast, which was celebrated every year at the court of Bisnagar, at which all the governors of provinces, commanders of fortified places, all the governors and judges of towns, and the Brahmins most celebrated for their learning, were obliged to be present; and some lived so far off that they were four months in coming. This assembly, composed of innumerable multitudes of Indians, met in a plain of vast extent, as far as the eye could reach. In the centre of this plain was a square of great length and breadth, closed on one side by a large scaffolding of nine stories, supported by forty pillars, raised for the king and his court, and those strangers whom he admitted to audience once a week. Inside, it was adorned and furnished magnificently; and on the outside were painted fine landscapes, wherein all sorts of beasts, birds, and insects, even flies and gnats, were drawn as naturally as possible. Other scaffolds of at least four or five stories, and painted almost all alike, formed the other three sides.

On each side of the square, at some little distance from each other, were ranged a thousand elephants, sumptuously harnessed, each having upon his back a square wooden castle, finely gilt, in which were musicians and actors. The trunks, ears, and bodies of these elephants were painted with cinnabar and other colours, representing grotesque figures.

But what Prince Houssain most of all admired was to see the largest of these elephants stand with his four feet on a post fixed into the earth, two feet high, playing and beating time with his trunk to the music. Besides this, he admired another elephant as big, standing on a board, which was laid across a strong beam about ten feet high, with a great weight at the other end which balanced him, while he kept time with the music by the motions of his body and trunk.

Prince Houssain might have made a longer stay in the kingdom and court of Bisnagar, where he would have seen other wonders, till the last day of the year, whereon he and his brothers had appointed to meet. But he was so well satisfied with what he had seen, and his thoughts ran so much upon the Princess Nouronnihar, that he fancied he should be the more easy and happy the nearer he was to her. After he had paid the master of the khan for his apartment, and told him the hour when he might come for the key, without telling him how he should go, he shut the door, put the key on the outside, and spreading the carpet, he and the officer he had brought with him sat down on it, and, as soon as he had wished, were transported to the inn at which he and his brothers were to meet, where he passed for a merchant till they came.

Prince Ali, the second brother, travelled into Persia with a caravan, and after four months' travelling arrived at Schiraz, which was then the capital of the kingdom of Persia, and having on the way made friends with some merchants, passed for a jeweller, and lodged in the same khan with them.

The next morning, while the merchants were opening their bales of merchandise, Prince Ali took a walk into that quarter of the town where they sold precious stones, gold and silver work, brocades, silks, fine linens, and other choice and valuable merchandise, which was at Schiraz called the bezestein. It was a spacious and well-built place, arched over, and supported by large pillars; along the walls, within and without, were shops. Prince Ali soon rambled through the bezestein, and with admiration judged of the riches of the place by the prodigious quantities of most precious merchandise there exposed to view.

But among all the criers who passed backwards and forwards with several sorts of things to sell, he was not a little surprised to see one who held in his hand an ivory tube about a foot in length and about an inch thick, and cried it at thirty purses. At first he thought the crier mad, and to make sure, went to a shop, and said to the merchant, who stood at the door, 'Pray, sir, is not that man mad? If he is not, I am very much deceived.'

'Indeed, sir,' answered the merchant, 'he was in his right senses yesterday, and I can assure you he is one of the ablest criers we have, and the most employed of any when anything valuable is to be sold; and if he cries the ivory tube at thirty purses, it must be worth as much, or more, for some reason or other which does not appear. He will come by presently, and we will call him; in the meantime sit down on my sofa and rest yourself.'

Prince Ali accepted the merchant's obliging offer, and presently the crier passed by. The merchant called him by his name; and pointing to the prince, said to him, 'Tell that gentleman, who asked me if you were in your right senses, what you mean by crying that ivory tube, which seems not to be worth much, at thirty purses: I should be very much amazed myself, if I did not know you were a sensible man.'

The crier, addressing himself to Prince Ali, said, 'Sir, you are not the only person that takes me for a madman on account of this tube; you shall judge yourself whether I am or no, when I have told you its peculiarity. First, sir,' pursued the crier, presenting the ivory tube to the prince, 'observe that this tube is furnished with a glass at both ends; by looking through one of them you see whatever object you wish to behold.'

'I am,' said the prince, 'ready to make you all proper reparation for the scandal I have thrown on you, if you will make the truth of what you say appear'; and as he had the ivory tube in his hand, he said, 'Show me at which of these ends I must look.' The crier showed him, and he looked through, wishing at the same time to see the sultan, his father. He immediately beheld him in perfect health, sitting on his throne, in the midst of his council. Afterwards, as there was nothing in the world so dear to him, after the sultan, as the Princess Nouronnihar, he wished to see her, and saw her laughing, and in a pleasant humour, with her women about her.

Prince Ali needed no other proof to persuade him that this tube was the most valuable thing, not only in the city of Schiraz, but in all the world; and he believed that, if he should neglect it, he would never meet again with such another rarity. He said to the crier, 'I am very sorry that I should have entertained so bad an opinion of you, but hope to make you amends by buying the tube, so tell me the lowest price the seller has fixed upon it. Come with me, and I will pay you the money.' The crier assured him that his last orders were to take no less than forty purses; and, if he disputed the truth of what he said, he would take him to his employer. The prince believed him, took him to the khan where he lodged, counted out the money, and received the tube.

Prince Ali was overjoyed at his bargain; and persuaded himself that, as his brothers would not be able to meet with anything so rare and marvellous, the Princess Nouronnihar would be his wife. He thought now of visiting the court of Persia incognito, and seeing whatever was curious in and about Schiraz, till the caravan with which he came returned back to the Indies. When the caravan was ready to set out, the prince joined them, and arrived without any accident or trouble at the place of rendezvous, where he found Prince Houssain, and both waited for Prince Ahmed.

Prince Ahmed took the road to Samarcand; and the day after his arrival there went, as his brothers had done, into the bezestein. He had not walked long before he heard a crier, who had an artificial apple in his hand, cry it at five-and-thirty purses. He stopped the crier, and said to him, 'Let me see that apple, and tell me what virtue or extraordinary property it has, to be valued at so high a rate.'

'Sir,' said the crier, putting it into his hand, 'if you look at the outside of this apple, it is very ordinary; but if you consider the great use and benefit it is to mankind, you will say it is invaluable. He who possesses it is master of a great treasure. It cures all sick persons of the most mortal diseases, fever, pleurisy, plague, or other malignant distempers; and, if the patient is dying, it will immediately restore him to perfect health; and this is done after the easiest manner in the world, merely by the patient smelling the apple.'

'If one may believe you,' replied Prince Ahmed, 'the virtues of this apple are wonderful, and it is indeed valuable: but what ground has a plain man like myself, who may wish to become the purchaser, to be persuaded that there is no deception or exaggeration in the high praise you bestow on it?'

'Sir,' replied the crier, 'the thing is known and averred by the whole city of Samarcand; but, without going any further, ask all these merchants you see here, and hear what they say; several of them would not have been alive this day if they had not made use of this excellent remedy. It is the result of the study and experience of a celebrated philosopher of this city, who applied himself all his life to the knowledge of plants and minerals, and at last performed such surprising cures in this city as will never be forgotten; but he died suddenly himself, before he could apply his own sovereign remedy, and left his wife and a great many young children behind him in very indifferent circumstances; to support her family, and provide for her children, she has resolved to sell it.'

While the crier was telling Prince Ahmed the virtues of the artificial apple, a great many persons came about them, and confirmed what he said; and one among the rest said he had a friend dangerously ill, whose life was despaired of, which was a favourable opportunity to show Prince Ahmed the experiment. Upon which Prince Ahmed told the crier he would give him forty purses if he cured the sick person by letting him smell at it.

The crier, who had orders to sell it at that price, said to Prince Ahmed, 'Come, sir, let us go and make the experiment, and the apple shall be yours; it is an undoubted fact that it will always have the same effect as it already has had in recovering from death many sick persons whose life was despaired of.'

The experiment succeeded, and the prince, after he had counted out to the crier forty purses, and the other had delivered the apple to him, waited with the greatest impatience for the first caravan that should return to the Indies. In the meantime he saw all that was curious in and about Samarcand, especially the valley of Sogda, so called from the river which waters it, and is reckoned by the Arabians to be one of the four paradises of this world, for the beauty of its fields and gardens and fine palaces, and for its fertility in fruit of all sorts, and all the other pleasures enjoyed there in the fine season.

At last Prince Ahmed joined the first caravan that returned to the Indies, and arrived in perfect health at the inn where the Princes Houssain and Ali were waiting for him.

Prince Ali, who was there some time before Prince Ahmed, asked Prince Houssain, who got there first, how long he had been there; he told him three months: to which he replied, 'Then certainly you have not been very far.'

'I will tell you nothing now,' said Prince Houssain, 'but only assure you I was more than three months travelling to the place I went to.'

'But then,' replied Prince Ali, 'you made a short stay there.'

'Indeed, brother,' said Prince Houssain, 'you are mistaken: I resided at one place over four or five months, and might have stayed longer.'

'Unless you flew back,' replied Prince Ali again, 'I cannot comprehend how you can have been three months here, as you would make me believe.'

'I tell you the truth,' added Prince Houssain, 'and it is a riddle which I shall not explain till our brother Ahmed comes; then I will let you know what curiosity I have brought home from my travels. I know not what you have got, but believe it to be some trifle, because I do not see that your baggage is increased.'

'And pray what have you brought?' replied Prince Ali, 'for I can see nothing but an ordinary piece of carpet, with which you cover your sofa, and as you seem to make what you have brought a secret, you cannot take it amiss that I do the same.'

'I consider the rarity which I have purchased,' replied Prince Houssain, 'to excel all others whatever, and should not have any objection to show it you, and make you agree that it is so, and at the same time tell you how I came by it, without being in the least apprehensive that what you have got is better. But we ought to wait till our brother Ahmed arrives, that we may all communicate our good fortune to each other.'

Prince Ali would not enter into a dispute with Prince Houssain, but was persuaded that, if his perspective glass were not preferable, it was impossible it should be inferior, and therefore agreed to wait till Prince Ahmed arrived, to produce his purchase.

When Prince Ahmed came, they embraced and complimented each other on the happiness of meeting together at the place they set out from. Then Prince Houssain, as the elder brother, said, 'Brothers, we shall have time enough hereafter to entertain ourselves with the particulars of our travels: let us come to that which is of the greatest importance for us to know; let us not conceal from each other the curiosities we have brought home, but show them, that we may do ourselves justice beforehand and see to which of us the sultan our father may give the preference.

'To set the example,' continued Prince Houssain, 'I will tell you that the rarity which I have brought from my travels to the kingdom of Bisnagar, is the carpet on which I sit, which looks but ordinary and makes no show; but, when I have declared its virtues to you, you will be struck with admiration, and will confess you never heard of anything like it. Whoever sits on it as we do, and desires to be transported to any place, be it ever so far off, is immediately carried thither. I made the experiment myself before I paid down the forty purses, and when I had fully satisfied my curiosity at the court of Bisnagar, and had a mind to return, I made use of no other means than this wonderful carpet for myself and servant, who can tell you how long we were coming hither. I will show you both the experiment whenever you please. I expect you to tell me whether what you have brought is to be compared to this carpet.'

Here Prince Houssain ended, and Prince Ali said, 'I must own, brother, that your carpet is one of the most surprising things imaginable, if it has, as I do not doubt in the least, that property you speak of. But you must allow that there may be other things, I will not say more, but at least as wonderful, in another way; and to convince you there are, here is an ivory tube, which appears to the eye no more a rarity than your carpet. It cost me as much, and I am as well satisfied with my purchase as you can be with yours; and you will be so just as to own that I have not been cheated, when you know by experience that by looking at one end you see whatever you wish to behold. Take it,' added Prince Ali, presenting the tube to him, 'make trial of it yourself.'

Prince Houssain took the ivory tube from Prince Ali, and clapped that end to his eye which Prince Ali showed him, to see the Princess Nouronnihar, and to know how she was, when Prince Ali and Prince Ahmed, who kept their eyes fixed upon him, were extremely surprised to see his countenance change suddenly with extraordinary pain and grief. Prince Houssain would not give them time to ask what was the matter, but cried out, 'Alas! princes, to what purpose have we undertaken long and fatiguing journeys? In a few moments our lovely princess will breathe her last. I saw her in her bed, surrounded by her women and attendants, who were all in tears. Take the tube, behold for yourselves the miserable state she is in.'

Prince Ali took the tube out of Prince Houssain's hand and after he had looked, presented it to Prince Ahmed.

When Prince Ahmed saw that the Princess Nouronnihar's end was so near, he addressed himself to his two brothers, and said, 'Princes, the Princess Nouronnihar, the object of all our vows, is indeed at death's door; but provided we make haste and lose no time, we may preserve her life.' Then he took out the artificial apple, and showing it to the princes his brothers, said to them, 'This apple which you see here cost as much as either the carpet or tube. The opportunity now presents itself to show you its wonderful virtue. Not to keep you longer in suspense, if a sick person smells it, though in the last agonies, it restores him to perfect health immediately. I have made the experiment, and can show you its wonderful effect on the Princess Nouronnihar, if we make all haste to assist her.'

'If that is all,' replied Prince Houssain, 'we cannot make more haste than by transporting ourselves instantly into her room by the means of my carpet. Come, lose no time; sit down on it by me; it is large enough to hold us all three: but first let us give orders to our servants to set out immediately, and join us at the palace.'

As soon as the order was given, Prince Ali and Prince Ahmed went and sat down by Prince Houssain, and all three framed the same wish, and were transported into the Princess Nouronnihar's chamber.

The presence of the three princes, who were so little expected, frightened the princess's women and attendants, who could not comprehend by what enchantment three men should be among them; for they did not know them at first, and the attendants were ready to fall upon them, as people who had got into a part of the palace where they were not allowed to come; but they presently recollected and found their mistake.

Prince Ahmed no sooner saw himself in Nouronnihar's room, and perceived the princess dying, than he rose off the tapestry, as did also the other two princes, and went to the bed-side, and put the apple under her nose. Some moments after, the princess opened her eyes, and turned her head from one side to another, looking at the persons who stood about her; she then rose up in the bed, and asked to be dressed, just as if she had awaked out of a sound sleep. Her women informed her, in a manner that showed their joy, that she was obliged to the three princes her cousins, and particularly to Prince Ahmed, for the sudden recovery of her health. She immediately expressed her joy to see them, and thanked them all together, and afterwards Prince Ahmed in particular, and they then retired.

While the princess was dressing, the princes went to throw themselves at the sultan their father's feet, and pay their respects to him. The sultan received and embraced them with the greatest joy, both for their return and for the wonderful recovery of the princess his niece, whom he loved as if she had been his own daughter, and who had been given over by the physicians. After the usual compliments, the princes presented each the curiosity which he had brought: Prince Houssain his carpet, which he had taken care not to leave behind him in the princess's chamber; Prince Ali his ivory tube, and Prince Ahmed the artificial apple; and after each had commended his present, when they put it into the sultan's hands, they begged him to pronounce their fate, and declare to which of them he would give the Princess Nouronnihar for a wife, according to his promise.

The Sultan of the Indies having kindly heard all that the princes had to say, without interrupting them, and being well informed of what had happened in relation to the Princess Nouronnihar's cure, remained some time silent, as if he were thinking what answer he should make. At last he broke silence, and said to them in terms full of wisdom, 'I would declare for one of you, my children, with a great deal of pleasure, if I could do so with justice; but consider whether I can. It is true, Prince Ahmed, the princess my niece is obliged to your artificial apple for her cure, but let me ask you, whether you could have been so serviceable to her if you had not known by Prince Ali's tube the danger she was in, and if Prince Houssain's carpet had not brought you to her so soon?

'Your tube, Prince Ali, informed you and your brothers that you were likely to lose the princess your cousin, and so far she is greatly obliged to you. You must also grant that that knowledge would have been of no service without the artificial apple and the carpet.

'And for you, Prince Houssain, consider that it would have been of little use if you had not been acquainted with the princess's illness by Prince Ali's tube, and Prince Ahmed had not applied his artificial apple. Therefore, as neither the carpet, the ivory tube, nor the artificial apple has the least preference one over the other, but, on the contrary, there is a perfect equality, I cannot grant the princess to any one of you, and the only fruit you have reaped from your travels is the glory of having equally contributed to restore her to health.

'If this be true,' added the sultan, 'you see that I must have recourse to other means to determine with certainty in the choice I ought to make among you, and as there is time enough between this and night, I will do it to-day. Go, and get each of you a bow and arrow, and repair to the great plain outside the city, where the horses are exercised. I will soon come to you, and I declare I will give the Princess Nouronnihar to him that shoots the farthest.

'I do not, however, forget to thank you all in general, and each in particular, for the presents you brought me. I have a great many rarities in my museum already, but nothing that comes up to the carpet, the ivory tube, and the artificial apple, which shall have the first place among them, and shall be preserved carefully, not only for show, but to make an advantageous use of them upon all occasions.'

The three princes had nothing to say against the decision of the sultan. When they were out of his presence, they each provided themselves with a bow and arrow, which they delivered to one of their officers, and went to the plain appointed, followed by a great concourse of people.

The sultan did not make them wait long; and as soon as he arrived, Prince Houssain, as the eldest, took his bow and arrow, and shot first. Prince Ali shot next, and much beyond him; and Prince Ahmed last of all; but it so happened, that nobody could see where his arrow fell; and, notwithstanding all the search of himself and everybody else, it was not to be found far or near. And though it was believed that he shot the farthest, and that he therefore deserved the Princess Nouronnihar, it was necessary that his arrow should be found, to make the matter evident and certain; so, notwithstanding his remonstrances, the sultan determined in favour of Prince Ali, and gave orders for preparations to be made for the wedding, which was celebrated a few days afterwards with great magnificence.

Prince Camaralzaman and the Princess of China

E. Dixon

ABOUT TWENTY DAYS' sail from the coast of Persia, in the Islands of the Children of Khaledan, there lived a king who had an only son, Prince Camaralzaman. He was brought up with all imaginable care; and when he came to a proper age, his father appointed him an experienced governor and able tutors. As he grew up he learned all the knowledge which a prince ought to possess, and acquitted himself so well that he charmed all that saw him, and particularly the sultan his father.

When the prince had attained the age of fifteen years, the sultan, who loved him tenderly, and gave him every day new marks of his affection, had thoughts of giving him a still greater one, by resigning to him his throne, and he acquainted his grand vizier with his intentions. 'I fear,' said he, 'lest my son should lose in the inactivity of youth those advantages which nature and education have given him; therefore, since I am advanced in age, and ought to think of retirement, I have thoughts of resigning the government to him, and passing the remainder of my days in the satisfaction of seeing him reign. I have undergone the fatigue of a crown a long while, and think it is now proper for me to retire.'

The grand vizier did not wholly dissuade the sultan from such a proceeding, but sought to modify his intentions. 'Sir,' replied he, 'the prince is yet but young, and it would not be, in my humble opinion, advisable to burden him with the weight of a crown so soon. Your majesty fears, with great reason, his youth may be corrupted in indolence, but to remedy that do not you think it would be proper to marry him? Your majesty might then admit him to your council, where he would learn by degrees the art of reigning, and so be prepared to receive your authority whenever in your discernment you shall think him qualified.'

The sultan found this advice of his prime minister highly reasonable, therefore he summoned the prince to appear before him at the same time that he dismissed the grand vizier.

The prince, who had been accustomed to see his father only at certain times, without being sent for, was a little startled at this summons; when, therefore, he came before him, he saluted him with great respect, and stood with his eyes fixed on the ground.

The sultan perceiving his constraint, said to him in a mild way,

'Do you know, son, for what reason I have sent for you?'

The prince modestly replied, 'God alone knows the heart; I shall hear it from your majesty with pleasure.'

'I sent for you,' said the sultan, 'to inform you that I have an intention of providing a proper marriage for you; what do you think of it?'

Prince Camaralzaman heard this with great uneasiness: it so surprised him, that he paused and knew not what answer to make. After a few moments' silence, he replied, 'Sir, I beseech you to pardon me if I seem surprised at the declaration you have made to me. I did not expect such proposals to one so young as I am. It requires time to determine on what your majesty requires of me.'

Prince Camaralzaman's answer extremely afflicted his father. He was not a little grieved to see what an aversion he had to marriage, yet would not charge him with disobedience, nor exert his paternal authority. He contented himself with telling him he would not force his inclinations, but give him time to consider the proposal.

The sultan said no more to the prince: he admitted him into his council, and gave him every reason to be satisfied. At the end of the year he took him aside, and said to him, 'My son, have you thoroughly considered what I proposed to you last year about marrying? Will you still refuse me that pleasure I expect from your obedience, and suffer me to die without it?'

The prince seemed less disconcerted than before, and was not long answering his father to this effect: 'Sir, I have not neglected to consider your proposal, but after the maturest reflection find myself more confirmed in my resolution to continue as I am, so that I hope your majesty will pardon me if I presume to tell you it will be in vain to speak to me any further about marriage.' He stopped here, and went out without staying to hear what the sultan would answer.

Any other monarch would have been very angry at such freedom in a son, and would have made him repent it, but the sultan loved him, and preferred gentle methods before he proceeded to compulsion. He communicated this new cause of discontent to his prime minister. 'I have followed your advice,' said he, 'but Camaralzaman is further than ever from complying with my desires. He delivered his resolution in such free terms that it required all my reason and moderation to keep my temper. Tell me, I beseech you, how I shall reclaim a disposition so rebellious to my will?'

'Sir,' answered the grand vizier, 'patience brings many things about that before seemed impracticable, but it may be this affair is of a nature not likely to succeed in that way. Your majesty would have no cause to reproach yourself if you gave the prince another year to consider the matter. If, in this interval he returns to his duty, you will have the greater satisfaction, and if he still continues averse to your proposal when this is expired, your majesty may propose to him in full council that it is highly necessary for the good of the state that he should marry, and it is not likely he will refuse to comply before so grave an assembly, which you honour with your presence.'

The year expired, and, to the great regret of the sultan, Prince Camaralzaman gave not the least proof of having changed his mind. One day, therefore, when there was a great council held, the prime vizier, the other viziers, the principal officers of the crown, and the generals of the army being present, the sultan began to speak thus to the prince: 'My son, it is now a long while since I have expressed to you my earnest desire to see you married; and I imagined you would have had more consideration for a father, who required nothing unreasonable of you, than to oppose him so long. But after so long a resistance on your part, which has almost worn out my patience, I have thought fit to propose the same thing once more to you in the presence of my council. I would have you consider that you ought not to have refused this, not merely to oblige a parent; the well-being of my dominions requires it; and the assembly here present joins with me to require it of you. Declare yourself, then; that, according to your answer, I may take the proper measures.'

The prince answered with so little reserve, or rather with so much warmth, that the sultan, enraged to see himself thwarted in full council, cried out, 'Unnatural son! have you the insolence to talk thus to your father and sultan?' He ordered the guards to take him away, and carry him to an old tower that had been unoccupied for a long while, where he was shut up, with only a bed, a little furniture, some books, and one slave to attend him.

Camaralzaman, thus deprived of liberty, was nevertheless pleased that he had the freedom to converse with his books, and that made him look on his imprisonment with indifference. In the evening he bathed and said his prayers; and after having read some chapters in the Koran, with the same tranquility of mind as if he had been in the sultan's palace, he undressed himself and went to bed, leaving his lamp burning by him all the while he slept.

In this tower was a well, which served in the daytime for a retreat to a certain fairy, named Maimoune, daughter of Damriat, king or head of a legion of genies. It was about midnight when Maimoune sprang lightly to the mouth of the well, to wander about the world after her wonted custom, where her curiosity led her. She was surprised to see a light in Prince Camaralzaman's chamber, and entered, without stopping, over the slave who lay at the door.

Prince Camaralzaman had but half-covered his face with the bedclothes, and Maimoune perceived the finest young man she had seen in all her rambles through the world. 'What crime can he have committed,' said she to herself, 'that a man of his high rank can deserve to be treated thus severely?' for she had already heard his story, and could hardly believe it.

She could not forbear admiring the prince, till at length, having kissed him gently on both cheeks and in the middle of the forehead without waking him, she took her flight into the air. As she mounted high to the middle region, she heard a great flapping of wings, which made her fly that way; and when she approached, she knew it was a genie who made the noise, but it was one of those that are rebellious. As for Maimoune, she belonged to that class whom the great Solomon compelled to acknowledge him.

This genie, whose name was Danhasch, knew Maimoune, and was seized with fear, being sensible how much power she had over him by her submission to the Almighty. He would fain have avoided her, but she was so near him that he must either fight or yield. He therefore broke silence first.

'Brave Maimoune,' said he, in the tone of a suppliant, 'swear to me that you will not hurt me; and I swear also on my part not to do you any harm.'

'Cursed genie,' replied Maimoune, 'what hurt canst thou do me? I fear thee not; but I will grant thee this favour; I will swear not to do thee any harm. Tell me then, wandering spirit, whence thou comest, what thou hast seen, and what thou hast done this night.'

'Fair lady,' answered Danhasch, 'you meet me at a good time to hear something very wonderful. I come from the utmost limits of China, which look on the last islands of this hemisphere. But, charming Maimoune,' said Danhasch, who so trembled with fear at the sight of this fairy that he could hardly speak, 'promise me at least that you will forgive me, and let me go on after I have satisfied your demands.'

'Go on, go on, cursed spirit,' replied Maimoune; 'go on and fear nothing. Dost thou think I am as perfidious an elf as thyself, and capable of breaking the solemn oath I have made? Be sure you tell nothing but what is true, or I shall clip thy wings, and treat thee as thou deservest.'

Danhasch, a little heartened at the words of Maimoune, said, 'My dear lady, I will tell you nothing but what is strictly true, if you will but have the goodness to hear me. The country of China, from whence I come, is one of the largest and most powerful kingdoms of the earth. The king of this country is at present Gaiour, who has an only daughter, the finest maiden that ever was seen in the world since it was a world. Neither you nor I, nor your class nor mine, nor all our respective genies, have expressions strong enough, nor eloquence sufficient to describe this brilliant lady. Any one that did not know the king, father of this incomparable princess would scarcely be able to imagine the great respect and kindness he shows her. No one has ever dreamed of such care as his to keep her from every one but the man who is to marry her: and, that the retreat which he has resolved to place her in may not seem irksome to her, he has built for her seven palaces, the most extraordinary and magnificent that ever were known.

'The first palace is of rock crystal, the second of copper, the third of fine steel, the fourth of brass, the fifth of touchstone, the sixth of silver, and the seventh of massy gold. He has furnished these palaces most sumptuously, each in a manner suited to the materials that they are built of. He has filled the gardens with grass and flowers, intermixed with pieces of water, water- works, fountains, canals, cascades, and several great groves of trees, where the eye is lost in the prospect, and where the sun never enters, and all differently arranged. King Gaiour, in a word, has shown that he has spared no expense.

'Upon the fame of this incomparable princess's beauty, the most powerful neighbouring kings sent ambassadors to request her in marriage. The King of China received them all in the same obliging manner; but as he resolved not to compel his daughter to marry without her consent, and as she did not like any of the suitors, the ambassadors were forced to return as they came: they were perfectly satisfied with the great honours and civilities they had received.'

'"Sir," said the princess to the king her father, "you have an inclination to see me married, and think to oblige me by it; but where shall I find such stately palaces and delicious gardens as I have with your majesty? Through your good pleasure I am under no constraint, and have the same honours shown to me as are paid to yourself. These are advantages I cannot expect to find anywhere else, to whatsoever husband I should give my hand; men love ever to be masters, and I do not care to be commanded."

'At last there came an embassy from the most rich and potent king of all. This prince the King of China recommended to his daughter as her husband, urging many powerful arguments to show how much it would be to her advantage to accept him, but she intreated her father to dispense with her accepting him for the same reasons as before, and at last lost all the respect due to the king her father: "Sir," said she, in anger, "talk to me no more of this or any other match, unless you would have me plunge this poniard in my bosom, to deliver myself from your importunities."

'The king, greatly enraged, said "Daughter, you are mad, and I must treat you as such." In a word, he had her shut up in a single apartment of one of his palaces, and allowed her only ten old women to wait upon her and keep her company, the chief of whom had been her nurse. And in order that the kings his neighbours, who had sent embassies to him on this account, might not think any more of her, he despatched envoys to them severally, to let them know how averse his daughter was to marriage; and as he did not doubt that she was really mad, he charged them to make known in every court that if there were any physician that would undertake to come and cure her, he should, if he succeeded, marry her for his pains.

'Fair Maimoune,' continued Danhasch, 'all that I have told you is true; and I have not failed to go every day regularly to contemplate this incomparable beauty, to whom I would be very sorry to do the least harm, notwithstanding my natural inclination to mischief. Come and see her, I conjure you; it would be well worth your while; I am ready to wait on you as a guide, and you have only to command me. I doubt not that you would think yourself obliged to me for the sight of a princess unequalled for beauty.'

Instead of answering Danhasch, Maimoune burst out into violent laughter, which lasted for some time; and Danhasch, not knowing what might be the occasion of it, was astonished beyond measure. When she had laughed till she could laugh no more, she cried, 'Good, good, very good! you would have me believe all you have told me: I thought you intended to tell me something surprising and extraordinary, and you have been talking all this while of a mad woman. What would you say, cursed genie, if you had seen the beautiful prince that I have just come from seeing? I am confident you would soon give up the contest, and not pretend to compare your choice with mine.'

'Agreeable Maimoune,' replied Danhasch, 'may I presume to ask you who is this prince you speak of?'

'Know,' answered Maimoune, 'the same thing has happened to him as to your princess. The king his father would have married him against his will; but, after much importunity, he frankly told him he would have nothing to do with a wife. For this reason he is at this moment imprisoned in an old tower which I make my residence, and whence I came but just now from admiring him.'

'I will not absolutely contradict you,' replied Danhasch; 'but, my pretty lady, you must give me leave to be of opinion, till I have seen your prince, that no mortal upon earth can come up to the beauty of my princess.'

'Hold thy tongue, cursed sprite,' replied Maimoune. 'I tell thee once more that that can never be.'

'I will not contend with you,' said Danhasch; 'but the way to be convinced whether what I say is true or false is to accept the proposal I made you to go and see my princess, and after that I will go with you to your prince.'

'There is no need I should take so much pains' replied Maimoune; 'there is another way to satisfy us both; and that is for you to bring your princess, and place her in my prince's room; by this means it will be easy for us to compare them together and determine the dispute.'

Danhasch consented to what Maimoune had proposed, and determined to set out immediately for China upon that errand. But Maimoune told him she must first show him the tower whither he was to bring the princess. They flew together to the tower, and when Maimoune had shown it to Danhasch, she cried, 'Go, fetch your princess, and do it quickly, for you shall find me here: but listen, you shall pay the wager if my prince is more beautiful than your princess, and I will pay it if your princess is more beautiful than my prince.'

Danhasch left Maimoune, and flew towards China, whence he soon returned with incredible speed, bringing the fair princess along with him, asleep. Maimoune received him, and introduced him into the tower of Prince Camaralzaman, where they placed the princess still asleep.

At once there arose a great contest between the genie and the fairy about their respective beauty. They were some time admiring and comparing them without speaking: at length Danhasch broke silence, and said to Maimoune, 'You see, as I have already told you, my princess is handsomer than your prince; now, I hope, you are convinced of it.'

'Convinced of it!' replied Maimoune; 'I am not convinced of it, and you must be blind if you cannot see that my prince is far handsomer. The princess is fair, I do not deny; but if you compare them together without prejudice, you will quickly see the difference.'

'Though I should compare them ever so often,' said Danhasch, 'I could never change my opinion. I saw at first sight what I see now, and time will not make me see differently: however, this shall not hinder my yielding to you, charming Maimoune, if you desire it.'

'Yield to me as a favour? I scorn it,' said Maimoune: 'I would not receive a favour at the hand of such a wicked genie; I refer the matter to an umpire, and if you will not consent I shall win by your refusal.'

Danhasch no sooner gave his consent than Maimoune stamped with her foot; the earth opened, and out came a hideous, humpbacked, squinting, and lame genie, with six horns on his head, and claws on his hands and feet. As soon as he had come forth, and the earth had closed up, he, perceiving Maimoune, cast himself at her feet, and then rising up on one knee asked her what she would please to do with him.

'Rise, Caschcasch,' said Maimoune, 'I brought you hither to determine a difference between me and Danhasch. Look there, and tell me, without partiality, which is the handsomest of those two that lie asleep, the young man or the young lady.'

Caschcasch looked at the prince and princess with great attention, admiration and surprise; and after he had considered them a good while, without being able to determine which was the handsomer, he turned to Maimoune, and said, 'Madam, I must confess I should deceive you and betray myself, if I pretended to say that one was a whit handsomer than the other: the more I examine them, the more it seems to me that each possesses, in a sovereign degree, the beauty which is betwixt them. But if there be any difference, the best way to determine it is to awaken them one after the other, and by their conduct to decide which ought to be deemed the most beautiful.'

This proposal of Caschcasch's pleased equally both Maimoune and Danhasch. Maimoune then changed herself into a gnat, and leaping on the prince's neck stung him so smartly that he awoke, and put up his hand to the place; but Maimoune skipped away, and resumed her own form, which, like those of the two genies, was invisible, the better to observe what he would do.

In drawing back his hand, the prince chanced to let it fall on that of the Princess of China, and on opening his eyes, was exceedingly surprised to perceive a lady of the greatest beauty. He raised his head and leaned on his elbow, the better to consider her. She was so beautiful that he could not help crying out, 'What beauty! my heart! my soul!' In saying which he kissed her with so little caution that she would certainly have been awaked by it, had she not slept sounder than ordinary, through the enchantment of Danhasch.

He was going to awaken her at that instant, but suddenly refrained himself. 'Is not this she,' said he, 'that the sultan my father would have had me marry? He was in the wrong not to let me see her sooner. I should not have offended him by my disobedience and passionate language to him in public, and he would have spared himself the confusion which I have occasioned him.'

The prince began to repent sincerely of the fault he had committed, and was once more upon the point of waking the Princess of China. 'It may be,' said he, recollecting himself, 'that the sultan my father has a mind to surprise me with this young lady. Who knows but he has brought her himself, and is hidden behind the curtains to make me ashamed of myself. I will content myself with this ring, as a remembrance of her.'

He then gently drew off a fine ring which the princess had on her finger, and immediately put on one of his own in its place. After this he fell into a more profound sleep than before through the enchantment of the genies.

As soon as Prince Camaralzaman was in a sound sleep, Danhasch transformed himself, and went and bit the princess so rudely on the lip that she forthwith awoke, started up, and opening her eyes, was not a little surprised to see a beautiful young prince. From surprise she proceeded to admiration, and from admiration to a transport of joy.

'What,' cried she, 'is it you the king my father has designed me for a husband? I am indeed most unfortunate for not knowing it before, for then I should not have made him so angry with me. Wake then, wake!'

So saying, she took Prince Camaralzaman by the arm and shook him so that he would have awaked, had not Maimoune increased his sleep by enchantment. She shook him several times, and finding he did not wake, she seized his hand, and kissing it eagerly, perceived he had a ring upon his finger which greatly resembled hers, and which she was convinced was her own, by seeing she had another on her finger instead of it. She could not comprehend how this exchange could have been made. Tired with her fruitless endeavours to awaken the prince, she soon fell asleep.

When Maimoune saw that she could now speak without fear of awaking the princess, she cried to Danhasch, 'Ah, cursed genie dost thou not now see what thy contest has come to? Art thou not now convinced how much thy princess is inferior to my prince? But I pardon thee thy wager. Another time believe me when I assert anything.' Then turning to Caschcasch, 'As for you,' said she, 'I thank you for your trouble; take the princess, you and Danhasch, and convey her back whence he has taken her.' Danhasch and Caschcasch did as they were commanded, and Maimoune retired to her well.

Prince Camaralzaman on waking next morning looked to see if the lady whom he had seen the night before were there. When he found she was gone, he cried out, 'I thought indeed this was a trick the king my father designed to play me. I am glad I was aware of it.' Then he waked the slave, who was still asleep, and bade him come and dress him, without saying anything. The slave brought a basin and water, and after he had washed and said his prayers, he took a book and read for some time.

After this, he called the slave, and said to him, 'Come hither, and look you, do not tell me a lie. How came that lady hither, and who brought her?'

'My lord,' answered the slave with great astonishment, 'I know not what lady your highness speaks of.'

'I speak,' said the prince, 'of her that came, or rather, that was brought hither.'

'My lord,' replied the slave, 'I swear I know of no such lady; and how should she come in without my knowledge, since I lay at the door?'

'You are a lying rascal,' replied the prince, 'and in the plot to vex and provoke me the more.' So saying, he gave him a box on the ear which knocked him down; and after having stamped upon him for some time, he at length tied the well-rope under his arms, and plunged him several times into the water, neck and heels. I will drown thee,' cried he, 'if thou dost not tell me speedily who this lady was, and who brought her.'

The slave, perplexed and half-dead, said within himself, 'The prince must have lost his senses through grief.' 'My lord, then,' cried he, in a suppliant tone, 'I beseech your highness to spare my life, and I will tell you the truth.'

The prince drew the slave up, and pressed him to tell him. As soon as he was out of the well, 'My lord,' said he trembling, 'your highness must perceive that it is impossible for me to satisfy you in my present condition; I beg you to give me leave to go and change my clothes first.'

'I permit you, but do it quickly,' said the prince, 'and be sure you conceal nothing.'

The slave went out, and having locked the door upon the prince, ran to the palace just as he was. The king was at that time in discourse with his prime vizier, to whom he had just related the grief in which he had passed the night on account of his son's disobedience and opposition to his will. The minister endeavoured to comfort his master by telling him that the prince himself had given him good cause to be angry. 'Sir,' said he, 'your majesty need not repent of having treated your son after this sort. Have but patience to let him continue a while in prison, and assure yourself his temper will abate, and he will submit to all you require.'

The grand vizier had just made an end of speaking when the slave came in and cast himself at the king's feet. 'My lord,' said he, 'I am very sorry to be the messenger of ill news to your majesty, which I know must create you fresh affliction. The prince is distracted, my lord; and his treatment to me, as you may see, too plainly proves it.' Then he proceeded to tell all the particulars of what Prince Camaralzaman had said to him, and the violence with which he had been treated.

The king, who did not expect to hear anything of this afflictive kind, said to the prime minister, 'This is very melancholy, very different from the hopes you gave me just now: go immediately, without loss of time, see what is the matter, and come and give me an account.'

The grand vizier obeyed instantly; and coming into the prince's chamber, he found him sitting on his bed in good temper, and with a book in his hand, which he was reading.

After mutual salutations, the vizier sat down by him, and said, 'My lord, I wish that a slave of yours were punished for coming to frighten the king your father.'

'What,' replied the prince, 'could give my father alarm? I have much greater cause to complain of that slave.'

'Prince,' answered the vizier, 'God forbid that the news which he has told your father concerning you should be true; indeed, I myself find it to be false, by the good temper I observe you in.'

'It may be,' replied the prince, 'that he did not make himself well understood; but since you are come, who ought to know something of the matter, give me leave to ask you who was that lady who was here last night?'

The grand vizier was thunderstruck at this question; however, he recovered himself and said, 'My lord, be not surprised at my astonishment at your question. Is it possible that a lady, or any other person in the world, should penetrate by night into this place, without entering at the door and walking over the body of your slave? I beseech you, recollect yourself, and you will find it is only a dream which has made this impression on you.'

'I give no ear to what you say,' said the prince, raising his voice; 'I must know of you absolutely what is become of the lady; and if you hesitate to obey me, I shall soon be able to force you to obey me.'

At these stern words the grand vizier began to be in greater confusion than before, and was thinking how to extricate himself. He endeavoured to pacify the prince by good words, and begged of him, in the most humble and guarded manner, to tell him if he had seen this lady.

'Yes, yes,' answered the prince, 'I have seen her, and am very well satisfied you sent her. She played the part you had given her admirably well, for I could not get a word out of her. She pretended to be asleep, but I was no sooner fallen into a slumber than she arose and left me. You know all this; for I doubt not she has been to make her report to you.'

'My lord,' replied the vizier, 'nothing of this has been done which you seem to reproach me with; neither your father nor I have sent this lady you speak of; permit me therefore to remind your highness once more that you have only seen this lady in a dream.'

'Do you come to affront and contradict me,' said the prince in a great rage, 'and to tell me to my face that what I have told you is a dream?' At the same time he took him by the beard, and loaded him with blows as long as he could stand.

The poor grand vizier endured with respectful patience all the violence of his lord's indignation, and could not help saying within himself, 'Now am I in as bad a condition as the slave, and shall think myself happy if I can, like him, escape from any further danger.' In the midst of repeated blows he cried out for but a moment's audience, which the prince, after he had nearly tired himself with beating him, consented to give.

'I own, my prince,' said the grand vizier, dissembling, 'there is something in what your highness suspects; but you cannot be ignorant of the necessity a minister is under to obey his royal master's orders; yet, if you will but be pleased to set me at liberty, I will go and tell him anything on your part that you shall think fit to command me.'

'Go then,' said the prince, 'and tell him from me that if he pleases I will marry the lady he sent me. Do this quickly, and bring me a speedy answer.' The grand vizier made a profound reverence, and went away, not thinking himself altogether safe till he had got out of the tower, and shut the door upon the prince.

He came and presented himself before the king, with a countenance that sufficiently showed he had been ill-used, which the king could not behold without concern. 'Well,' said the king, 'in what condition did you find my son?'

'Sir,' answered the vizier, 'what the slave reported to your majesty is but too true.' He then began to relate his interview with Camaralzaman, how he flew into a passion upon his endeavouring to persuade him it was impossible that the lady he spoke of should have got in; the ill-treatment he had received from him; how he had been used, and by what means he made his escape.

The king, the more concerned as he loved the prince with excessive tenderness, resolved to find out the truth of this matter, and therefore proposed himself to go and see his son in the tower, accompanied by the grand vizier.

Prince Camaralzaman received the king his father in the tower with great respect. The king sat down, and, after he had made his son the prince sit down by him, put several questions to him, which he answered with great good sense. The king every now and then looked at the grand vizier, as intimating that he did not find his son had lost his wits, but rather thought he had lost his.

The king at length spoke of the lady to the prince. 'My son,' said he, 'I desire you to tell me what lady it was that came here, as I have been told.'

'Sir,' answered Camaralzaman, 'I beg of your majesty not to give me more vexation on that head, but rather to oblige me by letting me have her in marriage: this young lady has charmed me. I am ready to receive her at your hands with the deepest gratitude.'

The king was surprised at this answer of the prince, so remote, as he thought, from the good sense he had shown before. 'My son,' said he to him, 'you fill me with the greatest astonishment imaginable by what you now say to me; I declare to you by my crown, that is to devolve upon you after me, I know not one word of the lady you mention; and if any such has come to you, it was altogether without my knowledge. But how could she get into this tower without my consent? For whatever my grand vizier told you, it was only to appease you: it must therefore be a mere dream; and I beg of you not to believe otherwise, but to recover your senses.'

'Sir,' replied the prince, 'I should be for ever unworthy of your majesty's favour, if I did not give entire credit to what you are pleased to say; but I humbly beseech you at the same time to give a patient hearing to what I shall say to you, and then to judge whether what I have the honour to tell you be a dream or not.'

Then Prince Camaralzaman related to the king his father after what manner he had been awakened, and the pains he took to awaken the lady without effect, and how he had made the exchange of his ring with that of the lady: showing the king the ring, he added, 'Sir, your majesty must needs know my ring very well, you have seen it so often. After this, I hope you will be convinced that I have not lost my senses, as you have been almost made to believe.'

The king was so perfectly convinced of the truth of what his son had been telling him, that he had not a word to say, remaining astonished for some time, and not being able to utter a syllable.

'Son,' at length replied the king, 'after what I have just heard, and what I see by the ring on your finger, I cannot doubt but that you have seen this lady. Would I knew who she was, and I would make you happy from this moment, and I should be the happiest father in the world! But where shall I find her, and how seek for her? How could she get in here without my consent? Why did she come? These things, I must confess, are past my finding out.' So saying, and taking the prince by the hand, 'Come then, my son,' he said, 'let us go and be miserable together.'

The king then led his son out of the tower, and conveyed him to the palace, where he no sooner arrived than in despair he fell ill, and took to his bed; the king shut himself up with him, and spent many a day in weeping, without attending to the affairs of his kingdom.

The prime minister, who was the only person that had admittance to him, came one day and told him that the whole court, and even the people, began to murmur at not seeing him, and that he did not administer justice every day as he was wont to do. 'I humbly beg your majesty, therefore,' proceeded he, 'to pay them some attention; I am aware your majesty's company is a great comfort to the prince, but then you must not run the risk of letting all be lost. Permit me to propose to your majesty to remove with the prince to the castle in a little island near the port, where you may give audience to your subjects twice a week only; during these absences the prince will be so agreeably diverted with the beauty, prospect, and good air of the place, that he will bear them with the less uneasiness.'

The king approved this proposal; and after the castle, where he had not resided for some time, had been furnished, he removed thither with the prince; and, excepting the times that he gave audience, as aforesaid, he never left him, but passed all his time by his son's pillow, endeavouring to comfort him in sharing his grief.

Whilst matters passed thus, the two genies, Danhasch and Caschcasch, had carried the Princess of China back to the palace where the king her father had shut her up.

When she awoke the next morning, and found by looking to the right and left that Prince Camaralzaman was not by, she cried out with a loud voice to her women. Her nurse, who presented herself first, desired to be informed what she would please to have, and if anything disagreeable had happened to her.

'Tell me,' said the princess, 'what is become of the young man whom I love with all my soul?'

'Madam,' replied the nurse, 'we cannot understand your highness, unless you will be pleased to explain yourself.'

'A young man, the best and most amiable,' said the princess 'whom I could not awake; I ask you where he is?'

'Madam,' answered the nurse, 'your highness asks these questions to jest with us. I beseech you to rise.'

'I am in earnest,' said the princess, 'and I must know where this young man is.'

'Madam,' insisted the nurse, 'how any man could come without our knowledge we cannot imagine, for we all slept about the door of your chamber, which was locked, and I had the key in my pocket.'

At this the princess lost all patience, and catching her nurse by the hair of her head, and giving her two or three sound cuffs, she cried, 'You shall tell me where this young man is, old sorceress, or I will beat your brains out.'

The nurse struggled to get from her, and at last succeeded; when she went immediately, with tears in her eyes, to complain to the queen her mother, who was not a little surprised to see her in this condition, and asked who had done this.

'Madam,' began the nurse, 'you see how the princess has treated me; she would certainly have murdered me, if I had not had the good fortune to escape out of her hands.' She then began to tell what had been the cause of all that violent passion in the princess. The queen was surprised to hear it, and could not guess how she came to be so senseless as to take that for a reality which could be no other than a dream. 'Your majesty must conclude from all this, madam,' continued the nurse, 'that the princess is out of her senses. You will think so yourself if you go and see her.'

The queen ordered the nurse to follow her; and they went together to the princess's palace that very moment.

The Queen of China sat down by her daughter's bed-side, immediately upon her arrival in her apartment; and after she had informed herself about her health, she began to ask what had made her so angry with her nurse, that she should have treated her in the manner she had done. 'Daughter,' said she, 'this is not right; and a great princess like you should not suffer herself to be so transported by passion.'

'Madam,' replied the princess, 'I plainly perceive your majesty is come to mock me; but I declare I will never let you rest till you consent I shall marry the young man. You must know where he is, and therefore I beg of your majesty to let him come to me again.'

'Daughter,' answered the queen, 'you surprise me; I know nothing of what you talk of.' Then the princess lost all respect for the queen: 'Madam,' replied she, 'the king my father and you persecuted me about marrying, when I had no inclination; I now have an inclination, and I will marry this young man I told you of, or I will kill myself.'

Here the queen endeavoured to calm the princess by soft words. 'Daughter,' said she, 'how could any man come to you?' But instead of hearing her, the princess interrupted her, and flew out into such violence as obliged the queen to leave her, and retire in great affliction to inform the king of all that had passed.

The king hearing it had a mind likewise to be satisfied in person; and coming to his daughter's apartment, asked her if what he had just heard was true. 'Sir,' replied the princess, 'let us talk no more of that; I only beseech your majesty to grant me the favour that I may marry the young man. He was the finest and best made youth the sun ever saw. I entreat you, do not refuse me. But that your majesty may not longer doubt whether I have seen this young man, whether I did not do my utmost to awake him, without succeeding, see, if you please, this ring.' She then reached forth her hand, and showed the king a man's ring on her finger. The king did not know what to make of all this; but as he had shut her up as mad, he began to think her more mad than ever: therefore, without saying anything more to her, for fear she might do violence to herself or somebody about her, he had her chained, and shut up more closely than before, allowing her only the nurse to wait on her, with a good guard at the door.

The king, exceedingly concerned at this indisposition of his daughter, sought all possible means to get her cured. He assembled his council, and after having acquainted them with the condition she was in, 'If any of you,' said he, 'is capable of undertaking her cure, and succeeds, I will give her to him in marriage, and make him heir to my dominions and crown after my decease.'

The desire of marrying a handsome young princess, and the hopes of one day governing so powerful a kingdom as that of China, had a strange effect on an emir, already advanced in age, who was present at this council. As he was well skilled in magic, he offered to cure the king's daughter, and flattered himself he should succeed.

'I consent,' said the king, 'but I forgot to tell you one thing, and that is, that if you do not succeed you shall lose your head. It would not be reasonable that you should have so great a reward, and yet run no risk on your part; and what I say to you,' continued the king, 'I say to all others that shall come after you, that they may consider beforehand what they undertake.'

The emir, however, accepted the condition, and the king conducted him to where the princess was. She covered her face as soon as she saw them come in, and cried out, 'Your majesty surprises me by bringing with you a man whom I do not know, and by whom my religion forbids me to let myself be seen.'

'Daughter,' replied the king, 'you need not be scandalized, it is only one of my emirs who is come to demand you in marriage.'

'It is not, I perceive, the person that you have already given me, and whose faith is plighted by the ring I wear,' replied the princess; 'be not offended that I will never marry any other.'

The emir expected the princess would have said or done some extravagant thing, and was not a little disappointed when he heard her talk so calmly and rationally; for then he understood what was really the matter. He dared not explain himself to the king, who would not have suffered the princess to give her hand to any other than the person to whom he wished to give her with his own hand. He therefore threw himself at his majesty's feet, and said, 'After what I have heard and observed, sir, it will be to no purpose for me to think of curing the princess, since I have no remedies suited to her malady, for which reason I humbly submit my life to your majesty's pleasure.' The king, enraged at his incapacity and the trouble he had given him, caused him immediately to be beheaded.

Some days afterwards, his majesty, unwilling to have it said that he had neglected his daughter's cure, put forth a proclamation in his capital, to the effect that if there were any physician, astrologer, or magician, who would undertake to restore the princess to her senses, he need only come, and he should be employed, on condition of losing his head if he miscarried. He had the same published in the other principal cities and towns of his dominions, and in the courts of the princes his neighbours.

The first that presented himself was an astrologer and magician, whom the king caused to be conducted to the princess's prison. The astrologer drew forth out of a bag he carried under his arm an astrolabe, a small sphere, a chafing dish, several sorts of drugs for fumigations, a brass pot, with many other things, and desired he might have a fire lighted.

The princess demanded what all these preparations were for.

'Madam,' answered the astrologer, 'they are to exorcise the evil spirit that possesses you, to shut him up in this pot, and throw him into the sea.'

'Foolish astrologer,' replied the princess, 'I have no occasion for any of your preparations, but am in my perfect senses, and you alone are mad. If your art can bring him I love to me, I shall be obliged to you; otherwise you may go about your business, for I have nothing to do with you.'

'Madam,' said the astrologer, 'if your case be so, I shall desist from all endeavours, believing that only the king your father can remedy your disaster.' So putting up his apparatus again, he marched away, very much concerned that he had so easily undertaken to cure an imaginary malady.

Coming to give an account to the king of what he had done, he began thus boldly: 'According to what your majesty published in your proclamation, and what you were pleased to confirm to me yourself, I thought the princess was distracted, and depended on being able to recover her by the secrets I have long been acquainted with, but I soon found that your majesty alone is the physician who can cure her, by giving her in marriage the person whom she desires.'

The king was very much enraged at the astrologer, and had his head cut off upon the spot. Not to make too long a story of it, a hundred and fifty astrologers, physicians, and magicians all underwent the same fate, and their heads were set up on poles on every gate of the city.

The Princess of China's nurse had a son whose name was Marzavan, and who had been foster-brother to the princess, and brought up with her. Their friendship was so great during their childhood, and all the time they had been together, that they treated each other as brother and sister as they grew up, even some time after their separation.

This Marzavan, among other studies, had from his youth been much addicted to judicial astrology, geomancy, and the like secret arts, wherein he became exceedingly skilful. Not content with what he had learned from masters, he travelled as soon as he was able to bear the fatigue, and there was hardly any person of note in any science or art but he sought him in the most remote cities, and kept company with him long enough to obtain all the information he desired, so great was his thirst after knowledge.

After several years' absence in foreign parts on this account, he returned to the capital city of his native country, China, where seeing so many heads on the gate by which he entered, he was exceedingly surprised; and coming home he demanded for what reason they had been placed there, but more especially he inquired after the princess his foster-sister, whom he had not forgotten. As he could not receive an answer to one inquiry without the other, he heard at length a general account with much sorrow, waiting till he could learn more from his mother, the princess's nurse.

Although the nurse, mother to Marzavan, was very much taken up with the princess, she no sooner heard that her dear son had returned than she found time to come out, embrace him, and converse with him a little. Having told him, with tears in her eyes, what a sad condition the princess was in, and for what reason the king her father had shut her up, he desired to know of his mother if she could not procure him a private sight of her royal mistress, without the king's knowing it. After some pause, she told him she could say nothing for the present, but if he would meet her the next day at the same hour, she would give him an answer.

The nurse knowing that none could approach the princess but herself without leave of the officer who commanded the guard at the gate, addressed herself to him, who she knew had been so lately appointed that he could know nothing of what had passed at the court of China. 'You know,' said she to him, 'I have brought up the princess, and you may likewise have heard that I had a daughter whom I brought up along with her. This daughter has since been married; yet the princess still does her the honour to love her, and would fain see her, but without anybody's perceiving her coming in or out.'

The nurse would have gone on, but the officer cried, 'Say no more; I will with pleasure do anything to oblige the princess; go and fetch your daughter, or send for her about midnight, and the gate shall be open to you.'

As soon as night came, the nurse went to look for her son Marzavan, and having found him, she dressed him so artificially in women's clothes that nobody could know he was a man. She carried him along with her, and the officer verily believing it was her daughter, admitted them together.

The nurse, before she presented Marzavan, went to the princess, and said, 'Madam, this is not a woman I have brought to you; it is my son Marzavan in disguise, newly arrived from his travels, and he having a great desire to kiss your hand, I hope your highness will admit him to that honour.'

'What! my brother Marzavan,' said the princess, with great joy: 'come hither,' cried she, 'and take off that veil; for it is not unreasonable, surely, that a brother and a sister should see each other without covering their faces.'

Marzavan saluted her with profound respect, when she, without giving him time to speak, cried out, 'I am rejoiced to see you returned in good health, after so many years' absence without sending the least account all the while of your welfare, even to your good mother.'

'Madam,' replied Marzavan, 'I am infinitely obliged to your highness for your goodness in rejoicing at my health: I hoped to have heard a better account of yours than what to my great affliction I am now witness of. Nevertheless, I cannot but rejoice that I am come seasonably enough to bring your highness that remedy of which you stand so much in need; and though I should reap no other fruit of my studies and long voyage, I should think myself fully recompensed.'

Speaking these words, Marzavan drew forth out of his pocket a book and other things, which he judged necessary to be used, according to the account he had had from his mother of the princess's illness. The princess, seeing him make all these preparations, cried out, 'What! brother, are you then one of those that believe me mad? Undeceive yourself and hear me.'

The princess then began to relate to Marzavan all the particulars of her story, without omitting the least circumstance, even to the ring which was exchanged for hers, and which she showed him.

After the princess had done speaking, Marzavan, filled with wonder and astonishment, continued for some time with his eyes fixed on the ground, without speaking a word; but at length he lifted up his head and said, 'If it be as your highness says, which I do not in the least doubt, I do not despair of procuring you the satisfaction you desire; but I must first entreat your highness to arm yourself with patience for some time longer, till I shall return after I have travelled over kingdoms which I have not yet visited; and when you hear of my return, be assured that the object of your wishes is not far off.' So saying, Marzavan took leave of the princess, and set out next morning on his intended journey.

He travelled from city to city, from province to province, and from island to island, and in every place he passed through he could hear of nothing but the Princess Badoura (which was the Princess of China's name), and her history.

About four months afterwards, Marzavan arrived at Torf, a seaport town, great and populous, where he no more heard of the Princess Badoura, but where all the talk was of Prince Camaralzaman, who was ill, and whose history very much resembled hers. Marzavan was extremely delighted to hear this, and informed himself of the place where the prince was to be found. There were two ways to it; one by land and sea, the other by sea only, which was the shortest way.

Marzavan chose the latter, and embarking on board a merchant ship, he arrived safe in sight of the capital; but, just before it entered the port, the ship struck against a rock through the unskilfulness of the pilot, and foundered. It went down in sight of Prince Camaralzaman's castle, where were at that time the king and his grand vizier.

Marzavan could swim very well, and immediately on the ship's sinking cast himself into the sea, and got safe to the shore under the castle, where he was soon relieved by the grand vizier's order. After he had changed his clothes and been well treated, and had recovered, he was introduced to the grand vizier, who had sent for him.

Marzavan being a young man of good air and address, this minister received him very civilly; and when he heard him give such just and fitting answers to what was asked of him, conceived a great esteem for him. He also gradually perceived that he possessed a great deal of knowledge, and therefore said to him, 'From what I can understand, I perceive you are no common man; you have travelled a great way: would to God you had learned any secret for curing a certain sick person, who has greatly afflicted this court for a long while!'

Marzavan replied that if he knew what malady it was, he might perhaps find a remedy for it.

Then the grand vizier related to him the whole story of Prince Camaralzaman from its origin, and concealed nothing; his birth, his education, the inclination the king his father had to see him married early, his resistance and extraordinary aversion to marriage, his disobeying his father in full council, his imprisonment, his pretended extravagancies in prison, which were afterwards changed into a violent madness for a certain unknown lady, who, he pretended, had exchanged a ring with him; though, for his part, he verily believed there was no such person in the world.

Marzavan gave great attention to all the grand vizier said; and was infinitely rejoiced to find that, by means of his shipwreck, he had so fortunately lighted on the person he was looking after. He saw no reason to doubt that Prince Camaralzaman was the man, and the Princess of China the lady; therefore, without explaining himself further to the vizier, he desired to see him, that he might be better able to judge of his illness and its cure. 'Follow me,' said the grand vizier, 'and you will find the king with him, who has already desired that I should introduce you.'

The first thing that struck Marzavan on entering the prince's chamber was to find him upon his bed languishing, and with his eyes shut. Although he saw him in that condition, and although the king his father was sitting by him, he could not help crying out, 'Was there ever a greater resemblance!' He meant to the Princess of China; for it seems the princess and prince were much alike.

The words of Marzavan excited the prince's curiosity so far that he opened his eyes and looked at him. Marzavan, who had a ready wit, laid hold of that opportunity, and made his compliment in verse extempore: but in such a disguised manner, that neither the king nor grand vizier understood anything of the matter. However, he represented so nicely what had happened to him with the Princess of China, that the prince had no reason to doubt that he knew her, and could give him tidings of her. This made him so joyful, that the effects of it showed themselves in his eyes and looks.

After Marzavan had finished his compliment in verse which surprised Prince Camaralzaman so agreeably, his highness took the liberty to make a sign to the king his father, to go from the place where he was, and let Marzavan sit by him.

The king, overjoyed at this alteration, which gave him hopes of his son's speedy recovery, quitted his place, and taking Marzavan by the hand, led him to it. Then his majesty demanded of him who he was, and whence he came. And upon Marzavan's answering that he was a subject of China and came from that kingdom, the king cried out, 'Heaven grant that you may be able to cure my son of this profound melancholy, and I shall be eternally obliged to you; all the world shall see how handsomely I will reward you.' Having said thus, he left the prince to converse at full liberty with the stranger, whilst he went and rejoiced with the grand vizier.

Marzavan leaning down to the prince, spoke low in his ear, thus: 'Prince,' said he, 'it is time you should cease to grieve. The lady for whom you suffer is the Princess Badoura, daughter of Gaiour, King of China. This I can assure your highness from what she has told me of her adventure, and what I have learned of yours. She has suffered no less on your account than you have on hers.' Here he began to relate all that he knew of the princess's story, from the night of their extraordinary interview.

He omitted not to acquaint him how the king had treated those who had failed in their pretensions to cure the princess of her indisposition. 'But your highness is the only person,' added he, 'that can cure her effectually, and may present yourself without fear. However, before you undertake so great a voyage, I would have you perfectly recovered, and then we will take such measures as are necessary. Think then immediately of the recovery of your health.'

This discourse had a marvellous effect on the prince. He found such great relief that he felt he had strength to rise, and begged leave of his father to dress himself, with such an air as gave the old king incredible pleasure.

The king could not refrain from embracing Marzavan, without inquiring into the means he had used to produce this wonderful effect, and soon after went out of the prince's chamber with the grand vizier to publish this agreeable news. He ordered public rejoicings for several days together, and gave great largesses to his officers and the people, alms to the poor, and caused the prisoners to be set at liberty throughout his kingdom. The joy was soon general in the capital and every corner of his dominions.

Prince Camaralzaman, though extremely weakened by almost continual want of sleep and long abstinence from almost all food, soon recovered his health. When he found himself in a condition to undertake the voyage, he took Marzavan aside, and said, 'Dear Marzavan, it is now time to perform the promise you have made me. I burn with impatience to see the charming princess, and if we do not set out on our journey immediately I shall soon relapse into my former condition. One thing still troubles me,' continued he, 'and that is the difficulty I shall meet with in getting leave of my father to go. This would be a cruel disappointment to me, if you do not contrive a way to prevent it. You see he scarcely ever leaves me.'

At these words the prince fell to weeping: and Marzavan said, 'I foresaw this difficulty; let not your highness be grieved at that, for I will undertake to prevent it. My principal design in this voyage was to deliver the Princess of China from her malady, and this from all the reasons of mutual affection which we have borne to each other from our birth, besides the zeal and affection I otherwise owe her; and I should be wanting in my duty to her, if I did not do my best endeavour to effect her cure and yours, and exert my utmost skill. This then is the means I have contrived to obtain your liberty. You have not stirred abroad for some time, therefore let the king your father understand you have a mind to take the air, and ask his leave to go out on a hunting party for two or three days with me. No doubt he will grant your request; when he has done so, order two good horses to be got ready, one to mount, the other to change, and leave the rest to me.'

Next day Prince Camaralzarnan took his opportunity. He told the king he was desirous to take the air, and, if he pleased, would go and hunt for two or three days with Marzavan. The king gave his consent, but bade him be sure not to stay out above one night, since too much exercise at first might impair his health, and a too long absence create his majesty uneasiness. He then ordered him to choose the best horses in his stable, and himself took particular care that nothing should be wanting. When all was ready, his majesty embraced the prince, and having recommended the care of him to Marzavan, he let him go. Prince Camaralzaman and Marzavan were soon mounted, when, to amuse the two grooms that led the fresh horses, they made as if they would hunt, and so got as far off the city and out of the road as was possible. When night began to approach, they alighted at a caravansera or inn, where they supped, and slept till about midnight; then Marzavan awakened the prince without awakening the grooms, and desired his highness to let him have his suit, and to take another for himself, which was brought in his baggage. Thus equipped, they mounted the fresh horses, and after Marzavan had taken one of the groom's horses by the bridle, they set out as hard as their horses could go.

At daybreak they were in a forest, where, coming to the meeting of four roads, Marzavan desired the prince to wait for him a little, and went into the forest. He then killed the groom's horse, and after having torn the prince's suit, which he had put off, he besmeared it with blood and threw it into the highway.

The prince demanded his reason for what he had done. He told his highness he was sure the king his father would no sooner find that he did not return, and come to know that he had departed without the grooms, than he would suspect something, and immediately send people in quest of them. 'They that come to this place,' said he, 'and find these blood-stained clothes, will conclude you are devoured by wild beasts, and that I have escaped to avoid the king's anger. The king, persuading himself that you are dead will stop further pursuit, and we may have leisure to continue our journey without fear of being followed. I must confess,' continued Marzavan, 'that this is a violent way of proceeding, to alarm an old father with the death of his son, whom he loves so passionately; but his joy will be the greater when he hears you are alive and happy.'

'Brave Marzavan,' replied the prince,' I cannot but approve such an ingenious stratagem, or sufficiently admire your conduct: I am under fresh obligations to you for it.'

The prince and Marzavan, well provided with cash for their expenses, continued their journey both by land and sea, and found no other obstacle but the length of time which it necessarily took up. They, however, arrived at length at the capital of China, where Marzavan, instead of going to his lodgings, carried the prince to a public inn. They tarried there incognito for three days to rest themselves after the fatigue of the voyage; during which time Marzavan caused an astrologer's dress to be made for the prince. The three days being expired, the prince put on his astrologer's habit; and Marzavan left him to go and acquaint his mother, the Princess Badoura's nurse, of his arrival, to the end that she might inform the Princess.

Prince Camaralzaman, instructed by Marzavan as to what he was to do, and provided with all he wanted as an astrologer, came next morning to the gate of the king's palace, before the guards and porters, and cried aloud, 'I am an astrologer, and am come to effect a cure on the estimable Princess Badoura, daughter of the most high and mighty monarch Gaiour, King of China, on the conditions proposed by his majesty, to marry her if I succeed, or else to lose my life for my fruitless and presumptuous attempt.'

Besides the guards and porters at the gate, this drew together a great number of people about Prince Camaralzaman. No physician, astrologer, nor magician had appeared for a long time, deterred by the many tragic examples of ill success that appeared before their eyes; it was therefore thought that there were no more men of these professions in the world, or that there were no more so mad as those that had gone before them.

The prince's good mien, noble air, and blooming youth made everybody that saw him pity him. 'What mean you, sir,' said some that were nearest to him, 'thus to expose a life of such promising expectation to certain death? Cannot the heads you see on all the gates of this city deter you from such an undertaking? Consider what you do: abandon this rash attempt, and be gone.'

The prince continued firm, notwithstanding all these remonstrances; and as he saw nobody come to introduce him, he repeated the same cry with a boldness that made everybody tremble. Then they all cried, 'Let him alone, he is resolved to die; God have mercy upon his youth and his soul!' He then proceeded to cry out a third time in the same manner, when the grand vizier came in person, and introduced him to the King of China.

As soon as the prince came into the king's presence, he bowed and kissed the ground. The king, who, of all that had hitherto presumptuously exposed their lives on this occasion, had not seen one worthy to cast his eyes upon, felt real compassion for Prince Camaralzaman on account of the danger he was about to undergo. But as he thought him more deserving than ordinary, he showed him more honour, and made him come and sit by him. 'Young man,' said he, 'I can hardly believe that you, at this age, can have acquired experience enough to dare attempt the cure of my daughter. I wish you may succeed; and would give her to you in marriage with all my heart, with the greatest joy, more willingly than I should have done to others that have offered themselves before you; but I must declare to you at the same time, with great concern, that if you do not succeed in your attempt, notwithstanding your noble appearance and your youth you must lose your head.'

'Sir,' replied the prince, 'I am under infinite obligations to your majesty for the honour you design me, and the great goodness you show to a stranger; but I desire your majesty to believe that I would not have come from so remote a country as I have done, the name of which perhaps may be unknown in your dominions, if I had not been certain of the cure I propose. What would not the world say of my fickleness, if, after such great fatigues and dangers as I have undergone on this account, I should abandon the enterprise? Even your majesty would soon lose that esteem you have conceived for me. If I must die, sir, I shall die with the satisfaction of not having lost your esteem after I have merited it. I beseech your majesty therefore to keep me no longer impatient to display the certainty of my art.'

Then the king commanded the officer who had the custody of the princess to introduce Prince Camaralzaman into her apartment: but before he would let him go, he reminded him once more that he was at liberty to renounce his design; yet the prince paid no heed, but, with astonishing resolution and eagerness, followed the officer.

When they came to a long gallery, at the end of which was the princess's apartment, the prince, who saw himself so near the object of the wishes which had occasioned him so many tears, pushed on, and got before the officer.

The officer, redoubling his pace, with much ado got up with him. 'Whither away so fast?' cried he, taking him by the arm; 'you cannot get in without me: and it would seem that you have a great desire for death thus to run to it headlong. Not one of all those many astrologers and magicians I have introduced before made such haste as yourself to a place whither I fear you will come but too soon.'

'Friend,' replied the Prince, looking earnestly at the officer, and continuing his pace, 'this was because none of the astrologers you speak of were so sure of their art as I am of mine: they were certain, indeed, that they would die if they did not succeed, but they had no certainty of their success. On this account they had reason to tremble on approaching the place whither I go, and where I am sure to find my happiness.' He had just spoken these words as he was at the door. The officer opened it, and introduced him into a great hall, whence was an entrance into the princess's chamber, divided from it only by a piece of tapestry.

Prince Camaralzaman stopt before he entered, speaking softly to the officer for fear of being heard in the princess's chamber. 'To convince you,' said he, 'that there is neither presumption, nor whim, nor youthful conceit in my undertaking, I leave it to your own desire whether I should cure the princess in your presence, or where we are, without going any further?'

The officer was amazed to hear the prince talk to him with such confidence: he left off insulting him, and said seriously, 'It is no matter whether you do it here or there, provided the business is done: cure her how you will, you will get immortal honour by it, not only in this court, but over all the world.'

The prince replied, 'It will be best then to cure her without seeing her, that you may be witness of my skill: notwithstanding my impatience to see a princess of her rank, who is to be my wife, yet, out of respect to you, I will deprive myself of that pleasure for a little while.' He was furnished with everything suitable for an astrologer to carry about him; and taking pen, ink, and paper out of his pocket, he wrote a letter to the princess.

When the prince had finished his letter, he folded it up, and enclosed in it the princess's ring, without letting the officer see what he did. When he had sealed it, he gave it to him: 'There, friend,' said he, 'carry it to your mistress; if it does not cure her as soon as she reads it, and sees what is inclosed in it, I give you leave to tell everybody that I am the most ignorant and impudent astrologer that ever was, is, or shall be.'

The officer, entering the Princess of China's chamber, gave her the packet he received from Prince Camaralzaman. 'Madam,' said he, 'the boldest astrologer that ever lived, if I am not mistaken, has arrived here, and pretends that on reading this letter and seeing what is in it you will be cured; I wish he may prove neither a liar nor an impostor.'

The Princess Badoura took the letter, and opened it with a great deal of indifference, but when she saw the ring, she had not patience to read it through; she rose hastily, broke the chain that held her, ran to the door and opened it. She knew the prince as soon as she saw him, and he knew her; they at once embraced each other tenderly, without being able to speak for excess of joy: they looked on one another a long time, wondering how they met again after their first interview. The princess's nurse, who ran to the door with her, made them come into her chamber, where the Princess Badoura gave the prince her ring, saying, 'Take it; I cannot keep it without restoring yours, which I will never part with; neither can it be in better hands.'

The officer immediately went to tell the King of China what had happened. 'Sir,' said he, 'all the astrologers and doctors who have hitherto pretended to cure the princess were fools in comparison with the last. He made use neither of schemes nor spells or perfumes, or anything else, but cured her without seeing her.' Then he told the king how he did it. The monarch was agreeably surprised at the news, and going forthwith to the princess's chamber embraced her: he afterwards embraced the prince, and, taking his hand, joined it to the princess's.

'Happy stranger,' said the king, 'whoever you are, I will keep my word, and give you my daughter to marry; though, from what I see in you, it is impossible for me to believe that you are really what you appear to be, and would have me believe you.'

Prince Camaralzaman thanked the king in the most humble tones, that he might the better show his gratitude. 'As for my person,' said he, 'I must own I am not an astrologer, as your majesty very judiciously guessed; I only put on the habit of one, that I might succeed more easily in my ambition to be allied to the most potent monarch in the world. I was born a prince, and the son of a king and queen; my name is Camaralzaman; my father is Schahzaman, who now reigns over the islands that are well known by the name of the Islands of the Children of Khaledan.' He then told him his history.

When the prince had done speaking, the king said to him, 'This history is so extraordinary that it deserves to be known to posterity; I will take care it shall be; and the original being deposited in my royal archives, I will spread copies of it abroad, that my own kingdoms and the kingdoms around me may know it.'

The marriage was solemnized the same day, and the rejoicings for it were universal all over the empire of China. Nor was Marzavan forgotten: the king immediately gave him an honourable post in his court, and a promise of further advancement; and held continual feastings for several months, to show his joy.

The Loss of the Talisman

E. Dixon

SOON AFTER HIS marriage Prince Camaralzaman dreamt one night that he saw his father Schahzaman on his death-bed, and heard him speak thus to his attendants: 'My son, my son, whom I so tenderly loved, has abandoned me.' He awoke with a great sigh, which aroused the princess, who asked him the cause of it. Next morning the princess went to her own father, and finding him alone kissed his hand and thus addressed herself to him: 'Sir, I have a favour to beg of your majesty; it is that you will give me leave to go with the prince my husband to see King Schahzaman, my father-in-law.'

'Daughter,' replied the king, 'though I shall be very sorry to part with you for so long a time, your resolution is worthy of you: go, child, I give you leave, but on condition that you stay no longer than a year in King Schahzaman's court.'

The princess communicated the King of China's consent to Prince Camaralzaman, who was transported with joy to hear it.

The King of China gave orders for preparations to be made for the journey; and when all things were ready, he accompanied the prince and princess several days' journey on their way. They parted at length with great weeping on all sides: the king embraced them, and having desired the prince to be kind to his daughter, and to love her always, he left them to proceed on their journey, and, to divert his thoughts, hunted all the way home.

Prince Camaralzaman and the Princess Badoura travelled for about a month, and at last came to a meadow of great extent, planted with tall trees, forming an agreeable shade. The day being unusually hot, Camaralzaman thought it best to encamp there. They alighted in one of the finest spots, and the prince ordered his servants to pitch their tents, and went himself to give directions. The princess, weary with the fatigue of the journey, bade her women untie her girdle, which they laid down by her, and when she fell asleep, her attendants left her by herself.

Prince Camaralzaman having seen all things in order came to the tent where the princess was sleeping; he entered, and sat down without making any noise, intending to take a nap himself; but observing the princess's girdle lying by her, he took it up, and looked at the diamonds and rubies one by one. In doing this, he saw a little purse hanging to it, sewed neatly on to the stuff, and tied fast with a ribbon; he felt it, and found there was something solid inside it. Desirous to know what it was, he opened the purse, and took out a cornelian, engraven with unknown figures and characters. 'This cornelian,' said the prince to himself, 'must be something very valuable, or my princess would not carry it with so much care.' It was Badoura's talisman, which the Queen of China had given her daughter as a charm, to keep her, as she said, from any harm as long as she had it about her.

The prince, the better to look at the talisman, took it out to the light, the tent being dark; and while he was holding it up in his hand, a bird darted down from the air and snatched it away from him.

Imagine the concern and grief of Prince Camaralzaman when he saw the bird fly away with the talisman. He was more troubled at it than words can express, and cursed his unseasonable curiosity, by which his dear princess had lost a treasure that was so precious and so much valued by her.

The bird having got her prize settled on the ground not far off, with the talisman in her mouth. The prince drew near, in hopes she would drop it; but, as he approached, the bird took wing, and settled again on the ground further off. Camaralzaman followed, and the bird, having swallowed the talisman, took a further flight: the prince still followed; the further she flew, the more eager he grew in pursuing her. Thus the bird drew him along from hill to valley, and valley to hill all day, every step leading him further away from the field where he had left his camp and the Princess Badoura; and instead of perching at night on a bush where he might probably have taken her, she roosted on a high tree, safe from pursuit. The prince, vexed to the heart for taking so much pains to no purpose, thought of returning to the camp; 'but,' said he to himself, 'which way shall I return? Shall I go down the hills and valleys which I passed over? Shall I wander in darkness? and will my strength bear me out? How dare I appear before my princess without her talisman?' Overwhelmed with such thoughts, and tired with the pursuit, he lay down under a tree, where he passed the night.

He awoke the next morning before the bird had left the tree, and, as soon as he saw her on the wing, followed her again that whole day, with no better success, eating nothing but herbs and fruits all the way. He did the same for ten days together, pursuing the bird, and keeping his eye upon her from morning to night, always lying under the tree where she roosted. On the eleventh day the bird continued flying, and came near a great city. When the bird came to the walls, she flew over them and the prince saw no more of her; so he despaired of ever recovering the Princess Badoura's talisman.

Camaralzaman, whose grief was beyond expression, went into the city, which was built by the seaside, and had a fine port; he walked up and down the streets without knowing where he was, or where to stop. At last came to the port, in as great uncertainty as ever what he should do. Walking along the river-side, he perceived the gate of a garden open, and an old gardener at work. The good man looked up and saw that he was a stranger and a Mussulman, so he asked him to come in, and to shut the door after him.

Camaralzaman entered, and, as the gardener bade him shut the door, demanded of the gardener why he was so cautious.

'Because,' replied the old man, 'I see you are a stranger newly arrived, and a Mussulman, and this city is inhabited for the most part by idolaters, who have a mortal aversion to us Mussulmans, and treat those few of us that are here with great barbarity. I suppose you did not know this, and it is a miracle that you have escaped as you have thus far, these idolaters being very apt to fall upon the Mussulmans that are strangers, or to draw them into a snare, unless those strangers know how to beware of them.'

Camaralzaman thanked the honest gardener for his advice, and the safety he offered him in his house: he would have said more, but the good man interrupted him, saying, 'You are weary, and must want to refresh yourself. Come in and rest.' He conducted him into his little hut, and after the prince had eaten heartily of what he set before him, he requested him to relate how he came there.

Camaralzaman complied with his request, and when he had ended his story, he asked him which was the nearest way to the king his father's territories; 'for it is in vain,' said he, 'for me to think of finding my princess where I left her, after wandering eleven days from the spot. Ah!' continued he, 'how do I know she is alive?' and so saying, he burst into tears.

The gardener replied that there was no possibility of his going thither by land, the roads were so difficult and the journey so long; besides, he must necessarily pass through the countries of so many barbarous nations that he would never reach his father's. It was a year's journey from the city where he was to any country inhabited only by Mussulmans; the quickest passage for him would be to go to the Isle of Ebony, whence he might easily transport himself to the Isles of the Children of Khaledan: a ship sailed from the port every year to Ebony, and he might take that opportunity of returning to those islands. 'The ship departed,' said the gardener, 'but a few days ago: if you had come a little sooner you might have taken your passage in it. If you will wait the year round until it makes the voyage again, and will stay with me in my house, such as it is, you will be as welcome to it as to your own.'

Prince Camaralzaman was glad he had met with such a place of refuge, in a place where he had no acquaintances. He accepted the offer, and lived with the gardener till the time came that the ship was to sail to the Isle of Ebony. He spent his time in working all day in the garden, and all night in sighs, tears and complaints, thinking of his dear Princess Badoura.

We must leave him in this place, to return to the princess, whom we left asleep in her tent.

The princess slept a long time, and, when she awoke, wondered that Prince Camaralzaman was not with her; she called her women, and asked them if they knew where he was. They told her they saw him enter the tent, but did not see him go out again. While they were talking to her, she took up her girdle, found the little purse open, and the talisman gone. She did not doubt but that Camaralzaman had taken it to see what it was, and that he would bring it back with him. She waited for him impatiently till night, and could not imagine what made him stay away from her so long.

When it was quite dark, and she could hear no news of him, she fell into violent grief; she cursed the talisman, and the man that made it. She could not imagine how her talisman should have caused the prince's separation from her: she did not however lose her judgment, and came to a courageous decision as to what she should do.

She only and her women knew of the prince's being gone; for his men were asleep in their tents. The princess, fearing they would betray her if they had any knowledge of it, moderated her grief, and forbade her women to say or do anything that might create the least suspicion. She then laid aside her robe, and put on one of Prince Camaralzaman's, being so like him that next day, when she came out, his men took her for him.

She commanded them to pack up their baggage and begin their march; and when all things were ready, she ordered one of her women to go into her litter, she herself mounting on horseback, and riding by her side.

They travelled for several months by land and sea; the princess continuing, the journey under the name of Camaralzaman. They took the Isle of Ebony on their way to the Isles of the Children of Khaledan. They went to the capital of the Isle of Ebony, where a king reigned whose name was Armanos. The persons who first landed gave out that the ship carried Prince Camaralzaman, who was returning from a long voyage and was driven in there by a storm, and the news of his arrival was presently carried to the court.

King Armanos, accompanied by most of his courtiers, went immediately to meet the prince, and met the princess just as she was landing, and going to the lodging that had been taken for her. He received her as the son of a king who was his friend, and conducted her to the palace, where an apartment was prepared for her and all her attendants, though she would fain have excused herself, and have lodged in a private house. He showed her all possible honour, and entertained her for three days with extraordinary magnificence. At the end of this time, King Armanos, understanding that the princess, whom he still took for Prince Camaralzaman, talked of going on board again to proceed on her voyage, charmed with the air and qualities of such an accomplished prince as he took her to be, seized an opportunity when she was alone, and spoke to her in this manner: 'You see, prince, that I am old, and cannot hope to live long; and, to my great mortification, I have not a son to whom I may leave my crown. Heaven has only blest me with one daughter, the Princess Haiatalnefous whose beauty cannot be better matched than with a prince of your rank and accomplishments. Instead of going home, stay and marry her from my hand, with my crown, which I resign in your favour. It is time for me to rest, and nothing could be a greater pleasure to me in my retirement than to see my people ruled by so worthy a successor to my throne.'

The King of the Isle of Ebony's generous offer to bestow his only daughter in marriage, and with her his kingdom, on the Princess Badoura, put her into unexpected perplexity. She thought it would not become a princess of her rank to undeceive the king, and to own that she was not Prince Camaralzaman, but his wife, when she had assured him that she was he himself, whose part she had hitherto acted so well. She was also afraid refuse the honour he offered her, lest, as he was much bent upon the marriage, his kindness might turn to aversion and hatred, and he might attempt something even against her life. Besides, she was not sure whether she might not find Prince Camaralzaman in the court of King Schahzaman his father.

These considerations, added to the prospect of obtaining a kingdom for the prince her husband, in case she found him again, determined her to accept the proposal of King Armanos, and marry his daughter; so after having stood silent for some minutes, she with blushes, which the king took for a sign of modesty, answered, 'Sir, I am infinitely obliged to your majesty for your good opinion of me, for the honour you do me, and the great favour you offer me, which I cannot pretend to merit, and dare not refuse.

'But, sir,' continued she, 'I cannot accept this great alliance on any other condition than that your majesty will assist me with your counsel, and that I do nothing without first having your approbation.'

The marriage treaty being thus concluded and agreed on, the ceremony was put off till next day. In the mean time Princess Badoura gave notice to her officers, who still took her for Prince Camaralzaman, of what she was going to do so that they might not be surprised at it, assuring them that the Princess Badoura consented. She talked also to her women, and charged them to continue to keep the secret.

The King of the Isle of Ebony, rejoicing that he had got a son-in-law so much to his satisfaction, next morning summoned his council, and acquainted them with his design of marrying his daughter to Prince Camaralzaman, whom he introduced to them; and having made him sit down by his side, told them he resigned the crown to the prince, and required them to acknowledge him for king, and swear fealty to him. Having said this, he descended from his throne, and the Princess Badoura, by his order, ascended it. As soon as the council broke up, the new king was proclaimed through the city, rejoicings were appointed for several days, and couriers despatched all over the kingdom to see the same ceremonies observed with the same demonstrations of joy.

As soon as they were alone, the Princess Badoura told the Princess Haiatalnefous the secret, and begged her to keep it, which she promised faithfully to do.

'Princess,' said Haiatalnefous, 'your fortune is indeed strange, that a marriage, so happy as yours was, should be shortened by so unaccountable an accident. Pray heaven you may meet with your husband again soon, and be sure that I will religiously keep the secret committed to me. It will be to me the greatest pleasure in the world to be the only person in the great kingdom of the Isle of Ebony who knows what and who you are, while you go on governing the people as happily as you have begun. I only ask of you at present to be your friend.' Then the two princesses tenderly embraced each other, and after a thousand expressions of mutual friendship lay down to rest.

While these things were taking place in the court of the Isle of Ebony, Prince Camaralzaman stayed in the city of idolaters with the gardener, who had offered him his house till the ship sailed.

One morning when the prince was up early, and, as he used to do, was preparing to work in the garden, the gardener prevented him, saying, 'This day is a great festival among the idolaters, and because they abstain from all work themselves, so as to spend the time in their assemblies and public rejoicings, they will not let the Mussulmans work. Their shows are worth seeing. You will have nothing to do to-day: I leave you here. As the time approaches in which the ship is accustomed to sail for the Isle of Ebony, I will go and see some of my friends, and secure you a passage in it.' The gardener put on his best clothes, and went out.

When Prince Camaralzaman was alone, instead of going out to take part in the public joy of the city, the solitude he was in brought to his mind, with more than usual violence, the loss of his dear princess. He walked up and down the garden sighing and groaning, till the noise which two birds made on a neighbouring tree tempted him to lift up his head, and stop to see what was the matter.

Camaralzaman was surprised to behold a furious battle between these two birds, fighting one another with their beaks. In a very little while one of them fell down dead at the foot of a tree; the bird that was victorious took wing again, and flew away.

In an instant, two other large birds, that had seen the fight at a distance, came from the other side of the garden, and pitched on the ground one at the feet and the other at the head of the dead bird: they looked at it some time, shaking their heads in token of grief; after which they dug a grave with their talons, and buried it.

When they had filled up the grave with the earth they flew away, and returned in a few minutes, bringing with them the bird that had committed the murder, the one holding one of its wings in its beak, and the other one of its legs; the criminal all the while crying out in a doleful manner, and struggling to escape. They carried it to the grave of the bird which it had lately sacrificed to its rage, and there sacrificed it in just revenge for the murder it had committed. They killed the murderer with their beaks. They then opened it, tore out the entrails, left the body on the spot unburied, and flew away.

Camaralzaman remained in great astonishment all the time that he stood beholding this sight. He drew near the tree, and casting his eyes on the scattered entrails of the bird that was last killed, he spied something red hanging out of its body. He took it up, and found it was his beloved Princess Badoura's talisman, which had cost him so much pain and sorrow and so many sighs since the bird snatched it out of his hand. 'Ah, cruel monster!' said he to himself, still looking at the bird, 'thou tookest delight in doing mischief, so I have the less reason to complain of that which thou didst to me: but the greater it was, the more do I wish well to those that revenged my quarrel on thee, in punishing thee for the murder of one of their own kind.'

It is impossible to express Prince Camaralzaman's joy: 'Dear princess,' continued he to himself, 'this happy minute, which restores to me a treasure so precious to thee, is without doubt a presage of our meeting again, perhaps even sooner than I think.'

So saying, he kissed the talisman, wrapped it up in a ribbon, and tied it carefully about his arm. Till now he had been almost every night a stranger to rest, his trouble always keeping him awake, but the next night he slept soundly: he rose somewhat later the next morning than he was accustomed to do, put on his working clothes, and went to the gardener for orders. The good man bade him root up an old tree which bore no fruit.

Camaralzaman took an axe, and began his work. In cutting off a branch of the root, he found that his axe struck against something that resisted the blow and made a great noise. He removed the earth, and discovered a broad plate of brass, under which was a staircase of ten steps. He went down, and at the bottom saw a cavity about six yards square, with fifty brass urns placed in order around it, each with a cover over it. He opened them all, one after another, and there was not one of them which was not full of gold-dust. He came out of the cave, rejoicing that he had found such a vast treasure: he put the brass plate over the staircase, and rooted up the tree against the gardener's return.

The gardener had learned the day before that the ship which was bound for the Isle of Ebony would sail in a few days, but the exact time was not yet fixed. His friend promised to let him know the day, if he called upon him on the morrow; and while Camaralzaman was rooting up the tree, he went to get his answer. He returned with a joyful countenance, by which the prince guessed that he brought him good news. 'Son,' said the old man (so he always called him, on account of the difference of age between him and the prince), 'be joyful, and prepare to embark in three days, for the ship will then certainly set sail: I have arranged with the captain for your passage.'

'In my present situation,' replied Camaralzaman, 'you could not bring me more agreeable news; and in return, I have also tidings that will be as welcome to you; come along with me, and you shall see what good fortune heaven has in store for you.'

The prince led the gardener to the place where he had rooted up the tree, made him go down into the cave, and when he was there showed him what a treasure he had discovered, and thanked Providence for rewarding his virtue, and the labour he had done for so many years.

'What do you mean?' replied the gardener: 'do you imagine I will take these riches as mine? They are yours: I have no right to them. For fourscore years, since my father's death, I have done nothing but dig in this garden, and could not discover this treasure, which is a sign that it was destined for you, since you have been permitted to find it. It suits a prince like you, rather than me: I have one foot in the grave, and am in no want of anything. Providence has bestowed it upon you, just when you are returning to that country which will one day be your own, where you will make a good use of it.'

Prince Camaralzaman would not be outdone in generosity by the gardener. They had a long dispute about it. At last the prince solemnly protested that he would have none of it, unless the gardener would divide it with him and take half. The good man, to please the prince, consented; so they parted it between them, and each had twenty-five urns.

Having thus divided it, 'Son,' said the gardener to the prince, 'it is not enough that you have got this treasure; we must now contrive how to carry it so privately on board the ship that nobody may know anything of the matter, otherwise you will run the risk of losing it. There are no olives in the Isle of Ebony, and those that are exported hence are wanted there; you know I have plenty of them; take what you will; fill fifty pots, half with the gold dust, and half with olives, and I will get them carried to the ship when you embark.'

Camaralzaman followed this good advice, and spent the rest of the day in packing up the gold and the olives in the fifty pots, and fearing lest the talisman, which he wore on his arm, might be lost again, he carefully put it into one of the pots, marking it with a particular mark, to distinguish it from the rest. When they were all ready to be shipped, the prince retired with the gardener, and talking together, he related to him the battle of the birds, and how he had found the Princess Badoura's talisman again. The gardener was equally surprised and joyful to hear it for his sake.

Whether the old man was quite worn out with age, or had exhausted himself too much that day, he had a very bad night; he grew worse the next day, and on the third day, when the prince was to embark, was so ill that it was plain he was near his end. As soon as day broke, the captain of the ship came in person with several seamen to the gardener's; they knocked at the garden-door, and Camaralzaman opened it to them. They asked him where the passenger was that was to go with him. The prince answered, 'I am he; the gardener who arranged with you for my passage is ill, and cannot be spoken with: come in, and let your men carry those pots of olives and my baggage aboard. I will only take leave of the gardener, and follow you.'

The seamen took up the pots and the baggage, and the captain bade the prince make haste, for the wind being fair they were waiting for nothing but him.

When the captain and his men were gone, Camaralzaman went to the gardener, to take leave of him, and thank him for all his good offices: but he found him in the agonies of death, and had scarcely time to bid him rehearse the articles of his faith, which all good Mussulmans do before they die, when the gardener expired in his presence.

The prince being under the necessity of embarking immediately hastened to pay the last duty to the deceased. He washed his body, buried him in his own garden (for the Mahometans had no cemetery in the city of the idolaters, where they were only tolerated), and as he had nobody to assist him it was almost evening before he had put him in the ground. As soon as he had done it he ran to the water- side, carrying with him the key of the garden, intending, if he had time, to give it to the landlord; otherwise to deposit it in some trusty person's hand before a witness, that he might leave it when he was gone. When he came to the port, he was told the ship had sailed several hours before he came and was already out of sight. It had waited three hours for him, and the wind standing fair, the captain dared not stay any longer.

It is easy to imagine that Prince Camaralzaman was exceedingly grieved to be forced to stay longer in a country where he neither had nor wished to have any acquaintance: to think that he must wait another twelvemonth for the opportunity he had lost. But the greatest affliction of all was his having let go the Princess Badoura's talisman, which he now gave over for lost. The only course that was left for him to take was to return to the garden to rent it of the landlord, and to continue to cultivate it by himself, deploring his misery and misfortunes. He hired a boy to help him to do some part of the drudgery; and that he might not lose the other half of the treasure, which came to him by the death of the gardener, who died without heirs, he put the gold-dust into fifty other pots, which he filled up with olives, to be ready against the time of the ship's return.

While Prince Camaralzaman began another year of labour, sorrow and impatience, the ship, having a fair wind, continued her voyage to the Isle of Ebony, and happily arrived at the capital.

The palace being by the sea-side, the new king, or rather the Princess Badoura, espying the ship as she was entering the port, with all her flags flying, asked what vessel it was; she was told that it came annually from the city of the idolaters, and was generally richly laden.

The princess, who always had Prince Camaralzaman in her mind amidst the glories which surrounded her, imagined that the prince might be on board, and resolved to go down to the ship and meet him. Under presence of inquiring what merchandise was on board, and having the first sight of the goods, and choosing the most valuable, she commanded a horse to be brought, which she mounted, and rode to the port, accompanied by several officers in waiting, and arrived at the port just as the captain came ashore. She ordered him to be brought before her, and asked whence he came, how long he had been on his voyage, and what good or bad fortune he had met with: if he had any stranger of quality on board, and particularly with what his ship was laden.

The captain gave a satisfactory answer to all her demands; and as to passengers, assured her that there were none but merchants in his ship, who were used to come every year and bring rich stuffs from several parts of the world to trade with, the finest linens painted and plain, diamonds, musk, ambergris, camphor, civet, spices, drugs, olives, and many other articles.

The Princess Badoura loved olives extremely: when she heard the captain speak of them, she said, 'Land them, I will take them off your hands: as to the other goods, tell the merchants to bring them to me, and let me see them before they dispose of them, or show them to any one else.'

The captain, taking her for the King of the Isle of Ebony, replied, 'Sire, there are fifty great pots of olives, but they belong to a merchant whom I was forced to leave behind. I gave him notice myself that I was waiting for him, and waited a long time; but as he did not come, and the wind was good, I was afraid of losing it, and so set sail.'

The princess answered, 'No matter; bring them ashore; we will make a bargain for them.'

The captain sent his boat aboard, and in a little time it returned with the pots of olives. The princess demanded how much the fifty pots might be worth in the Isle of Ebony. 'Sir,' said the captain, 'the merchant is very poor, and your majesty will do him a singular favour if you give him a thousand pieces of silver.'

'To satisfy him,' replied the princess, 'and because you tell me he is poor, I will order you a thousand pieces of gold for him, which do you take care to give him.' The money was accordingly, paid, and the pots carried to the palace in her presence.

Night was drawing on when the princess withdrew into the inner palace, and went to the Princess Haiatalnefous' apartment, ordering the fifty pots of olives to be brought thither. She opened one, to let the Princess Haiatalnefous taste them, and poured them into a dish. Great was her astonishment when she found the olives mingled with gold-dust. 'What can this mean?' said she, 'it is wonderful beyond comprehension.' Her curiosity increasing, she ordered Haiatalnefous' women to open and empty all the pots in her presence; and her wonder was still greater, when she saw that the olives in all of them were mixed with gold-dust; but when she saw her talisman drop out of that into which the prince had put it, she was so surprised that she fainted away. The Princess Haiatalnefous and her women restored the Princess Badoura by throwing cold water on her face. When she recovered her senses, she took the talisman and kissed it again and again; but not being willing that the Princess Haiatalnefous's women, who were ignorant of her disguise, should hear what she said, she dismissed them.

'Princess,' said she to Haiatalnefous, as soon as they were gone, 'you, who have heard my story, surely guessed that it was at the sight of the talisman that I fainted. This is the talisman, the fatal cause of my losing my dear husband Prince Camaralzaman; but as it was that which caused our separation, so I foresee it will be the means of our meeting again soon.'

The next day, as soon as it was light, she sent for the captain of the ship; and when he came she spoke to him thus: 'I want to know something more of the merchant to whom the olives belong, that I bought of you yesterday. I think you told me you had left him behind you in the city of the idolaters: can you tell me what he is doing there?'

'Yes, sire,' replied the captain, 'I can speak on my own knowledge. I arranged for his passage with a very old gardener, who told me I should find him in his garden, where he worked under him. He showed me the place, and for that reason I told your majesty he was poor. I went there to call him. I told him what haste I was in, spoke to him myself in the garden, and cannot be mistaken in the man.'

'If what you say is true,' replied the Princess Badoura, 'you must set sail this very day for the city of idolaters, and fetch me that gardener's man, who is my debtor; else I will not only confiscate all your goods and those of your merchants, but your and their lives shall answer for his. I have ordered my seal to be put on the warehouses where they are, which shall not be taken off till you bring me that man. This is all I have to say to you; go, and do as I command you.'

The captain could make no reply to this order, the disobeying of which would be a very great loss to him and his merchants. He told them about it, and they hastened him away as fast as they could after he had laid in a stock of provisions and fresh water for his voyage. They were so diligent, that he set sail the same day. He had a prosperous voyage to the city of the idolaters, where he arrived in the night. When he was as near to the city as he thought convenient, he would not cast anchor, but let the ship ride off the shore; and going into his boat, with six of his stoutest seamen, he landed a little way off the port, whence he went directly to Camaralzaman's garden.

Though it was about midnight when he arrived there, the prince was not asleep. His separation from the fair Princess of China his wife afflicted him as usual. He cursed the minute in which his curiosity tempted him to touch the fatal girdle.

Thus did he pass those hours which are devoted to rest, when he heard somebody knock at the garden door. He ran hastily to it, half-dressed as he was; but he had no sooner opened it, than the captain and his seamen took hold of him, and carried him by force on board the boat, and so to the ship, and as soon as he was safely lodged, they set sail immediately, and made the best of their way to the Isle of Ebony.

Hitherto Camaralzaman, the captain, and his men had not said a word to one another; at last the prince broke silence, and asked the captain, whom he recognized, why they had taken him away by force? The captain in his turn demanded of the prince whether he was not a debtor of the King of Ebony?

'I the King of Ebony's debtor!' replied Camaralzaman in amazement; 'I do not know him, I never had anything to do with him in my life, and never set foot in his kingdom.'

The captain answered, 'You should know that better than I; you will talk to him yourself in a little while: till then, stay here and have patience.'

Though it was night when he cast anchor in the port, the captain landed immediately, and taking Prince Camaralzaman with him hastened to the palace, where he demanded to be introduced to the king.

The Princess Badoura had withdrawn into the inner palace; however, as soon as she had heard of the captain's return and Camaralzaman's arrival, she came out to speak to him. As soon as she set her eyes on the prince, for whom she had shed so many tears, she knew him in his gardener's clothes. As for the prince, who trembled in the presence of a king, as he thought her, to whom he was to answer for an imaginary debt, it did not enter into his head that the person whom he so earnestly desired to see stood before him. If the princess had followed the dictates of her inclination, she would have run to him and embraced him, but she put a constraint on herself, believing that it was for the interest of both that she should act the part of a king a little longer before she made herself known. She contented herself for the present with putting him into the hands of an officer, who was then in waiting, with a charge to take care of him till the next day.

When the Princess Badoura had provided for Prince Camaralzaman, she turned to the captain, whom she was now to reward for the important service he had done her. She commanded another officer to go immediately and take the seal off the warehouse where his and his merchants' goods were, and gave him a rich diamond, worth much more than the expense of both his voyages. She bade him besides keep the thousand pieces of gold she had given him for the pots of olives, telling him she would make up the account with the merchant herself.

This done, she retired to the Princess of the Isle of Ebony's apartment, to whom she communicated her joy, praying her to keep the secret still. She told her how she intended to manage to reveal herself to Prince Camaralzaman, and to give him the kingdom.

The Princess of the Isle of Ebony was so far from betraying her, that she rejoiced and entered fully into the plan.

The next morning the Princess of China ordered Prince Camaralzaman to be apparelled in the robes of an emir or governor of a province. She commanded him to be introduced into the council, where his fine person and majestic air drew all the eyes of the lords there present upon him.

The Princess Badoura herself was charmed to see him again, as handsome as she had often seen him, and her pleasure inspired her to speak the more warmly in his praise. When she addressed herself to the council, having ordered the prince to take his seat among the emirs, she spoke to them thus: 'My lords, this emir whom I have advanced to the same dignity with you is not unworthy the place assigned him. I have known enough of him in my travels to answer for him, and I can assure you he will make his merit known to all of you.'

Camaralzaman was extremely amazed to hear the King of the Isle of Ebony, whom he was far from taking for a woman, much less for his dear princess, name him, and declare that he knew him, while he thought himself certain that he had never seen him before in his life. He was much more surprised when he heard him praise him so excessively. Those praises, however, did not disconcert him, though he received them with such modesty as showed that he did not grow vain. He prostrated himself before the throne of the king, and rising again, 'Sire,' said he, 'I want words to express my gratitude to your majesty for the honour you have done me: I shall do all in my power to render myself worthy of your royal favour.'

From the council-board the prince was conducted to a palace, which the Princess Badoura had ordered to be fitted up for him; where he found officers and domestics ready to obey his commands, a stable full of fine horses, and everything suitable to the rank of an emir. Then the steward of his household brought him a strong box full of gold for his expenses.

The less he understood whence came his great good fortune, the more he admired it, but never once imagined that he owed it to the Princess of China.

Two or three days after, the Princess Badoura, that he might be nearer to her, and in a more distinguished post, made him high treasurer, which office had lately become vacant. He behaved himself in his new charge with so much integrity, yet obliging everybody, that he not only gained the friendship of the great but also the affections of the people, by his uprightness and bounty.

Camaralzaman would have been the happiest man in the world, if he had had his princess with him. In the midst of his good fortune he never ceased lamenting her, and grieved that he could hear no tidings of her, especially in a country where she must necessarily have come on her way to his father's court after their separation. He would have suspected something had the Princess Badoura still gone by the name of Camaralzaman, but on her accession to the throne she changed it, and took that of Armanos, in honour of the old king her father-in-law. She was now known only by the name of the young King Armanos. There were very few courtiers who knew that she had ever been called Camaralzaman, which name she assumed when she arrived at the court of the Isle of Ebony, nor had Camaralzaman so much acquaintance with any of them yet as to learn more of her history.

The princess fearing he might do so in time, and desiring that he should owe the discovery to herself only, resolved to put an end to her own torment and his; for she had observed that as often as she discoursed with him about the affairs of his office, he fetched such deep sighs as could be addressed to nobody but her. She herself also lived under such constraint that she could endure it no longer.

The Princess Badoura had no sooner made this decision with the Princess Haiatalnefous, than she took Prince Camaralzaman aside, saying, 'I must talk with you about an affair, Camaralzaman, which requires much consideration, and on which I want your advice. Come hither in the evening, and leave word at home that you will not return; I will take care to provide you a bed.'

Camaralzaman came punctually to the palace at the hour appointed by the princess; she took him with her into the inner apartment, and having told the chief chamberlain, who was preparing to follow her, that she had no occasion for his service, and that he should only keep the door shut, she took him into a different apartment.

When the prince and princess entered the chamber she shut the door, and, taking the talisman out of a little box, gave it to Camaralzaman, saying, 'It is not long since an astrologer presented me with this talisman; you being skilful in all things, may perhaps tell me its use.'

Camaralzaman took the talisman, and drew near a lamp to look at it. As soon as he recollected it, with an astonishment which gave the princess great pleasure, 'Sire,' said he to the princess, 'your majesty asked me what this talisman is good for. Alas! it is only good to kill me with grief and despair, if I do not quickly find the most charming and lovely princess in the world to whom it belonged, whose loss it occasioned by a strange adventure, the very recital of which will move your majesty to pity such an unfortunate husband and lover, if you would have patience to hear it.'

'You shall tell me that another time,' replied the princess; 'I am very glad to tell you I know something of it already; stay here a little, and I will return to you in a moment.'

At these words she went into her dressing-room, put off her royal turban, and in a few minutes dressed herself like a woman; and having the girdle round her which she wore on the day of their separation, she entered the chamber.

Prince Camaralzaman immediately knew his dear princess, ran to her, and tenderly embraced her, crying out, 'How much I am obliged to the king, who has so agreeably surprised me!'

'Do not expect to see the king any more,' replied the princess, embracing him in her turn, with tears in her eyes; 'you see him in me: sit down, and I will explain this enigma to you.'

They sat down, and the princess told the prince the resolution she came to, in the field where they encamped the last time they were together, as soon as she perceived that she waited for him to no purpose; how she went through with it till she arrived at the Isle of Ebony, where she had been obliged to marry the Princess Haiatalnefous, and accept the crown which King Armanos offered her as a condition of the marriage: how the princess, whose merit she highly extolled, had kept the secret, and how she found the talisman in the pots of olives mingled with the gold dust, and how the finding it was the cause of her sending for him to the city of the idolaters.

The Princess Badoura and Prince Camaralzaman rose next morning as soon as it was light, but the princess would no more put on her royal robes as king; she dressed herself in the dress of a woman, and then sent the chief chamberlain to King Armanos, her father-in- law to desire he would be so good as to come to her apartment.

When the king entered the chamber, he was amazed to see there a lady who was unknown to him, and the high treasurer with her, who was not permitted to come within the inner palace. He sat down and asked where the king was.

The princess answered, 'Yesterday I was king, sir, and to-day I am the Princess of China, wife of the true Prince Camaralzaman, the true son of King Schahzaman. If your majesty will have the patience to hear both our stories, I hope you will not condemn me for putting an innocent deceit upon you.' The king bade her go on, and heard her discourse from the beginning to the end with astonishment. The princess on finishing it said to him, 'Sir, in our religion men may have several wives; if your majesty will consent to give your daughter the Princess Haiatalnefous in marriage to Prince Camaralzaman, I will with all my heart yield up to her the rank and quality of queen, which of right belongs to her, and content myself with the second place. If this precedence was not her due, I would, however, give it her, after she has kept my secret so generously.'

King Armanos listened to the princess with astonishment, and when she had done, turned to Prince Camaralzaman, saying, 'Son, since the Princess Badoura your wife, whom I have all along thought to be my son-in-law, through a deceit of which I cannot complain, assures me that she is willing, I have nothing more to do but to ask you if you are willing to marry my daughter and accept the crown, which the Princess Badoura would deservedly wear as long as she lived, if she did not quit it out of love to you.'

'Sir,' replied Prince Camaralzaman, 'though I desire nothing so earnestly as to see the king my father, yet the obligation I am under to your majesty and the Princess Haiatalnefous are so weighty, I can refuse her nothing.' Camaralzaman was proclaimed king, and married the same day with all possible demonstrations of joy.

Not long afterwards they all resumed the long interrupted journey to the Isles of the Children of Khaledan, where they were fortunate enough to find the old King Schahzaman still alive and overjoyed to see his son once more; and after several months' rejoicing, King Camaralzaman and the two queens returned to the Island of Ebony, where they lived in great happiness for the remainder of their lives.

Tale of Ali Bin Bakkar and of Shams Al-Nahar

Richard F. Burton

IT HATH REACHED me, O august King, that in days of yore and in times and ages long gone before, during the Caliphate of Harun al-Rashid, there was a merchant who named his son Abú al-Hasan Ali bin Táhir; and the same was great of goods and grace, while his son was fair of form and face and held in favour by all folk. He used to enter the royal palace without asking leave, for all the Caliph's concubines and slave-girls loved him, and he was wont to be companion with Al-Rashid in his cups and recite verses to him and tell him curious tales and witty. Withal he sold and bought in the merchants' bazar, and there used to sit in his shop a youth named Ali bin Bakkár, of the sons of the Persian Kings who was formous of form and symmetrical of shape and perfect of figure, with cheeks red as roses and joined eyebrows; sweet of speech, laughing-lipped and delighting in mirth and gaiety. Now it chanced one day, as the two sat talking and laughing behold, there came up ten damsels like moons, every one of them complete in beauty and loveliness, and elegance and grace; and amongst them was a young lady riding on a she-mule with a saddle of brocade and stirrups of gold. She wore an outer veil of fine stuff, and her waist was girt with a girdle of gold-embroidered silk; and she was even as saith the poet,

> "Silky her skin and silk that zoned waist;
> Sweet voice; words not o'er many nor too few:
> Two eyes quoth Allah 'Be,' and they became;
> And work like wine on hearts they make to rue:
> O love I feel! grow greater every night:
> O solace! Doom-day bring our interview."

And when the cortège reached Abu al-Hasan's shop, she alighted from her mule, and sitting down on the front board, saluted him, and he returned her salam. When Ali bin Bakkar saw her, she ravished his understanding and he rose to go away; but she said to him, "Sit in thy place. We came to thee and thou goest away: this is not fair!" Replied he, "O my lady, by Allah, I flee from what I see; for the tongue of the case saith,

> 'She is a sun which towereth high a-sky;
> So ease thy heart with cure by Patience lent:
> Thou to her skyey height shalt fail to fly;
> Nor she from skyey height can make descent.'"

When she heard this, she smiled and asked Abu al-Hasan, "What is the name of this young man?"; who answered, "He is a stranger;" and she enquired, "What countryman is he?"; whereto the merchant replied, "He is a descendant of the Persian Kings; his name is Ali son of Bakkar and the stranger deserveth honour." Rejoined she, "When my damsel comes to thee, come thou at once to us and bring him with thee, that we may entertain him in our abode, lest he blame us and say, 'There is no hospitality in the people of Baghdad'; for niggardliness is the worst fault a man can have. Thou hearest what I say to thee and, if thou disobey me, thou wilt incur my displeasure and I will never again visit thee or salute thee." Quoth Abu al-Hasan, "On my head and my eyes: Allah preserve me from thy displeasure, fair lady!" Then she rose and went her way. Such was her case; but as regards Ali bin Bakkar he remained in a state of bewilderment. Now after an hour the damsel came to Abu al-Hasan and said to him, "Of a truth my lady Shams Al-Nahar, the favourite of the Commander of the Faithful, Harun al-Rashid, biddeth thee to her, thee and thy friend, my lord Ali bin Bakkar." So he rose and, taking Ali with him, followed the girl to the Caliph's palace, where she carried them into a chamber and made them sit down. They talked together awhile, when behold, trays of food were set before them, and they ate and washed their hands. Then she brought them wine, and they drank deep and made merry; after which she bade them rise and carried them into another chamber, vaulted upon four columns, furnished after the goodliest fashion with various kinds of furniture, and adorned with decorations as it were one of the pavilions of Paradise. They were amazed at the rarities they saw; and, as they were enjoying a review of these marvels, suddenly up came ten slave-girls, like moons, swaying and swimming in beauty's pride, dazzling the sight and confounding the sprite; and they ranged themselves in two ranks as if they were of the black-eyed Brides of Paradise. And after a while in came other ten damsels, bearing in their hands lutes and divers instruments of mirth and music; and these, having saluted the two guests, sat down and fell to tuning their lute-strings. Then they rose and standing before them, played and sang and recited verses: and indeed each one of them was a seduction to the servants of the Lord. Whilst they were thus busied there entered other ten damsels like unto them, high-bosomed maids and of an equal age, with black-eyes and cheeks like the rose, joined eyebrows and looks languorous; a very fascination to every faithful wight and to all who looked upon them a delight; clad in various kinds of coloured silks, with ornaments that amazed man's intelligence. They took up their station at the door, and there succeeded them yet other ten damsels even fairer than they, clad in gorgeous array, such as no tongue can say; and they also stationed themselves by the doorway. Then in came a band of twenty damsels and amongst them the lady, Shams al-Nahar hight, as she were the moon among the stars swaying from side to side, with luring gait and in beauty's pride. And she was veiled to the middle with the luxuriance of her locks, and clad in a robe of azure blue and a mantilla of silk embroidered with gold and gems of price; and her waist was girt with a zone set with various kinds of precious stones. She ceased not to advance with her graceful and coquettish swaying, till she came to the couch that stood at the upper end of the chamber and seated herself thereon. But when Ali bin Bakkar saw her, he versified with these verses,

"Source of mine evils, truly, she alone 's,
Of long love-longing and my groans and moans;

> *Near her I find my soul in melting mood,*
> *For love of her and wasting of my bones."*

And finishing his poetry he said to Abu al-Hasan, "Hadst thou Dealt more kindly with me thou haddest forewarned me of these things ere I came hither, that I might have made up my mind and taken patience to support what hath befallen me." And he wept and groaned and complained. Replied Abu al-Hasan, "O my brother, I meant thee naught but good; but I feared to tell thee this, lest such transport should betide thee as might hinder thee from foregathering with her, and be a stumbling-block between thee and her. But be of good cheer and keep thine eyes cool and clear; for she to thee inclineth and to favour thee designeth." Asked Ali bin Bakkar, "What is this young lady's name?" Answered Abu al-Hasan, "She is hight Shams al-Nahar, one of the favourites of the Commander of the Faithful, Harun al-Rashid, and this is the palace of the Caliphate." Then Shams al-Nahar sat gazing upon the charms of Ali bin Bakkar and he upon hers, till both were engrossed with love for each other. Presently she commanded the damsels, one and all, to be seated, each in her rank and place, and all sat on a couch before one of the windows, and she bade them sing; whereupon one of them took up the lute and began caroling,

> *"Give thou my message twice*
> *Bring clear reply in trice!*
> *To thee, O Prince of Beau*
> *-ty with complaint I rise:*
> *My lord, as heart-blood dear*
> *And Life's most precious prize!*
> *Give me one kiss in gift*
> *Or loan, if thou devise:*
> *And if thou crave for more*
> *Take all that satisfies.*
> *Thou donn'st me sickness-dress*
> *Thee with health's weed I bless."*

Her singing charmed Ali bin Bakkar, and he said to her, "Sing me more of the like of these verses." So she struck the strings and began to chaunt these lines,

> *"By stress of parting, O beloved one,*
> *Thou mad'st these eyelids torment-race to run:*
> *Oh gladness of my sight and dear desire,*
> *Goal of my wishes, my religion!*
> *Pity the youth whose eyne are drowned in tears*
> *Of lover gone distraught and clean undone."*

When she had finished her verses, Shams al-Nahar said to another damsel, "Let us hear something from thee!" So she played a lively measure and began these couplets,

> *"His looks have made me drunken, not his wine;*
> *His grace of gait disgraced sleep to these eyne:*

> *Dazed me no cup, but cop with curly crop;*
> *His gifts overcame me not the gifts of vine:*
> *His winding locks my patience-clue unwound:*
> *His robed beauties robbed all wits of mine."*

When Shams Al-Nahar heard this recital from the damsel, she sighed heavily and the song pleased her. Then she bade another damsel sing; so she took the lute and began chanting,

> *"Face that with Sol in Heaven lamping vies;*
> *Youth-tide's fair fountain which begins to rise;*
> *Whose curly side-beard writeth writ of love,*
> *And in each curl concealeth mysteries:*
> *Cried Beauty, 'When I met this youth I knew*
> *'Tis Allah's loom such gorgeous robe supplies.'"*

When she had finished her song, Ali bin Bakkar said to the slave-maiden nearest him, "Sing us somewhat, thou O damsel." So she took the lute and began singing,

> *"Our trysting-time is all too short*
> *For this long coyish coquetry:*
> *How long this 'Nay, Nay!' and 'Wait, wait?'*
> *This is not old nobility!*
> *And now that Time deigns lend delight*
> *Profit of th' opportunity."*

When she ended, Ali bin Bakkar followed up her song with flowing tears; and, as Shams al-Nahar saw him weeping and groaning and complaining, she burned with love-longing and desire; and passion and transport consumed her. So she rose from the sofa and came to the door of the alcove, where Ali met her and they embraced with arms round the neck, and fell down fainting in the doorway; whereupon the damsels came to them and carrying them into the alcove, sprinkled rose-water upon them both. When they recovered, they found not Abu al-Hasan who had hidden himself by the side of a couch, and the young lady said, "Where is Abu al-Hasan?" So he showed himself to her from beside the couch and she saluted him, saying, "I pray Allah to give me the means of requiting thee, O kindest of men!" Then she turned to Ali bin Bakkar and said to him, "O my lord, passion hath not reached this extreme pass with thee without my feeling the like; but we have nothing to do save to bear patiently what calamity hath befallen us." Replied he, "By Allah, O my lady, union with thee may not content me nor gazing upon thee assuage the fire thou hast lighted, nor shall leave me the love of thee which hath mastered my heart but with the leaving of my life." So saying, he wept and the tears ran down upon his cheeks like thridded pearls; and when Shams al-Nahar saw him weep, she wept for his weeping. But Abu al-Hasan exclaimed, "By Allah, I wonder at your case and am confounded at your condition; of a truth, your affair is amazing and your chance dazing. What! this weeping while ye are yet together: then how will it be what time ye are parted and far separated?" And he continued, "Indeed, this is no tide for weeping and wailing, but a season for meeting and merry-making; rejoice, therefore, and take your pleasure and shed no more tears!" Then Shams al-Nahar signed to a slave-girl, who arose and presently returned with handmaids bearing a table, whose dishes of silver were full of various rich viands. They set the table before the pair and Shams al-Nahar began to eat and to place tid-bits in the mouth of Ali bin Bakkar; and they ceased not so doing till they were satisfied, when the table was removed and they washed their hands. Then the waiting-women fetched censers with all manner of incense, aloe-wood and ambergris and mixed scents; and sprinkling-flasks full of rose-water were also brought and they were fumigated and perfumed. After this the slaves set on vessels of graven gold, containing all kinds of sherbets, besides fruits fresh and dried, that heart can desire and eye delight in; and lastly one brought a flagon of carnelion full of old wine. Then Shams al-Nahar chose out ten handmaids to attend on them and ten singing women; and, dismissing the rest to their apartments, bade some of those who remained strike the lute. They did as she bade them and one of them began to sing,

> *"My soul to him who smiled back my salute,*
> *In breast reviving hopes that were no mo'e: The hand o' Love my secret brought*
> *to light,*
> *And censor's tongues what lies my ribs below: My tear-drops ever press twixt*
> *me and him,*
> *As though my tear-drops showing love would flow."*

When she had finished her singing, Shams al-Nahar rose and, filling a goblet, drank it off, then crowned it again and handed it to Ali bin Bakkar – And Shahrazad perceived the dawn of day and ceased saying her permitted say.

When it was the One Hundred and Fifty-fourth Night,

She said, it hath reached me, O auspicious King, that Shams al-Nahar filled a goblet and handed it to Ali bin Bakkar; after which she bade another damsel sing; and she began singing these couplets,

> *"My tears thus flowing rival with my wine,*
> *Pouring the like of what fills cup to brink: By Allah wot I not an run these eyne*
> *Wi' wine, or else it is of tears I drink."*

And when she ended her recitation, Ali bin Bakkar drained his cup and returned it to Shams al-Nahar. She filled it again and gave it to Abu al-Hasan who tossed it off. Then she took the lute, saying, "None shall sing over my cup save myself;" so she screwed up the strings and intoned these verses,

> *"The tears run down his cheeks in double row,*
> *And in his breast high flameth lover-lowe:*
> *He weeps when near, a-fearing to be far;*
> *And, whether far or near, his tear-drops flow."*

And the words of another,

> *"Our life to thee, O cup-boy Beauty-dight!*
> *From parted hair to calves; from black to white:*

Sol beameth from thy hands, and from thy lips
Pleiads, and full Moon through thy collar's night,
Good sooth the cups, which made our heads fly round,
Are those thine eyes pass round to daze the sight:
No wonder lovers hail thee as full moon
Waning to them, for self e'er waxing bright:
Art thou a deity to kill and quicken,
Bidding this fere, forbidding other wight?
Allah from model of thy form made Beau
-ty and the Zephyr scented with thy sprite.
Thou art not of this order of human
-ity but angel lent by Heaven to man."

When Ali bin Bakkar and Abu al-Hasan and those present heard Shams al-Nahar's song, they were like to fly for joy, and sported and laughed; but while they were thus enjoying themselves lo! up came a damsel, trembling for fear and said, "O my lady, the Commander of the Faithful's eunuchs are at the door, Afíf and Masrúr and Marján and others whom wot I not." When they heard this they were like to die with fright, but Shams al-Nahar laughed and said, "Have no fear!" Then quoth she to the damsel, "Keep answering them whilst we remove hence." And she caused the doors of the alcove to be closed upon Ali and Abu al-Hasan, and let down the curtains over the entrance (they being still within); after which she shut the door of the saloon and went out by the privy wicket into the flower-garden, where she seated herself on a couch she had there and made one of the damsels knead her feet. Then she dismissed the rest of her women to their rooms and bade the portress admit those who were at the door; whereupon Masrur entered, he and his company of twenty with drawn swords. And when they saluted her, she asked, "Wherefore come ye?"; whereto they answered, "The Commander of the Faithful saluteth thee. Indeed he is desolated for want of thy sight; he letteth thee know that this be to him a day of joy and great gladness and he wisheth to seal his day and complete his pleasure with thy company at this very hour. So say, wilt go to him or shall he come to thee?" Upon this she rose and, kissing the earth, replied, "I hear and I obey the commandment of the Prince of True Believers!" Then she summoned the women guards of her household and other slave-damsels, who lost no time in attending upon her and made a show of obeying the Caliph's orders. And albeit everything about the place was in readiness, she said to the eunuchs, "Go to the Commander of the Faithful and tell him that I await him after a little space, that I may make ready for him a place with carpets and other matters." So they returned in haste to the Caliph, whilst Shams al-Nahar, doffing her outer gear, repaired to her lover, Ali bin Bakkar, and drew him to her bosom and bade him farewell, whereat he wept sore and said, "O my lady, this leave-taking will cause the ruin of my very self and the loss of my very soul; but I pray Allah grant me patience to support the passion wherewith he hath afflicted me!" Replied she, "By Allah, none shall suffer perdition save I; for thou wilt fare forth to the bazar and consort with those that shall divert thee, and thy life will be sound and thy love hidden forsure; but I shall fall into trouble and tristesse nor find any to console me, more by token that I have given the Caliph a tryst, wherein haply great peril shall betide me by reason of my love for thee and my longing for thee and my grief at being parted from thee. For with what tongue shall I sing and with what heart shall I present myself before the Caliph? and with what speech shall I company the Commander of the Faithful in his cups? and with what eyes shall I look upon a place where thou art absent? and with what taste shall I drink wine of which thou drinkest not?" Quoth Abu al-Hasan, "Be not troubled but take patience and be not remiss in entertaining the Commander of the Faithful this night, neither show him any neglect, but be of good heart." Now at this juncture, behold, up came a damsel, who said to Shams al-Nahar, "O my lady, the Caliph's pages are come." So she hastily rose to her feet and said to the maid, "Take Abu al-Hasan and his friend and carry them to the upper balcony giving upon the garden and there leave them till darkness come on; when do thou contrive to carry them forth." Accordingly the girl led them up to the balcony and, locking the door upon them both, went her way. As they sat looking on the garden lo! the Caliph appeared escorted by near an hundred eunuchs, with drawn swords in hand and girt about with a score of damsels, as they were moons, all clad in the richest of raiment and on each one's head was a crown set with jewels and rubies; while each carried a lighted flambeau. The Caliph walked in their midst, they encompassing him about on all sides, and Masrur and Afíf and Wasíf went before him and he bore himself with a graceful gait. So Shams al-Nahar and her maidens rose to receive him and, meeting him at the garden-door, kissed ground between his hands; nor did they cease to go before him till they brought him to the couch whereon he sat down, whilst all the waiting-women who were in the garden and the eunuchs stood before him and there came fair handmaids and concubines holding in hand lighted candles and perfumes and incense and instruments of mirth and music. Then the Sovereign bade the singers sit down, each in her place, and Shams al-Nahar came up and, seating herself on a stool by the side of the Caliph's couch, began to converse with him; all this happening whilst Abu al-Hasan and Ali bin Bakkar looked on and listened, unseen of the King. Presently the Caliph fell to jesting and toying with Shams al-Nahar and both were in the highest spirits, glad and gay, when he bade them throw open the garden pavilion. So they opened the doors and windows and lighted the tapers till the place shone in the season of darkness even as the day. Then the eunuchs removed thither the wine-service and (quoth Abu al-Hasan) "I saw drinking-vessels and rarities whose like mine eyes never beheld, vases of gold and silver and all manner of noble metals and precious stones, such as no power of description can describe, till indeed it seemed to me I was dreaming, for excess of amazement at what I saw!" But as for Ali bin Bakkar, from the moment Shams al-Nahar left him, he lay strown on the ground for stress of love and desire; and, when he revived, he fell to gazing upon these things that had not their like and saying to Abu al-Hasan, "O my brother, I fear lest the Caliph see us or come to know of our case; but the most of my fear is for thee. For myself, of a truth I know that I am about to be lost past recourse, and the cause of my destruction is naught but love and longing and excess of desire and distraction, and disunion from my beloved after union with her; but I beseech Allah to deliver us from this perilous predicament." And they ceased not to look out of the balcony on the Caliph who was taking his pleasure, till the banquet was spread before him, when he turned to one of the damsels and said to her, "O Gharám, let us hear some of thine enchanting songs." So she took the lute and tuning it, began singing,

> "The longing of a Bedouin maid, whose folks are far away,
> Who yearns after the willow of the Hejaz and the bay, —

Whose tears, when she on travellers lights, might for their water serve
And eke her her passion, with its heat, their bivouac-fire purvey, —
Is not more fierce nor ardent than my longing for my love,
Who deems that I commit a crime in loving him alway."

Now when Shams al-Nahar heard these verses she slipped off the stool whereon she sat and fell to the earth fainting and became insensible to the world around her; upon which the damsels came and lifted her up. And when Ali bin Bakkar saw this from the balcony he also slipped down senseless, and Abu al-Hasan said, "Verily Fate hath divided love-desire equally upon you twain!" As he spoke lo! in came the damsel who had led them up to the balcony and said to him, "O Abu al-Hasan, arise thou and thy friend and come down, for of a truth the world hath waxed strait upon us and I fear lest our case be discovered or the Caliph become aware of you; unless you descend at once we are dead ones." Quoth he, "And how shall this youth descend with me seeing that he hath no strength to rise?" Thereupon the damsel began sprinkling rose-water on Ali bin Bakkar till he came to his senses, when Abu al-Hasan lifted him up and the damsel made him lean upon her. So they went down from the balcony and walked on awhile till the damsel opened a little iron door, and made the two friends pass through it, and they came upon a bench by the Tigris' bank. Thereupon the slave-girl clapped her hands and there came up a man with a little boat to whom said she, "Take up these two young men and land them on the opposite side." So both entered the boat and, as the man rowed off with them and they left the garden behind them, Ali bin Bakkar looked back towards the Caliph's palace and the pavilion and the grounds; and bade them farewell with these two couplets,

"I offered this weak hand as last farewell,
While to heart-burning fire that hand is guided: O let not this end union! Let not this
Be last provision for long road provided!"

Thereupon the damsel said to the boatman, "Make haste with them both." So he plied his oars deftly (the slave-girl being still with them) – And Shahrazad perceived the dawning day and ceased saying her permitted say.

When it was the One Hundred and Fifty-fifth Night,

She said, it hath reached me, O auspicious King, that the boatman rowed them towards the other bank till they reached it and landed, whereupon she took leave of them, saying, "It were my wish not to abandon you, but I can go no farther than this." Then she turned back, whilst Ali bin Bakkar lay prostrate on the ground before Abu al-Hasan and by no manner of means could he rise, till his friend said to him, "Indeed this place is not sure and I fear lest we lose our lives in this very spot, by reason of the lewd fellows who infest it and highwaymen and men of lawlessness." Upon this Ali bin Bakkar arose and walked a little but could not continue walking. Now Abu al-Hasan had friends in that quarter; so he made search for one of them, in whom he trusted, and who was of his intimates, and knocked at the door. The man came out quickly and seeing them, bade them welcome and brought them into his house, where he seated them and talked with them and asked them whence they came. Quoth Abu al-Hasan, "We came out but now, being obliged thereto by a person with whom I had dealings and who hath in his hands dirhams of mine. And it reached me that he designed to flee into foreign parts with my monies; so I fared forth to-night in quest of him, taking with me for company this youth, Ali bin Bakkar; but, when we came hoping to see the debtor, he hid from us and we could get no sight of him. Accordingly we turned back, empty-handed without a doit, but it was irksome to us to return home at this hour of the night; so weeting not whither to go, we came to thee, well knowing thy kindness and wonted courtesy." "Ye are welcome and well come!" answered the host, and studied to do them honour; so the twain abode with him the rest of their night and as soon as the daylight dawned, they left him and made their way back without aught of delay to the city. When they came to the house of Abu al-Hasan, he conjured his comrade to enter; so they went in and lying down on the bed, slept awhile. As soon as they awoke, Abu al-Hasan bade his servants spread the house with rich carpets, saying in his mind, "Needs must I divert this youth and distract him from thinking of his affliction, for I know his case better than another." Then he called for water for Ali bin Bakkar who, when it was brought, rose up from his bed and making his ablutions, prayed the obligatory prayers which he had omitted for the past day and night; after which he sat down and began to solace himself by talking with his friend. When Abu al-Hasan saw this, he turned to him and said, "O my lord, it were fitter for thy case that thou abide with me this night, so thy breast may be broadened and the distress of love-longing that is upon thee be dispelled and thou make merry with us, so haply the fire of thy heart may thus be quenched." Ali replied, "O my brother, do what seemeth good to thee; for I may not on any wise escape from what calamity hath befallen me; so act as thou wilt." Accordingly, Abu al-Hasan arose and bade his servants summon some of the choicest of his friends and sent for singers and musicians who came; and meanwhile he made ready meat and drink for them; so they sat eating and drinking and making merry through the rest of the day till nightfall. Then they lit the candles, and the cups of friendship and good fellowship went round amongst them and the time passed pleasantly with them. Presently, a singing-woman took the lute and began singing,

> "I've been shot by Fortune, and shaft of eye
> Down struck me and parted from fondest friend:
> Time has proved him foe and my patience failed,
> Yet I ever expected it thus would end."

When Ali bin Bakkar heard her words, he fell to the earth in a swoon and ceased not lying in his fainting fit till day-break; and Abu al-Hasan despaired of him. But, with the dawning, he came to himself and sought to go home; nor could his friend hinder him, for fear of the issue of his affair. So he made his servants bring a she-mule and, mounting Ali thereon, carried him to his lodgings, he and one of his men. When he was safe at home, Abu al-Hasan thanked Allah for his deliverance from that sore peril and sat awhile with him, comforting him; but Ali could not contain himself, for the violence of his love and longing. So Abu al-Hasan rose to take leave of him and return to his own place. – And Shahrazad perceived the dawn of day and ceased to say her permitted say.

When it was the One Hundred and Fifty-sixth Night,

She said, it hath reached me, O auspicious King, that when Abu al-Hasan rose to take leave of him, Ali son of Bakkar exclaimed, "O my brother, leave me not without news." "I hear and obey," replied the other; and forthwith went away and, repairing to his shop, opened it and sat there all day, expecting news of Shams al-Nahar. But none came. He passed the night in his own house and, when dawned the day, he walked to Ali bin Bakkar's lodging and went in and found him thrown on his bed, with his friends about him and physicians around him prescribing something or other, and the doctors feeling his pulse. When he saw Abu al-Hasan enter he smiled, and the visitor, after saluting him, enquired how he did and sat with him till the folk withdrew, when he said to him, "What plight is this?" Quoth Ali bin Bakkar, "It was bruited abroad that I was ill and my comrades heard the report; and I have no strength to rise and walk so as to give him the lie who noised abroad my sickness, but continue lying strown here as thou seest. So my friends came to visit me; say, however, O my brother, hast thou seen the slave-girl or heard any news of her?" He replied, "I have not seen her, since the day we parted from her on Tigris' bank;" and he presently added, "O my brother, beware thou of scandal and leave this weeping." Rejoined Ali, "O my brother, indeed, I have no control over myself;" and he sighed and began reciting,

> "She gives her woman's hand a force that fails the hand of me,
> And with red dye on wrist she gars my patience fail and flee:
> And for her hand she fears so sore what shafts her eyes discharge,
> She's fain to clothe and guard her hand with mail-ring panoply:
> The leach in ignorance felt my pulse the while to him I cried,
> 'Sick is my heart, so quit my hand which hath no malady:'
> Quoth she to that fair nightly vision favoured me and fled,
> 'By Allah picture him nor add nor 'bate in least degree!'
> Replied the Dream, 'I leave him though he die of thirst,' I cry,
> 'Stand off from water-pit and say why this persistency.'
> Rained tear-pearls her Narcissus-eyes, and rose on cheek belit
> She made my sherbet, and the lote with bits of hail she bit."

And when his recital was ended he said, "O Abu al-Hasan, I am smitten with an affliction from which I deemed myself in perfect surety, and there is no greater ease for me than death." Replied he, "Be patient, haply Allah will heal thee!" Then he went out from him and repairing to his shop opened it, nor had he sat long, when suddenly up came the handmaid who saluted him. He returned her salam and looking at her, saw that her heart was palpitating and that she was in sore trouble and showed signs of great affliction: so he said to her, "Thou art welcome and well come! How is it with Shams al-Nahar?" She answered, "I will presently tell thee, but first let me know how doth Ali bin Bakkar." So he told her all that had passed and how his case stood, whereat she grieved and sighed and lamented and marvelled at his condition. Then said she, "My lady's case is still stranger than this; for when you went away and fared homewards, I turned back, my heart beating hard on your account and hardly crediting your escape. On entering I found her lying prostrate in the pavilion, speaking not nor answering any, whilst the Commander of the Faithful sat by her head not knowing what ailed her and finding none who could make known to him aught of her ailment. She ceased not from her swoon till midnight, when she recovered and the Prince of the Faithful said to her, 'What harm hath happened to thee, O Shams al-Nahar, and what hath befallen thee this night?' Now when she heard the Caliph's words she kissed his feet and said, 'Allah make me thy ransom, O Prince of True Believers! Verily a sourness of stomach lighted a fire in my body, so that I lost my senses for excess of pain, and I know no more of my condition.' Asked the Caliph, 'What hast thou eaten to-day?'; and she answered, 'I broke my fast on something I had never tasted before.' Then she feigned to be recovered and calling for a something of wine, drank it, and begged the Sovereign to resume his diversion. So he sat down again on his couch in the pavilion and the sitting was resumed, but when she saw me, she asked me how you fared. I told her what I had done with you both and repeated to her the verses which Ali bin Bakkar had composed at parting-tide, whereat she wept secretly, but presently held her peace. After awhile, the Commander of the Faithful ordered a damsel to sing, and she began reciting,

> 'Life has no sweet for me since forth ye fared;
> Would Heaven I wot how fare ye who forsake:
> 'Twere only fit my tears were tears of blood,
> Since you are weeping for mine absence sake.'

But when my lady heard this verse she fell back on the sofa in a swoon," – And Shahrazad perceived the dawn of day and ceased saying her permitted say.

When it was the One Hundred and Fifty-seventh Night,

She said, it hath reached me, O auspicious King, that the slave-girl continued to Abu al-Hasan, "But when my lady heard this verse, she fell back on the sofa in a swoon, and I seized her hand and sprinkled rose-water on her face, till she revived, when I said to her, 'O my lady, expose not thyself and all thy palace containeth. By the life of thy beloved, be thou patient!' She replied, 'Can aught befal me worse than death which indeed I seek, for by Allah, my ease is therein?' Whilst we were thus talking, another damsel sang these words of the poet,

'Quoth they, 'Maybe that Patience lend thee ease!'

Quoth I, 'Since fared he where is Patience' place? Covenant he made 'twixt me and him, to cut the cords of Patience at our last embrace!'

And as soon as she had finished her verse Shams al-Nahar swooned away once more, which when the Caliph saw, he came to her in haste and commanded the wine to be removed and each damsel to return to her chamber. He abode with her the rest of the night, and when dawned the day, he sent for chirurgeons and leaches and bade them medicine her, knowing not that her sickness arose from love and longing. I tarried with her till I deemed her in a way of recovery, and this is what kept me from thee. I have now left her with a number of her body-women, who were greatly concerned for her, when she bade me go to you two and bring her news of Ali bin Bakkar and return to her with the tidings." When Abu al-Hasan heard her story, he marvelled and said, "By Allah, I have acquainted thee with his whole case; so now return to thy mistress; and salute her for me and diligently exhort her to have patience and say to her, 'Keep thy secret!'; and tell her that I know all her case which is indeed hard and one which calleth for nice conduct." She thanked him and taking leave of him, returned to her mistress. So far concerning her; but as regards Abu al-Hasan, he ceased not to abide in his shop till the end of the day, when he arose and shut it and locked it and betaking himself to Ali bin Bakkar's house knocked at the door. One of the servants came out and admitted him; and when Ali saw him, he smiled and congratulated himself on his coming, saying, "O Abu al-Hasan, thou hast desolated me by thine absence this day; for indeed my soul is pledged to thee during the rest of my time." Answered the other, "Leave this talk! Were thy healing at the price of my hand, I would cut it off ere thou couldst ask me; and, could I ransom thee with my life, I had already laid it down for thee. Now this very day, Shams al-Nahar's handmaid hath been with me and told me that what hindered her coming ere this was the Caliph's sojourn with her mistress; and she acquainted me with everything which had betided her." And he went on to repeat to him all that the girl had told him of Shams al-Nahar; at which Ali bin Bakkar lamented sore and wept and said to him, "Allah upon thee, O my brother, help me in this affliction and teach me what course I shall take. Moreover, I beg thee of thy grace to abide with me this night, that I may have the solace of thy society." Abu al-Hasan agreed to this request, replying that he would readily night there; so they talked together till even-tide darkened, when Ali bin Bakkar groaned aloud and lamented and wept copious tears, reciting these couplets,

> "Thine image in these eyne, a-lip thy name,
> My heart thy home; how couldst thou disappear?
> How sore I grieve for life which comes to end,
> Nor see I boon of union far or near."
> And these the words of another,
> "She split my casque of courage with eye-swords that sorely smite;
> She pierced my patience' ring-mail with her shape like cane-spear light:
> Patched by the musky mole on cheek was to our sight displayed
> Camphor set round with ambergris, light dawning through the night.
> Her soul was sorrowed and she bit carnelion stone with pearls
> Whose unions in a sugared tank ever to lurk unite:
> Restless she sighed and smote with palm the snows that clothe her breast,
> And left a mark whereon I looked and ne'er beheld such sight,
> Pens, fashioned of her coral nails with ambergris for ink,
> Five lines on crystal page of breast did cruelly indite:
> O swordsmen armed with trusty steel! I bid you all beware
> When she on you bends deadly glance which fascinates the sprite:
> And guard thyself, O thou of spear! whenas she draweth near
> To tilt with slender quivering shape, likest the nut-brown spear."

And when Ali bin Bakkar ended his verse, he cried out with a great cry and fell down in a fit. Abu al-Hasan thought that his soul had fled his body and he ceased not from his swoon till day-break, when he came to himself and talked with his friend, who continued to sit with him till the forenoon. Then he left him and repaired to his shop; and hardly had he opened it, when lo! the damsel came and stood by his side. As soon as he saw her, she made him a sign of salutation which he returned; and she delivered to him the greeting message of her mistress and asked, "How doth Ali bin Bakkar?" Answered he, "O handmaid of good, ask me not of his case nor what he suffereth for excess of love-longing; he sleepeth not by night neither resteth he by day; wakefulness wasteth him and care hath conquered him and his condition is a consternation to his friend." Quoth she, "My lady saluteth thee and him, and she hath written him a letter, for indeed she is in worse case than he; and she entrusted the same to me, saying, 'Do not return save with the answer; and do thou obey my bidding.' Here now is the letter, so say, wilt thou wend with me to him that we may get his reply?" "I hear and obey," answered Abu al-Hasan, and locking his shop and taking with him the girl he went, by a way different from that whereby he came, to Ali bin Bakkar's house, where he left her standing at the door and walked in. – And Shahrazad perceived the dawn of day and ceased to say her permitted say.

When it was the One Hundred and Fifty-eighth Night,

She said, it hath reached me, O auspicious King, that Abu al-Hasan went with the girl to the house of Ali son of Bakkar, where he left her standing at the door and walked in to his great joy. And Abu al-Hasan said to him, "The reason of my coming is that such an one hath sent his handmaid to thee with a letter, containing his greeting to thee and mentioning therein that the cause of his not coming to thee was a matter that hath betided him. The girl standeth even now at the door: shall she have leave to enter?"; and he signed to him that it was Shams al-Nahar's slave-girl. Ali understood his signal and answered, "Bring her in," and when he saw her, he shook for joy and signed to her, "How doth thy lord?; Allah grant him health and healing!" "He is well," answered she and pulling out the letter gave it to him. He took it and kissing it, opened and read it; after which he handed it to Abu al-Hasan, who found these verses written therein,

> "This messenger shall give my news to thee;
> Patience what while my sight thou canst not see:
> A lover leav'st in love's insanity,
> Whose eyne abide on wake incessantly:
> I suffer patience-pangs in woes that none
> Of men can medicine – such my destiny!
> Keep cool thine eyes; ne'er shall my heart forget,
> Nor without dream of thee one day shall be.
> Look what befel thy wasted frame, and thence
> Argue what I am doomed for love to dree!

"And afterwards:

> Without fingers I have written to thee, and without tongue I have spoken to thee
> to resume my case, I have an eye wherefrom sleeplessness departeth not
> and a heart whence sorrowful thought stirreth not
> It is with me as though health I had never known
> nor in sadness ever ceased to wone
> nor spent an hour in pleasant place
> but it is as if I were made up of pine and of the pain of passion and chagrin
> Sickness unceasingly troubleth
> and my yearning ever redoubleth
> desire still groweth
> and longing in my heart still gloweth
> I pray Allah to hasten our union
> and dispel of my mind the confusion

And I would fain thou favour me
with some words of thine
that I may cheer my heart in pain and repine
Moreover, I would have thee put on a patience lief,
until Allah vouchsafe relief
And His peace be with thee."

When Ali bin Bakkar had read this letter he said in weak accents and feeble voice, "With what hand shall I write and with what tongue shall I make moan and lament? Indeed she addeth sickness to my sickness and draweth death upon my death!" Then he sat up and taking in hand ink-case and paper, wrote the following reply, "In the name of Allah, the Compassionating, the Compassionate! Thy letter hath reached me, O my lady, and hath given ease to a sprite worn out with passion and love-longing, and hath brought healing to a wounded heart cankered with languishment and sickness; for indeed I am become even as saith the poet,

'Straitened bosom; reveries dispread;*
Slumberless eyelids; body wearied; Patience cut short; disunion longsomest;
Reason deranged and heart whose life is fled!'

And know that complaining is unavailing; but it easeth him whom love-longing disordereth and separation destroyeth and, with repeating, 'Union,' I keep myself comforted and how fine is the saying of the poet who said,

'Did not in love-plight joys and sorrows meet,*
How would the message or the writ be sweet?'"

When he had made an end of this letter, he handed it to Abu al-Hasan, saying, "Read it and give it to the damsel." So he took it and read it and its words stirred his soul and its meaning wounded his vitals. Then he committed it to the girl, and when she took it Ali bin Bakkar said to her, "Salute thy lady for me and acquaint her with my love and longing and how passion is blended with my flesh and my bones; and say to her that in very deed I need a woman who shall snatch me from the sea of destruction and save me from this dilemma; for of a truth Fortune oppresseth me with her vicissitudes; and is there any helper to free me from her turpitudes?" And he wept and the damsel wept for his weeping. Then she took leave of him and went forth and Abu al-Hasan went out with her and farewelled her. So she ganged her gait and he returned to his shop, which he opened and sat down there, as was his wont – And Shahrazad perceived the dawn of day and ceased saying her permitted say.

When it was the One Hundred and Fifty-ninth Night,

She said, it hath reached me, O auspicious King, that Abu al-Hasan farewelled the slave-girl and returned to his shop which he opened and sat down there according to his custom; but as he tarried, he found his heart oppressed and his breast straitened, and he was perplexed about his case. So he ceased not from melancholy the rest of that day and night, and on the morrow he betook himself to Ali bin Bakkar, with whom he sat till the folk withdrew, when he asked him how he did. Ali began to complain of desire and to descant upon the longing and distraction which possessed him, and repeated these words of the poet.

*"Men have 'plained of pining before my time,
Live and dead by parting been terrified:
But such feelings as those which my ribs immure
I have never heard of, nor ever espied."*

And these of another poet,

*"I have borne for thy love what never bore
For his fair, Kays the 'Daft one' hight of old:
Yet I chase not the wildlings of wold and wild
Like Kays, for madness is manifold."*

Thereupon quoth Abu al-Hasan, "Never did I see or hear of one like unto thee in thy love! When thou sufferest all this transport and sickness and trouble being enamoured of one who returneth thy passion, how would it be with thee if she whom thou lovest were contrary and contumelious, and thy case were discovered through her perfidy?" "And Ali the son of Bakkar" (says Abu al-Hasan) "was pleased with my words and he relied upon them and he thanked me for what I had said and done. I had a friend" (continued Abu al-Hasan), "to whom I discovered my affair and that of Ali and who knew that we were intimates; but none other than he was acquainted with what was betwixt us. He was wont to come to me and enquire how Ali did and after a little, he began to ask me about the damsel; but I fenced him off, saying, 'She invited him to her and there was between him and her as much as can possibly take place, and this is the end of their affair; but I have devised me a plan and an idea which I would submit to thee.'" Asked his friend, "And what is that?" Answered Abu al-Hasan, "I am a person well known to have much dealing among men and women, and I fear, O my brother, lest the affair of these twain come to light and this lead to my death and the seizure of my goods and the rending of my repute and that of my family. Wherefore I have resolved to get together my monies and make ready forthright and repair to the city of Bassorah and there abide, till I see what cometh of their case, that none may know of me; for love hath lorded over both and correspondence passeth between them. At this present their go-between and confidante is a slave-girl who hath till now kept their counsel, but I fear lest haply anxiety get the better of her and she discover their secret to some one and the matter, being bruited abroad, might bring me to great grief and prove the cause of my ruin; for I have no excuse to offer my accusers." Rejoined his friend, "Thou hast acquainted me with a parlous affair, from the like of which the wise and understanding will shrink with fear. Allah avert from thee the evil thou dreadest with such dread and save thee from the consequences thou apprehendest! Assuredly thy recking is aright." So Abu al-Hasan returned to his place and began ordering his affairs and preparing for his travel; nor had three days passed ere he made an end of his business and fared forth Bassorah-wards. His friend came to visit him three days after but finding him not, asked of him from the neighbours who answered, "He set out for Bassorah three days ago, for he had dealings with its merchants and he is gone thither to collect monies from his debtors; but he will soon return." The young man was confounded at the news and knew not whither to wend; and he said in his mind, "Would I had not parted from Abu al-Hasan!" Then he bethought him of some plan whereby he should gain access to Ali bin Bakkar; so he went to his lodging, and said to one of his servants, "Ask leave for me of thy lord that I may go in and salute him." The servant entered and told his master and presently returning, invited the man to walk in. So he entered and found Ali bin Bakkar thrown back on the pillow and saluted him. Ali returned his greeting and bade him welcome; whereupon the young man began to excuse himself for having held aloof from him all that while and added, "O my lord, between Abu al-Hasan and myself there was close friendship, so that I used to trust him with my secrets and could not sever myself from him an hour. Now it so chanced that I was absent three days' space on certain business with a company of my friends; and, when I came back and went to him, I found his shop locked up; so I asked the neighbours about him and they replied, 'He is gone to Bassorah.' Now I know he had no surer friend than thou; so, by Allah, tell me what thou knowest of him." When Ali bin Bakkar heard this, his colour changed and he was troubled and answered, "I never heard till this day of his departure and, if the case be as thou sayest, weariness is come upon me." And he began repeating,

> "For joys that are no more I wont to weep,
> While friends and lovers stood by me unscattered;
> This day when disunited me and them
> Fortune, I weep lost loves and friendship shattered."

Then he hung his head ground-wards in thought awhile and presently raising it and looking to one of his servants, said, "Go to Abu al-Hasan's house and enquire anent him whether he be at home or journeying abroad. If they say, 'He is abroad'; ask whither he be gone." The servant went out and returning after a while said to his master, "When I asked for Abu al-Hasan, his people told me that he was gone on a journey to Bassorah; but I saw a damsel standing at the door who, knowing me by sight, though I knew her not, said to me, 'Art thou not servant to Ali bin Bakkar?' 'Even so,' answered I; and she rejoined, 'I bear a message for him from one who is the dearest of all folk to him.' So she came with me and she is now standing at the door." Quoth Ali bin Bakkar, "Bring her in." The servant went out to her and brought her in, and the man who was with Ali looked at her and found her pretty. Then she advanced to the son of Bakkar and saluted him. – And Shahrazad perceived the dawn of day and ceased to say her permitted say,

When it was the One Hundred and Sixtieth Night, she said, it hath reached me, O auspicious King, that when the slave-girl came in to Ali bin Bakkar, she advanced to him and saluted him and spake with him secretly; and from time to time during the dialogue he exclaimed with an oath and swore that he had not talked and tattled of it. Then she took leave of him and went away. Now Abu al-Hasan's friend was a jeweller, and when she was gone, he found a place for speech and said to Ali bin Bakkar, "Doubtless and assuredly the Caliph's household have some demand upon thee or thou hast dealings therewith?" "Who told thee of this?" asked Ali; and the jeweller answered, "I know it by yonder damsel who is Shams al-Nahar's slave-girl; for she came to me a while since with a note wherein was written that she wanted a necklace of jewels; and I sent her a costly collar." But when Ali bin Bakkar heard this, he was greatly troubled, so that the jeweller feared to see him give up the ghost, yet after a while he recovered himself and said, "O my brother, I conjure thee by Allah to tell me truly how thou knowest her." Replied he, "Do not press this question upon me;" and Ali rejoined, "Indeed, I will not turn from thee till thou tell me the whole truth." Quoth the jeweller, "I will tell thee all, on condition that thou distrust me not, and that my words cause thee no restraint; nor will I conceal aught from thee by way of secret but will discover to thee the truth of the affair, provided that thou acquaint me with the true state of thy case and the cause of thy sickness." Then he told him all that had passed from first to last between Abu al-Hasan and himself, adding, "I acted thus only out of friendship for thee and of my desire to serve thee;" and assured him that he would keep his secret and venture life and good in his service. So Ali in turn told him his story and added, "By Allah, O my brother, naught moved me to keep my case secret from thee and from others but my fear lest folk should lift the veils of protection from certain persons." Rejoined the jeweller, "And I desired not to foregather with thee but of the great affection I bear thee and my zeal for thee in every case, and my compassion for the anguish thy heart endureth from severance. Haply I may be a comforter to thee in the room of my friend, Abu al-Hasan, during the length of his absence: so be thou of good cheer and keep thine eyes cool and clear." Thereupon Ali thanked him and repeated these couplets,

> "An say I, 'Patient I can bear his faring,'
> My tears and sighings give my say the lie;
> How can I hide these tears that course adown
> This plain, my cheek, for friend too fain to fly?"

Then he was silent awhile, and presently said to the jeweller "Knowest thou what secret the girl whispered to me?" Answered he, "Not I, by Allah, O my lord!" Quoth Ali, "She fancied that I directed Abu al-Hasan to go to Bassorah and that I had devised this device to put a stop to our correspondence and consorting. I swore to her that this was on nowise so; but she would not credit me and went away to her mistress, persisting in her injurious suspicions; for she inclined to Abu al-Hasan and gave ear to his word." Answered the young jeweller, "O my brother, I understood as much from the girl's manner; but I will win for thee thy wish, Inshallah!" Rejoined Ali bin Bakkar, "Who can be with me in this and how wilt thou do with her, when she shies and flies like a wildling of the wold?" Cried the jeweller "By Allah, needs must I do my utmost to help thee and contrive to scrape acquaintance with her without exposure or mischief!" Then he asked leave to depart and Ali bin Bakkar said, "O my brother, mind thou keep my counsel;" and he looked at him and wept. The jeweller bade him good-bye and fared forth. – And Shahrazad perceived the dawn of day and ceased saying her permitted say.

When it was the One Hundred and Sixty-first Night, she said, it hath reached me, O auspicious King, that the jeweller bade him good-bye and fared forth not knowing what he should do to win for him his wishes; and he ceased not walking, while over-musing the matter, till he spied a letter lying in the road. He took it up and looked at its direction and superscription, then read it and behold, it ran: "From the least worthy of lovers to the most worthy of beloveds." So he opened it and found these words written therein,

> "A messenger from thee came bringing union-hope,
> But that he erred somehow with me the thought prevailed;

So I rejoiced not; rather grew my grief still more;
Weeting my messenger of wits and wit had failed.

"But afterwards: Know, O my lord! that I ken not the reason why our correspondence between thee and me hath been broken off: but, if the cruelty arise from thy part, I will requite it with fidelity, and if thy love have departed, I will remain constant to my love of the parted, for I am with thee even as says the poet,

'Be proud; I'll crouch! Bully; I'll bear! Despise; I'll pray!
Go; I will come! Speak; I will hear! Bid; I'll obey!'"

As he was reading lo! up came the slave-girl, looking right and left, and seeing the paper in the jeweller's hand, said to him, "O my master, this letter is one I let fall." He made her no answer, but walked on, and she walked behind him, till he came to his house, when he entered and she after him, saying, "O my master, give me back this letter, for it fell from me." Thereon he turned to her and said, "O handmaid of good, fear not neither grieve, for verily Allah the Protector loveth those who protect; but tell me in truthful way thy case, as I am one who keepeth counsel. I conjure thee by an oath not to hide from me aught of thy lady's affairs; for haply Allah shall help me to further her wishes and make easy by my hand that which is hard." When the slave-girl heard these words she said, "O my lord, indeed a secret is not lost whereof thou art the secretist; nor shall any affair come to naught for which thou strivest. Know that my heart inclineth to thee and would interest thee with my tidings, but do thou give me the letter." Then she told him the whole story, adding, "Allah is witness to whatso I say." Quoth he, "Thou hast spoken truly, for I am acquainted with the root of the matter." Then he told her his tale of Ali bin Bakkar and how he had learned his state of mind; and related to her all that had passed from first to last, whereat she rejoiced; and they two agreed that she should take the letter and carry it to Ali and return and acquaint the jeweller with all that happened. So he gave her the letter and she took it and sealed it up as it was before, saying, "My mistress Shams al-Nahar gave it to me sealed; and when he hath read it and given me its reply, I will bring it to thee." Then she took leave and repaired to Ali bin Bakkar, whom she found waiting, and gave him the letter. He read it and writing a paper by way of reply, gave it to her; and she carried it to the jeweller, who tore asunder the seal and read it and found written therein these two couplets,

"The messenger, who kept our commerce hid,
Hath failed, and showeth wrath without disguise;
Choose one more leal from your many friends
Who, truth approving, disapproves of lies.
"To proceed: Verily, I have not entered upon perfidy
nor have I abandoned fidelity
I have not used cruelty
neither have I out off lealty
no covenant hath been broken by me
nor hath love-tie been severed by me
I have not parted from penitence

nor have I found aught but misery and ruin after severance
I know nothing of that thou avouchest
nor do I love aught but that which thou lovest
By Him who knoweth the secret of hidden things none discover
I have no desire save union with my lover
and my one business is my passion to conceal
albeit with sore sickness I ail.
This is the exposition of my case and now all hail!"

When the jeweller read this letter and learnt its contents he wept with sore weeping, and the slave-girl said to him, "Leave not this place till I return to thee; for he suspecteth me of such and such things, in which he is excusable; so it is my desire to bring about a meeting between thee and my mistress, Shams al-Nahar, howsoever I may trick you to it. For the present I left her prostrate, awaiting my return with the reply." Then she went away and the jeweller passed the night with a troubled mind. And when day dawned he prayed his dawn-prayer and sat expecting the girl's coming; and behold, she came in to him rejoicing with much joy and he asked her, "What news, O damsel?" She answered, "After leaving thee I went to my mistress and gave her the letter written by Ali bin Bakkar; and, when she read it and understood it, she was troubled and confounded; but I said to her, 'O my lady, have no fear of your affair being frustrated by Abu al-Hasan's disappearance, for I have found one to take his place, better than he and more of worth and a good man to keep secrets.' Then I told her what was between thyself and Abu al-Hasan and how thou camest by his confidence and that of Ali bin Bakkar and how that note was dropped and thou camest by it; and I also showed her how we arranged matters betwixt me and thee." The jeweller marvelled with much wonder, when she resumed, "And now my mistress would hear whatso thou sayest, that she may be assured by thy speech of the covenants between thee and him; so get thee ready to go with me to her forthwith." When the jeweller heard the slave-girl's words, he saw that the proposed affair was grave and a great peril to brave, not lightly to be undertaken or suddenly entered upon, and he said to her, "O my sister, verily, I am of the ordinary and not like unto Abu al-Hasan; for he being of high rank and of well-known repute, was wont to frequent the Caliph's household, because of their need of his merchandise. As for me, he used to talk with me and I trembled before him the while. So, if thy mistress would speak with me, our meeting must be in some place other than the Caliph's palace and far from the abode of the Commander of the Faithful; for my common sense will not let me consent to what thou proposest." On this wise he refused to go with her and she went on to say that she would be surety for his safety, adding, "Take heart and fear no harm!" and pressed him to courage till he consented to accompany her; withal, his legs bent and shivered and his hands quivered and he exclaimed, "Allah forbid that I should go with thee! Indeed, I have not strength to do this thing!" Replied she, "Hearten thy heart, if it be hard for thee to go to the Caliph's palace and thou canst not muster up courage to accompany me, I will make her come to thee; so budge not from thy place till I return to thee with her." Then the slave-girl went away and was absent for a while, but a short while, after which she returned to the jeweller and said to him, "Take thou care that there be with thee none save thyself, neither man-slave nor girl-slave." Quoth he, "I have but a negress, who is in years and who waiteth on me." So she arose and locked the door between his negress and the jeweller and sent his man-servants out of the place; after which she fared forth and presently returned, followed by a lady who, entering the house, filled it with the sweet scent of her perfumes. When the jeweller saw her, he sprang up and set her a couch and a cushion; and she sat down while he seated himself before her. She abode awhile without speaking till she had rested herself, when she unveiled her face and it seemed to the jeweller's fancy as if the sun had risen in his home. Then she asked her slave-girl, "Is this the man of whom thou spakest to me?" "Yes," answered she; whereupon the lady turned to the jeweller and said to him, "How is it with thee?" Replied he, "Right well! I pray Allah for thy preservation and that of the Commander of the Faithful." Quoth she, "Thou hast moved us to come to thee and possess thee with what we hold secret." Then she questioned him of his household and family; and he disclosed to her all his circumstance and his condition and said to her, "I have a house other than this; and I have set it apart for gathering together my friends and brethren; and there is none there save the old negress, of whom I spoke to thy handmaid." She asked him on what wise he came first to know how the affair began and the matter of Abu al-Hasan and the cause of his way-faring: accordingly he told her all he knew and how he had advised the journey. Thereupon she bewailed the loss of Abu al-Hasan and said to the jeweller, "Know, O such an one, that men's souls are active in their lusts and that men are still men; and that deeds are not done without words nor is end ever reached without endeavour. Rest is won only by work." – And Shahrazad perceived the dawn of day and ceased to say her permitted say.

When it was the One Hundred and Sixty-second Night, she said, it hath reached me, O auspicious King, that Shams al-Nahar thus addressed the jeweller, "Rest is gained only by work and success is gendered only by help of the generous. Now I have acquainted thee with our affair and it is in thy hand to expose us or to shield us; I say no more, because thy generosity requireth naught. Thou knowest that this my handmaiden keepeth my counsel and therefore occupieth high place in my favour; and I have selected her to transact my affairs of importance. So let none be worthier in thy sight than she and acquaint her with thine affair; and be of good cheer, for on her account thou art safe from all fear, and there is no place shut upon thee but she shall open it to thee. She shall bring thee my messages to Ali bin Bakkar and thou shalt be our intermediary." So saying, she rose, scarcely able to rise, and fared forth, the jeweller faring before her to the door of her house, after which he returned and sat down again in his place, having seen of her beauty and heard of her speech what dazzled him and dazed his wit, and having witnessed of her grace and courtesy what bewitched his sprite. He sat musing on her perfections till his mind waxed tranquil, when he called for food and ate enough to keep soul and body together. Then he changed his clothes and went out; and, repairing to the house of the youth Ali bin Bakkar, knocked at the door. The servants hastened to admit him and walked before him till they had brought him to their master, whom he found strown upon his bed. Now when he saw the jeweller, he said to him, "Thou hast tarried long from me, and that hath heaped care upon my care." Then he dismissed his servants and bade the doors be shut; after which he said to the jeweller, "By Allah, O my brother, I have not closed my eyes since the day I saw thee last; for the slave-girl came to me yesterday with a sealed letter from her mistress Shams al-Nahar;" and went on to tell him all that had passed with her, adding, "By the Lord, I am indeed perplexed concerning mine affair and my patience faileth me: for Abu al-Hasan was a comforter who cheered me because he knew the slave-girl." When the jeweller heard his words, he laughed; and Ali said, "Why dost thou laugh at my words, thou on whose coming I congratulated myself and to whom I looked for provision against the shifts of fortune?" Then he sighed and wept and repeated these couplets,

> "Full many laugh at tears they see me shed
> Who had shed tears an bore they what I bore;
> None feeleth pity for th' afflicted's woe,
> Save one as anxious and in woe galore:
> My passion, yearning, sighing, thought, repine
> Are for me cornered in my heart's deep core:
> He made a home there which he never quits,
> Yet rare our meetings, not as heretofore:
> No friend to stablish in his place I see;
> No intimate but only he and – he."

Now when the jeweller heard these lines and understood their significance, he wept also and told him all that had passed betwixt himself and the slave-girl and her mistress since he left him. And Ali bin Bakkar gave ear to his speech, and at every word he heard his colour shifted from white to red and his body grew now stronger and then weaker till the tale came to an end, when he wept and said, "O my brother, I am a lost man in any case: would mine end were nigh, that I might be at rest from all this! But I beg thee, of thy favour, to be my helper and comforter in all my affairs till Allah fulfil whatso be His will; and I will not gainsay thee with a single word." Quoth the jeweller, "Nothing will quench thy fire save union with her whom thou lovest; and the meeting must be in other than this perilous place. Better it were in a house of mine where the girl and her mistress met me; which place she chose for herself, to the intent that ye twain may there meet and complain each to other of what you have suffered from the pangs of love." Quoth Ali bin Bakkar, "O good Sir, do as thou wilt and with Allah be thy reward!; and what thou deemest is right do it forthright: but be not long in doing it, lest I perish of this anguish." "So I abode with him (said the jeweller) that night conversing with him till the morning morrowed," – And Shahrazad perceived the dawn of day and ceased saying her permitted say.

When it was the One Hundred and Sixty-third Night,

She said, it hath reached me, O auspicious King, that the jeweller continued: "So I abode with him that night conversing with him till the morning morrowed, when I prayed the dawn-prayers and, going out from him, returned to my house. Hardly had I settled down when the damsel came up and saluted me; and I returned her salutation and told her what passed between myself and Ali bin Bakkar, and she said, 'Know that the Caliph hath left us and there is no one in our place and it is safer for us and better.' Replied I, 'Sooth thou sayest; yet is it not like my other house which is both fitter and surer for us;' and the slave-girl rejoined 'Be it as thou seest fit. I am now going to my lady and will tell her what thou sayest and acquaint her with all thou hast mentioned.' So she went away and sought her mistress and laid the project before her, and presently returned and said to me, 'It is to be as thou sayest: so make us ready the place and expect us.' Then she took out of her breast-pocket a purse of dinars and gave this message, 'My lady saluteth thee and saith to thee, 'Take this and provide therewith what the case requireth.' But I swore that I would accept naught of it; so she took the purse and returning to her mistress, told her, 'He would not receive the money, but gave it back to me.' 'No matter,' answered Shams al-Nahar. As soon as the slave-girl was gone" (continued the jeweller), "I arose and betook myself to my other house and transported thither all that was needful, by way of vessels and furniture and rich carpets; and I did not forget china vases and cups of glass and gold and silver; and I made ready meat and drink required for the occasion. When the damsel came and saw what I had done, it pleased her and she bade me fetch Ali bin Bakkar; but I said, 'None shall bring him save thou.' Accordingly she went to him and brought him back perfectly dressed and looking his best. I met him and greeted him and then seated him upon a divan befitting his condition, and set before him sweet-scented flowers in vases of china and vari-coloured glass. Then I set on a tray of many-tinted meats such as broaden the breast with their sight, and sat talking with him and diverting him, whilst the slave-girl went away and was absent till after sundown-prayers, when she returned with Shams al-Nahar, attended by two maids and none else. Now as soon as she saw Ali bin Bakkar and he saw her, he rose and embraced her, and she on her side embraced him and both fell in a fit to the ground. They lay for a whole hour insensible; then, coming to themselves, they began mutually to complain of the pains of separation. Thereupon they drew near to each other and sat talking charmingly, softly, tenderly; after which they somewhat perfumed themselves and fell to thanking me for what I had done for them. Quoth I, 'Have ye a mind for food?' 'Yes,' quoth they. So I set before them a small matter of food and they ate till they were satisfied and then washed their hands; after which I led them to another sitting-room and brought them wine. So they drank and drank deep and inclined to each other; and presently Shams al-Nahar said to me, 'O my master, complete thy kindness by bringing us a lute or other instrument of mirth and music that the measure of our joy may be fully filled.' I replied, 'On my head and eyes!' and rising brought her a lute, which she took and tuned; then laying it in her lap she touched it with a masterly touch, at once exciting to sadness and changing sorrow to gladness; after which she sang these two couplets,

> 'My sleeplessness would show I love to bide on wake;
> And would my leanness prove that sickness is my make: And tear-floods course
> adown the cheeks they only scald;
> Would I knew union shall disunion overtake!'

Then she went on to sing the choicest and most affecting poesy to many and various modes, till our senses were bewitched and the very room danced with excess of delight and surprise at her sweet singing; and neither thought nor reason was left in us. When we had sat awhile and the cup had gone round amongst us, the damsel took the lute and sang to a lively measure these couplets,

> My love a meeting promised me and kept it faithfully,
> One night as many I shall count in number and degree:
> O Night of joyance Fate vouchsafed to faithful lovers tway,
> Uncaring for the railer loon and all his company!

My lover lay the Night with me and clipt me with his right,
While I with left embraced him, a-faint for ecstasy;
And hugged him to my breast and sucked the sweet wine of his lips,
Full savouring the honey-draught the honey-man sold to me.'

Whilst we were thus drowned in the sea of gladness" (continued the jeweller) "behold, there came in to us a little maid trembling and said, 'O my lady, look how you may go away for the folk have found you out and have surrounded the house; and we know not the cause of this!' When I heard her words, I arose startled and lo! in rushed a slave-girl who cried, 'Calamity hath come upon you.' At the same moment the door was burst open and there rushed in upon us ten men masked in kerchiefs with hangers in their hands and swords by their sides, and as many more behind them. When I saw this, the world was straitened on me for all its wideness, and I looked to the door but saw no issue; so I sprang from the terrace into the house of one of my neighbours and there hid myself. Thence I found that folk had entered my lodgings and were making a mighty hubbub; and I concluded that the Caliph had got wind of us and had sent his Chief of the Watch to seize us and bring us before him. So I abode confounded and ceased not remaining in my place, without any possibility of quitting it till midnight. And presently the house-master arose, for he had heard me moving, and he feared with exceeding great fear of me; so he came forth from his room with drawn brand in hand and made at me, saying, 'Who is this in my house?' Quoth I, 'I am thy neighbour the jeweller;' and he knew me and retired. Then he fetched a light and coming up to me, said, 'O my brother, indeed that which hath befallen thee this night is no light matter to me.' I replied, 'O my brother, tell me who was in my house and entered it breaking in my door; for I fled to thee not knowing what was to do.' He answered, 'Of a truth the robbers who attacked our neighbours yesterday and slew such an one and took his goods, saw thee on the same day bringing furniture into this house; so they broke in upon thee and stole thy goods and slew thy guests.' Then we arose" (pursued the jeweller), "I and he, and repaired to my house, which we found empty without a stick remaining in it; so I was confounded at the case and said to myself, 'As for the gear I care naught about its loss, albeit I borrowed part of the stuff from my friends and it hath come to grief; yet is there no harm in that, for they know my excuse in the plunder of my property and the pillage of my place. But as for Ali bin Bakkar and the Caliph's favourite concubine, I fear lest their case get bruited abroad and this cause the loss of my life.' So I turned to my neighbour and said to him, 'Thou art my brother and my neighbour and wilt cover my nakedness; what then dost thou advise me to do?' The man answered, 'What I counsel thee to do is to keep quiet and wait; for they who entered thy house and took thy goods have murdered the best men of a party from the palace of the Caliphate and have killed not a few of the watchmen: the government officers and guards are now in quest of them on every road and haply they will hit upon them, whereby thy wish will come about without effort of thine.'" The jeweller hearing these words returned to his other house, that wherein he dwelt, – and Shahrazad perceived the dawn of day and ceased to say her permitted say.

When it was the One Hundred and Sixty-fourth Night, she said, it hath reached me, O auspicious King, that when the jeweller heard these words he returned to his other house wherein he dwelt, and said to himself, "Indeed this that hath befallen me is what Abu al-Hasan feared and from which he fled to Bassorah. And now I have fallen into it." Presently the pillage of his pleasure-house was noised abroad among the folk, and they came to him from all sides and places, some exulting in his misfortune and others excusing him and condoling with his sorrow; whilst he bewailed himself to them and for grief neither ate meat nor drank drink. And as he sat, repenting him of what he had done, behold one of his servants came in to him and said, "There is a person at the door who asketh for thee; and I know him not." The jeweller went forth to him and saluted him who was a stranger; and the man whispered to him, "I have somewhat to say between our two selves." Thereupon he brought him in and asked him, "What hast thou to tell me?" Quoth the man, "Come with me to thine other house;" and the jeweller enquired, "Dost thou then know my other house?" Replied the other, "I know all about thee and I know that also whereby Allah will dispel thy dolours." "So I said to myself" (continued the jeweller) "'I will go with him whither he will;' and went out and walked on till we came to my second house; and when the man saw it he said to me, 'It is without door or doorkeeper, and we cannot possibly sit in it; so come thou with me to another place.' Then the man continued passing from stead to stead (and I with him) till night overtook us. Yet I put no question to him of the matter in hand and we ceased not to walk on, till we reached the open country. He kept saying, 'Follow me,' and quickened his pace to a trot, whilst I trotted after him heartening my heart to go on, until we reached the river, where he took boat with me, and the boatman rowed us over to the other bank. Then he landed from the boat and I landed after him: and he took my hand and led me to a street which I had never entered in all my days, nor do I know in what quarter it was. Presently the man stopped at the door of a house, and opening it entered and made me enter with him; after which he locked the door with an iron padlock, and led me along the vestibule, till he brought me in the presence of ten men who were as though they were one and the same man; they being brothers. We saluted them" (continued the jeweller) "and they returned our greeting and bade us be seated; so we sat down. Now I was like to die for excess of weariness; but they brought me rose-water and sprinkled it on my face; after which they gave me a sherbet to drink and set before me food whereof some of them ate with me. Quoth I to myself, 'Were there aught harmful in the food, they would not eat with me.' So I ate, and when we had washed our hands, each of us returned to his place. Then they asked me, 'Dost thou know us?' and I answered, 'No! nor in my life have I ever seen you; nay, I know not even him who brought me hither.' Said they, 'Tell us thy tidings and lie not at all.' Replied I, 'Know then that my case is wondrous and my affair marvellous; but wot ye anything about me?' They rejoined, 'Yes! it was we took thy goods yesternight and carried off thy friend and her who was singing to him.' Quoth I, 'Allah let down His veil over you! Where be my friend and she who was singing to him?' They pointed with their hands to one side and replied, 'Yonder, but, by Allah, O our brother, the secret of their case is known to none save to thee, for from the time we brought the twain hither up to this day, we have not looked upon them nor questioned them of their condition, seeing them to be persons of rank and dignity. Now this and this only it was that hindered our killing them: so tell us the truth of their case and thou shalt be assured of thy safety and of theirs.' When I heard this" (continued the jeweller) "I almost died of fright and horror, and I said to them, 'Know ye, O my brethren, that if generosity were lost, it would not be found save with you; and had I a secret which I feared to reveal, none but your breasts would conceal it.' And I went on exaggerating their praises in this fashion, till I saw that frankness and readiness to speak out would profit me more than concealing facts; so I told them all that had betided me to the very end of the tale. When they heard it, they said, 'And is this young man Ali Bakkar-son and this lady Shams al-Nahar?' I replied, 'Yes.' Now this was grievous to them and they rose and made their excuses to the two and then they said to me, 'Of what we took from thy house part is spent, but here is what is left of it.' So speaking, they gave me back most of my goods and they engaged to return them to their places in my house, and to restore me the rest as soon as they could. My heart was set at ease till they split into two parties, one with me and the other against me; and we fared forth from that house and such was my case. But as regards Ali bin Bakkar and Shams al-Nahar; they were well-nigh dying for excess of fear, when I went up to them and saluting them, asked, 'What happened to the damsel and the two maids, and where be they gone?', and they answered only, 'We know nothing of them.' Then we walked on and stinted not till we came to the river-bank where the barque lay; and we all boarded it, for it was the same which had brought me over on the day before. The boatman rowed us to the other side; but hardly had we landed and taken seat on the bank to rest, when a troop of horse swooped down on us like eagles and surrounded us on all sides and places, whereupon the robbers with us sprang up in haste like vultures, and the boat put back for them and took them in and the boatman pushed off into mid-stream, leaving us on the river bank, unable to move or to stand still. Then the chief horseman said to us, 'Whence be ye!'; and we were perplexed for an answer, but I said" (continued the jeweller), "'Those ye saw with us are rogues; we know them not. As for us, we are singers, and they intended taking us to sing for them, nor could we get free of them, save by subtlety and soft words; so on this occasion they let us go, their works being such as you have seen.' But they looked at Shams al-Nahar and Ali bin Bakkar and said to me, 'Thou hast not spoken sooth but, if thy tale be true, tell us who ye are and whence ye are; and what be your place and in what quarter you dwell.' I knew not what to answer them, but Shams al-Nahar sprang up and approaching the Captain of the horsemen spoke with him privily, whereupon he dismounted from his steed and, setting her on horse-back, took the bridle and began to lead his beast. And two of his men did the like with the youth, Ali bin Bakkar, and it was the same with myself. The Commandant of the troop ceased not faring on with us, till they reached a certain part of the river bank, when he sang out in some barbarous jargon and there came to us a number of men with two boats. Then the Captain embarked us in one of them (and he with us) whilst the rest of his men put off in the other, and rowed on with us till we arrived at the palace of the Caliphate where Shams al-Nahar landed. And all the while we endured the agonies of death for excess of fear, and they ceased not faring till they came to a place whence there was a way to our quarter. Here we landed and walked on, escorted by some of the horsemen, till we came to Ali bin Bakkar's house; and when we entered it, our escort took leave of us and went their way. We abode there, unable to stir from the place and not knowing the difference between morning and evening; and in such case we continued till the dawn of the next day. And when it was again nightfall, I came to myself and saw Ali bin Bakkar and the women and men of his household weeping over him, for he was stretched out without sense or motion. Some of them came to me and thoroughly arousing me said, 'Tell us what hath befallen our son and say how came he in this plight?' Replied I, 'O folk, hearken to me!'" – And Shahrazad perceived the dawn of day and ceased saying her permitted say.

When it was the One Hundred and Sixty-fifth Night, she said, it hath reached me, O auspicious King, that the jeweller answered them, "'O folk, hearken to my words and give me no trouble and annoyance! but be patient and he will come to and tell you his tale for himself.' And I was hard upon them and made them afraid of a scandal between me and them, but as we were thus, behold, Ali bin Bakkar moved on his carpet-bed, whereat his friends rejoiced and the stranger folk withdrew from him; but his people forbade me to go away. Then they sprinkled rose-water on his face and he presently revived and sensed the air; whereupon they questioned him of his case, and he essayed to answer them but his tongue could not speak forthright and he signed to them to let me go home. So they let me go, and I went forth hardly crediting my escape and returned to my own house, supported by two men. When my people saw me thus, they rose up and set to shrieking and slapping their faces; but I signed to them with my hand to be silent and they were silent. Then the two men went their way and I threw myself down on my bed, where I lay the rest of the night and awoke not till the forenoon, when I found my people gathered round me and saying, 'What calamity befel thee, and what evil with its mischief did fell thee?' Quoth I 'Bring me somewhat to drink.' So they brought me drink, and I drank of it what I would and said to them, 'What happened, happened.' Thereupon they went away and I made my excuses to my friends, and asked if any of the goods that had been stolen from my other house had been returned. They answered, 'Yes! some of them have come back; by token that a man entered and threw them down within the doorway and we saw him not.' So I comforted myself and abode in my place two days, unable to rise and leave it; and presently I took courage and went to the bath, for I was worn out with fatigue and troubled in mind for Ali bin Bakkar and Shams al-Nahar, because I had no news of them all this time and could neither get to Ali's house nor, out of fear for my life, take my rest in mine own. And I repented to Almighty Allah of what I had done and praised Him for my safety. Presently my fancy suggested to me to go to such and such a place and see the folk and solace myself; so I went on foot to the cloth-market and sat awhile with a friend of mine there. When I rose to go, I saw a woman standing over against me; so I looked at her, and lo! it was Shams al-Nahar's slave-girl. When I saw her, the world grew dark in my eyes and I hurried on. She followed me, but I was seized with affright and fled from her, and whenever I looked at her, a trembling came upon me whilst she pursued me, saying. 'Stop, that I may tell thee somewhat!' But I heeded her not and never ceased walking till I reached a mosque, and she entered after me. I prayed a two-bow prayer, after which I turned to her and, sighing, said, 'What cost thou want?' She asked me how I did, and I told her all that had befallen myself and Ali bin Bakkar and besought her for news of herself. She answered, 'Know that when I saw the robbers break open thy door and rush in, I was in sore terror, for I doubted not but that they were the Caliph's officers and would seize me and my mistress and we should perish forthwith: so we fled over the roofs, I and the maids; and, casting ourselves down from a high place, came upon some people with whom we took refuge; and they received us and brought us to the palace of the Caliphate, where we arrived in the sorriest of plights. We concealed our case and abode on coals of fire till nightfall, when I opened the river-gate and, calling the boatman who had carried us the night before, said to him, 'I know not what is become of my mistress; so take me in the boat, that we may go seek her on the river: haply I shall chance on some news of her. Accordingly he took me into the boat and went about with me and ceased not wending till midnight, when I spied a barque making towards the water gate, with one man rowing and another standing up and a woman lying prostrate between them twain. And they rowed on till they reached the shore when the woman landed, and I looked at her, and behold, it was Shams al-Nahar. Thereupon I got out and joined her, dazed for joy to see her after having lost all hopes of finding her alive.'" – And Shahrazad perceived the dawn of day and ceased saying her permitted say.

When it was the One Hundred and Sixty-sixth Night, she said, it hath reached me, O auspicious King, that the slave-girl went on telling the jeweller, "'I was dazed for joy to see her, after having lost all hopes of finding her alive. When I came up to her, she bade me give the man who had brought her thither a thousand gold pieces; and we carried her in, I and the two maids, and laid her on her bed; where she passed that night in a sorely troubled state; and, when morning dawned, I forbade the women and eunuchs to go in to her, or even to draw near her for the whole of that day; but on the next she revived and somewhat recovered and I found her as if she had come out of her grave. I sprinkled rose-water upon her face and changed her clothes and washed her hands and feet; nor did I cease to coax her, till I brought her to eat a little and drink some wine, though she had no mind to any such matter. As soon as she had breathed the fresh air and strength began to return to her, I took to upbraiding her, saying, 'O my lady, consider and have pity on thyself; thou seest what hath betided us: surely, enough and more than enough of evil hath befallen thee; for indeed thou hast been nigh upon death. She said, 'By Allah, O good damsel, in sooth death were easier to me than what hath betided me; for it seemed as though I should be slain and no power could save me. When the robbers took us from the jeweller's house they asked me, Who mayest thou be? and hearing my answer, 'I am a singing girl, they believed me. Then they turned to Ali bin Bakkar and made enquiries about him, 'And who art thou and what is thy condition?; whereto he replied, 'I am of the common kind. So they took us and carried us along, without our resisting, to their abode; and we hurried on with them for excess of fear; but when they had us set down with them in the house, they looked hard at me and seeing the clothes I wore and my necklaces and jewellery, believed not my account of myself and said to me, 'Of a truth these necklaces belong to no singing-girl; so be soothfast and tell us the truth of thy case. I returned them no answer whatever, saying in my mind, 'Now will they slay me for the sake of my apparel and ornaments; and I spoke not a word. Then the villains turned to Ali bin Bakkar, asking, 'And thou, who art thou and whence art thou? for thy semblance seemeth not as that of the common kind. But he was silent and we ceased not to keep our counsel and to weep, till Allah softened the rogues' hearts to pity and they said to us, 'Who is the owner of the house wherein we were?' We answered, 'Such an one, the jeweller; whereupon quoth one of them, 'I know him right well and I wot the other house where he liveth and I will engage to bring him to you this very hour. Then they agreed to set me in a place by myself and Ali bin Bakkar in a place by himself, and said to us, 'Be at rest ye twain and fear not lest your secret be divulged; ye are safe from us. Meanwhile their comrade went away and returned with the jeweller, who made known to them our case, and we joined company with him; after which a man of the band fetched a barque, wherein they embarked us all three and, rowing us over the river, landed us with scant ceremony on the opposite bank and went their ways. Thereupon up came a horse-patrol and asked us who we were; so I spoke with the Captain of the watch and said to him, 'I am Shams al-Nahar, the Caliph's favourite; I had drunken strong wine and went out to visit certain of my acquaintance of the wives of the Wazirs, when yonder rogues came upon me and laid hold of me and brought me to this place; but when they saw you, they fled as fast as they could. I met these men with them: so do thou escort me and them to a place of safety and I will requite thee as I am well able to do. When the Captain of the watch heard my speech, he knew me and alighting, mounted me on his horse; and in like manner did two of his men with Ali bin Bakkar. So I spoke to her' (continued the handmaid) 'and blamed her doings, and bade her beware, and said to her, 'O my lady, have some care for thy life!' But she was angered at my words and cried out at me; accordingly I left her and came forth in quest of thee, but found thee not and dared not go to the house of Ali bin Bakkar; so stood watching for thee, that I might ask thee of him and wot how it goes with him. And I pray thee, of thy favour, to take of me some money, for thou hast doubtless borrowed from thy friends part of the gear and as it is lost, it behoveth thee to make it good with folk.' I replied, 'To hear is to obey! go on;' and I walked with her till we drew near my house, when she said to me, 'Wait here till I come back to thee.'" – And Shahrazad perceived the dawn of day and ceased to say her permitted say.

When it was the One Hundred and Sixty-seventh Night, she said, it hath reached me, O auspicious King, that after the slave-girl had addressed the jeweller, "'Wait here till I come back to thee!' she went away and presently returned with the money, which she put" (continued the jeweller) "into my hand, saying, 'O my master, in what place shall we meet?' Quoth I, 'I will start and go to my house at once and suffer hard things for thy sake and contrive how thou mayst win access to him, for such access is difficult at this present.' Said she, 'Let me know some spot, where I shall come to thee,' and I answered, 'In my other house, I will go thither forthright and have the doors mended and the place made safe again, and henceforth we will meet there.' Then she took leave of me and went her way, whilst I carried the money home, and counting it, found it five thousand dinars. So I gave my people some of it and to all who had lent me aught I made good their loss, after which I arose and took my servants and repaired to my other house whence the things had been stolen; and I brought builders and carpenters and masons who restored it to its former state. Moreover, I placed my negress-slave there and forgot the mishaps which had befallen me. Then I fared forth and repaired to Ali bin Bakkar's house and, when I reached it, his slave-servants accosted me, saying, 'Our lord calleth for thee night and day, and hath promised to free whichever of us bringeth thee to him; so they have been wandering about in quest of thee everywhere but knew not in what part to find thee. Our master is by way of recovering strength, but at times he reviveth and at times he relapseth; and whenever he reviveth he nameth thee, and saith, 'Needs must ye bring him to me, though but for the twinkling of an eye;' and then he sinketh back into his torpor.' Accordingly" (continued the jeweller) "I accompanied the slave and went in to Ali bin Bakkar; and, finding him unable to speak, sat down at his head, whereupon he opened his eyes and seeing me, wept and said, 'Welcome and well come!' I raised him and making him sit up, strained him to my bosom, and he said, 'Know, O my brother, that, from the hour I took to my bed, I have not sat up till now: praise to Allah that I see thee again!' And I ceased not to prop him and support him until I made him stand on his feet and walk a few steps, after which I changed his clothes and he drank some wine: but all this he did for my satisfaction. Then, seeing him somewhat restored, I told him what had befallen me with the slave-girl (none else hearing me), and said to him, 'Take heart and be of good courage, I know what thou sufferest.' He smiled and I added, 'Verily nothing shall betide thee save what shall rejoice thee and medicine thee.' Thereupon he called for food, which being brought, he signed to his pages, and they withdrew. Then quoth he to me, 'O my brother, hast thou seen what hath befallen me?'; and he made excuses to me and asked how I had fared all that while. I told him everything that had befallen me, from beginning to end, whereat he wondered and calling his servants, said, 'Bring me such and such things.' They brought in fine carpets and hangings and, besides that, vessels of gold and silver, more than I had lost, and he gave them all to me; so I sent them to my house and abode with him that night. When the day began to yellow, he said to me, 'Know thou that as to all things there is an end, so the end of love is either death or accomplishment of desire. I am nearer unto death, would I had died ere this befel!; and had not Allah favoured us, we had been found out and put to shame. And now I know not what shall deliver me from this my strait, and were it not that I fear Allah, I would hasten my own death; for know, O my brother, that I am like bird in cage and that my life is of a surety perished, choked by the distresses which have befallen me; yet hath it a period stablished firm and an appointed term.' And he wept and groaned and began repeating,

'Enough of tears hath shed the lover-wight,
When grief outcast all patience from his sprite:
He hid the secrets which united us,
But now His eye parts what He did unite!'"

When he had finished his verses, the jeweller said to him, "O my lord, I now intend returning to my house." He answered, "There be no harm in that; go and come back to me with news as fast as possible, for thou seest my case." "So I took leave of him" (continued the jeweller) "and went home, and hardly had I sat down, when up came the damsel, choked with long weeping. I asked, 'What is the matter'?; and she answered, 'O my lord, know then that what we feared hath befallen us; for, when I left thee yesterday and returned to my lady, I found her in a fury with one of the two maids who were with us the other night, and she ordered her to be beaten. The girl was frightened and ran away; but, as she was leaving the house, one of the door-porters and guards of the gate met her and took her up and would have sent her back to her mistress. However, she let fall some hints, which were a disclosure to him; so he cajoled her and led her on to talk, and she tattled about our case and let him know of all our doings. This affair came to the ears of the Caliph, who bade remove my mistress, Shams al-Nahar, and all her gear to the palace of the Caliphate; and set over her a guard of twenty eunuchs. Since then to the present hour he hath not visited her nor hath given her to know the reason of his action, but I suspect this to be the cause; wherefore I am in fear for my life and am sore troubled, O my lord, knowing not what I shall do, nor with what contrivance I shall order my affair and hers; for she hath none by her more trusted or more trustworthy than myself.'" – And Shahrazad perceived the dawn of day and ceased saying her permitted say.

When it was the One Hundred and Sixty-eighth Night,

She said, it hath reached me, O auspicious King, that the slave-girl thus addressed the jeweller, "'And in very sooth my lady hath none by her more trusted or more trustworthy in matter of secrecy than myself. So go thou, O my master, and speed thee without delay to Ali bin Bakkar; and acquaint him with this, that he may be on his guard and ward; and, if the affair be discovered, we will cast about for some means whereby to save our lives.' On this" (continued the jeweller), "I was seized with sore trouble and the world grew dark in my sight for the slave-girl's words; and when she was about to wend, I said to her, 'What reckest thou and what is to be done?' Quoth she, 'My counsel is that thou hasten to Ali bin Bakkar, if thou be indeed his friend and desire to save him; thine be it to carry him this news at once without aught of stay and delay, or regard for far and near; and mine be it to sniff about for further news.' Then she took her leave of me and went away: so I rose and followed her track and, betaking myself to Ali bin Bakkar, found him flattering himself with impossible expectations. When he saw me returning to him so soon, he said, 'I see thou hast come back to me forthwith and only too soon.' I answered, 'Patience, and cut short this foolish connection and shake off the pre-occupation wherein thou art, for there hath befallen that which may bring about the loss of thy life and good.' Now when he heard this, he was troubled and strongly moved; and he said to me, 'O my brother, tell me what hath happened.' Replied I, 'O my lord, know that such and such things have happened and thou art lost without recourse, if thou abide in this thy house till the end of the day.' At this, he was confounded and his soul well-nigh departed his body, but he recovered himself and said to me, 'What shall I do, O my brother, and what counsel hast thou to offer.' Answered I, 'My advice is that thou take what thou canst of thy property and whom of thy slaves thou trustest, and flee with us to a land other than this, ere this very day come to an end.' And he said, 'I hear and I obey.' So he rose, confused and dazed like one in epilepsy, now walking and now falling, and took what came under his hand. Then he made an excuse to his household and gave them his last injunctions, after which he loaded three camels and mounted his beast; and I did likewise. We went forth privily in disguise and fared on and ceased not our wayfare the rest of that day and all its night, till nigh upon morning, when we unloaded and, hobbling our camels, lay down to sleep. But we were worn with fatigue and we neglected to keep watch, so that there fell upon us robbers, who stripped us of all we had and slew our slaves, when these would have beaten them off, leaving us naked and in the sorriest of plights, after they had taken our money and lifted our beasts and disappeared. As soon as they were gone, we arose and walked on till morning dawned, when we came to a village which we entered, and finding a mosque took refuge therein for we were naked. So we sat in a corner all that day and we passed the next night without meat or drink; and at day-break we prayed our dawn-prayer and sat down again. Presently behold, a man entered and saluting us prayed a two-bow prayer, after which he turned to us and said, 'O folk, are ye strangers?' We replied, 'Yes: the bandits waylaid us and stripped us naked, and we came to this town but know none here with whom we may shelter.' Quoth he, 'What say ye? will you come home with me?' And" (pursued the jeweller) "I said to Ali bin Bakkar, 'Up and let us go with him, and we shall escape two evils; the first, our fear lest some one who knoweth us enter this mosque and recognise us, so that we come to disgrace; and the second, that we are strangers and have no place wherein to lodge.' And he answered helplessly, 'As thou wilt.' Then the man said to us again, 'O ye poor folk, give ear unto me and come with me to my place,' and I replied, 'Hearkening and obedience;' whereupon he pulled off a part of his own clothes and covered us therewith and made his excuses to us and spoke kindly to us. Then we arose and accompanied him to his house and he knocked at the door, whereupon a little slave-boy came out and opened to us. The host entered and we followed him; when he called for a bundle of clothes and muslins for turbands, and gave us each a suit and a piece; so we dressed and turbanded ourselves and sat us down. Presently, in came a damsel with a tray of food and set it before us, saying, 'Eat.' We ate some small matter and she took away the tray: after which we abode with our host till nightfall, when Ali bin Bakkar sighed and said to me, 'Know, O my brother, that I am a dying man past hope of life and I would charge thee with a charge: it is that, when thou seest me dead, thou go to my parent and tell her of my decease and bid her come hither that she may be here to receive the visits of condolence and be present at the washing of my corpse, and do thou exhort her to bear my loss with patience.' Then he fell down in a fainting fit and, when he recovered he heard a damsel singing afar off and making verses as she sang. Thereupon he addressed himself to give ear to her and hearken to her voice; and now he was insensible, absent from the world, and now he came to himself; and anon he wept for grief and mourning at the love which had befallen him. Presently, he heard the damsel who was singing repeat these couplets,

> 'Parting ran up to part from lover-twain
> Free converse, perfect concord, friendship fain:
> The Nights with shifting drifted us apart,
> Would heaven I wot if we shall meet again:
> How bitter after meeting 'tis to part,
> May lovers ne'er endure so bitter pain!
> Death-grip, death-choke, lasts for an hour and ends,
> But parting-tortures aye in heart remain:
> Could we but trace where Parting's house is placed,
> We would make Parting eke of parting taste!'

When Ali son of Bakkar heard the damsel's song, he sobbed one sob and his soul quitted his body. As soon as I saw that he was dead" (continued the jeweller), "I committed his corpse to the care of the house-master and said to him 'Know thou, that I am going to Baghdad, to tell his mother and kinsfolk, that they may come hither and conduct his burial.' So I betook myself to Baghdad and, going to my house, changed my clothes; after which I repaired to Ali bin Bakkar's lodging. Now when his servants saw me, they came to me and questioned me of him, and I bade them ask permission for me to go in to his mother. She gave me leave; so I entered and saluting her, said, 'Verily Allah ordereth the lives of all creatures by His commandment and when He decreeth aught, there is no escaping its fulfilment; nor can any soul depart but by leave of Allah, according to the Writ which affirmeth the appointed term.' She guessed by these words that her son was dead and wept with sore weeping, then she said to me, 'Allah upon thee! tell me, is my son dead?' I could not answer her for tears and excess of grief, and when she saw me thus, she was choked with weeping and fell to the ground in a fit. As soon as she came to herself she said to me, 'Tell me how it was with my son.' I replied, 'May Allah abundantly compensate thee for his loss!' and I told her all that had befallen him from beginning to end. She then asked, 'Did he give thee any charge?'; and I answered, 'Yes,' and told her what he had said, adding, 'Hasten to perform his funeral.' When she heard these words, she swooned away again; and, when she recovered, she addressed herself to do as I charged her. Then I returned to my house; and as I went along musing sadly upon the fair gifts of his youth, behold, a woman caught hold of my hand;" – And Shahrazad perceived the dawn of day and ceased to say her permitted say.

When it was the One Hundred and Sixty-ninth Night, she said, it hath reached me, O auspicious King, that the jeweller thus continued: "A woman caught hold of my hand; and I looked at her and lo! it was the slave-girl who used to come from Shams al-Nahar, and she seemed broken by grief. When we knew each other we both wept and ceased not weeping till we reached my house, and I said to her, 'Knowest thou the news of the youth, Ali bin Bakkar?' She replied, 'No, by Allah!'; so I told her the manner of his death and all that had passed, whilst we both wept; after which quoth I to her, 'How is it with thy mistress?' Quoth she, 'The Commander of the Faithful would not hear a single word against her; but, for the great love he bore her, saw all her actions in a favourable light, and said to her, 'O Shams al-Nahar, thou art dear to me and I will bear with thee and bring the noses of thy foes to the grindstone. Then he bade them furnish her an apartment decorated with gold and a handsome sleeping-chamber, and she abode with him in all ease of life and high favour. Now it came to pass that one day, as he sat at wine according to his custom, with his favourite concubines in presence, he bade them be seated in their several ranks and made Shams al-Nahar sit by his side. But her patience had failed and her disorder had redoubled upon her. Then he bade one of the damsels sing: so she took a lute and tuning it struck the chords, and began to sing these verses,

> 'One craved my love and I gave all he craved of me,
> And tears on cheek betray how 'twas I came to yield:
> Tear-drops, meseemeth, are familiar with our case,
> Revealing what I hide, hiding what I revealed:
> How can I hope in secret to conceal my love,
> Which stress of passion ever showeth unconcealed:
> Death, since I lost my lover, is grown sweet to me;
> Would I knew what their joys when I shall quit the field!

Now when Shams al-Nahar heard these verses sung by the slave-girl, she could not keep her seat; but fell down in a fainting-fit whereupon the Caliph cast the cup from his hand and drew her to him crying out; and the damsels also cried out, and the Prince of True Believers turned her over and shook her, and lo and behold! she was dead. The Caliph grieved over her death with sore grief and bade break all the vessels and dulcimers and other instruments of mirth and music which were in the room; then carrying her body to his closet, he abode with her the rest of the night. When the day broke, he laid her out and commanded to wash her and shroud her and bury her. And he mourned for her with sore mourning, and questioned not of her case nor of what caused her condition. And I beg thee in Allah's name' (continued the damsel) 'to let me know the day of the coming of Ali bin Bakkar's funeral procession that I may be present at his burial.' Quoth I, 'For myself, where thou wilt thou canst find me; but thou, where art thou to be found, and who can come at thee where thou art?' She replied, 'On the day of Shams al-Nahar's death, the Commander of the Faithful freed all her women, myself among the rest; and I am one of those now abiding at the tomb in such a place.' So I rose and accompanied her to the burial-ground and piously visited Shams al-Nahar's tomb; after which I went my way and ceased not to await the coming of Ali bin Bakkar's funeral. When it arrived, the people of Baghdad went forth to meet it and I went forth with them: and I saw the damsel among the women and she the loudest of them in lamentation, crying out and wailing with a voice that rent the vitals and made the heart ache. Never was seen in Baghdad a finer funeral than his; and we ceased not to follow in crowds till we reached the cemetery and buried him to the mercy of Almighty Allah; nor from that time to this have I ceased to visit the tombs of Ali son of Bakkar and of Shams al-Nahar. This, then, is their story, and Allah Almighty have mercy upon them!" And yet is not their tale (continued Shahrazad) more wonderful than that of King Shahriman. The King asked her "And what was his tale?" – And Shahrazad perceived the dawn of day and ceased saying her permitted say.

The Lovers of Bassorah

Richard F. Burton

THE CALIPH HARUN AL-RASHID was sleepless one night; so he sent for Al-Asma'i and Husayn al-Khalí'a and said to them, "Tell me a story you twain and do thou begin, O Husayn." He said, "'Tis well, O Commander of the Faithful;" and thus began: Some years ago, I dropped down stream to Bassorah, to present to Mohammed bin Sulayman al-Rabí'í a Kasidah or elegy I had composed in his praise; and he accepted it and bade me abide with him. One day, I went out to Al-Mirbad, by way of Al-Muháliyah; and, being oppressed by the excessive heat, went up to a great door, to ask for drink, when I was suddenly aware of a damsel, as she were a branch swaying, with eyes languishing, eye brows arched and finely pencilled and smooth cheeks rounded clad in a shift the colour of a pomegranate flower, and a mantilla of Sana'á work; but the perfect whiteness of her body overcame the redness of her shift, through which glittered two breasts like twin granadoes and a waist, as it were a roll of fine Coptic linen, with creases like scrolls of pure white paper stuffed with musk Moreover, O Prince of True Believers, round her neck was slung an amulet of red gold that fell down between her breasts, and on the plain of her forehead were browlocks like jet. Her eyebrows joined and her eyes were like lakes; she had an aquiline nose and thereunder shell-like lips showing teeth like pearls. Pleasantness prevailed in every part of her; but she seemed dejected, disturbed, distracted and in the vestibule came and went, walking upon the hearts of her lovers, whilst her legs made mute the voices of their ankle-rings; and indeed she was as saith the poet,

> *"Each portion of her charms we see*
> *Seems of the whole a simile"*

I was overawed by her, O Commander of the Faithful, and drew near her to greet her, and behold, the house and vestibule and highways breathed fragrant with musk. So I saluted her and she returned my salaam with a voice dejected and heart depressed and with the ardour of passion consumed. Then said I to her, "O my lady, I am an old man and a stranger and sore troubled by thirst. Wilt thou order me a draught of water, and win reward in heaven?" She cried, "Away, O Shaykh, from me! I am distracted from all thought of meat and drink." – And Shahrazad perceived the dawn of day and ceased to say her permitted say.

When it was the Six Hundred and Ninety-fourth Night,

She pursued, It hath reached me, O auspicious King, that the damsel said, "O Shaykh, I am distracted from all thought of meat and drink." Quoth I (continued Husayn), "By what ailment, O my lady?" and quoth she, "I love one who dealeth not justly by me and I desire one who of me will none. Wherefore I am afflicted with the wakefulness of those who wake star-gazing." I asked, "O my lady, is there on the wide expanse of earth one to whom thou hast a mind and who to thee hath no mind?" Answered she, "Yes; and this for the perfection of beauty and loveliness and goodliness wherewith he is endowed." "And why standeth thou in this porch?" enquired I. "This is his road," replied she, "and the hour of his passing by." I said, "O my lady, have ye ever foregathered and had such commerce and converse as might cause this passion?" At this she heaved a deep sigh; the tears rained down her cheeks, as they were dew falling upon roses, and she versified with these couplets,

> "We were like willow-boughs in garden shining
> And scented joys in happiest life combining;
> Whenas one bough from other self would rend
> And oh! thou seest this for that repining!"

Quoth I, "O maid, and what betideth thee of thy love for this man?"; and quoth she, "I see the sun upon the walls of his folk and I think the sun is he; or haply I catch sight of him unexpectedly and am confounded and the blood and the life fly my body and I abide in unreasoning plight a week or e'en a se'nnight." Said I, "Excuse me, for I also have suffered that which is upon thee of love-longing and distraction of soul and wasting of frame and loss of strength; and I see in thee pallor of complexion and emaciation, such as testify of the fever-fits of desire. But how shouldst thou be unsmitten of passion and thou a sojourner in the land of Bassorah?" Said she, "By Allah, before I fell in love of this youth, I was perfect in beauty and loveliness and amorous grace which ravished all the Princes of Bassorah, till he fell in love with me." I asked, "O maid, and who parted you?"; and she answered, "The vicissitudes of fortune, but the manner of our separation was strange; and 'twas on this wise. One New Year's day I had invited the damsels of Bassorah and amongst them a girl belonging to Siran, who had bought her out of Oman for four score thousand dirhams. She loved me and loved me to madness and when she entered she threw herself upon me and well nigh tore me in pieces with bites and pinches. Then we withdrew apart, to drink wine at our ease, till our meat was ready and our delight was complete, and she toyed with me and I with her, and now I was upon her and now she was upon me. Presently, the fumes of the wine moved her to strike her hand on the inkle of my petticoat-trousers, whereby it became loosed, unknown of either of us, and my trousers fell down in our play. At this moment he came in unobserved and, seeing me thus, was wroth at the sight and made off, as the Arab filly hearing the tinkle of her bridle." – And Shahrazad perceived the dawn of day and ceased saying her permitted say.

When it was the Six Hundred and Ninety-fifth Night,

She resumed, It hath reached me, O auspicious King, that the maiden said to Husayn al-Khali'a, "When my lover saw me playing, as I described to thee, with Siran's girl, he went forth in anger. And 'tis now, O Shaykh, three years ago, and since then I have never ceased to excuse myself to him and coax him and crave his indulgence, but he will neither cast a look at me from the corner of his eye, nor write me a word nor speak to me by messenger nor hear from me aught." Quoth I, "Harkye maid, is he an Arab or an Ajam?"; and quoth she, "Out on thee! He is of the Princes of Bassorah." "Is he old or young?" asked I; and she looked at me laughingly and answered, "Thou art certainly a simpleton! He is like the moon on the night of its full, smooth-cheeked and beardless, nor is there any defect in him except his aversion to me." Then I put the question, "What is his name?" and she replied, "What wilt thou do with him?" I rejoined, "I will do my best to come at him, that I may bring about reunion between you." Said she, "I will tell thee on condition that thou carry him a note;" and I said "I have no objection to that." Then quoth she, "His name is Zamrah bin al-Mughayrah, hight Abú al-Sakhá, and his palace is in the Mirbad." Therewith she called to those within for inkcase and paper and tucking up her sleeves, showed two wrists like broad rings of silver. She then wrote after the Basmalah as follows, "My lord, the omission of blessings at the head of this my letter shows mine insufficiency, and know that had my prayer been answered, thou hadst never left me; for how often have I prayed that thou shouldest not leave me, and yet thou didst leave me! Were it not that distress with me exceedeth the bounds of restraint, that which thy servant hath forced herself to do in writing this writ were an aidance to her, despite her despair of thee, because of her knowledge of thee that thou wilt fail to answer. Do thou fulfil her desire, my lord, of a sight of thee from the porch, as thou passest in the street, wherewith thou wilt quicken the dead soul in her. Or, far better for her still than this, do thou write her a letter with thine own hand (Allah endow it with all excellence!), and appoint it in requital of the intimacy that was between us in the nights of time past, whereof thou must preserve the memory. My lord, was I not to thee a lover sick with passion? An thou answer my prayer, I will give to thee thanks and to Allah praise; and so The Peace!" Then she gave me the letter and I went away. Next morning I repaired to the door of the Viceroy Mohammed bin Sulayman, where I found an assembly of the notables of Bassorah, and amongst them a youth who adorned the gathering and surpassed in beauty and brightness all who were there; and indeed the Emir Mohammed set him above himself. I asked who he was and behold, it was Zamrah himself: so I said in my mind, "Verily, there hath befallen yonder unhappy one that which hath befallen her!" Then I betook myself to the Mirbad and stood waiting at the door of his house, till he came riding up in state, when I accosted him and invoking more than usual blessings on him, handed him the missive. When he read it and understood it he said to me, "O Shaykh, we have taken other in her stead. Say me, wilt thou see the substitute?" I answered, "Yes." Whereupon he called out a woman's name, and there came forth a damsel who shamed the two greater lights; swelling-breasted, walking the gait of one who hasteneth without fear, to whom he gave the note, saying, "Do thou answer it." When she read it, she turned pale at the contents and said to me, " O old man, crave pardon of Allah for this that thou hast brought." So I went out, O Commander of the Faithful, dragging my feet and returning to her asked leave to enter. When she saw me, she asked, "What is behind thee?"; and I answered, "Evil and despair." Quoth she, "Have thou no concern of him. Where are Allah and His power?" Then she ordered me five hundred dinars and I took them and went away. Some days after I passed by the place and saw there horsemen and footmen. So I went in and lo! these were the companions of Zamrah, who were begging her to return to him; but she said, "No, by Allah, I will not look him in the face!" And she prostrated herself in gratitude to Allah and exultation over Zamrah's defeat. Then I drew near her, and she pulled out to me a letter, wherein was written, after the Bismillah, "My lady, but for my forbearance towards thee (whose life Allah lengthen!) I would relate somewhat of what betided from thee and set out my excuse, in that thou transgressedst against me, whenas thou wast manifestly a sinner against thyself and myself in breach of vows and lack of constancy and preference of another over us; for, by Allah, on whom we call for help against that which was of thy free will, thou didst transgress against the love of me; and so The Peace!" Then she showed me the presents and rarities he had sent her, which were of the value of thirty thousand dinars. I saw her again after this, and Zamrah had married her. Quoth Al-Rashid, "Had not Zamrah been beforehand with us, I should certainly have had to do with her myself."

Ma'aruf the Cobbler and His Wife

Richard F. Burton

THERE DWELT ONCE upon a time in the God-guarded city of Cairo a cobbler who lived by patching old shoes. His name was Ma'aruf and he had a wife called Fatimah, whom the folk had nicknamed "The Dung;" for that she was a whorish, worthless wretch, scanty of shame and mickle of mischief. She ruled her spouse and abused him; and he feared her malice and dreaded her misdoings; for that he was a sensible man but poor-conditioned. When he earned much, he spent it on her, and when he gained little, she revenged herself on his body that night, leaving him no peace and making his night black as her book; for she was even as of one like her saith the poet:

> *How manifold nights have I passed with my wife*
> *In the saddest plight with all misery rife:*
> *Would Heaven when first I went in to her*
> *With a cup of cold poison I'd ta'en her life.*

One day she said to him, "O Ma'aruf, I wish thee to bring me this night a vermicelli-cake dressed with bees' honey." He replied, "So Allah Almighty aid me to its price, I will bring it thee. By Allah, I have no dirhams to-day, but our Lord will make things easy." Rejoined she, – And Shahrazad perceived the dawn of day and ceased to say her permitted say.

When it was the Nine Hundred and Ninetieth Night,

She resumed, It hath reached me, O auspicious King, that Ma'aruf the Cobbler said to his spouse, "By Allah, I have no dirhams to-day, but our Lord will make things easy to me!" She rejoined, "I wot naught of these words; look thou come not to me save with the vermicelli and bees' honey; else will I make thy night black as thy fortune whenas thou fellest into my hand." Quoth he, "Allah is bountiful!" and going out with grief scattering itself from his body, prayed the dawn-prayer and opened his shop. After which he sat till noon, but no work came to him and his fear of his wife redoubled. Then he arose and went out perplexed as to how he should do in the matter of the vermicelli-cake, seeing he had not even the wherewithal to buy bread. Presently he came to the shop of the Kunafah-seller and stood before it, whilst his eyes brimmed with tears. The pastry-cook glanced at him and said, "O Master Ma'aruf, why dost thou weep? Tell me what hath befallen thee." So he acquainted him with his case, saying, "My wife would have me bring her a Kunafah; but I have sat in my shop till past mid-day and have not gained even the price of bread; wherefore I am in fear of her." The cook laughed and said, "No harm shall come to thee. How many pounds wilt thou have?" "Five pounds," answered Ma'aruf. So the man weighed him out five pounds of vermicelli-cake and said to him, "I have clarified butter, but no bees' honey. Here is drip-honey, however, which is better than bees' honey; and what harm will there be, if it be with drip-honey?" Ma'aruf was ashamed to object, because the pastry-cook was to have patience with him for the price, and said, "Give it me with drip-honey." So he fried a vermicelli-cake for him with butter and drenched it with drip-honey, till it was fit to present to Kings. Then he asked him, "Dost thou want bread and cheese?"; and Ma'aruf answered, "Yes." So he gave him four half dirhams worth of bread and one of cheese, and the vermicelli was ten nusfs. Then said he, "Know, O Ma'aruf, that thou owest me fifteen nusfs; so go to thy wife and make merry and take this nusf for the Hammam; and thou shalt have credit for a day or two or three till Allah provide thee with thy daily bread. And straiten not thy wife, for I will have patience with thee till such time as thou shalt have dirhams to spare." So Ma'aruf took the vermicelli-cake and bread and cheese and went away, with a heart at ease, blessing the pastry-cook and saying, "Extolled be Thy perfection, O my Lord! How bountiful art Thou!" When he came home, his wife enquired of him, "Hast thou brought the vermicelli-cake?"; and, replying "Yes," he set it before her. She looked at it and seeing that it was dressed with cane-honey, said to him, "Did I not bid thee bring it with bees' honey? Wilt thou contrary my wish and have it dressed with cane-honey?" He excused himself to her, saying, "I bought it not save on credit;" but said she, "This talk is idle; I will not eat Kunafah save with bees' honey." And she was wroth with it and threw it in his face, saying, "Begone, thou pimp, and bring me other than this !" Then she dealt him a buffet on the cheek and knocked out one of his teeth. The blood ran down upon his breast and for stress of anger he smote her on the head a single blow and a slight; whereupon she clutched his beard and fell to shouting out and saying, "Help, O Moslems!" So the neighbours came in and freed his beard from her grip; then they reproved and reproached her, saying, "We are all content to eat Kunafah with cane-honey. Why, then, wilt thou oppress this poor man thus? Verily, this is disgraceful in thee!" And they went on to soothe her till they made peace between her and him. But, when the folk were gone, she sware that she would not eat of the vermicelli, and Ma'aruf, burning with hunger, said in himself, "She sweareth that she will not eat; so I will e'en eat." Then he ate, and when she saw him eating, she said, "Inshallah, may the eating of it be poison to destroy the far one's body." Quoth he, "It shall not be at thy bidding," and went on eating, laughing and saying, "Thou swarest that thou wouldst not eat of this; but Allah is bountiful, and to-morrow night, an the Lord decree, I will bring thee Kunafah dressed with bees' honey, and thou shalt eat it alone." And he applied himself to appeasing her, whilst she called down curses upon him; and she ceased not to rail at him and revile him with gross abuse till the morning, when she bared her forearm to beat him. Quoth he, "Give me time and I will bring thee other vermicelli-cake." Then he went out to the mosque and prayed, after which he betook himself to his shop and opening it, sat down; but hardly had he done this when up came two runners from the Kazi's court and said to him, "Up with thee, speak with the Kazi, for thy wife hath complained of thee to him and her favour is thus and thus." He recognised her by their description; and saying, "May Allah Almighty torment her!" walked with them till he came to the Kazi's presence, where he found Fatimah standing with her arm bound up and her face-veil besmeared with blood; and she was weeping and wiping away her tears. Quoth the Kazi, "Ho man, hast thou no fear of Allah the Most High? Why hast thou beaten this good woman and broken her forearm and knocked out her tooth and entreated her thus?" And quoth Ma'aruf, "If I beat her or put out her tooth, sentence me to what thou wilt; but in truth the case was thus and thus and the neighbours made peace between me and her." And he told him the story from first to last. Now this Kazi was a benevolent man; so he brought out to him a quarter dinar, saying, "O man, take this and get her Kunafah with bees' honey and do ye make peace, thou and she." Quoth Ma'aruf, "Give it to her." So she took it and the Kazi made peace between them, saying, "O wife, obey thy husband; and thou, O man, deal kindly with her." Then they left the court, reconciled at the Kazi's hands, and the woman went one way, whilst her husband returned by another way to his shop and sat there, when, behold, the runners came up to him and said, "Give us our fee." Quoth he, "The Kazi took not of me aught; on the contrary, he gave me a quarter dinar." But quoth they "'Tis no concern of ours whether the Kazi took of thee or gave to thee, and if thou give us not our fee, we will exact it in despite of thee." And they fell to dragging him about the market; so he sold his tools and gave them half a dinar, whereupon they let him go and went away, whilst he put his hand to his cheek and sat sorrowful, for that he had no tools wherewith to work. Presently, up came two ill-favoured fellows and said to him, "Come, O man, and speak with the Kazi; for thy wife hath complained of thee to him." Said he, "He made peace between us just now." But said they, "We come from another Kazi, and thy wife hath complained of thee to our Kazi." So he arose and went with them to their Kazi, calling on Allah for aid against her; and when he saw her, he said to her, "Did we not make peace, good woman?" Whereupon she cried, "There abideth no peace between me and thee." Accordingly he came forward and told the Kazi his story, adding, "And indeed the Kazi Such-an-one made peace between us this very hour." Whereupon the Kazi said to her, "O strumpet, since ye two have made peace with each other, why comest thou to me complaining?" Quoth she, "He beat me after that;" but quoth the Kazi, "Make peace each with other, and beat her not again, and she will cross thee no more." So they made peace and the Kazi said to Ma'aruf, "Give the runners their fee." So he gave them their fee and going back to his shop, opened it and sat down, as he were a drunken man for excess of the chagrin which befel him. Presently, while he was still sitting, behold, a man came up to him and said, "O Ma'aruf, rise and hide thyself, for thy wife hath complained of thee to the High Court and Abú Tabak is after thee." So he shut his shop and fled towards the Gate of Victory. He had five nusfs of silver left of the price of the lasts and gear; and therewith he bought four worth of bread and one of cheese, as he fled from her. Now it was the winter season and the hour of mid-afternoon prayer; so, when he came out among the rubbish-mounds the rain descended upon him, like water from the mouths of water-skins, and his clothes were drenched. He therefore entered the 'Adiliyah, where he saw a ruined place and therein a deserted cell without a door; and in it he took refuge and found shelter from the rain. The tears streamed from his eyelids, and he fell to complaining of what had betided him and saying, "Whither shall I flee from this whore? I beseech Thee, O Lord, to vouchsafe me one who shall conduct me to a far country, where she shall not know the way to me!" Now while he sat weeping, behold, the wall clave and there came forth to him therefrom one of tall stature, whose aspect caused his body-pile to bristle and his flesh to creep, and said to him, "O man, what aileth thee that thou disturbest me this night? These two hundred years have I dwelt here and have never seen any enter this place and do as thou dost. Tell me what thou wishest and I will accomplish thy need, as ruth for thee hath got hold upon my heart." Quoth Ma'aruf, "Who and what art thou?"; and quoth he, "I am the Haunter of this place." So Ma'aruf told him all that had befallen him with his wife and he said, "Wilt

thou have me convey thee to a country, where thy wife shall know no way to thee?"
"Yes," said Ma'aruf; and the other, "Then mount my back." So he mounted on his back
and he flew with him from after supper-tide till daybreak, when he set him down on
the top of a high mountain – And Shahrazad perceived the dawn of day and ceased
saying her permitted say.

When it was the Nine Hundred and Ninety-first Night,

She said, it hath reached me, O auspicious King, that the Marid having taken up
Ma'aruf the Cobbler, flew off with him and set him down upon a high mountain and
said to him, "O mortal, descend this mountain and thou wilt see the gate of a city.
Enter it, for therein thy wife cannot come at thee." He then left him and went his way,
whilst Ma'aruf abode in amazement and perplexity till the sun rose, when he said to
himself, "I will up with me and go down into the city: indeed there is no profit in my
abiding upon this highland." So he descended to the mountain-foot and saw a city girt
by towering walls, full of lofty palaces and gold-adorned buildings which was a delight
to beholders. He entered in at the gate and found it a place such as lightened the
grieving heart; but, as he walked through the streets the townsfolk stared at him as a
curiosity and gathered about him, marvelling at his dress, for it was unlike theirs.
Presently, one of them said to him, "O man, art thou a stranger?" "Yes." "What
countryman art thou?" "I am from the city of Cairo the Auspicious." "And when didst
thou leave Cairo?" "I left it yesterday, at the hour of afternoon-prayer." Whereupon the
man laughed at him and cried out, saying, "Come look, O folk, at this man and hear
what he saith!" Quoth they, "What doeth he say?"; and quoth the townsman, "He
pretendeth that he cometh from Cairo and left it yesterday at the hour of afternoon-
prayer!" At this they all laughed and gathering round Ma'aruf, said to him, "O man, art
thou mad to talk thus? How canst thou pretend that thou leftest Cairo at mid-afternoon
yesterday and foundedst thyself this morning here, when the truth is that between our
city and Cairo lieth a full year's journey?" Quoth he, "None is mad but you. As for me,
I speak sooth, for here is bread which I brought with me from Cairo, and see, 'tis yet
new." Then he showed them the bread and they stared at it, for it was unlike their
country bread. So the crowd increased about him and they said to one another, "This
is Cairo bread: look at it;" and he became a gazing-stock in the city and some believed
him, whilst others gave him the lie and made mock of him. Whilst this was going on,
behold, up came a merchant riding on a she-mule and followed by two black slaves,
and brake a way through the people, saying, "O folk, are ye not ashamed to mob this
stranger and make mock of him and scoff at him?" And he went on to rate them, till he
drave them away from Ma'aruf, and none could make him any answer. Then he said to
the stranger, "Come, O my brother, no harm shall betide thee from these folk. Verily
they have no shame." So he took him and carrying him to a spacious and richly-
adorned house, seated him in a speak-room fit for a King, whilst he gave an order to
his slaves, who opened a chest and brought out to him a dress such as might be worn
by a merchant worth a thousand. He clad him therewith and Ma'aruf, being a seemly
man, became as he were consul of the merchants. Then his host called for food and
they set before them a tray of all manner exquisite viands. The twain ate and drank
and the merchant said to Ma'aruf, "O my brother, what is thy name?" "My name is
Ma'aruf and I am a cobbler by trade and patch old shoes." "What countryman art
thou?" "I am from Cairo." "What quarter?" "Dost thou know Cairo?" "I am of its
children. I come from the Red Street." "And whom dost thou know in the Red Street?"

"I know such an one and such an one," answered Ma'aruf and named several people to him. Quoth the other, "Knowest thou Shaykh Ahmad the druggist?" "He was my next neighbour, wall to wall." "Is he well?" "Yes." "How many sons hath he?" "Three, Mustafà, Mohammed and Ali." "And what hath Allah done with them?" "As for Mustafà, he is well and he is a learned man, a professor: Mohammed is a druggist and opened him a shop beside that of his father, after he had married, and his wife hath borne him a son named Hasan." "Allah gladden thee with good news!" said the merchant; and Ma'aruf continued, "As for Ali, he was my friend, when we were boys, and we always played together, I and he. We used to go in the guise of the children of the Nazarenes and enter the church and steal the books of the Christians and sell them and buy food with the price. It chanced once that the Nazarenes caught us with a book; whereupon they complained of us to our folk and said to Ali's father: An thou hinder not thy son from troubling us, we will complain of thee to the King. So he appeased them and gave Ali a thrashing; wherefore he ran away none knew whither and he hath now been absent twenty years and no man hath brought news of him." Quoth the host, "I am that very Ali, son of Shaykh Ahmad the druggist, and thou art my playmate Ma'aruf." So they saluted each other and after the salam Ali said, "Tell me why, O Ma'aruf, thou camest from Cairo to this city." Then he told him all that had befallen him of ill-doing with his wife Fatimah the Dung and said, "So, when her annoy waxed on me, I fled from her towards the Gate of Victory and went forth the city. Presently, the rain fell heavy on me; so I entered a ruined cell in the Adiliyah and sat there, weeping; whereupon there came forth to me the Haunter of the place, which was an Ifrit of the Jinn, and questioned me. I acquainted him with my case and he took me on his back and flew with me all night between heaven and earth, till he set me down on yonder mountain and gave me to know of this city. So I came down from the mountain and entered the city, when people crowded about me and questioned me. I told them that I had left Cairo yesterday, but they believed me not, and presently thou camest up and driving the folk away from me, carriedst me this house. Such, then, is the cause of my quitting Cairo; and thou, what object brought thee hither?" Quoth Ali, "The giddiness of folly turned my head when I was seven years old, from which time I wandered from land to land and city to city, till I came to this city, the name whereof is Ikhtiyán al-Khatan. I found its people an hospitable folk and a kindly, compassionate for the poor man and selling to him on credit and believing all he said. So quoth I to them: I am a merchant and have preceded my packs and I need a place wherein to bestow my baggage. And they believed me and assigned me a lodging. Then quoth I to them: Is there any of you will lend me a thousand dinars, till my loads arrive, when I will repay it to him; for I am in want of certain things before my goods come? They gave me what I asked and I went to the merchants' bazar, where, seeing goods, I bought them and sold them next day at a profit of fifty gold pieces and bought others. And I consorted with the folk and entreated them liberally, so that they loved me, and I continued to sell and buy, till I grew rich. Know, O my brother, that the proverb saith, The world is show and trickery: and the land where none wotteth thee, there do whatso liketh thee. Thou too, an thou say to all who ask thee, I'm a cobbler by trade and poor withal, and I fled from my wife and left Cairo yesterday, they will not believe thee and thou wilt be a laughing-stock among them as long as thou abidest in the city; whilst, an thou tell them, An Ifrit brought me hither, they will take fright at thee and none will come near thee; for they will say, This man is possessed of an Ifrit and harm will betide whoso approacheth him. And such public report will be dishonouring both to thee and to me, because they ken I come from Cairo." Ma'aruf asked: "How then shall I do?"; and Ali answered, "I will tell thee how thou shalt do, Inshallah! To-morrow I will give thee a thousand dinars and a she-mule to ride and a black slave, who shall walk before thee and guide thee to the gate of the merchants' bazar; and do thou go into them. I will be there sitting amongst them, and when I see thee, I will rise to thee and salute thee with the salam and kiss thy hand and make a great man of thee. Whenever I ask thee of any kind of stuff, saying, Hast thou brought with thee aught of such a kind? do thou answer, "Plenty." And if they question me of thee, I will praise thee and magnify thee in their eyes and say to them, Get him a store-house and a shop. I also will give thee out for a man of great wealth and generosity; and if a beggar come to thee, bestow upon him what thou mayst; so will they put faith in what I say and believe in thy greatness and generosity and love thee. Then will I invite thee to my house and invite all the merchants on thy account and bring together thee and them, so that all may know thee and thou know them," – And Shahrazad perceived the dawn of day and ceased to say her permitted say.

When it was the Nine Hundred and Ninety-second Night,

She continued, It hath reached me, O auspicious King, that the merchant Ali said to Ma'aruf, "I will invite thee to my house and invite all the merchants on thy account and bring together thee and them, so that all may know thee and thou know them, whereby thou shalt sell and buy and take and give with them; nor will it be long ere thou become a man of money." Accordingly, on the morrow he gave him a thousand dinars and a suit of clothes and a black slave and mounting him on a she-mule, said to him, "Allah give thee quittance of responsibility for all this, inasmuch as thou art my friend and it behoveth me to deal generously with thee. Have no care; but put away from thee the thought of thy wife's misways and name her not to any." "Allah requite thee with good!" replied Ma'aruf and rode on, preceded by his blackamoor till the slave brought him to the gate of the merchants' bazar, where they were all seated, and amongst them Ali, who when he saw him, rose and threw himself upon him, crying, "A blessed day, O Merchant Ma'aruf, O man of good works and kindness!" And he kissed his hand before the merchants and said to them, "Our brothers, ye are honoured by knowing the merchant Ma'aruf." So they saluted him, and Ali signed to them to make much of him, wherefore he was magnified in their eyes. Then Ali helped him to dismount from his she-mule and saluted him with the salam; after which he took the merchants apart, one after other, and vaunted Ma'aruf to them. They asked, "Is this man a merchant?;" and he answered, "Yes; and indeed he is the chiefest of merchants, there liveth not a wealthier than he; for his wealth and the riches of his father and forefathers are famous among the merchants of Cairo. He hath partners in Hind and Sind and Al-Yaman and is high in repute for generosity. So know ye his rank and exalt ye his degree and do him service, and wot also that his coming to your city is not for the sake of traffic, and none other save to divert himself with the sight of folk's countries: indeed, he hath no need of strangerhood for the sake of gain and profit, having wealth that fires cannot consume, and I am one of his servants." And he ceased not to extol him, till they set him above their heads and began to tell one another of his qualities. Then they gathered round him and offered him junkets and sherbets, and even the Consul of the Merchants came to him and saluted him; whilst Ali proceeded to ask him, in the presence of the traders, "O my lord, haply thou hast brought with thee somewhat of such and such a stuff?"; and Ma'aruf answered,"Plenty." Now Ali had that day shown him various kinds of costly clothes and had taught him the names of the different stuffs, dear and cheap. Then said one of the merchants, "O my lord, hast thou brought with thee yellow broad cloth?": and Ma'aruf said, "Plenty"! Quoth another, "And gazelles' blood red?"; and quoth the Cobbler, "Plenty"; and as often as he asked him of aught, he made him the same answer. So the other said, "O Merchant Ali had thy countryman a mind to transport a thousand loads of costly stuffs, he could do so"; and Ali said, "He would take them from a single one of his store-houses, and miss naught thereof." Now whilst they were sitting, behold, up came a beggar and went the round of the merchants. One gave him a half dirham and another a copper, but most of them gave him nothing, till he came to Ma'aruf who pulled out a handful of gold and gave it to him, whereupon he blessed him and went his ways. The merchants marvelled at this and said, "Verily, this is a King's bestowal for he gave the beggar gold without count, and were he not a man of vast wealth and money without end, he had not given a beggar a handful of gold." After a while, there came to him a poor woman and he gave her a handful of gold; whereupon she went away, blessing him, and told the other beggars, who came to him, one after other, and he gave them each a handful of gold, till he disbursed the thousand dinars. Then he struck hand upon hand and said, "Allah is our sufficient aid and excellent is the Agent!" Quoth the Consul, "What aileth thee, O Merchant Ma'aruf?"; and quoth he, "It seemeth that the most part of the people of this city are poor and needy; had I known their misery I would have brought with me a large sum of money in my saddle-bags and given largesse thereof to the poor. I fear me I may be long abroad and 'tis not in my nature to baulk a beggar; and I have no gold left: so, if a pauper come to me, what shall I say to him?" Quoth the Consul, "Say, Allah will send thee thy daily bread!"; but Ma'aruf replied, "That is not my practice and I am care-ridden because of this. Would I had other thousand dinars, wherewith to give alms till my baggage come!" "Have no care for that," quoth the Consul and sending one of his dependents for a thousand dinars, handed them to Ma'aruf, who went on giving them to every beggar who passed till the call to noon-prayer. Then they entered the Cathedral-mosque and prayed the noon-prayers, and what was left him of the thousand gold pieces he scattered on the heads of the worshippers. This drew the people's attention to him and they blessed him, whilst the merchants marvelled at the abundance of his generosity and openhandedness. Then he turned to another trader and borrowing of him other thousand ducats, gave these also away, whilst Merchant Ali looked on at what he did, but could not speak. He ceased not to do thus till the call to mid-afternoon prayer, when he entered the mosque and prayed and distributed the rest of the money. On this wise, by the time they locked the doors of the bazar, he had borrowed five thousand sequins and given them away, saying to every one of whom he took aught, "Wait till my baggage come when, if thou desire gold I will give thee gold, and if thou desire stuffs, thou shalt have stuffs; for I have no end of them." At eventide Merchant Ali invited Ma'aruf and the rest of the traders to an entertainment and seated him in the upper end, the place of honour, where he talked of nothing but cloths and jewels, and whenever they made mention to him of aught, he said, "I have plenty of it." Next day, he again repaired to the market-street where he showed a friendly bias towards the merchants and borrowed of them more money, which he distributed to the poor: nor did he leave doing thus twenty days, till he had borrowed threescore thousand dinars, and still there came no baggage, no, nor a burning plague. At last folk began to clamour for their money and say, "The merchant Ma'aruf's baggage cometh not. How long will he take people's monies and give them to the poor?" And quoth one of them, "My rede is that we speak to Merchant Ali." So they went to him and said, "O Merchant Ali, Merchant Ma'aruf's baggage cometh not." Said he, "Have patience, it cannot fail to come soon." Then he took Ma'aruf aside and said to him, "O Ma'aruf, what fashion is this? Did I bid thee brown the bread or burn it? The merchants clamour for their coin and tell me that thou owest them sixty thousand dinars, which thou hast borrowed and given away to the poor. How wilt thou satisfy the folk, seeing that thou neither sellest nor buyest?" Said Ma'aruf, "What matters it; and what are threescore thousand dinars? When my baggage shall come, I will pay them in stuffs or in gold and silver, as they will." Quoth Merchant Ali, "Allah is Most Great! Hast thou then any baggage?"; and he said, "Plenty." Cried the other, "Allah and the Hallows requite thee thine impudence! Did I teach thee this saying, that thou shouldst repeat it to me? But I will acquaint the folk with thee." Ma'aruf rejoined, "Begone and prate no more! Am I a poor man? I have endless wealth in my baggage and as soon as it cometh, they shall have their money's worth two for one. I have no need of them." At this Merchant Ali waxed wroth and said, "Unmannerly wight that thou art, I will teach thee to lie to me and be not ashamed!" Said Ma'aruf, "E'en work the worst thy hand can do! They must wait till my baggage come, when they shall have their due and more." So Ali left him and went away, saying in himself, "I praised him whilome and if I blame him now, I make myself out a liar and become of those of whom it is said:- -Whoso praiseth and then blameth lieth twice." And he knew not what to do. Presently, the traders came to him and said, "O Merchant Ali, hast thou spoken to him?" Said he, "O folk, I am ashamed and, though he owe me a thousand dinars, I cannot speak to him. When ye lent him your money ye consulted me not; so ye have no claim on me. Dun him yourselves, and if he pay you not, complain of him to the King of the city, saying: He is an impostor who hath imposed upon us. And he will deliver you from the plague of him." Accordingly, they repaired to the King and told him what had passed, saying, "O King of the age, we are perplexed anent this merchant, whose generosity is excessive; for he doeth thus and thus, and all he borroweth, he giveth away to the poor by handsful. Were he a man of naught, his sense would not suffer him to lavish gold on this wise; and were he a man of wealth, his good faith had been made manifest to us by the coming of his baggage; but we see none of his luggage, although he avoucheth that he hath baggage-train and hath preceded it. Now some time hath past, but there appeareth no sign of his baggage-train, and he oweth us sixty thousand gold pieces, all of which he hath given away in alms." And they went on to praise him and extol his generosity. Now this King was a very covetous man, a more covetous than Ash'ab; and when he heard tell of Ma'aruf's generosity and openhandedness, greed of gain got the better of him and he said to his Wazir, "Were not this merchant a man of immense wealth, he had not shown all this munificence. His baggage-train will assuredly come, whereupon these merchants will flock to him and he will scatter amongst them riches galore. Now I have more right to this money than they; wherefore I have a mind to make friends with him and profess affection for him, so that, when his baggage cometh whatso the merchants would have had I shall get of him; and I will give him my daughter to wife and join his wealth to my wealth." Replied the Wazir, "O King of the age, methinks he is naught but an impostor, and 'tis the impostor who ruineth the house of the covetous;" – And Shahrazad perceived the dawn of day and ceased saying her permitted say.

When it was the Nine Hundred and Ninety-third Night,

She pursued, It hath reached me, O auspicious King, that when the Wazir said to the King, "Methinks he is naught but an impostor, and 'tis the impostor who ruineth the house of the covetous;" the King said, "O Wazir, I will prove him and soon know if he be an impostor or a true man and whether he be a rearling of Fortune or not." The Wazir asked, "And how wilt thou prove him?"; and the King answered, "I will send for him to the presence and entreat him with honour and give him a jewel which I have. An he know it and wot its price, he is a man of worth and wealth; but an he know it not, he is an impostor and an upstart and I will do him die by the foulest fashion of deaths." So he sent for Ma'aruf, who came and saluted him. The King returned his salam and seating him beside himself, said to him, "Art thou the merchant Ma'aruf?" and said he, "Yes." Quoth the King, "The merchants declare that thou owest them sixty thousand ducats. Is this true?" "Yes," quoth he. Asked the King, "Then why dost thou not give them their money?"; and he answered, "Let them wait till my baggage come and I will repay them twofold. An they wish for gold, they shall have gold; and should they wish for silver, they shall have silver; or an they prefer for merchandise, I will give them merchandise; and to whom I owe a thousand I will give two thousand in requital of that wherewith he hath veiled my face before the poor; for I have plenty." Then said the King, "O merchant, take this and look what is its kind and value." And he gave him a jewel the bigness of a hazel-nut, which he had bought for a thousand sequins and not having its fellow, prized it highly. Ma'aruf took it and pressing it between his thumb and forefinger brake it, for it was brittle and would not brook the squeeze. Quoth the King, "Why hast thou broken the jewel?"; and Ma'aruf laughed and said, "O King of the age, this is no jewel. This is but a bittock of mineral worth a thousand dinars; why dost thou style it a jewel? A jewel I call such as is worth threescore and ten thousand gold pieces and this is called but a piece of stone. A jewel that is not of the bigness of a walnut hath no worth in my eyes and I take no account thereof. How cometh it, then, that thou, who art King, stylest this thing a jewel, when 'tis but a bit of mineral worth a thousand dinars? But ye are excusable, for that ye are poor folk and have not in your possession things of price." The King asked, "O merchant, hast thou jewels such as those whereof thou speakest?"; and he answered, "Plenty." Whereupon avarice overcame the King and he said, "Wilt thou give me real jewels?" Said Ma'aruf, "When my baggage-train shall come, I will give thee no end of jewels; and all that thou canst desire I have in plenty and will give thee, without price." At this the King rejoiced and said to the traders, "Wend your ways and have patience with him, till his baggage arrive, when do ye come to me and receive your monies from me." So they fared forth and the King turned to his to his Wazir and said to him, Pay court to Merchant Ma'aruf and take and give with him in talk and bespeak him of my daughter, Princess Dunyá, that he may wed her and so we gain these riches he hath." Said the Wazir, "O King of the age, this man's fashion misliketh me and methinks he is an impostor and a liar: so leave this whereof thou speakest lest thou lose thy daughter for naught." Now this Minister had sued the King aforetime to give him his daughter to wife and he was willing to do so, but when she heard of it she consented not to marry him. Accordingly, the King said to him, "O traitor, thou desirest no good for me, because in past time thou soughtest my daughter in wedlock, but she would none of thee; so now thou wouldst cut off the way of her marriage and wouldst have the Princess lie fallow, that thou mayst take her; but hear from me one word. Thou hast no concern in this matter.

How can he be an impostor and a liar, seeing that he knew the price of the jewel, even that for which I bought it, and brake it because it pleased him not? He hath jewels in plenty, and when he goeth in to my daughter and seeth her to be beautiful she will captivate his reason and he will love her and give her jewels and things of price: but, as for thee, thou wouldst forbid my daughter and myself these good things." So the Minister was silent, for fear of the King's anger, and said to himself, "Set the curs on the cattle!" Then with show of friendly bias he betook himself to Ma'aruf and said to him, "His Highness the King loveth thee and hath a daughter, a winsome lady and a lovesome, to whom he is minded to marry thee. What sayst thou?" Said he, "No harm in that; but let him wait till my baggage come, for marriage-settlements on Kings' daughters are large and their rank demandeth that they be not endowed save with a dowry befitting their degree. At this present I have no money with me till the coming of my baggage, for I have wealth in plenty and needs must I make her marriage-portion five thousand purses. Then I shall need a thousand purses to distribute amongst the poor and needy on my wedding-night, and other thousand to give to those who walk in the bridal procession and yet other thousand wherewith to provide provaunt for the troops and others; and I shall want an hundred jewels to give to the Princess on the wedding-morning and other hundred gems to distribute among the slavegirls and eunuchs, for I must give each of them a jewel in honour of the bride; and I need wherewithal to clothe a thousand naked paupers, and alms too needs must be given. All this cannot be done till my baggage come; but I have plenty and, once it is here, I shall make no account of all this outlay." The Wazir returned to the King and told him what Ma'aruf said, whereupon quoth he, "Since this is his wish, how canst thou style him impostor and liar?" Replied the Minister, "And I cease not to say this." But the King chid him angrily and threatened him, saying, "By the life of my head, an thou cease not this talk, I will slay thee! Go back to him and fetch him to me and I will manage matters with him myself." So the Wazir returned to Ma'aruf and said to him, "Come and speak with the King." "I hear and I obey," said Ma'aruf and went in to the King, who said to him, "Thou shalt not put me off with these excuses, for my treasury is full; so take the keys and spend all thou needest and give what thou wilt and clothe the poor and do thy desire and have no care for the girl and the handmaids. When the baggage shall come, do what thou wilt with thy wife, by way of generosity, and we will have patience with thee anent the marriage-portion till then, for there is no manner of difference betwixt me and thee; none at all." Then he sent for the Shaykh Al-Islam and bade him write out the marriage-contract between his daughter and Merchant Ma'aruf, and he did so; after which the King gave the signal for beginning the wedding festivities and bade decorate the city. The kettle drums beat and the tables were spread with meats of all kinds and there came performers who paraded their tricks. Merchant Ma'aruf sat upon a throne in a parlour and the players and gymnasts and effeminates and dancing-men of wondrous movements and posture-makers of marvellous cunning came before him, whilst he called out to the treasurer and said to him, "Bring gold and silver." So he brought gold and silver and Ma'aruf went round among the spectators and largessed each performer by the handful; and he gave alms to the poor and needy and clothes to the naked and it was a clamorous festival and a right merry. The treasurer could not bring money fast enough from the treasury, and the Wazir's heart was like to burst for rage; but he dared not say a word, whilst Merchant Ali marvelled at this waste of wealth and said to Merchant Ma'aruf, "Allah and the Hallows visit this upon on thy head-sides! Doth it not suffice thee to squander the traders' money, but thou must squander that of the King to boot?" Replied Ma'aruf, "'Tis none of thy concern: whenas my baggage shall come, I will requite the King manifold." And he went on lavishing money and saying in himself, "A burning plague! What will happen will happen and there is no flying from that which is fore-ordained." The festivities ceased not for the space of forty days, and on the one-and-fortieth day, they made the bride's cortège and all the Emirs and troops walked before her. When they brought her in before Ma'aruf, he began scattering gold on the people's heads, and they made her a mighty fine procession, whilst Ma'aruf expended in her honour vast sums of money. Then they brought him in to Princess Dunya and he sat down on the high divan; after which they let fall the curtains and shut the doors and withdrew, leaving him alone with his bride; whereupon he smote hand upon hand and sat awhile sorrowful and saying, "There is no Majesty and there is no Might save in Allah, the Glorious, the Great!" Quoth the Princess, "O my lord, Allah preserve thee! What aileth thee that thou art troubled?" Quoth he, "And how should I be other than troubled, seeing that thy father hath embarrassed me and done with me a deed which is like the burning of green corn?" She asked, "And what hath my father done with thee? Tell me!"; and he answered, "He hath brought me in to thee before the coming of my baggage, and I want at very least an hundred jewels to distribute among thy handmaids, to each a jewel, so she might rejoice therein and say, My lord gave me a jewel on the night of his going in to my lady. This good deed would I have done in honour of thy station and for the increase of thy dignity; and I have no need to stint myself in lavishing jewels, for I have of them great plenty." Rejoined she, "Be not concerned for that. As for me, trouble not thyself about me, for I will have patience with thee till thy baggage shall come, and as for my women have no care for them. Rise, doff thy clothes and take thy pleasure; and when the baggage cometh we shall get the jewels and the rest." So he arose and putting off his clothes sat down on the bed and sought love-liesse and they fell to toying with each other. He laid his hand on her knee and she sat down in his lap and thrust her lip like a tit-bit of meat into his mouth, and that hour was such as maketh a man to forget his father and his mother. So he clasped her in his arms and strained her fast to his breast and sucked her lip, till the honey-dew ran out into his mouth; and he laid his hand under her left-armpit, whereupon his vitals and her vitals yearned for coition. Then he clapped her between the breasts and his hand slipped down between her thighs and she girded him with her legs, whereupon he made of the two parts proof amain and crying out, "O sire of the chin-veils twain!" applied the priming and kindled the match and set it to the touch-hole and gave fire and breached the citadel in its four corners; so there befel the mystery concerning which there is no enquiry: and she cried the cry that needs must be cried. – And Shahrazad perceived the dawn of day and ceased to say her permitted say.

When it Was the Nine Hundred and Ninety-fourth Night,

She resumed, It hath reached me, O auspicious King, that while the Princess Dunyá cried the cry which must be cried, Merchant Ma'aruf abated her maidenhead and that night was one not to be counted among lives for that which it comprised of the enjoyment of the fair, clipping and dallying *langue fourrée* and futtering till the dawn of day, when he arose and entered the Hammam whence, after donning a suit for sovrans suitable he betook himself to the King's Divan. All who were there rose to him and received him with honour and worship, giving him joy and invoking blessings upon him; and he sat down by the King's side and asked, "Where is the treasurer?" They answered, "Here he is, before thee," and he said to him, "Bring robes of honour for all the Wazirs and Emirs and dignitaries and clothe them therewith." The treasurer brought him all he sought and he sat giving to all who came to him and lavishing largesse upon every man according to his station. On this wise he abode twenty days, whilst no baggage appeared for him nor aught else, till the treasurer was straitened by him to the uttermost and going in to the King, as he sat alone with the Wazir in Ma'aruf's absence, kissed ground between his hands and said, "O King of the age, I must tell thee somewhat, lest haply thou blame me for not acquainting thee therewith. Know that the treasury is being exhausted; there is none but a little money left in it and in ten days more we shall shut it upon emptiness." Quoth the King, "O Wazir, verily my son-in-law's baggage-train tarrieth long and there appeareth no news thereof." The Minister laughed and said , Allah be gracious to thee, O King of the age! Thou art none other but heedless with respect to this impostor, this liar. As thy head liveth, there is no baggage for him, no, nor a burning plague to rid us of him! Nay, he hath but imposed on thee without surcease, so that he hath wasted thy treasures and married thy daughter for naught. How long therefore wilt thou be heedless of this liar?" Then quoth the King, "O Wazir, how shall we do to learn the truth of his case?"; and quoth the Wazir, "O King of the age, none may come at a man's secret but his wife; so send for thy daughter and let her come behind the curtain, that I may question her of the truth of his estate, to the intent that she may make question of him and acquaint us with his case." Cried the King, "There is no harm in that; and as my head liveth, if it be proved that he is a liar and an impostor, I will verily do him die by the foulest of deaths!" Then he carried the Wazir into the sitting-chamber and sent for his daughter, who came behind the curtain, her husband being absent, and said, "What wouldst thou, O my father?" Said he "Speak with the Wazir." So she asked, "Ho thou, the Wazir, what is thy will?"; and he answered, "O my lady, thou must know that thy husband hath squandered thy father's substance and married thee without a dower; and he ceaseth not to promise us and break his promises, nor cometh there any tidings of his baggage; in short we would have thee inform us concerning him." Quoth she, "Indeed his words be many, and he still cometh and promiseth me jewels and treasures and costly stuffs; but I see nothing." Quoth the Wazir, "O my lady, canst thou this night take and give with him in talk and whisper to him: Say me sooth and fear from me naught, for thou art become my husband and I will not transgress against thee. So tell me the truth of the matter and I will devise thee a device whereby thou shalt be set at rest. And do thou play near and far with him in words and profess love to him and win him to confess and after tell us the facts of his case." And she answered, "O my papa, I know how I will make proof of him." Then she went away and after supper her husband came in to her, according to his wont, whereupon Princess Dunya rose to him and took him under the armpit and wheedled him with winsomest wheedling (and all-sufficient are woman's wiles whenas she would aught of men); and she ceased not to caress him and beguile him with speech sweeter than the honey till she stole his reason; and when she saw that he altogether inclined to her, she said to him, "O my beloved, O coolth of my eyes and fruit of my vitals, Allah never desolate me by less of thee nor Time sunder us twain me and thee! Indeed, the love of thee hath homed in my heart and the fire of passion hath consumed my liver, nor will I ever forsake thee or transgress against thee. But I would have thee tell me the truth, for that the sleights of falsehood profit not, nor do they secure credit at all seasons. How long wilt thou impose upon my father and lie to him? I fear lest thine affair be discovered to him, ere we can devise some device and he lay violent hands upon thee? So acquaint me with the facts of the case for naught shall befal thee save that which shall begladden thee; and, when thou shalt have spoken sooth, fear not harm shall betide thee. How often wilt thou declare that thou art a merchant and a man of money and hast a luggage-train? This long while past thou sayest, My baggage! my baggage! but there appeareth no sign of thy baggage, and visible in thy face is anxiety on this account. So an there be no worth in thy words, tell me and I will contrive thee a contrivance whereby by thou shalt come off safe, Inshallah!" He replied, "I will tell thee the truth, and then do thou whatso thou wilt." Rejoined she, "Speak and look thou speak soothly; for sooth is the ark of safety, and beware of lying, for it dishonoureth the liar and God-gifted is he who said:

'Ware that truth thou speak, albe sooth when said
Shall cause thee in threatenèd fire to fall:
And seek Allah's approof, for most foolish he
Who shall anger his Lord to make friends with thrall."

He said, "Know, then, O my lady, that I am no merchant and have no baggage, no, nor a burning plague; nay, I was but a cobbler in my own country and had a wife called Fatimah the Dung, with whom there befel me this and that." And he told her his story from beginning to end; whereat she laughed and said, "Verily, thou art clever in the practice of lying and imposture!" Whereto he answered, "O my lady, may Allah Almighty preserve thee to veil sins and countervail chagrins!" Rejoined she, "Know, that thou imposedst upon my sire and deceivedst him by dint of thy deluding vaunts, so that of his greed for gain he married me to thee. Then thou squanderedst his wealth and the Wazir beareth thee a grudge for this. How many a time hath he spoken against thee to my father, saying, Indeed, he is an impostor, a liar! But my sire hearkened not to his say, for that he had sought me in wedlock and I consented not that he be baron and I femme. However, the time grew longsome upon my sire and he became straitened and said to me, Make him confess. So I have made thee confess and that which was covered is discovered. Now my father purposeth thee a mischief because of this; but thou art become my husband and I will never transgress against thee. An I told my father what I have learnt from thee, he would be certified of thy falsehood and imposture and that thou imposest upon Kings' daughters and squanderest royal wealth: so would thine offence find with him no pardon and he would slay thee sans a doubt: wherefore it would be bruited among the folk that I married a man who was a liar, an impostor, and this would smirch mine honour. Furthermore an he kill thee, most like he will require me to wed another, and to such thing I will never consent; no, not though I die! So rise now and don a Mameluke's dress and take these fifty thousand dinars of my monies, and mount a swift steed and get thee to a land whither the rule of my father doth not reach. Then make thee a merchant and send me a letter by a courier who shall bring it privily to me, that I may know in what land thou art, so I may send thee all my hand can attain. Thus shall thy wealth wax great and if my father die, I will send for thee, and thou shalt return in respect and honour; and if we die, thou or I and go to the mercy of God the Most Great, the Resurrection shall unite us. This, then, is the rede that is right: and while we both abide alive and well, I will not cease to send thee letters and monies. Arise ere the day wax bright and thou be in perplexed plight and perdition upon thy head alight!" Quoth he, "O my lady, I beseech thee of thy favour to bid me farewell with thine embracement;" and quoth she, "No harm in that." So he embraced her and knew her carnally; after which he made the Ghusl-ablution; then, donning the dress of a white slave, he bade the syces saddle him a thoroughbred steed. Accordingly, they saddled him a courser and he mounted and farewelling his wife, rode forth the city at the last of the night, whilst all who saw him deemed him one of the Mamelukes of the Sultan going abroad on some business. Next morning, the King and his Wazir repaired to the sitting-chamber and sent for Princess Dunya who came behind the curtain; and her father said to her, "O my daughter, what sayst thou?" Said she, "I say, Allah blacken thy Wazir's face, because he would have blackened my face in my husband's eyes!" Asked the King, "How so?"; and she answered, "He came in to me yesterday; but, before I could name the matter to him, behold, in walked Faraj the Chief Eunuch, letter in hand, and said: Ten white slaves stand under the palace window and have this letter, saying: Kiss for us the hands of our lord, Merchant Ma'aruf, and give him this letter, for we are of his Mamelukes with the baggage, and it hath reached us that he hath wedded the King's daughter, so we are come to acquaint him with that which befel us by the way. Accordingly I took the letter and read as follows: From the five hundred Mamelukes to his highness our lord Merchant Ma'aruf. But further. We give thee to know that, after thou quittedst us, the Arabs came out upon us and attacked us. They were two thousand horse and we five hundred mounted slaves and there befel a mighty sore fight between us and them. They hindered us from the road thirty days doing battle with them and this is the cause of our tarrying from thee." – And Shahrazad perceived the dawn of day and ceased saying her permitted say.

When it was the Nine Hundred and Ninety-fifth Night,

She said, it hath reached me, O auspicious King, that Princess Dunya said to her sire, "My husband received a letter from his dependents ending with: The Arabs hindered us from the road thirty days which is the cause of our being behind time. They also took from us of the luggage two hundred loads of cloth and slew of us fifty Mamelukes. When the news reached my husband, he cried, Allah disappoint them! What ailed them to wage war with the Arabs for the sake of two hundred loads of merchandise? What are two hundred loads? It behoved them not to tarry on that account, for verily the value of the two hundred loads is only some seven thousand dinars. But needs must I go to them and hasten them. As for that which the Arabs have taken, 'twill not be missed from the baggage, nor doth it weigh with me a whit, for I reckon it as if I had given it to them by way of an alms. Then he went down from me, laughing and taking no concern for the wastage of his wealth nor the slaughter of his slaves. As soon as he was gone, I looked out from the lattice and saw the ten Mamelukes who had brought him the letter, as they were moons, each clad in a suit of clothes worth two thousand dinars, there is not with my father a chattel to match one of them. He went forth with them to bring up his baggage and hallowed be Allah who hindered me from saying to him aught of that thou badest me, for he would have made mock of me and thee, and haply he would have eyed me with the eye of disparagement and hated me. But the fault is all with thy Wazir, who speaketh against my husband words that besit him not." Replied the King, "O my daughter, thy husband's wealth is indeed endless and he recketh not of it; for, from the day he entered our city, he hath done naught but give alms to the poor. Inshallah, he will speedily return with the baggage, and good in plenty shall betide us from him." And he went on to appease her and menace the Wazir, being duped by her device. So fared it with the King; but as regards Merchant Ma'aruf he rode on into waste lands, perplexed and knowing not to what quarter he should betake him; and for the anguish of parting he lamented and in the pangs of passion and love-longing he recited these couplets:

> Time falsed our Union and divided who were one in tway;
> And the sore tyranny of Time doth melt my heart away:
> Mine eyes ne'er cease to drop the tear for parting with my dear;
> When shall Disunion come to end and dawn the Union-day?
> O favour like the full moon's face of sheen, indeed I'm he
> Whom thou didst leave with vitals torn when faring on thy way.
> Would I had never seen thy sight, or met thee for an hour;
> Since after sweetest taste of thee to bitters I'm a prey.
> Ma'aruf will never cease to be enthralled by Dunyá's charms
> And long live she albe he die whom love and longing slay,
> O brilliance, like resplendent sun of noontide, deign them heal
> His heart for kindness and the fire of longing love allay!
> Would Heaven I wot an e'er the days shall deign conjoin our lots,
> Join us in pleasant talk o' nights, in Union glad and gay:
> Shall my love's palace hold two hearts that savour joy, and I
> Strain to my breast the branch I saw upon the sand-hill sway?
> O favour of full moon in sheen, never may sun o' thee
> Surcease to rise from Eastern rim with all-enlightening ray!
> I'm well content with passion-pine and all its bane and bate
> For luck in love is evermore the butt of jealous Fate.

And when he ended his verses, he wept with sore weeping, for indeed the ways were walled up before his face and death seemed to him better than dreeing life, and he walked on like a drunken man for stress of distraction, and stayed not till noontide, when he came to a little town and saw a plougher hard by, ploughing with a yoke of bulls. Now hunger was sore upon him; and he went up to the ploughman and said to him, "Peace be with thee!"; and he returned his salam and said to him, "Welcome, O my lord! Art thou one of the Sultan's Mamelukes?" Quoth Ma'aruf, "Yes;" and the other said "Alight with me for a guest-meal." Whereupon Ma'aruf knew him to be of the liberal and said to him, "O my brother, I see with thee naught with which thou mayst feed me: how is it, then, that thou invitest me?" Answered the husbandman, "O my lord, weal is well nigh. Dismount thee here: the town is near hand and I will go and fetch thee dinner and fodder for thy stallion." Rejoined Ma'aruf, "Since the town is near at hand, I can go thither as quickly as thou canst and buy me what I have a mind to in the bazar and eat." The peasant replied, "O my lord, the place is but a little village and there is no bazar there, neither selling nor buying. So I conjure thee by Allah, alight here with me and hearten my heart, and I will run thither and return to thee in haste." Accordingly he dismounted and the Fellah left him and went off to the village, to fetch dinner for him whilst Ma'aruf sat awaiting him. Presently he said in himself, "I have taken this poor man away from his work; but I will arise and plough in his stead, till he come back, to make up for having hindered him from his work." Then he took the plough and starting the bulls, ploughed a little, till the share struck against something and the beasts stopped. He goaded them on, but they could not move the plough; so he looked at the share and finding it caught in a ring of gold, cleared away the soil and saw that it was set centre-most a slab of alabaster, the size of the nether millstone. He strave at the stone till he pulled it from its place, when there appeared beneath it a souterrain with a stair. Presently he descended the flight of steps and came to a place like a Hammam, with four daïses, the first full of gold, from floor to roof, the second full of emeralds and pearls and coral also from ground to ceiling; the third of jacinths and rubies and turquoises and the fourth of diamonds and all manner other preciousest stones. At the upper end of the place stood a coffer of clearest crystal, full of union-gems each the size of a walnut, and upon the coffer lay a casket of gold, the bigness of a lemon. When he saw this, he marvelled and rejoiced with joy exceeding and said to himself, "I wonder what is in this casket?" So he opened it and found therein a seal-ring of gold, whereon were graven names and talismans, as they were the tracks of creeping ants. He rubbed the ring and behold, a voice said, "Adsum! Here am I, at thy service, O my lord! Ask and it shall be given unto thee. Wilt thou raise a city or ruin a capital or kill a king or dig a river-channel or aught of the kind? Whatso thou seekest, it shall come to pass, by leave of the King of All-might, Creator of day and night." Ma'aruf asked, "O creature of my lord, who and what art thou?"; and the other answered, "I am the slave of this seal-ring standing in the service of him who possesseth it. Whatsoever he seeketh, that I accomplish for him, and I have no excuse in neglecting that he biddeth me do; because I am Sultan over two-and-seventy tribes of the Jinn, each two-and-seventy thousand in number every one of which thousand ruleth over a thousand Marids, each Marid over a thousand Ifrits, each Ifrit over a thousand Satans and each Satan over a thousand Jinn: and they are all under command of me and may not gainsay me. As for me, I am spelled to this seal-ring and may not thwart whoso holdeth it. Lo! thou hast gotten hold of it and I am become thy slave; so ask what thou wilt, for I hearken to thy word and obey thy bidding; and if thou have need of me at any time, by land or by sea rub the signet-ring and thou wilt find me with thee. But beware of rubbing it twice in succession, or thou wilt consume me with the fire of the names graven thereon; and thus wouldst thou lose me and after regret me. Now I have acquainted thee with my case and – the Peace!" – And Shahrazad perceived the dawn of day and ceased to say her permitted say.

When it was the Nine Hundred and Ninety-sixth Night,

She continued, it hath reached me, O auspicious King, that when the Slave of the Signet-ring acquainted Ma'aruf with his case, the Merchant asked him, "What is thy name?" and the Jinni answered, "My name is Abú al-Sa'ádát." Quoth Ma'aruf, "O Abú al-Sa'ádát what is this place and who enchanted thee in this casket?"; and quoth he, "O my lord, this is a treasure called the Hoard of Shaddád son of Ad, him who the base of Many-columned Iram laid, the like of which in the lands was never made.' I was his slave in his lifetime and this is his seal-ring, which he laid up in his treasure; but it hath fallen to thy lot." Ma'aruf enquired, "Canst thou transport that which is in this hoard to the surface of the earth?"; and the Jinni replied, "Yes! Nothing were easier." Said Ma'aruf, "Bring it forth and leave naught." So the Jinni signed with his hand to the ground, which clave asunder, and he sank and was absent a little while. Presently, there came forth young boys full of grace, and fair of face bearing golden baskets filled with gold which they emptied out and going away, returned with more; nor did they cease to transport the gold and jewels, till ere an hour had sped they said, "Naught is left in the hoard." Thereupon out came Abú al-Sa'ádát and said to Ma'aruf, "O my lord, thou seest that we have brought forth all that was in the hoard." Ma'aruf asked, "Who be these beautiful boys?" and the Jinni answered, "They are my sons. This matter merited not that I should muster for it the Marids, wherefore my sons have done thy desire and are honoured by such service. So ask what thou wilt beside this." Quoth Ma'aruf, "Canst thou bring me he-mules and chests and fill the chests with the treasure and load them on the mules?" Quoth Abú al-Sa'ádát, "Nothing easier," and cried a great cry; whereupon his sons presented themselves before him, to the number of eight hundred, and he said to them, "Let some of you take the semblance of he-mules and others of muleteers and handsome Mamelukes, the like of the least of whom is not found with any of the Kings; and others of you be transmewed to muleteers, and the rest to menials." So seven hundred of them changed themselves into bât-mules and other hundred took the shape of slaves. Then Abú al-Sa'ádát called upon his Marids, who presented themselves between his hands and he commanded some of them to assume the aspect of horses saddled with saddles of gold crusted with jewels. And when Ma'aruf saw them do as he bade he cried, "Where be the chests?" They brought them before him and he said, "Pack the gold and the stones, each sort by itself." So they packed them and loaded three hundred he-mules with them. Then asked Ma'aruf, "O Abú al-Sa'ádát, canst thou bring me some loads of costly stuffs?"; and the Jinni answered, "Wilt thou have Egyptian stuffs or Syrian or Persian or Indian or Greek?" Ma'aruf said, "Bring me an hundred loads of each kind, on five hundred mules;" and Abú al-Sa'ádát, "O my lord accord me delay that I may dispose my Marids for this and send a company of them to each country to fetch an hundred loads of its stuffs and then take the form of he-mules and return, carrying the stuffs." Ma'aruf enquired, "What time dost thou want?"; and Abú al-Sa'ádát replied, "The time of the blackness of the night, and day shall not dawn ere thou have all thou desirest." Said Ma'aruf, "I grant thee this time," and bade them pitch him a pavilion. So they pitched it and he sat down therein and they brought him a table of food. Then said Abú al-Sa'ádát to him, "O my lord, tarry thou in this tent and these my sons shall guard thee: so fear thou nothing; for I go to muster my Marids and despatch them to do thy desire." So saying, he departed, leaving Ma'aruf seated in the pavilion, with the table before him and the Jinni's sons attending upon him, in the guise of slaves and servants and suite. And while he sat in this state behold, up came the husband man, with a great porringer of lentils and a nose-bag full of barley and seeing the pavilion pitched and the Mamelukes standing, hands upon breasts, thought that the Sultan was come and had halted on that stead. So he stood openmouthed and said in himself, "Would I had killed a couple of chickens and fried them red with clarified cow-butter for the Sultan!" And he would have turned back to kill the chickens as a regale for the Sultan; but Ma'aruf saw him and cried out to him and said to the Mamelukes, "Bring him hither." So they brought him and his porringer of lentils before Ma'aruf, who said to him, "What is this?" Said the peasant, "This is thy dinner and thy horse's fodder! Excuse me, for I thought not that the Sultan would come hither; and, had I known that, I would have killed a couple of chickens and entertained him in goodly guise." Quoth Ma'aruf, "The Sultan is not come. I am his son-in-law and I was vexed with him. However he hath sent his officers to make his peace with me, and now I am minded to return to city. But thou hast made me this guest-meal without knowing me, and I accept it from thee, lentils though it be, and will not eat save of thy cheer." Accordingly he bade him set the porringer amiddlemost the table and ate of it his sufficiency, whilst the Fellah filled his belly with those rich meats. Then Ma'aruf washed his hands and gave the Mamelukes leave to eat; so they fell upon the remains of the meal and ate; and, when the porringer was empty, he filled it with gold and gave it to the peasant, saying, "Carry this to thy dwelling and come to me in the city, and I will entreat thee with honour." Thereupon the peasant took the porringer full of gold and returned to the village, driving the bulls before him and deeming himself akin to the King. Meanwhile, they brought Ma'aruf girls of the Brides of the Treasure, who smote on instruments of music and danced before him, and he passed that night in joyance and delight, a night not to be reckoned among lives. Hardly had dawned the day when there arose a great cloud of dust which presently lifting, discovered seven hundred mules laden with stuffs and attended by muleteers and baggage-tenders and cresset-bearers. With them came Abú al-Sa'ádát, riding on a she-mule, in the guise of a caravan-leader, and before him was a travelling-litter, with four corner-terminals of glittering red gold, set with gems. When Abú al-Sa'ádát came up to the tent, he dismounted and kissing the earth, said to Ma'aruf, "O my lord, thy desire hath been done to the uttermost and in the litter is a treasure-suit which hath not its match among Kings' raiment: so don it and mount the litter and bid us do what thou wilt." Quoth Ma'aruf, "O Abú al-Sa'ádát, I wish thee to go to the city of Ikhtiyan al-Khatan and present thyself to my father-in-law the King; and go thou not in to him but in the guise of a mortal courier;" and quoth he, "To hear is to obey." So Ma'aruf wrote a letter to the Sultan and sealed it and Abú al-Sa'ádát took it and set out with it; and when he arrived, he found the King saying, "O Wazir, indeed my heart is concerned for my son-in-law and I fear lest the Arabs slay him. Would Heaven I wot whither he was bound, that I might have followed him with the troops! Would he had told me his destination!" Said the Wazir, "Allah be merciful to thee for this thy heedlessness! As thy head liveth, the wight saw that we were awake to him and feared dishonour and fled, for he is nothing but an impostor, a liar." And behold, at this moment in came the courier and kissing ground before the King, wished him permanent glory and prosperity and length of life. Asked the King, "Who art thou and what is thy business?" "I am a courier," answered the Jinni, "and thy son-in-law who is come with the baggage sendeth me to thee with a letter, and here it is!" So he took the letter and read therein these words, "After salutations galore to our uncle the glorious King! Know that I am at hand with the baggage-train: so come thou forth to meet me with the troops." Cried the King, "Allah blacken thy brow, O Wazir! How often wilt thou defame my son-in-law's name and call him liar and impostor? Behold, he is come with the baggage-train and thou art naught but a traitor." The Minister hung his head ground-wards in shame and confusion and replied, "O King of the age, I said not this save because of the long delay of the baggage and because I feared the loss of the wealth he hath wasted." The King exclaimed, "O traitor, what are my riches! Now that his baggage is come he will give me great plenty in their stead." Then he bade decorate the city and going in to his daughter, said to her, "Good news for thee! Thy husband will be here anon with his baggage; for he hath sent me a letter to that effect and here am I now going forth to meet him." The Princess Dunyá marvelled at this and said in herself, "This is a wondrous thing! Was he laughing at me and making mock of me, or had he a mind to try me, when he told me that he was a pauper? But Alhamdolillah, Glory to God, for that I failed not of my duty to him!" On this wise fared it in the palace; but as regards Merchant Ali, the Cairene, when he saw the decoration of the city and asked the cause thereof, they said to him, "The baggage-train of Merchant Ma'aruf, the King's son-in-law, is come." Said he, "Allah is Almighty! What a calamity is this man! He came to me, fleeing from his wife, and he was a poor man. Whence then should he get a baggage-train? But haply this is a device which the King's daughter hath contrived for him, fearing his disgrace, and Kings are not unable to do anything. May Allah the Most High veil his fame and not bring him to public shame!" – And Shahrazad perceived the dawn of day and ceased saying her permitted say.

When it was the Nine Hundred and Ninety-seventh Night,

She pursued, It hath reached me, O auspicious King, that when Merchant Ali asked the cause of the decorations, they told him the truth of the case; so he blessed Merchant Ma'aruf and cried, "May Allah Almighty veil his fame and not bring him to public shame!" And all the merchants rejoiced and were glad for that they would get their monies. Then the King assembled his troops and rode forth, whilst Abú al-Sa'ádát returned to Ma'aruf and acquainted him with the delivering of the letter. Quoth Ma'aruf, "Bind on the loads;" and when they had done so, he donned the treasure-suit and mounting the litter became a thousand times greater and more majestic than the King. Then he set forward; but, when he had gone half-way, behold, the King met him with the troops, and seeing him riding in the Takhtrawan and clad in the dress aforesaid, threw himself upon him and saluted him, and giving him joy of his safety, greeted him with the greeting of peace. Then all the Lords of the land saluted him and it was made manifest that he had spoken the truth and that in him there was no lie. Presently he entered the city in such state procession as would have caused the gall-bladder of the lion to burst for envy and the traders pressed up to him and kissed his hands, whilst Merchant Ali said to him, "Thou hast played off this trick and it hath prospered to thy hand, O Shaykh of Impostors! But thou deservest it and may Allah the Most High increase thee of His bounty!"; whereupon Ma'aruf laughed. Then he entered the palace and sitting down on the throne said, "Carry the loads of gold into the treasury of my uncle the King and bring me the bales of cloth." So they brought them to him and opened them before him, bale after bale, till they had unpacked the seven hundred loads, whereof he chose out the best and said, "Bear these to Princess Dunyá that she may distribute them among her slavegirls; and carry her also this coffer of jewels, that she may divide them among her handmaids and eunuchs." Then he proceeded to make over to the merchants in whose debt he was stuffs by way of payment for their arrears, giving him whose due was a thousand, stuffs worth two thousand or more; after which he fell to distributing to the poor and needy, whilst the King looked on with greedy eyes and could not hinder him; nor did he cease largesse till he had made an end of the seven hundred loads, when he turned to the troops and proceeded to apportion amongst them emeralds and rubies and pearls and coral and other jewels by handsful, without count, till the King said to him, "Enough of this giving, O my son! There is but little left of the baggage." But he said, "I have plenty." Then indeed, his good faith was become manifest and none could give him the lie; and he had come to reck not of giving, for that the Slave of the Seal-ring brought him whatsoever he sought. Presently, the treasurer came in to the King and said, "O King of the age, the treasury is full indeed and will not hold the rest of the loads.

Where shall we lay that which is left of the gold and jewels?" And he assigned to him another place. As for the Princess Dunya when she saw this, her joy redoubled and she marvelled and said in herself, "Would I wot how came he by all this wealth!" In like manner the traders rejoiced in that which he had given them and blessed him; whilst Merchant Ali marvelled and said to himself, "I wonder how he hath lied and swindled, that he hath gotten him all these treasures? Had they come from the King's daughter, he had not wasted them on this wise! But how excellent is his saying who said:

> When the Kings' King giveth, in reverence pause
> And venture not to enquire the cause:
> Allah gives His gifts unto whom He will,
> So respect and abide by His Holy Laws!"

So far concerning him; but as regards the King, he also marvelled with passing marvel at that which he saw of Ma'aruf's generosity and open-handedness in the largesse of wealth. Then the Merchant went in to his wife, who met him, smiling and laughing-lipped and kissed his hand, saying, "Didst thou mock me or hadst thou a mind to prove me with thy saying: I am a poor man and a fugitive from my wife? Praised be Allah for that I failed not of my duty to thee! For thou art my beloved and there is none dearer to me than thou, whether thou be rich or poor. But I would have thee tell me what didst thou design by these words." Said Ma'aruf, "I wished to prove thee and see whether thy love were sincere or for the sake of wealth and the greed of worldly good. But now 'tis become manifest to me that thine affection is sincere and as thou art a true woman, so welcome to thee! I know thy worth." Then he went apart into a place by himself and rubbed the seal-ring, whereupon Abu al-Sa'adat presented himself and said to him, "Adsum, at thy service! Ask what thou wilt." Quoth Ma'aruf, "I want a treasure-suit and treasure-trinkets for my wife, including a necklace of forty unique jewels." Quoth the Jinni, "To hear is to obey," and brought him what he sought, whereupon Ma'aruf dismissed him and carrying the dress and ornaments in to his wife, laid them before her and said, "Take these and put them on and welcome!" When she saw this, her wits fled for joy, and she found among the ornaments a pair of anklets of gold set with jewels of the handiwork of the magicians, and bracelets and earrings and a belt such as no money could buy. So she donned the dress and ornaments and said to Ma'aruf, "O my lord, I will treasure these up for holidays and festivals." But he answered, "Wear them always, for I have others in plenty." And when she put them on and her women beheld her, they rejoiced and bussed his hands. Then he left them and going apart by himself, rubbed the seal-ring whereupon its slave appeared and he said to him, "Bring me an hundred suits of apparel, with their ornaments of gold." "Hearing and obeying," answered Abu al-Sa'adat and brought him the hundred suits, each with its ornaments wrapped up within it. Ma'aruf took them and called aloud to the slave-girls, who came to him and he gave them each a suit: so they donned them and became like the black-eyed girls of Paradise, whilst the Princess Dunya shone amongst them as the moon among the stars. One of the handmaids told the King of this and he came in to his daughter and saw her and her women dazzling all who beheld them; whereat he wondered with passing wonderment. Then he went out and calling his Wazir, said to him, "O Wazir, such and such things have happened; what sayst thou now of this affair?" Said he, "O King of the age, this be no merchant's fashion; for a merchant keepeth a piece of linen by him for years and selleth it not but at a profit. How should a merchant have generosity such as this generosity, and whence should he get the like of these monies and jewels, of which but a slight matter is found with the Kings? So how should loads thereof be found with merchants? Needs must there be a cause for this; but, an thou wilt hearken to me, I will make the truth of the case manifest to thee." Answered the King, "O Wazir, I will do thy bidding." Rejoined the Minister, "Do thou foregather with thy son-in-law and make a show of affect to him and talk with him and say: O my son-in-law, I have a mind to go, I and thou and the Wazir but no more, to a flower-garden that we may take our pleasure there. When we come to the garden, we will set on the table wine, and I will ply him therewith and compel him to drink; for, when he shall have drunken, he will lose his reason and his judgment will forsake him. Then we will question him of the truth of his case and he will discover to us his secrets, for wine is a traitor and Allah-gifted is he who said:

> When we drank the wine, and it crept its way
> To the place of Secrets, I cried, "O stay!"
> In my fear lest its influence stint my wits
> And my friends spy matters that hidden lay.

When he hath told us the truth we shall ken his case and may deal with him as we will; because I fear for thee the consequences of this his present fashion: haply he will covet the kingship and win over the troops by generosity and lavishing money and so depose thee and take the kingdom from thee." "True," answered the King. – And Shahrazad perceived the dawn of day and ceased to say her permitted say.

When it was the Nine Hundred and Ninety-eighth Night,

She resumed, It hath reached me, O auspicious King, that when the Wazir devised this device the King said to him, "Thou hast spoken sooth!"; and they passed the night on this agreement. And when morning morrowed the King went forth and sat in the guest-chamber, when lo, and behold! the grooms and serving-men came in to him in dismay. Quoth he, "What hath befallen you?"; and quoth they, "O King of the age, the Syces curried the horses and foddered them and the he-mules which brought the baggage; but, when we arose in the morning, we found that thy son-in-law's Mamelukes had stolen the horses and mules. We searched the stables, but found neither horse nor mule; so we entered the lodging of the Mamelukes and found none there, nor know we how they fled." The King marvelled at this, unknowing that the horses and Mamelukes were all Ifrits, the subjects of the Slave of the Spell, and asked the grooms, "O accursed how could a thousand beasts and five hundred slaves and servants flee without your knowledge?" Answered they, "We know not how it happened," and he cried, "Go, and when your lord cometh forth of the Harim, tell him the case." So they went out from before the King and sat down bewildered, till Ma'aruf came out and, seeing them chagrined enquired of them, "What may be the matter?" They told him all that had happened and he said, "What is their worth that ye should be concerned for them? Wend your ways." And he sat laughing and was neither angry nor grieved concerning the case; whereupon the King looked in the Wazir's face and said to him, "What manner of man is this, with whom wealth is of no worth? Needs must there be a reason for this?" Then they talked with him awhile and the King said to him, "O my son-in-law, I have a mind to go, I, thou and the Wazir, to a garden, where we may divert ourselves." "No harm in that," said Ma'aruf. So they went forth to a flower-garden, wherein every sort of fruit was of kinds twain and its waters were flowing and its trees towering and its birds carolling. There they entered a pavilion, whose sight did away sorrow from the soul, and sat talking, whilst the Minister entertained them with rare tales and quoted merry quips and mirth-provoking sayings and Ma'aruf attentively listened, till the time of dinner came, when they set on a tray of meats and a flagon of wine. When they had eaten and washed hands, the Wazir filled the cup and gave it to the King, who drank it off; then he filled a second and handed it to Ma'aruf, saying, "Take the cup of the drink to which Reason boweth neck in reverence." Quoth Ma'aruf, "What is this, O Wazir?"; and quoth he, "This is the grizzled virgin and the old maid long kept at home, the giver of joy to hearts, whereof saith the poet:

> *The feet of sturdy Miscreants went trampling heavy tread,*
> *And she hath ta'en a vengeance dire on every Arab's head.*
> *A Káfir youth like fullest moon in darkness hands her round*
> *Whose eyne are strongest cause of sin by him inspiritèd.*

And Allah-gifted is he who said:

> *'Tis as if wine and he who bears the bowl,*
> *Rising to show her charms for man to see,*
> *Were dancing undurn-Sun whose face the moon*
> *Of night adorned with stars of Gemini.*
> *So subtle is her essence it would seem*
> *Through every limb like course of soul runs she.*
> *And how excellent is the saying of the poet:*
> *Slept in mine arms full Moon of brightest blee*
> *Nor did that sun eclipse in goblet see:*
> *I nighted spying fire whereto bow down*
> *Magians, which bowed from ewer's lip to me.*

And that of another:

> *It runs through every joint of them as runs*
> *The surge of health returning to the sick.*

And yet another:

> *I marvel at its pressers, how they died*
> *And left us aqua vitae – lymph of life!*

And yet goodlier is the saying of Abu Nowas:

> *Cease then to blame me, for thy blame doth anger bring*
> *And with the draught that maddened me come med'cining:*
> *A yellow girl whose court cures every carking care;*
> *Did a stone touch it would with joy and glee upspring:*

She riseth in her ewer during darkest night
The house with brightest, sheeniest light illumining:
And going round of youths to whom the world inclines
Ne'er, save in whatso way they please, their hearts shall wring.
From hand of coynted lass begarbed like yarded lad,
Wencher and Tribe of Lot alike enamouring,
She comes: and say to him who dares claim lore of love
Something hast learnt but still there's many another thing.

But best of all is the saying of Ibn al-Mu'tazz:

On the shady woody island His showers Allah deign
Shed on Convent hight Abdún drop and drip of railing rain:
Oft the breezes of the morning have awakened me therein
When the Dawn shows her blaze, ere the bird of flight was fain;
And the voices of the monks that with chants awoke the walls
Black-frocked shavelings ever wont the cup amorn to drain.
'Mid the throng how many fair with languour-kohl'd eyes
And lids enfolding lovely orbs where black on white was lain,
In secret came to see me by shirt of night disguised
In terror and in caution a-hurrying amain!
Then I rose and spread my cheek like a carpet on his path
In homage, and with skirts wiped his trail from off the plain.
But threatening disgrace rose the Crescent in the sky
Like the paring of a nail yet the light would never wane:
Then happened whatso happened: I disdain to kiss and tell
So deem of us thy best and with queries never mell.

And gifted of God is he who saith:

In the morn I am richest of men
And in joy at good news I start up
For I look on the liquid gold
And I measure it out by the cup.
And how goodly is the saying of the poet:
By Allah, this is th' only alchemy
All said of other science false we see!
Carat of wine on hundredweight of woe
Transmuteth gloomiest grief to joy and glee.
And that of another:
The glasses are heavy when empty brought
Till we charge them all with unmixèd wine.
Then so light are they that to fly they're fain
As bodies lightened by soul divine.
And yet another:
Wine-cup and ruby-wine high worship claim;
Dishonour 'twere to see their honour waste:

Bury me, when I'm dead, by side of vine
Whose veins shall moisten bones in clay misplaced;
Nor bury me in wold and wild, for I
Dread only after death no wine to taste."

And he ceased not to egg him on to the drink, naming to him such of the virtues of wine as he thought well and reciting to him what occurred to him of poetry and pleasantries on the subject, till Ma'aruf addressed himself to sucking the cup-lips and cared no longer for aught else. The Wazir ceased not to fill for him and he to drink and enjoy himself and make merry, till his wits wandered and he could not distinguish right from wrong. When the Minister saw that drunkenness had attained in him to utterest and the bounds transgressed, he said to him, "By Allah, O Merchant Ma'aruf, I admire whence thou gottest these jewels whose like the Kings of the Chosroës possess not! In all our lives never saw we a merchant that had heaped up riches like unto thine or more generous than thou, for thy doings are the doings of Kings and not merchants' doings. Wherefore, Allah upon thee, do thou acquaint me with this, that I may know thy rank and condition." And he went on to test him with questions and cajole him, till Ma'aruf, being reft of reason, said to him, "I'm neither merchant nor King," and told him his whole story from first to last. Then said the Wazir, "I conjure thee by Allah, O my lord Ma'aruf, show us the ring, that we may see its make." So, in his drunkenness, he pulled off the ring and said, "Take it and look upon it." The Minister took it and turning it over, said, "If I rub it, will its slave appear?" Replied Ma'aruf, "Yes. Rub it and he will appear to thee, and do thou divert thyself with the sight of him." Thereupon the Wazir rubbed the ring and behold forthright appeared the Jinni and said, "Adsum, at thy service, O my lord! Ask and it shall be given to thee. Wilt thou ruin a city or raise a capital or kill a king? Whatso thou seekest, I will do for thee, sans fail." The Wazir pointed to Ma'aruf and said, "Take up yonder wretch and cast him down in the most desolate of desert lands, where he shall find nothing to eat nor drink, so he may die of hunger and perish miserably, and none know of him." Accordingly, the Jinni snatched him up and flew with him betwixt heaven and earth, which when Ma'aruf saw, he made sure of destruction and wept and said, "O Abu al-Sa'adat, whither goest thou with me?" Replied the Jinni, "I go to cast thee down in the Desert Quarter, O ill-bred wight of gross wits. Shall one have the like of this talisman and give it to the folk to gaze at? Verily, thou deservest that which hath befallen thee; and but that I fear Allah, I would let thee fall from a height of a thousand fathoms, nor shouldst thou reach the earth, till the winds had torn thee to shreds." Ma'aruf was silent and did not again bespeak him till he reached the Desert Quarter and casting him down there, went away and left him in that horrible place. – And Shahrazad perceived the dawn of day and ceased saying her permitted say.

When it was the Nine Hundred and Ninety-ninth Night,

She said, it hath reached me, O auspicious King, that the Slave of the Seal-ring took up Ma'aruf and cast him down in the Desert Quarter where he left him and went his ways. So much concerning him; but returning to the Wazir who was now in possession of the talisman, he said to the King, "How deemest thou now? Did I not tell thee that this fellow was a liar, an impostor, but thou wouldst not credit me?" Replied the King, "Thou wast in the right, O my Wazir, Allah grant thee weal! But give me the ring, that I may solace myself with the sight." The Minister looked at him angrily and spat in his face, saying, "O lack-wits, how shall I give it to thee and abide thy servant, after I am become thy master? But I will spare thee no more on life." Then he rubbed the seal-ring and said to the Slave, "Take up this ill-mannered churl and cast him down by his son-in-law the swindler-man." So the Jinni took him up and flew off with him, whereupon quoth the King to him, "O creature of my Lord, what is my crime?" Abu al-Sa'adat replied, "That wot I not, but my master hath commanded me and I cannot cross whoso hath compassed the enchanted ring." Then he flew on with him, till he came to the Desert Quarter and, casting him down where he had cast Ma'aruf left him and returned. The King hearing Ma'aruf weeping, went up to him and acquainted him with his case; and they sat weeping over that which had befallen them and found neither meat nor drink. Meanwhile the Minister, after driving father-in-law and son-in-law from the country, went forth from the garden and summoning all the troops held a Divan, and told them what he had done with the King and Ma'aruf and acquainted them with the affair of the talisman, adding, "Unless ye make me Sultan over you, I will bid the Slave of the Seal-ring take you up one and all and cast you down in the Desert Quarter where you shall die of hunger and thirst." They replied, "Do us no damage, for we accept thee as Sultan over us and will not anywise gainsay thy bidding." So they agreed, in their own despite, to his being Sultan over them, and he bestowed on them robes of honour, seeking all he had a mind to of Abu al-Sa'adat, who brought it to him forthwith. Then he sat down on the throne and the troops did homage to him; and he sent to Princess Dunya, the King's daughter, saying, "Make thee ready, for I mean to come in unto thee this night, because I long for thee with love."

When she heard this, she wept, for the case of her husband and father was grievous to her, and sent to him saying, "Have patience with me till my period of widowhood be ended: then draw up thy contract of marriage with me and go in to me according to law." But he sent back to say to her, "I know neither period of widowhood nor to delay have I a mood; and I need not a contract nor know I lawful from unlawful; but needs must I go in unto thee this night." She answered him saying, "So be it, then, and welcome to thee!"; but this was a trick on her part. When the answer reached the Wazir, he rejoiced and his breast was broadened, for that he was passionately in love with her. He bade set food before all the folk, saying, "Eat; this is my bride-feast; for I purpose to go in to the Princess Dunya this night." Quoth the Shaykh al-Islam, "It is not lawful for thee to go in unto her till her days of widowhood be ended and thou have drawn up thy contract of marriage with her." But he answered, "I know neither days of widowhood nor other period; so multiply not words on me." The Shaykh al-Islam was silent, fearing his mischief, and said to the troops, "Verily, this man is a Kafir, a Miscreant, and hath neither creed nor religious conduct." As soon as it was evenfall, he went in to her and found her robed in her richest raiment and decked with her goodliest adornments. When she saw him, she came to meet him, laughing and said, "A blessed night! But hadst thou slain my father and my husband, it had been more to my mind." And he said, "There is no help but I slay them." Then she made him sit down and began to jest with him and make show of love caressing him and smiling in his face so that his reason fled; but she cajoled him with her coaxing and cunning only that she might get possession of the ring and change his joy into calamity on the mother of his forehead: nor did she deal thus with him but after the rede of him who said:

I attained by my wits
What no sword had obtained,

And return wi' the spoils
Whose sweet pluckings I gained.

When he saw her caress him and smile upon him, desire surged up in him and he besought her of carnal knowledge; but, when he approached her, she drew away from him and burst into tears, saying, "O my lord, seest thou not the man looking at us? I conjure thee by Allah, screen me from his eyes! How canst thou know me what while he looketh on us?" When he heard this, he was angry and asked, "Where is the man?"; and answered she, "There he is, in the bezel of the ring! putting out his head and staring at us." He thought that the Jinni was looking at them and said laughing, "Fear not; this is the Slave of the Seal-ring, and he is subject to me." Quoth she, "I am afraid of Ifrits; pull it off and throw it afar from me." So he plucked it off and laying it on the cushion, drew near to her, but she dealt him a kick, her foot striking him full in the stomach, and he fell over on his back senseless; whereupon she cried out to her attendants, who came to her in haste, and said to them, "Seize him!" So forty slavegirls laid hold on him, whilst she hurriedly snatched up the ring from the cushion and rubbed it; whereupon Abu al-Sa'adat presented himself, saying, "Adsum, at thy service O my mistress." Cried she, "Take up yonder Infidel and clap him in jail and shackle him heavily." So he took him and throwing him into the Prison of Wrath returned and reported, "I have laid him in limbo." Quoth she, "Whither wentest thou with my father and my husband?"; and quoth he, "I cast them down in the Desert Quarter." Then cried she, "I command thee to fetch them to me forthwith." He replied, "I hear and I obey," and taking flight at once, stayed not till he reached the Desert Quarter, where he lighted down upon them and found them sitting weeping and complaining each to other. Quoth he, "Fear not, for relief is come to you"; and he told them what the Wazir had done, adding, "Indeed I imprisoned him with my own hands in obedience to her, and she hath bidden me bear you back." And they rejoiced in his news. Then he took them both up and flew home with them; nor was it more than an hour before he brought them in to Princess Dunya, who rose and saluted sire and spouse. Then she made them sit down and brought them food and sweetmeats, and they passed the rest of the night with her. On the next day she clad them in rich clothing and said to the King, "O my papa, sit thou upon thy throne and be King as before and make my husband thy Wazir of the Right and tell thy troops that which hath happened. Then send for the Minister out of prison and do him die, and after burn him, for that he is a Miscreant, and would have gone in unto me in the way of lewdness, without the rites of wedlock and he hath testified against himself that he is an Infidel and believeth in no religion. And do tenderly by thy son-in-law, whom thou makest thy Wazir of the Right." He replied, "Hearing and obeying, O my daughter. But do thou give me the ring or give it to thy husband." Quoth she, "It behoveth not that either thou or he have the ring. I will keep the ring myself, and belike I shall be more careful of it than you. Whatso ye wish seek it of me and I will demand it for you of the Slave of the Seal-ring. So fear no harm so long as I live and after my death, do what ye twain will with the ring." Quoth the King, "This is the right rede, O my daughter," and taking his son-in-law went forth to the Divan. Now the troops had passed the night in sore chagrin for Princess Dunya and that which the Wazir had done with her, in going in to her after the way of lewdness, without marriage-rites, and for his ill-usage of the King and Ma'aruf, and they feared lest the law of Al-Islam be dishonoured, because it was manifest to them that he was a Kafir. So they assembled in the Divan and fell to reproaching the Shaykh al-Islam, saying, "Why didst thou not forbid him from going in to the Princess in the way of lewdness?" Said he, "O folk, the man is a Miscreant and hath gotten possession of the ring and I and you may not prevail against him. But Almighty Allah will requite him his deed, and be ye silent, lest he slay you." And as the host was thus engaged in talk, behold the King and Ma'aruf entered the Divan. – And Shahrazad perceived the dawn of day and ceased to say her permitted say.

When it was the Thousandth Night,

She continued, It hath reached me, O auspicious King, that when the troops sorely chagrined sat in the Divan talking over the ill-deeds done by the Wazir to their Sovran, his son-in-law and his daughter, behold, the King and Ma'aruf entered. Then the King bade decorate the city and sent to fetch the Wazir from the place of duresse. So they brought him, and as he passed by the troops, they cursed him and abused him and menaced him, till he came to the King, who commanded to do him dead by the vilest of deaths. Accordingly, they slew him and after burned his body, and he went to Hell after the foulest of plights; and right well quoth one of him:

The Compassionate show no ruth to the tomb where his bones shall lie
And Munkar and eke Nakír ne'er cease to abide thereby!

The King made Ma'aruf his Wazir of the Right and the times were pleasant to them and their joys were untroubled. They abode thus five years till, in the sixth year, the King died and Princess Dunya made Ma'aruf Sultan in her father's stead, but she gave him not the seal-ring. During this time she had conceived by him and borne him a boy of passing loveliness, excelling in beauty and perfection, who ceased not to be reared in the laps of nurses till he reached the age of five, when his mother fell sick of a deadly sickness and calling her husband to her, said to him, "I am ill." Quoth he, "Allah preserve thee, O dearling of my heart!" But quoth she, "Haply I shall die and thou needest not that I commend to thy care thy son: wherefore I charge thee but be careful of the ring, for thine own sake and for the sake of this thy boy." And he answered, "No harm shall befal him whom Allah preserveth!" Then she pulled off the ring and gave it to him, and on the morrow she was admitted to the mercy of Allah the Most High, whilst Ma'aruf abode in possession of the kingship and applied himself to the business of governing. Now it chanced that one day, as he shook the handkerchief and the troops withdrew to their places that he betook himself to the sitting-chamber, where he sat till the day departed and the night advanced with murks bedight. Then came in to him his cup-companions of the notables according to their custom, and sat with him by way of solace and diversion, till midnight, when they craved permission to withdraw. He gave them leave and they retired to their houses; after which there came in to him a slave-girl affected to the service of his bed, who spread him the mattress and doffing his apparel, clad him in his sleeping-gown. Then he lay down and she kneaded his feet, till sleep overpowered him; whereupon she withdrew to her own chamber and slept. But suddenly he felt something beside him in the bed and awaking started up in alarm and cried, "I seek refuge with Allah from Satan the stoned!" Then he opened his eyes and seeing by his side a woman foul of favour, said to her, "Who art thou?" Said she, "Fear not, I am thy wife Fatimah al-Urrah." Whereupon he looked in her face and knew her by her loathly form and the length of her dog-teeth: so he asked her, "Whence camest thou in to me and who brought thee to this country?" "In what country art thou at this present?" "In the city of Ikhtiyan al-Khatan. But thou, when didst thou leave Cairo?" "But now." "How can that be?" "Know," said she, "that, when I fell out with thee and Satan prompted me to do thee a damage, I complained of thee to the magistrates, who sought for thee and the Kazis enquired of thee, but found thee not. When two days were past, repentance gat hold upon me and I knew that the fault was with me; but penitence availed me not, and I abode for some days weeping for thy loss, till what was in my hand failed and I was obliged to beg my bread. So I fell to begging of all, from the courted rich to the contemned poor, and since thou leftest me, I have eaten of the bitterness of beggary and have been in the sorriest of conditions. Every night I sat beweeping our separation and that which I suffered, since thy departure, of humiliation and ignominy, of abjection and misery." And she went on to tell him what had befallen her, whilst he stared at her in amazement, till she said, "Yesterday, I went about begging all day but none gave me aught; and as often as I accosted any one and craved of him a crust of bread, he reviled me and gave me naught. When night came, I went to bed supperless, and hunger burned me and sore on me was that which I suffered: and I sat weeping when, behold, one appeared to me and said, O woman why weepest thou? Said I, erst I had a husband who used to provide for me and fulfil my wishes; but he is lost to me and I know not whither he went and have been in sore straits since he left me. Asked he, What is thy husband's name? and I answered, His name is Ma'aruf. Quoth he, I ken him. Know that thy husband is now Sultan in a certain city, and if thou wilt, I will carry thee to him. Cried I, I am under thy protection: of thy bounty bring me to him! So he took me up and flew with me between heaven and earth, till he brought me to this pavilion and said to me: Enter yonder chamber, and thou shalt see thy husband asleep on the couch. Accordingly I entered and found thee in this state of lordship. Indeed I had not thought thou wouldst forsake me, who am thy mate, and praised be Allah who hath united thee with me!" Quoth Ma'aruf, "Did I forsake thee or thou me? Thou complainedst of me from Kazi to Kazi and endedst by denouncing me to the High Court and bringing down on me Abú Tabak from the Citadel: so I fled in mine own despite."

And he went on to tell her all that had befallen him and how he was become Sultan and had married the King's daughter and how his beloved Dunya had died, leaving him a son who was then seven years old. She rejoined, "That which happened was fore-ordained of Allah; but I repent me and I place myself under thy protection beseeching thee not to abandon me, but suffer me eat bread, with thee by way of an alms." And she ceased not to humble herself to him and to supplicate him till his heart relented towards her and he said, "Repent from mischief and abide with me, and naught shall betide thee save what shall pleasure thee: but, an thou work any wickedness, I will slay thee nor fear any one. And fancy not that thou canst complain of me to the High Court and that Abu Tabak will come down on me from the Citadel; for I am become Sultan and the folk dread me: but I fear none save Allah Almighty, because I have a talismanic ring which when I rub, the Slave of the Signet appeareth to me. His name is Abu al-Sa'adat, and whatsoever I demand of him he bringeth to me. So, an thou desire to return to thine own country, I will give thee what shall suffice thee all thy life long and will send thee thither speedily; but, an thou desire to abide with me, I will clear for thee a palace and furnish it with the choicest of silks and appoint thee twenty slave-girls to serve thee and provide thee with dainty dishes and sumptuous suits, and thou shalt be a Queen and live in all delight till thou die or I die. What sayest thou of this?" "I wish to abide with thee," she answered and kissed his hand and vowed repentance from frowardness. Accordingly he set apart a palace for her sole use and gave her slave-girls and eunuchs, and she became a Queen. The young Prince used to visit her as he visited his sire; but she hated him for that he was not her son; and when the boy saw that she looked on him with the eye of aversion and anger, he shunned her and took a dislike to her. As for Ma'aruf, he occupied himself with the love of fair handmaidens and bethought him not of his wife Fatimah the Dung, for that she was grown a grizzled old fright, foul-favoured to the sight, a bald-headed blight, loathlier than the snake speckled black and white; the more that she had beyond measure evil entreated him aforetime; and as saith the adage, "Ill-usage the root of desire disparts and sows hate in the soil of hearts;" and God-gifted is he who saith:

> Beware of losing hearts of men by thine injurious deed;
> For when Aversion takes his place none may dear Love restore:
> Hearts, when affection flies from them, are likest unto glass
> Which broken, cannot whole be made, – 'tis breached for evermore.

And indeed Ma'aruf had not given her shelter by reason of any praiseworthy quality in her, but he dealt with her thus generously only of desire for the approval of Allah Almighty. – Here Dunyazad interrupted her sister Shahrazad, saying, "How winsome are these words of thine which win hold of the heart more forcibly than enchanters' eyne; and how beautiful are these wondrous books thou hast cited and the marvellous and singular tales thou hast recited!" Quoth Shahrazad, "And where is all this compared with what I shall relate to thee on the coming night, an I live and the King deign spare my days?" So when morning morrowed and the day brake in its sheen and shone, the King arose from his couch with breast broadened and in high expectation for the rest of the tale and saying, "By Allah, I will not slay her till I hear the last of her story;" repaired to his Durbár while the Wazir, as was his wont, presented himself at the Palace, shroud under arm. Shahriyar tarried abroad all that day, bidding and forbidding between man and man; after which he returned to his Harim and, according to his custom went in to his wife Shahrazad.

When it was the Thousand and First Night,

Dunyazad said to her sister, "Do thou finish for us the History of Ma'aruf!" She replied, "With love and goodly gree, an my lord deign permit me recount it." Quoth the King, "I permit thee; for that I am fain of hearing it." So she said: It hath reached me, O auspicious King, that Ma'aruf would have naught to do with his wife by way of conjugal duty. Now when she saw that he held aloof from her bed and occupied himself with other women, she hated him and jealousy gat the mastery of her and Iblis prompted her to take the seal-ring from him and slay him and make herself Queen in his stead. So she went forth one night from her pavilion, intending for that in which was her husband King Ma'aruf; and it chanced by decree of the Decreer and His written destiny, that Ma'aruf lay that night with one of his concubines; a damsel endowed with beauty and loveliness, symmetry and a stature all grace. And it was his wont, of the excellence of his piety, that, when he was minded to have to lie with a woman, he would doff the enchanted seal-ring from his finger, in reverence to the Holy Names graven thereon, and lay it on the Pillow, nor would he don it again till he had purified himself by the Ghusl-ablution. Moreover, when he had lain with a woman, he was used to order her go forth from him before daybreak, of his fear for the seal-ring; and when he went to the Hammam he locked the door of the pavilion till his return, when he put on the ring, and after this, all were free to enter according to custom. His wife Fatimah the Dung knew of all this and went not forth from her place till she had certified herself of the case. So she sallied out, when the night was dark, purposing to go in to him, whilst he was drowned in sleep, and steal the ring, unseen of him. Now it chanced at this time that the King's son had gone out, without light, to the Chapel of Ease for an occasion, and sat down over the marble slab of the jakes in the dark, leaving the door open. Presently, he saw Fatimah come forth of her pavilion and make stealthily for that of his father and said in himself, "What aileth this witch to leave her lodging in the dead of the night and make for my father's pavilion? Needs must there be some reason for this:" so he went out after her and followed in her steps unseen of her. Now he had a short sword of watered steel, which he held so dear that he went not to his father's Divan, except he were girt therewith; and his father used to laugh at him and exclaim, "Mahallah! This is a mighty fine sword of thine, O my son! But thou hast not gone down with it to battle nor cut off a head therewith." Whereupon the boy would reply, "I will not fail to cut off with it some head which deserveth cutting." And Ma'aruf would laugh at his words. Now when treading in her track, he drew the sword from its sheath and he followed her till she came to his father's pavilion and entered, whilst he stood and watched her from the door. He saw her searching about and heard her say to herself, "Where hath he laid the seal-ring?"; whereby he knew that she was looking for the ring and he waited till she found it and said, "Here it is." Then she picked it up and turned to go out; but he hid behind the door. As she came forth, she looked at the ring and turned it about in her grasp. But when she was about to rub it, he raised his hand with the sword and smote her on the neck; and she cried a single cry and fell down dead. With this Ma'aruf awoke and seeing his wife strown on the ground, with her blood flowing, and his son standing with the drawn sword in his hand, said to him, "What is this, O my son?" He replied, "O my father, how often hast thou said to me, Thou hast a mighty fine sword; but thou hast not gone down with it to battle nor cut off a head. And I have answered thee, saying, I will not fail to cut off with it a head which deserveth cutting. And now, behold, I have therewith cut off for thee a head well worth the cutting!" And he told him what had passed. Ma'aruf sought for the seal-ring, but found it not; so he searched the dead woman's body till he saw her hand closed upon it; whereupon he took it from her grasp and said to the boy, "Thou art indeed my very son, without doubt or dispute; Allah ease thee in this world and the next, even as thou hast eased me of this vile woman! Her attempt led only to her own destruction, and Allah-gifted is he who said:

> *When forwards Allah's aid a man's intent,*
> *His wish in every case shall find consent:*
> *But an that aid of Allah be refused,*
> *His first attempt shall do him damagement."*

Then King Ma'aruf called aloud to some of his attendants, who came in haste, and he told them what his wife Fatimah the Dung had done and bade them to take her and lay her in a place till the morning. They did his bidding, and next day he gave her in charge to a number of eunuchs, who washed her and shrouded her and made her a tomb and buried her. Thus her coming from Cairo was but to her grave, and Allah-gifted is he who said:

> We trod the steps appointed for us:
> And he whose steps are appointed must tread them.
> He whose death is decreed to take place in our land shall not die in any land but that.

And how excellent is the saying of the poet:

> I wot not, whenas to a land I fare,
> Good luck pursuing, what my lot shall be.
> Whether the fortune I perforce pursue
> Or the misfortune which pursueth me.

After this, King Ma'aruf sent for the husbandman, whose guest he had been, when he was a fugitive, and made him his Wazir of the Right and his Chief Counsellor. Then, learning that he had a daughter of passing beauty and loveliness, of qualities nature-ennobled at birth and exalted of worth, he took her to wife; and in due time he married his son. So they abode awhile in all solace of life and its delight and their days were serene and their joys untroubled, till there came to them the Destroyer of delights and the Sunderer of societies, the Depopulator of populous places and the Orphaner of sons and daughters. And glory be to the Living who dieth not and in whose hand are the Keys of the Seen and the Unseen!"

Conclusion

NOW, DURING THIS time, Shahrazad had borne the King three boy children: so, when she had made an end of the story of Ma'aruf, she rose to her feet and kissing ground before him, said, "O King of the time and unique one of the age and the tide, I am thine handmaid and these thousand nights and a night have I entertained thee with stories of folk gone before and admonitory instances of the men of yore. May I then make bold to crave a boon of Thy Highness?" He replied, "Ask, O Shahrazad, and it shall be granted to thee." Whereupon she cried out to the nurses and the eunuchs, saying, "Bring me my children." So they brought them to her in haste, and they were three boy children, one walking, one crawling and one sucking. She took them and setting them before the King, again kissed the ground and said, "O King of the age, these are thy children and I crave that thou release me from the doom of death, as a dole to these infants; for, an thou kill me, they will become motherless and will find none among women to rear them as they should be reared." When the King heard this, he wept and straining the boys to his bosom, said, "By Allah, O Shahrazad, I pardoned thee before the coming of these children, for that I found thee chaste, pure, ingenuous and pious! Allah bless thee and thy father and thy mother and thy root and thy branch! I take the Almighty to witness against me that I exempt thee from aught that can harm thee." So she kissed his hands and feet and rejoiced with exceeding joy, saying, The Lord make thy life long and increase thee in dignity and majesty!"; presently adding, "Thou marvelledst at that which befel thee on the part of women; yet there betided the Kings of the Chosroës before thee greater mishaps and more grievous than that which hath befallen thee, and indeed I have set forth unto thee that which happened to Caliphs and Kings and others with their women, but the relation is longsome and hearkening groweth tedious, and in this is all sufficient warning for the man of wits and admonishment for the wise." Then she ceased to speak, and when King Shahriyar heard her speech and profited by that which she said, he summoned up his reasoning powers and cleansed his heart and caused his understanding revert and turned to Allah Almighty and said to himself, "Since there befel the Kings of the Chosroës more than that which hath befallen me, never, whilst I live, shall I cease to blame myself for the past. As for this Shahrazad, her like is not found in the lands; so praise be to Him who appointed her a means for delivering His creatures from oppression and slaughter!" Then he arose from his séance and kissed her head, whereat she rejoiced, she and her sister Dunyazad, with exceeding joy.

When the morning morrowed, the King went forth and sitting down on the throne of the Kingship, summoned the Lords of his land; whereupon the Chamberlains and Nabobs and Captains of the host went in to him and kissed ground before him. He distinguished the Wazir, Shahrazad's sire, with special favour and bestowed on him a costly and splendid robe of honour and entreated him with the utmost kindness, and said to him, "Allah protect thee for that thou gavest me to wife thy noble daughter, who hath been the means of my repentance from slaying the daughters of folk. Indeed I have found her pure and pious, chaste and ingenuous, and Allah hath vouchsafed me by her three boy children; wherefore praised be He for his passing favour." Then he bestowed robes of honour upon his Wazirs, and Emirs and Chief Officers and he set forth to them briefly that which had betided him with Shahrazad and how he had turned from his former ways and repented him of what he had done and purposed to take the Wazir's daughter, Shahrazad, to wife and let draw up the marriage-contract with her. When those who were present heard this, they kissed the ground before him and blessed him and his betrothed Shahrazad, and the Wazir thanked her. Then Shahriyar made an end of his sitting in all weal, whereupon the folk dispersed to their dwelling-places and the news was bruited abroad that the King purposed to marry the Wazir's daughter, Shahrazad. Then he proceeded to make ready the wedding gear, and presently he sent after his brother, King Shah Zaman, who came, and King Shahriyar went forth to meet him with the troops.

Furthermore, they decorated the city after the goodliest fashion and diffused scents from censers and burnt aloes-wood and other perfumes in all the markets and thoroughfares and rubbed themselves with saffron, what while the drums beat and the flutes and pipes sounded and mimes and mountebanks played and plied their arts and the King lavished on them gifts and largesse; and in very deed it was a notable day. When they came to the palace, King Shahriyar commanded to spread the tables with beasts roasted whole and sweetmeats and all manner of viands and bade the crier cry to the folk that they should come up to the Divan and eat and drink and that this should be a means of reconciliation between him and them. So, high and low, great and small came up unto him and they abode on that wise, eating and drinking, seven days with their nights. Then the King shut himself up with his brother and related to him that which had betided him with the Wazir's daughter, Shahrazad, during the past three years and told him what he had heard from her of proverbs and parables, chronicles and pleasantries, quips and jests, stories and anecdotes, dialogues and histories and elegies and other verses; whereat King Shah Zaman marvelled with the uttermost marvel and said, "Fain would I take her younger sister to wife, so we may be two brothers-german to two sisters-german, and they on like wise be sisters to us; for that the calamity which befel me was the cause of our discovering that which befel thee and all this time of three years past I have taken no delight in woman, save that I lie each night with a damsel of my kingdom, and every morning I do her to death; but now I desire to marry thy wife's sister Dunyazad."

When King Shahriyar heard his brother's words, he rejoiced with joy exceeding and arising forthright, went in to his wife Shahrazad and acquainted her with that which his brother purposed, namely that he sought her sister Dunyazad in wedlock; whereupon she answered, "O King of the age, we seek of him one condition, to wit, that he take up his abode with us, for that I cannot brook to be parted from my sister an hour, because we were brought up together and may not endure separation each from other. If he accept this pact, she is his handmaid." King Shahriyar returned to his brother and acquainted him with that which Shahrazad had said; and he replied, "Indeed, this is what was in my mind, for that I desire nevermore to be parted from thee one hour. As for the kingdom, Allah the Most High shall send to it whomso He chooseth, for that I have no longer a desire for the kingship." When King Shahriyar heard his brother's words, he rejoiced exceedingly and said, "Verily, this is what I wished, O my brother. So Alhamdolillah – Praised be Allah – who hath brought about union between us." Then he sent after the Kazis and Olema, Captains and Notables, and they married the two brothers to the two sisters. The contracts were written out and the two Kings bestowed robes of honour of silk and satin on those who were present, whilst the city was decorated and the rejoicings were renewed.

The King commanded each Emir and Wazir and Chamberlain and Nabob to decorate his palace and the folk of the city were gladdened by the presage of happiness and contentment. King Shahriyar also bade slaughter sheep and set up kitchens and made bride-feasts and fed all comers, high and low; and he gave alms to the poor and needy and extended his bounty to great and small. Then the eunuchs went forth, that they might perfume the Hammam for the brides; so they scented it with rosewater and willow-flower-water and pods of musk and fumigated it with Kákilí eagle-wood and ambergris. Then Shahrazad entered, she and her sister Dunyazad, and they cleansed their heads and clipped their hair. When they came forth of the Hammam-bath, they donned raiment and ornaments; such as men were wont prepare for the Kings of the Chosroës; and among Shahrazad's apparel was a dress purfled with red gold and wrought with counterfeit presentments of birds and beasts. And the two sisters encircled their necks with necklaces of jewels of price, in the like whereof Iskander rejoiced not, for therein were great jewels such as amazed the wit and dazzled the eye; and the imagination was bewildered at their charms, for indeed each of them was brighter than the sun and the moon.

Before them they lighted brilliant flambeaux of wax in candelabra of gold, but their faces outshone the flambeaux, for that they had eyes sharper than unsheathed swords and the lashes of their eyelids bewitched all hearts. Their cheeks were rosy red and their necks and shapes gracefully swayed and their eyes wantoned like the gazelle's; and the slave-girls came to meet them with instruments of music. Then the two Kings entered the Hammam-bath, and when they came forth, they sat down on a couch set with pearls and gems, whereupon the two sisters came up to them and stood between their hands, as they were moons, bending and leaning from side to side in their beauty and loveliness. Presently they brought forward Shahrazad and displayed her, for the first dress, in a red suit; whereupon King Shahriyar rose to look upon her and the wits of all present, men and women, were bewitched for that she was even as saith of her one of her describers:

> *A sun on wand in knoll of sand she showed,*
> *Clad in her cramoisy-hued chemisette:*
> *Of her lips' honey-dew she gave me drink*
> *And with her rosy cheeks quencht fire she set.*

Then they attired Dunyazad in a dress of blue brocade and she became as she were the full moon when it shineth forth. So they displayed her in this, for the first dress, before King Shah Zaman, who rejoiced in her and well-nigh swooned away for love-longing and amorous desire; yea, he was distraught with passion for her, whenas he saw her, because she was as saith of her one of her describers in these couplets:

> *She comes apparelled in an azure vest*
> *Ultramarine as skies are deckt and dight:*
> *I view'd th' unparallel'd sight, which showed my eyes*
> *A Summer-moon upon a Winter-night.*

Then they returned to Shahrazad and displayed her in the second dress, a suit of surpassing goodliness, and veiled her face with her hair like a chin-veil. Moreover, they let down her side-locks and she was even as saith of her one of her describers in these couplets:

> *O hail to him whose locks his cheeks o'ershade,*
> *Who slew my life by cruel hard despight:*
> *Said I, "Hast veiled the Morn in Night?" He said,*
> *"Nay I but veil Moon in hue of Night."*

Then they displayed Dunyazad in a second and a third and a fourth dress and she paced forward like the rising sun, and swayed to and fro in the insolence of beauty; and she was even as saith the poet of her in these couplets:

> *The sun of beauty she to all appears*
> *And, lovely coy she mocks all loveliness:*
> *And when he fronts her favour and her smile*
> *A-morn, the sun of day in clouds must dress.*

Then they displayed Shahrazad in the third dress and the fourth and the fifth and she became as she were a Bán-branch snell or a thirsting gazelle, lovely of face and perfect in attributes of grace, even as saith of her one in these couplets:

> She comes like fullest moon on happy night.
> Taper of waist with shape of magic might:
> She hath an eye whose glances quell mankind,
> And ruby on her cheeks reflects his light:
> Enveils her hips the blackness of her hair;
> Beware of curls that bite with viper-bite!
> Her sides are silken-soft, that while the heart
> Mere rock behind that surface 'scapes our sight:
> From the fringed curtains of her eyne she shoots
> Shafts that at furthest range on mark alight.

Then they returned to Dunyazad and displayed her in the fifth dress and in the sixth, which was green, when she surpassed with her loveliness the fair of the four quarters of the world and outvied, with the brightness of her countenance, the full moon at rising tide; for she was even as saith of her the poet in these couplets:

> A damsel 'twas the tirer's art had decked with snare and sleight,
> And robed with rays as though the sun from her had borrowed light:
> She came before us wondrous clad in chemisette of green,
> As veilèd by his leafy screen Pomegranate hides from sight:
> And when he said, "How callest thou the fashion of thy dress?"
> She answered us in pleasant way with double meaning dight,
> We call this garment crève-coeur; and rightly is it hight,
> For many a heart wi' this we brake and harried many a sprite."

Then they displayed Shahrazad in the sixth and seventh dresses and clad her in youth's clothing, whereupon she came forward swaying from side to side and coquettishly moving and indeed she ravished wits and hearts and ensorcelled all eyes with her glances. She shook her sides and swayed her haunches, then put her hair on sword-hilt and went up to King Shahriyar, who embraced her as hospitable host embraceth guest, and threatened her in her ear with the taking of the sword; and she was even as saith of her the poet in these words:

> Were not the Murk of gender male,
> Than feminines surpassing fair,
> Tirewomen they had grudged the bride,
> Who made her beard and whiskers wear!

Thus also they did with her sister Dunyazad, and when they had made an end of the display the King bestowed robes of honour on all who were present and sent the brides to their own apartments. Then Shahrazad went in to King Shahriyar and Dunyazad to King Shah Zaman and each of them solaced himself with the company of his beloved consort and the hearts of the folk were comforted. When morning morrowed, the Wazir came in to the two Kings and kissed ground before them; wherefore they thanked him and were large of bounty to him. Presently they went forth and sat down upon couches of Kingship, whilst all the Wazirs and Emirs and Grandees and Lords of the land presented themselves and kissed ground. King Shahriyar ordered them dresses of honour and largesse and they prayed for the permanence and prosperity of the King and his brother. Then the two Sovrans appointed their sire-in-law the Wazir to be Viceroy in Samarcand and assigned him five of the Chief Emirs to accompany him, charging them attend him and do him service. The Minister kissed the ground and prayed that they might be vouchsafed length of life: then he went in to his daughters, whilst the Eunuchs and Ushers walked before him, and saluted them and farewelled them. They kissed his hands and gave him joy of the Kingship and bestowed on him immense treasures; after which he took leave of them and setting out, fared days and nights, till he came near Samarcand, where the townspeople met him at a distance of three marches and rejoiced in him with exceeding joy. So he entered the city and they decorated the houses and it was a notable day. He sat down on the throne of his kingship and the Wazirs did him homage and the Grandees and Emirs of Samarcand and all prayed that he might be vouchsafed justice and victory and length of continuance. So he bestowed on them robes of honour and entreated them with distinction and they made him Sultan over them. As soon as his father-in-law had departed for Samarcand, King Shahriyar summoned the Grandees of his realm and made them a stupendous banquet of all manner of delicious meats and exquisite sweetmeats. He also bestowed on them robes of honour and guerdoned them and divided the kingdoms between himself and his brother in their presence, whereat the folk rejoiced. Then the two Kings abode, each ruling a day in turn, and they were ever in harmony each with other while on similar wise their wives continued in the love of Allah Almighty and in thanksgiving to Him; and the peoples and the provinces were at peace and the preachers prayed for them from the pulpits, and their report was bruited abroad and the travellers bore tidings of them to all lands.

In due time King Shahriyar summoned chroniclers and copyists and bade them write all that had betided him with his wife, first and last; so they wrote this and named it "The Stories of the Thousand Nights and A Night." The book came to thirty volumes and these the King laid up in his treasury. And the two brothers abode with their wives in all pleasance and solace of life and its delights, for that indeed Allah the Most High had changed their annoy into joy; and on this wise they continued till there took them the Destroyer of delights and the Severer of societies, the Desolator of dwelling-places and Garnerer of grave-yards, and they were translated to the ruth of Almighty Allah; their houses fell waste and their palaces lay in ruins and the Kings inherited their riches. Then there reigned after them a wise ruler, who was just, keen-witted and accomplished and loved tales and legends, especially those which chronicle the doings of Sovrans and Sultans, and he found in the treasury these marvellous stories and wondrous histories, contained in the thirty volumes aforesaid. So he read in them a first book and a second and a third and so on to the last of them, and each book astounded and delighted him more than that which preceded it, till he came to the end of them. Then he admired whatso he had read therein of description and discourse and rare traits and anecdotes and moral instances and reminiscences and bade the folk copy them and dispread them over all lands and climes; wherefore their report was bruited abroad and the people named them "The marvels and wonders of the Thousand Nights and A Night."

This is all that hath come down to us of the origin of this book, and Allah is All-knowing. So Glory be to Him whom the shifts of Time waste not away, nor doth aught of chance or change affect His sway: whom one case diverteth not from other case and Who is sole in the attributes of perfect grace. And prayer and peace be upon the Lord's Pontiff and Chosen One among His creatures, our lord MOHAMMED the Prince of mankind through whom we supplicate Him for a goodly and a godly

THE
END

Biographies

Richard F. Burton

Born in Torquay, England, Sir Richard Francis Burton (1821–90) lived a remarkable life. Much of his childhood was spent in France and Italy, encouraging Burton's talent for languages. Fluent in numerous languages and dialects before the age of 20, he went on to master at least 26 languages in his lifetime. Best known as a scholar and explorer, Burton was also a soldier, translator, poet, fencer, spy, ethnologist and diplomat. He wrote extensively about his travels, which included journeying to Mecca during a time when it was still forbidden to Europeans, as well as an expedition to find the source of the Nile, where Burton became the first European to see Lake Tanganiyaka, one of the Great African Lakes. Burton's work, which included translations of *The Kama Sutra* and *The Book of the Thousand Nights and a Night,* often scandalised Victorian society for its depiction of sex and sexuality, as well as his criticism of Britain's colonial policies.

E. Dixon

E. Dixon, about whom we know little else, was the editor and arranger of *Fairy Tales from the Arabian Nights* in 1893, along with illustrations by John D. Batten.

Andrew and Nora Lang

Scottish writer and critic Andrew Lang (1844–1912) was born and raised in Selkirk. In 1875 he married Leonora 'Nora' Blanche Alleyne (1851–1933), who would become his collaborator on many works. Although Lang worked variously as a historian, journalist, poet, and anthropologist, his greatest legacy has been his works on folklore, mythology, and religion. Among these are the *Fairy Books*, 25 volumes of folk and fairy tales published Lang published with his wife, including *The Arabian Nights Entertainments* (1898), their adaptation of the One Thousand Nights and a Night folk tales. While many volumes in the series list Lang alone as the editor, it was in fact Nora who translated and adapted these works. Lang later acknowledged his wife's significant contribution in the preface to *The Lilac Fairy Book (1910)*, crediting almost all of the series to 'the work of Mrs. Lang', and later volumes also listed her as an author.

Wen-chin Ouyang *(foreword)*

Wen-chin Ouyang FBA is Professor of Arabic and Comparative Literature at SOAS, University of London. Born in Taiwan and raised in Libya, she completed her BA in Arabic at Tripoli University and PhD in Middle Eastern Studies at Columbia University in New York City. She is the author of *Literary Criticism in Medieval Arabic-Islamic Culture: The Making of a Tradition* (1997), *Poetics of Love in the Arabic Novel (2012)* and *Politics of Nostalgia in the Arabic Novel* (2013). She has also published widely on *The Thousand and One Nights*, often in comparison with classical and modern Arabic narrative traditions, European and Hollywood cinema, magic realism, and Chinese storytelling. She founded and co-edits *Edinburgh Studies in Classical Arabic Literature*. She has been the Editor-in-Chief of *Middle Eastern Literatures* since 2011. She also co-chairs the Editorial Committee of Legenda *Studies in Comparative Literature*. She was a member of the judging panel for Man Booker

International Prize for Fiction 2013-15. A native speaker of Arabic and Chinese, she has been working towards Arabic-Chinese comparative literary and cultural studies, including Silk Road Studies.

Kate Douglas Wiggin and Nora A. Smith

Sisters and frequent collaborators Kate Douglas Wiggin (née Smith, 1856–1923) and Nora Archibald Smith (1859–1934) spent most of their childhood in Hollis, Maine. Although the girls' education was somewhat inconsistent, it was more than many women had access to at that time. In 1973, their family moved to California, where both women became became involved in the developing kindergarten movement. Wiggin opened the Silver Street Free Kindergarten, the first free kindergarten west of the Rocky Mountains, in 1878, and was soon joined by Smith. Together, they founded the California Kindergarten Training School. The sisters were both avid writers, publishing fictional as well as scholarly works independently and as co-authors. Most notably, Wiggin's novel *Rebecca of Sunnybrook Farm* (1903) has gone on to become a beloved children's classic.

Sources

***Fairy Tales from the Arabian Nights*, edited and arranged by E. Dixon**
Originally Published by J.M. Dent and Co, London, 1893

***The Arabian Nights Entertainments*, selected and edited by Andrew and Nora Lang** Originally Published by Longmans, Green and Co, 1898

***The Arabian Nights: their best-known tales*, edited by Kate Douglas Wiggin and Nora A. Smith** Originally Published by Charles Scribner's Sons, New York City, 1909

***The Book of the Thousand Nights and a Night*, Volumes 1–10, translated by Richard F. Burton** Originally Published by the Burton Club, USA, circa 1903–1920

FLAME TREE PUBLISHING
Short Story Series
New & Classic Writing

Flame Tree's Gothic Fantasy books offer a carefully curated series of new titles, each with combinations of original and classic writing:

Chilling Horror • Chilling Ghost • Science Fiction
Murder Mayhem • Crime & Mystery • Swords & Steam
Dystopia Utopia • Supernatural Horror • Lost Worlds
Time Travel • Heroic Fantasy • Pirates & Ghosts • Agents & Spies
Endless Apocalypse • Alien Invasion • Robots & AI • Lost Souls
Haunted House • Cosy Crime • American Gothic • Urban Crime
Epic Fantasy • Detective Mysteries • Detective Thrillers
A Dying Planet • Bodies in the Library • Footsteps in the Dark

Also, new companion titles offer rich collections of classic fiction, myths and tales in the gothic fantasy tradition:

H.G. Wells • Lovecraft • Sherlock Holmes
Edgar Allan Poe • Bram Stoker • Mary Shelley
Charles Dickens Supernatural • Heroes & Heroines Myths &
Tales • Witches, Wizards, Seers & Healers Myths & Tales
African Myths & Tales • Celtic Myths & Tales • Greek Myths & Tales
Norse Myths & Tales • Chinese Myths & Tales • Japanese Myths & Tales
Irish Fairy Tales • King Arthur & The Knights of the Round Table
Alice's Adventures in Wonderland • The Divine Comedy
Hans Christian Andersen Fairy Tales • Brothers Grimm
The Wonderful Wizard of Oz • The Age of Queen Victoria

Available from all good bookstores, worldwide, and online at
flametreepublishing.com

See our new fiction imprint
FLAME TREE PRESS | FICTION WITHOUT FRONTIERS
New and original writing in Horror, Crime, SF and Fantasy

And join our monthly newsletter with offers and more stories:
FLAME TREE FICTION NEWSLETTER
flametreepress.com

GOTHIC FANTASY

For our books, calendars, blog
and latest special offers please see:
flametreepublishing.com